PRAISE FOR THE HEARTWARMING
NOVELS OF LINDA LAEL MILLER

SPRINGWATER WEDDING

"Fans will be thrilled to join the action, suspense, and romance portrayed in [Linda Lael Miller's contemporary fiction]."

—*Romantic Times*

"Pure delight from the beginning to the satisfying ending. . . . Miller is a master craftswoman at creating unusual story lines [and] charming characters."

—*Rendezvous*

"Miller's strength is her portrayal of the history and traditions that distinguish Springwater and its residents."

—*Publishers Weekly*

"*Springwater Wedding* is the perfect recipe for love. . . . Miller writes with a warm and loving heart."

—*BookPage*

COURTING SUSANNAH

"Enjoyable. . . . Linda Lael Miller provides her audience with a wonderful look at an Americana romance."

—Harriet Klausner, *Midwest Book Review*

TWO BROTHERS

"A fun read, full of Ms. Miller's simmering sensuality and humor, plus two fabulous brothers who will steal your heart."

—*Romantic Times*

"Excellent, believable stories. . . . Miller has created two sensational heroes and their equally fascinating heroines."

—*Rendezvous*

"Great western romance. . . . *The Lawman* is a five-star tale. . . . *The Gunslinger* is an entertaining, fun-to-read story. . . . Both novels are excellent."

—*Affaire de Coeur*

ONE WISH

"[A] story rich in tenderness, romance, and love. . . . An excellent book from an author destined to lead the romance genre into the next century."

—*Rendezvous*

"An author who genuinely cares about her characters, Miller also expresses the exuberance of Western life in her fresh, human, and empathetic prose and lively plot."

—*Booklist*

"Another triumph. . . . *One Wish* shows why Linda Lael Miller has remained one of the giantesses of the industry for the past decade."

—Harriet Klausner, Barnesandnoble.com

Books by Linda Lael Miller

Banner O'Brien
Corbin's Fancy
Memory's Embrace
My Darling Melissa
Angelfire
Desire and Destiny
Fletcher's Woman
Lauralee
Moonfire
Wanton Angel
Willow
Princess Annie
The Legacy
Taming Charlotte
Yankee Wife
Daniel's Bride
Lily and the Major
Emma and the Outlaw
Caroline and the Raider
Pirates
Knights
My Outlaw

The Vow
Two Brothers
Springwater
Springwater Seasons series:
  Rachel
  Savannah
  Miranda
  Jessica
A Springwater Christmas
One Wish
The Women of Primrose
Creek series:
  Bridget
  Christy
  Skye
  Megan
Courting Susannah
Springwater Wedding
My Lady Beloved
  (writing as Lael St. James)
My Lady Wawyard
  (writing as Lael St. James)

LINDA LAEL MILLER

The WOMEN of PRIMROSE CREEK

BRIDGET   CHRISTY   SKYE   MEGAN

POCKET BOOKS
New York   London   Toronto   Sydney   Singapore

An *Original* Publication of POCKET BOOKS

 POCKET BOOKS, a division of Simon & Schuster, Inc.
1230 Avenue of the Americas, New York, NY 10020

Bridget, *Christy*, *Skye* and *Megan* copyright
© 2000 by Linda Lael Miller

ISBN: 0-7434-3660-1

First Pocket Books printing March 2002

10 9 8 7 6 5 4 3 2 1

POCKET and colophon are registered trademarks of Simon & Schuster, Inc.

Front cover illustration by Lisa Litwack;
photo credit: Yuen Lee/Photonica

For information regarding special discounts for bulk purchases, please contact Simon & Schuster Special Sales at 1-800-456-6798 or business@simonandschuster.com

Printed in the U.S.A.

These titles were previously published individually by Pocket Books

Contents

Bridget

For Anita Carter,
the sweetest voice in any choir,
with love

Midsummer 1867

Primrose Creek, Nevada

Chapter

1

❧

Trace was on foot when she saw him again, carrying a saddle over one shoulder, a gloved hand grasping the horn. His hat was pushed to the back of his head, and his pale, sun-streaked hair caught the sunlight. His blue-green eyes flashed bright as sun on water, and the cocky grin she knew oh-so-well curved his mouth. Oh, yes. Even from the other side of Primrose Creek, Bridget knew right off who he was—trouble.

She had half a mind to go straight into the cabin for Granddaddy's shotgun and send him packing. Might have done it, too, if she hadn't known he was just out of range. The scoundrel had probably figured out what she was thinking, for she saw that lethal grin broaden for a moment, before he tried, without success, to look serious again. He knew he was safe, right enough, long as he kept his distance.

She folded her arms. "You just turn yourself right

around, Trace Qualtrough, and head back to wherever you came from," she called.

No effect. That was Trace for you, handsome as the devil himself and possessed of a hide like a field ox. Now, he just tipped the brim of that sorry-looking hat and set his saddle down on the stream bank, as easily as if it weighed nothing at all. Bridget, a young widow who'd spent three months on the trail from St. Louis, with no man along to attend to the heavier chores, knew better.

"Now, Bridge," he said, "that's no way to greet an old friend."

Somewhere inside this blatantly masculine man was the boy she had known and loved. The boy who had taught her to swim, climb trees, and ride like an Indian. The boy she'd laughed with and loved with an innocent ferocity that sometimes haunted her still, in the dark of night, after more than a decade.

Bridget stood her ground, though a fickle part of her wanted to splash through the creek and fling her arms around his neck in welcome, and hardened her resolve. This was not the Trace she remembered so fondly. This was the man who'd gotten her husband killed, sure as if he'd shot Mitch himself. "You just get! Right now."

He had the effrontery to laugh as he bent to hoist the saddle up off the ground. Bridget wondered what had happened to his horse even as she told herself it didn't matter to her. He could walk all the way back to Virginia as far as she cared, long as he left.

"I'm staying," he said, and started through the knee-deep, sun-splashed water toward her without even taking off his boots. "Naturally, I'd rather I was welcome, but your taking an uncharitable outlook on the matter won't change anything."

Bridget's heart thumped against the wall of her chest; she told herself it was pure fury driving her and paced the creek's edge to prove it so. "I declare you are as impossible as ever," she accused.

He laughed again. "Yes, ma'am." Up close, she saw that he'd aged since she'd seen him last, dressed in Yankee blue and riding off to war, with Mitch following right along. There were squint lines at the corners of his blue-green eyes, and his face was leaner, harder than before, but the impact of his personality was just as jarring. Bridget felt weakened by his presence, in a not unpleasant way, and that infuriated her.

Mitch, she thought, and swayed a little. Her bridegroom, her beloved, the father of her three-year-old son, Noah. Her lifelong friend—and Trace's. Mitch had traipsed off to war on Trace's heels, like a child dancing after a piper, certain of right and glory. And he'd died for that sweet, boyish naïveté of his.

"I've got nothing to say to you," Bridget said to him.

He took off his hat and swiped it once lightly against his thigh, in a gesture that might have been born of either annoyance or simple frustration, the distinction being too fine to determine. "Well," he replied, in a quiet voice that meant he was digging in to outstubborn her, should things come to that pass, "*I've* got plenty to say to *you,* Bridget McQuarry, and you're going to hear me out."

His gaze strayed over her shoulder to take in the cabin, such as it was. The roof of the small stone structure had fallen in long before Bridget and Skye, her younger sister, and little Noah had finally arrived at Primrose Creek just two months before, after wintering at Fort Grant, a cavalry installation at the base of the

Sierras. Right away, Bridget had taken the tarp off the Conestoga and draped it over the center beam, but it made a wretched substitute. Rain caused it to droop precariously and often dripped through the worn cloth to plop on the bed and table and sizzle on the stove.

Trace let out a low whistle. "I didn't get here any too soon," he said.

Just then, Skye came bounding around the side of the cabin, an old basket in one hand, face alight with pleasure. She was sixteen, Skye was, and all the family Bridget had left, except for her son and a pair of snooty cousins who'd passed the war years in England. No doubt, Christy and Megan had been sipping tea, having themselves fitted for silken gowns, and playing lawn tennis, while Bridget and their granddaddy tried in vain to hold on to the farm in the face of challenges from Yankees and Rebels alike.

Good riddance, she thought. The last time she'd seen Christy, the two of them had fought in the dirt like a pair of cats; they'd been like oil and water the whole of their lives, Christy and Bridget, always tangling over something.

"Trace!" Skye whooped, her dark eyes shining.

He laughed, scooped her into his arms, and spun her around once. "Hello, monkey," he said, with a sort of fond gruffness in his voice, before planting a brotherly kiss on her forehead.

Bridget stood to one side, watching and feeling a little betrayed. She and Skye were as close as two sisters ever were, but if you looked for a resemblance, you'd never guess they were related. Just shy of twenty-one, Bridget was small, with fair hair and skin, and her eyes were an intense shade of violet, "Irish blue," Mitch had called them. She gave an appearance of china-doll fragility, most likely because of her diminutive size, but this was deceptive; she was as agile and wiry as a panther cub, and just about as delicate.

Skye, for her part, was tall, a late bloomer with long, gangly legs and arms. Her hair was a rich chestnut color, her wide-set eyes a deep and lively brown, her mouth full and womanly. She was awkward and somewhat dreamy, and though she was always eager to help, Bridget usually just went ahead and did most things herself. It was easier than explaining, demonstrating, and then redoing the whole task when Skye wasn't around.

"You'll stay, won't you?" Skye demanded, beaming up at Trace. "Please, say you'll stay!"

He didn't so much as glance in Bridget's direction, which, she assured herself impotently, was a good thing for *him.* "I'm not going anywhere."

Behind the cabin, in the makeshift corral Bridget had constructed from barrels and fallen branches, the new horse neighed. He was her one great hope of earning a living, that spectacular black and white paint. She'd swapped both oxen for him, barely a week before, when a half dozen Paiute braves had paid her an alarming visit. His name, rightfully enough, was Windfall, for she'd certainly gotten the best of the trade. Granddaddy would have been proud.

People would pay good money to have their mares bred to a magnificent horse like Windfall.

Her little mare, Sis, tethered in the grassy shade of a wild oak tree nearby, replied to the stallion's call with a companionable nicker.

A muscle pulsed in Trace's jaw. Even after all that time and trouble, flowing between them like a river, she could still read him plain as the *Territorial Enterprise*. If there were horses around, Trace was invariably drawn to them. He was known for his ability to train untrainable animals, to win their trust and even their affection. All of which made her wonder that much more how he'd come to be walking instead of riding.

"Where's the boy?" he asked. "I'd like to see him."

Bridget sighed. Maybe if he got a look at Noah, he'd leave. If there was any justice in the world, the child's likeness to his martyred father would be enough to shame even Trace into moving on. "He's inside, taking his nap," she said shortly, and gestured toward the cabin.

"What happened to your horse?" Skye wanted to know. Skye had many sterling traits, but minding her tongue wasn't among them.

"That's a long story," Trace answered. He was already on his way toward the open door of the cabin, and Skye hurried along beside him. "It ends badly, too." He paused at the threshold to kick off his wet boots.

"Tell me," Skye insisted. Her delight caused a bittersweet spill in Bridget's heart; the girl had been withdrawn and sorrowful ever since they'd buried Granddaddy and headed west to claim their share of the only thing he'd had left to bequeath: a twenty-five-hundred-acre tract of land in the high country of Nevada, sprawled along both sides of a stream called Primrose Creek. Too much loss. They had all seen too much loss, too much grief.

Trace stepped over the high threshold and into the tiny house, just as if he had the right to enter. The place was twelve by twelve, reason enough for him to move on, even if he'd been an invited guest. Which, of course, he wasn't. "He took off," he said. "Nothing but a knot-head, that horse."

Bridget, following on their heels, didn't believe a word of it, but she wasn't about to stir up another argument by saying so. Trace would have known better than to take up with a stupid horse, though she wasn't so sure about his taste in women. He'd probably lost the animal in a game of some sort, for he was inclined to take reckless chances and always had been.

Noah, a shy but willful child, so like Mitch, with his wavy brown hair and mischievous hazel eyes, that it still struck Bridget like a blow whenever she looked at him, sat up in the middle of the big bedstead, rubbing his eyes with plump little fists and then peering at Trace in the dim, cool light.

"Papa," he said. "That's my papa."

A strained silence ensued. Bridget merely swallowed hard and looked away. She would have corrected her son, but she didn't trust herself to speak.

Trace crossed the small room and reached out for the boy, who scrambled readily into his arms. The little traitor.

"Well," Trace said, his voice thick with apparent emotion. "Hullo, there."

"He calls everybody 'Papa,'" Bridget blurted, and then, mortified, turned to the stove and busied herself with pots and kettles, so Trace wouldn't see her expression.

Trace chuckled and set his hat on the boy's head, covering him to the shoulders, and Noah's delighted giggle echoed from inside. "Does he, now?"

"Some of the folks in town think Bridget is a fallen woman," Skye announced. "On account of her name still being McQuarry, even though she was married to

Mitch. I told her she ought to explain how he was a distant cousin, but—"

"*Skye,*" Bridget fretted, without turning around. It was too early to fix supper, and yet there she was, ladling bear fat into a pan to fry up greens and onions and what was left of the cornmeal mush they'd had for breakfast.

Trace came to stand beside her, her son crowing in his arms, evidently delighted at being swallowed up in a hat. "He sure does take after Mitch," Trace said. His voice was quiet, low.

Bridget didn't dare even to glance up at him. "More so every day," she agreed, striving for a light note. "I wouldn't say he's easygoing like Mitch was, though. He's got himself a strong will, and something of a temper, too."

"That," Trace said, "would have come from you."

"Skye," Bridget said crisply, as though he hadn't spoken, "go and catch a chicken if you can. And take Noah with you, please."

Skye obeyed without comment, though she might reasonably have pointed out that the two tasks just assigned were in direct conflict with each other. Noah protested a bit, though, not wanting to be parted from Trace—or, perhaps, his hat.

Then they were alone in the small, shadowy space, side by side. Bridget could feel Trace's gaze resting on her face, but meeting his eyes took some doing. Every time she looked at him, it weakened her somehow, made her want to sit down and fan herself like some scatter-brained girl at a cotillion.

"Why did you come here?" she demanded.

His expression was solemn and, at the same time,

intractable. "Because I promised Mitch I would," he said. "Two days before he was drowned, he got your letter telling him Noah had been born. He was happy, of course, but it was hard for him, being so far away. After a while, he turned reflective." Trace paused, rubbed the back of his neck with one hand. "He made me swear I'd look after you, if he didn't make it home."

Bridget knew the details of Mitch's drowning—Trace had described the scene to her in a letter, his words so vivid that she sometimes forgot that she hadn't been there, hadn't witnessed the tragedy herself—but the mention of his death brought stinging tears to her eyes all the same. "Damn you," she whispered. "Haven't you done enough?"

He took the spatula from her hand and, grasping her shoulders gently, turned her to face him. "What the devil do you mean by that?" he demanded in a hoarse whisper.

"You *know* what I mean," Bridget hissed back. "If it hadn't been for you, Mitch would never have gone to war. Noah and I wouldn't have to make our way without him. How dare you come here, like some storybook knight in shining armor, when—when—"

"When it was all my fault?" he asked in that same low tone. The words were knife-sharp, for all their softness, honed to a dangerous edge.

It was no use trying to hide her tears, so she didn't make the attempt. For some reason, it seemed all right to cry in front of Trace, though she'd taken great care in the years since the war began to make sure she was alone when she could no longer control her emotions. "Yes!" she cried. *"Yes! Mitch wasn't like you. He was guileless and sweet, and he believed everyone else was just as good, just as honest, just as kind. He would have done practically anything you asked him to, and *damn you*, Trace, you had to know that!"

Trace shoved a hand through that shaggy, light-streaked hair of his. He needed barbering in the worst way, clean clothes, and a bath, too, and for all that, Bridget felt the ancient shame, the powerful, secret pull toward him. She had never confessed that weakness to anyone, could barely acknowledge it to herself.

"Mitch had a mind of his own," he rasped. In his eyes, the ghosts of a hundred fallen soldiers flickered, one of them his best friend from earliest memory. "You make him sound like some kind of idiot. I didn't make him join the fight—he knew it was something he had to do. Hell, we all did."

They stared at each other for a long moment, like winter-starved bears fixing to tie in, tooth and claw. The air seemed to buzz and crackle at Bridget's ears, and she could feel her own heartbeat thundering in every part of her body. She told herself it was anger and nothing else. *Nothing else.*

"He had a wife and a child," she said finally. Shakily. "Granddaddy needed him on the farm. *We* needed him."

"Sweet Lord in heaven, Bridget," Trace reasoned with weary patience, "just about *everybody* had to leave something or someone behind, Federals and Rebs alike. Did you think you were the only one who made sacrifices?"

Sacrifices? What did he know about sacrifices, with his ready smile and the whole of his life still ahead of him? Bridget wanted to slap the man, but she managed to hold on to her dignity. It wouldn't do to set a bad example for Skye and Noah by resorting to violence, however great the temptation. She sniffed. "I should have known that you wouldn't accept responsibility."

He leaned in until his nose was barely an inch from hers. His eyes seemed to flash with blue and green sparks. "I'll 'accept responsibility' for anything that's my doing," he snapped, "but I'll be *damned* if I'll let you blame the whole war on me!"

"I don't see how you can stop me," Bridget pointed out. "And I'll thank you not to use profane language in my house."

Color surged up Trace's neck and flared along his beard-stubbled jaw. "You haven't changed, you know that?" And then, just as suddenly as his whole countenance had turned to fury, he grinned, all jovial good nature. "It's good to know that some things—and some people—stay the same."

Bridget was reconsidering her previous decision not to slap him. "You can't stay here," she insisted. "It's simply out of the question." She looked around at the humble dwelling, with its dirt floor and oil-barrel cookstove, perhaps a little desperately. Even the bed had been scavenged along the westward trail, left behind by some other family. "This place is hardly big enough for Skye and Noah and me as it is—there'll be talk in town—"

"I'll make camp down by the creek," he said. "And if folks have anything to say about my being here, you just send them to me." He heaved a sigh. "Now, I think I'll go out and have a look at those horses of yours, if that's all right with you."

"As if you cared one whit about my opinion on anything," Bridget huffed.

He was still grinning. It was an unfair advantage,

that disarming smile of his, bright as noonday sun spilling across clear water. "I've missed you," he said, and then he turned, and when Bridget let herself look, he was gone.

Damned if it wasn't Sentinel, his own horse, penned in behind Bridget's tumbledown shack of a house. At the sight of Trace, the stallion tossed his head and ambled over to greet him with a hard nuzzle to the shoulder.

Trace stroked the stallion's white-splashed brow and spoke in a low voice. "I was afraid our paths might never cross again, fella," he confided. The goose egg on the back of his head pulsed, a reminder of the morning ten days before, when a pack of renegade Paiutes had jumped him in camp. One of them had knocked him out cold, probably with the butt of an army rifle, before he had time to think, but he supposed he ought to be grateful they hadn't relieved him of his boots, saddle, and watch while he was still facedown in the dirt. Not to mention his hair.

Sentinel blew affectionately, and Trace chuckled. "Looks like Miss Bridget's gone to no little trouble to keep you here," he observed, looking askance at the flimsy arrangement of branches and barrels posing as a corral fence. "I guess we oughtn't to tell her you could have gotten out of this with one good kick. You were waiting for me, weren't you, boy?"

Again, the horse nickered, as if to reply in the affirmative.

Trace glanced toward the house; even from outside, he could hear Bridget banging pots and kettles around. He turned his head, saw Skye and Noah chasing a squawking chicken around in the high grass, and smiled at the sight. *You did good, Mitch,* he thought. *He's a fine boy, your Noah.*

"Skye!" Bridget called. She was probably in the dooryard, but Trace couldn't see her for the cabin. "Stop that nonsense before you run the meat right off that bird!"

Trace looked heavenward. *I'll do my best,* he promised. Then he turned back to the horse and patted its long, glistening neck. "You and I, we'll just pretend we're strangers for a while," he said quietly.

The paint pawed the ground with one foreleg and flung his head, but Trace knew he'd go along with the plan, insofar as a horse could be expected to do.

Obediently, Skye closed in on the chicken and held it in both arms, and even from that distance, Trace could make out the bleak expression in her eyes. He moved toward her.

"I don't want to kill it," she confessed, and bit her lower lip. When she grew to be a woman—she was still just a girl in Trace's eyes, and maybe she always would be—she would make some lucky man an exceptional wife.

"I'll do it," he said. "You take the boy inside before he meets up with a rattler."

Skye nodded and smiled up at him with her eyes. "Thanks, Trace," she said softly, and leaned down to take Noah's small hand. Then, tentatively, she touched Trace's arm. "I'm glad you're here. Bridget is, too, even if she can't make herself admit it. You won't let her run you off, will you?"

He glanced toward the cabin, with its pitiful canvas roof. Bridget had gone back inside to slam things around some more. That woman was hell on hardware. "She always make this much noise when she cooks?"

Skye laughed and shook her head. "No, sir. That particular commotion is in your honor for sure and certain," she said, and set off through the high, sweet grass, the boy scrambling along behind her.

That night, sitting on stumps and crates under a black sky prickled with stars, they ate fried chicken for supper, along with cornmeal cakes and greens, and Trace could not recall a finer meal. He probably hadn't had home-cooked food since before he joined the army, though he'd developed a taste for it as a boy. All the while he was growing up, he'd eaten with the McQuarrys whenever he was invited, which was often. Even back then, before she picked up and left, his mother hadn't troubled herself much where such things were concerned. Tillie Qualtrough had been a loose woman, plain and simple, and she'd taken to camp following long before the war came and made a profitable enterprise of the habit.

All things taken into consideration, though, he couldn't see any sense in faulting Tillie for the choices she'd made. She'd been alone in the world, with nothing to trade on but her looks. She'd done what she had to, that was all, and despite her circumstances, which would have turned a lot of people bitter, she'd been kind-hearted and quick to laugh.

"That's a fine stallion you've got there," Trace observed, when he'd eaten all he decently could. It seemed a safe topic to him, unrelated as it was to Mitch or to his staying on at Primrose Creek. "Where'd you get him?"

Bridget's face softened at the mention of the animal;

ever since she was a little girl, she'd loved critters the way some people do art or music or going to church. "I swapped the oxen for him," she said, obviously proud of the deal. "I mean to breed him to my mare, Sis, and some others and eventually start myself a horse ranch."

Trace raised his blue enamel coffee mug to his mouth, more because he wanted to hide his smile than because he needed any more of the brew. He'd be awake half the night as it was, remembering. Regretting. "I see," he said. "I guess you wouldn't consider plain farming."

She sat up straight on the crate she'd taken for a chair, her half-filled plate forgotten on her lap. "Farming," she scoffed. "This is timber country. Mining country. *Ranch* country."

"We've got a nice vegetable patch, though," Skye put in, and there was an anxious note in her voice, putting Trace in mind of somebody stepping between two opposing forces in the faint hope of keeping them from colliding. "Potatoes. Squash—" Her words fell away, like pebbles vanishing down the side of a precipice.

"You might not turn a profit for some time," Trace observed, watching Bridget. "How do you intend to eat this winter?"

He knew he'd touched a nerve, for all that she tried to disguise the fact with her trademark bravado. "We might sell some of the timber. Mr. Jake Vigil is building a house and a sawmill at the edge of town, and he'll be wanting trees."

Trace assessed the towering ponderosa pines and firs surrounding them, blue-black shadows marching as far as the eye could see, in every direction. "Doesn't look to me like he'd have any trouble getting all the lumber he want-

ed," he said. He didn't mean there wouldn't be a market
for McQuarry timber—not exactly, anyway—but Bridget
took it that way and ruffled her feathers like a little par-
tridge, making it necessary to take another sip of coffee.

"We have flour and salt. We have a shotgun for hunting, and thanks to a friend in town, we've got enough
chickens to provide eggs and"—she looked down at her
food—"the occasional feast. We will do just fine, thank
you."

Trace suppressed a sigh. He'd known this encounter wouldn't be easy, but he'd been afoot for the
best part of a week, and before that he'd spent so
much time in the saddle that for a while there, he'd
thought he might turn bow-legged. He was in no
mood to grapple with a stiff-backed little spitfire like
Bridget McQuarry.

You promised, Mitch's memory reminded him.

Yes, damn it, I promised. And I'll keep my word.

"I'll need some timber for that roof," he said in
measured tones. "You have a saw? An ax, at least?"

Bridget pursed her lips, just briefly, but she looked
pretty, even in a sour pose. Motherhood lent her a softness of the sort a man can't really help noticing, no matter how hard he might try. "We can build our own roof,"
she said. "Skye and I will do it ourselves."

Trace rolled his eyes, but he kept a hold on his
patience. Skye offered no comment but busied herself
gathering up a fretful Noah and herding him inside to be
swabbed down and put to bed. "And a fine job you've
done, too," he said dryly, nodding to indicate the canvas
stretched across the top of the house. "Roof building, I
mean."

Even in the thickening twilight, he saw her color

heighten. It made something grind painfully, deep inside him, seeing that. Instead of speaking, though, she just got up and started collecting the tin plates.

"Why can't you just admit that you need help?" he asked, very quietly.

She straightened, and he saw—or thought he saw— tears glimmering in her eyes. "Oh, I can admit that, Mr. Qualtrough," she said. "I've got a child and a young sister to feed and clothe. I have this house and this land and two horses and nothing else. I need help, all right. I just don't need it from you."

He sighed again. "You hate me that much?"

"No," she answered, stiffening that ramrod spine of hers. "I'm completely indifferent."

"You have to have a roof, Bridget. My being here would mean protection for Skye and Noah, if you won't accept it for yourself. And somebody has to train that stallion. You're good with horses, you always were, but you're too small to handle him, and you know it."

She was silent.

He pressed the advantage. "This is what Mitch wanted," he said reasonably. "How can I ignore that? How can you?"

The plates rattled in her hands, and she wouldn't look at him. "You'll train the stallion—put on a roof— build a barn?"

"That and more," he agreed.

She caught her upper lip between her teeth, something she'd done ever since he could remember. And that was a long time, since the McQuarry farm had bordered the little patch of no-account land where Trace and his mother had lived in what had once been slave quarters.

"No. Nothing more. You do those things, and we'll be all right. It'll ease your conscience, and you'll move on like you ought."

He stood, faced her, cupped her chin in one hand. "What are you so scared of, Bridge?" he asked. "You must know you have nothing to fear from me, not on your account and not on Skye's."

Her eyes flashed in the starlight; for a moment, he thought she was going to insult his honor by saying she *was* afraid of him, but when it came down to cases, she nodded. "I know that," she whispered. "It's just that— well, every time I look at you, I think of Mitch. I think of how he might have stayed home—"

Trace let her chin go. "Stayed home and done what?" he asked, at the edge of his patience. "Planted cotton and corn and sweet potatoes? Milked cows?"

Bridget pulled away. "There is no use in our discussing this," she said, her tone on the peevish side. Then she snatched the coffee mug out of his hand, turned, and strode toward the cabin. If the boy hadn't been asleep by then, or close to it, anyway, he knew she'd have slammed the door smartly behind her.

He watched as the lanterns winked out inside the house, first one, and then the other, and the sight gave him a lonely feeling, as if he were set apart from everything warm and sweet and good. It wasn't the first time he'd felt like that; as a boy, he'd yearned to be one of the McQuarrys, instead of some long-gone stranger's illegitimate son. During the war, far from the land and the people he knew, he'd ached inside, ached to go back to the Shenandoah Valley. After Mitch was drowned in the river that day, his horse shot out from under him, things had been a whole lot worse.

For a long time, he just sat there, mourning. Then, slowly, he turned his back on the cabin and headed for the makeshift camp he'd set up a hundred yards away, in the shelter of several tall oak trees growing alongside the creek. Rummaging in his saddlebags, he got out his spare shirt and a sliver of yellow soap. He kicked off his boots, still damp from his crossing earlier in the day, and then, downstream a little way, where he was sure he was out of sight of the house, he shed his clothes and waded, teeth chattering, into the icy waters of Primrose Creek. He made necessarily quick work of his bath, dried off with his dirty shirt, and pulled his trousers back on, his mind occupied, the whole time, with Bridget.

God only knew what she'd say when he told her they were getting married.

Chapter

2

Bridget did not receive the news with any discernible grace.

"Married?" She whooped, the next morning, as though he'd asked her to walk the ridgepole of a barn with a milk bucket balanced on her nose. She was poking around in the grass, looking for eggs and carefully setting the ones she found into an old basket. "Why, I'd sooner be tied to the hind legs of a bobcat and chewed free again."

He felt himself flush hotly, from the neck up. Some women—lots of them, maybe, given the number of men killed on both sides of the war—would have counted him good husband material. After all, he was still young at twenty-four, and he was no coward, no shirker, no stranger to hard work. He had a few dollars in good federal gold hidden in the bottom of one saddlebag, and he cut a fine figure, if he did say so himself. Once, he thought, with a rueful glance toward the pitiful corral, where the stallion watched him even then, he'd even had a pretty good horse.

She smiled, no doubt amused to see him tangled in his own tongue. "I thought you'd have started on the roof by now," she said. She shaded her eyes and looked up at the sky, assessing it as if it had something to prove to her. "We're burning daylight, you know. Breakfast will be ready in half an hour."

He swallowed hard and finally got past the lump in his throat. "I've got the ring," he said, and produced the small golden band from the pocket of his trousers as proof. It caught the early-morning sunshine as he held it up for her to see, a small and perfect circle, gleaming between his thumb and index finger.

She bent, picked up an egg, inspected it solemnly, frowned, and then threw it. It smacked against the trunk of a nearby birch tree. "You never did lack for confidence," she observed lightly, without looking at him. Her whole countenance was telling him she'd already lost interest in anything he had to say. "You can take that ring, Trace Qualtrough, and—" Just then, Noah exploded through the cabin doorway, half dressed—and the wrong half, at that—with Skye in pursuit. Bridget straightened to face Trace again. "And give it to someone else."

"I don't plan on marrying anybody else," he rasped. It was a private conversation, and he didn't want Noah and Skye to overhear. "You're going to be my wife, and I'm going to be your husband, and that, damn it all to hell, is the end of it!"

Bridget spoke through clenched teeth and a brittle smile. Skye captured Noah and hauled him back inside. "While it may be true, Mr. Qualtrough, that women have few, if any, legal rights in this country, if they can be forced into making wedding vows, I have yet to hear of it!"

He leaned down, caught the fresh-air, green-grass, lantern-smoke scent of her. Indignant as he was at the moment, and he was fit to yell, it was all he could do not to wrench her up onto her toes and kiss her, good and proper. Fact was, he'd wanted to do exactly that ever since she turned thirteen and started pinning her hair up, had even given in to the temptation once. "You're mighty choosy, it seems to me, for a woman alone in Indian country!" He'd struck his mark, he could see that by the brief widening of her blue eyes, but he wasn't proud of the victory.

"If you want a wife," she retorted, for she'd always been one to regroup quickly, "then go into town and find yourself one. Let's see—there's Bertha, the store-keeper's sister. She's twice your size, has a beard, and speaks nothing but German, but I imagine she can cook. Or maybe you'd like Shandy Wheaton. She's pock-marked, poor thing, missing a few teeth. But then, you're pretty enough for the both of you."

If he hadn't been standing right at the tips of Bridget's toes already, he'd have taken another step toward her. "Now, you listen to me. Mitch was the best friend I ever had. I would have died in his place if I'd been given the choice. He asked me to look out for you and Noah, and out here that means marrying you, ornery though you may be. So you might just as well get used to the idea, Bridget: you'll be wearing this ring before the leaves change colors!"

She glared at him for a long moment. He really thought she was going to slap him, and he would have welcomed the blow, if only because it would break the tension. Instead, she simply turned her back on him and stormed toward the cabin.

He swore under his breath, kicked up a clod of dirt, and went to the creek's edge, where he crouched to splash water on his face. The wedding band, back in his pocket, seemed to burn right through the fabric of his pants, like a tiny brand. Any sensible man would reclaim his horse, leave what money he had with Bridget, and ride out without looking back, but Trace wasn't just any man, and where Bridget was concerned, he wasn't particularly sensible, either.

Still sitting on his haunches beside the stream, skin and hair dripping, he turned his gaze toward the house, squinting against the polished-brass glimmer of the summer sun. *I've never given up on anything in my life,* he told Bridget silently, *and I'm not going to start now.*

Skye was perched on an upturned crate at the table, which had once been a spool for wire cable, her chin propped in one hand, her eyes misty with dreams. "I'd marry Trace if he asked me," she said. Bridget hadn't told her about the ridiculous proposal; she'd evidently been spying. If the child had one besetting sin, it was that: she was a snoop.

"Nonsense. You're just sixteen—far too young to be a bride."

"You were only seventeen when you married Mitch."

"I was—" Bridget's voice snagged in her throat. *I was too young. I had a head full of dreams and fancies.* She sighed. *I wanted to keep Mitch from going to war.*

Fortunately, before Skye could pursue the subject further, Trace rapped at the door and stepped inside without waiting for a by-your-leave. Just like him.

"Mornin', monkey," he said, ruffling Skye's hair. Noah stood a few feet away, watching him shyly, but with a hopeful expression in his eyes that hurt Bridget's heart. "Hullo, cowboy," Trace said.

Noah beamed. "Hullo," he replied in a staunch little voice. "Do you have a horse? You can't be a cowboy if you don't got a horse."

Out of the corner of her eye, Bridget saw Trace's gaze slide in her direction, glance off again. "No, sir," he said, squatting down to look into Noah's face. "I reckon I can't. Need some cows, too, if you're going to be particular about it."

Noah frowned. "We got horses. Two of them. But Mama gets our milk from town, so we don't have no cows."

"We don't have *any* cows," Bridget corrected automatically. Perhaps Noah was destined to be raised in the wilderness, with few playmates and little opportunity for culture, but that didn't mean he had to grow up to be an unlettered ruffian. She had had tutors during her girlhood on the prosperous McQuarry farm, as had Skye and their cousins, Megan and Christy, and she'd saved her schoolbooks, brought them along so she could teach her son to read and write when the time came.

"That's what I *said*, Mama," Noah replied, with an air of worldly patience. "We don't have no cows."

Trace laughed and mussed Noah's hair. Skye grinned, her eyes shining. And Bridget turned her back on all of them and made herself very busy with breakfast.

Trace dragged one arm across his brow and then glanced ruefully at the resultant sweat and grime. There ended the sorry story of his spare shirt; he'd head into town, once he'd finished sawing down and trimming the large cedar tree he'd chosen for roof lumber, and outfit himself with some new clothes. If he didn't, he'd soon have little choice but to strip himself bare, soap up his duds, and walk around in the altogether until they'd dried. The image made him grin—it was almost worth doing, it would annoy Bridget so much.

Finally, the cedar was ready to come down. After making sure no one was close by, he gave it a hard shove and watched as it fell gracefully to the ground, lushly scented, limbs billowing like a dancer's skirts. He mourned the tree's passing for a moment, then set aside the ax, took up a saw with Gideon McQuarry's initials carved into the handle, and began the pitch-sticky job of cutting away branches.

As he worked, he thought of the old man, Bridget and Skye's grandfather, and smiled. Gideon had been as much an original creation as Adam in the Garden, a tall, lanky man with eyes that missed very little and a mind that missed even less. Most of the time, his manner had been gruff, even abrupt, and yet there'd been a well of kindness hidden in that crusty old heart. Gideon had taught Trace to ride and shoot, right along with Mitch and later Bridget as well. By that time, Gideon's beloved wife, Rebecca, had passed on, and his two sons—J.R., Bridget and Skye's father, and Eli, Megan and Christy's—had fought a duel over the same mistress and accomplished nothing except to inflict each other with duplicate shoulder wounds and permanently alienate their wives. They'd gone their separate ways that very day, Eli and J.R. had, and Gideon had said he was glad Rebecca hadn't lived to see her own sons make fools of themselves in front of the whole county. Then he'd wiped his eyes on the sleeve of his shirt and turned his back to the road.

Bridget's mother, Patricia, always given to the vapors, weakened after that and eventually died. Jenny, who was Megan and Christy's mother, showed more spirit; she hooked up with a rich Englishman, applied for a divorce on grounds of desertion and disgrace, and left Virginia behind forever.

Gideon had grieved anew over that parting, not because of Jenny's going, for he'd never thought she had much substance to her character on any account, but because he feared he would never see Megan and Christy again. And he'd been right, as it turned out. When Trace had finally returned to Virginia, after a year spent flat on his back in an Atlanta hospital, recovering from a wound that nearly cost him a leg, he'd found Gideon dead and buried beside Rebecca. Eli and J.R. had been there, too, one having died for the Union cause, one for the Confederate. Bridget, long since widowed, had packed up the wagon, according to the neighbors, and headed west to Nevada, bound for a place called Primrose Creek, to claim her and Skye's share of the land Gideon had left them. The once-thriving farm, home to the McQuarry family since the Revolutionary War, had fallen into the hands of strangers.

Trace stopped swinging the ax to wipe his brow again and was grateful when he saw Skye coming toward him with a bucket and a ladle.

"I thought you might be thirsty," she said.

He chuckled hoarsely. He *was* thirsty. He was also relieved to turn his thoughts from the devastation he'd seen in Virginia. With Gideon and Mitch both dead, Bridget gone, and the big house at once forever changed and eternally the same, in his memory at least, it had seemed to him that the whole of creation ought to creak to a halt, like an old wagon wheel in need of greasing. It had been a while before he'd set out to find his best friend's wife and honor what he considered a sacred promise.

"Thanks," he said, and took a ladle full of water. He drank that and spilled a second down the back of his neck.

Skye looked as if she were working up her courage for something; he knew that expression. Skye had been tagging along behind him and Bridget and Mitch ever since she could walk. He braced himself.

"If Bridget won't have you," she said, all in a rush, "then I will."

Whatever he'd been expecting the child to say, that hadn't been it. For a few moments, he just gaped at her, while his mind groped for words that wouldn't inflict some hidden and maybe lasting wound. "If you were a few years older," he said, finally, "I'd be glad to take you up on that offer. Time you finish growing up, though, I'll just be old Trace. You'll have a dozen fellas singing under your window every night of the year."

Her lower lip trembled, and her eyes darkened. "You don't want me," she accused.

Don't cry, he pleaded silently. *Please, don't cry.* He could not bear it when a female broke down and wept.

"No," he said, because he couldn't think of anything else to say. "No, honey, I don't want you. And if I did, somebody would have to shoot me."

She bit her lower lip, looked away, looked back with a challenge snapping in her eyes. She had the same passion in her as Bridget did, he thought, the same fire. He could imagine a legion of boys and men warming up for their serenades.

By force of will, he kept himself from grinning at the picture. He took another ladle of water from the bucket, which she'd set at his feet, and drank, watching her over the enamel brim.

Skye put her hands on her hips. "You don't want to marry Bridget because of any promise to Mitch," she said. "You've loved her all along. Even when your closest friend was courting her. Even when she was his wife—"

"That will be enough," he interrupted. It wasn't true. He'd liked Bridget, that was all. And sure, he'd thought she was pretty. But love? He knew better than to fall into a trap like that.

Skye blinked, then thrust out her chin. "I saw you kiss her, the day before the wedding, in the kitchen garden."

He couldn't refute that charge; he hadn't known anyone else was around, and neither had Bridget. He'd kissed her, all right, and she'd kissed him back, and he wondered if she remembered. Though an excuse came readily to mind, that he'd merely been wishing Bridget a lifetime of happiness on the eve of her marriage to his friend, he didn't offer it. He would have choked on the first word, because he'd meant to do exactly what he did. To this day, he didn't know what had possessed him.

Suddenly, tears glistened in Skye's lashes, and she thrust out a disgusted sigh. "I'm sorry," she told him, and put a hand briefly to her mouth. "I shouldn't have said that."

"You shouldn't have been sneaking around eavesdropping on people, either," Trace pointed out.

"I was only twelve, for heaven's sake."

He chuckled.

She slumped a little. "I don't know what gets into me sometimes."

He pushed a dark curl back from her cheek, where it had gotten itself stuck in a stray tear. "I reckon it's all pretty normal," he said gently. "The time'll come, sweetheart, when you'll turn red to think of asking me to marry you, if you remember it at all."

She went ahead and blushed right then. "I'm already embarrassed," she said, and sat down on a nearby tree stump. "You're not going to tell anyone, are you?"

"Our secret," he promised.

She was visibly relieved, and her smile was tremulous and beautiful, like sunshine after a thunderstorm or candlelight flickering in the dark. "You're a good man. Why doesn't Bridget see that?"

"She'll come around," he said.

"Do you love her?"

Trace wondered if a tactful McQuarry had ever drawn breath. He doubted it. "I feel something. Maybe it's friendship. Maybe it's regret, because she lost a husband and I lost a good friend. Whatever it is, I reckon it might grow into love, given enough time."

Skye plunked her knobby elbows on her knobby knees and rested her chin in both palms, regarding him carefully. "Bridget cried, you know. After you kissed her that day in Grandma's garden, and she sent you away, she sat down on that old stone bench and cried till I thought I'd have to let on that I was watching and put my arm around her or something. Then Granddaddy caught me looking and pulled me back into the house by my ear. He told me that eavesdroppers always hear ill of themselves, and I had to help Caney peel potatoes all afternoon." Caney Blue was the family cook; she, too, had been gone when Trace got back to Virginia. To that day, he thought of the spirited black woman whenever he came within smelling distance of hot apple pie.

"He was quite a man, your grandfather."

Skye sighed. "I miss him so much. He was more like a daddy than Daddy ever was."

"I know," Trace answered gently. Gideon had been a father to him as well, in all the most important ways.

"You know what he was trying to do, don't you? Leaving half this land to Bridget and me and half to Christy and Megan?"

Trace nodded. "It was the greatest sorrow of his life, except for losing your grandmother, to see his family torn apart the way it was. You and Bridget and Christy and Megan have the same blood in your veins, whatever your differences might be. Gideon wanted the four of you to patch things up and get on with your lives, so he left you this land, probably figuring you'd have to get along if you were neighbors."

Skye nodded, but a melancholy aspect had overtaken her. "I don't reckon our cousins will ever come back from England. They've probably got all sorts of beaus and pretty dresses and hair ribbons." She paused, sighed dramatically. "I bet they go dancing every single night."

Trace allowed himself only the slightest smile. "Is that the sort of life you'd like to live, monkey?"

She pondered the question. "Sometimes I think it is," she confessed. Then she shrugged. "Other times, I just figure I want to stay right here forever." She took in the incredible vista of mountains and timber by spreading her arms, as if to embrace it all. "This place is beautiful, don't you think?"

It wasn't gentle, rolling Virginia, but Nevada had a magnificence all its own. It was a new place, made for a new beginning. "Yes," he said, and meant it. "This is as fine a land as God ever turned His hand to."

Quicksilver—with Bridget-like speed—Skye's agile mind careened off in another direction. "We didn't even know Granddaddy owned these twenty-five hundred acres."

Trace thought back. "I don't recall that he ever mentioned the place."

"The lawyer said he got them when an old friend defaulted on a debt. I guess that cabin we're living in now must have belonged to that poor man, whoever he was." She stood, with a resigned sigh, and smoothed her skirts. "I'd better get back. Bridget wants to work with the horse, and I promised to look after Noah so he won't try to help."

Trace had bent to put the ladle back in the bucket, and he was reaching for the ax handle when Skye's announcement stopped him in mid-motion. "What did you say?"

"I said—"

"Not the stallion," he said quickly. Damn, he should have warned them. He should have told them that Sentinel had been mistreated by his last owner, that he had injured at least half a dozen seasoned cowboys, that only he, Trace, had managed to win the animal's trust. "She wouldn't try to work with the stallion?"

"Sure she would," said Skye, sounding baffled by the question. "Why would she want to train Sis? She's been riding that mare ever since Granddaddy gave it to her for her fifteenth birthday."

Trace was already running toward the house, his

mind full of bloody, broken-bone images, leaping over fallen logs, nearly landing on his face when he caught the toe of one boot under a root, and half deafened by the sound of his own heartbeat drumming in his ears. Sentinel was a fine horse, the best, but he was dangerous and bad-tempered, too. That was surely why those thieving Paiutes had been willing to trade the critter for a pair of worn-out oxen; they hadn't been able to tame him, either. And if a pack of Indians, every one of them riding from the time they could hold on to a horse's mane, couldn't break the paint to ride, Bridget certainly wouldn't be able to do it.

"Bridget!" he yelled, as he sprinted across the meadow toward the house. Sure enough, she was standing by that matchstick corral, with a halter draped over one arm. Noah was beside her, holding on to her skirt and peering up at the horse.

She turned at the sound of her name, and, of all things to notice at a time like that, he took in the fact that she'd done something to her dress, sewn a V right up the center of the skirt and snipped it away to fashion a trouser-like get-up. He shouted her name again.

She watched him for a few moments, as though she thought he might flap his arms and take flight or something, then turned and shooed Noah away from her side. One small finger caught in his mouth, the boy went reluctantly toward Skye, who was following Trace at a much slower pace.

Bridget moved the branches that served as fence rails and approached the stallion, raising the halter. Sentinel danced backward and tossed his head. Even from that distance, Trace could see that the beast's eyes were rolled upward in either fury or panic. The last time the horse had looked like that, he'd caved in a man's rib cage with his front hooves and would have killed him if Trace hadn't interceded.

"Bridget!" Trace roared. He felt as he sometimes did in dreams, as though he were running in mud. Working hard and getting nowhere.

She turned to look at him again, and the stallion reared against the sky, his forelegs slicing at the air, and let out a long, whinnying shriek that turned Trace's blood cold as creek water.

No, he screamed, only to realize that he hadn't spoken at all. Hadn't made a sound. *No.*

When Sentinel brought his hooves down, he missed Bridget by inches. Then he reared again and sprang like a jackrabbit, straight over Bridget's head, racing wildly toward the creek. She fell, and, for a heart-stopping moment, Trace thought she'd been struck after all. Noah scrambled toward his mother, screaming, and he and Trace reached her at the same instant.

No blood. She was looking at him. Blinking. Pale.

She sat up to draw the boy into her arms and whisper into his gossamer hair. "Hush, now, darling. I'm not hurt. I'm fine." She met Trace's gaze over Noah's head and repeated herself distractedly. "I'm fine."

Trace, on one knee in the grass, felt like shaking her. At the same time, he would have given anything to pull her close and comfort her the same way she was comforting Noah. Well, sort of the same way.

"Are you out of your mind?" he spat. "That horse could have—"

"But he didn't," Bridget interrupted softly. "Catch him for me, Trace—bring him back. Please?"

He'd never been able to deny her anything, not even

when they were kids, and she knew it. "We are not through talking about this," he snapped. But then he got to his feet and went after the stallion.

He found the animal a mile downstream, high on the opposite bank, caught in a blackberry thicket. Trace spent an hour freeing the frightened horse, then led him into the water to wash off his scratched legs and pick out half a dozen more thorns. All the while, he scolded the stallion, but his voice was quiet and even, and when Trace headed back toward the cabin, Sentinel followed him, docile as an old dog.

Bridget was waiting in the dooryard, one hand shielding her eyes as she watched man and horse cross Primrose Creek.

"How did you do that?" she asked, none too graciously, either, for somebody who had done a damn fool thing like trying to put a halter on a half-wild horse.

Trace set his back teeth before answering. His boots were full of water, his pants were soaked to his thighs, and he'd nearly lost the woman he'd sworn to protect, not to mention a perfectly good stallion. He was not in a cordial state of mind. "How," he drawled, "did I do *what?*"

She retreated half a step, though she probably wasn't aware of it. "You're angry," she said. It might have been a marvel, if you went by the surprise in her voice.

"You're damned right I'm angry," he growled. "Fact is, I'm *so* angry that it would be better if you and I didn't talk just now."

"But—"

"Bridget, if I get started yelling, I don't rightly know when I'll stop again," he said, and went way out around her. Sentinel ambled along behind him, nickering a cheerful greeting as they passed the mare.

There was no sense in putting the stallion back in Bridget's corral, so Trace drove a stake into the ground and used his rope as a tether. Then, since he still didn't dare open his mouth around Bridget, he headed back to the cedar tree and swung the ax with a new vigor.

He was drenched in sweat and nearly ready to collapse when he became aware that he wasn't alone. Expecting to see Skye with another bucket of water, he was caught off-guard when he found himself facing Bridget again.

"I've made dinner," she said quietly. "You must be hungry."

He ran an arm across his mouth, inwardly testing his temper. He figured he could speak without raising his voice. "Yes," he said. Better to err on the side of caution.

"Thank you for fetching back my horse."

Trace had to bite his tongue, figuratively anyway, to keep from correcting her on the point of ownership. "We had an agreement, Bridget. *I'm* supposed to train the stallion, remember?"

She wrapped her arms around her middle, as though chilled, and sighed. "How do you do it, Trace? How do you—well—make a friend out of a wild horse the way you do?"

He felt a stab of guilt, but it was quickly quelled. If he admitted that Sentinel was his horse, he realized, she'd believe him, but she would be furious, and there would be one fewer reason for him to stay on at Primrose Creek. Her pride, at once the taproot of her strength and the source of many of her sorrows, might even prevent her from accepting further help of any sort. If he left, there was a very good chance that she and

Skye and little Noah would either freeze or starve over the coming winter. Or get themselves carried off by Indians.

"I don't know how I do it," he replied honestly. "It's a knack, I guess. Gideon used to say I was part gypsy." He gave a rueful, tilted grin and shrugged slightly, thinking of his scandalous birth. "For all I know, he was right."

Her cornflower-blue eyes widened a little; he sensed a softening in her and feared it was pity. There were things he wanted from her, it was true—their old easy camaraderie, for example—but not sympathy. "Do you ever wonder about him? Your father?"

He shook his head and folded his arms, perhaps to form a barrier of sorts. He wasn't sure. "No." That was a lie, of course. He'd wondered about him a thousand times and even asked Gideon if he knew who the man was. And Gideon had laid one big, callused hand on his shoulder and put his greatest hope and worst fear to rest in the space of two sentences. *"I'm not him,"* he'd said. *"Nor is either of my sons."*

"I heard my daddy and my uncle Eli talking about him one day. Your father, I mean. They said he was a Northerner." She paused, lowered her eyes, then met his gaze squarely. "He was killed in a bar fight when you were little."

Trace's jaw hardened painfully, and the pit of his stomach knotted. "You knew that? All this time, you knew, and you never told me?"

She spread her hands. "How could I? You had all these grand visions of how he was going to come back and marry your mother—"

He turned his back on her, on the dreams of a lonely

little boy. Flinched when he felt her hand come to rest lightly on his shoulder.

"Do you think we could start over?" she asked softly. "Oh, Trace, we were such good friends once upon a time—"

Such good friends. He'd have cut his heart out of his chest and handed it to her, if she'd asked it of him. Ironic that Skye, sixteen and innocent, had been the one to see into the dark passages of his soul with perfect clarity, and thereby forced him to see, too. If he hadn't loved Miss Skye McQuarry like a sister, he would have been furious with her.

"Trace?"

He made himself face Bridget, put out his hand. "Friends," he said, and all the while, he was conscious of the wedding band in the depths of his pants pocket—where it was likely to remain.

Chapter
3

The truce held until after the midday meal, when Trace announced that he was going to town and wanted to take Noah along with him. He'd borrow the mare, if Bridget didn't mind.

She didn't mind, not about the mare, anyway. Letting her son out of her sight, however, was evidently another thing entirely. Bridget, seated on an upturned crate across the table from Trace, straightened her spine with the same dignity she might have exhibited at home, presiding over Sunday dinner at her grandmother's fine mahogany dining table. "My son will stay right here," she said, her blue eyes snapping with challenge. "Primrose Creek is a tent town, full of saloons and inebriated drifters and loose women. Let me assure you, it is no place for a child."

Skye groaned right out loud at this pronouncement, and, out of the corner of his eye, Trace saw Noah's face fall with disappointment. If it hadn't been for those factors, he might have laughed at Bridget's statement. "The boy was born smack in the middle of a war," he pointed out reasonably. "He made the trip out here, none the worse for wear. And I hardly think you need to concern yourself that he might take up with 'loose women'—not just yet, anyhow."

Bridget glared at him. Obviously, she did not like discussing the subject of a visit to Primrose Creek in front of her son, but he wasn't about to back down without a tussle. Noah didn't belong only to her, he belonged to Mitch, too. And Mitch, Trace knew, would not have wanted his boy brought up to be timid, particularly in a place that demanded strength and courage of a person, be they man, woman, or child.

"The subject," she said, "is closed."

Trace stood up. "I'm going to town, and Noah is going with me." It was all a bluff, because if Bridget held her ground, he wouldn't override her wishes, but the issue was an important one, and he could be every bit as stubborn as she was. "I reckon we'll be back before you manage to have me arrested." With that, he carried his plate and fork to the wash basin, deposited them there, and started for the door.

Skye looked from her fuming sister to Trace and back again. "I want to go, too," she said. There was a note of shaky determination in her voice, and she stood. "May I go with you?" she asked Trace.

He nodded and extended a beckoning hand to the boy. Waited.

Noah hesitated, reading his mother carefully, then edged toward Trace.

Bridget stood, blushed furiously, and then sat down

again. "I'll expect you back here before sundown," she said.

"You could come with us," Skye suggested quickly. Trace could tell that the girl wanted to walk over and lay a reassuring hand on Bridget's shoulder, but she didn't move. "It's not far to town. You and I could walk. Maybe pick some wildflowers for the supper table—"

Bridget merely shook her head, and though she said nothing more, the look she gave Trace just before he turned away said plainly that the fires of hell itself could not surpass what she would do to him if anything happened to Noah or Skye.

Outside, he saddled the mare and helped Skye to mount, hoisting Noah up to sit in front of her. She looked confused. "I don't mind walking, Trace," she said. "I walk all over the place, all the time." She bit her lip briefly, averted her eyes for a moment, and Trace guessed by her guilty manner that she'd been to town on her own, probably on more than one occasion, with Bridget none the wiser. "I mean—"

"I know what you mean," he said sternly. "You go ahead. I'll ride the stallion."

Her eyes went wide. "But he's not even halter-broke—"

"We have an understanding, he and I," Trace said easily. Then, using Bridget's rope halter in place of a bridle, he swung up onto Sentinel's bare back and urged him forward with a feather-light motion of his knees.

Skye's mouth was wide open. "I'll be jiggered," she said. "That horse is close kin to the devil, and here you are riding him like he was a pony at a fair!"

Trace laughed. "Come on," he replied. "You heard your sister. If we're not back here by sundown, she'll hang my hide out like a hog's and scrape off the bristles."

He'd gotten a look at the settlement of Primrose Creek the day before, passing through on his way to find Bridget and the boy, but he hadn't lingered long. It was typical of mining and timber towns all across the West, with whiskey flowing free and good sense at a premium. Even armed with a .44 as he was, a man was at a distinct disadvantage without a horse under him; Trace never ran from trouble, but he wasn't one to seek it out, either.

"You stay close to me," Trace told Skye, as they both dismounted in front of the general store, a building with a temporary air about it, as though it might be planning to pick itself up some dark night and go sneaking off into the countryside. The merchandise—as well as the clientele—was visible through the cracks in the walls.

Skye nodded and turned to help Noah out of the saddle, only to find him with one small foot in the stirrup, set on getting down on his own. It gave Trace an odd sense of pride, witnessing the enterprise, as though he'd had something to do with the making and raising of this boy.

Trace waited, held out a restraining arm when Skye would have taken her nephew by the waist and set him on his feet. Then Noah was standing on the ground, gazing up at him with an expression so reminiscent of Mitch that, for a moment, his throat closed up tight. After a hard swallow and a long study of the horizon, Trace was able to look down into those bright, eager eyes again. "Now, you listen to me, boy," he said, not unkindly, but at the same time making it clear that he would brook no nonsense. "You don't go wandering off anywhere. You and I, we're partners, and we've got a lady to look after. That means we have to stick together."

Skye rolled her eyes. "I come here all the time," she hissed.

"If I catch you at it," Trace answered under his breath, "I'll paddle your backside."

Skye colored, and that reminded him of her sister. No telling how long Bridget would hold this little escapade against him, for all her pretty words about what good friends they'd been back in the old days.

"You wouldn't dare," Skye said.

"Try me," Trace responded.

The general store turned out to be remarkably well stocked for such a rustic establishment: there were blankets and boots and ready-made shirts and good denim pants, made to last. While Skye admired a shelf full of books, handling one and then another as reverently as if they'd been printed in letters of fire on Mount Olympus, and Noah squatted to brush aside some sawdust and set a red and blue striped top to spinning on the floor, Trace selected two sets of everyday clothes and set them on the counter, which was really only a pair of rough-hewn boards stretched between two fifty-gallon barrels.

The storekeeper, a burly gray-haired man with a wiry white beard, smiled broadly and greeted him in a strong German accent. Trace couldn't help thinking of the woman Bridget had mentioned, the one twice his size, and wondering if he'd get a look at her. He figured a female who didn't speak English might not be a bad bargain; a man could get some peace, keeping company with somebody like that. Unless, of course, she talked as much as most women did. It was bad enough when you could understand what they were saying. Being nagged in another language would be worse still, because there'd be no way to fight back.

"Something else for you?" the storekeeper asked, interrupting Trace's runaway train of thought. He'd said his name was Gus.

Trace indicated Skye and the boy, both lost in pursuits of their own. "We'll be wanting that toy," he said. "And one of those books, into the bargain." He paused, thought of Bridget again, remembered how she'd loved to curl up in the porch swing on a hot summer afternoon back home in Virginia and lose herself in some story or another. Times like that, he and Mitch hadn't been able to coerce her to ride or fish or climb trees with them, no matter what they said or did.

He smiled at the memory of a time when Bridget's life—all their lives—had been simple. Safe. "Better make that two," he added.

Gus beamed, pleased, and gestured toward the shelf. "You choose, yes?"

"Yes," Trace agreed, and stepped up beside Skye. "Which one?" he asked in a quiet voice.

She looked bewildered. "Which—?"

"Which book, monkey," he prompted with a grin. "Or don't you accept presents from men who turn down your marriage proposals?"

Her cheeks turned a fetching shade of pink, but she smiled. "Presents? But it isn't Christmas or anything—"

He sighed, examined the titles. For a place like Primrose Creek, the selection was impressive; obviously, not all the miners and lumbermen spent their wages on whiskey and women. "Go ahead," he said. "You can have any one you want."

She took a blue clothbound volume off the shelf

and clutched it to her chest as if she thought he might change his mind and take it away. He chose a second book, one with a bright red cover and gold print on the spine; it was a love story, and there was a horse in it. Just the kind of thing Bridget would enjoy.

"We—we had to leave Granddaddy's books when we came out here," Skye told him, and he was touched to see tears in her eyes. "All we brought with us was the Bible, the one that's got all the McQuarrys' names written inside, clear back to the first war with England. Bridget said we had to take useful things, food and blankets and warm clothes and the like—"

Trace touched her nose with the tip of his finger. "It must have been real hard, leaving home," he said.

She nodded, blinked, and looked away.

He understood about that and gave her the time and privacy to collect herself while he selected other things from the shelves: flour, yeast, sugar, coffee, and all manner of other staples. After making arrangements for Gus to bring the foodstuffs as far as the creek's edge in his buckboard, they left the general store.

A portly middle-aged man wearing a nickel-plated star on his vest was admiring the stallion. "Fine horse you've got here," he said. "Care to sell him?"

"No," Trace answered, too quickly. Then, "You'd have to speak to Bridget McQuarry is what I mean. It's her horse."

The marshall put out one hand. "My name's Flynn. Sam Flynn. I don't believe I've seen you around Primrose Creek up to now."

"Trace Qualtrough," Trace replied. "I just got here yesterday."

Flynn assessed him thoughtfully. "You just passing through?"

Trace shook his head. "I mean to tie the knot with the Widow McQuarry," he said. Might as well spread the word; it was bound to happen, after all, and folks would find out eventually, anyhow.

The lawman chuckled. "Well, now," he said. "That will come as bad news to the gentlemen of our fine town." He glanced apologetically at Skye and tugged at the brim of his hat, and Trace could have sworn the older man colored up a little, under all the beard stubble and hard experience. "I hope you don't think I meant any disrespect for your sister, miss," he went on. "It's just that she's got plenty of admirers around here, whether she knows it or not."

Skye nodded. Her eyes were twinkling when she looked at Trace. "Sounds like you've got some competition," she said.

About that time, Noah lifted one foot over a puddle of horse piss and stomped.

Skye wrinkled her nose, scooped the boy up, and set him in the mare's saddle. "Now, look at you," she fretted. "You're getting a bath as soon as we get home, Noah McQuarry. And, phew, you stink."

Trace grinned. The boy smelled, and that was a fact, but such escapades rarely proved fatal. "Glad to meet you, Marshal," he said, and, after tying the string-bound parcel containing his new clothes, the books, and Noah's top behind Sis's saddle, swung up onto Sentinel's back.

"Looks as if you might be a fair hand with a horse," Flynn observed. "There's work around here for a man who knows one end of a critter from the other."

"I've got a roof to build," Trace replied. "After that, though, I might be looking to make wages."

The marshall raised a hand in farewell. "I'll see that word gets around. Not that folks haven't already noticed you're here, of course. Don't wait too long on that wedding, Mr. Qualtrough. We're mostly men here in Primrose Creek, but there are a few ladies who've come to save our sinful souls. One or two of them might take it upon themselves to make judgments."

Skye glowered. "Those old crows," she muttered. "They'll be lucky to save their *own* souls." Trace had heard her, and he was pretty sure the marshal had, too. The lawman's smile confirmed it.

Trace grinned back. "I'll keep your words in mind," he promised, and then they headed toward home. They crossed the creek just as the setting sun was spilling crimson and orange and deep violet light over the cold, shallow waters.

Bridget was standing in the dooryard with her hands on her hips. She looked both testy and confounded; testy because she'd probably expected them to spend half the night reveling in one of the tent saloons, confounded because Trace was riding the stallion she believed to be untamed.

"Noah needs a bath," Skye said immediately. "He stepped—*stomped*—right into a puddle of—" She paused. "Well, a puddle. And Trace bought me a book, all my own. Noah got a top, and—" She glanced back at Trace, caught the look he gave her, and fell silent. He supposed she was both grateful for the book and afraid he'd tell Bridget that she'd been to Primrose Creek before on her own.

Bridget laughed and shook her head when she

caught a whiff of Noah. "Put some water on to heat," she told her sister cheerfully. "I'll scrub him down before supper."

Skye nodded and, after collecting the precious parcel from behind the mare's saddle, led the boy inside. Bridget took a light hold on the cheek piece of Sis's bridle, and, for what seemed a long while to Trace, he and Bridget just gazed at each other.

It was Bridget who broke the silence. "Noah had a good time," she said quietly. "I haven't seen his eyes shine like that since—well, since last Christmas at Fort Grant, when one of the soldiers carved a little horse for him."

Trace waited. When Bridget had something on her mind, it was better to let her have her say, all in one piece.

"He's missed having a man around," she went on, and he could tell she'd swallowed her pride, that she wanted to look away and wouldn't let herself. "I was just—I was so afraid. Of his going to town, I mean. I don't think I could bear losing him."

"It's all right, Bridget," Trace said, and, swinging one leg over the stallion's glistening neck, slid to the ground. "Noah's your son. I shouldn't have brought up the subject of going to town in front of him—it wasn't fair—and I'm sorry for that." He was standing very close to her now and wondered how he'd gotten there, since he had no memory of the steps in between. She smelled of green grass and clear creek water and supper, and her proximity filled him with a sweet, mysterious ache, partly pain, partly glory, that he did not choose to explore. "Mind you, I still think it's wrong to shelter the boy too much. Mitch wouldn't like it."

She let that pass. "You've been kind to Skye, as well as to Noah. I'm grateful for that."

He nodded an acknowledgment, held his tongue. He couldn't think of anything he wanted to say that wouldn't get her all riled up again, like as not, and he just didn't have the stamina to hold his own in a skirmish. They just stood there, for a long moment, looking at each other, thinking their own separate thoughts.

"I'll tend to Sis," she finally said, and walked away, leaving him standing there, staring after her. She had already removed the mare's saddle and bridle and left her to graze in the high grass before he took a single step. He might not have had the presence of mind to do that much if the stallion hadn't butted him between the shoulder blades and damn near knocked him to his knees.

Gus, the storekeeper, appeared on the far side of the creek, despite the settling twilight, waved a meaty hand in cheerful greeting, and began unloading boxes and bags from the back of his buckboard. Bridget smiled somewhat nervously and started toward him. She didn't have the money to pay for supplies, and she didn't dare take anything on a note of promise. She might very well need to run up a bill over the winter months, and it was vital to keep the ledger clear in the meantime.

Since Gus's last name was unpronounceable, nobody ever used it. It made for a unique sort of slap-dash familiarity that would have been improper in most any other place or situation. "Gus," she called, stopping at the edge of the creek. "What are you doing?"

"I bring you groceries, missus," he said. His face was round as a dinner plate, and his eyes were a bright, childlike blue. His white beard made him resemble St. Nicholas. "I could carry them over, but my sister, Bertha, she don't like the night dark. I got to get back to her."

Bridget was at a complete loss, but not for long. "But I didn't order groceries."

He set the last box on the rocky ground, and the buckboard tilted dangerously when he climbed up to take the reins. Bridget's heart went out to the gray mule in the harness; Gus must have weighed almost as much as he did. "Your feller, he make business with Gus. Good night, missus."

"But—"

"I tell Bertha you say hullo," he called, already headed back toward town. He didn't even turn around, just waved one big hand again, this time in farewell, and drove on.

Trace, after eating a light supper of bread and cold chicken, had gone back out to hack at the fallen cedar tree, taking a lantern along to provide the necessary light, and Skye, having washed the dishes and sung a freshly bathed Noah to sleep, was settled at the table, her head bent over the book Trace had bought her. Bridget did not want to walk into the woods—the prospect of time alone with Trace was simply too disturbing—and she wasn't about to drag Skye away from her reading.

Never one to leave work undone if there was a spare minute in her day, she sat down on the bank, unlaced her shoes, and removed them, along with her stockings. Then she tied her skirts into a big knot, roughly on a level with her knees, and waded into the creek. No sense leaving the food where it might be stolen.

One, two, three crossings, and then she was finished, and Trace was standing at the edge of the yard, watching her. She hadn't heard him approaching, hadn't seen the lantern. A guilty thrill rushed through her, seeming to come up from the ground, through her body, out the top of her head, because her legs were bare. Quickly, but not quickly enough, she untied the fabric of her skirt and shook it into place, as glad of the darkness as she'd ever been of anything. He had surely seen her limbs, but he didn't need to know about the heat in her face and the strange riot among her senses.

"You shouldn't have done this," she said.

"What?" he asked. His voice was hoarse, and he sounded honestly puzzled.

"You shouldn't have bought all this food. I can't repay you, and I don't like being obliged."

He sighed. "You're not obliged, Bridge," he said. "I'm your friend, remember? I believe it was only this morning that we agreed on that."

She couldn't be angry with him. He was generous; it was his nature. Besides, he'd made Skye and Noah so happy. "Yes," she said. "We agreed." He handed her the lantern, bent to lift one of the crates with an exaggerated grunt. "You carried this stuff across the creek? Remind me not to arm wrestle you."

Bridget laughed. "Oh, I will. If indeed the subject ever comes up."

He carried the box inside, set it on the floor beside the stove. He refused any help, over Bridget's protests, and went back for the others. Bridget occupied herself putting the treasures in their right places—sugar, coffee, flour, salt. Tea. Spices and butter. Dried peas and salt pork. Canned meats and vegetables. Two bars of soap, one for laundry, one for bathing. Kerosene for the lamps. It had been so long since she had had such luxuries, all at once, that she was very nearly overcome.

Skye didn't look up from her book even once during the entire interlude, and that made Bridget smile. She, too, had missed reading, missed it desperately. She'd been through the Bible twice since leaving home—skipping Leviticus and Lamentations both times, with apologies to the Lord—and she was ready for a story she hadn't heard, read, or been told beside a campfire. Perhaps, when Skye had been through that lovely cloth-bound volume of epic poetry two or three times, she would make Bridget the loan of it.

She became aware of Trace very suddenly, knew he was standing just inside the cabin, though she had neither heard nor seen him after he brought in the last box. A moment passed before she thought it prudent to turn around and face him.

He was there, just where she knew he'd be, his fair hair golden in the light of the lamp Skye was reading by.

Guilt swamped her, for surely the things she was feeling were sinful, especially when all tangled up with the deep and private fury he roused in her. She thought, God help her, of what it would be like to tell him her secrets, to cry, at long last, because Mitch and Granddaddy were both dead, and her home, her heritage, her birthplace, was gone forever. She wanted to confess that she'd been scared—no, terrified—more times than she could count, but she hadn't shown it, hadn't dared, because Skye and Noah had no one to depend on but her. Not even the day those Paiutes came, riding their short-legged, shaggy ponies, armed with bows and arrows and hatchets. She'd nearly swooned when she'd looked up from the clothes she was washing in the creek to see them on the other side of the water, watching her with fierce, expressionless faces.

She'd been so frightened that she hadn't even noticed the paint stallion they were leading, magnificent as he was. All she'd been able to think of was her sister and her son and all the dreadful stories she'd heard about women and children at the mercy of savages.

Then one of the men had ridden across the water and indicated the oxen, the two tired beasts who'd pulled the wagon all the way from Virginia to the mountains of Nevada, with a thrust of his spear.

"Take them," she had said. "If you want them, take them." She'd given Skye strict orders to stay out of sight if the Indians ever came, no matter what happened, to take Noah and climb out over the low place in the back wall and hide in the root cellar until she was sure it was safe to come out. Despite Bridget's explicit instructions, Skye had walked right up to Bridget's side, bold as you please, and solemnly handed her Granddaddy's shotgun. And scared as she was, Bridget had thought to herself, *She's growing up*. Then, *Oh, God, please—let her grow up*.

The Paiutes had looked askance at the shotgun, and little wonder. They were equipped with army carbines, in addition to their knives, bows, and spears. They'd spoken to one another in a quick, clipped, and guttural language, and then they'd laughed.

Bridget had cocked the shotgun. Told them to take the oxen and get out.

Miraculously, they complied, and when they went,

taking the oxen with them, they left the stallion behind. . . .

"Bridget?" The sound of Trace's voice brought her out of the disturbing reverie.

She blinked. "Oh. Yes. Yes?"

"I just wanted to say good night." Dear heaven, but he was a fine-looking man; he had always been half scoundrel, half archangel, and that had never changed.

She wet her lips and deliberately remembered Mitch. How he'd loved her. How he'd trusted her. How he'd died to defend her and Noah and all the things he'd believed in. "Good night," she said, barely breathing the word, and then the door was shut fast, and he was gone.

Bridget swallowed hard and wondered why she wanted to cover her face with both hands and weep inconsolably. To distract herself, she walked over to Skye and laid a hand lightly on her silken brown hair. "It's time to rest," she said softly. "Besides, you'll spoil your eyesight, reading for so long in such poor light."

Skye looked up, blinked. Made the transition from the world inside the pages to the one around her, the roofless cabin, the bed she shared with both Bridget and Noah, when at home she'd had a large room all her own. They all had, Skye, Christy, Megan, and Bridget herself. Oh, but everything had been so different before the war. Everything.

"What?" Skye asked.

Bridget bent to kiss the top of her sister's head. "Time to put out the lamp and go to bed," she said. "Morning will be here almost before you close your eyes."

Skye sighed dreamily. "Do you suppose Megan and

Christy have ever seen a real knight? Being in England, they might have—"

Bridget smiled. "I suppose so. But I don't think knights wear shining armor these days."

Her sister sighed again, though this time she sounded a little forlorn. "I wish we had knights. Here in Nevada, I mean."

Oddly, Bridget thought of Trace, almost said there might be one or two around. Wearing ordinary clothes, of course. Building roofs and training wild horses. "Silly," she said, and laughed. "You'll meet a nice man, when the time is right, and you won't care *that*"—she snapped her fingers—"about knights in England."

Skye looked miserable. "I asked Trace to marry me today," she said.

Bridget was taken aback. "Oh, Skye."

"I thought if you didn't want him, well, I'd take him. I mean, I think he's nice, and he's handsome, too."

Bridget was careful not to smile. "And what did he say?"

"That I'm too young. That I'll have men singing under my window someday, and that if he said yes, he ought to be shot."

Bridget bit the inside of her lower lip. "I see." She went toward the bed, unbuttoning her bodice as she walked. "Well, I'd say he was right on all counts. You are too young. You will have all manner of suitors. And I would most certainly have shot him. Come to bed, Skye. You'll have time to read tomorrow, after the chores."

"Do you think he's handsome?"

Bridget had stopped talking, stopped thinking, stopped breathing. There was a book lying on her pillow, a red leather book with golden print embossed on the cover. "Wh-what did you say?" she asked. She must have started drawing in air again at some point, she reasoned, or she wouldn't have been able to speak. Her hand trembled as she reached out for the treasure.

Skye had put out the lantern and was now standing on the opposite side of the bed, pulling on her night-dress. In the spill of moonlight seeping through the canvas roof, Bridget saw that her sister was smiling.

"He bought that for you," she said. "It's a present. I thought I'd die, waiting for you to notice."

Bridget's knees felt unsteady; she turned her back to Skye, sat down on the edge of the mattress, one hand to her mouth, the other clutching the book to her chest. She hadn't looked at the title, had no idea of the subject, but it didn't matter. It was a *book*. Tears brimmed in her eyes.

"It's a love story," Skye whispered, climbing carefully into bed, lest she awaken Noah. "Very tragic. There's a horse, and somebody dies. I'm not sure who, though I don't imagine it's the horse. It will make you cry, though."

Bridget said nothing. She was, after all, already crying, but there was absolutely no point in calling attention to the fact.

Trace, her heart called, through the darkness that separated them. *Oh, Trace.*

Chapter

4

Trace had already carried water in from the creek and gotten the fire going in the stove by the time Bridget opened her eyes the next morning. Skye and Noah were still sleeping, Skye fitfully, Noah with a sweet-dream smile touching just the corner of his small mouth.

"Morning," Trace said, quiet and gruff-voiced. It wasn't yet dawn, but his grin flashed like light off a mirror. "I was beginning to think you meant to pass the whole day right there in bed."

Bridget knew he was teasing, but she was mildly chagrined all the same. She arose quickly, pulled on her worn wrapper, and stepped into her shoes without fastening the buttons. The dirt floor was always cold until the sun got a good start, and she wasn't one for going about barefoot, anyway. There were too many perils, from sharp stones to snakebite, and a simple puncture wound from a nail or other rusted object might bring on lockjaw.

She shifted her thoughts to the bracing aroma of hot, fresh coffee scenting the crisp predawn air. She knew without looking that there was dew on the grass, for the sun was still mostly huddled behind the hills to the east, and the ground was surely hard and cold. She felt a pang of guilt for her lack of hospitality, necessary though it was.

"Did you sleep well?" she asked, taking a sip from the mug of coffee he'd poured for her.

Trace's mouth tilted upward at one corner, but his eyes were solemn, in a gentle, uncomplaining sort of way. "I've slept in worse places than green mountain grass, Bridge," he assured her.

She was filled with a swift, consuming desire to know all his experiences, large and small, and told herself it was because what Trace had endured, Mitch had, too. "Where?"

He drew a deep, slow breath and expelled it slowly. "In rocky fields. Inside the trunks of trees, under them on the ground, and up in the branches. Barns and burned-out houses and, once or twice, a chicken coop."

Bridget had already wrinkled her nose and grimaced before she realized the expression could be construed as rude. "A *chicken coop?*"

Trace chuckled, a man-sound that Bridget had sorely missed after he and Mitch and Granddaddy had all gone. "It wasn't so bad," he reflected, and this time, there was real humor in his eyes. "Fact is, we counted ourselves lucky to bunk there, given that the sky was dumping icy rain and there wasn't any other shelter for about ten miles in any direction."

She felt a small crinkle form between her eyebrows. " 'We'? Was Mitch with you?" It was so important to know, though she couldn't have explained why in a month of full moons.

He nodded. "Mitch and nine other men." A distant look entered his eyes, threw shadows. "One of them was bleeding pretty bad. We tried to keep him alive, but he was gone by morning."

Bridget touched his forearm. "I'm sorry, Trace."

"It's all right," he answered. "It's all right," he said again. But then he turned his back and went to the door to watch the sunlight spill over the waters of the creek. Bridget knew that was what he was doing because it was a spectacular, sometimes even dazzling sight, and she'd done the same on many a morning herself.

She didn't cross to him but busied herself with the assemblage of breakfast—cornmeal mush, molasses, one of the precious tins of pears Trace had bought in town the day before at Gus's mercantile. "Thank you for the book," she said, shy as a schoolgirl acknowledging a valentine. She wondered what it was about Trace that kept her off-balance, sometimes bold, sometimes reticent, and always confused. Why, if she hadn't known better, she might have thought . . .

No.

He didn't turn around, and the cool breeze felt good, filling the cabin with sweet freshness and a multitude of sounds—birds singing, the creek telling its old, old story, the horses greeting one another in snuffles and muted whinnies.

Bridget felt a swell of love for the place, rising up from the core of her being, and all of a sudden, she knew that however much she missed Virginia—and the memory of it would always be a tender bruise pressed deep into her heart—Primrose Creek was home now.

She set the cast-iron kettle on top of the stove, hoisted up one of the buckets, and filled the pot with water. She was making no effort to be quiet now, for there was work to be done, and Skye's help would be needed.

"I was glad to do it," Trace said belatedly. "I'll see to the stock while you and Skye are getting dressed." With that, he was gone.

Skye grumbled something from the direction of the bedstead, and Bridget smiled to herself. Skye was not at her best in the mornings. Noah, on the other hand, was wide awake from the instant he opened his eyes, and he was already bouncing in the middle of the straw-filled mattress.

"I didn't wet!" he crowed. "I didn't wet!"

"Good thing for you," Skye grumbled. More than once, they'd had to carry the mattress outside to air in the sunshine.

"I'm proud of you, Noah," Bridget said.

By midmorning, Bridget and Skye were toiling in the vegetable garden, and Trace's ax echoed rhythmically through the woods. Noah was sitting on the ground, spinning his top on the surface of a flat rock, and the sun was high and hot.

"Mama?" Noah said in a tone of gleeful wonder, and in the odd stillness that followed, in the space of a single heartbeat, Bridget heard it. A brief, ominous, hissing rattle. She raced toward her son, stumbling over furrows and flailing through waist-high stalks of corn, and it seemed as though she traveled a great distance in that flicker of time.

A small rattlesnake was coiled on the ground, just to Noah's left. Bridget didn't reason, she didn't scream; she simply acted on instinct. She snatched up the snake in her right hand, feeling a fiery sting midway between her wrist and elbow as soon as she did so, and hurled the creature away, into the pile of rocks to one side of the garden. The bite on her forearm burned like a splash of acid; a sickening heat surged through her body, brought out a clammy sweat. Nausea roiled in her stomach, and the ground tilted at wild angles.

"Take him inside," she gasped to Skye, swaying a little but keeping her feet. "Take Noah inside. Now!"

Skye obeyed—she was a sobbing blur to Bridget by then—and ran stumbling across the clearing, battling through brambles and high grass, shrieking Trace's name.

Bridget pulled off her sunbonnet and tried to make a tourniquet of sorts with the ties. Then she leaned over and threw up in the dirt.

Trace appeared in the throbbing, thundering void, lifted her into his arms, carried her inside to the bed.

"Lie still," she heard him say. His voice seemed to come from the far end of a long chimney pipe or the depths of a well. "Just lie still."

Bridget closed her eyes, felt herself slipping toward the darkness, and opened them again. She could not, *would not* die. Noah needed her. Skye needed her. Devil take it, she needed herself.

Trace was not part of the equation—or was he?

"It hurts," she said.

"I don't doubt that," Trace said. "And I'm about to do something that's going to hurt more. Shut your eyes, and do your best to relax."

She tried but got no further than the shutting-her-eyes part; before she could follow through and relax, something hot and sharp sliced into the swelling wound where the snake had bitten her. She swooned, for the first time in her life, and found sanctuary in the cool gloom of some strange inner landscape.

Trace loosened the tourniquet on Bridget's upper arm; he'd replaced her bonnet strings with his leather belt. He'd drawn as much of the poison as he could, and now came the hardest part. The waiting.

"Will she die?" Skye whispered. She didn't worry that Noah would overhear, for the boy had curled up on the bed beside Bridget, close as he could get, and fallen asleep. It was as though the child thought he could save his mother by holding on tight.

"No," Trace said, and it was a vow before God. "No. Bridget isn't going to die."

"It happened so fast," Skye murmured, gazing at her sister with fear-glazed eyes. "I don't know why she didn't use the hoe. She's killed a lot of snakes since we took to the trail."

"I don't reckon she took time to consider her choices, honey. She was thinking about Noah." He sat down carefully on the edge of the bed, took one of Bridget's still, pale hands in his. The sight and feel of the calluses on her palms and fingers jabbed at his awareness, made an ache behind his eyes. She'd been reared to be a lady, the well-bred and educated wife of some prosperous Virginian, with servants at her beck and call, linen sheets on her bed, fine china and silver gracing her table. Instead, she'd wound up in a broken-down cabin, all but alone in the middle of Indian country, with a lifetime of hardship and struggle ahead of her. "Is there any whiskey around here?"

Skye glared at him and set her hands—which were

probably just as work-worn as Bridget's—on her hips. "No," she said, peevish. "And this is no time to be drinking anyhow, Trace Qualtrough. I don't know what you could be thinking of."

He would have laughed if he hadn't been so afraid Bridget would never open her eyes. "It's good for cleaning wounds," he told her gently. "How about carbolic acid? Or quinine?"

She shook her head. "No," she fretted, "and there's no doctor in Primrose Creek, either. Gus might have some medicine at the mercantile, though."

The store had been well stocked, Trace reflected. He was pretty sure he'd gotten most of the venom out of Bridget's snakebite, but he didn't like to leave her. Her forehead was hot as an oven brick, and it wasn't a good sign, her not waking yet. Nonetheless, he shook his head and replied, "I'll go. You stay right here next to Bridget. Talk to her, so she knows she isn't alone." *So she won't slip away.*

Skye cast a glance toward the open door. "No," she said. "No, *I'll* go—I'll take Sis and be back in no time at all."

"Skye—" Trace began. He wasn't inclined to argue. Skye was a vulnerable young woman, and Primrose Creek was a dangerous place.

She'd backed all the way to the threshold. "You can't stop me," she said. And then she bolted.

He should have chased her, brought her back, he knew, but he was bound to Bridget somehow, as surely as if there had been a short but strong cord stretched taut between them. "Be careful," he muttered, and set his jaw when he heard Skye and the little mare crossing the creek with a lot of splashing, yelling, and whinnying.

Then he laid the back of his right hand to Bridget's forehead and thought, couldn't help thinking, what it would mean to lose her. In the hard years since he and Mitch had ridden away to war, he'd sustained himself with the simple knowledge of Bridget's existence, recalling the sound of her laughter, the fire of her temper, the deep blue of her eyes. To him, she'd symbolized everything good about home. Whatever the distance between them, real and figurative, he'd carried her with him every step of the way, a secret saint hidden away in his heart.

"Don't go," he whispered.

Her lashes fluttered, and she murmured something, but she hadn't heard him. She was wandering through the red mists of a fever, he knew, perhaps lost, seeking a way out. She would live if she could, no doubt of that. Bridget McQuarry might have been a little thing, small-boned and fragile-looking as a canary bird, but she had the spirit of a Roman warhorse.

He brushed his lips across the backs of her knuckles and settled in to keep his vigil.

She dreamed she was back in Virginia. It was twilight, and the cicadas and fireflies were out. A jagged shard of moon hung in the sky, transparent as a thin layer of mica, and the collapse of the Union was still far off, a troublesome possibility, a topic men discussed after supper, while they smoked their cigars and drank their brandy.

Bridget sat in the swinging bench on the veranda; she heard the familiar creak of the supporting chains as she rocked and dreamed. It was getting chilly, but she didn't want to go inside, not yet. She wrapped her arms around her middle and went on savoring it all: the scent of the lush flower garden her late grandmother had started as a bride, the distant lowing of the cows, and the nickering of horses. The house, a three-story structure of whitewashed wood, with green shutters at each of its many windows, brimmed with light and noise and family behind her—she heard her cousin Christy pounding doggedly at the ancient organ in the parlor, heard Skye and Megan chasing each other through the downstairs rooms, squealing with delight.

And Mitch was beside her on the swing, hidden in shadow, holding her hand. She was completely happy in those moments, though even then she knew that the sturdiest of blessings could be snatched away in the blink of an eye.

She had only to think of her grandmother's passing to be reminded that life was a fleeting and ofttimes frail gift. Rebecca had gone riding one perfect summer morning, and when Bridget saw her again, Granddaddy was carrying her across the meadow toward the house, tears shining on his face. Something had spooked Rebecca McQuarry's prize gelding; she'd been thrown and struck her head on a stone. She was already gone when Granddaddy and Uncle Eli found her.

"Bridget?"

She started a little; she'd thought Mitch was beside her, there in the swing, but the voice belonged to Trace Qualtrough. She fidgeted with the soft organza of her dress. Where was Mitch?

He took her hand, Trace did. "Don't go," he said.

Her heart flailed, like a wounded bird trying to take wing. She picked up the ivory-handled fan lying in her lap and stirred the air in front of her face, for it felt uncommonly warm all of the sudden. "Go? Don't be silly, Trace. Where would I go?"

His hold tightened on her hand, a firm grip but not a painful one. "There's nobody I care about more than you, Bridget," he said. "God help me, it's always been that way."

She frowned, but something caught up her spirit and carried it skyward in a dizzying rush. Her heart pounded, and the fan picked up speed. She started to speak, had to clear her throat and start again. "You don't mean it."

"I do mean it. Right or wrong, it's so."

Didn't he know she was going to marry Mitch? That had always been understood. Mitch needed her; he'd said so himself, a thousand times. She was his strength, she was his soul. She was his honor, and all his courage came from her. He could not imagine a life without her at his side.

"Mitch," she said, a little desperately. "I've got to marry Mitch. I promised."

"You don't love him. You know you don't."

It was true, Trace was everything to her that she was to Mitch, but she could not allow that to be so. She'd long since decided that. "No," she whispered. "Please— no."

If he'd kissed her then, she would have been lost, but he didn't. He touched her hand to the side of his face, held it there lightly for a mere moment and for the length of eternity, and then he stood up, said good night, and walked away without looking back.

And there would be another time when he didn't come back. A time when she needed him more than she ever had or ever would. A time when he'd failed her.

*   *   *

"Bridget?" She didn't open her eyes, though he sensed that she was beginning to awaken. Skye had gone to town and returned with both whiskey and carbolic acid, bought from Gus on credit, and Trace had treated Bridget's wound with the latter several times, in the hope of staving off infection. Her skin had blazed with heat all day, but now, with evening creeping across the land, shadow by shadow, a deep chill had seeped into her, and that scared Trace more than the fever had.

"She's not getting better," Skye breathed, "is she?" She looked stricken, and little wonder. Bridget was surely one of the cornerstones of her life: sister, mother, friend. "She's—she's shivering."

Trace nodded. Then, on an impulse, he wrapped Bridget in bed quilts, gathered her up in his arms, and carried her over to the stove. There he sat, rocking her back and forth, staring down into her face with fierce concentration. Willing her to hold on.

Skye made supper, fed Noah, put him to bed, and lay down beside the child in her clothes.

Trace did not relinquish his hold on Bridget but held her through the night.

It was almost dawn when, at last, she opened her eyes, blinked, and stared at him with something resembling amazement. "The snake—?" Terror seized her; she struggled to sit up. *"Noah!"*

He held her firmly. "Noah is fine," he said. "You're the one who was bitten."

She gnawed at her lower lip, and he could see that she was debating with herself: believe, don't believe. "My son—where—?"

"He's sound asleep. He and Skye."

She let her head rest against his shoulder, and even though he knew it was weakness, not affection, that made her snuggle in close like that, he treasured the sensation. He'd come so near to losing her.

"Are you hungry?" he asked. He might have had sandpaper in his throat, the way he sounded.

She shook her head. Then, very softly, "You saved me, didn't you?"

He grinned; couldn't help it. She was *alive*. "I wouldn't put it that way, exactly. There's still some swelling, and I reckon you're sore as all get-out, whether you'll admit as much or not. You're going to have to rest for a few days."

She blinked, stiffened in protest. "A few days?" she echoed. He might have said she'd never walk again, if you went by her tone. "That's impossible! There's the gardening to do, and the cooking—"

He laid a fingertip to her lips to silence her. "We won't starve, Bridget."

"But winter is coming, and—"

"And I'm here. So is Skye. You could still get in trouble with that bite if you don't take care of yourself. Where would Noah and Skye be then?"

That gave her pause, though it was obvious that she wasn't one bit pleased at the prospect of giving in.

As a lady of leisure, in fact, Bridget was hopeless. She let Trace put her in bed and cover her up, let Skye bring her tea and Noah tell her stories, but her eyes were big and frightened, and in between long slides into healing sleep, she fussed and fretted.

Trace worked all day, cutting wood for the roof, but he came in often to check on Bridget. Skye looked after Noah, and the two of them weeded the garden and carried water and kept Bridget company whenever she was awake.

Trace took a bath in the creek at sundown, put on clean clothes, and went into the cabin. Skye had made a simple but flavorful hash for supper, and he managed to pester Bridget into taking a couple of bites. There were big dark circles under her eyes, and her skin was bluish-pale, like thin milk. He knew she was in pain, knew also that he would never hear her say so. The bite was still angry, but the swelling was going down, and there was no sign of infection.

He made a brew of hot water, molasses, and whiskey and brought it to her. It had a lot more kick than tea, and it might dull the pain a little.

She sniffed the concoction and scrunched up her face.

"Drink it," Trace commanded. He wanted to reach out, brush a tendril of pale gold hair back from her forehead, but that would be pushing his luck. She was skittish as a filly about to be ridden for the first time, and the mere suggestion that she might need anyone's help—his in particular—was bound to scare her half to death.

She took a cautious sip, coughed, tried to push the mug back into his hand.

"Drink," he repeated.

"Where are Noah and Skye?" She was stalling.

He took the cup, held it gently to her mouth. Reluctantly, she sipped and swallowed. "They're right here, darlin'. Sitting at the table, playing cards." Poker, to be exact. He'd taught them himself—well, he'd taught Skye, anyhow; Noah still had a way to go—while Bridget was asleep, but it was probably better not to go into too much detail just then. He grinned at her, made her drink more and then more of the whiskey mixture, but slowly.

"Trace?" She'd taken half the drink, and she was already getting heavy-eyed.

"Um?" He set the cup aside, tucked the covers under her chin.

"Thanks."

He leaned down and kissed her lightly on the forehead, the same way he might have kissed Skye. The result was a tangle of emotions and sensations that fairly took his breath away, though he was pretty sure he'd managed to hide his reactions. "Anytime," he replied. "But I'll thank you not to go grabbing up any more rattlers."

Her eyes shone, though she could barely keep them open. "You'll be—you'll be close by?"

He wanted to kiss her again, but he didn't dare because he knew it wouldn't be the same kind of kiss as before. So he nodded instead. "I brought my bedroll in and laid it out over there by the stove. Go to sleep, Bridget. You need to sleep."

A smile wobbled on her mouth, vanished. "I *hate* to sleep," she said.

He knew it was true. She was a vital person, energetic, fully alive. Even her stillness was vibrant, and she begrudged every idle moment. "Look at it this way," he teased. "The sooner you go to sleep, the sooner it will be morning."

She managed a small, strangled laugh, and he knew he'd turned a corner, that somehow his whole life had pivoted on that tiny sound. "That's what I tell Noah," she said.

He raised an eyebrow. "Well, then," he said, "it must be true."

She smiled again and closed her eyes, none too soon. The tenderness he felt toward her was overwhelming, bound to show in his face, and he didn't want her to see it, lest she retreat again.

When Bridget awakened the next morning, a burning ache throbbed in her arm, but she would have celebrated if she'd had the strength. She was alive, thanks to Trace. On the crate next to the bed, a fruit jar spilled over with colorful wildflowers, reds and violets, yellows and whites, and the new book was there, too, promising so much.

The tarp had been drawn back from the roof, halfway at least, and Trace, shirtless and sweating, grinned down at her from the rafters. "Hullo, Sleeping Beauty," he said.

She swallowed hard. Trace had been twelve or so the last time she'd seen him without a shirt; she'd come upon him and Mitch down at the swimming hole. This was disturbingly different. "What are you doing up there?"

Even from that distance, the mischief was clearly visible in his eyes. "Now, what kind of question is that?" he countered. "I'm fixing to put on that roof I promised you."

She felt self-conscious, lying there in bed, gazing up at Trace and his naked chest. "Put on a shirt," she said, sitting up. "You'll get sunburned."

Again, that lethal grin. "Watch out," he warned. "You keep talking like that, I might get the idea that you care."

She blushed. "Stop looking at me. How on earth am I supposed to get up with you staring at me like that?"

He laughed. The sun shone around him like an aura. "You're not," he said. "Supposed to get up, I mean."

Bridget sighed. "In the meantime, you plan on nailing up beams and shingles right over my head?"

He pretended to consider the matter seriously. "I guess we'll have to put you outside, by the creek." Again, that light in his eyes. That grin. "Skye and I have rigged up a place."

The mere thought of getting outside raised Bridget's flagging spirits. She smiled. "Really?"

"Really," he replied, and dropped into the cabin, agile as some sort of jungle creature. "If you're ready, I'll take you out there right now."

Bridget couldn't help staring at him, and she was mortified by her own wantonness. What kind of woman was she, looking at a man's bare chest? A man, no less, who was not her husband.

Not Mitch.

He seemed to read her thoughts, and a sad smile rested on his mouth and settled in around his eyes. He lifted her out of bed, quilts and all, and somehow managed to hand her the book he'd bought for her in town a few days before. The breeze and sunlight were like the touch of a healing hand, and Bridget gasped in delighted surprise when she saw the hammock. He'd tied an old blanket securely between two small but sturdy birch trees, a stone's throw from the creek's edge. Skye and Noah were further down the bank, each holding an improvised fishing pole, and both of them beamed when they saw Bridget.

It was heaven, lying there in that hammock, shaded

by the dancing shadows of leaves, lulled by the sound of flowing water. Bridget read, dozed, and read again. Noah and Skye continued to fish, and Trace worked on the roof, driving in wooden pegs with Granddaddy's hammer.

"Look, Mama!" Bridget had nodded off, but the sound of her son's voice and the feel of something cold and slick against the back of her hand brought her awake. "I caught a fish!" he crowed.

Sure enough, Noah had a fine, gleaming trout on the hook. She laughed and leaned over to kiss his cheek soundly. "Why, it's nearly as big as the whale that swallowed poor Jonah," she observed.

Noah nodded. "Nobody helped me, neither. I did it all by myself."

Bridget ruffled his shining hair, thought of Mitch. Some of the sparkle faded from Noah's catch, from the sun-spattered creek, from the comforting sound of Trace's roof building. "Your papa would be so proud," she said softly.

Noah's small brow knitted into a frown. "I want Trace to be my papa," he said.

The remark didn't surprise Bridget, but it did sting. "Sweetheart," she said, fighting a silly, weak impulse to break down and cry. "Oh, sweetheart. Things don't work that way. Your papa was a man named Mitch McQuarry, and even though he's gone, he'll always be your father."

Noah let the fish fall to his side, and there was something so disconsolate in the motion that Bridget yearned to gather him in and hold him close. She restrained herself, though; Noah might be a small boy, but he wasn't a baby. To patronize him would serve no purpose but to undermine his dignity. "Where is he? My papa, I mean?"

"We've talked about that before, Noah," Bridget reminded him. She had to look away, dash at her cheek with the back of one hand. "He's in heaven."

"Is he coming back?"

She met her son's gaze. "No, darling. People like to stay in heaven when they get there. It's a wonderful place."

"Could we go there? You and me and Skye and Trace? Could we go and find my papa?"

Bridget swallowed, glanced at the creek, and made herself look at Noah again. Her eyes were still dazzled; she could not make out his features. "All of us will go there, someday," she told him carefully. "But not anytime soon." *And not together.*

Noah digested that. "Oh," he said. Then, quicksilver, he held his gleaming trout high above his head again and whooped, "Look, Trace, I caught a fish, all by my own self!"

Chapter

5

Marshal Sam Flynn showed up the next day, stood with his head back and his thumbs hooked into his gun-belt, squinting as he admired the new roof on the McQuarry cabin. "Yes, sir," he called to Trace, who was straddling the ridgepole. "That's a fine job of work. Jake Vigil sees that, he'll be after you to turn a hand to that sawmill he's trying to get built."

Bridget had mentioned a sawmill, but Trace had seen no sign of one during his brief visit to Primrose Creek the day he'd bought the groceries. "He got a planer?" Trace called back. He had plenty of rough timber. What he needed was lumber, cut to measured lengths and planed smooth, if he was going to get Bridget's place in any kind of shape; besides the roof, she needed bed-rooms added on, and a barn. A real corral.

"Steam-operated," Sam answered, sounding as proud as if the machine were his own. "Has one com-ing, anyhow. I reckon it's someplace between here and

San Francisco. Jake's got a good bit of lumber laid by, though. Had it planed over in Virginia City. He might be willing to make a trade for some labor."

Trace reached for his shirt, discarded earlier when the sun was high, stuck the handle of the hammer through his belt, and made for the edge of the roof. From there, it was an easy jump to the ground. "I'm obliged, Sam," he said, and thrust out a hand.

The marshal shook it. His horse, an overfed sorrel with ears like a mule's, snuffled behind him.

Trace grinned. "This a social call, or did my wasted youth finally catch up to me?"

Sam chortled. "If you got a wasted youth, it's bound to turn up on your doorstep one of these days." He swept off his sweat-stained hat and thrust the splayed fingers of his left hand through thinning hair. "Fact is, though, I came out here to bring a letter for Mizz McQuarry. Come all the way from England, and from the looks of the envelope, it's been one hell of a trip."

Trace frowned as he accepted the thin scrap of translucent vellum. Bridget had been recovering from the snakebite for a full week, and although he knew she'd enjoyed being waited on and fussed over for the first few days, she did not have the temperament to be an invalid. In fact, she was as cantankerous as a mother bear missing a cub. Trace cherished a slight hope that the letter might cheer her, but at the same time, he knew it must have come from one or both of her estranged cousins, whom she viewed as virtual deserters.

He slapped the letter thoughtfully against his palm. "Water your horse, Sam, and sit a spell." He indicated the upended rain barrel he'd taken off the broken-down Conestoga while scrounging for tools. By then, the wagon had somehow gotten itself overturned on a steep hillside, and it wasn't good for much of anything now besides firewood. Bridget was probably asleep, and he knew she'd kill him if he invited the marshal inside while she was in repose. He'd been treading carefully around her, in order to preserve the delicate peace, and neither one of them had ventured to mention his proposal of marriage. "I'll let Bridget know you're here."

"I can see that for myself," Bridget said clearly, and he turned to see her standing in the cabin doorway. She'd put on her yellow calico dress and caught her long, long hair back at the nape, and she looked thin and pale and incredibly young. "Come inside, Mr. Flynn. I'll make some coffee."

Sam doffed his hat and smiled, but Trace could see that the other man had taken note of Bridget's malaise. "I'm obliged, ma'am," he said, "but I can't stay. I just came to bring this here letter. Got some rowdies in town, and I don't want to leave them to it for too long."

She managed a smile, but she was holding the door frame with one hand, as though unsteady, and the blue shadows under her eyes made Trace want to go off in search of a doctor. He'd just decided that he'd drag one back from Virginia City if he had to when she answered. "I can't imagine who'd be writing to me," she said.

"Come all the way from England," the marshal said, for the second time. "I hope it brings you good news, ma'am."

Bridget's smile had already faded. "England?" she said, and started toward them. She stopped uncertainly in the middle of the dooryard. Sam, busy hauling himself up into the saddle, didn't see the expression on her face, but Trace did, and he almost wished he didn't have to give her the letter.

He went toward her, placed the envelope in her hand, and supported her by slipping an arm loosely around her waist.

She studied the elegant, faded handwriting, the stamp, the words *McQuarry Farm* and *Virginia* crossed out, replaced with *Primrose Creek, Nevada.* "It's—it's from Christy," she said. He couldn't tell much from the tone of her voice, but her lingering weakness gave him worry enough to last a lifetime. "She—she must have thought we were all still at the farm—"

"Come inside, Bridget," Trace said firmly, after sparing a wave for the departing marshal. "You'll be wanting some privacy, and you need to sit down."

She allowed him to steer her back into the cabin and seat her at the table, and that, too, was troublesome proof of her frailty. Skye and Noah were somewhere nearby, fishing for trout, and the house was quiet. She'd shown a fondness for tea since her encounter with the snake, and Trace went about brewing a batch, using a plain cooking pot to boil the water while she sat there, staring at the letter as if she thought it might sprout wings and fly out the window.

"Our parting was not a pleasant one, you know," she said, so softly that he almost didn't hear her.

"I know," he replied quietly. "I was there, remember? People change. Situations change."

Bridget was silent for a long time, and when she spoke, it was as if she hadn't heard a word he said. Didn't recall that he'd helped haul the two of them apart. "We had a dreadful row, Christy and I, that last day. Things were said—"

He would have crossed the room and laid a hand to her shoulder, if he hadn't guessed that she didn't want to be touched. "Maybe it's time to forget old differences. Family is family, after all."

She was watching him; he felt her gaze, in that uncanny way, even before he turned and met her eyes. "Uncle Eli went with the Confederate side. Christy said our daddy, Skye's and mine, was a traitor for taking up the Union cause. Said he was a disgrace to the whole state of Virginia and ought to be hanged."

Trace sighed. "Bridge," he said. The water wasn't quite hot, but he dumped a couple of spoonfuls of loose tea in, anyhow. "She was a kid. You were a kid. The country had just snapped in two like a dry twig. A lot of folks said a lot of things they didn't mean."

She bit her lower lip, reached for the letter, lying travel-worn on the table before her, drew back her hand again. "I told her I hated her, Trace," she said. She closed her eyes tightly for a moment, and when she opened them again, her gaze was fixed on something far away. "I spat on her skirt."

"If I recall it correctly," he said, "you went at her with your claws out. She gave as good as she got, and I suppose the two of you would have killed each other if your granddaddy and I hadn't dragged you apart."

She blushed. Set her jaw. "I vowed I'd never forgive her," she said.

He leaned down, peered doubtfully into the can of hot water and floating tea leaves, and stirred the concoction once with a wooden spoon. "Some promises," he answered distractedly, "really ought to be broken." He knew immediately that he'd made a mistake, but it was too late.

"Yes," she said. "Like the one you made to Mitch, for instance."

"That," he replied after a beat, "was different."

She thumped her fingers lightly on top of the letter; that was still as close as she'd gotten to opening the thing. One eyebrow was raised, and there was a triumphant tilt to one corner of her mouth. "I'm not so sure of that," she said thoughtfully, but she didn't pursue the subject any further.

He was grateful for her restraint; as it was, he felt like a trout wriggling on a hook about half the time. Not that he'd have left, no matter how good a case she made. She had to marry somebody sooner or later, and it might just as well be him.

He sloshed some of the tea into a mug and set it before her. "I'll be on the roof," he said, and headed outside.

She looked into the mug, furrowed her brow, and then smiled to herself. "Make sure you wear your shirt," she said. "You'll be peeling like an onion if you don't be careful."

He sighed, winked somewhat dispiritedly, and left the cabin.

Bridget waited until Trace was overhead again, hammering away at the shingles he'd fashioned from thick pieces of tree bark. Although she wasn't quite ready to tell him so outright, she was glad he was around. If he hadn't been there when she was bitten by that rattler, she would surely be dead, and Skye and Noah would have been left alone.

Skye was strong, in her own way, and resourceful; she would have found a way to provide for herself and her nephew, but Bridget shuddered at the predicament the girl would have been in—a woman's options were narrow, after all, especially in a place like Primrose Creek. She could enter into an immediate and probably loveless marriage or trade her favors for food and shelter; the line between those two situations was thin indeed. Thanks to Trace, though, Skye could grow to full womanhood and choose a husband for herself when the time came.

You're stalling, Bridget scolded herself. Then, with her hands trembling a little, she picked up the envelope, turned it over, and broke the once-fancy wax seal covering the edge of the flap.

The single page inside bore an embossed crest in the upper left-hand corner, and beneath that was a date— approximately six months before—and *Fieldcrest,* the name of Christy and Megan's stepfather's estate.

Bridget sniffed once and gave the sheet of fine paper a nearly imperceptible snap before reading on.

> *Dear Bridget,*
>
> *I direct this letter to you because I know you must be managing everything and everyone around you, like always. My regards to Skye.*
>
> *Word of Grandfather's death reached us just this morning. His lawyer wrote to inform us of his passing, or we would not have known. I should have expected to hear such news from you—had you been anyone else at all.*
>
> *According to Grandfather's man-of-law, Megan and I have inherited half of a tract of land he referred to as Primrose Creek, way out in the West somewhere, with the other half going to you*

and Skye—as well, it would seem, as the farm itself and all of Grandmother's lovely things.

In any case, having no use for such a distant and desolate expanse, my sister and I would like to sell our share of the property. We have expressed our wishes to Grandfather's representative in Richmond, but following a long discussion, we came to the decision that it was only honorable to offer our acreage to you before turning to strangers. We would expect a fair price, of course.

Please reply at your earliest convenience. Both Megan and I are eager to make plans.

Sincerely,
Christina McQuarry

Bridget might have crumpled the missive and flung it across the room if it hadn't been the second or third letter she'd ever received. A muddle of emotions simmered and stewed within her—anger at some of the things Christy had implied, sorrow that her once big family had been so diminished, the very real fear that her cousins would sell the land on the other side of the creek to someone who would cut off the water supply somewhere upstream, or chop down all the trees to sell for timber, or scrape away the topsoil to dig for silver, gold, or copper. . . .

"You got a letter?" The voice was Skye's.

Bridget looked up, blinked. Her sister was standing in the doorway, and the light came from behind, leaving her face in shadow. "Yes," she said, a little wearily, and took a cautious sip of Trace's tea. "Where is Noah?"

"He's on the roof with Trace," Skye said. Then,

quickly, "And don't start worrying. Trace tied a rope around his middle."

Bridget rolled her eyes. Better not to think about that just now. "It's from Christy," she said, and held out the letter.

Skye was at her side, snatching the page from her fingers, in a fraction of a moment. "Holy boot grease," she said.

Bridget let that pass. "They want to sell their share of the land," she said, unnecessarily, for Skye was probably on her second pass through the letter by then. "Somehow, we've got to raise enough money to buy it."

Skye sank onto her customary crate, just to the left of where Bridget sat. Overhead, the hammer thwacked, and Trace and Noah carried on a running conversation. "How are we going to do that?" she asked.

It was a more than reasonable question. It had taken practically everything Bridget had, everything she could sell or swap, beg or promise, just to get this far. She had no money, none at all, and Grandmother's silver teapot and jade brooch, the last of their inheritance, had gone for last winter's room and board at Fort Grant. "I don't know," she confessed at some length. "But I'll find a way."

Skye watched her intently. "There aren't many folks willing to live way out here," she said. "Probably, that land will just stay empty, like it is now."

It wasn't *entirely* empty; there had been an Indian village on that site, long ago, and an ancient lodge still stood on the hillside opposite the cabin, hidden from view by a stand of birches, oaks, and cottonwoods. "It's fine land, Skye. Someone is going to want it. And what if it's the wrong someone?"

Skye said nothing. They both knew that certain sorts of neighbors might well represent a danger to them, once Trace had done his self-imposed penance and moved on. And Bridget had no doubt that he *would* move on, when the old restlessness set in. For that reason, and several others, she must not allow herself to care for him.

Carefully, Bridget folded the page, returned it to its envelope, got the McQuarry Bible out of its square pine box, and tucked the letter inside. When she turned around, she caught Skye watching her with a thoughtful smile.

Bridget pressed her lips together, smoothed the skirts of her calico dress, and went outside to shade her eyes with one hand and look up. Noah was wielding the hammer, his tongue pressed into one cheek, while Trace supervised. It was an ordinary scene, a man and a boy working together, but the sight filled Bridget with a strange, bittersweet poignancy. In one and the same moment, she wished Trace had never come to Primrose Creek and rejoiced that he had.

He looked up, probably expecting her to demand that he bring Noah down from there *this instant,* and she wanted to do just that, wanted it the way parched ground wants water, but she held her tongue. Made herself go inside.

By suppertime, Trace's back, chest, arms, and shoulders were painfully red and hot to the touch.

"I warned you," Bridget fussed, getting out the jug of cider vinegar she kept for flavoring dandelion greens and the like. "Wear your shirt, I said. But you're so hard-headed, and you just wouldn't listen—"

He laughed, though it was perfectly obvious that he

was suffering. "I figure if I go down and lie in the creek for a while, I'll be fine."

"You'll take a chill, going from one extreme to the other like that," she said. "Sit down, and let me tend to you."

He looked at the vinegar and the handkerchief she'd gotten from the trunk she and Skye used in place of a bureau and narrowed his eyes dubiously. "Is that going to hurt?"

"Now is a fine time to ask that," Bridget responded.

He flinched when she dampened the handkerchief and touched it gently to the broiled flesh on his left shoulder. "You seem to be feeling better," he said. "Nothing like tormenting me to brighten your day."

She shook her head but could not maintain her serious expression. She laughed. "I *warned* you," she reminded him. "You're going to be sore for a couple of days, Trace, and you'll be lucky if you sleep tonight."

He was looking at her; his eyes were turquoise in the fading light. They'd had supper—fresh trout and greens and some of Skye's rock-hard biscuits—and the cabin had taken on a cozy aspect, what with the new roof and the lamplight and the lingering aroma of a good dinner. Skye and Noah were sitting together on the high threshold, watching the first stars come out.

"I'll be going into town again tomorrow," he said. "I want to speak to Jake Vigil, see if I can swap for some good lumber. Build a corral and some shelter for the horses."

She nodded; her throat felt thick, for some odd reason, and anything she tried to say would have come out as a croak.

"I was wondering if you wouldn't like to go along,"

he went on. He was not a shy man; Trace had always been the boldest of the three of them, dreaming up all sorts of mischief and then cajoling Mitch and Bridget into going along. And yet there was boyish uncertainty about him now, arousing an unwelcome tenderness in Bridget. "Just for an outing, I mean."

A refusal sprang to the tip of her tongue, but she bit it back. Both Skye and Noah had turned in the doorway to watch her, plainly awaiting her answer, and the truth of it was, Bridget was sick and tired of staying at home. She would assess the growth of Primrose Creek for herself, find out if there was a church yet, and a bank. Most definitely a bank.

"Yes," she said. "I'd like that."

Trace had gone back to sleeping by the creek, making a bed of the hammock he'd fashioned for Bridget's convalescence, and he reached for his shirt as soon as Bridget had finished dousing him with vinegar, pulled it on gingerly, leaving the buttons undone. Bridget had been able to avoid looking at his chest throughout the exercise, but now, all of a sudden, it drew her gaze, once, twice, a third time.

She finally had to turn away. "Good night, Trace," she said.

He was close behind her, so close. She felt his warm breath caress her nape. "Good night," he answered.

The storm rolled in after midnight, sundering the sky into blackened pieces, shaking the new roof over their heads. Lightning illuminated the landscape with an eerie clarity, and the horses shrieked in terror. Commanding Skye to stay inside with Noah, Bridget pulled on her wrapper, slipped her feet into unlaced shoes, and dashed out. Just across the creek, a giant ponderosa pine exploded into flames, flaring up like a torch.

Bridget turned, stumbled around the house to the corral, where Sis was kept, the stallion being tethered some distance away. The mare was in a frenzy, running back and forth in the small space, flinging her head, screaming and sweat-soaked.

"Easy, girl," Bridget said. "Easy."

She could hear the stallion between claps of thunder, but she knew Trace was with him.

Sis, probably recognizing Bridget's voice, or perhaps her scent, calmed down slightly. Nickered.

"Come here, Sis," Bridget said, holding out a hand to the frightened animal. "It's me. See? It's Bridget. And I'm not going to let anything happen to you."

Just then, the rain began, falling lightly at first, then with growing force. Trace appeared at Bridget's side just as she got a halter on Sis and fastened it. He was leading the stallion. "Is there a place we can take them?" he yelled over the roar of the rain.

The animals, overheated just moments before, were soaked.

Bridget thought of the old Indian lodge across the creek and pointed with one hand. "Over there!" she shouted back. The downpour had, at least, extinguished the flaming pine tree. "Back behind those trees. I'll show you!"

Trace caught her arm. "No," he told her. "The creek will be running pretty fast. You go inside!"

She shook her head. "These are my horses," she said stubbornly.

Trace threw up his free hand in a flash of frustration,

but he let her lead the way to the creek, where she hiked her nightdress and wrapper up to her knees and tied them into a knot. The stream was indeed swollen, and between bolts of lightning, the surrounding countryside was darker than dark. Twice, while they were crossing, each of them leading a half-panicked horse, blue-gold light danced across the opposite bank.

It would have been a beautiful thing to see, Bridget thought, if it hadn't come so close to the water. The creek was without question the worst place they could possibly be in such weather, and the trees they were headed toward were the second worst.

The lodge had a hide roof and sturdy walls, though. When she and Skye and Noah had arrived at Primrose Creek in their ox-drawn wagon, she had considered taking the place for their home. In the end, she'd chosen the cabin because it had stone walls and was closer to the creek.

Bridget's feet and legs were numb by the time they got to the other side, and her shoes were probably ruined. The rain came down in torrents, making a sound on the water that might have been mistaken for the roar of a raging fire. They made their slippery way up the hillside and finally, finally, found the lodge itself.

Trace tied the stallion at one end of the long structure and then secured Sis at the other, while Bridget groped for something they could use to wipe down the horses. Being careful not to think too much about rats and spiders and other creatures that might take refuge in such places, Bridget picked up a length of what felt like leather—no doubt it was part of the roof—and used that to dry the shivering mare as best she could. When she'd finished, she found her way to Trace, gave him the hide, and waited while he attended to the stallion.

Neither Bridget nor Trace spoke at all—they were both too spent to make idle conversation—until they were standing face to face, visible to each other only because of intermittent explosions of lightning. When he put his hands on her shoulders, pulled her close, and lowered his mouth to hers, it seemed perfectly natural.

Bridget was fairly certain her eyes were closed, and yet it seemed to her that the whole world burst into flames in the space of that kiss. A bolt of lightning coursed through her, delving deep into the earth, like roots of fire, shooting out through the top of her head like the tail of a rocket. She was dazed when Trace drew back; she swayed slightly, and he steadied her.

"We'd better get back," he said.

Bridget couldn't speak at all. She let him take her hand, though, and lead her out of the lodge, down the bank, across water that blazed with reflected lightning. She stumbled once, in the middle of the creek, went clear under, and came up laughing. She couldn't get any wetter than she already was.

Lamplight glowed from the cabin doorway; they followed it, Trace setting Bridget over the threshold before stepping inside himself, fastening the door behind him.

"Good thing you got the roof done," Skye said.

Bridget and Trace looked at each other, dripping wet, and laughed like a pair of fools.

"Look at you," Skye went on, all but shaking her finger. "You'll be down with pneumonia before morning if we don't do something."

Bridget was, all of a sudden, at a loss for what to do. It seemed she'd spent all her wits on getting the horses in out of the storm. Trace appeared to be equally bewildered; his lips—had he truly kissed her?—had turned blue, and his teeth were chattering.

Fortunately, Skye was more than ready to take charge. "Trace, you stay here by the stove, and I'll get you a blanket to wrap up in. You'll want to get out of those clothes first, of course." She took Bridget's arm. "I've laid out a dry nightgown for you and a towel for drying your hair." Then, sternly, "Trace, you keep your back turned."

He made a sound that might have been a groan or a raw-throated laugh. "Where's that whiskey?" he asked.

A few minutes later, when Trace had stripped and wrapped himself in one of several old quilts they'd brought from the farm, and she had gotten into her thickest flannel nightdress, they sat side by side in front of the inadequate little stove, sipping coffee laced with molasses and strong whiskey. Skye was there, alternately brushing and toweling Bridget's long hair, so neither of them raised the subject of the kiss stolen in the dark ruin across the creek.

Bridget wasn't sure she could have brought the subject up, anyhow. She felt strangely shy, as though that kiss had been her first ever. As though it had been not just a kiss but an introduction to the fullness of womanhood, complete in itself. Never, not once, had Mitch's kisses affected her that way—but it was better not to follow such thoughts.

"Are we still going to town tomorrow?" Noah wanted to know.

Trace chuckled. "If the rain lets up," he said, "I suppose we'll go ahead."

Noah turned his hazel eyes to Bridget. "You'll come,

too, won't you, Mama?" He looked so hopeful. And so like Mitch.

She reached out, laid her hand on his silky hair. "Yes, sweetheart. I'll go, too. Now, hadn't you better get back in bed? If you don't get your rest, you might be too tired to make a trip to town."

Noah nodded in eager agreement, leaned forward, and gave Bridget a good-night smack on the cheek.

Out of the corner of her eye, she saw Trace's crooked smile. "That was pretty sly," he murmured, when Skye was busy settling Noah down for what remained of the night.

She merely smiled and took another sip of the medicinal coffee.

Trace ran a hand through his hair and gazed at the stove. "I'll get started on the barn as soon as I can," he said. "In the meantime, we'll use the place over there. I'll nail up the tarp to reinforce that roof."

She didn't want him to talk about roofs and barns and canvas tarps. She wanted him to explain how he'd had the audacity to kiss her that way, and why it had changed her forever. She laid a hand on his arm, the one covered by the soft fabric of the old quilt. "Trace?"

He met her gaze, waited.

And Skye came back, clucking like a mother hen trying to herd scattered chicks back to the nest. "Really, Bridget. You have so much hair—it'll be a *week* before it's dry."

Trace and Bridget were still staring at each other, in stricken silence now, and Bridget was certain her own expression must be as thunderstruck as Trace's.

Chapter

6

When he finally stretched out on the pallet of quilts and blankets Skye had made for him in front of the stove, Trace didn't expect to sleep. His clothes, draped over the edge of the spool table, would surely be dry by morning, and, thanks to the whiskey, the aching chill of wind and rain and creek water had left his flesh. No, it was the memory of the kiss he'd stolen from Bridget that would keep him awake; he could feel the heat of it lingering on his mouth, and the force of the emotions raised by her response still reverberated through his very bones.

He stared up at the underside of the roof he'd finished none too soon, listening to the soft patter of the rain, and wished that Bridget were there beside him, his to hold. He closed his eyes with a sigh, and in the next instant, he was asleep and dreaming. The confounding thing was that he knew he was actually lying on the floor of a cabin in the high country of Nevada, but his mind and spirit had strayed back to an earlier time in his life, and he could do nothing else but follow.

Mitch was up ahead, mounted on the fine black gelding Gideon had given him only a few months before, leading a charge across some swift and nameless river, sword raised and gleaming in the midday sun. Trace had fallen behind, some twenty minutes before, when his own spotted horse, also bred on the McQuarrys' farm, had picked up a stone and turned up lame.

By the time Trace had removed the stone and caught up with the other troops, Mitch was almost out of sight. Trace stood in the stirrups, just in time to see the gelding catch a sniper's bullet square in the side of its neck. The animal shrieked in terror and pain and flailed wildly, while Mitch tried in vain to control it. A crimson foam churned atop the water, and more shots were fired.

In the chaos that followed, Mitch somehow lost his seat in the saddle, disappeared under the water. Trace, oblivious to the shower of Rebel bullets pocking the surface of the river, struggled to reach his friend. The spotted mare balked, and there were other men shot, other horses as well, blocking the way.

Then, at last, he reached the drowning gelding, dove beneath the surface of the water, found Mitch floating motionless, eyes wide open, arms spread as if to receive his fate. His right foot had slipped through the stirrup, and he hadn't been able to pull free before he ran out of air.

Trace drew his knife, severed the stirrup from the saddle, and hauled Mitch to the surface.

The shooting had stopped, but Trace barely noticed. He dragged his best friend out of the river, laid him face down on the bank, and bore down on his back with both hands in an effort to force the water from Mitch's lungs. He was aware of a dull throbbing in his right thigh, but it would be some time before he realized he'd been wounded.

The barrel of a rifle prodded his shoulder; he looked up to see a young Reb standing over him, scared half to death but determined to do his duty. "He's dead, mister. And you're a prisoner now, so get to your feet if you can."

Trace wrenched Mitch over onto his back, yelled at him to blink or get up or just breathe. By then, though, Mitch's lips had turned a blue-gray color, and his eyes were empty. Trace swallowed a scream of protest and pain, swayed to his feet, and hoisted his friend off the ground, carrying him over one shoulder.

"You got to leave him here, Yank," the boy persisted. He couldn't have been more than sixteen, that kid in the ill-fitting gray woolen jacket; he still had spots on his face.

Trace glared at his unlikely captor. "I mean to bury him," he said. "If you want to stop me, you'd best just shoot me right here."

The boy's gaze dropped to Trace's bloody leg. "Looks like somebody already done that," he said, without triumph. He prodded Trace with the rifle barrel again, but cautiously. "They ain't gonna let you bury him. There's too many others that need burying."

Trace gripped the rifle barrel and forced it aside, twisting it out of the boy's grasp in the process. It clattered to the wet, smooth pebbles on the riverbank, where it lay, unclaimed. "You wave that thing in my face again," he said fiercely, "and I'm going to jam it in one end of you and out the other." Then he started up the slope to the grassy meadow above, and the Confederates made way for him to pass.

Someone brought him a shovel; he began to dig the grave. He was in a strange state of mind, half outside himself, a step behind, like his own hapless ghost. He thought he might have gone wild with the force of his grief, if only he could catch up to himself.

They let him dig and dig, those Rebs, and at some point, a couple of them joined in. When the hole was deep enough, Trace wrapped Mitch's body in a blanket someone had brought, got down into the grave himself and lay his lifeless friend at his feet as gently as if he'd been a sleeping baby.

"Good-bye," he said, and then his knees gave way, and his mind went dark, one shadow at a time.

"Trace?" A hand rested firmly on his shoulder, gave him a shake. "Trace, wake up. You're dreaming."

He opened his eyes and looked up to see Bridget bending over him, hair trailing to her waist. "I'm sorry," he murmured, and made to sit up. She stepped back so he could.

She sat down on one of the crate chairs, her hands folded in her lap. The rain had stopped, and the moon must have come out, too, because no lamps were burning, and he could see her so plainly, in her white flannel night-dress. "You were calling to Mitch," she said, very softly.

He sighed, shoved a hand through his hair. For some reason, he couldn't look at her. "Yeah," he said. "I didn't mean to wake you."

"You didn't," she replied. "I was thinking about— about tonight."

The kiss. He would have preferred to talk about Mitch. "I shouldn't have done that."

"No, you shouldn't have," she agreed readily. "And I shouldn't have responded the way I did. It's just that— it's just that I've been so lonely."

"I know," he said. "I know."

She straightened her spine a little. "Do you suppose the horses are all right?"

He grinned, relieved at the change of subject, though a part of him was mighty disappointed that she could dismiss a kiss like that one so easily. "They're in out of the rain. For tonight, that's enough."

She smiled a small, wobbly smile. "Thank you, Trace. I don't know what I would have done if you hadn't been here—the tarp would never have kept out a storm like that, and heaven only knows what would have happened to Sis and the stallion."

He wanted to touch her cheek, her hand, her shoulder, but he didn't dare. He'd stepped out of line as it was, kissing her the way he had, and he was cold again, as cold as if he'd really been in that bloody river so far away, trying desperately, hopelessly, to save his best friend.

"Go back to bed, Bridget," he said hoarsely.

She hesitated, then rose, put more wood into the stove, and watched him for a long time in pensive silence. Finally, she spoke. "Did he suffer? Mitch, I mean?"

Trace bit his lower lip, held her gaze. "I don't think so," he said. "There was a gash in the back of his head. He must have struck it on a rock when he was thrown."

"You did everything you could, Trace," she whispered. "I know you did."

It came upon him suddenly sometimes, took him by surprise even in the broad light of day, the knowledge that Mitch was dead, that he'd never see him again. After the dream, though, the grief was worse, as fresh as if the incident had happened only hours ago, instead of years. "That's kind of you, Mrs. McQuarry," he said, and wondered at the edge in his voice even as he spoke, "considering your stated opinion that I'm to blame for what happened." In truth, he blamed himself. And he was beginning to suspect that he hadn't come to Primrose Creek set on marrying Bridget because of any promise to Mitch but for reasons of his own. Selfish ones.

She paled; he saw that in the dim light, hated himself for it. And then she said something he'd never have expected to hear her say. "I was wrong, Trace. I'm sorry. Mitch was a man, not a little boy, and he wouldn't have gone to war if he hadn't wanted to."

There was nothing he could say to that. It was wholly true. Though amiable and maybe even naive, Mitch had been eager for adventure. He'd have joined the fighting even if Trace had refused to go along; it was just that neither of them had really expected to die. They'd been so young, with their blood pulsing in their veins, convinced they would go home triumphant one day, together, and tell stories about their experiences until they were both too old to rightly recall any of it.

Only it hadn't happened that way.

Trace lay down. The dirt floor was hard, even wrapped in quilts the way he was, and the cold seemed to seep through his skin.

"First thing, after I get the barn built," he said, turning away from Bridget and dragging the covers up to his ear, "I mean to put a bedroom on the back of this cabin. You and I aren't sleeping out here once we're married."

He waited for her protest, but she said nothing at all. He heard her cross the room, get back into bed, and sigh.

When Bridget awakened the next morning, with burning eyes and an irritating stuffiness in her nose, Trace had already left the house. She was fairly certain he'd gone to fetch the horses back from the lodge across the creek, and a glance out the front window confirmed the fact. He was leading Sis by her halter, while Windfall followed amenably.

The air was golden, scrubbed clean by last night's storm, and the creek was a ribbon of bright silver, light in motion. It was only then, watching the man and the two horses coming up the near bank, that she realized why the stallion obeyed Trace so readily.

She went outside and watched, arms folded loosely in front of her, while Trace put both Sis and the stallion out to graze, each tethered to a separate line.

"What's his true name?" she asked, when Trace finally came to stand before her, looking like a Norse god in the dazzling glow of the morning sun. "The stallion, I mean."

Trace watched her solemnly for a few moments, then he flashed that illegal grin. "I call him Sentinel," he said.

She set her hands on her hips and tried to be annoyed, but she just couldn't manage it. Not on such a beautiful day. "Why didn't you tell me he was yours in the first place?"

He scratched the back of his head, narrowed his eyes to a good-natured squint. "That would have been one less reason to stay here," he said, "and I do mean to stay. Besides, I reckoned you'd figure it out on your own sooner or later, given that I showed up here on foot, carrying my saddle. Those Paiutes jumped me, one fine morning before I'd had my coffee, and relieved me of the horse. Evidently, they couldn't handle him and decided to pass the problem on to you." He stopped smiling. "The thing that troubles me about that is, it means they were watching this place. I'd be willing to bet they knew you and Skye and the boy were here alone, and they sure as hell had their eye on those oxen for a while, too."

Bridget had imagined the Indians watching her and Skye as they went about their chores, watching Noah, but until now, she'd never allowed herself to entertain the thought for too long. It was too frightening. "If that's so, then by now they know you're here."

He scanned the surrounding countryside, as though he expected the pack of renegades to come shrieking out of the timber, mounted on their war ponies and waving tomahawks over their heads. "Maybe it's just that I didn't get much rest last night," he said, "but I've got a real uneasy feeling just now. You keep Skye and Noah close by until it's time to leave for town."

Bridget nodded, unconsciously wringing the fabric of her skirt with both hands. "You'd best move your things into the cabin," she said.

"I'll do that," he replied.

As he walked away to gather up his rain-soaked belongings, Bridget harbored the notion that he might have been trying to scare her so she would let him stay inside the house. Instantly, she dismissed the idea. Trace was certainly no model of decorum, but he'd never use fear to get what he wanted. Anyway, the small hairs on her nape were standing up.

They left for Primrose Creek an hour later, Skye and Noah riding bareback on Sis, Trace on the stallion, with Bridget side-saddle in front of him. She tried to ignore the way it made her feel, having Trace's arms around her that way, however loosely, but the effort proved useless. Ever since he'd kissed her the night before—and honesty compelled her to consider the fact that she had most definitely kissed him back—she'd had a strange, boneless feeling, as though some slow, sweet fever had taken root inside her, causing her to melt away, digit by digit, limb by limb.

It was an exceedingly peculiar sensation, one she had never experienced before, even in her most intimate moments with Mitch. There had been few enough of those, of course, since her bridegroom had gone away to war barely a week after their wedding, leaving her pregnant with a child he would never see.

She had been filled with tenderness for Mitch. With Trace, it was something else entirely—a deep and violent yearning to touch him, to surrender to him, to lie beneath him. But there was the fury, too—always the fury. Where had he been when the world was crumbling around her, when the farm was overrun with carpetbaggers and Granddaddy was dying and she'd needed his help? Where?

Heat thrummed in her face, and she was glad her back was turned to him, because he would have seen too much if he'd been able to look at her straight on.

Water dappled the mud-and-manure streets of Primrose Creek, standing in dirty puddles big as lakes. The tents all had a sodden look about them, their tops weighted and dripping, but the townspeople seemed exuberant, and Bridget thought she understood their cheerful mood. There was something about a storm like last night's that made a person feel as though the world had been washed and polished, groomed for a new start.

Jake Vigil's grand mansion was at the far end of town, and the sawmill was beyond, just a long log structure, really, with a crudely lettered sign on the roof announcing lumber for sale. Jake himself was a tower of a man, standing well over six feet, broad-shouldered and square-jawed, with thoughtful hazel eyes and a head full of curly brown hair. Handsome as he was, Mr. Vigil was shy, at least around anyone in a skirt. Just seeing Bridget and Skye made him flush crimson and look away quickly, as if he'd found them somehow, well, indisposed.

Trace dismounted and introduced himself. He and Vigil shook hands, and then they vanished inside the mill building, deep in discussion.

Bridget took that opportunity to look around for a bank. Most likely, she wouldn't be able to get a loan anyhow, especially now that she wouldn't have the stallion for collateral, but she had to do something. Granddaddy had meant the Primrose Creek tract to stay in the family, her share and Skye's, and Christy and Megan's, too.

"What are you looking for?" Skye asked, always curious.

"A bank," Bridget said. "I thought if—"

"You thought if you borrowed money and paid Christy and Megan for their land, they'd never have cause to come out here and live across the creek from us."

Bridget was affronted, though not, if the truth were known, precisely justified in her response. She did cherish a certain secret worry that their cousins would come to Primrose Creek to claim their inheritance, unlikely as it seemed. The old feud would surely start up again. "You can't seriously think they'll *ever* set foot in a place like this," she said, as much to convince herself as Skye. Her conscience was troubling her a little, for she knew full well that Gideon hadn't meant for Christy and Megan to sell their land. He might even have put something in his will that would prevent it.

"They don't truly belong in England," Skye said. "The farm was home to them, just like it was to us. But now that's gone, and *this* is home."

Bridget rolled her eyes. "Can you really picture those two here, mincing down the street in their satin slippers, pressing their linen handkerchiefs to their pert little noses?" She was convinced she was safe in making the obvious assumption, for she truly couldn't imagine Christy and Megan in these surroundings.

Skye looked obstinate. "They'll come to Primrose Creek, Bridget. Just you wait and see. And you'd better be nice to them, too."

Before Bridget was forced to offer a reply, she spotted a sign hanging outside an especially ragged tent just down the road. *Preaching, this Sunday,* it read. Well, if there wasn't a bank, at least there was a church of sorts. The mining town might have stumbled unwittingly into the path of civilization after all.

Trace came out of the mill, notable for its lack of a shrieking saw if nothing else, looking very pleased with himself.

"We'll have a barn in no time at all," he said, "and a bedroom right after that."

Skye looked from Trace to Bridget, blushed a little, and then smiled. "You're adding a room?"

Trace nodded, as though there were nothing unusual or improper about discussing such accommodations in front of a young girl and a child. Not to mention his best friend's widow. "Come next spring," he said easily, "I'll build one for you, too, little sister, and one for Noah here."

Skye beamed at the prospect, then lapsed into a frown. "I'll be almost seventeen then. Ready to marry up with somebody and have my own place, next to Bridget's."

He chuckled. "Don't be in such a hurry, monkey," he said. "You'll be a long time married, after all."

Bridget glanced away. Her face felt hot again. "Is there a bank in this town?" she asked, maybe with just a hint of testiness in her voice.

"Now, Mrs. McQuarry," Trace drawled, pushing his hat to the back of his head and looking up at her with eyes full of mischief, "what in all the blue-skied world would you want with such an institution as that?"

She stiffened. She hated it when he called her "Mrs. McQuarry" in that particular tone, as though she were a young girl playing house and serving make-believe tea in miniature cups, instead of a woman grown, with a child to raise. "That ought to be perfectly obvious, *Mr. Qualtrough*. I want to borrow a sum of money and buy the land across the creek before our cousins sell it to someone—er—undesirable."

He was holding the cheek piece of the stallion's bridle, his shoulder touching Bridget's right knee and part of her thigh. She wished he wouldn't stand so close; it made her feel as if she were caught in the middle of the creek, with lightning striking all around her. "Gideon meant that land for Christy and Megan. I reckon you ought to leave them to decide what to do with it."

Bridget set her jaw, released it with an effort. "Christy asked me to buy the land," she said. "Read the letter if you don't believe me."

"Oh, I believe you, all right," Trace said, tugging the brim of his hat forward a little so it shaded his eyes. "But I figure you'd better just wait and see what happens before you go taking on any debts. You know Christy's impetuous; she might have changed her mind by now, and Megan would have had a thing or two to say about it, too, since half that tract is hers."

There was no sense in arguing, especially when Skye was right there, listening in, ready to take Trace's side in the matter. "It would appear that there is a church here," she said, because the silence had stretched to an uncomfortable length.

"Good," Trace said, grinning again. "We can get married proper-like."

"I have no intention of marrying you," Bridget informed him, out of pique and habit.

He just looked at her, with the memory of that kiss laughing in his eyes. His expression said, *Think what you like.* And he took the stallion's reins in one hand and headed for the tent in question.

"We'd like to get married," Trace said, when a white-haired man came out of the church tent, smiling at the prospect of welcoming stray sheep into the fold.

The reverend looked at Skye, then at Bridget, obviously puzzled.

"This one," Trace told him helpfully, laying a hand on Bridget's thigh, big as life, right there in front of God and everybody. He was just lucky she didn't have a riding quirt in her hand. "I figure we ought to get the words said as soon as possible, on account of we're living in sin."

Bridget's mouth dropped open. Skye giggled behind one hand, while Noah reached out both arms for Trace and said, "Papa, papa."

Trace took the boy from the saddle and settled him on one of his shoulders. The reverend took a handkerchief from the pocket of his frayed black waistcoat and wiped his brow.

"You can see," Trace added in a confidential tone, "that it's urgent."

"Yes, indeed," said the reverend. "Yes, indeed. Well, come inside, all of you, and let's attend to this matter."

"Now, wait just one moment," Bridget protested. "I ought to have something to say about this, it seems to me, and I—"

Skye and Trace and Noah all turned their gazes in her direction at once. She thought of unfriendly Indians and thunderstorms, snakebites and starvation, and knew in that moment that she *had* to agree to the marriage if she were going to live in the same skin with her conscience.

"All right," she said. "All right. But I would like a word with my future husband before the ceremony. *Alone.*"

Beaming, Skye sprang down from Sis's back, tied her to the nearest hitching post, and, collecting Noah from Trace's shoulders, followed the reverend into the church tent.

Trace put his hands on Bridget's waist and lifted her down, and just that much contact took her breath away, so that it was a moment or two before she could speak.

"Now, you listen to me, Trace Qualtrough," she whispered in a burst, waggling a finger under his nose. "We might be man and wife after this, but that does *not* mean that you will—that I will allow you to—"

He chuckled, bent to place a light, teasing kiss on her mouth, effectively silencing her. "I understand," he said. "We'll wait until you're ready or until that bedroom is finished, whichever comes first."

Bridget's mouth opened again; he closed it with a slight upward pressure from the fingertips of his right hand.

"This isn't a game, Bridget. I want a real wife. A home. Children."

She swallowed. "Children?" She hadn't thought much about that since Mitch was killed, though she'd wanted a big family before he died, for she hadn't expected to marry again.

"A whole passel of them," he said.

"Good heavens," Bridget said, and fanned her face with one hand.

He laughed again, took her arm, and propelled her toward the doorway of the church tent. "Now, don't go fretting yourself," he teased in an undertone. "I'll wait as long as a week."

It happened in a whirl of small events that all fit together to seal Bridget's fate, once and for all. The pastor of Primrose Creek's first church introduced himself as "Reverend Taylor, just Taylor." There were rows of benches, and someone had erected a modest pulpit of raw, unpainted wood.

Skye stood at Bridget's side, to serve as her maid of honor, and Noah, settled comfortably on Trace's hip, was the best man. The reverend cleared his throat and opened his prayer book with a solemnity suitable for such an occasion.

Bridget thought of running, just turning on her heel and fleeing, more than once, but the ceremony was over before she'd gotten up the nerve. Reverend Taylor pronounced her and Trace husband and wife, and Trace leaned down and touched his mouth to Bridget's.

The powerful, heated shock of that second kiss turned her already riotous senses to an indescribable muddle of wildly varying sensations. She had never guessed that a simple peck on the lips could provoke such havoc; this was very different from the quiet tenderness she'd felt when Mitch kissed her. Very different indeed.

She looked down at the golden band Trace had slipped onto her left-hand ring finger and was amazed. Trace had showed her that ring only a few days before and told her with certainty that they were about to be married. She hadn't believed him, but here she was, with a husband and a new name. She'd make an entry in the McQuarry Bible as soon as she got home.

After the wedding, Trace bought dinner for the four of them in the mess tent next to Jake Vigil's sawmill, surrounded by lumbermen and miners, drifters and farmers. Bridget thought they must all know she'd gone ahead and married Trace Qualtrough even though she'd sworn she could not be persuaded. The food, venison stew and fresh bread with lots of butter, was delicious, but Bridget didn't eat much. She was thinking about the coming night, her wedding night, wondering if Trace would honor his promise to wait until she was ready.

Even in her agitated state, Bridget noticed the way the men crowding the tent kept stealing sidelong glances at Skye, and that brought all her protective instincts to the fore. Very likely, these men knew Trace had been staying at the cabin and had concluded that the McQuarry women must be loose.

It ought to be obvious to these men that Skye was far too young and too innocent for courting, but even if they had noticed, they did not seem to be dissuaded. One of them, a young man in workman's clothes, had the nerve to approach the table. He had dark hair and green eyes, and Bridget supposed he was handsome enough, but he didn't look as though he had good prospects.

He cleared his throat and reddened a little when Skye looked up at him and smiled questioningly. The onlookers—and that included virtually everyone else in the mess tent—hooted and elbowed one another.

"My name's Tom Barkley," the boy said.

Skye glanced at Bridget, then met Barkley's green gaze. "Skye McQuarry."

More hoots and howls. Tom turned and took in the whole place with an angry gesture of one hand—the hand that held his slouch hat. "You all tend to your own business," he said, "and I'll tend to mine."

"Do something," Bridget whispered, elbowing Trace.

He reached for another piece of bread and buttered it calmly. "About what?" he asked, though he knew perfectly well.

"There's a dance on Saturday night," Tom said to Skye. "I would count it an honor if you'd let me bring you."

Bridget opened her mouth, fell silent when Trace's hand came to rest lightly on her forearm.

Skye averted her gaze for a few moments, then looked up into Tom's earnest, youthful face and nodded. "I'd like that," she said.

A great tension seemed to leave Tom at her agreement; his serious expression turned to a smile that even

Bridget would have had to admit was endearing. If anyone would have asked her, that is. Nobody did.

"I'll come by for you at six o'clock," Tom Barkley
said.

Skye regarded him steadily. "I—I don't really know
how to dance."

Tom's grin broadened. "That's all right," he said generously. "Neither do I. I reckon we can work it out
together."

Bridget cast a quick, sidelong glance in her husband's direction.

"Your baby sister is old enough to have callers," he
said very quietly. "Loosen your grip, if you don't want
to drive her off."

Bridget sighed, folded her hands in her lap, and waited for the meal to end. All she wanted now was to go
home, push up her sleeves, and deal with whatever was
going to happen next.

Chapter

7

*T*race acted as if nothing much had happened when they got home; without a word about the wedding, he put the horses to pasture and proceeded to pace off the area of the barn, pounding stakes into the ground to mark the corners. Bridget stood watching him until he looked her way and waved, and then she turned on one heel and fled into the cabin.

Noah was sitting on the floor, playing with the top Trace had bought for him, and Skye was on her knees in front of the trunk, pawing through the assorted garments inside.

"That blue silk," she said in a distracted tone of voice. "You brought that, didn't you? You didn't leave it behind in Virginia?"

Bridget felt a pang of nostalgia. Trace was right; Skye was no longer a little girl, and it was natural for her to have suitors. Knowing those things did nothing to ease Bridget's aching heart, however. She had been as

115

much a mother to Skye as an elder sister, and she loved her with a fierce intensity. "It's there somewhere," she said.

Skye found the gown, held it up by the shoulders. "It ought to fit, if I let it out a little and take down the hem." She met Bridget's gaze at last, clutching the simple dress against her chest as though it were woven of golden thread and trimmed in pearls. "I can wear it, can't I? Please?"

Bridget swallowed. She cared nothing about the dress, but her sister's well-being was another matter. "Yes," she said. "You can wear it. But don't you think—well—shouldn't you get to know Mr. Barkley a little better, before you go off to a dance with him?"

Skye's lovely face darkened. She got to her feet, holding the gown carefully the whole time. "How can I get to know the man at all if I can't talk to him?" she countered. She had an obstinate glint in her eyes, and her chin jutted out a little way. "I'm going to that dance, even if you won't let me borrow this dress."

"It's yours," Bridget said gently. Things would change between Skye and herself, after this day. There would be more callers, more dances, more dangers than a girl of sixteen could imagine. All the same, Skye would need her sister less and less, from now on, until finally she wouldn't need her at all.

The thought made a lonely ache in Bridget's chest. Trace was right; she had to let go of Skye, but it was one of the hardest things she'd ever had to do. Even worse, it wouldn't be long before Noah, too, was grown.

Skye must have seen something in the expression on Bridget's face, for she sighed, crossed the room, and embraced her quickly but with real affection. "You've always protected me, looked after me, worried about me," she said, tears glistening at the roots of her lashes. "I'll always be grateful. But don't you see, Bridge? It's your turn to be happy. For once in your life, think of yourself."

Bridget sniffled, summoned up a wavery smile. "I'm married," she said. "Oh, Skye, what on earth possessed me to take Trace Qualtrough for a husband?"

Skye laughed and kissed Bridget's forehead. "I think you showed a great deal of discernment, choosing him. It surprised me a little, to tell the truth—I was afraid you'd either never marry again or hitch yourself to somebody who wanted taking care of." She paused, blushing a little when she saw Bridget's face quicken with amused interest. "You know, because you're so strong and everything. Let him love you, Bridge. Please, just set your pride aside and let Trace love you."

Bridget was forced to turn away then. Love had nothing to do with her marriage to Trace; she'd loved one man in her life, and that was Mitch. To let those feelings die would be a cruelty, an unthinkable betrayal. No, her union with Trace was merely one of convenience. "You'd best get started on that dress," she said, tying on an apron, "if you expect to have it ready by Saturday."

Skye let out a long sigh.

Noah had gone to the doorway, where the afternoon sun shone around him. "Listen, Mama. There's wagons coming."

Sure enough, the faint sound of creaking wheels and horses' hooves found its way across the creek. "That would be the lumber Trace ordered for the barn," Bridget said. *And the bedroom,* added a voice in her mind.

How long, she wondered, without examining her reasons too closely, did it take to build a barn?

To Skye's delight, Tom Barkley was driving one of the two huge wagons; he and Mr. Vigil drove right across the creek without even pausing, calling to their reluctant teams and slapping down the reins.

"Tom here had himself an idea," Mr. Vigil said, cocking a thumb in the other man's direction, when Bridget joined the visitors and her husband—*her husband*—on the future site of the barn. "Said we ought to have the Saturday night dance out here, at your place. Some of us could come early and help you raise the walls." He looked up, assessed the sky. "Sooner you have shelter for your stock, the better. The weather can change pretty quickly around here. Turn nasty, the way it did last night."

Bridget gnawed on her lower lip. A barn could go up pretty quickly when folks lent a hand, and that meant she might find herself sharing a room with Trace far sooner than she'd expected. An unseemly thrill raced through her, chased by a sense of delicious alarm. She didn't dare glance in Trace's direction, because she knew he'd be looking at her, reading her mind. Grinning.

"We'd be obliged for any help," she heard Trace say.

It was settled, as easily as that. Trace and Mr. Vigil and Tom set themselves to unloading the lumber and two kegs of nails, and then the visitors took their leave, rattling away in their huge, empty wagons.

Stacks of fragrant timber stood all around.

"I suppose you think you're pretty clever," Bridget said to Trace under her breath as the two of them stood side by side, waving Tom and Jake Vigil out of sight.

"You'll have that barn finished in a fraction of the time with so much help. And how did you pay for all this?"

Trace laughed. "I can't figure out whether you're pleased or ready to tie into me with your claws out. As for the lumber, I made a swap with Jake. His pinewood for my help finishing his mill."

"You amaze me," Bridget confessed.

And Trace laughed again. "Just you wait," he said. "There are more surprises ahead."

Saturday morning brought seventeen men, armed with saws and hammers, chisels and measuring sticks. The barn seemed to take shape before Bridget's very eyes; every time she ventured to peer around the corner of the cabin, another wall was framed. By late afternoon, the walls were up, and the roof was being nailed into place.

Skye changed into her carefully altered dancing gown well beforehand, put her hair up, let it down, put it up again. She paced and waited and watched the progress of the sun as it descended in the western skies, as if by watching she could hurry it along. Bridget hid her smile and concentrated on keeping track of Noah; he wanted very much to participate in the barn building, but he was forbidden to go near the project. Even Trace had agreed to that; it was simply too dangerous.

Skye was visibly relieved when sunset finally settled over the land, and Bridget herself felt a certain sweet excitement. Now, the horses would have stalls, walls to keep out wolves and at least discourage unfriendly Indians, a thick roof to shelter them from rain and wind and snow. She could get a cow. Plant a field of hay next summer. . . .

But it wasn't the practicality of having a barn that made her want to sing, and she knew it. It was the idea of dancing with Trace, being held in his arms, looking up into his eyes. She'd hardly thought of anything else since their wedding three days before, even though Trace had been nothing if not a gentleman. He hadn't even tried to kiss her, as a matter of fact.

She wasn't sure how she felt about that. On the one hand, she'd have been furious if he made any untoward advances. On the other, she was indignant that he *hadn't*.

As evening approached, guests began to arrive, in wagons, in buggies, on foot, and on horseback. Lanterns were lit, and the musicians—miners with fiddles and a dark-skinned man with a guitar—set themselves up to play in the pitch-scented confines of the new barn. There were a few women, grim-faced and clearly on the lookout for sin run amok, but most of the revelers were men. When the music started, a spirited jig, they danced with one another. Skye and Mr. Barkley joined in, laughing at their own stumbling efforts to get in step, and Bridget looked on, clapping in time to the music, Noah at her side.

Trace came up behind her, mussed Noah's hair with one hand.

"Well, Mrs. Qualtrough," Trace said. "What do you think of your barn?"

Mrs. Qualtrough. Now, wasn't that something? A sweet quiver started in the pit of her stomach and radiated outward, into every part of her. "It's very sturdy," she allowed.

He grinned. "That it is," he said. "Plenty of lumber left, too. I can start building on to the house right away."

Bridget knew he was trying to get a rise out of her, and she was darned if she'd let him succeed. He'd shaken her up enough as it was.

It was about time somebody turned the tables on Trace Qualtrough. "Yes," she said, watching the dancers, clapping her hands, smiling. "And I've been thinking. You're doing all the work. You ought to have that room to yourself."

He took her elbow, turned her to face him, and pulled her into his arms. Noah was already at the other end of the barn by that time—the older he got, the faster he moved, it seemed to Bridget—watching the fiddlers ply their bows, and a dizzy feeling made her head light. The musicians took up a reel, and Trace spun both of them into its midst without missing a step.

"That wasn't our agreement," he pointed out.

Bridget beamed up at him, but the familiar anger, never far from the surface, was crackling inside her. "Are you saying that I must pay for this barn with my favors?"

He wasn't even pretending to smile by then, but he kept up with the lively tune spilling from the fiddles and the guitar, and made Bridget keep up, too. "You know damn well that isn't what I meant," he said. "You're my wife. I told you, I want a real marriage—complete with kids."

"What about Mitch?"

He stopped, pulled her out of the barn to stand with him under a drapery of sparkling stars. "Mitch," he said, his face close to hers, "is dead. It's about time you accepted that."

Bridget wanted to slug him, because deep down, she knew he was right, and it was too painful a thing to admit.

"Do you think I need reminding of that? He's lying in the ground somewhere, while we're—we're—" She gestured toward the barn, spilling light and music. *"Dancing."*

He took her by the sides of her waist and dragged her hard against him. "What's wrong with that, Bridget?" he demanded. "Husbands and wives dance together."

She was breathless. He was, well, hard. Everywhere. The warm summer night seemed even warmer, all of a sudden. She pulled away. "You didn't come home," she seethed, and suddenly tears were streaming down her face. "You wrote me a letter to tell me my husband was dead, but *you didn't come home*. Damn you, I watched the road for you, every day and every night—"

Trace stared at her, obviously shocked. "Is that what's got you riled?" he asked. "I was in a prison hospital, Bridget. I nearly lost my leg."

It was her turn to be stunned. "But you didn't mention that, in the letter—"

"Damn it, Bridget," Trace went on, "Mitch was my best friend, and losing him was probably the worst thing that ever happened to me. I was thinking about that, and besides, it was three months before I could bribe a Reb into posting that letter." He closed his eyes for a moment, and when he spoke again, his voice was lower, softer. "When are we going to let the past rest with Mitch and move on?"

Bridget swallowed; she was still reeling. "You were shot? Thrown into prison?"

"Yes," he snapped. He was holding her firmly by the upper arms, and she knew he wanted to shake her. She also knew he wouldn't. "And don't pretend you don't know I was in love with you. In case you've forgotten, I begged you not to marry Mitch."

She closed her eyes, remembering that interlude in her grandmother's fragrant garden. Absorbing the dual realization that she had indeed known how Trace felt, and that she'd denied it ever since. Moreover, she'd disavowed her own passions as well.

Trace went on, his words picking up steam as his temper rose. He was relentless. "And what's more, you loved me in return. You married Mitch because you thought you could keep him from going to war that way. You thought you could *save* him, Bridget, and that's a damn pitiful reason to marry anybody!"

Tears burned behind Bridget's eye sockets. "Stop it."

"I won't stop it," Trace said, holding her wrists now. "I loved you then, and I love you now, and I'm not about to let you cling to a dead man's coattails until it's too late. I'm through living out that lie, Bridget, and so are you!"

Shame filled her, for she could not refute what Trace had said. She had always cared for him. She always would. But she had sworn her loyalty to Mitch, she had borne his son, all the while loving another man. His best friend. It was that she had to make up for: the deception. Mitch had died believing she loved him.

Trace caught her face between his hands, leaned in, and kissed her, hard. She melted, opened her mouth to him, opened her soul. Too soon, he set her away from him with a swiftness that was at once unwilling and resolute. His breathing was quick and ragged, and Bridget, with one palm resting against his chest, could feel his heart pounding. "Enough," he said. "Enough." He might have been speaking to himself, as well as to her. When he met her eyes, she was chilled by the sorrow she saw in his face. "I love you, and I want you. Oh, God, how I want you. But when you come to my bed, Bridget, you have to come alone. You can't bring Mitch with you."

The implication stung fiercely. She drew back her hand, ready to slap Trace hard across the face, but in the end, she couldn't make herself do it.

It was then, as they stood facing each other, their fractured dreams lying between them, that the raid began.

It started with a single, blood-chilling shriek, swelling out of the darkness like a gust of the devil's breath. In the next moment, Indians came from every direction, mounted on their shaggy, hungry ponies, spears and rifles in hand. Trace shouted a warning to the people in the barn—not that one was necessary—grabbed Bridget by the arm, and hurled her under the nearest wagon.

"Stay there!" he ordered.

Noah. Skye. Bridget went out the other side and raced toward the barn.

She heard the horse, felt the thunder rising up out of the ground, reverberating through her lower limbs like an earthquake, and then a steel-hard arm encircled her waist, and she was dragged up onto the back of a horse. She tried to scream, but the sound lodged in her throat.

The Indian growled something at her in his own language, but Bridget understood, all the same. He was warning her to be silent, and when he pressed the blade of his knife to the side of her neck a second later, she knew he meant it.

Dazed, sick with horror, Bridget watched as the beautiful new barn went up in flames. *Noah!* She screamed inwardly. *Skye!*

Gunfire erupted all around them after that, and out of the corner of one eye, Bridget saw that the house was on fire as well. *Trace,* she pleaded silently, *Trace.*

Fear gnawed at Bridget's insides, brought a sticky sweat out all over her body. Crimson reflections danced off the flesh of Indians and horses, and there was so much noise, yelling and shooting. So much fire.

Bridget squinted, her eyes burning in the thickening smoke of her burning hopes, searching in vain for even a glimpse of her son, her sister, and Trace. Oh, God, where was Trace? Had they killed him, these marauding savages—not Paiutes, Bridget could see, but rogues and outlaws of many different tribes.

The man who held her prisoner tightened his grip and shouted something to the others. Then he spurred the pony hard with his heels, and they were jolting away, into the night. Into the terrifying unknown.

Bridget was numb where her own fate was concerned; she could not think beyond the terror that she would never see her family again. *Oh, God,* she prayed, *don't let them be dead. I can't bear to lose any of them.*

It seemed to Bridget that they rode endlessly, on and on, and at a teeth-clattering speed. Uphill, down again, through dark, gloomy trees, smelling incongruously of Christmas. Finally, toward dawn, they reached a camp of sorts, a smoky place, ripe with the smells of untanned animal hides, horses, and human beings.

When Bridget was flung to the ground, she scrambled immediately to her feet, running among the horses, searching desperately for her sister or her son. The renegades laughed at her efforts, and one of them put his foot out to make hard contact with her shoulder and send her sprawling.

She got up immediately and hurtled toward the offender, furious as a scalded cat. Like everyone else, she'd wondered, from time to time, if she were capable of killing. Now, she knew the answer.

She scrabbled halfway up the raider's leg, clawing her way toward his face.

He swore—she didn't need to know his language to recognize a curse—and kicked her again, this time harder. She struck the ground, felt a stone or a horse's hoof stab at her left temple, and lost consciousness.

"Mizz Qualtrough?" The voice was feminine, a cautious whisper. A moment passed before Bridget realized the other person was speaking English. "Mizz Qualtrough, are you all right?"

Bridget opened her eyes. Her headache pulsed through her entire body, in time with her runaway heartbeat, and she found that she was seated on the ground, tied at the wrists and ankles with painfully tight rawhide, the rough bark of a tree biting into her back. She wanted to throw up but somehow managed to control the impulse.

"Mizz Qualtrough?"

She peered at her fellow captive—Miss Florence Coffin, until then a member of the Primrose Creek faction who pretty much kept to themselves. Bridget had always considered them somewhat standoffish, but such things hardly mattered in their present circumstances.

Florence looked some the worse for wear, with her hair straggling and her dress torn, but her chin was up, and her eyes snapped with the determination to survive, no matter what.

"Miss Coffin," Bridget finally acknowledged, straining her neck to look around. "Are there others?"

"I don't think so," the other woman said. "And given the situation, I think you ought to call me Flossie."

Bridget smiled to herself, in spite of everything, because she had never once imagined this usually dour woman as a Flossie. Of course, she'd only seen her at a distance, and they'd never spoken. "My name is Bridget," she said.

"I know," replied Flossie with a sigh. "What do you suppose they mean to do with us?"

The possibilities didn't bear thinking about, but Bridget thought of them all the same, and bile rushed into the back of her throat, burning like acid. Again, she wanted to vomit; again, she stifled the impulse. "Let's concentrate on getting out of here," she said when she could manage to speak. "They probably mean to trade us for something. Horses, maybe, or food."

Flossie looked skeptical. She'd heard the same terrifying stories of slavery, rape, scalping, and all-over tattooing as Bridget had, no doubt, but she kept her spine straight. You had to admire a person with that much gumption. "Let's hope you're right."

"Did—did you see—was anyone killed?"

"I don't know," Flossie replied, and now her gaze was gentle. Why, Bridget wondered, had she ever imagined these townswomen, however distant, as anything other than ordinary human beings, trying to make their way in a difficult world? "Seems likely, with all that shooting, that somebody's got to be dead."

Bridget couldn't answer, and for a while, she and Flossie just sat there in silence, wrestling with their own thoughts. The birds began to chirp a morning song, and as light spilled across the camp, they saw that there were no tepees or lodges, just a campfire, a closely guarded band of some two dozen grazing horses, and about half that many Indians, all in various states of drunkenness. If there were other captives, they were somewhere out of sight.

Hatred spilled through Bridget's heart, cold and bracing. Her headache eased a little, and so did the nausea centered in her middle. If they'd harmed any of the people she loved, Skye and Noah and, yes, Trace, she'd see every one of these miscreants in hell, even if she had to lead them there by the hand, one by one.

As if discerning her thoughts, one of the men got up and staggered toward her, a foul grin creasing his filthy, painted face. Only then, in the light of day, did she see that the man was white, merely posing as an Indian. A quick glance around the camp confirmed that most of the others were, too.

Bridget was sure this particular scoundrel was the one who had kicked her to the ground, and she glared at him.

"Well, now, pretty lady," he drawled, showing rotted teeth. "I reckon somebody will pay a good price for you. And you'll only be a little the worse for wear."

Bridget tried to kick at him, but her feet were still bound.

He laughed, pulled a knife, and held it close to Bridget's face for a moment, no doubt expecting the gesture to subdue her into cowed silence. It didn't work, for Bridget was past caution; she had nothing to lose at this point, and she meant to go for broke.

"Leave us alone," Flossie said.

"Shut up," said the man without so much as glancing toward her. Then he proceeded to cut Bridget's bonds, freeing her feet first and then her hands. "I believe I'll just take you out into the woods a little way," he said. "Teach you how to behave like a lady."

There was a sound, only a slight cracking, but it drew Bridget's awareness like metal shavings rushing toward a magnet, and she caught the merest glint of fair hair, just out of the corner of one eye. She gave none of this away by her bearing, however, and, gathering as much spittle as her dry mouth would provide, spat into her tormenter's face.

The man drew back his arm to strike her, and Bridget was getting ready to spit again, when suddenly the camp was filled with men and horses. The "Indians," taken by surprise and still reeling from a night of revelry and thieving, fled in every direction, like chickens with a fox in their midst.

Bridget didn't take time to assess the situation; she snatched up the knife her would-be assailant had dropped and hurried to cut Flossie loose and drag her out of the fray.

She saw the paint stallion in the center of the skirmish, with Trace on its bare, glistening back, wielding the butt of a rifle like some sort of medieval weapon. He was covered in soot, from the top of his head to the soles of his boots, and his shirt was soaked through with sweat. Their eyes met, and as the other men, Jake Vigil among them, along with the marshal and Tom Barkley and a number of posse members, rode down the rest of the outlaws, he reined the paint in her direction, bent down, and lifted her up in front of him.

He looked a sight, and she was absolutely certain she'd never seen a more beautiful one.

"Fancy meeting you here, Mrs. Qualtrough," he said with a grin.

The grin told her that Skye and Noah were safe; she let her forehead rest against his shoulder for a long moment, then looked up into his eyes. "I've been a fool," she said.

He touched his mouth to hers, but only lightly. After all, they were in the middle of a crowd. "And?" he prompted.

She flushed a little. "And I love you."

"And?" he persisted.

"And—"

He waited. He wasn't going to make it easy, that was plain.

Bridget swallowed, glanced around, and lowered her eyes briefly before meeting his gaze again, steadily. "And the sooner you finish that bedroom, the sooner we can start having babies."

He kissed her again, this time on the bridge of the nose. "Oh, I don't think we need to wait quite that long," he responded, in a gruff tone meant for her ears alone.

"Skye and Noah—?"

"Skye and Noah are fine, and you know it," he said. "Unlike you, they stayed put and hid, just like I told them to."

"The house and barn?"

He sighed. "Gone. But we'll start over. There's still time enough to get some sort of shelter built before winter."

"Where will we stay in the meantime?" She hooked a finger idly between two of the buttons on his shirt.

"I reckon we'll have to sleep in that old lodge for a while, anyhow. The marshal sent them back to town for the night. His wife will see to them."

Bridget nodded, looked deep into her husband's eyes. "I've always loved you," she said.

He smiled. "I know." His arms tightened around her, and she settled close against him, a strong woman content to be held and soothed and protected. For a while, anyway.

"Trace?" She did not look up at him this time, for she felt suddenly shy.

"Yes?" His voice was low, and it echoed through her like a caress.

She kissed the hollow beneath his left ear. "Let's go home."

Epilogue

Bridget McQuarry Qualtrough would certainly not have been the first bride to lie with her husband, beneath a blue canopy of sky and a fragrant arch of pine branches, but she might well have been the happiest. They made their bed in the tall grass, near the creek, where Trace had set up his lean-to when he first arrived, and their privacy was complete, Skye and Noah having gone to town to spend a day and a night with the marshal and his wife.

He kissed her, gently, almost reverently, and smoothed her hair back from her face with a light pass of his hand. "Bridget," he said, as though tasting her name, marveling over it, and then he grinned. He took her breath away, even covered in sweat and soot as he was. "I'm about to make love to you," he announced. "Unless you have an objection, of course."

Bridget's face heated, but she shook her head. She might have been a virgin, she had so little experience. "I'm not sure just how—"

133

He laid an index finger to her lips. "Everything will be perfect," he said, and the promise sent waves of desire rolling through her, heating her blood, making her body restless. "Let me prove it."

She swallowed, then nodded.

He was fiddling with the buttons at the front of her dress, which was no cleaner than his clothes were.

She trembled. "What—?"

Trace smiled, smoothed one side of her bodice away, revealing the thin camisole beneath. Her breast strained against the fabric, reaching for him, and he smiled at that, bent his head, and touched the nipple with his tongue, leaving a wet spot on the linen.

Bridget groaned and arched her back.

"Oh, yes," Trace whispered. "Yes." Then he uncovered her breasts entirely, worked the soiled dress skillfully down over her hips. He fell to her hungrily, and she cried out in welcome, both hands cupped behind his head, pressing him close.

Trace took his time, attending to each breast in its turn, extracting whimpers and pleas from an increasingly frenzied Bridget. All the while, he was undoing the ribbons that held her now-crumpled camisole closed, and when he slid one hand down the front of her drawers to caress her private place, she nearly went mad with the want of him.

"Please, Trace," she whispered.

He kissed his way down her breastbone and made a circle around her navel with the tip of his tongue. His low groan echoed in her very bones, but he did not increase his pace. Instead, he pushed his palm through the damp nest of curls at the juncture of her thighs and began a slow, light rubbing motion.

Bridget strained against his hand, gasped when she felt his fingers slide inside her. And still it continued; he returned to her mouth, kissed her deeply, demandingly. She thought her heart would burst, it was racing so fast, and a pressure was building under Trace's palm that threatened an incomprehensibly sweet mayhem.

She had never known, never guessed. . . .

"Oh," she cried as fresh, delicious shock rocketed through her veins. *"Please—"*

He continued to kiss her, continued to ply her toward absolute madness. And then the sky split apart, and the earth trembled, and Bridget clung to Trace with both arms and sobbed while her body convulsed in ecstasy.

He brought her down slowly, as slowly as he had raised her to heaven, and when she lay still at last, dazed and breathing hard, he kissed and nibbled and teased her back to the same heated state of delicious madness she'd been in before. This time when she begged, however, he parted her legs and mounted her, and just when she thought she might claw his bare back to ribbons in her desperation, he entered her. The thrust was powerful but exquisitely controlled, as were the ones to follow, and Bridget rode back up through the clouds, careened past stars and planets, and returned to herself only when a long, timeless interval had passed.

"I love you," she said, curled against his chest, when the faculty of speech came back. "I want to spend the rest of my life with you."

He rolled onto his side, and she lay on her back in the fragrant grass, naked and free. He took a blade of that grass and teased her nipple with it, grinning. "I believe that can be arranged, Mrs. Qualtrough. And just in case I haven't said it yet, I love you, too. I think I always have."

She gave a soft moan. He was going to excite her all over again. "If you leave me, Trace Qualtrough, I swear by all that's holy, I'll come after you and bring you home."

He replaced the blade of grass with his tongue. "Don't you worry," he said. "I'm not going anyplace. Ever."

She closed her eyes. Gasped with pleasure as he suckled again. "Promise?"

"Promise," he replied, at his leisure.

She smiled and, with a long, crooning sigh, gave herself up to her husband's lovemaking. One thing about Trace Qualtrough—he always kept his word.

Christy

For Ramona Stratton, with love.
From here out, it's all good.

Prologue

Fort Grant, Nevada
1868

With no small amount of trepidation, Christy McQuarry peered through the late Mrs. Royd's limp lace curtains, assessing the man sent to fetch them home to Primrose Creek. It had been alarming enough, during the long, dull winter passed at Fort Grant, to consider putting herself, Caney, and especially Megan, her younger sister, in the charge of some mere passerby for the remainder of the journey. A grizzled old prospector, for example, or one of the seedy-looking scouts who came and went on occasion, foul-smelling and full of horrendous tales involving Indians and outlaws. For some indefinable reason, she found this particular man, fair-haired and blue-eyed, insolently handsome in his ordinary but obviously clean clothes and well-worn hat, almost equally disturbing. He rode a splendid cocoa-brown stallion with a pale mane and tail, and a .45 caliber pistol rested low and easy on his left hip, seemingly as much a part of him as a finger or a foot.

"I don't like him," she confided to Caney Blue, the tall and angular black woman who had worked on the McQuarry farm, back in Virginia, for as long as Christy's memory reached. Which, since she was nearly twenty, was a considerable distance. "He's too handsome. Too sure of himself."

Caney was smiling her broad and luminous smile, watching as the man dismounted and offered a hand and a grin to the aging army officer who had gone out to greet him. "That so?" she said, her dark eyes following the man as he spoke with the colonel in the street just beyond the window of the modest parlor. There was precisely one house at Fort Grant, if indeed such a rustic structure could be described as a house, and it belonged to the recently widowed commander of the installation, Colonel Webley Royd, who had kindly given the place over to the women upon their arrival the previous October with the first flurries of snow. "Well, I think he's right purty. And I like a man who thinks well of himself."

A star-shaped badge glinted on the front of the visitor's shirt, and Christy clamped her back teeth together for a moment, without quite knowing why a stranger should affect her so. She might have been struck by a runaway freight car, so great and so confounding was the impact of merely *seeing* him. What would it be like to actually meet him? To travel in his company?

"Colonel Royd told me his name is Zachary Shaw," Megan put in eagerly, from her post on the other side of the window. Being just sixteen, she could not be expected, Christy supposed, to exhibit any real degree of good judgment. She had a headful of dreams, Megan did, and at the same time one of the finest minds Christy had ever encountered. She meant to see that her sister didn't waste that gift by settling for a house and a husband and a half dozen babies, which she feared Megan was wont to do. "He's a U.S. Marshal."

He's trouble, Christy thought to herself. At just that moment, as if to confirm this opinion, Marshal Zachary Shaw seemed to sense her perusal; his gaze met and captured hers through the gauzy veil of lace. Held it fast.

Infuriated, and stirred in a way that was not entirely proper, Christy glared at him, in hopes of hiding the fact that she could not look away until he chose to release her.

He grinned and tugged at the brim of his shapeless hat, and Christy felt a sudden, primitive sort of heat pounding in all her pulses, throbbing in her face.

"Well, I'll be," Caney remarked in a murmur. Caney could be damnably perceptive at times.

Christy somehow gathered the strength to step back from the window and whirl away on one heel. "He won't do," she blustered, pacing at the edge of a hand-hooked rug. "He simply won't do. He's arrogant, and almost certainly a rascal. We'll have to find someone else to escort us. Or make the trip on our own."

Megan turned to stare at her sister, appalled. With her auburn hair, flawless skin, and Irish-green eyes, Megan was a stunning beauty, though, despite her brilliance, a naive child in so many ways. From the day they left Virginia for the first time, amid the scandal of their parents' acrimonious divorce, life had consisted of one loss, one humiliation, one defeat after another, but things were going to be different from here on, if Christy had any say in the matter. And she had plenty.

"Christy!" Megan marveled. "You can't be serious—it's miles and miles to Primrose Creek, and there are wild animals, and road agents, and renegade Indians—"

Caney was already shaking her head. "You've done gone fool-headed if you think we're goin' up into them mountains on our own," she vowed. During the trip west, she'd often allowed Christy to help her tend the sick and injured, and once she'd even helped to deliver a baby. Caney had told Christy she had a gift for healing, but most of the time—like now—the woman treated her as if she were still a child.

Christy didn't relish the thought of another perilous journey herself, but pride usually compelled her to stand her ground in the face of any opposition, and that warm spring afternoon was no exception. "Good heavens," she said in a hissing whisper, "we traveled all the way from Virginia, didn't we?"

"We was with a wagon train," Caney pointed out, just as impatiently.

Megan's eyes were enormous with memories of the voyage, many of which were unpleasant ones. They'd been through so much in the past few years, first being dragged away from the family to England, then being sent back again over tempestuous seas, only to reach Virginia and find that their grandfather, Gideon McQuarry, had died, as had both their father and uncle, and the farm was gone forever. They were essentially penniless now, she and Megan, and the tract of land at Primrose Creek, an inheritance from Granddaddy, to be shared equally with their cousins, Bridget and Skye, represented their best hope of gaining a foothold.

"He looks strong," Megan said at last. Hopefully. "Marshal Shaw, I mean."

"Ain't that the truth of it," Caney commented, still watching him through the window. "Knows how to take care of himself, a body can see that right off."

"And us, too," Megan pressed.

Christy let out a long sigh. She would put aside her personal misgivings—hadn't she done that often enough to become expert at it?—and go along with what Megan and Caney wanted. "All right," she breathed. "All right. We'll travel with the marshal." *But no good will come of it,* she added, to herself.

Colonel Royd brought the lawman to supper that evening, and they all sat down to one of Caney's legendary fried chicken dinners. Although she tried not to fidget, Christy was unsettled throughout the meal, and her appetite, usually unshakable, was nonexistent. Little wonder; she was seated directly across from the marshal, by some contrivance of Caney's, and when he looked at her with those bright blue eyes, she felt as though her deepest secrets were written on her skin. Worse, he had taken notice of her discomfiture, and—just *imagine*—it made him smile a very small, very private, twitch-at-the-corner type of smile.

"Have you lived at Primrose Creek long, Mr. Shaw?" she asked, her hands knotted in her lap, just to show him he hadn't had any affect whatsoever upon her. Which, of course, he had.

He lifted one finely made shoulder in a semblance of a shrug. "No, ma'am," he said. "Fact is, I was just passing through, and I got into a poker game over at the Silver Spike. I lost, as it happens."

"You lost?" Christy echoed, mystified, and immediately wished she'd held her tongue. Odd, how this man perturbed her. If there was one thing Christy prided herself on, it was her ability to retain her emotional balance, yet he made her feel as though she were dancing on a rolling log in the middle of a raging river. "I don't see what that has to do with anything."

Again, that grin, so boyish and yet so grown-up. So certain of himself and his ability to make his way in the world. "No, ma'am," he said easily. "I don't reckon you would." He paused, took a breath and another of Caney's biscuits. His third, Christy noted. "My old friend Sam Flynn was wearing this badge then. He wanted to head down to Virginia City and try his luck in the mines for a year or so, but he couldn't find anybody willing to serve out his term. He suckered me into a poker game, and, well, like I said, I lost. Fact is, I'm not exactly sure he didn't stack the deck."

The colonel gave his booming laugh. He was a pleasant, somewhat corpulent man, fond of Caney's cooking. Indeed, he'd tried to persuade her to stay and keep house for him there at Fort Grant, and certainly Christy couldn't have blamed the woman if she'd agreed, considering that the position offered a salary along with room and board. All she and Megan had to offer was their friendship.

"That would be like Sam," Royd said, serving himself another helping of mashed potatoes. "If I were you, Shaw, I wouldn't look for him to come back—especially if he strikes it rich in the Comstock."

Mr. Shaw gave a rueful sigh. "If he doesn't show up when he's supposed to," he said, "I might just have to hunt him down and shoot him."

A brief silence descended, while everyone else at the table, Christy suspected, tried to decide whether or not he was serious. His expression, while affable enough and certainly polite, gave nothing away.

Then the colonel laughed again, thunderously, all but shaking the crockery on the table. Clearly, he thought the marshal was joking. Caney chuckled, a bit belatedly, and Megan twittered a little, her gaze resting adoringly upon Zachary Shaw.

Christy, however, was not amused, for it seemed to her that the marshal had spoken in all seriousness. "When will we set out for Primrose Creek?" she asked, without smiling.

"Dawn," Mr. Shaw answered. He wasn't smiling, either. It seemed to Christy in that moment that they understood each other, for good or for ill. "I'll want to load the wagon tonight. Everything is packed, I assume?"

"Such as it is," Caney put in, while Christy was strangling on a civil answer of her own.

"Good," he said, still watching Christy. His gaze had not strayed from her face, she realized, in some moments. "It's a hard trip, and it's dangerous. We'll be two days on the road, at the least. I'm in charge until we get there, and I'll thank everybody to remember that."

There was another silence, during which Christy tried to stare him down, let him know who was boss. In the end, though, it was she who looked away.

Zachary passed the night in the soldiers' barracks and soon found that he was the envy of every man there, just because he was squiring the women back up the mountain to Primrose Creek.

Lying on his back on a cot, his hands cupped behind his head as he settled in to sleep, he listened.

"That dark-haired one, Miss Christy," ventured one soldier, after the last lamp was extinguished, "she's pretty as a china doll. Mean, though."

Zachary felt a tightening in his gut, though he grinned into the darkness. "She's got the temperament of a wet cat, all right," he allowed.

Another voice piped up. "Ain't like we didn't try to court her, every last one of us. She's too fancy for the likes of us, though—made that right plain. In fact, she as good as told Jim Toth to his face that there's nobody here to suit her. Didn't she, Jim?"

"Yup," someone, probably Jim, replied mournfully. "She comes from money and property. All you got to do is look at her to know that. Said she's got to think of her future, and her sister's."

Zachary's smile faded, though he couldn't have said why he took to feeling gloomy all of a sudden. It wasn't as if he gave a damn about Christy McQuarry.

Chapter

1

"There it is," the marshal said, with obvious relief, doffing his hat to indicate a meandering stream, winking with silvery patches of sunlight as it flowed across the valley tucked amid the peaks of the High Sierras. Trees bristled on all sides, ponderosa pine and Douglas fir mostly, so dense that they appeared more blue than green, though there were splashes of aspen and maple, oak and cottonwood here and there. "That's Primrose Creek. The town's over yonder, about two miles southwest of here."

Christy stood in her stirrups and drew in a sharp breath. The air was soft with the promise of a warm summer, and the view was so spectacular that it made her heart catch and brought the sting of tears to her eyes.

Megan, riding beside her, drew in a breath and then exclaimed, "It's Beulah Land!" She pointed eagerly. "And look—that must be Bridget and Skye's house, there by the bend in the stream. Oh, Christy, isn't it grand?"

Some of Christy's own delight in their arrival faded. She and Megan had passed the war years in Great Britain, at the insistence of their mother, Jenny Davis McQuarry, who had kicked up considerable dust back in Virginia by leaving her drunken rounder of a husband, Eli, and running off with a titled Englishman. Jenny's new love, a relatively minor baron as it turned out, and not an earl as he had led her to believe, was nonetheless the master of Fieldcrest, a small estate in the heart of Devon. He had promptly sent both his bride's daughters off to St. Martha's, a boarding school outside London—over Jenny's anemic protests—and had never made a secret of the fact that he would have preferred to leave them behind with their ruffian relatives in the first place. When Jenny had died suddenly of a fever in the winter of 1866, he'd been quick to pack them off to America.

Christy would have been overjoyed to return, except that by then they had almost no family left; their father and Uncle J.R. had both been killed in the War between the States, and their passage had been booked when word of their beloved grandfather's death reached them in the form of a terse letter from Gideon McQuarry's lawyers. Already grief-stricken at her mother's passing, and now Gideon's, Christy had been in a private panic. She'd succeeded in putting on a brave front, for Megan's sake, and had impetuously written her cousin Bridget, an act she would soon regret, offering to sell their half of the inheritance, hers and Megan's, as outlined in the copy of Gideon McQuarry's will. There had not been enough time for a response from Bridget before their ship sailed, and, besides, she did not have the right to dispose of Megan's share of the bequest in the same way as her own. With only their clothes—including ugly school uniforms and a few ball gowns garnered from their mother's wardrobe—a set of china that had belonged to their grandmother Rebecca, and the few modest jewels Jenny had managed to acquire during her two tempestuous marriages, they crossed the sea and arrived in Virginia to find strangers living in the house they had loved. Granddaddy was buried in the family plot, alongside the beautiful wife who had died in a riding accident when the girls were small. Uncle J.R. rested beside his father, his grave marked with an impressive granite stone declaring him a Union hero. Christy and Megan's father, Eli, lay next to Rebecca, but a little apart from the others, or so it seemed to Christy. He had fought bravely, his wooden marker claimed, under the direct command of General Robert E. Lee.

There had been no reason to stay in Virginia, with everything and everyone they loved gone.

"Ma'am?" the marshal prompted, bringing Christy back from her musings with a snap. He was about thirty years of age, she estimated, though she'd been doing her best, ever since they'd left Fort Grant that morning not to think of him at all. He was easy in his skin, with a habit of whistling cheerfully, and just being near him made Christy feel breathless and off-balance, as though the ground had been jerked from beneath her feet. She had expected these emotions to pass while they were traveling together, especially since they had disagreed practically every time they had occasion to speak, but they had only intensified, and she blamed him entirely. "I reckon we ought to ride on down there and let them know you're here."

Behind Christy and the marshal, Caney waited at the reins of a wagon she'd driven all the way from Virginia. Also known as Miz Blue, Caney had been at the farm when Christy and Megan arrived from England; she and her man, Titus, had worked for Granddaddy as free people, since he'd never kept slaves. Recently widowed and "frightful lonesome," Caney had chosen to accompany them on the trip west to the spanking new state of Nevada—the state whose wealth of silver had helped to finance the Union cause. "Yez, Missy," she said now. "This here wagon seat be harder than the devil's heart. I want to sit me down someplace comfortable!"

Christy turned her head and gave her friend a narrow look. The daughter of a Baptist preacher, Caney had learned to read and write before she was six, and her grammar was as good as anybody's. Still, she liked to carry on like an ignorant bond servant once in a while, for reasons she had never troubled herself to share.

Caney met Christy's gaze straight on, and without flinching. Her mannish jaw was set, and her dark eyes glittered with challenge. "I will surely be glad to look upon Miss Bridget and Miss Skye again," she said. "They's my own precious babies, just like you and Miss Megan. Oh, I will be glad, indeed."

Megan was flushed and beaming at the prospect of a family reunion, and Marshal Zachary Shaw was obviously chafing to get on with whatever it was he did to keep the peace in the town of Primrose Creek. It seemed that Christy was quite alone in her reluctance to come face-to-face with their Yankee cousins. She hoped neither Caney nor Megan remembered the last time she and Bridget had been together; they'd gotten into a hissing, scratching, screeching fight, right there in the front yard at the farm, and would surely have killed each other if Uncle J.R. and a laughing Trace hadn't hauled them apart and held them till they were too exhausted from kicking and struggling to go at it again.

"I declare a place as grand as that *must* have a bathtub," Megan mused, squinting a little in the bright spring sunshine. Then, as if that decided the matter, she spurred the little pinto pony she was riding, on loan from the army as was the spirited sorrel gelding Christy had been assigned, down the trail toward the rambling log house, with its glistening glass windows and smoking chimneys. Caney headed that way, too, which left Christy alone on the ridge with Mr. Shaw.

She shifted uncomfortably in the saddle, while he swept off his disreputable leather hat to run one forearm across his forehead. In spite of herself, and all her efforts to ignore him, she was aware of the man in every sense. He was in his shirtsleeves, having shed his heavy coat earlier and bound it behind his saddle with strands of rawhide, and his suspenders were exposed. His shoulders and chest were broad, tapering to a lean waist, and his hair, the color of new straw, wanted cutting. His eyes seemed to see past all the barriers Christy had erected over the years, and that alone would have been reason enough to avoid him, but there was much more to the allure than that. Indeed, it had an almost mystical quality, not merely physical but a thing of the soul and the spirit as well.

"You'll be all right now," he said, and Christy couldn't tell whether he was making a statement or asking a question. In the end, she didn't care, or so she told herself. She just wanted to see the back of Zachary Shaw, once and for all. Bad enough she'd had to put up with him for three days and two nights on the trail.

"Yes," she replied, as stiffly as if she'd been addressing a scullery maid in the kitchen at Fieldcrest. "Thank you very much, Marshal. You may go now."

His eyes lighted with amazed amusement, and his mouth tilted upward in a cocky grin. "Well, now. That's mighty generous of you, Lady McQuarry," he teased. "Your giving me permission to leave your presence and all."

He'd made no secret of the fact that he thought she was high-handed and uppity, but Christy felt a flood of startled color surge into her face all the same. No matter what she said, he'd probably manage to misconstrue her words, make her seem condescending, even snobbish. Well, she wasn't going to let him have the satisfaction of upsetting her any more than he already had.

"Good day," she said, tartly this time.

He chuckled, shook his head again, reined his spectacular cocoa-colored stallion around, and rode off toward the southwest without slowing down or looking back. For some thoroughly unaccountable reason, she was disappointed.

Quite against her will, let alone her better judgment, Christy watched him until he disappeared into a grove of cottonwood trees, their leaves shimmering in the breeze like silver coins stitched to a gypsy's skirt, and she had an awful feeling that he knew it. Well, tit for tat, she thought. She'd certainly caught him watching *her* often enough during the trip from Fort Grant, his face a study in perplexed annoyance.

At last, she decided she'd been stalling in order to avoid the inevitable meeting with Bridget and rode slowly down the steep grade, following Megan, who was traveling at a lope now that she'd reached flatter ground, and Caney, rattling along in their ancient mule-drawn wagon, a relic of better days at the farm. There was no sense in putting it off any longer.

When proper greetings had been exchanged, she'd ride over and have a look at her and Megan's side of the creek, decide where they might put up a cabin of some sort to shelter them until they could afford a real house.

Bridget was standing in the doorway now, her abundant hair, as pale as Christy's was dark, swept up at her nape in a loose chignon. She was wearing a blue calico dress that matched her eyes—Christy's were charcoal gray—and she was sumptuously pregnant. She laughed as Megan jumped down from the pinto's back, hurrying toward her like a filly gamboling through a field, and took the girl in her arms. Then, weeping and exclaiming for joy, she turned to embrace Caney.

The merriment had already gone on for some time when Skye came rushing across the clearing, basket in hand, overjoyed to see Megan, her old playmate, and Caney, whom neither she nor Bridget had probably expected to see again, ever. Bridget's boy, Noah, stood staunchly at his mother's side. His resemblance to his late father, Bridget's first husband, Mitch, jarred Christy a little. He was four or five, and there was a spark of formidable intelligence in his eyes.

She managed to dismount, but her legs seemed to be sending roots deep into the ground, and she couldn't make herself take a single step forward. When she did contrive to move, it was only to turn and flee. She promptly came face-to-chest with Trace Qualtrough.

She'd known that he and Bridget were married—the marshal had told her in one of their brief, stilted conversations—but that didn't lessen the impact of actually seeing him again. The memory of their last meeting was as much a thorn in her side as that of the scene she and Bridget had made, brawling in the dirt like a pair of tavern wenches. She'd declared her eternal love and begged Trace to wait until she was older; she would come home from England then, and they would be wed. He'd smiled sadly, kissed her forehead, and said he didn't plan to take a wife, ever, and she'd felt as though he'd plunged a knife into her.

Older now, and handsomer than before, if that were possible, he nonetheless had no effect whatsoever on her emotions. She supposed she'd become jaded, reflecting on her father's wild and irresponsible ways and the unfriendly nature of her mother's second husband.

"Running away?" he teased, taking a gentle hold of her shoulders. Trace assessed her with brotherly dispatch and pulled a face. "That isn't like you, Christy. Besides, I believe you might be able take Bridget this time, her being pregnant and all. You'd want to watch out, though. She bites."

Christy laughed, almost giddy with relief that her little-girl adoration for this man was gone. Perhaps the old animosity between herself and Bridget would prove as fleeting, and they could become friends. Or at least establish a truce of some kind. "Have you forgotten that we were practically children at the time?"

"Not for a moment," he replied, and took her elbow lightly in one hand. "Come on. Let's get this done. Bridget's dreading it as much as you are."

To her credit, Bridget met them halfway, wiping her hands unconsciously on her apron as she approached. Her expression was solemn, even wary, but not unfriendly. "Come inside," she said in a quiet voice. "You must be longing for a cup of hot tea."

Christy had been braced for censure; their legendary catfight notwithstanding, she and Bridget had never been close, as Skye and Megan were. Long before their fathers had taken separate sides on the questions of states' rights and secession, they'd bickered over dolls, ponies, lemon tea cakes, and, in time, matters of decorum. Bridget had been a veritable hoyden, a blight upon the McQuarry name, while Christy had endeavored to behave as a lady—most of the time. The only thing they'd had in common, besides the proud, stubborn blood of Gideon and Rebecca McQuarry simmering in their veins, was a deep interest in horses. Both had been expert riders almost from the moment they could sit a horse, and at that point, where they might have found an affinity, they'd become rivals instead.

"Thank you," Christy murmured with a nod. She hadn't enjoyed real tea since she'd left England, for such luxuries were still rare in Virginia and impossibly dear when they could be found. It made her grind her teeth just to think of how poor she and Megan really were, but if she had her way, they'd never have to fear poverty again.

Bridget linked her arm through Christy's and tugged her toward the open doorway. "Tell me," she began, "about the farm. Are the new people diligent? The barn wanted painting when we left—"

The inside of the house was cool and spacious and smelled pleasantly of baking bread. There was a good stove at one end of the large central room, and three doorways led into other parts of the house. A gigantic rock fireplace stood opposite the kitchen area, faced with handmade rocking chairs and a cushioned bench, and just looking around spawned a bittersweet mixture of sorrow and pleasure in Christy. Pleasure because the place reminded her so much of the farmhouse back home in Virginia, and sorrow because it wasn't her house at all, but Bridget's.

Always, Bridget.

"Christy?" Bridget spoke gently. Cautiously.

She glanced back and smiled to see that she and Bridget were alone. Convenient, she thought. No doubt, the others considered themselves peacemakers, even diplomats, giving the two cousins a chance to work out their long-standing differences by staying clear for a while.

"They've put on a new roof," she said, referring to the new residents at the family farm, as though the thread of the conversation had not been dropped. "And I do believe they mean to shore up the stables before there's any painting done."

Bridget ducked her head, sniffled slightly. Of course, she still missed the homeplace, as did Christy. It was a part of them both, that faraway land of gentle hills and blue-green rivers, and it probably always would be. The deed had borne a McQuarry name since the Revolution, though now it belonged to Northerners, fast-talking carpetbaggers who'd strolled in and claimed the place for back taxes.

"Do sit down and rest yourself," Bridget said, without looking at Christy. She hurried to the stove, while Christy took a seat in one of the rocking chairs and stared into the dying fire.

"When is your baby due?" she asked presently. It had taken her that long to come up with a safe topic.

Bridget raised a happy clatter with the teapot, and

there was a note of eager anticipation in her voice when she replied. "June," she said. "I'm hoping for a girl, though Trace thinks we ought to have several more sons first, so that our daughters will have older brothers to look after them."

Christy ached with envy, not because Bridget was well married, not even because she was expecting her second child. She was sure to find a husband of her own in a place where women were regarded as a rare treasure, and she would almost certainly have babies, too, in good time. But it was evident that Bridget and Trace had married for love, for passion; she could not expect the same good fortune. No, for Megan's sake, and for her own, Christy was determined to marry for much more practical reasons.

She sat up a little straighter in the rocking chair. "This is a fine home, Bridget," she said. "You've done well."

"Trace deserves most of the credit for the house," Bridget replied lightly, stretching to take a china teapot down from a shelf. "He built it with his own hands. The barn, too."

Christy tilted her head back and looked up at the sturdy log rafters. Perhaps one day, she reflected, this ranch would be to Bridget and Trace's children and grandchildren what the farm had been to several generations of McQuarrys. What legacy might she, Christy, leave to her own descendants?

"Sugar?" Bridget said. "Milk?" It was a moment before Christy, weary of the road, realized her cousin was asking what she took in her tea.

"Just milk," Christy replied. "Please." She studied Bridget as she sat down in the next rocker.

Bridget's spoon rattled as she stirred sugar into her tea. She bit her lower lip once, started to speak, and stopped herself.

"You received my letter?" Christy guessed. "Asking you to buy Megan's and my share of the land?" She paused, savored another sip of tea, stalling. "It was a mistake to make such an offer. I was distraught. I'm—I'm sorry."

Bridget nodded. "I understand," she said. "Still, I'm prepared to pay a fair price. If you're ever of a mind to sell."

Christy set her teacup atop the small table between the two chairs. It nettled her that Bridget not only had Trace, Noah, and the unborn baby but this grand house as well. Even as she spoke, she knew she was being unfair, but she couldn't help herself. Things were so complicated when it came to anything concerning Bridget. "You're not content with the twelve hundred and fifty acres you have here?"

Bridget sat up a little straighter, and a blue tempest ignited in her eyes. "It is not a matter of contentment," she said. "Furthermore, Trace and I own only half of the property, as Skye inherited an equal share. I merely assumed that since you'd written—"

"I told you—I've changed my mind," Christy said as she pushed back her chair a little more forcibly than was required and got to her feet.

Bridget closed her eyes for a moment, in a bid for patience. "Christy, please. Sit down. Hear me out."

Christy began to pace the length of the huge hearth, her arms wrapped tightly around her middle. "You might as well know it right now. I mean to use that land—my share, anyhow—as a dowry of sorts."

Bridget's mouth dropped open. She looked purely confounded. "A *dowry?*"

"Yes," Christy replied. "Even rich men expect them, you know. In fact, they seem to prefer property over gold or currency, in these uncertain times." She stopped, met Bridget's bewildered gaze. "I mean to marry a wealthy man, for Megan's sake and my own." She threw the words at her cousin's feet like a gauntlet. "The richest one available. Who would that be, Bridget?"

Her cousin's jaw line clamped down hard while she made a visible effort to contain her legendary temper. "If you want to keep the land, that's your right. But only a fool marries for money. I've held many an opinion where you're concerned, Christy McQuarry, but I *never* thought you were a fool."

Christy felt color rise to her face. "I'm not you, Bridget. Lucky stars don't tangle themselves in my hair or fall at my feet—I have to fight for the things I want."

Bridget's own expression softened from anger to sadness. "Christy," she said softly. "It must have been hard, coming home from England—"

"Damn England," Christy spat. "We were miserable there—shunted off and forgotten. Made to feel like poor relations, even beggars."

"Christy," Bridget repeated. "Oh, Christy."

"Don't," Christy said before her cousin could go on. She didn't want Bridget's concern, damn it. Didn't want her pity. She had swallowed enough of her pride already. "You've always been fortune's favorite. You were Granddaddy's favorite, too. And Mitch's. And—Trace's."

"Granddaddy loved you," Bridget insisted. "He was heartbroken to lose you and Megan. He never forgave

Jenny for taking you away, or Uncle Eli for letting you go."

Christy did not reply; she would have choked on the painful lump that had risen in her throat. She had never doubted her grandfather's love, as she had her mother's and certainly that of Eli McQuarry, her wild and reckless father. Nor did it particularly trouble her that she would have to make her own way in a world that would grant her no special concessions whatsoever. She had the grit, the strength, the intelligence, and, yes, the beauty to get what she wanted—and she would not be turned from her course.

"Christy," Bridget said once more when she started for the door.

But Christy kept walking and did not look back.

The town of Primrose Creek was hardly more than a cow path with a wide spot, to Zachary's way of thinking, but it had its own sturdy log jailhouse and four saloons. He supposed that said something about a place, that it boasted a hoosegow and more than one watering hole, but no schoolhouse and no real church, either. The Methodists and Baptists held services in borrowed tents, but a hard rain or a high wind could send them scrambling for the shelter of the Silver Spike, the Golden Garter, the Rip-Snorter, or Diamond Lil's.

Truth to tell, this state of affairs hadn't troubled him much; he wasn't a religious man, despite his good Christian raising, nor was he especially fond of liquor, and had heretofore concerned himself with neither churches nor beer halls. He was even-natured, for the most part, a man with simple wants and wishes. He had a way with horses and little else, and he made a point of minding his own business. Moreover, something had gone cold within him the day Jessie died in his arms, so while he enjoyed a sporting woman as well as the next man, he never thought about settling down.

Now something had changed, and there was no denying it, much as he would have liked to do just that. Some inner foundation had shifted, sent cracks streaking through the walls he'd erected to last a lifetime.

Feeling a chill—spring weather in the Sierras was a fickle thing—he shoved a piece of wood into the stove near his desk and prodded it into flames with the poker. A day ago, he'd showed up at Fort Grant, looking to do his duty as marshal, fetch a gaggle of women safely up the trail, and be done with it. He'd gone, however grudgingly, but the man who'd ridden back up the track wasn't the same as the one who'd ridden down it. And what had wreaked all this havoc? One look at Miss Christy McQuarry, that was what.

He'd seen pretty girls before, of course, even out there in the back of beyond, but Christy—Miss McQuarry—was more than pretty. She was beautiful. That first sight of her, with her gleaming dark hair and charcoal-gray eyes, her perfect skin and slim, womanly figure, had struck him with the force of a log shooting off one end of a flume, and he was still reeling. God in heaven, he even liked fighting with her.

He rubbed his beard-stubbled chin and squinted into the cracked shaving mirror next to the window. He didn't *look* all that different, but he was thinking some crazy thoughts, that was for sure. He wanted to dance, for God's sake, and not with one of the ladies who plied their trade over at the Golden Garter, either. He wanted an excuse to put his arms around Christy McQuarry, that was a fact, and the music was optional. Furthermore, he'd started to imagine what it would be like, living in a real house with curtains at the windows, raising a passel of kids, just as his own mother and father had done.

He made twenty dollars a month, he reminded himself, and that was when the town council had the funds to pay him, which was only intermittently. He felt his forehead with the back of one hand and grinned ruefully at his own image in the looking glass. No fever.

At least, not in his head.

Christy faced the ramshackle structure with as much courage as she could muster. According to Trace, the place had originally been a Paiute lodge. It had a leaky hide roof, stitched more with daylight than rawhide, and he and Bridget had kept horses there in inclement weather. They'd lived in the place, too, while their house was being built, but Christy took small comfort in that knowledge.

"You must be outta yo' head," Caney said, hands on her hips. "Miss Bridget and Mister Trace have that nice house over yonder, and you want to live here?"

Christy turned to face the woman she considered her only true friend, exasperating as she was. "Go ahead and stay with them, if that's what you want," she replied, keeping her voice crisp.

"Well, I ought to, that's fo' sure. They got real beds over there. They got windows and a roof that don't show no sky through it—"

Determined, Christy began sweeping out the rock-lined fire pit in the center of the building, using a broom she'd improvised herself from twigs and slender branches, and she was brisk about it. "Fine. You're getting old, and you need your comforts. Besides, you got spoiled living at Fort Grant all winter."

Caney rose to the bait like a trout leaping for a fly, and Christy, having her back to the woman now, smiled to herself. "What you mean, I'm gettin' old and spoilt? I ain't but forty-two, and I can do the work of any two mule-skinners. Got you and Miss Megan across all them plains and mountains, didn't I?"

"You did," Christy said, and pressed her lips together.

"You think I ain't got the gumption to sleep in a place like this? Laid my head down in many a worse one, I have."

Christy smiled, swept, and said nothing.

"Drat it all," Caney groused. "You know dern well Miss Megan will stay here if you do, out of plain loyalty, and that leaves me with no choice at all, because I wouldn't sleep a wink for thinkin' of the wolves and the outlaws and the Injuns gettin' to you, after all I done went through to bring you here—"

Shame jabbed at Christy's conscience; she'd promised herself that she wouldn't be like her mother, wouldn't use other people to get her own way, wouldn't use another's weakness to her advantage, and here she was, doing precisely those things. "I'm sorry," she said, turning and meeting Caney's level gaze. "I shouldn't have said anything. I was trying to influence you—"

Caney gave a guffaw of laughter. "Were you, now?" she said, her bright jet eyes twinkling. "Well, two can play at that, young lady."

Christy pretended to swat at her friend with the

makeshift broom. "You were pulling my leg the whole time."

" 'Course I was," Caney said, grinning now. "If you're set on stayin' here, then I will, too." She looked up at the deer hides sagging overhead. "We gonna live in this place, Miss Christy, we gotta put us some boards up there, and some tar paper, too, if we can get it. You have any of that money left? What you got for your mama's watch and pearls back in Richmond?"

Christy sank onto a bale of hay and sighed. "It took every penny to buy the mules and food and sign on with the wagon train. I'll take the cameo into town tomorrow. Surely some miner will want it for a present." Tears stung behind her eyes at the prospect of yet another stranger taking possession of one of Jenny's belongings, but she would not shed them. She had certainly had her differences with her mother, but she'd loved her. In spite of everything, the losses, the separations, the grim, unhappy days at St. Martha's, and the even unhappier visits to Fieldcrest, she'd loved her.

Caney's large, slender hand came to rest on Christy's shoulder. "Life'd be some easier for you if it weren't for that McQuarry pride of yours," she said quietly. "Now, let's gather some firewood and carry in the trunks from that wagon out there. We push some of these bales together, we can make us some beds. Better'n sleepin' under the wagon like we did whilst we was travelin'."

Christy laid her hand over Caney's, squeezed. "What's wrong with me, Caney?" she whispered. "Why can't I be beholden to Bridget or anybody else, even for something as basic as a real roof over my head?"

"I done told you already," Caney said. "It's that ole

devil, pride. You got it from your granddaddy—he sure had him plenty, ole Mister Gideon McQuarry. Turns a body cussed, that's fo' sure. But it makes you strong, too. Keeps you goin' right on when other folks would lay down and whimper."

Christy blinked a few times, stood up, and went back to her sweeping. When that was done, she and Caney brought in the trunks and pushed bales together to make three beds. There were plenty of quilts, hand-stitched by Rebecca McQuarry herself, and knitted woolen blankets, for Caney had rescued them from the laundry before she'd left the farm. They spread them over the prickly surfaces of the hay and made jokes about princesses and peas.

By the time Megan returned, accompanied by Skye, twilight was falling, and there was a cheerful blaze crackling in the middle of the lodge. The mules had been let out to pasture, along with horses borrowed from the army, their things had been brought in from the wagon, and Caney had a pot of beans, dried ones left over from the journey west, simmering on the fire.

Megan gleamed as though she'd been polished, and her bright red-gold hair caught the firelight. She and Skye were both barefoot, having waded across the stream, and carried their shoes by the laces. "I had a real bath," Megan said, as proudly as if she'd never taken one before. "I used hot water and store-bought soap, too, and I didn't even have to hurry in case it got cold, because Bridget kept filling up the tea kettle and warming it on the stove."

Christy, seated on yet another bale of hay, smiled and leaned forward to stir the beans with a wooden spoon. "Well, now. I'm sure you must be entirely too fine to keep company with the likes of Caney and me. I expect you'd rather spend the night with Skye."

Megan was clearly torn between a perfectly natural yearning for creature comforts—she had done without them for a long time, without a single complaint—and a strong devotion to her older sister, and it moved Christy deeply, seeing that. Forced her to look down at the fire for a moment and swallow hard.

"Bridget sent you a dried apple pie," Skye put in quickly, as if fearing the silence, and set a covered basket on the dirt floor, close to Christy's right foot. "She can't bake a decent cake to save her life, but she's got a way with pie dough."

Christy spoke carefully. Quietly. "Please tell her I said thank you," she told the girl gently, then shifted her gaze to Megan. "You go on across the creek with Skye, now. The two of you have been apart for a long time— you must have a lot of giggling to catch up on."

Megan looked doubtful, and at the same time full of hope. "You're sure?" Her voice was small. "You wouldn't mind?"

"I won't be alone, Megan," Christy pointed out tenderly. "I've got Caney to keep me company."

Megan hesitated just a moment longer, then bent and kissed Christy on the cheek. "I'll be back first thing in the morning," the girl promised earnestly. "You'll be needing a lot of help. Maybe I can catch us some fish for supper."

Christy reached out, patted her sister's hand. As children, Megan and Skye had been thicker than the proverbial thieves. She wasn't about to let her own problems with Bridget come between them. "That would be a fine thing," she said.

With that, the girls vanished into the night again, and their happy chatter trailed behind them like music.

"You did the right thing, lettin' that girl go like that. I know you worry about her whenever she's out of your sight," Caney observed, taking the spoon from Christy's hands and serving up a plate of beans for each of them.

"She'll be safe with Trace and Bridget," Christy said. Safer, certainly, than in an old Indian lodge with no door and no windows and only the flimsiest excuse for a roof.

The two women ate in companionable silence, both of them sick to death of boiled beans, and Caney insisted on carrying the dishes down to the creek for washing. When she returned, Christy had put on a nightgown, unpinned her waist-length hair, and begun to brush it with long, rhythmic strokes. She'd lit a kerosene lamp against the descending darkness and set the basket containing Bridget's pie inside one of the recently emptied trunks, in hopes of discouraging mice. It would be a fine treat for breakfast.

Caney undressed in the shadows and donned her own night dress, a fancy red taffeta affair trimmed in lace. It had been given to her by a sick woman she and Christy had tended while they were crossing the plains with the wagon train. The lady, one Lottie Benson, accompanied by a man she said was her brother, must certainly have had a story to tell, but Christy hadn't dared to ask her. Besides, it was kind of fun, just speculating.

"I reckon you know that good-lookin' marshal has an eye for you?" Caney asked, stretching out on her spiky bed with a long-suffering sigh.

The idea warmed Christy in a way no nightgown, taffeta or flannel, could have done. She blew out the lamp and lay down to take her night's rest. "Nonsense," she said. "You're imagining things."

Caney sighed again, a comfortable, settling-in sigh. "We'll see 'bout that," she replied. "We'll just see."

Chapter

2

Christy awakened early the following morning, while Caney was still snoring quietly on the other side of the fire. She dressed in haste, attended to a brief bit of business in the woods, and went down to the creek to wash her face and hands. Although there was smoke curling from both chimneys rising from Bridget's roof, she saw no other sign that anyone was up and about.

She returned to the lodge, brushed her hair and wound it into a loose knot at the back of her head, then brought the small velvet pouch containing her mother's jewelry from its hiding place in the false bottom of one of the trunks. She spilled the meager contents into one palm—the cameo brooch she meant to sell that very day, a pearl and diamond ring, a pair of sapphire ear bobs, and a garnet necklace.

A sob rose in her throat, but she did not make a sound. Nonetheless, the silent cry reverberated through her spirit and found its place there, among her dreams and wishes and private sorrows. She closed her hand around the jewels for a moment—they were only trinkets, really, and she should not let herself be sentimental about them—and then resolutely tucked everything back into the bag except the cameo. When the pouch was hidden again, she rose from her knees, slipped the brooch into her skirt pocket, and set about brewing the morning coffee.

Caney awakened with a stretch and a crow of exuberance. "Now, then," she said, "it's a brand new morning, praise be to God, and I'm here to see it and set my feet on the ground!"

Christy smiled. Whenever she got to railing against the fate that had brought her to this pass of destitution, Caney always said or did something that brought her around. Heaven knew, there were plenty of other women in the world in far worse straits than she was— women with no friends, no land, no jewelry to pawn. The brothels of the West were full of such unfortunates—and just the thought of them was enough to give Christy nightmares. "I have business in town," she said simply, fetching Bridget's pie from its place of protection in the cedar-lined trunk. "I'll see about lumber and tar paper for the roof."

Caney sat up, looking rumpled in her red taffeta nightgown. "I'd best go with you," she said.

Christy shook her head, averted her eyes. It was bad enough, practically begging for what they needed. The prospect of Caney or anyone else she cared about looking on was beyond endurance. "You stay here. There's plenty to keep you busy, and anyway, this is something I need to do alone."

Caney understood pride, and she nodded solemnly.

"All right, then," she said with reluctance, and produced a small, familiar derringer from her ancient valise. Granddaddy had given it to her years before, Christy knew, so she could protect herself when she was away from home. "You take this along. Just in case."

Christy accepted the pistol, more at ease with it than she would have expected, and slipped it into her pocket alongside the brooch. She had never fired a gun and hoped she wouldn't be called upon to do so, that day or any other, but these were dangerous times, and a woman alone was unquestionably vulnerable.

"You gonna walk to town?" Caney wanted to know. "I could saddle up one of them army horses for you, quick as that." She snapped her fingers and, after pawing through a trunk, ferreted out a well-worn dress of yellow calico. "You run into some bad-tempered critter or a band of Injuns, you'll have a fightin' chance on horseback—"

"The marshal said it was two miles into Primrose Creek. That is hardly any distance at all. Besides, I need to stretch my legs."

Caney gave up, but she wasn't happy about it. "Well, you just better be back here afore noon, missy, or I'll come lookin' for you myself, you hear?"

"I hear," Christy said with a laugh. After a cup of coffee and a slice of Bridget's more than passable dried apple pie, she set out for town, following the rutted trail that passed for a road.

The countryside between the McQuarry land and the town itself was forested, though not densely so, and Christy walked with her shoulders back, her head up, and her arms swinging, lest some cougar or mama bear catch sight of her and mistake her for easy prey. She imagined a highwayman or a hostile native behind every tree trunk and boulder, but she reached the edge of town after an estimated three-quarters of an hour, and stood at the foot of the main thoroughfare, taking it all in.

There were tents everywhere, and the noise of steam-powered saws clawed at her eardrums. She counted four saloons and several rustic storefronts, but as far as she could make out, there wasn't a single church or schoolhouse.

The road was rutted, though here and there an effort had been made to fill the potholes with small stones and sawdust, and she would have to be careful not to drag her hems through mud or step in a pile of horse manure. She lifted her chin and proceeded toward the mercantile, a two-story structure with a false facade and a distinct list to the lefthand side. The plank walls were chinked with a mixture of mud and plaster, and an enormous and exceedingly ugly black dog lay curled in front of the door.

Christy paused at the edge of the slanted board sidewalk and assessed the creature.

"He's just for show," a familiar voice put in from behind her. Marshal Zachary Shaw; she knew even before she turned to look at him. "Old Rufus there, he hasn't got a tooth in his head, nor a mean thought, either."

Skirts in hand, Christy schooled her expression to one of polite reserve. "Good morning, Marshal," she said, noting that he was freshly shaven and sporting clean clothes. His badge gleamed on the well-worn buckskin of his vest. She glanced at the dog—she should have guessed it was harmless, since it hadn't even troubled itself to bark at her—still snoozing on the doorstep. "How comforting to know you're around to keep us all safe."

He merely grinned at the mild jibe and hooked his thumbs in the front of his gun belt. It was just plain bad luck that he was so fine to look at, worse still that the pull she felt toward him was something as ancient as the stars. "You can count on me, ma'am."

She remembered the brooch in her pocket and her morning's mission. She had to get it over with, and quickly. Too much delay would only make matters worse. "If you'll excuse me—"

He nodded, and when she turned to head into the general store, intent upon speaking with the merchant, she collided with a man roughly as tall and substantial as a tree trunk. Looking up, she saw a square, handsome face, a head of curly brown hair, and a pair of concerned hazel eyes. His hands, big as stove lids, clasped her shoulders lest she fall.

"Are you all right?" he demanded. "Did I hurt you?"

Christy blinked, still a bit stunned.

"I don't reckon she'll have any scars to show for meeting you, Jake," Mr. Shaw put in. He had stepped onto the sidewalk now, and, disconcertingly, his presence had far more of an impact on Christy's senses than the close proximity of the man he'd called Jake. "Christy McQuarry, meet Jake Vigil. He owns Vigil Timber and Mining. Jake, Miss McQuarry."

"Mr. Vigil," Christy said, somewhat shyly.

The lumberman finally realized that he was still holding on to her shoulders and dropped his hands to his sides. He was dressed all in buckskins, Christy noted, and burly as an ox. Color throbbed in his neck and along his jawline. "Miss McQuarry," he said, and gulped.

"Jake here is a genuine timber baron," Zachary said easily.

Mr. Vigil shook his head, still blushing. Christy thought it was charming that such a strong man could be so modest, even retiring. "I reckon I'd better be getting back to the mill," he blurted, and, in his apparent confusion, he raised a hand to tip a nonexistent hat. Then, still red as a pepper, he fled, nearly stumbling over the dog, which had repositioned itself in the shade of the horse trough in front of the store.

Zachary watched his friend's retreat with a look of sympathetic amusement. For his own part, he was completely at ease, his hat pushed to the back of his head, one arm braced almost negligently against the post supporting the small roof that served as an awning above the door of the mercantile. "Poor Jake," he said. "He gets his feet tangled in his tongue whenever he runs across a pretty lady."

Christy ducked her head to hide a blush of her own and was irritated with herself for succumbing even that much to Mr. Shaw's rascally charms. "Unlike some men," she replied, "who always seem to have a glib remark waiting on the tip of their tongue."

He grinned, undaunted. "He's a rich man, Jake is. You see that mansion on the other side of the mill? That's his. Lives in it all by his lonesome."

Christy's heartbeat quickened, but at the same time, she felt a little sick to her stomach. Had she mentioned her plans to marry for security to Zachary Shaw at some point? She was certain she hadn't.

"Is that so?" she replied, bluffing. "And what makes you think I'm interested in the state of Mr. Vigil's bank account?"

He leaned close, spoke in a low voice meant to nettle. "Oh, I just guessed," he drawled. The nerve. "A plain woman can do real well for herself out here, Miss McQuarry. A beautiful one—like you—can name her price."

Christy wasn't sure whether she'd just been complimented or insulted—a little of both, she suspected, but mainly the latter. And she was riled. Hard put, in fact, not to give Zachary a tongue-lashing he'd never forget. "I do hope, Mr. Shaw, that you are not insinuating—"

He tugged his hat brim forward again so it shadowed his eyes. "I'm not insinuating anything. I'm saying it straight out. You could have any man in this town, and Jake Vigil would probably suit you just fine. He's got a big house and money, and he'll let you do all the talking, like as not." With that, the marshal of Primrose Creek thrust himself away from the support pole and strode away, leaving Christy to stare after him in frustration.

"I can help you, miss?"

Christy turned and saw a man as big as Mr. Vigil looming in the doorway. He was obviously the store's proprietor, for he wore a white apron over his shirt and trousers, a visor, and an air of genial authority.

"I am Gus," he said.

Christy had recovered enough to remember the reason for her errand by then, and she put out a hand, which Gus politely shook. She introduced herself and, at Gus's invitation, followed him inside. The interior of the store was rustic but clean and fairly well supplied for a frontier enterprise. The good, earthy smells of coffee beans, wood smoke, fresh sawdust, and new leather greeted her, and she breathed them in appreciatively.

It would have been wrong, though, to pretend that she was in a position to purchase anything of substance, so Christy approached the counter, several boards stretched between two giant barrels, and laid her mother's brooch in plain view.

"I have fallen upon difficult times, Mr.—er—Gus," she said forthrightly, keeping her spine very straight and her chin high. "I was hoping you might—perhaps—sell this for me, on consignment?" In the end, she couldn't bring herself to ask this kindly man to purchase the cameo outright.

Gus examined the piece carefully, frowning thoughtfully as he did so. "It is beautiful thing, no?"

"Yes," Christy agreed, and blinked.

"Miners and lumbermen, they all the time ask me for pretty things to give their womens. Perhaps I make a present to my sister, Bertha, to make her smile."

Tears burned behind Christy's eyes. Her mother had treasured that brooch, a gift from Christy and Megan's father on their wedding day, and she had worn it often. There were many, many memories attached to that piece and all the others. "It is very old. And very valuable."

Gus, still pondering the cameo, slapped down a meaty hand with such force that Christy jumped. "I buy," he said. "Fifty dollars."

Fifty dollars! It was a fortune, surely enough to put a real roof on the lodge, and maybe a door, too. "Th-thank you," Christy said, and turned crimson. She was wildly relieved, and at the same time, she felt as though she'd sold a part of herself along with the trinket.

Gus dropped the cameo into the pocket of his apron, then carefully counted out the agreed sum in coins of gold and silver. Christy thanked him again, scooped up the small fortune, and turned to make for the door, just in case he was inclined to change his mind.

"Miss," he called, just as she reached the threshold.

Christy's stomach dropped, and it was all she could do to turn around and meet the storekeeper's friendly gaze instead of running like a thief. "Yes?"

"You want Mama's pin back again, you come to Gus. He'll save it for you."

"But your sister—"

Gus shrugged massive shoulders. "Bertha is simple woman. She like plain things best."

Christy couldn't speak; it had been a long time since she had encountered such generosity. She nodded once, quickly, and dashed out the door, lest she break down and blather like a ninny. The black dog sat on its haunches on the sidewalk and gave a low, sorrowful whimper as she passed.

Five minutes later, she was standing in front of Jake Vigil's house, gaping. The white-clapboard structure was twice the size of the farmhouse back home, and it had gabled windows, each one boasting dark blue shutters, and a veranda that surrounded it like the deck railing of a Mississippi riverboat. A white picket fence enclosed it all, and there were fledgling rosebushes planted on either side of the stone steps.

After admiring the place as long as she dared, Christy turned and headed for the sawmill, where she had legitimate business. She intended to buy materials for a roof, and nobody, not even Zachary Shaw, could find fault with that. Not that she intended to give him the opportunity.

Jake Vigil greeted her with surprised pleasure. On his own ground, in the office of his thriving lumber business, he was far more at ease. He invited Christy to sit down and even offered her coffee, which she politely refused.

"I'm here to place an order," she announced. She had hated parting with her mother's brooch, even temporarily, but there was a certain exhilaration in achieving the purpose she had set for herself. "For a roof. I'll take tar paper, too, if you can get it."

Mr. Vigil perched on a corner of his large and cluttered desk, regarding her thoughtfully. "A roof?" No doubt, if he had recognized the name *McQuarry,* he'd assumed she was staying with Bridget and Trace.

"For the Indian lodge, out by Primrose Creek," she said, and squirmed only a little under his pensive gaze.

"The Indian lodge?"

Christy suppressed a sigh. Did the man echo *everything* that was said to him? Perhaps he was stupid—but how could that be? He'd built an empire, apparently under his own power. "My sister, Megan, and I are cousins to Mrs. Qualtrough and *her* sister, Skye. We inherited half the tract, specifically twelve hundred and fifty acres on this side of the stream. As Trace and Bridget already have a houseful, well, it seemed more prudent to restore the lodge as best we can and live there until other arrangements can be made."

She had to look away briefly when she uttered the last part.

"Jupiter's ghost," he marveled in a voice that would have shaken Mount Olympus itself. "You can't live in that—that hut!"

She leaned forward in her chair. She clasped her pride like a lifeline. "I assure you, Mr. Vigil, we can. And we shall, for the time being, at least."

He shook his head in frank amazement. "I'll be deuced," he said. "What does Trace have to say about this plan of yours?"

"A great deal, I'm sure," Christy replied, gathering her skirts and rising from her chair with as much grace and dignity as she could manage. "However, he is Bridget's husband, not mine, and I am under no constraints to obey him. Now, Mr. Vigil, will you or will you not sell me the materials I require for a roof?"

He muttered something, then nodded. "I'll have the things you need delivered first thing tomorrow morning."

"Thank you," Christy said with a brisk note in her voice. They agreed upon a price—one that fortunately left her with a few dollars to spare—and then she took her leave.

As she'd promised Caney, she was home before noon. Megan was down by the creek, fishing for supper, and from the looks of the mess of trout she held up for Christy to see, it would be a feast. Caney was a few yards downstream, beating laundry against a large, flat rock. Seeing Christy, they both smiled, and though Megan went right on fishing, Caney wrung out the petticoat she'd been washing, draped it over a bush, and plodded up the bank.

"Well?" she asked, without preamble.

"I got fifty dollars for it," Christy whispered. "And we'll have all the necessary supplies for our roof by tomorrow."

Caney narrowed her eyes and let her hands rest on her wide hips. "There's somethin' you ain't tellin' me, missy. Now, just what would that be?"

Christy drew a deep breath and let it out slowly.

"Today I met the man I'm going to marry," she said, and tried very hard to smile.

Two wagons, one loaded with timber and one with great rolls of tar paper, each rig drawn by four sturdy mules, rolled up to the lodge the next day around eight, when Christy, Caney, and Megan were all busy clearing ground for a garden. Although Trace had lent them the use of a plow and even harnessed one of the work horses to it, the labor was hard, and all three women were sweating and covered in dirt from head to foot.

Christy was alarmed when she recognized one of the drivers, for he was none other than Marshal Shaw. He looked her over, from tousled hair to muddy hem, and grinned. Driving the wagon beside his was a tall, powerfully built black man, a stranger who probably worked for Mr. Vigil. Several men on horseback rode in behind them.

"What are you doing here?" she demanded, swiping at a persistent fly. Out of the corner of her eye, she saw Caney and Megan exchange a glance.

"Just lending a hand wherever I can," Shaw answered smoothly. "This is Malcolm Hicks," he said, indicating his silent companion, who jumped down from the wagon seat, nodded once, and started pulling on a pair of heavy leather gloves. "He's the foreman over at the mill. I figured he could use some help unloading the wagons." The riders got down from their horses and left them to graze in the deep grass.

"Why don't you git down and help me, then," Hicks grumbled to Zachary, rounding the rig, lowering the tailgate, and grasping a stack of planks. " 'Stead of just settin' up there yammerin'."

Shaw grinned, secured the brake lever and the reins, and did as he was told. "Don't mind Malcolm," he whispered to Christy moments later as he passed too close, balancing three heavy boards on one shoulder. The four other men were busy, too. "He's not the sociable sort."

Christy said nothing. She wasn't going to give Zachary the pleasure of knowing he'd succeeded in throwing her off balance again. And she would have died before letting him so much as guess that just being near him made her heartbeat quicken and her breath turn shallow.

"You reckon he's married?" Caney inquired much later, when all the lumber was neatly stacked beside the lodge. A third wagon had arrived, filled with tools and kegs of nails and other bits and pieces, and the riders unloaded those things, too. Hicks and the marshal were supervising.

"Do you mean Mr. Hicks?" Christy asked distractedly, wiping the back of her neck with a wadded sunbonnet. She was tired, hot, and almost desperate enough to swallow her pride and ask Bridget if she could make use of her bathtub, just this once.

"*Yes,* I mean Mr. Hicks," Caney retorted impatiently. "It's a cinch I ain't sweet on the marshal, fetchin' though he is. I'm old enough to be his mama. 'Sides, I like my men dark-skinned and serious."

Christy sighed. Mr. Hicks certainly met Caney's requirements on both counts. Except for the remark he'd made to Zachary about helping to unload the lumber, he hadn't said a single word the whole time he was there, nor had he spared so much as a smile for any of them. "For heaven's sake," she said. "You don't even know the man. He could be a fiend."

Caney was still watching Mr. Hicks in a most frank and forward fashion. "I know all I needs to, 'cept for one thing—if 'n he's got him a wife—and I mean to find that out right quick."

"How?"

"I'm goin' over the creek and ask Bridget, that's how," Caney replied. Then she brushed her hands against her skirts, adjusted the old floppy brimmed hat she wore to keep the sun off her head, and set herself for the Qualtrough place.

Megan had gone back to picking rocks out of the garden plot and carrying them to the growing pile beside the lodge's southern wall, and Skye and Noah had come to help. At the rate the three of them were going, they'd have enough stones for a fireplace every bit as grand as Bridget's before sunset, even if they *were* prattling the whole time.

Megan had always had exceptional hearing, and she was something of an eavesdropper, too, despite all her sterling qualities. Straightening, hands resting on her slender hips, she smiled. "Wouldn't that be something," she said, "if our Caney got herself another husband!"

Christy blew out a long breath, causing tendrils of sweat-dampened hair to dance against her forehead. Then, without answering, she marched over, took up the reins again, and urged the plow horse back into motion.

By nightfall, she was so dirty that she feared her skin would never be the same, her feet and legs were aching, and her palms were covered with raw blisters. She'd barely touched her supper—a batch of fried chicken Bridget had kindly sent over in Skye's keeping—and she wanted nothing so much as to fold her arms, drop her head, and sob. She was too tired to bother with a bath, and too miserable not to, and when it came right down to it, she just couldn't bring herself to ask her cousin for anything more. It was galling enough that Bridget felt she had to provide meals for her indigent relations. She was probably over there in that warm, tidy house of hers, shaking her head and clucking her tongue. *That Christy,* she would be saying to Trace. *She's as stubborn as ever.*

Unable to bear the thought of going to bed in her present state, however, Christy gathered her nightgown, an old flour sack that served as a towel, and a bar of scented soap Skye had given Megan as a gift. She made her way down to the creek, found a place sheltered by trees and bushes, and stripped to the skin.

The water was bone-jarringly cold, but it numbed the soreness in Christy's muscles and soothed the insect bites covering her legs and arms. She washed her hair thoroughly, knowing it would be a trial to brush when she got back to the lodge, then bathed the rest of her body. She was about to brave the chilly air of an April night when she saw a bobbing lantern light and heard a rustling in the brush.

"Who's there?" she called. She tried to speak with authority, but she knew she lacked conviction.

"Don't fret," Megan replied, flailing through the greenery to plop down gratefully on a rock. "It's only me. Are you trying to catch pneumonia? This creek is fed by melting snow!" She tossed Christy the flour-sack towel and lowered her eyes while her sister got out of the water to dry off and put her nightgown on.

Christy's teeth were chattering. "I'm f-fine," she said.

Megan sighed. "You're not fine," she replied.

"You've run yourself ragged. Caney and I agree that you need to let up a little. Rest. Read. Go out riding like you used to do at home. Christy, I can't remember the last time I saw you smile—*really* smile, I mean."

Christy sighed. "I'll do those things when the work is done," she said.

Megan frowned, and a bit of her redhead's temper showed in her eyes, even in the unsteady light of the lamp. "I know what you're planning, Christy," she said, "and I'll have no part of it. I will not see my only sister work herself into an early grave on my account."

"Who says it's on your account?" Christy asked, but her voice was a little shaky. Bluffs didn't always work with Megan. "I'd like to live in a grand house, wear lovely clothes—"

"Which is why you've set your cap for Jake Vigil?"

"Who told you that?"

"Never mind who told me. Just don't throw your life away on my account. I'll never forgive you if you do."

"But your wonderful mind, Megan. College and travel and fine things—"

"Are you sure those aren't *your* dreams, Christy?" Megan interrupted. "Because they certainly aren't mine!"

Christy was dumbfounded and not a little wounded.

Megan was already turning to go off and leave her. "I'm getting married and having babies," she said. "That's what I want. A husband and a house and babies." With that, she was gone.

Christy dressed slowly and made her own way up the hillside, her footsteps guided by the light of the moon. When she reached the place that would be home, at least until she managed to marry Mr. Vigil, she found that

Megan had already gone to bed. If she wasn't sound asleep, she pretended to be.

Caney was sitting by the fire, sipping a last cup of coffee and reflecting.

"Mr. Malcolm Hicks had himself a wife once," she said, without looking at Christy. "Her name was Polly, and she died of the consumption three years ago."

Christy found her comb and began working the tangles out of her wet hair. She was so tired she thought sure she could have fallen asleep on her feet, like an old horse in a field, and the echo of her conversation with Megan down by the creek bounced painfully through her mind and heart. "Well, you certainly didn't waste any time finding out what you wanted to know."

"I never do," Caney replied, and pressed a plug of tobacco inside one cheek. "I figured on asking Bridget, but she was feeling poorly—mind you, that girl is carryin' twins, no matter what everybody else says—so I hunted up Trace. He claims the whole town thinks highly of Mr. Hicks."

Christy struggled patiently with a snarl in her hair, biting her lip against the pain. "Lord have mercy," she teased. "Lord have mercy on us all."

Zachary made his rounds, arrested a pair of drunken cowboys to keep them from shooting up the town, and locked them in the small enclosed room that served as the jailhouse's only cell. Untroubled by their descent into shame and degradation, they decided to sing and set every dog in Primrose Creek to howling in accompaniment. Coupled with the racket coming from the saloons, it was hardly noticeable.

He poured himself a cup of coffee, considered

adding a shot of whiskey, and decided against it. A couple of drinks, and he'd be singing along with his prisoners.

He set the cup down on a corner of his desk, loosened the strand of rawhide that secured his holster to his thigh, unbuckled his gun belt, and hung the whole works on a peg within easy reach of his chair. Miss Nelly would be upset if he didn't turn up before she blew out the lamps and put the cat out; she wanted all her regular boarders present and accounted for, but he didn't like leaving the singing cowboys unguarded. He wasn't worried that they'd escape—they were both so drunk that neither of them could have covered his ass with a ten-gallon hat—but Primrose Creek was a canvas and dry-wood town, cheroots were popular, and fire was a very real threat. He couldn't risk letting his guests roast like a couple of stuffed pigs, which meant he'd have to sleep in his chair.

Not, he thought with a low chuckle, that he was likely to do that. He hadn't slept a whole night through since he met Miss McQuarry, and the problem showed no signs of abating. He was a damn fool, that's what, contriving ways to meet up with her when she'd already made it plain that she wanted a life wholly different from anything he could have given her. It would have been safer, not to mention smarter, to drag a couple of sticks of flaming firewood out of the stove and juggle them.

He blew out the lamp on his desk, sat back in his chair, and put his feet up, resting the heels of his worn boots on a copy of the *Territorial Enterprise,* published down in Virginia City. She'd looked a sight that morning when he and Hicks and the others had delivered the lumber, he thought with an involuntary grin, cupping his hands behind his head. From the state of her dress, she might have caught fire and rolled on the ground to put herself out, and her hair had been filled with grass and plain old dirt and falling around her shoulders in loops. For a long moment, he hadn't been able to catch his breath, might have been sitting there in that wagon box still, staring like a dumbfounded fool, if Malcolm hadn't broken the spell by inviting him to help unload the lumber.

He sighed and closed his eyes as the cowboys launched into a sentimental piece about long-suffering mothers watching at the parlor window for their "darling boy" to come marching home from war. They were way off key, the fellows were, but the dogs were doing all right.

She's going to marry Jake Vigil and his sawmill and his big house, he told himself silently, and it didn't do any good at all, even though he knew every word was true. He'd better find a way to put her out of his mind, and soon, or he'd go crazy.

One of the songsters began to pound at the heavy wooden door of the cell. "Marshal!" he yelled. "Hey, Marshal, you out there?"

"What?" Zachary shouted back.

"Can't somebody shut up them damn dogs?"

Zachary laughed. Whatever happened with Miss McQuarry, he would still have the singular joys of his work.

Chapter

3

When Jake Vigil came to help put up the roof, he brought a crew of more than a dozen men along, and a handful of yellow and blue wildflowers to boot. While his workers swarmed over the lodge like bees on a piece of fallen fruit, Mr. Vigil approached Christy, his face flaming.

"These are for you," he said. "I reckon you know my intentions."

Christy was charmed, but at the same time, she felt a distinct stab of conscience. While marrying the timber baron would certainly serve many purposes, Jake certainly deserved a wife who genuinely loved him. She'd not felt any particular stirrings, the few times she'd seen him, and she feared she never would, no matter how long she lived or how kind and generous he might be or how many children she bore him. Megan's heated words of the night before beside the creek roared in her ears. *Are you sure these aren't your dreams, Christy?*

I'm getting married and having babies . . . that's what I want.

Well, she thought resolutely, Megan didn't know what she was throwing away, that was all. It was up to her, Christy, to behave in everyone's best interests.

Everyone's except Jake Vigil's, possibly.

Just then, catching a glimpse of a cocoa-colored stallion at the edge of the small clearing, she feared she would never be able to put Marshal Zachary Shaw's irritating personage completely out of her mind. So far, her efforts had certainly been unsuccessful.

"Mornin', Miss McQuarry," he said, as if drawn to her side by the power of her thoughts, catching the brim of his hat lightly and briefly between thumb and forefinger. He nodded to Mr. Vigil, who was still standing rooted to the grass, the mass of flowers beginning to faint in his large hand. "Jake."

Jake returned the nod, but he didn't look entirely pleased to see Zachary. "I reckon things must be pretty peaceful in town, Marshal, if you've got the time to come out here and socialize."

Christy's hand shook a little as she reached out to rescue the blossoms from Jake's fist. "I'll just put these in water," she said, and turned in haste toward the lodge.

Jake caught her arm in a gentle grasp, however, and stopped her. He cleared his throat and colored up again. "I'm holding a party over at my place on Saturday night. To welcome you and the other ladies to Primrose Creek. I hope you'll come."

Zachary was watching her closely and with benign interest. She did her best to ignore him, but it was difficult, as usual. If she'd been the least bit superstitious, she would have thought he'd cast a spell over her.

She kept her gaze trained on Jake's face. She would wear one of her mother's fancy ball gowns, she told herself, and make the most of the opportunity—and to the devil with Zachary Shaw. "I'm flattered, Mr. Vigil. Certainly, we'll be there." With that, she spun around and dashed, flowers in hand, toward the shadowy doorway of the lodge.

Using an enamel cup for a vase, Christy placed the bluebells and buttercups in the last of the drinking water and hoisted the bucket, with its familiar tin ladle. After filling the pail again at the edge of the creek, she carried it back up and set it on the tailgate of one of Mr. Vigil's wagons.

Already, Zachary and Mr. Hicks were measuring off a large log to be used as the center beam, while others set up sawhorses and began cutting thick planks of ponderosa pine to equal lengths. Trace arrived shortly, pushed up his sleeves, and joined in the work. Bridget came along, though she settled herself, at her husband's insistence, on a large, moss-covered stone in the shade. She looked bulky and overheated in her advanced state of pregnancy, but her smile was as serene as that of a Renaissance madonna, and joy glowed from within her, lucent and pure.

Christy watched her cousin for a long moment, full of wonder and no little envy—this, then, was how a woman looked when she bore the children of a man she truly loved—but quickly regained control of her emotions. She'd made her choice, to marry for sensible reasons, hoping that love and passion would come later, and practicality demanded that she stand by the decision. There was no use whatsoever in bemoaning any of the sacrifices; better to concentrate on the rewards. Better to remember how it was, first at that wretched school in England and then in Virginia, when they found everything changed and those Yankees living in Granddaddy's house. Her desolation had been complete, and though she believed she had hidden her fears from Megan, Caney had certainly understood. It had been Caney who gave them cots in her tiny shack of a house, Caney who fed them, Caney who suggested traveling west, taking up the bequest, and starting over fresh.

What would she have done without Caney? Shaking her head, Christy filled a clean cup from the ladle in the water bucket and carried it across the deep grass to where Bridget was sitting. "Sorry," she said with a small but sincere smile. "I haven't the makings for a proper cup of tea."

Bridget accepted the water with a grateful nod, taking the mug in both hands. "Thanks," she said. She inclined her head toward the lodge, surrounded by busy builders. The sounds of hammers and saws rose on the soft spring air. "Looks as though you'll have a proper roof by mid-afternoon," she commented, and made room for Christy to sit down beside her.

The rock was hard, and Christy squirmed a little, trying in vain to make herself comfortable.

Bridget's McQuarry-blue eyes were full of friendly amusement. "You might want to sit in the grass instead," she said. "It's softer. After all, I've got padding."

Christy laughed, searched Megan out in the crowd, and saw her sister handing nails to a good-looking young scoundrel with dark hair and a mischievous grin. Some of her pleasure in the day ebbed.

Bridget must have followed her gaze. "That's Caleb

Strand," she said. "He's nice, hardworking, and entirely harmless."

Christy sighed. Young Mr. Strand might be all those things, but she meant to keep an eye on him all the same. She knew what was good for Megan, and marriage to a lumberjack was not on the list. No, Megan would go to school, perhaps in San Francisco or Denver, when the necessary funds became available. Eventually, she would marry a man she loved, but one from a substantial family, and never lack for so much as a hairpin for as long as she lived.

"Megan," she said at last, "will not be staying on at Primrose Creek. Not for long, in any event."

Bridget looked surprised. "Whyever not? This is her home now, as well as yours."

No, Bridget, Christy wanted to say, *this is* your *home. I will always be your cousin, who came from far away.*

"There is nothing here for Megan," she said firmly, just as Zachary caught her eye again. Even though he wasn't looking at her, she couldn't seem to look away. "As beautiful as this place is, it's—well—remote."

Bridget bristled almost imperceptibly. "Don't you mean backward?"

"I didn't say that!" Christy protested. Zachary had set aside his hat or lost it somewhere, and his hair gleamed in the sunlight like spun gold. Even from that distance, she was struck in the midsection by the pure visceral impact of his grin, flashing white in his tanned face. At last, she managed to look away and met Bridget's gaze again. "Even you have to admit that Primrose Creek is hardly the place for a polished young lady."

Bridget rolled her eyes. "Jupiter's ghost, but you are impossible."

Christy sat up a little straighter and spoke just as one of the workmen came into range, looking for the bucket of drinking water with its community ladle. "I've seen the 'town' of Primrose Creek for myself, Bridget, and it's no fit habitation for anything but men and mules!"

The worker paused, gave Christy an indignant look, and walked away without touching the ladle.

Bridget hissed like water spilling from the spout of a kettle onto a hot stove. "Do you *want* people to dislike you, Christy—is that it? That way, you don't have to take the risk of caring for somebody, right?"

Christy felt a surge of temperament move through her, but she kept a tight hold on her composure. She studied her fingers, which were tightly interlaced. "What would you suggest I do? Marry my sister off to the highest bidder, just to prove I don't think she's too good for these—these people?"

"Why not?" Bridget asked in a sharp whisper. "Isn't that what you plan to do with your own life? Marry yourself off to the highest bidder?"

Christy was at once stricken and furious. It must have been a moment of weakness that made her blurt out her private thoughts to Bridget that first day at Primrose Creek, and now, of course, she wished she'd held her tongue. "My plans," she said, when she dared speak, "are my own business, Bridget Qualtrough, and I will thank you to tend to your knitting."

Some of the starch seemed to go out of Bridget; she wilted a little, as the thirsty wildflowers had done earlier. Cupping her chin in one hand, she sighed heavily.

"There we go, bickering again," she lamented. Her eyes were clear when she caught Christy's gaze and held it. "I just want you to be happy, that's all."

Christy's throat thickened. No one, she realized, had ever said that to her, save her beloved Granddaddy, of course. She swallowed painfully. "Different things please different people," she said at great length.

Bridget grasped her hand, squeezed it. "Christy, listen to me—"

But Christy could not afford to listen, to fall prey to a lot of romantic dreams. Her life was not like her cousin's, never had been and never would be. She shot to her feet and pulled her hand from Bridget's. "You have Trace," she said, watching as Bridget's son chased a butterfly through the high grass nearby, and Skye, in turn, chased him. "You have little Noah, and a new baby coming, and a fine house to live in. What could you possibly know about my situation?"

"Christy, I was *in* your situation. I was just as stubborn and just as proud. Just as foolish. That's how I know you'll be making a terrible mistake if you marry anyone for any reason but love." She paused, no doubt aware that her words, unwanted as they were, were sinking in. "It wouldn't be fair to Jake, either," she added, granting no quarter. "He's a good man, Christy, and he deserves a woman who wants him for himself."

"I'm sure I would grow quite fond of him over the years," Christy allowed, raising her chin and folding her arms. She would never give Jake Vigil cause to regret taking her for a wife. Not willingly, at least. She would cook and sew and clean and—well, better to think about the rest another time.

"Fond?" Bridget challenged in a taut whisper.

"You're going to be sharing his life. His bed. And believe me, *fond*ness will be small comfort—"

Christy put her hands over her ears. "Stop."

But Bridget went right on. "Have you ever experienced passion, Christy? Have you ever thought you'd lose your mind over a certain man's kisses and caresses?"

"*Stop.*" Christy was pleading by then. She had dreamed of just such kisses and caresses, it was true, but lately in her imaginings, the man holding her in his arms was Zachary Shaw.

"I won't," Bridget persisted. "What I've found with Trace—when we're alone together, I mean—is, well, it's magical. It's intoxicating. I never imagined—" She blushed. "I married Mitch McQuarry because I liked him so much, because I thought somehow having a wife and family might keep him home from the war. What I'm trying to say is, it wasn't like that with Mitch. It was tender. It was *fond*. And now that I understand what love—real love—between a man and a woman can mean—"

Christy looked away, still hugging herself, nearer tears than ever. She was innocent of any man's touch, fond or otherwise, but she grasped what Bridget was saying only too well. "I'd better send Megan to the creek for more water," she said, out of pure desperation. "The men will be needing lots of it, I think, working so hard in this heat."

"You're not going to listen, are you?" Bridget's voice was quiet. Angrily resigned. "You're just going to go charging right ahead and ruin not only your own life but Jake's, too. And probably Megan's for good measure. Well, don't come crying to me when you're trapped in a loveless marriage and wanting Zachary every day and every night until the day you die."

Christy stared at her cousin. "How—what—?"

"How did I know you were sweet on Zachary? I've got eyes in my head, Christy. I saw the way you look at him. And, I might add, I saw the way he looks at you."

Christy's traitorous and undisciplined heart skipped over a beat and landed, skidding, upon the next. She could not keep herself from searching Zachary out with her eyes, finding him. Sure enough, he was watching her. Standing stock still, with his hands on his hips and his blond hair shining and his expression solemn. Even sad.

"I'd best get home," Bridget said, rising with some difficulty from her perch on the mossy rock. "Noah is probably running wild, and poor Skye is so smitten with the little stinker, she'll be letting him get away with murder." She paused. "Think about what I said, Christy," she warned. *"Think* about it."

Christy did not answer. Couldn't answer. It was as though she and Zachary were linked by some fierce and fiery current; although well out of earshot, and certainly beyond his reach, he might have been touching Christy. Might have been caressing her cheeks with the sides of his thumbs, getting ready to kiss her—

With a violent effort, she wrenched her gaze free of his and turned away, bent on fetching more water, having completely forgotten that she'd meant for Megan to do that chore.

Dear God, Zachary wondered, why did he keep letting himself in for the kind of trouble a woman like Christy McQuarry could stir up? If he didn't stay away from her, he was bound to do something downright stupid, like haul her into his arms and kiss her so she stayed kissed. She'd probably shoot him for it, once she recovered, but it would almost be worth it.

He rubbed the back of his neck once, before turning to his work again. In the process, of course, he'd lose one of the best friends he had—Jake Vigil. For Jake was plainly just as taken with Miss McQuarry as he was.

For the remainder of that long, long day, he steered clear of Christy, working on top of the roof, once the joists and ridgepole had been lifted into place, on the strength of muttered curses, mules, steel cable, and a pulley the size of a wagon wheel, pounding nails with more force than the task required.

In the end, it was all for nothing, though, because when he climbed down the ladder, aching in every joint and longing for a hot bath and a double shot of whiskey, she was standing right there, with a ladle of water in one hand and fathoms of sorrow in her gray eyes. Without speaking, she handed him the ladle, and he took it and drank.

He nodded his thanks, and they just stood there, staring at each other, for a long time. And suddenly, he realized just how deep it went, what he felt for her. How it had taken root in his very soul.

"Mr. Shaw—I—"

He waited; he wanted to hear what she had to say, and, besides that, he was so shaken by his own realization that he didn't trust himself not to trip over his own tongue if he opened his mouth.

Her cheeks turned a delicious shade of apricot, and her eyes were the color of a cloudy sky. "I just wanted to tell you that—well—there's a whole pig cooking over at Bridget and Trace's place." She paused and flushed again, plainly at a loss. He wanted to grin, didn't dare. "There's going to be an outdoor supper. For everybody who helped with the roof."

He nodded, waited. A gentleman would probably have gotten her off the proverbial hook, but he was no gentleman and had never pretended to be.

"You're invited." She didn't look all that pleased and added reluctantly, "Same as everybody else."

He chuckled, thrust one hand through his hair, which was full of sweat and sawdust. "Well, now," he said, surprising himself that he could speak at all, let alone in a slow drawl, "I guess I've had more enthusiastic invitations in my time, but I do favor roasted pork, and I am about as hungry as I've ever been." He sketched a slight bow, one that would never pass muster in the gracious drawing rooms and parlors of the fancy folks back east and in England. "Thank you, Miss McQuarry. I'll be honored to attend."

She turned on one heel, without so much as a parting word, and walked away.

Damnation, he thought, enjoying the sway of her rounded hips and the fire of a dying sun in her ebony-dark hair. Here he'd made himself a sensible plan—to stay away from Christy—and as soon as he found himself face-to-face with her, he turned witless as a post. As for that other part, the part that would have him on one knee proposing marriage, well, it showed no signs of waning.

He was still watching her and pondering his own contradictory and misguided nature, when a hearty slap on the shoulder snapped him out of his reverie.

Jake Vigil laughed, a sound that had been known to

set boulders rolling downhill, but there wasn't a whole lot of humor in his face. In fact, his usually friendly eyes were cold as high-country creek water in January. "Looks like you and I have taken a shine to the same filly, my friend," he said.

Zachary almost conceded the match, then and there, for he knew he'd been dealt a losing hand when it came to Christy McQuarry, but there was something inside him that wouldn't stand still for that. He'd lost one woman, one he'd loved very much. He hadn't had a chance then, but this time he did, however slim. However fleetingly, he'd known when he looked into Christy's eyes that she was drawn to him. "Looks like it," he agreed grimly. "I don't mind saying I wish things were different, though."

Jake's gaze was following Christy as she went to each of the workmen, shook his hand, and extended smiling thanks. It made Zachary's gut clench, seeing her smile like that at anybody who wasn't him; he felt like a buck in springtime, looking for a fight.

"You'll find yourself a wife in time," Jake said, and his tone was not without sympathy. The West was a lonely place, and the companionship of a good woman was no small consideration. A beautiful, intelligent, and spirited one, like Christy, was of infinite worth. "I mean to have Miss McQuarry there gracing my front parlor before the first snow."

Zachary had a few thoughts along that line himself—places Christy might grace—and none of them had to do with a parlor. Not that he had one, living at Miss Nelly's the way he did. He put out a hand to his friend. "I wish you the best of luck," he said.

Jake frowned, shaking Zachary's hand in a distracted way. "But you don't mean to back down, do you?"

Zach grinned. "I'm sorry. That's something I never really got the knack of doing."

Jake's responding grin was genuine if a little slippery. "Me, either," he said. "Now, I believe I'm going to have myself some of that roast pig over at the Qualtroughs' place."

Zachary retrieved his hat from the low branch where he'd left it and settled it on his head. "Sounds good," he answered.

After everyone had eaten all the pork they could hold, seated around the big bonfire in front of Bridget and Trace's house, Malcolm Hicks brought out a fiddle and began to play. Christy had never seen such a transformation in a man. Dour and silent before, Mr. Hicks became animated the instant he lifted his bow; his teeth flashed in a brilliant smile, and his eyes danced with enjoyment.

Soon another man joined in, pulling a harmonica from his shirt pocket. Members of the gathered crowd, tired from their hard work and sated by a delicious meal, clapped in time and tapped their feet. Trace swept a laughing Caney into his arms and waltzed her once, twice, around the fire, double-time. Then Megan whirled by, beaming, with young Caleb. Christy took a step forward, only to find herself whisked into the embrace of Zachary Shaw, going for a dizzying spin.

She felt as if she'd taken a particularly bad spill from a horse; there was no breath at all in her lungs, and she was a little dazed into the bargain. She hadn't the sense to protest and wasn't sure she would have done so, even if she'd been able.

In a moment, they were outside the rim of firelight, in the darkness, and the sounds of the party seemed to come from far, far away. Without any warning whatsoever, Zachary pulled Christy against him, bent his head, and kissed her. She squirmed at first, but then she was lost, returning the kiss, responding shamelessly, body and soul.

Finally, he set her away from him, though his hands remained on her upper arms. "That's all I wanted to know," he said. Then, hoarsely, "Christy?"

She drew a deep breath in an attempt to steady herself, but she was hopelessly adrift. The kiss, like the dance, had sent her spinning. "Y-yes?"

"Remember that." Then, as though he hadn't behaved badly enough already, he kissed her again, as soundly as before and at greater length. "And that," he said, gasping a little, when it was over. Then he simply walked away, leaving her standing there in the tall grass, every part of her still pulsing with a desire that would never be fulfilled. And at last, at long, long last, Christy McQuarry broke down and cried.

"It's good to have a proper roof over our heads again, at least," Caney remarked that night, when she and Christy and Megan had returned to the lodge. They all regarded their hay bale beds without enthusiasm, though, and Christy couldn't help remembering crisp linen sheets and feather mattresses and plump pillows. The fire burned low, flinging shadows onto the log walls of the lodge, and, far away, a coyote called a plaintive song to the moon.

"Umm," said Christy, who did not want to talk. Her eyes were still puffy, despite all the icy creek water she'd splashed onto her face, and she was afraid something in her voice would betray her feelings if she said too much. She undressed as far as her bloomers and camisole and laid herself down with a sigh.

"We got a door, too," Caney went on. "Fancy that. Up to now, an Injun or an old bear could have walked right in here and said how-dya-do."

"Um-hmm," Christy replied.

Megan, too, had gotten hastily into bed, and within a few moments, she was snoring delicately, all danced out.

"He'll make you a fine husband."

If Caney didn't get an answer of some sort, she'd just go right on chattering, half the night. "Jake?" Christy asked sleepily.

"Zachary," Caney said with surety.

Christy's eyes flew open. "Nonsense. You know how I feel about him."

"Exactly," came the satisfied response. "I saw you go off in the dark with that marshal. So did most everybody else, I reckon. Did he steal a kiss?"

Two, Christy thought, reliving them both in the space of a moment and fairly melting in the heat. *That's all I wanted to know,* he'd said.

"Of course not," she lied.

Caney chuckled. "Well, he might as well have, 'cause everybody thinks he did. Jake Vigil was fit to bite nails in half, and there were a few other unhappy fellers in the crowd, too."

Christy's face flamed in the darkness. It was mortifying to imagine the others gossiping about her, even though the rumors were true. And if she'd ruined her chances with Mr. Vigil, she would never forgive herself.

* * *

Saturday took its sweet time coming, but it finally arrived, and Christy was ready for the party long before it was time to leave for town. Caney and Megan had fussed all afternoon with her hair, and she'd taken in her mother's yellow silk, the French design with the daring neckline and sumptuous lace, so that it fit her perfectly, showing her figure off to best advantage. Caney was wearing her "church dress," a black bombazine, its austerity partially relieved by a modest pendant her late husband, Titus, had given her. Megan, with her auburn hair, ivory skin, and meadow-green eyes, looked like a visiting angel or a wood nymph in her gown of light-weight wine-colored velvet, also salvaged from Jenny's wardrobe.

"Skye and I have been *perishing* to see the inside of Mr. Vigil's house!" Megan confided, flushed with excitement at the prospect of a social evening. It had been a long time since either she or Christy had attended any sort of dress-up affair. "It looks so grand from the outside."

"Don't it, now?" Caney ruminated, but she was watching Christy as she spoke, not Megan. "I reckon the bed's mighty cold of a night, though, if there's no love there to fill it."

Christy glared.

"What?" Megan asked. Bless her heart, she was genuinely puzzled. When she got no reply, she prattled on. "Skye's madly in love with Mr. Vigil. I'm not supposed to tell, but there it is, I told."

"I reckon that'll pass," Caney said, "and Miss Skye will find somebody else entirely." Her tone was firm, and her gaze, still fixed on Christy, did not so much as flicker. " 'Fact, why don't you go and see if Trace is about ready with that wagon, Miss Megan. I don't fancy walkin' to town, party or no party."

Megan glanced at Christy, then pulled a shawl over her shoulders and went outside to watch for Trace and Bridget, Skye, and little Noah.

"If you're about to preach to me, Caney Blue," Christy warned in a whisper, "you'd do well to think better of it. I have had this argument with Bridget, and I *will not* have it with you."

Caney was a model of exasperated disgust. "You're a stiff-necked McQuarry, that's what you are."

"We've already established that."

Caney shook a finger. "Don't you smart-mouth me, young lady. You don't choose to argue, that's just fine with me. But you ain't got no choice but to listen!"

Just when the woman would have launched into a loud and colorful, not to mention familiar, sermon, arms waving for emphasis, they heard the unmistakable sounds of a team and wagon, and Megan burst through the door, eyes shining with eager excitement. "They're here!" she cried.

Christy hoped her sister's lively state of mind had nothing to do with Mr. Caleb Strand, though she suspected he was indeed the reason for Megan's special, sparkling prettiness. "Thank heaven," Christy said in the face of Caney's scowl.

"You don't need to think this discussion is over, miss," that good woman warned forcefully, " 'cause it ain't."

Christy donned her own shawl, a gossamer affair of filmy antique lace, made for beauty rather than warmth. She picked up the lantern and started for the door.

"Let's not keep the Qualtroughs waiting," she said cheerfully.

The bed of the wagon was spacious and padded with fresh straw. Skye and Noah were already seated amid the spiky gold, smiling at the prospect of an evening of fun. Bridget was beside Trace in the box, and once again Christy noticed a glow about her cousin, as though she'd swallowed the moon whole.

Trace greeted the three women with a grin and a tilt of his hat, then climbed down from the wagon seat to help them aboard. Bridget held the reins competently while he lifted first Caney, then Megan, and finally Christy herself up into the fragrant straw. Noah scrambled up on his own. "We're going to be late!" he crowed.

"My goodness," Christy said, finding a place near Skye in the center of the wagon bed, "we'll be half an hour picking the hay from our hair."

Bridget chuckled but offered no comment. Caney and Megan settled themselves at the edge of the tailgate, which Trace had left suspended from its hinges, their limbs dangling over the ground.

"I reckon Mr. Hicks is goin' to be there," Caney said, making no effort whatsoever to hide her infatuation with a man she barely knew. She was going to get herself a reputation if she didn't take care.

Aren't you a fine one to talk, Christy scolded herself. *Heart all aflutter for one man and planning to marry another.* "Who will we see at this party?" she asked aloud.

"Everybody," Skye answered. She looked very grown-up in her pale blue taffeta dress. Her hair was pinned into a loose knot at the back of her head, and her dark brown eyes gleamed with delight. Christy wondered if her young cousin really was infatuated with Mr. Vigil and if she'd be hurt when he married.

"Including Zachary Shaw, I reckon," Caney put in, unsolicited.

Christy ignored her, or tried to, anyway. Caney Blue was not an easy woman to overlook, even in the best of circumstances. When she was determined to be heard, she was impossible.

"It's true that everyone will be there," Bridget put in, as Trace, beside her again, took up the reins and released the brake lever. "Out here, when there's a party, it's just assumed that all and sundry are welcome. You might see anyone from the governor to a fancy woman from the Golden Garter or Diamond Lil's."

Within a half hour, their way illumined by moonlight, the Qualtrough wagon took its place among a dozen others in front of Jake Vigil's magnificent house. Even in Virginia, the structure would have roused comment, with its leaded windows, sweeping veranda, and towering front door. Light gleamed through spotless glass, and the sounds of merriment and plenty spilled out into the night.

Christy drew a deep breath and let it out slowly, trying to collect herself. In truth, however, Caney's earlier comment echoed in her mind. *I reckon that bed's mighty cold of a night, if there's no love to fill it.*

Love, she scoffed, gathering her skirts after Trace had helped her down from the wagon. It was a fickle emotion, at best, dispensed by whimsical gods to the favored few. And what good had it done her mother, loving two men, both of whom had betrayed her in one way or another? No, indeed, there was no sense at all in placing too great a store by something so fragile and so fleeting.

Head high, shoulders squared, Christy walked resolutely toward the light and music. Toward the shining future that she had imagined for herself and for Megan, long ago, during those first terrible nights at St. Martha's school and many, many times since.

The inside of the house was beyond grand, with its gilded moldings, marble fireplaces, costly furniture, and mirrors fit to rival Versailles. Crystal chandeliers shimmered overhead, the flames of their candles flickering magically in every draft.

Jake Vigil greeted each of his guests personally, not excluding Christy, and it seemed he held her hand just a little longer than he had Bridget's. His hazel eyes held a quality of wonder, as though he saw only her and hadn't even noticed the grandeur around him.

The music was provided by Mr. Hicks and several friends, and the object of Caney's affections must have sensed her presence, for he raised his head, heretofore bent over his fiddle in concentration, and favored her with a brief, shy smile. That was enough for Caney; she was off to pursue the courtship.

Christy was startled back to attention when Mr. Vigil took her hand and placed it in the curve of his arm.

"You'll be wanting supper," he said. "The dining room is this way."

On the contrary, the *last* thing Christy wanted was food; she was far too worried about turning a corner and running into Zachary—when, precisely, had she begun to think of him as *Zachary* instead of *Mr. Shaw* or *the marshal*?—but she meant to make significant progress toward a successful marriage that evening, and if eating when she wasn't the least bit hungry was a part of it, she would endure.

"This is a splendid house," she said. "I must admit, I'm surprised to see such furnishings as these in a place as remote as Primrose Creek."

He frowned, but pleasantly, and led her toward a wide arched doorway. Beyond the threshold, people were gathered around a table that should have sagged, it held so many dishes. There were hams, a joint of beef, and mountains of fried chicken, along with all manner of sweets. "We're not so remote," he answered pleasantly. "San Francisco is only a few days from here in good weather, and there's talk that we'll be linked to the railroad soon."

The mention of San Francisco served to remind Christy of her mission, to send her sister to that great city, or one like it, for an education and a spectacular marriage. And that was a good thing, because she nearly collided with Zachary the moment she and Mr. Vigil stepped into the room.

He gave a slow whistle at the sight of her, Zachary did, and his eyes danced with mischief. Just then, someone drew Mr. Vigil away on some errand, and she was left with the man she least wanted to see.

"Go away," she whispered, snapping open her fan and waving it somewhat frantically back and forth under her chin.

He grinned, took in her gown, her carefully dressed hair, and the tasteful application of rouge on her mouth. "By all means," he said. "I wouldn't want to keep you from your work."

Chapter

4

I wouldn't want to keep you from your work.

Christy stared up at Zachary, aghast. Mr. Vigil's party spun at the edges of her vision, a dizzying whirl of color and sound and motion. Despite a deep personal aversion to violence of any kind, she was hard put not to slap the marshal across the face with enough force to set him back on the worn heels of his boots. "I beg your pardon?" she managed at last.

He looked mildly chagrined—and, unfortunately, breathtakingly handsome in his plain suit coat, cotton shirt, and trousers. He took her elbow in a light grasp, pulled her out of the center of the dining room and into a quieter corner. He thrust one hand through his hair, which somehow contrived to look perfect even though it was too long and mussed into the bargain.

"I'm sorry," he said. "It's just that—" He paused, and his jaw tightened momentarily while he struggled with some private emotion. "Christy, if you go through with

211

what I think you're planning on doing, you'll be marrying a house, not a man, and ruining not only your life but Jake's, too."

"I must say," Christy sputtered, her fan still generating a furious breeze, "that you have your share of brass, and more, speaking to me this way. How *dare* you?"

He took her upper arms in his hands then, firmly, but not in a way that was uncomfortable. "You know damn well what I'm talking about," he rasped. "There's something between us, for right or for wrong, for better or for worse, and I for one want to know what it is while there's still time to do something about it!"

Christy averted her eyes, unable to meet his gaze, unable to pull out of his arms. When she looked at him again, it was through a blur of tears. "Only fools marry for passion," she said softly. Sadly. "For—for love." Hadn't she seen that for herself? Not once but twice?

"No," he countered in an outraged whisper. "Only fools marry for any *other* reason."

She thought of her home, with its dirt floor and chinked log walls. She might have been content once never to have anything more than that, if she had true love. Now, though, she knew how rare that was, and in point of fact, she would have preferred to remain unmarried, had she been given a choice. However, a lady without a husband was in a precarious position, not only socially but economically, too. The brothels and fancy houses were filled with women who, without property or private funds or a man to provide for them, protect them—be he brother, husband, or father—had nowhere else to turn.

"Christy," Zachary said, with a gentle squeeze on her upper arms. "Listen to me. I'm not asking you to stop seeing Jake. I'm not asking you to run off with me, though I've got to admit the idea has a measure of appeal, for me, at least. All I'm saying is that you shouldn't hurry into anything as important, as permanent—"

She straightened her spine, raised her chin, and stepped back. "You don't understand," she accused quietly, proudly. "You'll never understand, because you're a man, and you can get anything you want in this world if you're willing to try hard enough."

"Not anything," he corrected her. Then, with a look of defeat in his usually dancing, mischievous eyes, he offered her a broken smile, turned, and walked away, leaving her standing there in a corner of Jake Vigil's opulent dining room, staring after him. She felt exactly as she had when she'd first realized that the South she'd known, beloved home, refuge of her heart, had been trampled into the ground. She'd lost virtually everything and everyone that was important to her— Granddaddy, her mother, her father and uncle, and the farm—oh, dear heaven, *the farm,* the most beautiful place on earth, hidden away in an especially verdant corner of the Shenandoah Valley.

Now, oddly, Zachary Shaw seemed to be the greatest loss of all.

"Christy?"

She turned to see Bridget standing beside her, her blue eyes troubled.

"Is everything all right?" her cousin asked quietly when Christy didn't speak.

Christy bit down hard on her lower lip, then rummaged up a smile from the part of her soul where she kept a secret and ever-dwindling store of them. Oh, but she was so bloody sick of putting on a brave face, making the best of things, carrying on in the face of every trial. "Everything is perfect," she said.

Bridget looked skeptical, and a little annoyed, but she didn't press the matter. It was plain from her expression that she had better things to do than try to coax the truth out of someone who did not wish to give it. "The fried chicken is excellent," she said, lifting her china plate slightly to exhibit an array of sumptuous food. Then her gaze rose over Christy's shoulder, and a warm smile spread across her face. "Here's Jake now, with your supper," she said. "I'll just go and find Trace. Make sure he's not talking politics with somebody."

She and Mr. Vigil exchanged brief pleasantries, and then Bridget disappeared into the crowd. Christy was surprised to find herself feeling almost as stricken as she had when Zachary Shaw had walked away.

"It's a nice night out," Mr. Vigil said, reddening from the neck up in a slow flood of color. He was extraordinarily shy, Christy thought, with a certain fondness. "Maybe you'd like to take your supper in the porch swing?"

Christy drew a mental deep breath and smiled with bright resolution. "That would be lovely," she said. She resisted an urge to look around for some sign of Zachary and took the plate from Jake's hand, fearing he was about to drop it on the Persian rug.

She was, in fact, aware of Zachary's gaze as she passed through the parlor with Jake. She could feel his regard through layers of fabric and flesh, muscle and bone. No force on earth could have made her seek him in that moment, and yet she was weak with the desire to do exactly that. Skye, too, was watching, her gaze fixed on Jake.

As Christy had noted on her first visit, the Vigil mansion was surrounded by a gracious veranda. On the moonward side, in the soft light from tall windows, the white bench swing swayed ever so slightly in the evening breeze. Although she was nervous, Christy knew she was perfectly safe in Jake's company, and she willingly took a seat at his bidding, her supper plate held carefully in her lap.

Jake joined her, his significant weight causing the wood and chain supports to complain a little. He did not meet her eyes but instead admired the spatter of bright silver stars winking in the sky. The clean scents of timber and freshly bathed and barbered man mingled pleasantly with those of party food and night air.

"It's been a long time since a pretty woman like you came through Primrose Creek," Jake said after a period of awkward silence. Even now, as he spoke, he didn't look at her but concentrated on the spectacular sky and the obviously painful task of courting. "A man gets lonesome. Begins to wonder why he's worked so hard, built himself a fine house—"

Christy waited, unable to speak and certainly unable to eat. She wanted to bolt to her feet and flee, but she remained. She had set her course, and she meant to follow it.

Jake cleared his throat. The poor man looked miserable, there in the lace-filtered light from the parlor windows behind them. "Things happen fast out here, ma'am," he said, and his voice was still gruff despite his efforts to the contrary. "What might take a year or two back east, well—what I'm trying to say is—"

Christy might not have loved Jake Vigil, but she certainly liked him. She was a good judge of character, normally, and all her instincts told her that this man was kind, honorable, and generous, as well as wealthy. He possessed all the qualities she sought in a husband—or, at least, most of them.

She took his hand, letting her plate rest untouched on her thighs, and encouraged him with a squeeze of her fingers.

"What I'm trying to say is, I'm the sort of man who needs a wife. I don't drink much, nor gamble, nor chase after women. I'd never beat you or force—force myself on you—" He nearly choked on this last, poor man. Christy's bruised and cautious heart warmed a little more. "I've got no debts to speak of, and plenty of money to provide for you and for our children. I'd like—" He swallowed, made another start. "I'd like your permission to court you proper, with an eye to our getting married soon as it's decent."

It was Christy's turn to swallow. This was what she'd wanted, what she'd aimed to achieve, but she had expected the matter to take longer and perhaps to be just a little more challenging. "You're welcome to come calling, Mr. Vigil."

He took her hand now and squeezed gently. "Jake," he said gruffly. "Please call me Jake."

She managed to look at him. "You know hardly anything at all about me," she said. "We're strangers."

He surprised her by raising her hand to his lips and brushing a light kiss across the backs of her knuckles. She felt nothing at all, though she knew that the same gesture from Zachary would have infused her with heat. "I'm an honest man," he said. "I'm thirty years old, and I've never been married. Never had the time. I thought when I built this house and ordered all those fancy things from San Francisco to fill it up, well, it would be like having a real home. What I learned was, it takes a wife to give a place life, and—in due time, of course—I'd like us to have a family."

Christy wanted a husband. She wanted a lovely home, too, and she *definitely* wanted children of her own. Jake, a fine man, had just declared his very respectable intentions, and yet she felt more sorrow than joy. Zachary's words in the dining room pulsed in her heart. *You'll be marrying a house, not a man, and ruining not only your own life but Jake's, too . . .*

She would *not* ruin Jake's life, she promised herself in that moment, nor her own. Her devotion, if not precisely genuine, would be unfailing and, in the spirit of Holy Scripture, her husband's heart would have cause to trust safely in her. "Yes," she said, practically forcing the word off her tongue. "Of course, we'll have children."

He smiled at her at long last, and she wished with all her soul that she might love him, that some benign force, dancing by on the scented breeze of a spring evening, would cause her truly to adore this shy, gentle man. "We're agreed, then?" he asked.

She nodded, looked away, then down at the plate of now-cold food resting forgotten on her lap. She had not eaten since breakfast, and yet she knew that one bite would send her dashing for the bushes.

The morning sunshine was like a spill of silvery fire on the waters of the creek, and Caney, crouched on the bank and busily scrubbing a pair of worn-out muslin bloomers, fairly pinned Christy to the trunk of a giant ponderosa pine, so intense was the look in her brown eyes. "That's just plain whorin'," she said, in her forth-right way. "I'll have no part of it, Christy McQuarry. Mind you remember that. You go ahead with this lame-brained scheme of yours, and I'll move on without lookin' back. Leave you to simmer in your own brew. Don't you think I won't, neither."

Christy, equally busy with a set of much-mended linen sheets, was tired of defending her decision. "You wouldn't leave Primrose Creek," she said, a little peev-ishly. "You've set your heart on marrying up with Mr. Hicks, and it appears that he means to stay right where he is."

"I can be married to Mr. Malcolm Hicks and still pick who I wants to socialize with, Miss Snippety-britches. And don't you go thinkin' you can sweet-talk me into keepin' house for you. I ain't about to do that. No, sir. I'll go on across the creek there and do for Trace and Miss Bridget and them babies, show you what's what."

Christy had secretly hoped to persuade Caney to come to work for her once she was Mrs. Jake Vigil, and she hadn't given up on the idea. Still, the idea of Caney abandoning her and Megan for Bridget brought stinging color to her cheeks and a flash of temper to her eyes. "Why don't you just go right on over there now," she replied, bluffing shamelessly, "if that's how you feel?"

A short, vibrant silence descended, and Caney relented first, if grudgingly. "Miss Megan needs me 'round here, since her own flesh and blood—you—don't have a lick of sense!"

Christy swished a soapy pillowcase in the water with perhaps more industry than was strictly necessary. After her marriage to Jake, she and Megan and Caney would live in a lovely, spacious house, where they belonged, where they were wanted and cared for and, most of all, safe. They would never want for anything again. Why couldn't Caney see that? Why couldn't Megan?

It galled Christy that Caney, whose opinion she valued above 'most every other, did not approve. "You're a free woman," she said tautly. "You may certainly do whatever you want."

Now, Caney looked more despondent than angry. "You ain't gonna change your mind, neither, are you? I swear I've seen bulls with thinner skulls than you got."

Christy merely shook her head. No, she wasn't going to change her mind. She sought her younger sister out with her eyes, found her carrying buckets of water uphill to the lodge for cooking and washing up. Megan had already fed the mules and worked several hours in the garden, and although she did not seem unhappy, Christy could imagine only too well how years of such drudgery would steal the hope from Megan's heart, the spark from her green eyes, making her old and frail long before her time.

Christy could not bear the prospect, neither for her sister nor for herself, nor for the children she hoped to raise in a loving and unshakably secure home. The sort of life they'd all had before their world was torn apart.

"Let the girl find her own way," Caney said softly, evidently having followed Christy's thoughtful gaze. "The good Lord's got a plan for her, same as everybody else."

Christy's jaw clenched, unclenched. The Lord. She'd seen *His* plans before—for her granddaddy, for her mother, for the South, for the farm generations of McQuarrys had labored to build. She wasn't about to trust Him with something so vitally important as her younger sister's fate—or her own, for that matter. She held her tongue, however, for she knew the subject of God and His doings was of utmost importance to Caney; the other woman would rise up fierce as a fire-breathing dragon if roused to defend her beliefs.

It almost seemed that Caney read her mind in that moment; she stood, wrung out the bloomers she'd been washing, and turned to drape them over some bushes to dry. "I am goin' to town," she announced stiffly. "Don't wait supper on me."

Christy offered no protest; in truth, she was glad of the promise of some time alone with her thoughts. She finished the laundry and got to her feet, her knees and back sore from hard work, her skirts wet through, her hair tumbling from its pins.

Megan was crossing the footbridge, probably planning to pay Skye a visit, and Caney had saddled one of the mules and ridden off in a cloud of indignation and dust. Wearily, Christy began making her way up the hill toward the lodge. She planned to come back for the wash in a couple of hours; in the meantime, she would search the woods and fields for wild strawberries or perhaps a honeycomb.

The bees were out in force, and she spotted a large hive in the crotch of a tree, but catching a glimpse of a black bear, far off in the distance, Christy decided against the enterprise and continued her search for berries. She'd wandered some distance from the lodge when she came across a patch and stooped to begin picking the small, tart berries, using the front of her skirt for a basket. She smiled as she worked, remembering a similar venture back home in Virginia during her early childhood, when Granddaddy had accused her of eating more berries than she brought home, then laughed and lifted her high by the waist and spun her around and around until she was swoon-headed with delight.

It was the snuffle of a horse that made her realize she wasn't alone; she had not heard hoofbeats or the jingle of bridle fittings. She looked up and saw a fierce-looking Indian woman, white-haired and wrinkled, glaring down at her from the back of a sleek buckskin mare. Dressed in worn leather, the visitor carried a spear in one hand, and her eyes were black, bright as a crow's.

Christy was so taken aback that for several moments she didn't notice that the old woman was carrying something besides the spear. Her first thought was that she must be trespassing, and she was about to apologize, when the ancient rider leaned down from her horse and held out a squirming, whimpering bundle.

"Make well," she said, in a tone that brooked no argument. "White man's medicine, make well."

Christy was at once attracted and repelled. Curiosity drove her forward; she held out her arms, forgetting all about the berries she'd gathered, and found herself holding an infant wrapped in a horse blanket. The child was barely conscious; heat radiated from its copper-colored flesh, and the thick head of dark hair was matted with sweat.

"Wait," she said when the spell was broken and she raised her eyes from the baby's face. "I can't—I'm not—"

"You *make well,*" the old one reiterated, poking a gnarled and warning finger at Christy, knotty as the trunk of a time-twisted tree.

"But—"

The woman reined her horse around, spurred it with the heels of her moccasins, and was gone, her waist-length braid bobbing along the length of her rigid spine.

Christy pushed back the blanket and gazed down at a round, glistening little face. She'd helped Caney with various doctoring tasks on the road west with the wagon train, set some broken bones, and even removed the occasional bullet from the leg or shoulder of some hapless traveler. But for all that, she didn't have the remotest idea how to help this child.

After turning around in a full circle, she finally got her bearings and started toward home. She was three-quarters of the way there before it came to her that the baby might be—probably was—suffering from scarlet fever. That represented an acute danger to Megan, who had never had the dreaded malady, and of course to Bridget's young son, Noah, and even her unborn baby. Christy could not rightly remember whether she had had the disease or not. If she had, she'd been very small at the time.

She stopped. What should she do? She wouldn't have been able to abandon a well child, let alone a sick one. But neither did she wish to put so many other people at risk. If only Caney hadn't gone storming off to town, she would surely have had a practical suggestion to offer.

She began walking again, cutting through trees and brush toward the road that led to Primrose Creek. There was no real doctor in the immediate area, as far as she knew, but with luck she might encounter Caney returning from her highly improper visit to Mr. Malcolm Hicks.

Instead, she ran into Trace, driving a buckboard loaded with building supplies. Seeing Christy, he grinned and drew back on the reins, bringing the team of mismatched horses to a stop. He set the brake lever with a motion of one foot. "Hullo," he said. His expression turned solemn when he realized she was carrying something in her arms, and he started to jump down in order to approach her. "There'll be a fellow out to collect those army horses," he said. "Name's Charlie Brimm. He's headed down Fort Grant way and said he'd be glad to take them back."

The two horses she and Megan had borrowed were the last thing she cared about just then. "Stop, Trace," she said clearly and very firmly. "Don't come any closer."

He frowned, pushed his hat to the back of his head. "What—?"

She folded back the saddle blanket, at least far enough to reveal the baby. "He—or she—is very ill. I think it might be scarlet fever."

Trace let out a long, low whistle. "Good Lord," he breathed. "Where did you get him?"

Christy explained hastily. "Is there a doctor *anywhere* nearby?" she asked desperately, just in case.

Trace shook his head. "Closest one is Doc Tatum, down at Fort Grant. And he's not going to come near a baby with scarlet fever, in case of an epidemic on his own ground. You might try the Arrons, though—up at the mission. The reverend used to practice medicine before he took up preaching to the heathens."

"Doctor Tatum would turn an ailing child away? I'll bet he'd tend a *white* child," Christy said shortly. She knew she was being unfair, but frustration and fear had never had a worthy effect on her character.

"That may be so," Trace allowed, and he looked as stricken by the knowledge as Christy felt. "Best try the

Arrons, though. I hear they did a lot of good a couple of years back when the diphtheria struck. Fact is, they'd probably take the little fellow in for good."

Would they? Christy wondered. Or would she and the child travel all that way, through unfamiliar and dangerous territory, only to be turned away? She had made the acquaintance of any number of dedicated missionaries in her travels up to then, but she had also run across a few who'd made her wonder if hellfire, or at least purgatory, wouldn't be preferable to an eternity spent in their company.

"You can't go alone," Trace said when she didn't speak. "I'll let Bridget know we'll be gone a day or two and ride over there with you myself."

Christy was shaking her head before he'd finished making the statement. "And take a chance on infecting Noah or the new baby? Absolutely not."

"Then what?"

"Caney and I will go. She's bound to be back from town soon."

"I wouldn't count on that," Trace replied with just the slightest hint of a grin touching one corner of his mouth. "I just saw her, heading out of town in a buggy with Malcolm. I believe they might be planning to have a picnic supper together somewhere private. Play hell finding them."

Only dogged determination kept Christy standing; she wanted to sit down by the wayside, the sick baby still in her arms, and wail disconsolately. As usual, though, she did not have that luxury. "I've got to do *something,*" she said, as much to herself as to Trace. "I can't just give up and let this child die—"

Trace was bringing the buckboard around in a broad,

noisy circle. "I'll head back and try to find Caney.
Megan can stay at our place until you get back."

"Thank you," Christy said with a long sigh. As Trace
and his team and wagon disappeared into a dusty cloud,
she found a seat on a fallen log and rocked the baby
back and forth, back and forth, singing a wordless lull-
aby.

Considerable time had passed, though Christy never
knew how much, before Trace returned, not with Caney
but with Marshal Zachary Shaw. The lawman rode that
magnificent brown-and-tan stallion of his and led a dappled gray mare, no doubt borrowed, behind him.

"Where," Christy demanded, standing up and then
sitting down again, "is Caney?"

"She's a mite busy," the marshal said, with a smile
that was civil and no more. "Man cut his arm half off in
Jake's mill about half an hour back. Caney's stitching
up the gash." He swung down from the saddle and came
toward her, apparently unconcerned about the possibilities of contagion. "Anyhow, the way to the mission isn't
safe for a couple of women traveling alone."

Trace took off his hat, wiped his forehead with one
arm, and watched the interchange carefully, like somebody staring up at the night sky on Independence Day,
anticipating fireworks. "Bridget and I will see to Megan
and Caney," he said. "You two had better get started
while you've still got a few hours of daylight left."

Had Christy not been wretched with worry over the
child, she would have marveled at her ill fortune. First,
she'd had to endure Zachary Shaw's company during
the long ride up the mountain from Fort Grant. Now, the
two of them would be on the trail together again, for
who knew how long, or under what circumstances, with

only a very sick infant for a chaperone. It seemed to her that she had quite enough problems, thank you very much, without having to deal with this particular man on top of everything else.

"Let's see," he said, and, to her surprise, reached out and took the baby from her arms as easily as if he'd already raised a houseful of them. He turned back a corner of the saddle blanket and spoke quietly. "Hullo there, buckaroo. I hear tell you've come for a visit. Feeling a little rough, are you?"

Christy's throat tightened with an emotion she couldn't define. "I guess we'd better get started," she said with resignation. Heaven only knew what this undertaking was going to do to her marriage plans. Jake was unlikely to approve of such a journey, no matter how noble her reasons for making it. It wasn't as if she had a viable choice, though, given the circumstances.

"I suppose he ought to have water," she said weakly.

Trace called out a farewell just then and rattled away toward home.

"I've got a canteen on my saddle," Zachary replied. "I'll hold him while you mount up, then I'll hand him over."

She gathered the gray's reins in one hand and climbed easily onto the animal's back. Zachary gave her the baby when she was settled in the saddle and then soaked what she hoped was a clean handkerchief in water from his canteen and passed that to her, too.

Christy put the end of the handkerchief gently into the child's mouth, and he whimpered fitfully and began to suckle weakly. Zachary gave her the canteen when she was ready to accept it and then reined his stallion toward the higher peaks to the west.

"We might reach the mission around midnight," he said, "if you can keep up."

Christy would not allow him to nettle her. She spurred the mare into a trot alongside Zachary. "Where did you learn to do that?" she asked.

"Do what?" he replied. His eyes were so blue it hurt to look into them, the way it sometimes hurt to look up at a vivid sky.

She kept the baby in a tight, careful grasp, controlling the reins with one hand. "You're at ease around babies. Why is that?"

He grinned, adjusted his hat. "I grew up in a big family. Five younger, five older. We all helped out."

She was grateful that the conversation had taken a relatively harmless turn. "Where? I mean, where did you live?"

"We started out in Sioux City, then moved on to Denver when I was fourteen," he answered. "Took two wagons just to haul us all. My father was a preacher, an undertaker, a blacksmith, and a sometime-dentist, too, when the situation called for it. We never had much, but we didn't do without anything, either."

"Your mother?"

"She's still in Denver. Lives with my eldest brother and his wife. The rest of us are scattered from one end of creation to the other."

Christy was struck by the easy affection in his voice and expression. Whatever the privations involved, the Shaw family had obviously been a happy one. She envied him that. "What made you leave Denver?"

They had reached a flat stretch of trail, and their horses moved naturally into a gallop. Zachary's eyes turned thoughtful, maybe even a little evasive, but in the end he answered. "A woman," he said.

Christy wished she hadn't asked. Had she truly imagined, for so much as a moment, that such a man might have reached adulthood without courting someone? Still, the thought of Zachary Shaw romancing anyone else was nearly intolerable, even though she most certainly didn't want him for herself. "Ah," she replied at some length. "I'm sorry. I didn't mean to pry."

"I don't mind telling you," he answered easily. "Her name was Jessie St. Clair. She and I were planning on being married. She went into the bank one day, to deposit the day's profits from her father's mercantile, and walked straight into the middle of a robbery." He paused. Looked away. "She was shot. Killed instantly."

Christy felt ill, not to mention guilty for resenting a dead woman, taken long before her time. "I'm so sorry," she said.

"Wasn't your fault," he replied flatly. "You going to be able to hold on to that baby? Or should I rig up some kind of sling?"

"I can hold him for a while," she answered. "Did you love her?" Now, what—*what*—had made her ask such a personal question?

He looked into her eyes, intensely and for a long time. "Yes," he said. "I loved her. Now, tell me exactly how you came by this baby. Trace's story was a little short on detail."

Christy explained how she'd been picking berries and encountered the old woman. "They'll kill me if this child dies, won't they?" she said. The realization, having nagged at her all along, finally struck home. "The Indians, I mean."

Zachary didn't smile, but he didn't look worried, either. "I reckon they'll try," he said.

They traveled mostly in silence after that and stopped beside a mountain spring several hours later to water the horses. While they were resting, he asked for her petticoat and quickly made a sturdy sling in which to carry the baby safely and without undue strain on Christy's arms and back. They had, by that time, discovered that the "little fellow" was a girl.

"I've been wondering about something," Zachary said when they were ready to move on. He had donned the sling himself, the baby couched comfortably inside, and mounted the stallion.

Christy sighed. "What?" She was tired, sore, and terribly afraid for the infant girl fate had put in her charge. She lifted herself into the saddle and took up the reins.

"Where did you learn to ride the way you do? You sit a horse like an Indian."

She smiled. Her eyes were hot with exhaustion, her heart ached, she was hungry, and it would be hours before they reached their destination. "I was raised on a farm in Virginia," she told him. "I can't remember a time when I wasn't around horses—in fact, I was probably riding before I could walk. My daddy would have seen to that."

"Tell me about him."

It was only fair. He'd volunteered considerable information about his own family, and she had no good reason not to speak of hers. "My daddy's name was Eli McQuarry. He was a rascal from the day he was born. He drank enough for himself and half the county and rode like the devil was after him most of the time. He and Uncle J.R. got into a duel over a woman, and right after that, Mama lit out for England with a man she met in Richmond. A baron. She dragged Megan and me right along with her." She'd revealed far more than she'd intended, but there was no help for it.

"Did you like living over there?"

She shook her head. "I was so homesick for Virginia, and for my granddaddy, that sometimes I thought I'd die of it."

His face and hair seemed gilded by the afternoon sunshine, and his profile glowed. He supported the baby girl, in her petticoat pouch, with one arm. "Are you still? Homesick, I mean?"

Christy examined her heart and took her time about it. "No," she said finally. "It's not the same anymore."

He shook his head in acknowledgment and turned to look at her, but she couldn't see his expression because most of his face was cast in shadow by the brim of his hat. "So Primrose Creek is home now?"

She didn't avert her eyes, though the temptation was strong. "Yes," she said. "Primrose Creek is home."

Christy's first glimpse of the lake, a sapphire in a setting of trees, mountains, and sky, quite literally took her breath away. She could not speak for a long time but simply stood in her stirrups, taking in the astounding vista before her. A sense of deep reverence came over her, and she wanted to weep, not from sorrow but from joy.

As the sun set the horizon ablaze, splashes of silver and crimson, gold and purple danced over the otherwise placid surface of the water.

Zachary, still carrying the baby, reined in beside her. "The locals call it Tahoe," he said. "That's a twist on a Washoe word whites can't pronounce. To a lot of Indians, it's simply 'Lake of the Sky.' "

Christy let out a long, tremulous breath. Indeed, the latter was a fitting description, for one might have thought the sky itself had come fluttering down to earth in silken billows of blue, to settle gracefully into the midst of grandeur. "I have never seen anything so beautiful," she managed. "Never."

She felt his smile before she caught sight of it out of the corner of her eye. "Makes a person think there must be a God," he said. "There's no other way to explain something like this."

"I never want to leave," Christy whispered, still spellbound. "I wish I could build a cabin right here and spend the rest of my life just looking."

Zachary chuckled, a low and masculine sound, probably common and yet seeming to belong only to him. Against his midsection, the baby began to whimper, like some small, desolate, wounded creature of the woods, driven out of its hiding place and into open and very dangerous territory.

"Shhh, now," he said to the baby, and, miraculously, the child quieted. His expression was serious when he turned to look at Christy. "Maybe you can have your wish, after a fashion," he said, with all the eagerness of someone about to be thrown from his horse in the middle of a cattle stampede. "This little bit of a lady needs to stop and rest. So do you, for that matter."

Christy couldn't refute his statement. They had been riding for hours, and the baby was surely not only gravely ill but exhausted as well. She, too, was tired, although she'd worked and driven the wagon many times in much worse condition. "I'll give the child more water," she said, "while you see to the horses and build a fire."

He grinned. "Yes, your ladyship," he said, and tugged at his hat brim.

She frowned, unamused. "Why do you always have to do that? Mock me as though I were some supercilious dowager ordering you about, I mean?"

The grin stuck and rose to dance in his eyes. "I like to watch your reaction," he answered, swinging easily down from the saddle to stand looking up at her. "Besides, you *do* have a tendency to give unnecessary instructions and unsolicited advice."

Christy made a point of refusing his help when she dismounted, not because she was angry—she wasn't particularly—but because she desperately needed to maintain some illusion of distance between them. When she was standing on the ground, facing Zachary, he carefully removed the sling from around his neck and handed her the baby.

"I'll make camp," he said.

Christy merely nodded, turned on one heel, and walked away. There was a small clearing a few yards away, full of deep, luscious grass and spring wildflowers. She found a bit of soft ground and knelt, laying the child down before her and tenderly unwrapping her from the ruined petticoat and the horse blanket beneath.

There were sores from one end of the tiny body to the other, and the little girl's flesh was so hot that Christy could have warmed her hands from several inches away. A sound of despair escaped her, and the baby opened luminous brown eyes to gaze up into her face. The little one's expression was wretched; though not more than eight or nine months old, this child knew she was likely to die and wanted very much to live.

Tears burning her eyes, Christy tore off a small piece of the petticoat sling, moistened it with canteen water, and carefully bathed the baby's sore-covered skin, hoping to ease the fever a little and somehow communicate her own determination to fight the disease to the end.

"She ought to have a name," Zachary said from behind her. "Don't you think?"

Christy had finished bathing the infant, fashioned a diaper of sorts from another piece of the petticoat, and wrapped the baby in the horse blanket. She had been kneeling there, facing the lake like a supplicant praying to a saint, holding the child in her arms, and she'd had no sense of the passage of time. Now, though, she heard the crackle of a small fire and smelled wood smoke. "Yes," she said. "A name."

Zachary helped her to her feet. "Any suggestions?"

Christy could not think beyond the strange turmoil inside her, a tempest made of hope that the baby would recover, fear of the repercussions if she didn't, regret of various kinds, and a very real attraction to Zachary Shaw that seemed a holy thing, like the lake itself. "Jenny," she said. "My—my mother was called Jenny."

He smoothed a tendril of hair at her temple, his touch light as the passing breeze. "Jenny it is, then," he agreed. " 'Course, we've got to remember that she belongs to somebody. No question about it, they'll be back to claim her once she's hale and hearty again."

It was bittersweet, the experience of caring for a child, naming her, with Zachary's help. Christy loved children of all ages, always had. At the same time, it hurt far more than she would ever have guessed, knowing this was all she would ever have of motherhood—with this man at her side, anyway. "Yes," she answered at long last, and felt the word catch in her throat.

He caressed her cheek. "Everything's going to be all right," he said quietly, and it seemed to Christy that he was talking about more than little Jenny's recovery. Then he walked away, pulled his rifle from its scabbard, laid his .45 on a fallen log near the fire. "I'll find us some supper," he said. "If you get any visitors in the meantime, make sure that pistol is within easy reach."

Christy looked askance at the gun. "I've never—"

"And you probably won't have to fire it. But if anything or anybody comes around bothering you, pick the thing up, point it at them, and, if you have to, pull the trigger."

She shivered. "All—all right. But hurry."

That wicked grin came again. "Are you going to miss me?"

"No," she lied. "I'm hungry, that's all."

Zachary laughed and disappeared into the timber on foot. The stallion and the mare were hobbled nearby, where they could graze in the sweet grass and drink from the lake.

Christy paced awhile, Jenny fitful in her arms, then sat down on the same log where the pistol rested, keeping a careful distance. She gave the baby as much water as she would take, rocked her, and sang soft snippets of lullabies she remembered from her own childhood.

Presently, she heard a shot in the near distance and moved a little closer to the pistol, in case the report had not been that of Zachary's rifle sighted in on their supper. Twenty minutes later, he reappeared, carrying the gun in one hand and two skinned rabbits in the other.

While he rigged up a spit over the fire and put the meat on to roast, Christy did her level best to think only of Jake Vigil. The trouble was, she couldn't call his image to mind, let alone the touch of his hand or the sound of his voice. She was full of Zachary, as full of him as the lake was of sky, and fearful that she would never exorcise him from her mind and spirit.

* * *

He watched Christy through his lashes while he whittled idly at a stick, beside the fire, thinking she looked like an angel, sitting there on that log, holding little Jenny with an air of weary defiance, as if to inform the universe that she would not surrender her charge, even to death. She'd eaten hardly anything, despite an earlier claim that she was hungry, and she looked like a waif in her rumpled dress with her glossy dark hair falling around her straight little shoulders.

He felt something powerful, and if it wasn't love, it was something damn close. It stirred an odd mingling of joy and despair within him, that mysterious sentiment, and scared the hell out of him, but he faced it squarely all the same. When he'd knelt beside Jessie in that Denver bank, holding her lifeless body in his arms, refusing to let go until his father and two of his older brothers came to pry him away, he'd sworn there would never be another woman for him.

There had been a few passing fancies, of course. Whores, good-hearted and otherwise, the occasional widow, even an unhappy wife or two. He'd always been able to tip his hat and ride away when it was over, without a second thought or a backward look. This time, he was going to get his heart broken, for sure and for certain, and probably for life. Watching Christy marry Jake Vigil would be almost as bad as feeling Jessie's life seep, crimson, into the front of his shirt and the legs of his trousers.

He'd given a lot of thought to the matter of Christy McQuarry, especially after seeing her step out onto the veranda with Jake the night before during that blasted party of his. It had been all he could do not to storm out there and fling Vigil over the porch railing, just as if he had the right. Just as if Jake wasn't one of his closest friends.

He sighed. It was going to happen, and he might as well accept the fact. Christy meant to hitch up with Jake, even though she didn't love him, because of the money and the house and the prestige of being married to a man of substance. It might have been easier if he thought her motivation was greed, and he had to admit the thought had crossed his mind. He could have despised her then—but he knew better. Christy had seen her world fold up and cave in on itself and gotten a taste of true devastation, and somewhere along the line she'd gotten the crazy idea that she could avoid further losses by cushioning herself with money.

He continued to whittle. Back in Primrose Creek, on his desk at the jailhouse, was a stack of wanted posters. He'd been studying them thoughtfully when Trace came to fetch him; some of the rewards amounted to a small fortune. If he talked fast enough, he might be able to chide the mayor and the town council into hiring a temporary deputy to make his rounds while he did a little bounty hunting. . . .

"Do you think she'll die?"

He looked up, caught off guard by the question. It was a moment before he realized she was talking about the child they'd dubbed Jenny. He cleared his throat before answering. "I reckon we need to be prepared for the possibility," he said. "But she's obviously a tough little character. A lot of babies wouldn't have made it this far."

"I keep thinking it was a mistake, taking her on a difficult journey like this," Christy fretted.

"What else could you have done?"

He watched her as she studied the child. Her heart was visible in her face, in the tremulous motion of her hand as she soothed the small brow. He ached with the need to spare her the sorrow she was courting and knew, at the same time, that it could not be done.

She didn't look up. "I don't know. There was no place in town where I could take her, and if I'd brought her back to the lodge, Megan might have become infected."

"What about you?"

At last, she met his eyes, looking puzzled and worn-out enough to drop. "I don't understand."

"Are you immune to scarlet fever, Christy?" The answer was more important to him than his next heartbeat. He wondered why he hadn't asked before and concluded that he'd been afraid of the answer.

He knew by her hesitation, by the way she ran the tip of her tongue nervously over her lips, by the wobbling smile that made a brief landing on her mouth before taking wing and disappearing, but he still held his breath until she spoke.

"I don't recall ever having it. There was an outbreak of diphtheria when we were traveling with the wagon train, and once, cholera. I helped Caney with the sick but never fell ill myself." She swallowed visibly. "And you, Zachary? Have you had it?"

He nodded. "Yep. We had an epidemic in Denver when I was a kid. Nobody died, not in our family, at least, but two of my sisters are hard of hearing, and my youngest brother was left with a weak heart." He gave her a few moments to collect herself, for she was plainly on the verge of panic. He set his whittling aside.

"Here," he said quietly. "Let me look after Miss Jenny for a while. You need to rest."

She hesitated, then surrendered the child and went down to the lake to splash her face and hands and stare out at the view.

Zachary put down a desire to follow and take Christy in his arms and hold her, but just barely. He got his canteen and ferreted a bent spoon out of the depths of his saddle bags, all the while holding the baby in one arm.

He was sitting under a tree, knees bent, with Jenny resting on his thighs while he fed her droplets of water from the spoon. He didn't hear Christy come back, he was so intent on the task.

"You're a good man, Zachary," she said, as though there had ever been any doubt.

He grinned ruefully. "Yeah. That and a nickel will get me a shot of whiskey at the Golden Garter." He gave Jenny more water. "I've only got one blanket," he said, braced for the inevitable protest. "We're going to have to share it, I guess."

Once again, she surprised him. "After this, my reputation will probably be in shreds anyway," she said. "But don't mistake me, Marshal. I still plan to marry Jake Vigil if he'll have me, and I'll countenance no nonsense from you."

He might have laughed, if it hadn't been for the fact that he wanted her so badly. "Jake is no fool," he said. "He'd have you if you grew another head. 'Course, he might shoot me just for being here, but I don't imagine you'd let a little thing like that spoil your wedding day."

She made everything infinitely worse by smiling down at him. "Thank you," she said. "Thank you for caring enough to escort Jenny and me to the mission. I know a lot of people wouldn't have."

Her gratitude undid him in a whole new way. Evidently, she was just brimming with ways to turn him inside out. "Some folks don't have much use for Indians," he allowed, looking at the child and feeling a profound mixture of fury and sorrow at the injustice of it all.

It was probably a good thing Christy was bound to marry Jake instead of him. Maybe in five years—maybe in a hundred—he'd be glad he'd been spared a lifetime of Christy McQuarry.

Zachary had made a bed for the three of them on a cushion of soft grass, using their saddle blankets as an improvised mattress. Christy and the baby were snuggled beneath his bedroll when he sat down on the ground to pull off his boots. Overhead, a sky full of stars gleamed and winked, like diamonds scattered across a length of midnight-blue velvet, and the light of a full-to-bursting moon shimmered upon the waters of the lake.

She did not expect to sleep, but gradually her exhaustion pulled her under, and she surrendered to it. The baby's cry awakened her to a crisp, dew-laden morning. Zachary had already left the bed, and she could hear a new fire crackling, smell smoke and something delicious cooking.

Jenny was still weak, still in grave danger. But she was alive, and that was cause for celebration. Surely it was a good sign, her surviving this long. After improvising another diaper to replace the wet one, then tucking the baby into bed again until the sun was higher and the air warmer, Christy washed her own face and hands at the lakeside. Zachary was standing near the fire, watching her.

"Sorry I can't offer you hot coffee," he said. He was holding a long stick over the fire, with a fish crisping on its pointed end. "But there's trout for breakfast."

They ate with their fingers, watching sunlight spill further and further over the lake, then Zachary smothered the fire with dirt and saddled the horses while Christy put on the sling and placed Jenny inside it. She could feel the heat of the baby's fever, surely higher than before, even through her clothes, and fresh fear loomed up inside her, sudden and fierce. She faced the terror, as she had done many times before in her life, stared it down, but the task wasn't an easy one, and it left her a little dizzy.

Soon, they were mounted again and riding around the northern rim of the lake at a good pace. The beauty of their surroundings gave Christy a certain solace, and by the time the mission came into view, she was feeling strong again.

The mission building was a simple log structure, with a crude wooden cross standing prominently on its roof, and while there was no sign of activity outside, smoke curled from one of its two chimneys, and the front door stood open to the crisp, clean morning air.

Christy glanced at Zachary, expecting to see her own relief reflected in his face. Instead, he looked solemn.

"Is something wrong?" she asked, frowning a little. Jenny fidgeted against her middle and gave a mewling cry.

Zachary removed his hat and replaced it in an agitated fashion. "I hope not," he said, but his eyes were narrowed as he regarded the mission, and there was a certain intensity in his bearing that made her very nervous. He pulled his rifle from the scabbard at the side of his saddle and cocked it before drawing the .45 and handing it to Christy.

"Stay behind me," he said.

Christy's throat tightened painfully, and her palm was already sweating around the handle of that dreadful pistol, but she nodded. "All right," she croaked, holding Jenny a little closer.

They rode single file down the trail leading to the mission. Christy was expecting disaster at every moment; she could barely breathe, and her heart was pounding, but she held on to the .45 and the baby and kept her horse close behind Zachary's.

In the dusty dooryard, Zachary raised one hand to Christy in a silent command to stay put and be quiet, and he dismounted with the merest squeak of leather. Slowly, watchfully, he approached the open door. By that time, Christy shared his concern; visitors were surely rare in this isolated if beautiful place, and it seemed to her that someone should have come out to greet them by now.

He glanced back at Christy once, then stepped over the high threshold. A full two minutes passed before he came outside again, and Christy knew by the look on his face that he didn't have good news.

Unconsciously, she stood in her stirrups and leaned forward, as if by doing so she'd be able to see inside the mission. Find something that would prove him wrong.

"Probably Paiutes," he said, breaking the awful silence. "This is their territory. Reverend and Mrs. Arron are both dead."

Christy grasped the saddle horn with both hands and

drew a slow, deep breath in an effort to steady herself. "Dear God," she whispered. "Are—are you sure?"

"Oh, yes," Zachary replied, leaning against the jamb of the door for a moment. "The reverend's got an arrow through his throat, and Mrs. Arron had her head beaten in with a rock."

Christy squeezed her eyes shut, fought back a rush of bile from her stomach. "What do we do now?" she whispered.

"Bury them," he said simply.

Belatedly, Christy realized that the Arrons' attackers might still be nearby, and she hastily looked back over one shoulder. The towering ponderosa pines, so magnificent before, now seemed sinister, as though they were concealing new violence.

"Stay outside," Zachary instructed. "Things are pretty ugly in here. I'll see to the bodies."

Christy was already climbing down from the saddle, one arm clenched tightly around the baby as she did so. "I've seen dead people before," she said staunchly. "I'll help."

He opened his mouth to warn her off again, then shook his head and retreated back into the mission. Christy followed and was nearly overwhelmed by the smell of death. The place was awash in blood, and the bodies were just as Zachary had described them, and so much worse.

Christy hastened outside, still carrying Jenny in the sling, and was violently ill, but she made herself go back into the cabin as soon as she'd regained her composure. Indian attacks were a grim reality of life on the frontier; she had seen atrocities before, when the wagon train had overtaken such horrors along the trail, but it wasn't the sort of discovery a person ever got used to. Faced with this carnage, she couldn't help imagining what vengeance the old Indian woman might bring down on her and Caney and, dear God, Megan, should she fail to save this baby.

When she rejoined Zachary, he had removed the arrow from the reverend's throat and wrapped both bodies in blankets. Without a word, Christy laid the baby on the Arrons' bed, placed pillows on either side for safety's sake, and then put water on the stove to heat. When it was hot, she found some rags and set herself to the task of cleaning up the evidence of murder.

Zachary was gone a long time, and when he returned, shovel in hand, his sleeves were rolled up and his clothes were dirty. He'd left his coat somewhere, and he looked haggard. Pale. He glanced around the cabin with weary appreciation.

"Thanks," he said. "I'm not sure I could have stomached any more just now."

Christy nodded, went to the stove, and poured him a cup of the coffee she'd made after setting the cabin to rights. Something had been puzzling her since their arrival inside the cabin. Mrs. Arron had shed lots of blood, but there had been hardly any in the place where the reverend lay.

"I'd say the reverend was shot someplace else," he said, as if reading her thoughts. "Whoever did it probably brought the body home before killing Mrs. Arron."

"So horrible," Christy murmured.

"How's the baby?"

"She still has a fever," Christy answered. "I was just about to bathe her with cool water again."

"I'll find the reverend's doctoring bag," Zachary said

between sips of coffee. "Must be some medicine around here someplace." He paused, nodded toward a window. "There's a cow grazing out there. I'll get some milk, and we'll try feeding Jenny with a spoon."

The image of him sitting under a tree spooning water into the child's mouth rose before her mind's eye. She bit down hard on her lower lip and nodded, then fled into the cabin's tiny lean-to bedroom to attend to Jenny. The child's small body was limp with fever, and when Christy lifted her into her arms, the dark eyes rolled back until she could see only the whites.

Zachary brought in the reverend's medical bag, and there was a small vial of quinine inside, but Caney had told her repeatedly never to give an unconscious person water or medicine. Terrified, she frantically peeled off the shirtwaist she'd borrowed from Mrs. Arron's modest wardrobe to serve as a nightgown for the baby, grasped the basin from the wash table, and began once again to swab the infant's hot, ravaged flesh with cool water. This seemed to revive Jenny some, and Christy took the opportunity to give the weary baby as much of the quinine as she could tolerate. All the while, she prayed silently for a miracle, prayed even though she didn't think anyone was listening, even though her granddaddy had died and the farm was gone, even though the South had fallen, even though she was going to marry a man she didn't love.

Christy had curled up on the Arrons' bed and fallen into a sound sleep, and the child was snuggled against her middle, kicking and waving small, plump arms. Her eyes were bright, and she managed a faltering baby smile as she looked up at Zachary.

He had to deal with a whole tangle of feelings before he dared speak. "So you're feeling better, are you?" he asked quietly. When he extended a hand toward the baby and she clasped his finger, a sheen of tears blurred his vision. Nightfall was hours away, and already it had been one hell of a day.

Christy stirred, stretched, awakening slowly.

Zachary's insides ground with the desire to undress this complicated, irritating woman, make love to her, start a baby of their own. The first of many.

She sat up, looking rumpled and alarmed and entirely delectable. "Wh-what time is it?"

"On toward four in the afternoon," he answered. "Looks like your partner here is on the mend."

The look on her face when she realized that Jenny's fever had broken was as magnificent as a sunrise. She touched the baby's face and beamed up at him. "She is! She *is* better!"

He bent, kissed the top of Christy's head. He'd probably regret it, sooner or later—most likely sooner—but for the moment, it didn't seem like too much to ask, even in a hopeless situation like theirs.

"I caught the cow," he said, and immediately felt like an idiot.

She smiled at his expression. "Good. Jenny needs milk, so she can get her strength back. Don't you, little one?"

Minutes later, in the main part of the cabin, he watched, stricken, as Christy sat in Mrs. Arron's rocking chair, patiently spooning milk onto the baby's tongue, a few drops at a time. When Jenny drifted off into a healthy, natural sleep, she gazed serenely down at the child's peaceful little face and continued to rock gently back and forth.

Zachary's throat hurt, and for one moment, he wondered if he was coming down with scarlet fever for the second time in his life. Then, with an inward smile, he told himself he was coming down with something, all right, and no amount of quinine was going to cure it.

Christy carried the baby into the bedroom when she fell asleep in her arms, then returned momentarily to stand looking out the window. "Do you think they're out there?"

She was referring to the Arrons' killers, of course. He sighed, poured himself more coffee. Left over from earlier in the day, it was already stale, but it packed enough of a wallop to keep him on his feet. "Oh, yeah," he said grimly. "They're out there, all right."

"You're sure they were Indians?"

"Renegades, probably. But Indians, yes. The arrow was Paiute."

"We're in danger, then."

There was no sense in dodging the truth. "Yes."

"They could have attacked us while we were on the trail. Or camped last night by the lake."

"Yes," he repeated. "But they didn't. Apparently, they were busy elsewhere."

Her eyes filled with tears, and she looked away, blinking rapidly. "It must have been horrible—"

There was nothing to say to that. The Arrons had suffered, though probably briefly, and the brutality of such an attack was hard to get past. He'd seen worse, of course, but some things a man kept to himself.

"They might kill us that way," she said.

"I'll look after you," he replied.

"The reverend probably made the same promise to his wife."

"Christy, we can't stay here the rest of our lives. We've got to go back to Primrose Creek *sometime*, even if it means facing down a band of Paiutes."

She shivered at the prospect, and she was a little pale, but her head was high and her shoulders were straight. She sat down in the rocking chair again, her legs curled beneath her. "You're right. But I'm scared."

"So am I, if it's any comfort," he said.

She gave another shaky smile. "It isn't," she replied. "When are we leaving?"

He thought. "Tomorrow morning, I guess. If the baby is well enough, that is."

She nodded. "In the meantime—"

"In the meantime, we stay here. You and Jenny can have the bed, and I'll sleep in a chair."

She looked away, started to say something, stopped herself. Met his gaze again. "What about the horses? Are they safe?"

"About as safe as can be expected. I fed and watered them and put them up in the barn with the Arrons' cow. The reverend had a couple of mares and a gelding, last I knew, but they're gone. No surprise there."

She swallowed in an obvious effort to control a surge of well-justified fright. "It doesn't seem right, for their killers to go unpunished."

"Once we get back, I'll report the Arrons' murders to the army. They'll send out a few patrols, but like as not, nothing will come of it. And if it does—" He paused. "A couple of years back, down near Denver, some Indians killed a family of settlers. The law-abiding white folks took up arms and went out to avenge their friends and neighbors. They wiped out a village full of innocent women and children. In time, the braves gathered a war party and retaliated—it seems they'd been off someplace hunting when the first raids were made. If the army hadn't interceded, God knows where it would have ended."

"I've read some dreadful things." She nodded, glanced uneasily toward the windows. "Things Indians will do, I mean."

He approached her, laid a hand on her shoulder. "I'll take you home tomorrow, Christy," he said gruffly. "And you'll get there in one piece. You have my word on that."

She touched his fingers with her own, lightly, and fire shot through him.

"I believe you," she said.

Christy made a supper of sorts from potatoes and onions found in the Arrons' root cellar, and she brewed fresh coffee. She'd fashioned diapers from a muslin bed sheet—tragically, it would never be missed—and given Jenny more milk and, once it had cooled, some of the water she'd used to boil the potatoes.

While she and Zachary ate, alone at the well-worn table where countless graces had surely been offered, Christy listened to the howls of distant coyotes and wondered, were they really coyotes, or Indians calling to each other?

"Christy," Zachary said.

He'd been reading her face. She looked at him, tried to smile. "What?"

"Don't let your imagination run away with you. Indians usually don't attack at night. Something about spirits and ancestors."

"Then why aren't we traveling now? Why wait for daylight?"

Zachary heaved a sigh, and she realized how spent he must be after discovering the bodies and burying both Reverend and Mrs. Arron without help. "We can't risk taking that baby over the trail so soon. It's a miracle she made it as it stands."

She considered that. Considered the two devout people who had spent their lives in service to others and died at the hands of savages for their trouble. Two lives taken, one spared. The unbelievable beauty of the landscape, the ugliness of a cabin splashed with blood. Sometimes it was hard to know whether to despair or be thankful—creation seemed to be one big paradox.

Indeed, the ways of the Lord were past finding out.

Chapter

6

Through most of the night, Christy lay in the Arrons' bed, staring up at the dark ceiling and following every sound she heard through a labyrinth of possible horrors. Occasionally, she heard a creak from Zachary's rocking chair, and each time she took fresh comfort in his presence. Although she was most definitely afraid, she felt safer with him than she would have with a whole platoon from Fort Grant.

When morning came, and it took its sweet time, Christy was numb with exhaustion, and she counted that as a blessing. The day ahead was sure to be a difficult one, and the effects of a sleepless night might serve as a sort of buffer to her already raw emotions.

Zachary turned the Arrons' cow loose before they rode out, and Christy stopped briefly beside the unknown couple's fresh graves. She did not pray for them in words, would not have known what to say. Instead, she imagined the pair rising into the light, hand in hand, and with that picture in her mind a certain peace came over her. Holding a rapidly recovering Jenny in the familiar sling, Christy turned her back on death and set her thoughts and her heart on life.

They camped beside the lake that night, and while Christy and Jenny slept, huddled together under the blanket he provided, Zachary sat up, keeping watch. It was cold, and they went without food, not daring to light a fire lest they attract unwanted attention. The following day, around noon, the town of Primrose Creek sprang up in the distance.

"Do you suppose she's still contagious?" Christy asked Zachary. Jenny was smiling up at her from inside the sling, eyes bright, even after sleeping on the ground with no fire to warm her and jostling along on the back of a horse for the better part of two days.

"I doubt it," Zachary answered. "What do you want to do with her?"

Christy's heart swelled in her chest, threatening to break right in two. "I suppose that old woman will come for her pretty soon. It's going to be hard to give her up."

"She belongs with her own people," Zachary said reasonably. "You know that."

She nodded, then looked directly into his eyes. "Knowing something isn't the same as believing it," she said.

"Amen to that," he replied, and both of them knew they weren't talking about Jenny anymore.

Caney came to meet them as they crossed the meadow toward the lodge. She wiped both hands on her apron and narrowed her eyes. "Ain't you a sight," she said to Christy in a scolding tone that conveyed an equal amount of relief, as she held out her arms. "Let's have a look-see at that baby."

Christy surrendered Jenny to her old friend, watched as Caney peeled back the sling and peered at the child for a long time before speaking again. "Well, now. First I've seen of scarlet fever in a while. But she's on her way back, that's for sure."

Christy got down from the mare's back, while Zachary remained mounted and silent. The brim of his hat cast his features into shadow, and so she could not see his eyes, but she was intensely aware of him, all the same. She could, in fact, feel his regard in every nook and corner of her being. "Is it safe to take her to the lodge with Megan there?"

Caney fixed her with a level gaze. "I reckon so, but it seems likely to me that this little papoose's own people will want her back sooner instead of later. Indians cherish their children, you know."

Biting her lower lip, Christy nodded. She had had Jenny in her care for such a short time, less than two days, in fact, and yet she'd become deeply and permanently attached to the child in that time. She wanted to keep her, raise her as her own, though she knew that was impossible.

Caney looked up at Zachary. "I appreciate your lookin' after my girl here," she said with a slight toss of her head to indicate Christy. "Bringin' her home safe and all."

"Ma'am," he affirmed, with a tug at his hat brim. That was all, just "Ma'am," and not a word to Christy. He simply bent from the saddle to gather the mare's dangling reins in one hand and rode away, headed toward town. He was out of sight before Christy realized that she hadn't thanked him.

"Come on back to the house now," Caney commanded gently, taking Christy's arm and at the same time retaining a secure hold on the baby. "I want to hear all about how you tended this baby. 'Sides, you're wanting a bath, a hot meal, and a good night's rest, by my reckoning."

Christy could only nod, and even as they started toward the lodge, she was still watching the place where Zachary had disappeared onto the road to town.

At home, Caney took care of her as though she were a child, sending Megan and Skye across the creek to borrow Bridget's bathtub. When she was clean and clad in a flannel nightgown, Christy consumed a bowl of stew, telling the grim story between bites. She climbed into her hay bale bed and fell into a deep and mercifully dreamless sleep.

When she awakened, it was morning, and Caney was singing to baby Jenny as she spooned something into her mouth. Jenny laughed up at her between bites, as if trying to join in. Christy's heart constricted, but she managed a smile and what she hoped was a cheerful tone.

"Good morning," she said.

Caney gave her a smile tinged with sadness. " 'Mornin', missy," she said. "This sweet thing here is in fine fettle today." She wriggled a small toe between two fingers, prompting more gurgling glee from Jenny. "Ain't you, darlin' girl?"

Christy was glad of Jenny's recovery, of course. It was something of a miracle, since scarlet fever was so often fatal, but it still meant letting go, and she wasn't looking forward to that. She'd had to let go of so much in her lifetime, so many people, so many places, so many things.

After dishing up a bowl of cornmeal flavored with molasses and handing it to Christy, Caney broached the subject they had both avoided until then. "You mean to tell me what really happened on that trip, or do I have to guess?"

Christy looked away, blinked, looked back. She knew Caney was asking if a romance had developed between her and Zachary, but she pretended not to understand. "I've already told you. The missionaries—the Arrons—were dead when we got there. Massacred. Zachary—Marshal Shaw—buried them, and we passed the night in their cabin. The morning after, we set out for home."

Caney's lips moved in what Christy knew was a private prayer for the Arrons, but the expression in her dark eyes was a relentless one. "Nothing happened? Between you and the marshal?"

A hot blush moved up Christy's neck to pulse in her cheeks. "Of course not," she said, perhaps too fiercely.

"It don't necessarily have to be physical, you know, for something to happen between a man and a woman. There's deeper things than makin' love, and I suspect you know that, even though you've been sheltered for most of your life. Things that fix one person in somebody's heart for good."

Christy shifted uncomfortably and lost all appetite for her cornmeal mush. The hay bales prickled her bottom and the backs of her thighs, even through her nightgown and the quilt beneath her. "I haven't changed my mind about marrying Jake, if that's what you're trying to find out."

Caney sighed, rocking the baby distractedly in her capable arms. "I reckon he might have changed his mind about you, though. Everybody in town knows you and the marshal were alone together all that time. A thing like that stirs up talk, Christy, right or wrong."

She nodded. What would she do if she'd alienated Jake for good? Too much depended on her making a successful marriage, and the timber baron was the only suitable candidate, for her present purposes, at least.

She was developing a headache and rubbed both temples in a vain attempt to forestall it. "Will you look after Jenny for me, Caney? Please? I need to speak with Mr. Vigil as soon as possible."

"I should say you do," Caney agreed, somewhat tartly. Her glance was fond, though, when she returned her attention to the baby. "So you're called Jenny, are you? Ain't that an interestin' thing? I knew another Jenny one time."

Christy ignored her friend's remark, arose, and pulled on a wrapper to go down to the creek and wash. When she returned, face and hands stinging from the cold water, mind jolted into complete wakefulness by that same chill, she dressed very carefully. She wore an apricot silk, which she knew was flattering, if a little frayed at the hem and cuffs, and pinned her hair up in a loose bun at the back of her head. Although she dared not paint her face, she did go so far as to put the merest touch of rouge on her mouth.

"I declare," Caney remarked, looking her over. "If I didn't know better, I'd think you were a hussy, plain and simple."

Color pounded in Christy's cheeks—no doubt, that would be an improvement, given the fact that she'd been pale since the harrowing discovery at the mission three days before—but she did not stoop to offer a retort. The look she gave Caney was eloquent enough, anyhow.

Leaving the lodge, Christy met Megan.

"Where are you going?" Megan asked, looking shocked. "You look like you're dressed for a dance, and here it is barely breakfast time!"

Given that Christy was trying hard to do the best thing for all of them, her sister's confrontational attitude irritated her not a little. "I have business in town," she said, perhaps a bit pettishly.

Megan's hands went to her hips. She was a McQuarry, after all, and she could be as hard-headed as any of the rest of them. "What sort of 'business' could you possibly have, wearing a dress like that and rouge on your mouth?"

"It needn't concern you," Christy said. "Now, please get out of my way. I have two miles to walk, and I'd like to get started." She tried not to think of the renegade Paiutes who had so ruthlessly murdered the Arrons, and how they might be lurking in the nearby woods, even now. She couldn't afford to let fear get the better of her; if anything, the grisly scene at the mission had left her more convinced than ever that Megan belonged in San Francisco or some other relatively civilized city.

Megan remained squarely in Christy's path. "You've set your cap for Jake Vigil," she accused, as though it were a sin.

Christy lifted her chin. Her face felt hot with indignation, and her tone was crisp. "What if I have?"

"He's the wrong man," Megan insisted. She looked like Granddaddy in that moment, with her green eyes snapping and her jaw set. "What's worse, you know it!"

"That," Christy said, trying to go around her sister, "will be quite enough."

Megan immediately blocked her way again. "If

you're doing *any part* of this on my account, Christy McQuarry," she said, "you're making a terrible mistake. I'm not a child, and I've got plans of my own!"

Christy was taken aback, to say the least. "What sort of plans?" she asked in a softer voice. *Dear God, don't let her say she wants to marry Caleb Strand or some other lumberjack. She's too young, too innocent, too fragile for such a life.*

"Never you mind what plans," Megan replied. "I'll tell you this much, though—they don't include teaching school, and I've had all the book-learning I want, so if you're thinking of putting me into another school like St. Martha's, forget it. I won't waste my time studying Latin and embroidery with a lot of stupid society girls!"

Megan's words struck Christy like a slap in the face. Her sister didn't know what she was saying, of course, what she would be giving up. Surely, she could not possibly understand what it meant to battle the soil and the elements for a living, to do for a husband and children day and night.

"Excuse me," Christy said, and swept past Megan to start the long and dusty walk to town. Megan didn't understand the situation, that was all. At sixteen, she was still more child than woman. In time, she would thank Christy for keeping everyone's best interests in mind and pursuing them despite everything.

Jake looked Christy over without smiling when she stepped into his office more than an hour later. Her shoes were pinching and her pride was stung, for a whole nest of reasons, and she was in no mood to put up with a lot of nonsense.

"Are you going to invite me to sit down, or must I stand throughout the interview?" she asked.

"Sit down," Jake said, still not smiling. He was dressed in work clothes—a blue chambray shirt, open at the throat, and well-fitted denim pants. He was very attractive—why didn't that move her, even a little? Why didn't she want him the way she wanted Zachary Shaw?

She sat, folded her hands in her lap. Her backbone was straight as a broomstick. She knew she looked her very best, even after a two-mile walk, but that was little comfort in the face of Jake's dark countenance. She'd planned a speech and rehearsed it as she marched along, as much to keep from thinking about Indians as to prepare herself, but now she couldn't remember a single word. Pity. She recalled the substance of the argument as very convincing.

"Well?" Jake prompted. He drew back the chair behind his desk with a grating sound and sat down. "I have a business to run here, Miss McQuarry. If you wouldn't mind getting to the point—"

"Nothing happened," she said, and immediately turned scarlet.

"You spent several days and nights in the mountains with another man. *That* happened."

"We had to go, don't you see?" Christy demanded, getting angry. She had not expected Jake to be so stubborn, any more than she had expected Megan to behave in a fashion that could only be described as ungrateful. "The baby had scarlet fever—she needed a real doctor. I was trying to get help for her, and Zachary—Marshal Shaw—would not permit me to make the journey alone."

Jake leaned forward in his chair, his eyes flashing. He looked even more handsome in a temper than usual, but Christy might have been looking at a fine stallion or a spectacular painting, for all the passion she felt. "*I* would have gone," he said.

"I know," Christy confessed, losing some of her aplomb. "It's just that it all seemed so urgent at the time, and Mr. Shaw was right there with a horse for me to ride—"

"I'll just bet he was," Jake said, but she could tell that he was beginning to relent a little. He desired her with the same intensity as she desired Zachary, that was plain. She hoped it would be enough to sustain them both through the long years ahead.

"We have an understanding, you and I," she said. "I would never do anything to compromise either your honor or mine."

He gave a great sigh and tilted his head back, as though to stretch his neck. When he looked at Christy again, his eyes were smiling. "I believe that," he said, and opened a drawer in his desk.

Christy stiffened but managed a somewhat rigid smile in return. "Thank you," she said in a rather pointed tone.

He laid a diamond ring between them; its many stones gleamed and glittered in the dusty light pouring in through the window behind and above his head. "I've had this awhile. In case I found somebody to marry."

He looked and sounded like a small boy, proudly revealing a treasure, and Christy felt a stab of guilty dread. "It's—it's beautiful," she said.

He picked it up, came around the side of the desk, and took her hand. She managed to smile when he slipped it onto her finger, but it burned her flesh like a brand. She felt like a harlot, accepting payment for some unseemly act.

"Now it's official," he said, patting her hand once. "Just in case anybody has any doubts."

"Yes," Christy said. "It's official." She was glad she was still sitting down, because she felt faint. *Don't do this,* screamed a voice in her mind, a voice she recognized as her own.

He dropped to one knee beside her, holding her hand. "You'll never regret marrying me, Christy," he promised huskily. "I swear it."

She could only nod. The truth was, she hadn't even gone through with the ceremony yet, and she was *already* full of regrets. She rose shakily to her feet.

"Are you all right?" Jake asked, frowning.

"Just—just happy," she said.

He beamed. "I'm glad. I'll have someone hitch up the buggy, and then I'll drive you home myself, if you're ready to leave."

"I'd like to l-look at the house," she murmured. She needed something, in those desperate moments, to sustain her, to help keep up her resolve. "You wouldn't mind, would you?"

He looked enormously pleased. "No," he said. "Of course not. You'll be wanting changes, I imagine."

She looked away, saw through the plain timber walls of Jake's office to the street and the marshal's office beyond. "I imagine," she agreed, almost sighing the words.

Jake didn't seem to notice her reticence. No doubt, he was only seeing what he wanted to see, like most other people. "I don't guess it would be entirely proper, our being alone in the house before we're actually married. It isn't locked, though. You just go right in."

She nodded, somehow found the door and opened it, stepped outside. The walk to Jake's house was a short one, but it might have been a hundred miles, or a thousand, her feet—not to mention her heart—were so heavy.

She entered the mansion through the kitchen, a huge room with an indoor water supply, a massive and gleaming stove, a big pinewood table with eight chairs, and cupboards with doors. The floor, fashioned of lacquered wood, was dusty but otherwise beautiful, and a good washing would make it shine.

From there, Christy proceeded to the dining room, which she had seen the night of Jake's party. The large parlor was just off the entryway, and it boasted a white marble fireplace that must have cost the earth, though there were only a few pieces of furniture. Christy tried to imagine herself sewing beside a winter fire while Jake read a newspaper in the chair next to hers, but she couldn't.

She explored his study next; it was opposite the parlor and lined with floor-to-ceiling bookshelves. It was enlightening to see that Jake enjoyed reading, and mildly comforting, too. At least they had that much in common. Surely, they could build on a shared love of books and other quiet joys.

The staircase was a wide and graceful curve of gleaming wooden steps, and Christy climbed slowly, as though on her way to her own hanging. Perhaps Megan, young as she was, was right. Perhaps she was taking too much upon herself and making a dreadful mistake in the process.

The upstairs hallway was long and wide, with three doors on one side, three at the other, and a double set at the far end. Christy peeked into each bedroom, all of which were empty, before coming to stand before the towering doors of what she knew must be Jake's room.

Heart thumping, feet leaden, she finally turned one of the brass knobs and pushed the door open a little way. She closed her eyes, took a deep breath, and stepped over the threshold. It should have been Jake's scent that came to meet her, but instead it was Zachary's.

A tear slipped down her right cheek. The bed was a four-poster, intricately carved and set high off the floor. There was another marble fireplace, this one green and black, and at least two of the paintings on the walls were European. The curtains were Irish lace, and there were two gigantic wardrobes against one wall. Another door led to an astounding discovery—a stationary bathtub, commode, and sink. A contrivance at the foot of the tub served as a hot water reservoir. Christy discovered that the hard way, by touching the glittering, rattly thing and burning her fingers.

She was startled, to say the least, when she turned from the splendid bathroom to find herself facing the last person in the world she wanted to see just then.

"Maybe you ought to lie down on the bed," Zachary said, his eyes flashing with blue fire. "Make sure the mattress is to your liking."

She considered turning her back on him and walking off without a word, but that would be too much like running away. "Do you always walk into other people's houses uninvited?"

"Do you?"

"There's a difference," Christy informed him, with all the dignity she could muster. "I'm going to live here."

"That's the difference, all right," he snapped back, his nose so close to hers that she feared her eyes would cross.

She struggled to hold on to her temper and to keep from bursting into tears. "What do you want?" she demanded, and realized too late that the question had been an unfortunate one.

"You," Zachary answered. "I want you. And damn it, Christy, you want me."

"You're wrong!"

He took hold of her upper arms and lifted her almost onto her toes. "No," he rasped, "*you* are. God in heaven, Christy, don't do this. Don't do it to yourself, don't do it to Jake, don't do it to me!"

She was trembling all over and torn shamefully between flinging her arms around his neck to hold on for dear life and boxing his ears with both fists. "Get out," she hissed. "*Now.*"

He thrust out a sigh, and his splendid shoulders sagged a little. He let his hands fall to his sides. "All right," he said. "All right." Then, in complete contrast to his words, he pulled her into his arms again and kissed her so hard that she feared her mouth would be bruised. Worse still, she reveled in that forbidden kiss, surrendered to it, even moaned a little because it roused such a ferocious wanting in her.

When he put her away from him, she realized she was weeping, something only he could make her do. "Good-bye, Zachary," she said. "*Good-bye.*"

He gazed at her for a long, telling moment, then turned and walked out. She heard his boot heels on the stairs and barely kept herself from running after him.

"Let this be over," she murmured to herself. "Please, God, let this be over."

"He's gone." Bridget seemed to take a sort of furious pleasure in delivering the news the next morning. "I hope you're happy now."

"Who's gone?" Christy asked, though she feared she knew.

"Zachary. He swore in a deputy yesterday afternoon and rode out with a wad of wanted posters in his saddle bags. Gus told Trace all about it last night at the town council meeting."

Wanted posters. She was sick at her stomach, and her knees felt weak. Zachary was going after outlaws, men sought for terrible crimes, and he might very well be killed. In those moments, she would have done almost anything to bring him back safe, but of course that was impossible. There was nothing she could do now but brazen things through. "That," she said, putting on a performance, "is no concern of mine. Zachary is a grown man, and he makes his own choices."

"That's true," Bridget said, still flushed with right-eous anger, "except that we both know why he's doing this—don't we, Christy?"

She turned her back on her cousin; that seemed preferable to snatching her hair out by the roots. "I can't imagine what you're talking about."

"I could fertilize my petunia patch with *that* answer," Bridget persisted. "So help me, God, Christy, if he's shot because of your fancies of wealth and comfort, there won't be a person in Primrose Creek who'll speak to you ever again!"

Christy closed her eyes, shaken through and

through, not by the prospect of ostracism—she'd experienced that at St. Martha's and survived just fine, thank you—but by an image of Zachary lying dead on some lonely trail, awash in his own blood. A chill went through her, and she hugged herself against it. When she offered no reply, Bridget spun her around to face her.

If Bridget hadn't been so completely pregnant, Christy might have forgotten all her personal compunctions concerning violence and tied in, kicking and scratching.

"Don't you *ever* do that again!" she cried. "You won't *always* be pregnant, you know!"

Bridget was undaunted and absolutely furious. "You're just like your father!" she spat.

"And you're just like yours!" Christy responded.

"Now, that's right grown-up," Caney put in from somewhere in the pulsing haze that seemed to surround the two cousins. "I reckon you'll be puttin' out your tongues next."

The reprimand dispelled some of the hostility, and Christy and Bridget stepped back from each other, although their fists were still clenched.

Caney stepped between them. "Bridget, you git on home before you work yourself up into a pet and cause that baby to let go afore its time. Christy, you go on with whatever you were up to before Bridget showed up, and hold your tongue. If you're like anybody, the pair of you, it's your old granddaddy, and that's your trouble right there. You're too much alike."

Too much like Bridget? Christy quelled an unladylike desire to spit, but she minded Caney's orders and continued with what she'd been doing—wringing out

Jenny's diapers and draping them over various bushes to dry in the hot, dazzling sunshine.

They arrived in the middle of the afternoon, at least twenty mounted Paiute braves, painted for war and armed with spears, bows, and rifles. The sight of them brought back bloody memories of Reverend and Mrs. Arron, butchered in the sanctity of their own home.

Caney usually kept a shotgun somewhere within reach, and that day was no exception. She picked up the weapon and cocked it, and that gesture, coupled with the hard set of her face, sent a clear message that she meant business. Megan stood gaping in awe, and when Christy had recovered enough to hear anything but the thundering beat of her own pulse, she caught her sister's delighted exclamation.

"Zounds! *Indians!*"

They were going to die, Christy thought, with a peculiar sense of calm that resonated within her like an arrow quivering in its target. They'd never see another sunrise, any of them. Never laugh or argue. Never taste fried chicken or cold spring water.

She walked toward the Indians, heard Megan's gasp and Caney's muttered curse, and was only mildly relieved to see the old woman who had brought her Jenny, riding to the fore, her long gray braid dangling over one shoulder.

"Singing Deer—she is well?"

Singing Deer, Christy repeated to herself. So that was Jenny's true name. "Yes," she said, though a lump had formed in her throat and her eyes burned so badly that they might have been on fire.

"Bring," commanded the ancient one. That she

enjoyed a position of authority in her tribe there could be no doubt. The painted braves, Christy realized, were in attendance to enforce her decrees, that was all, and probably would have preferred to be elsewhere.

Christy nodded, turned, and went into the lodge. Jenny—Singing Deer—was lying happily in a basket atop the bed, diapered and clean and very fascinated with the toes on her right foot. Christy had known this moment was coming, of course, but she still felt as though she'd been dealt a knee-breaking blow. In the short time she had had the child in her care, she had fallen in love with her. Now, she would probably never see her again.

Tenderly, she lifted Singing Deer from her basket, wrapped her in a clean blanket she could not really spare, and carried her outside.

The elderly woman leaned down to collect the child. Her granddaughter, perhaps, or even her great-granddaughter.

Christy surrendered her charge unflinchingly, although inside she was falling apart. "She likes potato broth," she said, without intending to speak at all. It was unlikely that the visitors understood what she'd said or would have cared if they had.

The woman nodded, her gaze level. She barked out a few words in the language of her people, and one of the braves thrust a feathered spear into the ground at Christy's feet with enough force to make her start. She sensed, rather than saw, that Caney had raised her shotgun, ready to fire.

"No!" Christy cried, with one look backward. "Caney, don't shoot!"

A brisk exchange took place between the woman and several of the fiercer braves. Then, at her command, the party turned their ponies and rode away, vanishing into the timber.

"Wait until I tell Skye about *this,*" Megan enthused, reaching for the staff of the spear with the obvious intention of pulling it up to use as an exhibit.

"Leave it," Christy said.

Megan looked at her in surprise. Caney was standing close by, one hand under Christy's left elbow, the other clasping the shotgun.

"But it's an Indian spear," Megan said, with as much wonder as if the thing were the Holy Cross itself.

"Exactly," Christy managed to gasp. Then she dropped to her knees in the tall grass, covered her face with both hands, and sobbed with sorrow and relief and any number of other emotions.

Caney was soon kneeling beside her, gathering her into her arms. "There, now. You go right ahead and cry, Miss Christy. You go right on ahead. Lord knows, you have all the reason in the world."

"Why can't I have the spear?" Megan persisted.

"Because it's a sign to other Indians, that's why," Caney replied. "I reckon it means 'stay away.' Now, go fetch me some creek water and a clean cloth. Can't you see your sister needs tendin'?"

Christy was beginning to recover a little; her sobs had turned to hiccoughs, and she didn't need to cling quite so tightly to Caney.

"What is it, child?" Caney asked with a gruff gentleness that made Christy want to start wailing again. "I know you didn't expect to keep that sweet little baby. You couldn't have."

Christy nodded. She'd known this would happen, of course, but that didn't make it one bit easier. She'd lost Jenny, and Zachary had ridden off somewhere, looking to get himself killed. The future looked bleak indeed, a long series of black and empty days and endless lonely nights.

Chapter

7

Jake Vigil proved to be a patient man. He waited through what remained of April and all of May. He brought Christy flowers he'd gathered himself, took her for moonlight drives in his smart, gleaming buggy, and sent all the way to Chicago for his wedding gift to her, a grand piano.

All that time, Christy was in torment, and not merely because of the fruitlessness of her continuing efforts to fall truly in love with her future husband. Zachary had been gone for weeks, and as far as she knew, no one had heard from him. Christy had bad dreams nearly every night, dreams in which Zachary had been shot dead by one of the monstrous men he was hunting.

One night in early June, when Caney was in town courting Mr. Hicks, Trace came running across the footbridge and up the hillside, shouting for Christy.

She had been sitting on a stone near the creek, brushing her hair and planning to retire early and read one of a stack of books she'd borrowed from Jake's library. Sometimes, though not always, filling her mind with someone else's words served as a talisman of sorts, keeping the nightmares at bay.

"What is it?" she asked, even though she thought she already knew.

Trace didn't wait for her to rise; he grabbed one of her hands and wrenched her to her feet. "Bridget's having pains, real close together. She says the baby's coming."

Christy drew a deep breath to steady herself, let it out slowly. She had assisted Caney in the delivery of several babies on the wagon train but never actually brought one into the world herself. "I'll go to her right now," she said calmly, though inwardly she was considerably less composed than she must have seemed to Trace. "You head into town and fetch Caney back. She'll be with Mr. Hicks."

Trace shook his head. "I'm not leaving my wife," he said, and it was plain by his tone that he meant it. "Skye's off somewhere, with Noah, like most times. She can go, soon as she gets back."

Christy followed him back across the creek and into the sprawling house. Bridget was still dressed and pacing back and forth in front of the hearth.

Although relations had been strained between the two cousins, to say the least, Christy put everything aside and took Bridget's arm. "Trace says it's time."

Bridget smiled weakly and nodded. "Yes," she said. "It's going to be quicker than it was with Noah, I think. I felt the first pain about an hour ago, and now they're pretty hard, with just a few seconds in between."

Christy returned her cousin's smile. "Let's get down to business, then," she said, and turned to address

Bridget's pale, wide-eyed husband. She had to admire him for insisting on staying, when he was obviously scared half out of his skin. "Trace, I'll need plenty of hot water. And you'll probably want to send Skye and Noah over to our place if they show up. There's no time to fetch Caney."

He nodded, grabbed up two buckets, and stumbled out of the cabin like a sleepwalker, headed for the creek.

Meanwhile, Christy escorted Bridget into the bedroom she and Trace shared, helped her out of her clothes, into a loose nightgown, and into bed.

"Are you scared?" Christy asked quietly, rolling up the sleeves of her dress. There was water in the pitcher on the washstand; she poured some into the basin and began to scrub her hands with yellow soap Bridget had probably made herself.

Bridget nodded. "A little," she confessed.

"I know how to do this," Christy said quietly in an effort to reassure her. "Caney taught me when we were with the wagon train."

Bridget nodded again. And then the pains intensified; she doubled up in bed and moaned aloud.

Christy examined her gently. It would not be long, judging by appearances. In fact, they'd be fortunate if Trace got the water heated in time to be of any help.

"H-have you and Jake set a date yet?" Bridget asked.

Christy ached. *Zachary,* her heart cried, in silent sorrow. For a while, she'd played a game with herself. If Zachary returned, either penniless or prospering, and if he still wanted her, she would take it as a sign from God and marry him in spite of everything. But he hadn't come back, and time was running out. Jake wasn't willing to wait forever.

"Yes," she said without meeting Bridget's eyes. "We'll be married this coming Sunday, before church. Reverend Taylor has already agreed to perform the ceremony."

Bridget gasped as a particularly grievous pain seized her, knotting her belly with such force that the musculature was visible even through the fabric of her nightgown. "You're—you're sure?"

"I'm sure," Christy said. It wasn't precisely true, of course, but the charade might as well begin now as on her wedding day, just a few days hence. "Now, let's talk about you. Would you like something to hold on to? I could tie sheets to the bedposts."

Bridget shook her head. "I-I don't think I'm going to need anything like that. The baby seems to have made up its mind."

Christy smiled. When she examined Bridget again, she saw the crown of a tiny head. "You *are* quick," she said.

Bridget lay back on her pillows, panting. "Trace—is so scared—"

"Don't worry about Trace," Christy said. "I gave him some busywork to keep him out from underfoot. He'll be all right."

Bridget's back arched, and she gave a rasping cry.

"Push," Christy ordered.

Bridget pushed.

"Again." A small, perfectly formed head appeared, sporting masses of spiky golden hair. Christy's heart soared, and she smiled, despite the inherent drama of the situation. "Almost finished, Bridge. One more push."

The baby slipped out with the next contraction, but

Bridget's belly was still distended. So Caney had been right; no surprise there. Bridget was indeed carrying twins.

"It's a boy," Christy said, making sure the baby's mouth and nose were clear and then tying off and severing the cord.

Bridget looked down, her face glistening with sweat. "Oh, God," she moaned, "there's another one."

"So it would appear," Christy replied, just as Trace bumbled into the room. "The water's about ready," he said.

Christy handed him his son, unwashed and hastily bundled into a towel, and turned back to Bridget, who was yelling in earnest by then.

His eyes widened with the realization that Bridget was about to give birth to a second baby. "Maybe it's crosswise," Trace said, looking down at his wife with a combination of joy, bewilderment, and worry, but keeping a secure hold on the babe in his arms.

Christy might have laughed if she hadn't been so busy. "Look after your son," she said. "We're a little busy with number two, here."

The girl arrived five minutes later, as blond and perfect as her brother, and Bridget finally was allowed to lie still, struggling for breath, mussed and bloody and beaming with happiness.

Christy attended to the necessary details, changed the bedsheets without dislodging Bridget, in just the way Caney had taught her to do, and quietly left the room so that Bridget and Trace could be alone with each other and the two new additions to the family.

She washed thoroughly at the kitchen washstand, though she supposed her dress was unsalvageable, and wept silently because no matter how many babies she bore Jake Vigil, she would never have what Bridget and Trace were sharing at that moment, in the very room where they had conceived their babies.

In time, she noticed the familiar McQuarry family Bible, a large volume, awaiting the day's date—June 10—and the names of the newcomers, now squalling lustily on the other side of the parlor wall. With a reflective smile, she sat down, placed the Bible in her lap, and opened it to the pages of records in front.

The tome had been printed during the American Revolution, and it had probably cost a fortune, books being rare and very precious in that time.

Thinking of home, of Granddaddy, of Virginia, Christy ran an index finger down the long, long list of names. Births, deaths, marriages. McQuarrys all. When she reached her own generation, her breath caught in her throat, and she blinked, certain that she could not have read the copperplate handwriting correctly.

But she had.

With a snap, Christy closed the McQuarry Bible on a secret that had been right there all the time, in plain English, and she was still staring into space, assimilating all the ramifications, when Trace came out, beaming with pride, to say Bridget and the babies were sleeping.

"Did—did you decide what to call them?" she asked.

He nodded, went to wash his hands, then poured coffee for them both and came to sit in the second rocking chair in front of the fireplace. "The boy is Gideon Mitchell, the girl Rebecca Christina."

Under any other circumstances, Christy might have resented the fact that Bridget had just laid claim to two of the best family names. Yet Bridget had given the girl

Christy's own, which was surely an olive branch of sorts, and Christy was still reeling from what she'd just discovered in the pages of the McQuarry Bible.

Granddaddy, she thought, with the beginnings of a smile, *you crafty old devil, you.*

Sunday morning arrived all too soon, and Christy, still keeping her discovery to herself, still debating over whether or not to reveal it to anyone, ever, dressed for her marriage with all the exuberance Marie Antoinette must have felt when grooming herself for the guillotine.

"You can still back out, you hear?" Caney hissed as she helped Christy with the pale blue silk gown they had altered to serve as a wedding dress. They were in a corner of Reverend Taylor's tent church, behind an improvised changing screen. The parishioners would not arrive until later, after the deed had been done.

Christy sighed. Zachary hadn't returned, which surely meant that she ought to go ahead with her plans. "Where is Megan?" she fussed. "I declare, if she's late, I'll wring her neck."

"Don't you fret, now. Miss Skye will bring her right along," Caney said. "It's a pity Miss Bridget can't be here, too, but with them babies so new and all—"

Christy didn't mind not having a large wedding; the two people she needed for support, Caney and Megan, would be there. As far as she was concerned, no other witnesses were necessary, or even desirable. She felt like someone about to commit a crime.

A stir beyond the changing screen alerted her to the arrival of her bridegroom; she peeked around and swallowed hard at the sight of Jake, so handsome in his new suit of clothes. He was accompanied by Trace, who would serve as his best man, and several of the men who worked with him in the timber enterprise.

Apparently sensing Christy's regard, he looked up, met her gaze, and smiled.

Christy dodged behind the screen again. How could she do this? How? Jake was a decent man; he deserved a woman who truly loved him. "Caney—" she began.

Caney's expression was eager. "What, baby?"

She thought of the big house, the money, the opportunities and security she and Megan would both enjoy because of this union. "Nothing," she said, sighing the word.

Overhead, an unseasonable rain began to patter on the roof of the large tent. The weather was certainly in keeping with Christy's state of mind.

The sound of a fiddle playing the opening strains of the wedding march signaled the beginning of the ceremony. Caney fussed with Christy's hair and dress for a few more seconds, then pushed her around the edge of the screen.

Megan was standing near the altar, looking like one of the Three Graces, a bouquet of yellow and pink wildflowers clasped in both hands. Reverend Taylor was in position, prayer book in hand, and Jake stood to his left, gazing fondly at Christy, urging her forward with his eyes.

She swallowed, hesitated, took one step and then another. Somehow reached his side, although she could not feel her feet touching the sawdust-covered floor, could not feel anything except her knotted stomach.

The rain pounded at the tent top, and thunder crashed high above their heads. Jake's arm brushed Christy's, and he smelled pleasantly of some fine gentleman's cologne. She squeezed her eyes shut and opened them again just as quickly. She prayed she wouldn't disgrace herself and Jake by fainting right there in front of God and creation.

"Dearly beloved," the reverend began solemnly, "we are gathered here—"

Christy bit her upper lip.

"—in the sight of God—"

"No!" she burst out. She looked up at Jake's bewildered face. "I'm sorry," she whispered. "I'm so sorry. But I can't do this. I can't!" With that, she lifted her skirts, turned, and fled between the rows of rough-hewn pews toward the large, open doorway of the tent. She ran out into the hammering rain, through the downpour, through the gummy mud and the puddles, utterly heedless of everything except the need to escape and with no particular destination in mind.

He was tired, he was wet to the skin, and, apparently, he was hallucinating. Christy was running toward him, head down, wearing what looked like a wedding gown. He reined in the stallion, waited, and watched. She hadn't seen him yet; that was the only conclusion he could draw with any certainty, for the moment at least.

As she neared, he stepped down from the saddle and flung the reins loosely over the hitching rail in front of Diamond Lil's. He'd been gone for weeks, sleeping on the ground, solemnly working his way through the stack of wanted posters he'd gathered from the walls of the marshal's office. He'd earned a considerable sum since he'd been away, but with all that time to think, he'd had no choice but to face things about himself that he might not have looked at otherwise.

First of all, he'd explored the troubling fact that he was not only willing to marry a woman who would have him only if he had money in the bank, but half crazed with the need, and he'd asked himself if he truly cared that much. The answer was yes, and that hadn't changed, but at some point he'd made a decision: he wouldn't sell his soul, not even for Christy. No matter how badly it hurt to turn away, he wasn't going to buy her love.

Now, watching her running toward him through the rain, he was thoroughly bemused. He was also fairly certain she was going to run right into Jack Findley's hay wagon and do herself serious injury.

He stepped into her path and caught her upper arms firmly in both hands, lest she fall. Rain danced all around them, falling hard enough to raise a crackling sound from the roofs of Primrose Creek's few buildings.

She looked up at him in disbelief. "Zachary?"

He smiled. "Yup," he said. "Somebody chasing you?"

She must have known he was teasing, but the expression in her eyes was bruised, wary. She shook her head. "I love you," she said.

He felt as though he'd fallen out of a hayloft and landed stomach-first on an anvil. "What?"

"I love you!" she yelled over the rain.

He laughed, mostly because he could not contain the swell of joy that rose up inside him as her words hit home. Just as quickly, he summoned up a stern expression. "What about Jake?"

"I can't marry him. You were right. It would be wrong, even cruel." Her hair was soaked, and if he bided his time, he figured he might see her dress turn transparent.

He took her arm and pulled her swiftly out of the street, along the board sidewalk of which the town council was justifiably proud, and into his office. Fortunately, the deputy was nowhere around.

He took a blanket from one of the cots in the jail cell and wrapped her in it. There was coffee on the stove; he poured her a cup and added a generous dollop of bourbon. "Drink that," he ordered.

To his eternal surprise, she obeyed without question, her hands shivering as she closed both of them around the mug and lifted it to her lips. She looked like a drowned kitten, standing there sipping the worst coffee west of the Missouri, but he didn't dare soften his heart. Not yet. She, and she alone, possessed the power to rip it right out of his chest.

"Now, tell me what you were doing running down the middle of the street in the rain, wearing that fancy dress?"

She was trembling. "Today was supposed—supposed to be my wedding day."

"But you called it off."

She flushed, nodded guiltily. "Yes. In the end, I couldn't go through with it. I couldn't marry anybody for money."

He took off his sodden canvas coat and hung it from a peg on the wall. He'd been on the trail awhile, and he needed clean clothes, a shave, and a haircut. Not to mention a good meal and about twelve hours of uninterrupted sleep. "I see," he said.

She set the cup aside, came toward him, laid both hands on his chest, and looked up into his face. "I've hurt Jake, and you, too. I'm sorry, Zachary."

It took all his restraint to keep from hauling her

against him and kissing her with all the accumulated passion of weeks on the road, when he'd hoped against hope that he'd get back to Primrose Creek before she went through with that fool scheme of hers.

"Now what?" he asked, mentally holding his breath.

"That's up to you," she answered, and he thought he saw her heart shining in those wondrous, stormy-sky eyes of hers. "If you can forgive me, then I'd like for us to start over. I don't care if we have to scrape for a living for the rest of our lives, as long as we can be together."

She didn't know about the money. Probably assumed he'd been unsuccessful, tracking stage robbers, murderers, and cattle rustlers. He felt light-headed with happiness and new hope.

"I love you, Christy," he said. "And whatever I have, whether it's a little or a lot, I want to share it with you. Will you marry me?"

A beatific smile spread from her eyes to the rest of her face and finally seemed to glow from the very center of her being. She blinked away rainwater—or maybe tears—and reached up to touch his face. "Yes," she said. "Yes, I'll marry you. When?"

"How about now?" he heard himself ask. "The reverend was all set for a hitching anyhow. Might as well be us."

She nodded her agreement, but that sad look had slipped into her eyes again.

"I don't feel right, being so happy, when Jake is so— so—"

"Listen to me," he said, holding her shoulders now. Oh, to peel away that wet dress and the equally wet underthings beneath it, but he *would* wait. If it killed him—and he thought it might—he would wait. "Jake will be hurting for a while, that's true. But you did the right thing, Christy, for both of you. Marrying him wouldn't have been any favor, when you claim it's me you love."

She stood on tiptoe and kissed his chin. "I *do* love you," she said.

He kissed her in earnest then.

They were married that evening, in the front room at Bridget and Trace's place on Primrose Creek, with Megan, Skye, and Caney all in attendance and all beaming with approval. They would spend their wedding night in Skye's room, while she and Megan and Caney "camped" in the lodge across the stream.

It pleased Christy that Bridget was there, looking on with a happy smile. They still had their differences, and probably always would, but Granddaddy's entry in the family Bible had changed things, at least on Christy's part. Tomorrow, or the next day, she would broach the subject with her cousin, but for now, all that mattered was Zachary and the vows that would bind them forever.

The bed was wide, with a feather mattress, and the sheets were fresh and crisp. Rain whispered at the window and sputtered on the small hearth as Zachary closed the door on the rest of the world, loosening his tie as he turned toward Christy.

He shrugged out of his coat and tossed it aside, then crossed to where she stood, took her into his arms, and kissed her softly at first, then with an intensity that grew by degrees until it was blazing within them both, fusing into a single flame.

"No second thoughts," he said sleepily, his mouth

still very close to hers, when the kiss was over, "about marrying a dirt-poor U.S. Marshal?"

She shook her head, sure of her answer. "No second thoughts. Kiss me again, Zachary. Now."

He chuckled and did as he was bidden. At the same time, he began unbuttoning the front of her dress—an ivory and lace affair borrowed from Bridget—and smoothed it down over her shoulders and arms. It caught at her waist and then dropped in a pool at her feet.

She trembled, standing there in her best underthings, so ready to give herself to this man and yet frightened because it was an utterly new experience, and she didn't know exactly what to expect.

"Don't be scared," he said in that same throaty voice. The firelight made an aura in his golden hair. "I'd never do anything to hurt you."

She inclined her head toward the closed door of the bedroom. "Do you think they—they know—?"

He laughed. "Yeah, they know."

She felt herself go crimson, not just in her face but all over. Of course, they were all aware of what was happening. What a foolish question. "Oh," she said.

"Forget about everybody else," Zachary said, and ran the backs of his fingers down her cheek, along her neck, over her collarbone, and onto the top of her breast. "Pretend there's nobody in the world but you and me."

It seemed easy enough to do, standing there in her drawers and camisole, with her husband's hand brushing and then claiming her breast in a delicate grasp that elicited a soft cry of pleasure. "You and me," she repeated drunkenly.

He blew out the lamp, so that the fire provided the

only light, and began unbuttoning his shirt. Christy didn't trust her knees to support her; she sat down on the edge of the bed and watched as her shadowy bridegroom kicked off his boots, shrugged out of his shirt, began to unfasten his trousers. He was naked as a savage when he came to her, raised her gently to her feet, and removed the last of her garments.

For a long moment, he weighed her breasts in his hands, gazing reverently into her face. "God in heaven, Christy," he rasped. "I love you. And I need you so much."

She was too moved to speak. Too anxious. Too hungry.

He kissed her again and thereby dispensed with the last of her equilibrium. If he hadn't laid her gently down on the bed, she would have fallen, weak as a thin reed in a high wind.

More kisses followed, each one deeper and longer than the last, and then Zachary brushed the tender place under her ear with his lips, tasted her neck and the ridge of her collarbone. Then—

Christy cried out in ecstasy and clasped her hands behind his head, holding him close to her breast, delighting in every motion of his lips and tongue.

In time, he attended her other breast in the same way, and he was in no hurry about it. Christy lay tossing and writhing beneath him, urging him on with desperate little pleas, but he would not be rushed.

"Please," she whimpered.

He ran the tip of his tongue around her navel, and her hips sprang high off the bed, seemingly of their own accord. "Not yet," he said. "You need—to be ready."

She had no idea what he meant by "ready." If this

state of frenzied wanting didn't qualify, there was no telling what she should expect.

She soon found out, and the pleasure was so fiery, so ferocious, that she turned her face into her pillow in order to muffle a moan that came from some heretofore uncharted region of her being. He drove her higher and higher, and on each plateau, just when she was sure she could not survive any more of this sweet tension, he added fuel to the fire.

Finally, in a devastating inner explosion, he brought her to a new place, a new part of herself that she had never known existed. The descent was excruciatingly slow, and she caught on small branches of delight as she passed, her hands damp where she clasped the rails of the headboard.

After what seemed like an eternity, Zachary poised himself over her, careful not to crush her with his weight. His eyes searched hers, asking a silent question, and she nodded, loving him as much for that question as she did for the answer.

He entered her carefully but in a single, decisive stroke. She clenched her fingers on his back at the brief pain, then was caught off guard by a fresh storm of sensation. Gratification took a long time, but when it came, it shattered them both, left them collapsed and breathless in each other's arms.

As tired as they were, the moon was setting when they finally slept.

Bridget was nursing little Gideon, her bosom covered by a baby blanket, while Rebecca, already fed, slept on her shoulder with an abandon only infants can manage. Summer sunshine glittered on the creek, and across the way, the sounds of hammers and saws punctuated the morning songs of birds and insects as work continued on the lodge, which was being turned into a real home, with rooms and floors and windows.

They had brought the two rocking chairs outside, and Christy was holding the family Bible on her lap. Her mother's cameo brooch, which Zachary had retrieved for her by paying her debt to Gus the storekeeper, was pinned to the bodice of her dress.

"I don't believe you," Bridget said, unsmiling.

"See for yourself," Christy replied, folding back the book's heavy cover.

Bridget leaned over, and her blue eyes widened as she read. Read again. "Saints in suspenders," she marveled in a stunned whisper. "We're *sisters?* The four of us are sisters?"

Christy sighed and closed the Bible. "Yes," she said with a little sniff. "But we don't have to tell anybody." She paused. "Do we?"

Skye

In memory of Stevie Jo Wiley Clark.
If there are horses in heaven,
and surely there must be,
then you are racing the wind.

Prologue

Primrose Creek, Nevada
Fall 1868

The first strains of "Lorena" swelled from Malcolm Hicks's fiddle like smoke from the charred hopes of six hundred thousand dead men, Union and Confederate alike, and all those who had watched in vain for their return. All else was quiet, there in the newly built Community Hall, with its wooden floor, sanded smooth and varnished to lend spring to the reels and glide to the waltzes. The dancers stood in respectful silence, some with tears in their eyes. A few kept a hand resting on their heart, but one or two had set their jaws, like mules balking on a lead line.

Jake Vigil was among the latter. When he was just seventeen, he'd made his way west from Missouri, on his own, and so considered himself neither Yank nor Rebel. The way he figured, it was a waste looking backward, most times, when the present and the future were all that mattered, but he also knew that sometimes a person didn't have a choice.

Just as he began edging toward the double doors of the hall, which stood open to an October night rimed in frost, his gaze snagged on Christy McQuarry Shaw, the woman who would have been his wife if she hadn't changed her mind at the altar a year before. Losing her that way, with pretty much the whole town looking on, had probably been the single greatest humiliation of his life, but now, having gotten some perspective on the matter, he knew that the marriage would have been a mistake for both of them.

Tonight, swollen with her first child and standing close to her husband, Zachary Shaw, their arms linked, Christy fairly shimmered with happiness. Jake smiled, perhaps a little sadly, just as the last notes of Malcolm's tune drifted away into the night, and turned to make his escape.

Almost immediately, he collided with a woman he had to strain to recognize, so different was she without her customary garb of trousers, hat, and shirt. Something leaped inside him right away when their eyes met. Hers were brown, alight with mischief and intelligence. Her hair was the color of polished mahogany and done up somehow at the back of her head, all loose and soft and shiny.

Skye McQuarry.

"I'm sorry," he said, grasping her shoulders to steady her. "I didn't mean—"

She smiled, and Jake let his hands drop to his sides, stung in some sweet, fundamental way, and retreated a step. "I know you didn't," she said, and Jake would have sworn the back of his neck was sweating.

He was still stunned and took her in again, in one dizzying visual gasp. She was delectable, with her womanly figure and perfect skin, and there was something downright magical in the way she smiled, sort of secret-like, as though she might be casting a spell that could never be broken.

Her dress was green, and the skirts rustled, even though she was standing still. Her collarbones showed, and part of her shoulders—those shoulders he had presumed to touch. Beyond all that lay the undiscovered landscape of her nature, and he sensed the almost infinite range of it, knew that merely getting to know her would be the work of a lifetime, an adventure filled with mystery and wonder, pleasure and pain.

He stepped back again, remembering Christy. Remembering Amanda.

"You're Bridget Qualtrough's kid sister," he said, that being the first coherent remark that came to his mind, and immediately felt stupid.

She laughed, glancing back over her shoulder once, as if pursued. The sound of her nervous joy made the pit of Jake's gut quiver in a way that Malcolm's skill with the fiddle never could have done. "I'm Bridget Qualtrough's sister, indeed. And I have a name of my own. It's Skye." She looked behind her again, and Jake caught sight of a scowling young soldier, watching both of them with narrowed eyes.

He wouldn't have believed the change in the girl if he hadn't been a witness to it himself. The Skye McQuarry he recalled was a quiet, shy lass, usually keeping her face hidden under the brim of an old hat. How could that little hoyden have transformed herself into this almost mythically beautiful young woman in the space of a few months? Well, however it had happened, he hadn't been the only one to take notice. The soldier—a corporal, he thought—was starting toward them.

Jake felt a surge of protective fury even before Skye spoke again, this time in a rather urgent whisper. "Please," she said. "Dance with me. Now." The dim light of the lanterns flickered in her hair, danced in her eyes, threw shadows across her breasts. He took her into his arms and began to imagine things no gentleman should.

He swallowed, flushed. "Is that man bothering you?" he asked.

Her smile was dazzling. Spring sunshine following a dark winter. "Not anymore," she said.

Jake shook his head once, dizzy. They were moving awkwardly; he supposed it could have been called dancing.

"I reckon I ought to get back to the mill," he said when he saw that the corporal had been deflected, at least for the time being.

She clung to his hand and the back of his upper arm. "You mustn't leave me just yet," she enjoined with a sort of cheerful desperation. "Corporal Shelby is a persistent man. He'll be back, pestering me again, if he sees you leave."

Her brother-in-law, Trace Qualtrough, certainly could have protected her adequately, as could Shaw, her cousin by marriage. Jake wondered briefly why she had turned to him instead, decided he was flattered, and put the question out of his mind. "All right," he said lamely, for he was no hand with women, and he never had been.

He reminded himself, in a sort of last-ditch effort,

that the other three members of that troublesome family were lookers, like Skye, infamous for their stubbornness and pride and all but impossible to manage. While Jake had put his disappointment over losing Christy behind him—for the most part, anyhow—and bore no grudges, he was about as inclined to have truck with another McQuarry female as a snakebitten man would be to hand-feed a rattler. It worried him no little bit, the way this woman had set things to stirring inside him all of a sudden.

She'd noticed his underlying discomfort with the situation, that was plain by the pink in her cheeks, but she didn't show him any quarter. That, too, was a McQuarry trait. No, she simply squared those fine shoulders and stood her ground, figuratively speaking. "We have something in common, Mr. Vigil," she said as Malcolm began to fiddle up a lively melody, accompanied now by a prospector with a washboard and a lumberjack blowing into an empty jug. "Besides knowing Christy, I mean. I've been tracking that wild bay stallion up in the hills, and Trace tells me you have, too. Well, you might as well know—it's only fair and honorable to tell you— that I plan on getting to him first."

Jake sighed. The idea of holding this particular woman in his arms, even for an innocent purpose, muddled his reason and filled him with a combination of anticipation and foreboding. He heard himself chuckle. *"You're* after the bay?" he marveled. "A little snippet of a thing like you? Why, you'll get yourself killed."

Her cheeks flamed, and her chin went up a notch. She stiffened a little, there in his arms, and his left hand went of its own accord to rest upon the small of her back, while the fingers of his right closed more tightly around hers. "I can ride as well as anybody in the state of Nevada," she said. "Man *or* woman, side-saddle or astride."

"Well, you ought to take up some womanly pursuits," he advised. "Maybe sewing—cooking—" His voice fell away. He'd forgotten, just for a moment, that Skye was, after all, a McQuarry.

He and Skye waltzed, while everyone else in the hall kicked up their heels in a lively square dance. Her eyes flashed as she looked up at him, not just with fury but with a bridled passion that roused still more strong and improper yearnings. "It just so happens," she said with a chill, "that I *can* sew and cook. I know how to tend children, too—I've been helping to raise my nephew, Noah, ever since he was born. Therefore, Mr. Vigil, you needn't worry yourself with regards to my aptitude for 'womanly pursuits.' "

He stared at her, dumbfounded. She'd always been just a kid to him, Bridget's sister, Christy's cousin. He couldn't think why he should care whether she was angry with him or not—he hadn't approached *her* this fine autumn evening, after all—but care he did, and it terrified him.

She heaved a sigh worthy of a stage actress. "There," she said, after scanning the milling crowd. "Corporal Shelby has left. I won't keep you any longer."

He didn't want to let her go. "Miss McQuarry?"

"What is it?" she asked, about to turn away.

"Stay away from that stallion."

Up went the chin. "Kindly do not order me about, Mr. Vigil," she said. "For one thing, it's rude. For another, it's a complete waste of time." With that, she turned on one delicate heel and swept away, into the flurry of calico and sateen, denim and homespun.

As Jake watched her go, it struck him that there must have been twenty men in that hall, apart from the pesky corporal, who would have given as many acres and a team of good horses for the privilege of sharing just one dance with such a woman. She had male kinfolk to look out for her. Why had she sought refuge with him, of all people?

While he was struggling with that question, another tune began, and he made for the doorway, lost in thought. All the laws of time and space and substance seemed to have been suspended; some dark and secret part of him began to open to the light. The process was painful, like the thawing of a frozen limb.

He was clear outside before he remembered her land, six-hundred-odd acres of prime timber and grassland, on the southwest bank of Primrose Creek. Skye, Bridget, Christy, and her sister, Megan, had inherited the large plot from their paternal grandfather, each one given an equal share. He nearly turned and went back.

He went over his contract with the railroad, too, as he walked aimlessly toward the mill, for the subject was never far from his mind, night or day. The deal was pivotal, and he'd staked everything he had on fulfilling it. Through a streak of hard luck, he'd lost a lot of his own timber to the random fires that plagued the area in the late summer, and much of the milling equipment he'd borrowed money to buy had either broken down or was yet to be delivered from San Francisco. It soured things, more than a little, to recall that he was a man with pressing problems—somehow, holding Skye McQuarry, he'd forgotten that for a little while, and in that blessed interval, he'd simply been a man.

Chapter

1

Primrose Creek, Nevada
Spring 1869

She stood facing him, hands on her hips, elbows jutting, feet firmly planted, as though to sprout roots and become a part of the landscape, like the giant pine trees around them. Her brown eyes flashed beneath the limp brim of that silly leather hat of hers, and tendrils of dark hair, its considerable length clasped at her nape with a gewgaw of some sort, danced against her smooth cheeks. In that moment, for all that she stood barely taller than his collarbone, Skye McQuarry seemed every bit as intractable to Jake Vigil as the Sierras themselves.

The last time they'd met, months before at a dance in town, she'd been a mite more gracious. Now, in her unwelcoming presence, Jake, well over six feet and brawny after years of swinging axes and working one end of a cross-cut saw fourteen hours a day, felt strangely like a schoolboy, hauled up in front of the class for some misdeed. It made him furious; he, too, set his feet, and he leaned in until their noses were only inches apart. He would have backed off if he hadn't been desperate, and never gone near her again, but there it was. He was fresh out of choices, or soon would be.

"Now, you listen to me, Miss McQuarry," he rasped, putting just the slightest emphasis on *McQuarry,* since the name alone, to him at least, conveyed volumes about ornery females. "I made you a reasonable offer. If you're holding out for more just because of that little bit of gold you've been panning out of the creek, you're making a foolish mistake."

Skye tilted her chin upward and held her ground. She couldn't have been more than eighteen, and though she was pretty as a primrose, she showed no signs of wilting, either from the unusually hot May sunshine or from the heat of his temper. "And if *you* think you're going to strip my land of timber—for any price—*you* are the one who's mistaken!" Amazingly, she stopped for a breath. "These trees haven't stood here for hundreds of years, Mr. Vigil, just so you can come along and whittle them to slivers for fancy houses and railroad ties and scatter the very dust of their bones across the floors of saloons—"

Jake was at the far reaches of his patience. He'd already explained to this hardheaded little hoyden that the land was *choked* with Ponderosa pine and Douglas fir, among other species, that thinning them would merely leave room for the others to thrive. He closed his eyes and searched his thoughts for an argument he hadn't already raised.

She took advantage of the brief silence and rushed on. "Furthermore, these are *living things*—I won't allow you to murder them for money!"

They were standing in the middle of a small clearing—Skye's portion of an enviable bequest—with tender spring grass at their feet and Primrose Creek glittering in the sunlight as it tumbled past. In every direction, the timber seemed to go on and on, dense as the hairs on a horse's hide, skirting the Sierras in shades of blue and green. It was in that tenuous moment of reflective silence that Jake remembered his own lost timber and was inspired to take another tack.

"It's only May," he pointed out, "and we went all of April without rain." He jabbed a finger toward the thickest stand of timber, where the trees stood cheek-to-jowl, their roots intertwined, competing for soil and sun and water. It was a natural invitation to fire on a truly horrendous scale, and Jake had seen enough flaming mountainsides to last him until the third Sunday of Never. "What do you think is going to happen to those precious trees of yours if we get a lightning storm?"

She paled at that, and, though he supposed he should have taken some satisfaction in the response, he didn't. "I'll *tell* you what, Miss McQuarry," he went on furiously. "They'll pass the sparks from one to another like old maids spreading gossip over the back fence!"

Her mouth—it was a lovely, soft mouth, he noticed, and not for the first time, either—opened and promptly closed again. Then, in the next moment, her gaze narrowed, and her brows drew closer together. Her hands sprang back to her hips. If he hadn't known she was a McQuarry, her countenance would have given her away all on its own. "You're just trying to scare me," she accused.

"Ask Trace," Jake challenged. Trace Qualtrough, the first outsider brave enough to marry into the hornets' nest of McQuarry women, was Skye's brother-in-law, having taken her elder sister, Bridget, to wife. Damn, but that family was complicated; it gave Jake a headache just trying to sort them out. They were hellions, every one of them, that much was certain; two pairs of sisters, first cousins, and the best land in the countryside was deed to them, free and clear.

In point of fact, Bridget and Christy didn't always get along with each other, but a grievance with one was a grievance with them all, and Jake knew—hell, *everybody* knew—they would stand shoulder-to-shoulder, like their trees, against any challenge from an outsider.

As easily as that, Jake let Christy sneak into his mind. Christy, who, with her younger sister, Megan, owned the land on the other side of Primrose Creek. Beautiful, spirited Christy. A long-buried ache twisted in his heart, and, employing his considerable will, he quelled it, retreated into the familiar state of numbness he'd been cultivating ever since he lost her.

"I don't need to ask Trace," Skye said, wrenching him back from his reveries as swiftly as if she'd grabbed the back of his collar and yanked him onto the balls of his feet. "This is *my* land. Granddaddy left it to me, and *I* decide what happens here."

Jake heaved a great sigh. He'd already tried buying Bridget's timber rights, and Megan's, too, and neither of them had given him a definitive answer, one way or the other. He'd be damned if he'd approach Christy with any such request, even if it meant bankruptcy—and it just might, if he couldn't fulfill the deal with the railroad. Besides, the finest stands of trees grew on Skye's share of the tract.

He was way behind schedule, and although he had

modest holdings of his own, he'd already harvested the best stands of timber, those that hadn't burned the previous summer. To cut any more before the trees had time to come back would be plain stupid; despite appearances to the contrary, the resources of the West were not inexhaustible, and Jake knew it.

He heaved a great sigh. "I never should have wasted my breath trying to reason with a—with a—"

Skye raised one delicate eyebrow. "With a woman?" she asked softly. Dangerously. No doubt, she was still bristling from their conversation at the dance, when he'd suggested she leave off chasing the stallion and turn her mind to more feminine pursuits, and she'd taken offense at the remark. Neither of them had caught the bay, as it happened, but Jake figured she hadn't given up on the idea any more than he had.

"With a McQuarry!" Jake snapped. He wanted to give his temper free rein and bellow like a bull, but he knew he couldn't afford the indulgence. He had to win this argument, and soon. The fact that it seemed impossible only made him more determined.

Her very expressive mouth curved into a smile that made Jake want to kiss her and, at one and the same time, turn right around and head for his horse. Damn if she wasn't even more confusing, even more hogheaded, than her cousin Christy, and that was saying something. "If that's supposed to be an insult, you'll have to do better. I'm *proud* of my name."

He looked around, maybe a little wildly, at the empty clearing. He couldn't remember when he'd been more exasperated with anybody, man or woman. "What are you going to use to build with, if you refuse to cut your precious trees?" It was a gamble; she had house-room at Trace and Bridget's place, everybody knew that, and as a single woman, she might elect to live right there until she married. On the other hand, she was who she was, a McQuarry female, and her people were an independent lot, making and following rules of their own. She'd probably live in a chicken coop if she took a notion.

For all of that, he could see that her confidence had ebbed again, the way it had when he mentioned the possibility of fire. Perhaps she was envisioning vast tracts of timber reduced to charred stumps and wisps of smoke in a matter of hours, as he was.

"I've got gold," she said. "I mean to buy lumber. To build my house, I mean."

Jake grinned without humor. He set his hands on his hips again, mirroring her stance; there wasn't another lumber yard within three hundred miles, and they both knew it. "Suppose I don't want to sell?" he inquired. He was being mulish, for sure and certain, but he couldn't seem to help himself. Something about this complicated woman set his nerves to singing, and not only was the music downright unsettling, but he felt compelled to dance to it.

Color surged up Skye's neck to pulse, apricot pink, beneath her high cheekbones. Jake felt a swift, grinding ache somewhere deep inside. "That's ridiculous," she cried. "Selling lumber is your business!"

"Exactly. And *I* decide when and if I'm willing to sell. Just like you."

From the look in her eyes, she wanted to kick him in the shins, but she must have found it within herself to forbear, for Jake remained unbruised. At least, on the outside. "You're doing this because you have a grudge against my cousin," she said, that obstinate chin jutting way out. "Christy married someone else, and you're taking it out on *me*."

Her words sent such a shock jolting through him that she might as well have struck him with a closed fist. The sensation was immediately, and mercifully, followed by a sort of thrumming numbness. "I don't do business that way," he insisted, but he'd taken too long to reply. He could see that by the narrowing of those brown eyes.

"Don't you?" she countered, folding her arms, and turned her back on him, big as life. He couldn't recall the last time someone had dared to do that.

He watched her in helpless irritation for several moments, then spun around, stormed over to his horse, a gray and white stallion he'd dubbed Trojan, and mounted. "You know where to find me," he said, and then he headed for town.

Skye waited until she was sure Jake Vigil was well out of sight before letting down her guard. With the back of one hand, she dashed at the tears of fury and frustration clinging to her cheeks. Maybe he was right, and she was being unreasonable, she thought. Maybe, by refusing to sell him so much as a twig of the timber growing on her land, she was punishing him for loving Christy the way he had.

The way he surely still did. She hadn't missed the way he'd reacted to the mention of her cousin.

Skye heaved a sigh and glanced up at the sun, the way someone else might have consulted a pocket watch. She'd best stop standing here and get on home; she'd promised Bridget she'd look after Noah and the babies

while she and Trace went to town to pick up a load of
supplies, and after that, she and her cousin Megan
planned to gather wildflowers to press in their remem-
brance books. No sense standing around mooning over
a man who would never see her as anything more than
an obstacle between him and six hundred and twenty-
five acres of prime timber.

She took one last, long look around at her land,
where she planned to build a little cabin all her own,
along with a good barn, and make a life for herself.
She'd been saving the money she'd made panning gold,
and pretty soon she'd be able to put up her buildings,
buy a mare in foal from Trace and Bridget, and start a
ranch all her own. The bay stallion, once she roped him
in, would give distinction to her brand.

Just a week before, she'd nearly captured the exquisite bay stallion, wild as a storm wind, up near the tree
line, but he was wily, and, in the end, he'd managed to
elude her. That hadn't dimmed her determination to
bring him in, though; she was set on the plan, and there
would be no going back.

Trace and Zachary had promised to help with the
building, and others would pitch in, too, Primrose Creek
being that kind of town, but what good was a lot of willing labor without boards to make walls and floors and
ceilings?

Head down, thoughts racing far ahead, like willful
children, Skye started back toward Bridget and Trace's
place, following the edge of the creek the way she
always did. She had a room of her own with them, but
the Qualtrough family was growing rapidly, and it
wouldn't be long until things got real crowded. Besides,
she couldn't help wanting to *begin* doing something

real, something that was her own. As things stood, she was merely marking time, waiting for something, *anything,* to happen.

Within a few minutes, Skye rounded a curve in the creek, and her sister and brother-in-law's holdings came into view. The structure, fashioned of hewn logs, was large and sturdy, built to last. The door stood open to the fresh spring air, welcoming. Her six-year-old nephew, Noah, was running in circles in the front yard, whooping and hollering like a Paiute on the warpath, and Bridget immediately appeared on the threshold, smiling and wiping flour-covered hands on a blue-and-white checked apron.

Bridget was a beauty, with her fair tresses, perfect skin, and cornflower blue eyes. She was a small woman, and she looked deceptively delicate, even fragile. Skye had seen her face down Indians, bears, and the Ladies Aid Society, all without turning a hair.

"Did I just see Jake Vigil ride up the bank on the other side of the creek?" she asked. As her son raced past, she reached out and snagged him by the shirt collar. "Merciful heavens, Noah," she said good-naturedly, "that will be enough. Try being a *quiet* Indian."

Skye shaded her eyes with one hand. "He wants to cut down my timber," she said, as if that were an answer to her sister's inquiry.

Bridget sighed. "And you refused."

"Of course I did," Skye retorted, a little impatiently perhaps.

Bridget set her hands on her hips. "Why?"

For a moment, Skye couldn't recall what her reasoning had been—being near Jake always addled her—but then it all came back to her, like a flash flood racing through a dry creekbed. "He means to raze every tree on my land to the ground, that's why."

"Nonsense," Bridget scoffed. Like the rest of the McQuarrys, Bridget was never hesitant to express a differing opinion. "Jake's a very intelligent man, and he wouldn't do any such thing."

Skye had heard about the way some of the mining companies were ravaging the countryside, down Virginia City way and in other parts of the state, too. Why would the lumber industry be any kinder? "In any case, I told him no. And do you know how he responded?"

Her sister waited, no doubt to indicate that indeed she didn't have the first idea.

"He won't sell me the lumber I need for my house and barn. Even though I have cash money to pay him!"

Bridget looked pleasantly impatient; she cocked her head to one side and studied her sister with amusement. "Sounds to me like you two have reached a standoff. Both of you are plain stubborn, and that's a fact."

Skye felt color thump beneath the skin covering her cheekbones. "If you feel that way, why don't you sell him some of *your* timber?"

"Maybe I will. I haven't decided the matter."

Before Skye was forced to answer, Trace came whistling around the corner of the house, leading a team of two bay mares hitched to the family buckboard. The wagon rattled and jostled behind them.

Noah raced toward his stepfather. "You're going to town!" he crowed. "Can I go? Can I go?"

Trace ruffled the boy's gleaming brown hair and crouched to meet his eyes. He was as devoted a father to Noah, his late and best friend Mitch's child, as he was to the twins Bridget had borne him just the year before. Gideon and Rebecca were their names, and they were sunny toddlers now, with fat little legs and ready smiles. "Well, now," he said very thoughtfully in a confidential tone of voice, rubbing his chin as he pondered the situation, "I was kind of counting on you to look out for the womenfolk while I'm gone. Your Aunt Skye and little Rebecca, I mean. And then there's Miss Christy and Miss Megan, over there across the creek." He paused, sighed at the sheer magnitude of the task. Skye noticed he didn't include Caney Blue, the forthright black woman who ran the cousins' household; even Noah wouldn't have believed *she* needed a caretaker. "Gideon isn't quite big enough to handle the job, you know. I mean, suppose something happens that only you could take care of?"

Noah's small chest swelled with pride. He saw the babies as his special charge, and now that they were ambulatory and usually heading in two directions at once, he liked to keep an eye on them. *Just the way I always looked after him,* Skye thought with a small, sad smile. He was growing up so fast, Noah was. Before she knew it, he'd be a grown man, leading a life of his own, maybe even riding away for good. It made her heart ache to think of that.

"I'll watch out for the whole passel of 'em," the little boy said staunchly.

Trace did a creditable job of hiding a smile, though Skye saw it plainly, lurking in his eyes. "I'd appreciate that," he said with a grave nod of his blond head. "You and I, we'll make our own trip to town tomorrow morning," he finished. "No women allowed."

Noah beamed. "No women," he confirmed.

"What are you teaching that boy?" Bridget demanded, but there was a note in her voice that sounded suspiciously like laughter.

Trace rose easily to his feet. "Never you mind," he told his wife, grinning and mussing Noah's hair once again. As if it wasn't trouble enough keeping that child tidy. "We had some things to discuss, Noah and I. Personal stuff."

"Man-to-man," said Noah.

Bridget smiled and shook her head as she reached back to untie her apron. Trace's gaze followed the rise of her shapely breasts with a glint of admiration, and something as tangible as heat lightning passed between them.

Skye averted her eyes. She loved her sister better than anyone else in the world—she might not have survived all the grief they'd endured back in Virginia if not for Bridget, not to mention the long journey west that followed, but there were times, all the same, when she envied her a little. It seemed to Skye that Bridget had everything: a handsome, dedicated husband; three healthy, beautiful children; a house and land and horses. Although women were denied the vote and men could legally lay claim to any property their brides brought into a marriage, Bridget remained the sole owner of the six hundred and twenty-five acres she'd inherited from Granddaddy, and she often bought and sold livestock on her signature alone. Trace had an interest in the horses, of course, and in the investments the two of them made together, but he let Bridget tend to her own affairs. The two of them were partners in the truest sense of the word.

"We won't be long," Bridget promised when Skye

joined her in the cool, shadowy interior of the house. The babies were in Noah's room, asleep in the little railed beds Trace had built for them, but they'd be awake soon enough, rambunctious as ever. "Is there anything you'd like us to bring back?"

Skye smiled ruefully. "A few wagonloads of lumber, perhaps?"

Bridget laughed and shook her head, draping her good shawl over her shoulders. She had crocheted the piece over the winter and liked to wear it because it made her feel dressed up. "I'm afraid you're going to have to give in and part with some of those trees," she said. "At least enough to provide logs for a cabin and some kind of shed."

Even that seemed like a travesty to Skye, who loved every pine and fir, every twig and branch on her property, but she gave a slight, rueful nod all the same. She longed for a home of her own, and besides, she suspected that Bridget was expecting another baby, even though she hadn't said anything to that effect.

Very soon, Skye knew, she would become a burden. An image of herself as a maiden aunt, scrawny and terse and disappointed, made her shiver.

Bridget laid a hand on her shoulder. "Brew yourself some tea, if the twins leave you time. That will make you feel better."

Tea was the balm for most every ailment and strife, as far as Bridget was concerned. Skye nodded again, managed a slight smile, and went to the door, where she and Noah stood waving until Bridget and Trace and their wagon had rattled across the creek, up the bank, and off toward town.

Noah resumed his chief-on-the-warpath game and

promptly woke the twins. Wails came from the children's bedroom, shared with their older brother, and Skye rushed to fetch them, one in each arm.

Gideon and Rebecca were golden, blue-eyed babies, good-natured and intelligent. Being just up from their naps, however, they were both wet and fitful.

Skye snatched up two clean diapers and carried her niece and nephew outside, where she laid them down in the soft, sweet grass growing by the creek, beneath her favorite aspen tree, and changed them. They were more comfortable after that, and thus more cheerful, and they sat crowing and gurgling in the shade while their young aunt washed her hands at the stream.

She was sitting cross-legged on the ground, tickling their noses with blades of grass and delighting in their amusement, when Megan came splashing across the creek, riding her small brown-and-white pinto mare, Speckles. A slender, vibrantly energetic redhead, Megan was Skye's confidant, and the two of them, the children of feuding brothers, had all but grown up together back in Virginia on their grandparents' prosperous farm. Unlike Bridget and Christy, who got along most of the time but rarely sought out each other's company—and that alone was an improvement, considering the way they'd scrapped as children—Megan and Skye were best friends as well as cousins. The two of them often panned for gold together, and Megan had used her share of the proceeds to buy Speckles.

Letting the mare's reins dangle, Megan plopped down in the grass and hoisted Gideon onto her lap.

"I had to get away," she confided in a dramatic whisper, as though her elder sister might hear her from way over there, on the other side of the water, up the hill and inside the house Trace and Zachary and their friends had made of an old Indian lodge with a room added on just for Megan. "Christy's in a pet." Megan brushed a wisp of copper-penny hair back from her forehead, and her green eyes sparkled with mingled love and irritation. "I declare, ever since she lost her waist, she's been impossible. We'll all be glad when that baby comes." Christy and Zachary's first child was due soon, any day, in fact, and while Skye knew they were both thrilled, it was also true that pregnancy didn't seem to do a lot for Christy's disposition. Zachary was the only one who could really manage her, and he'd been away a lot lately, with a posse, trying to track down whoever was robbing the freight wagons and stagecoaches between Virginia City and Primrose Creek.

"Bridget was like that," Skye confided. "Cranky, I mean. Last time she was expecting. It'll pass."

Megan sighed heavily. "I suppose," she said, and then lay back on the cushiony ground and held Gideon up with both hands, causing him to chortle with slobbery good cheer. "She still insists that I go to normal school and earn my teaching certificate so I can always have 'security.'" Rebecca, wanting to share in her brother's adventures, tugged at Megan's sleeve until she got a turn, too. "Why can't Christy understand that things are different now that we're finally safe, the four of us?" She paused and sighed in a typically theatrical manner. "I've grown up and changed my mind about a lot of things. I want to be a stage actress—that's so much more exciting, don't you think, than teaching school?"

They often commiserated, Skye and Megan, being great friends; sometimes Bridget was the object of their frustration, but more often it was Christy. Skye felt especially charitable toward her elder cousin that day, though in truth it worried her a little, for she seemed to know Megan less and less these days. The rest of the family thought her fascination with the stage would pass, but Skye feared it wouldn't.

"She wants you to have a good life, that's all. What's so terrible about going to normal school, anyway? If you get tired of performing, you'll have that to fall back on."

Megan sat up, sprigs of grass caught in her gleaming hair, and held Rebecca on her lap, while Skye held Gideon. Noah, meanwhile, climbed deftly into the lower limbs of a nearby tree. "I don't want to learn another thing," she said in a familiar tone of determination. "At least, not about reading and writing and arithmetic. I want to travel all over the world, acting in plays, wearing splendid, sweeping gowns of velvet and silk, with hoods and tassels, and then come back to Primrose Creek, build a grand house on my share of the land, and live out the rest of my days in glorious notoriety." She lowered her voice. "'*She* was once an actress,' people will say. I might even write my memoirs."

"Don't you want a husband?" Skye asked, though the question was rhetorical because she knew the answer. Skye had business interests of her own to pursue, of course, but she craved a home and a family too and found it hard to comprehend that Megan had decided upon an entirely different path, especially since the two of them had wanted the same things for most of their lives. Skye got a lonely feeling just thinking of the changes in her closest friend.

"Perhaps," Megan relented, though grudgingly, "but

not for a long, long time. He'd have to be older, with a great deal of money. An admirer, maybe, from my days on the stage."

Skye smiled. Megan was fond of Caleb Strand, a good-looking, dark-haired young man, employed as a sawyer with Jake Vigil's timber company, but he was only one of several suitors, and Megan treated all of them with affectionate disinterest. "What about your property? Surely you don't want to leave it." The McQuarrys were Irish at their roots, and love of the land was a part of them, body and spirit, like the penchant for horses and the willingness to put up a fight when one was called for.

Megan flushed slightly and brushed Rebecca's downy blond curls with her chin. "It'll be here when I get back, I reckon," she said. Her spring-green eyes, inherited from their beautiful grandmother, turned somber. "What about you, Skye? You'd like to marry, I know you would. And you could have a husband like that"—she snapped her fingers for emphasis—"if you weren't mooning over Jake Vigil all the time."

That morning's encounter with Mr. Vigil had all but convinced Skye that what she'd thought was love for him had probably been a mere infatuation. Still, trying not to think about him was like trying not to breathe, not to let her heart beat. Knowing she'd idealized him, in the privacy of her thoughts since that night he'd rescued her at the dance, from a mere and fallible man into some kind of noble personage didn't lessen the strength of her emotions at all. "I'm not doing any such thing," she protested.

Megan merely smiled.

"I'm not," Skye insisted. But she was—wasn't she?

Great Zeus and Jupiter, she wasn't sure of much of anything anymore.

"Oh, for pity's sake," Megan said. "Why don't you just rope him in and hog-tie him and be done with it? He's surely over his feelings for Christy by now. After all, it's been more than a year."

To Megan, and usually to Skye, too, a year was just shy of forever. That was one of the reasons Megan resisted going away to normal school and Skye wanted to start *living* like a grown woman. After all, she was eighteen. Lots of women had several children by that age.

Skye sighed. "That's just the trouble. I'm not so sure he *is* over her. The way he talks, *McQuarry* is another word for *obstinate.*"

Megan shrugged. In the town of Primrose Creek, the male population far outnumbered the female, and a pretty young woman could have her pick of husbands. Megan had often pointed out that fact to Skye, forever trying to play the matchmaker. "I don't suppose you noticed," she said, "but Mr. Kincaid was quite taken with you." Megan had introduced her to the shy lumberjack, a newcomer to Primrose Creek, after church the Sunday before. "You could do worse, you know. He's thirty, and his teeth are excellent. You did notice his teeth?"

Skye giggled. "You make him sound like a horse up for auction. How are his feet? Maybe I should get him by the shin and lift one up, just to make sure he's really sturdy."

"Good teeth are not to be sneezed at," Megan said.

"I should hope not," Skye agreed.

Megan laughed and pretended to strike her a blow to

the shoulder. This started a rough-and-tumble free-for-all, and soon all of them, babies, Noah, Megan, and Skye, were engaged in a lively mock wrestling match.

"Lord-a-mercy," boomed a familiar female voice, and everyone stopped to look up at Caney Blue. "What is all this carryin' on about?" the tall woman demanded, her dark eyes flashing with good humor. Caney had worked for the McQuarry family as a free woman, back in Virginia, along with her late husband, Titus. When Christy and Megan traveled west to claim their shares of the inheritance, Caney accompanied them. She'd been with them ever since, although she had plans to marry one Mr. Malcolm Hicks one day soon. Although obviously fond of her, Mr. Hicks had proven himself to be a hard man to wrestle down.

"Is Christy still in a snit?" Megan asked, getting to her feet. She was holding Rebecca with an easy grace that said she would be a good mother one day, whether she thought so at present or not. "I'm not going home until she's over it, if she is."

"She's laborin' to push out that baby," Caney said. "I was hopin' Trace would be around, so I could send him out lookin' for the marshal. It ain't gonna be long."

"Trace is in town," Skye said.

"Zounds!" Megan gasped at almost the same time, and her face went so pale that all her freckles seemed to pop out on little springs. "I'll go and fetch him right this moment!" With that, she thrust little Rebecca at Skye, gathered up Speckles' reins, and mounted in a single smooth motion. All of Gideon McQuarry's granddaughters were accomplished horsewomen. He'd seen to that, teaching them all to ride as soon as they could cling to a saddle horn.

Before anyone could even say good-bye, Megan and the mare were splashing across the creek and up the opposite bank, disappearing into the trees.

"Is there anything I can do?" Skye asked quietly of Caney. Instinctively, she'd gathered the twins and Noah close to her skirts, as though there were a storm approaching.

"You just say some prayers," Caney replied, unruffled. "I'll head on back. I reckon she'll be wanting me close by, Miss Christy will."

Skye nodded. Her throat felt thick, and she wanted to weep, though her emotions were rooted in happiness, not sorrow. To her, the birth of a child was the greatest possible miracle; she'd imagined herself bearing Mr. Vigil's babies a thousand times, for all the good pretending did. Well, it was time she got over that foolishness, wasn't it, and moved on.

"You'll send word if you need something?"

Caney was already headed back across the rustic footbridge Trace had constructed by binding several logs together to span the creek. "You'll hear me holler out if I do," she said.

Jake Vigil stood in his great, elaborate, empty house, gazing out the window at the naked flower gardens and trying to work out what had gone wrong between himself and Skye McQuarry. He was shy, it was true, but he was normally a persuasive man, able to make others see reason, even if they tended toward the hot-headed side, the way she did.

The faintest, most grudging of smiles curved his mouth as he remembered Skye standing there before him, arms akimbo, guarding her patch of ground. She was young, but she was pretty, and she was nubile. He remembered clearly how beautiful, how downright womanly, she'd been that night last fall at the dance, and because of that, he was able to see past her shapeless clothes and sloppy hat. Getting by her willful nature would take a little more doing.

They were at an impasse, he and the lovely Miss McQuarry. Sooner or later, someone would have to give in, and it damned well wasn't going to be him. One way or the other, he'd get what he wanted—with just one notable exception, he always had.

If he couldn't persuade Skye to sell him the timber rights he needed, he was bound to lose everything. He thrust a hand through his hair. It wouldn't be the first time he'd started over; at thirty-four years of age, Jake had taken his share of hard knocks and then some, and he knew he could survive just about anything. That didn't mean he relished the idea.

After some time had passed, he turned from the window and sank into the richly upholstered leather chair behind his broad mahogany desk. He tilted his head back and closed his eyes, thinking about Christy McQuarry—now Mrs. Zachary Shaw. The image of her had kept him awake nights for the better part of three months, and he'd consumed a river of whiskey in a vain effort to put her out of his mind. Now, all of a sudden, he couldn't quite recall what she looked like. His thoughts kept straying back to Skye, with her chestnut hair and flashing, intelligent brown eyes. She was infuriating; that was why he couldn't get her out of his mind, he decided. She reminded him a little of Amanda.

Amanda. Now, there was a lady he would just as soon never think of again. The last time he'd seen her, she'd shot him in the shoulder with a derringer and left him to bleed to death. Though she'd taken the opportunity to clean out his cash box before leaving, of course.

He smiled again. He sure did know how to pick his women. First Amanda, trouble on two very shapely legs but good at pretense, and after her, Christy, who'd lured him to the altar and then abandoned him there to take up with Zachary Shaw. His smile faded. He'd made up his mind on that rainy, dismal occasion of his thwarted marriage that he'd guard his heart from then on and content himself with the attentions of the sporting ladies, over at the Golden Garter and Diamond Lil's, and he meant to abide by the decision.

Whether he wanted to or not.

Chapter

2

"You could marry her," Malcolm Hicks said, sounding just as calm as if he'd suggested a sensible course of action. "Miss Skye, I mean."

Jake leaned against the framework of his office door, one arm braced at shoulder level, one thumb pressed against his chin. It was a stance he often assumed when he was flummoxed—which was more and more often, it seemed. His gaze sliced to Hicks, who was behind the desk, going over a ledger book. "I'd sooner court a prickly cactus than that woman. Besides, she probably wouldn't have me."

Malcolm wiped his pen thoughtfully and then laid it down on the blotter. A black man, born a slave on some steamy plantation in Georgia, he'd managed to get himself educated by hook and by crook, and because Caney Blue had come along and set about courting him first thing, he considered himself an expert on matters of the heart. "You're not only a damn fool," he said eas-

323

ily, "you're blind, too. That girl thinks you pull the moon behind you on a string. Everybody knows it but you."

A fist clenched around Jake's stomach, eased off again. He wanted to believe Malcolm, and, at one and the same time, he *didn't* want to. "She's a McQuarry," he said, as though that put the whole matter to rest. For him it did, to a large degree, though he could already tell that Malcolm wasn't going to accommodate him by agreeing.

Malcolm smiled and took up his pen again, pretending to ruminate. "That she surely is. They're thoroughbreds, them McQuarry women, and that's a fact. Miss Skye's strong and proud—she marries a weak man, she's going to be downright miserable to the end of her days, and so is he. Now, on the other hand, if she were to marry a fine, substantial feller such as you—"

"Forget it," Jake snapped. He was fresh out of patience, having used up a fair amount earlier in the day in the skirmish with that little troublemaker. He thrust himself away from the door frame. Away from the thought of being married to Skye McQuarry, with her lively intelligence, her fierce determination, her womanly body, and all the enticing mysteries of her spirit. He pointed to the open ledger. "You just keep your mind on the books. And while you're at it, find me a way to meet those notes of mine without supplying ten thousand railroad ties first."

Malcolm's smile went dark, a shadow falling across cold ground. "Ain't no way to do that," he said.

Jake sighed and left the room. He'd go back to the mill and work until his muscles hurt enough to take his thoughts off this new, strange soreness in the region of his heart, or better yet, maybe he'd take another crack at finding that bay stallion.

Skye lay on her belly in the high grass blanketing the ridge, watching as the magnificent stallion stood, head high, mane dancing against his sleek neck. He was long-legged and solid through the chest, built to outrun the wind. She smiled, but a little sadly. It was almost a travesty to capture such a splendid animal and break him to ride. Provided, of course, that he *could* be caught. Sometimes, watching him, Skye thought he wasn't real at all but an illusion, the mirage of a dream.

He raised his head and turned toward her, probably catching her scent on the breeze. For a long moment, they simply gazed at each other. Then, offering a loud whinny, as if in friendly challenge, he turned and loped away, disappearing into a tree-lined draw like a spirit.

Skye lingered there, in the spot where she'd crushed the grass, for a long while after he'd gone. It was something of a shock when she came to herself and realized that she'd stopped thinking about the stallion at some point, and Jake Vigil had sneaked into her mind instead.

She rolled over onto her back and gazed up at a blue and cloudless sky. She oughtn't to tarry. Christy had given birth to a baby boy the night before, and her husband, Zachary, still hadn't returned. Skye had promised to spell Caney and Megan for a while and sit with Christy and the new baby.

It would be hours until nightfall, but the moon was visible, transparent as cheesecloth, and she wondered if there would be any use in wishing on it. She'd already tried talking to stars, all to no avail. Jake might want the timber growing on her land, but beyond that, he'd probably never given her a thought.

She sighed, plucked a blade of grass, and clasped it lightly between her teeth. She supposed she could trade the timber for a wedding ring and hope Jake would come to love her in time, as such men, in such marriages, often came to love their wives, and vice versa, but the mere idea chafed her pride raw. It would be bad enough if he accepted such a proposal; if he were to turn her down, she'd be too mortified to set foot in the town of Primrose Creek ever again.

The sound of a wagon, echoing from below, distracted her from her musings; she sat up and turned in the opposite direction, squinting to make out the team of mules and the rig, lumbering along the narrow trail. A load of freight, probably bound for the general store or Mr. Vigil's lumber mill. He was forever sending to San Francisco or Denver or even Chicago for some fancy piece of equipment.

Skye blinked. She could make out Mr. Harriman's bulky shape, there in the wagon box, the reins clasped in his meaty hands. Beside him, a little boy sat clutching the hard board seat, white-knuckled, his brown hair gleaming in the sun. Even from far away, she could tell that the child was skinny and pale, and an ache of sympathy burrowed deep into an inner wall of her heart.

Poor little fellow. He seemed scared to death.

Frowning, Skye got to her feet, shook out her hopelessly rumpled homespun skirts, and headed for her cousin's house, which stood on a rise almost directly across the creek from Bridget and Trace's place. The Shaws' home, sporting a new roof and glass windows, not to mention wood floors and four separate and spacious rooms, in an area where rustic log cabins were the rule, was widely admired.

When she arrived, the front door was ajar, and although Caney wasn't visible, Skye could hear her inside, singing an old spiritual in that rich, melodic voice of hers. If Caney didn't marry Malcolm Hicks—which she fully intended to do—she might have made her living performing on a stage, as Megan wanted to do.

Skye tapped at the door frame and stepped inside. Caney was standing at the cookstove, with its gleaming chrome trim, stirring something savory in a pot. She smiled in greeting.

"Well, now, Miss Skye, you are a welcome sight."

Skye glanced uneasily toward the entrance to Christy and Zachary's room. "How is she?"

Caney sighed. "Pinin' something fierce, that girl, sure that Mr. Zachary won't be coming back to her, ever. Won't even name that baby boy."

"Where's Megan?" Skye asked. She was always half afraid, these days, of hearing that her cousin had taken to the road, in search of fame and adventure on the boards.

Caney flung her hands out wide and let them slap against her sides. "Heaven only knows. That girl's gonna get herself a reputation if she don't stop traipsin' to and fro the way she does. Always dreamin' and carryin' on like she's somebody out of one of them Shakespeare plays. Ophelia, she calls herself, or Lady Macbeth. I declare that chile gets too much sun."

Skye smiled. Megan did love to play a part, even if she was the only one in the show.

"Caney?" came a voice from the main bedroom. "Is that Zachary out there?"

Skye and Caney exchanged glances.

"No, miss," Caney called back. "It's your cousin Skye, come to sit with you awhile and admire that sweet boy-child of yours."

"Oh," Christy responded, plainly disappointed. Then, with an effort at cheer, she added, "Come in. Perhaps Caney wouldn't mind brewing us some tea before she goes to town."

Caney gestured for Skye to enter her cousin's room and then reached for the tea kettle.

Christy was propped up in bed, her dark hair spilling in ribbons and tangles of silk over the pillows at her back and down over her shoulders and breasts. Always fair-skinned, Christy was alarmingly pale now, and there was a look in her gray eyes that made Skye want to ride out and find Zachary Shaw herself, then skin him alive for being gone at a time like this in the first place. The new baby, an impossibly tiny bundle, lay in the curve of her arm, swaddled in a bright yellow blanket that Bridget had knitted during the winter.

"Let me see," Skye pleaded good-naturedly, stepping close to the bed.

Proudly, Christy turned back a fold of the blanket to reveal a dark-haired infant, contentedly sleeping. "Isn't he wonderful?" she whispered.

Skye drew up a chair and sat down. Her nod was a sincere one. "He's very fine indeed," she agreed. "Has he a name?" She knew he hadn't, but she hoped that raising the subject might turn Christy's thoughts in a more constructive direction.

Christy's face clouded, and, very gently, she covered the baby's head again. "We always argued about that, Zachary and I," she said, and gazed wistfully toward the window, as though she saw an angel hovering there, waiting to lead her home to heaven. "We'd settled on Elizabeth for a girl. If we had a son instead, I wanted to call him Zachary, of course. But my husband insists a boy ought to have a name all to himself, and not one he has to share with his father—"

"Christy," Skye interrupted, reaching out to squeeze her cousin's slender hand. It felt cool, even chilled. "Zachary's all right, you know. If anything had happened to him, someone would have come to tell us."

Christy sniffled. "I'm behaving like a hysterical fool, aren't I?"

Skye smiled. "No. You've had a baby, and you want your husband at your side; there's nothing wrong with that. But you'll make yourself sick if you worry too much."

"I can't seem to collect myself," Christy fretted. Then her deep gray eyes searched Skye's face. "We lost so many loved ones, didn't we? You and Bridget and Megan and me. Sometimes it seemed that the dying would never stop—" She paused, blinked back tears of panic. "You don't think fate would be so unkind—?"

Skye shook her head. "No. I'm sure Zachary will be back any time now. Then the two of you can add a brand-new name to the family Bible. Would you like me to bring it over?" The ancient, much-prized volume was in Bridget's keeping, but it belonged to the four of them, and Skye knew that every birth and marriage was faithfully inscribed, all the way back to the first owner, a young Irish immigrant named Robert Mc-Quarry, who had fought in the Revolutionary War and subsequently received a land grant from General George Washington himself. So, too, were deaths, of course, although fortunately there had been none of those since the four surviving McQuarrys had reached Primrose Creek.

Christy's expression changed slightly at the mention of the McQuarry Bible. She averted her eyes for a moment, then met Skye's gaze squarely. "Yes," she said. "Yes, do bring the Bible, please." She sighed, relaxed a little, then became fretful again, though less so. "I should be up out of this bed. I don't care what the doctors say—it can't be good to lie about like an invalid."

Skye suspected it was Christy's worry that was keeping her abed rather than any medical necessity. That indeed it would be the best thing for her cousin to get up, dress, and get some fresh air and sunshine. "I could fetch Bridget if you like," she said, all innocence. "You know, to look after you—"

Christy's color rose encouragingly, and a certain fire snapped in her gray eyes. "Don't you dare," she said with quiet ferocity. "I have enough to contend with, without her lecturing me." The cousins, while no longer the sworn enemies they'd once been, still tended to bristle a bit at any suggestion of one needing the other's help. Lately, though, it almost seemed as though they were in collusion about something, keeping an uneasy secret.

"Here, then," Skye said, hiding a smile as she stood and extended her arms. "Let me hold that second cousin of mine while you get up. Just don't move too quickly."

Christy surrendered the infant, somewhat reluctantly, but when Skye left the room with the baby in her arms, she could hear the other woman walking around in the bedroom.

"How did you do that?" Caney asked, seeming a little miffed that someone else had succeeded where she'd failed. "I've been tryin' to roust that girl all morning."

Skye smiled and sat down in a rocking chair facing the fireplace. Caney had a tray in her hands; she'd been about to serve tea in the bedroom. Now, she set it down on a sturdy little table within Skye's reach. "I threatened to go and get Bridget," she whispered in reply.

Caney laughed, low and soft. "I always maintained you was a clever girl," she said. "Panning for gold, mind you. Savin' up your money. Makin' your plans, bold as a man. I surely never seen the likes of this family."

The baby was a warm, sweet-scented parcel, and Skye felt a pang, turning back the blanket and gazing down into that tiny face. For a moment, for just the merest, most fleeting moment, she allowed herself to pretend that she and Jake were married, and the child was her own. Jacob, she'd have him christened, but they'd call him by his middle name, so as not to confuse him with his father . . .

"What thoughts are goin' through that mind of yours just now?" Caney asked with her particular brand of rough tenderness. She was reaching back to untie the laces of her apron, bent on going to town to meet with Mr. Hicks, no doubt. "You got a look in your eye that reminds me of your old granddaddy."

Skye must have blushed a little; her face felt warm. She watched as Caney poured her tea, something she wouldn't ordinarily have done, except that Skye's hands were full. "I guess I was just making a wish," she said in a small voice.

Caney patted her on top of the head, just as she used to do when Skye was little, getting underfoot in the kitchen or the laundry room on the family farm back home. "You'll have your day, child," she said. "You'll have your day. And right soon, I reckon."

It was then that Christy came out of the bedroom, clad in a faded-rose morning gown. Her gleaming dark hair trailed down her back, but she had brushed the tresses to a high shine, and there was a spark of spirit in her eyes.

"Well, look at you!" Caney crowed, pleased to see her charge up and about.

Christy whisked into the room, took the chair next to Skye's, and jutted out her chin. "It's not as if I were Lazarus coming from the grave," she pointed out.

Caney took the sleeping baby carefully from Skye's arms and laid him in the nearby cradle, a sturdy pinewood piece that Trace had made as a gift, to go along with Bridget's blanket. "I'll just be gettin' myself into town," Caney said. "I done made up a basket lunch for me and Mr. Hicks to share."

Christy rolled her beautiful storm-cloud eyes, but a smile played at the corners of her mouth. "Miz Caney Blue, you are without shame. Why don't you just propose to the man and get it over with?"

Caney and Skye both laughed. Christy was beginning to sound like her old self.

" 'Cause I don't figure on scarin' him off," Caney answered a moment later. "You got to be careful, wooin' a man. Feed him and the like. Get him gentled down a bit, so he's fit to keep in the house."

Christy and Skye looked at each other, smiling.

"Good luck to you, then," Christy told their friend cheerfully. "I've been trying to 'gentle down' my Zachary since I met him. It's hopeless—he's as wild as ever." From the glow in her eyes, she didn't mind too much.

Caney gave Skye a pointed look. "Maybe I wasn't talkin' to you, Miss Christy," she said. "Maybe I was tryin' to plant an idea somewheres else." She waggled a finger for emphasis. "You want a man, you don't get him by chasin' him off your land and tryin' to hide your real feelin's, even from yourself. Men are skittish creatures, and a woman's got to handle 'em just so."

Skye averted her eyes. Were her feelings for Jake as painfully obvious as that?

Christy stepped in, bless her, before Skye was forced to answer. "You'll stop by the marshal's office, won't you? See if there's been any word from Zachary?"

Caney nodded. "I'll do that first thing," she said, and then she fetched her bonnet and cloak and left the house to start the long walk to town.

"Her heart's in the right place," Christy said, and patted Skye's hand reassuringly before pouring a cup of tea for herself.

"Does *everybody* know?" Skye burst out, chagrined.

Christy arched one dark, perfect eyebrow and raised the china cup to her lips. There was an unsettling twinkle in her eyes. "That you're smitten with Jake? Oh, yes, I suppose they do. Primrose Creek isn't exactly a den of secrets, is it?"

Skye's eyes went wide, and she knew she was blushing. "But how could—I wasn't even sure myself—"

Christy smiled. "Nevertheless, word's gotten out." An expression of sadness moved in her eyes. "Poor Jake. I had no business using him the way I did—"

"You never loved him at all?"

Christy shook her head. "No. I thought I could learn to, though. Thought that would be the best thing for Megan and for me, if I married Jake Vigil. Trouble is, I didn't consider what my plans might do to him." She looked away, looked back. "He's a good man, Skye. If you truly care for him, the way I care for Zachary and Bridget cares for Trace, then go after him. Personally, I think you and Jake would make a wonderful couple."

"Great Zeus," Skye murmured, for this was more than Christy had ever said about her brief engagement to Jake, at least to her. She set her own cup aside.

Christy was quiet for a long moment, rocking, sipping tea, gazing off into the ether. Then she looked at Skye again, and her expression was solemn. "You won't forget? To bring the Bible over, I mean?"

Skye was caught off-guard by something in her cousin's tone, even though she'd been the one to suggest that Christy and Zachary make an entry to record the birth of their first child. "Sure," she said.

Christy turned thoughtful again. "Thank you," she replied in a distracted tone of voice. Finally, she returned from her wanderings. "You haven't read the inscriptions lately, have you?" she asked. Their granddaddy had always called the list of births the McQuarry Begats, and the deaths and marriages had their monikers, too.

It was an odd question, even coming from Christy. She frowned. She hadn't seen the records since Bridget had penned in Granddaddy's name as one of the departed, and that time her vision had been clouded by tears. "No. Christy, why?"

Like quicksilver, Christy changed the subject. "Has Jake declared himself?"

"Declared himself?" Skye scoffed, oddly relieved. Whatever Christy was alluding to concerning the entries in the family Bible, she wasn't sure she wanted to know it. "He thinks all the McQuarry women are trouble, plain and simple."

"You're trouble, all right, the whole bunch of you," put in a male voice from the direction of the doorway, "but I wouldn't call any of you plain, or simple, either."

"Zachary!" Christy cried in delight, standing so rapidly that she swayed and had to grasp the back of her chair for support.

Skye rose and steadied her by taking her elbow, watching as Zachary crossed the room toward his wife. He looked rumpled and unshaven, and devilishly handsome into the bargain. Drawing Christy up in his arms with a gentleness that made Skye's heart swell, he kissed her smartly. "I hear we have a son," he said, and his voice was gruff with emotion. "Sweetheart, I'm so sorry I wasn't here—"

By that time, Skye was almost to the threshold. She didn't bother to say good-bye, for Zachary and Christy Shaw were aware only of each other and the baby boy conceived of their passion.

Although she was happy for them, glad Zachary was back safe, there was a hollowness in her heart as she made her way down the slope and across the log bridge, headed for home.

Standing in the street, with the steam saws screaming in the mill behind him, Jake assessed the small boy standing before him with mingled amazement and rage. He was seven, he said, and the note pinned to his shabby coat confirmed that he was called Henry. The ordinary sounds of daily life in a bustling frontier town faded to a dull thrumming in Jake's ears as he regarded the child, unable—unwilling—to deny the reflection of his own features in that stubborn stance and small, upturned face. Grubby fists were clenched at the boy's sides, as if he expected to be sent away, and his hazel eyes snapped with obstinate dignity. Judging by the frail and spindly look of the lad, he'd gone a long while between meals more than just once or twice.

"Your mother sent you here?" It was a rhetorical question, really. The note, brief to the point of terseness, was signed in Amanda's hand. She'd been pregnant when she left Denver, and she'd never troubled herself to let Jake know. Now, tired of being "tied down," she was leaving the boy in his father's care.

Henry nodded his head. "Yes, sir. She did."

Jake folded his arms. "Where is she?"

"Last I seen her," Henry answered sturdily, though his voice trembled a little, "she was gettin' on a stage bound for San Francisco. Said there was a man there, goin' to marry her."

Jake closed his eyes. There weren't many women who would abandon their children, even in the worst of circumstances, but Amanda was about as motherly as a rabid she-weasel, and just as warmhearted. Typically, she'd chosen the worst possible time to take to her heels.

"If you don't want me," the boy said stalwartly, "I reckon I can make my own way."

Jake dropped to one knee and laid his hands gently on the small shoulders. "You're my son," he said, and had to clear his throat before he could go on. "Somehow, we'll work this through. In the meantime, you need something to eat and maybe a few hours of shut-eye."

The child looked so desperately relieved not to be turned away that Jake was forced to look to the side and blink a couple of times. Then he stood again. "Come along, then," he said in a hoarse voice. "Let's get you settled."

"That your place? Truly?" Henry asked a few minutes later, when they stood at the gate of Jake's grand and heretofore empty house. At Jake's nod, he gave a long, low whistle of exclamation through the gap between his front teeth.

They made their way to the kitchen, which was at the back of the house, and Henry gaped all the way. "This place is bigger'n anything I seen in Virginia City. Fancier, too. You got paintings of naked ladies?"

"That where you've been living? Virginia City?" Jake asked casually. He'd address the question of naked ladies later. Much later.

"Yup," the boy answered. "Mandy was servin' drinks there, at the Bucket of Blood."

Jake set his jaw. Serving drinks. He'd just bet. And how like Amanda to train her own child to call her by her first name. She'd probably told all her customers that Henry was her little brother and needed the poor kid's collaboration to keep up the pretense. "What about you? What did you do in Virginia City?"

"I went to school, some of the time leastways. Mostly, I just helped out at one of the livery stables. I didn't get a wage, exactly, but I had my meals with ole Squilly Bates, the blacksmith, and sometimes somebody would give me a nickel for groomin' a horse. I got a whole two bits once."

"So," Jake said, reaching the kitchen at last, pushing open the swinging door, "you're a workin' man. Where did you live?" He stepped into the pantry, came out with a wheel of cheese and a loaf of bread.

Henry's eyes widened at the sight of so much food, and he gulped visibly. Jake wasn't so sure, but he thought he'd heard the kid's stomach rumble. "I mostly just slept at the livery. In the hayloft. Mandy didn't really have no place to put me."

"I don't suppose she did," Jake murmured. When he'd met Amanda several years back in Denver, he'd mistaken her for an angel, and he'd fallen in love with her. She'd been raised like an alley cat, as it turned out, though she seemed determined to change, and Jake couldn't rightly fault a person for wanting to rise above a questionable past. After all, it wasn't her fault, her being born to a saloon girl, never knowing her father's name.

One fine day, though, she'd hauled off and shot him in the shoulder with his own derringer, then cleaned out his private safe for good measure. Any sensible person would have thought she couldn't possibly stoop any lower than to try and kill the man she claimed to adore—but she had. Later, he'd learned that she had a husband tucked away somewhere, and she'd had some scuffles with the law, too.

Now, faced with his son, he knew that she'd robbed him of far more than the contents of his wallet and wall safe.

Damn her, she'd given birth to a child, unquestionably *his* child, and never told him the boy existed. He'd have taken the boy gladly, raised him as best he could, if only he'd known. Just then, if he could have gotten his hands on her throat—well, it didn't bear thinking about, what he might have done.

Belatedly, and with no little awkwardness, he pumped water and washed his hands at the iron sink, then set to slicing the bread and cheese. There was no milk, so he filled a glass with water from the pump. "Wash up over there at the sink, and have a chair," he said with a nod toward the table.

Henry obeyed and was soon seated, trying his best not to shove cheese and bread into his mouth with both hands. Jake felt a surge of sorrow for all the boy had done without, followed by a jolt of anger toward Amanda that was as sharp and pure as the thin air on a mountaintop.

He asked himself what in hell he was going to do now and was stuck for an answer. He couldn't let his business fold like a house of cards and walk away, not with a son to take care of. No, for Henry's sake and his own, he had to turn things around. Somehow.

He heard the echo of Malcolm's voice. *You could marry her.*

Marry Skye McQuarry? Not if his only other choice for a bride was a whore from Diamond Lil's. All the same, the idea of taking Skye to wife, and hence to his bed, sent an aching charge through his system to spark friction in every nerve ending he possessed. He imagined her soft skin, unveiled to him, imagined the scent of her hair . . .

Damnation. If he got down on bended knee, she wouldn't have him. And even if she agreed to a wedding, on some reckless impulse, she was sure to drive him insane from the time he said "I do" to the day after his funeral. No doubt, he'd have much the same effect on her.

He sighed.

"Are you sorry I came here?" Henry asked, his second hefty slice of buttered bread poised between his mouth and the tabletop. " 'Cause I can light out any time you say. Or maybe you have chores I could do to earn my keep—"

Jake crossed the room and ruffled the boy's hair with one hand. He was not a sentimental man, but in that moment, he very nearly scooped Henry up into his arms and embraced him. "Listen," he said quietly. "You'll have chores to do—every kid ought to help out—but you don't have to sing for your supper around here, understand? This is your home."

Henry looked bewildered. "It's a good thing I don't have to sing," he said. "I sound 'bout like a frog when I try."

Jake laughed, and he realized it was the first time in many, many months. "You come by that honestly. I can't sing, either." He drew back a chair and sat down across from his son. *His son.* "You been using your mother's last name or mine?"

"I ain't required no last name, up to now," Henry replied. He'd reduced a large serving of yellow cheese to crumbs, and now he was looking at the remainder with an expression of longing. "Just Henry was all anybody needed to say. I knew they was talkin' to me."

Jake gave the boy more cheese. He'd have to lay in milk, and some eggs, too, among other things. Up to now, he'd taken most of his meals over at Diamond Lil's, but that would have to change. "I'd be real honored," he said, "if you'd call yourself Henry Vigil."

Henry blinked. "Really?"

Jake smiled, touched so deeply that it was a moment before he trusted himself to speak. "Really," he said.

*　　*　　*

Dawn had not yet spilled over the eastern mountains when Skye tumbled out of bed, got herself dressed in riding clothes, and headed for the barn, where she first fed all the animals, then saddled Bridget's mare, Sis. Riding astride, with a coil of rope secured to the saddle horn, she turned the little mare toward the high country, where she'd last seen the bay stallion. It was probably too much to hope that she would catch him, especially riding Sis, but she meant to try all the same.

The sun was full up by the time she found the stallion, and then it was his shrill cries of terror that drew her. She found him cornered in a canyon by a pack of wolves, and there she was, without a shotgun or even a derringer to scare the critters off with.

"Git!" she shouted to the wolves, and spurred Sis on with the heels of her boots. Sis was having none of it; she wheeled and tried to bolt in the other direction. Skye promptly brought her around again, keeping a short rein, lest the mare take the bit in her teeth and hightail it for the ranch.

Sis put up an argument and, with unaccustomed spirit, flung out both hind legs in a fairly respectable buck, landing in a spin. Skye sailed through the air and struck the ground with a bruising impact that stole her breath and made her see sparks of silver light. By the time she sat up, blinking the world back into view, and realized what a fix she'd gotten herself into, Sis was halfway home, and the wolves, all five of them, were taking more interest in her than in the stallion.

"Sweet Zeus," she swore, although she'd promised Bridget she'd break the habit of cussing, and she'd really tried, too. After gathering a rock in each hand, she scrabbled to her feet and faced her future, which did not look at all lengthy just then. Granddaddy's hat fell backward off her head, and her hair tumbled free of the few pins that held it. "You go on," she bluffed as the lead male, a scrawny, burr-covered beast with a grubby gray and white pelt, ambled toward her. "Git!"

The stallion had stopped carrying on and was awaiting his chance to make a run for it. The rest of the wolves, noting the leader's interest in this strange two-legged creature, had turned their massive heads, panting, to assess her.

Skye flung one of her precious rocks—they'd be on her before she could bend down to replace it with another—and took a stumbling step backward. "Help," she squeaked in a tiny voice, more because that was all she could think of than out of any expectation of rescue. "Somebody, *help.*"

All the wolves were advancing toward her now, and, behind them, the bay stallion pawed the ground, ready to bolt for the hills but wisely biding his time, lest the pack give chase. With him would go all hope of capture, but Skye figured that didn't matter much anyhow, since she was about to be good and dead. She took another step back, and threw the second and last rock.

The crack of a rifle shot came in the next instant and startled her every bit as much as it did the wolves and the stallion. *That was some rock,* she thought for a portion of a moment, before the animals scattered and headed for the hills. Two more bursts of gunfire pursued them, for good measure. If the fellow firing that rifle was really trying to hit one of them, though, he was a poor shot, for the bullets pinged off the rocks and splintered a patch of bark off a tree, and that was all.

Skye whirled, one hand raised to shade her eyes, and saw Jake Vigil, of all people, mounted on his own impressive stallion. Without so much as a howdy-do, he went after the bay, rope in hand, and lassoed him in one throw.

Skye was livid, forgetting all about the wolf pack. She'd tracked that horse for months, and she wasn't about to let anyone take him from her, now or ever.

"That," she said when she was within shouting distance, "is *my* horse."

Jake was standing on the ground by then, holding his own against the stallion, still straining to break free and run. "I don't see your brand on him anywhere, Miss McQuarry. And by the way, you're welcome."

Skye's face went crimson, she could feel it, and her heart was beating hard enough to stampede right out of her chest. She told herself it was because of the wolves and because of the stallion, but she knew, deep down, that neither had much to do with her present distress. "What are you doing out here?" she demanded. "This is *my* land."

"This is Bridget's land," Jake corrected her calmly, keeping the lead rope taut as the stallion began to settle down a little. "As for what I was doing, that should be obvious. I was tracking this stallion. In point of fact, I've been after him since he was a yearling—I believe I told you that once."

Skye found her leather hat, plunked it on her head, and promptly hurled it to the ground again. Then she stomped on it with one foot, just for good measure, and

Jake Vigil did the worst thing he possibly could have at that particular moment.

He threw back his handsome head and hooted with delight.

"Don't mention it," he said, as if she'd spoken, when at last he'd recovered himself, though there was laughter still lurking in his eyes. "Any time I can save your hide again, you just let me know."

Chapter

3

She'd made a perfect fool of herself, throwing her hat down like that, mashing the crown with one heel, but she didn't care. Damn Jake Vigil, anyhow, and damn whatever he thought of her as well, be it good or ill. She hadn't gone through all this, and nearly *died,* just so he could go merrily off with her horse.

"If you don't give me that animal right now, I'll have you arrested," she warned.

The stallion was frightened; no doubt, his nostrils were still full of the scent of wolf, and now he had a rope around his neck into the bargain. To him, one foe surely seemed as deadly as the other.

Jake worked deftly, gently, and spoke in a quiet voice as he calmed the poor beast. He didn't reply to Skye's challenge, which made her want to squash her hat into the dirt all over again.

"I can do it, too," she said. "My cousin is married to the marshal, you know."

He looked at her with an expression she couldn't read. He might have been seething, he might still have been laughing at her. Either one would be unacceptable. "Yes," he said evenly. "I know."

Skye regretted making such a silly statement and would have called it back if she could; surely, reminding Jake of the man Christy had married instead of him wouldn't help her case any. Besides, Zachary wasn't about to put a man in jail on her say-so, not for catching a wild horse before she did and refusing to hand it over, anyhow. In fact, she knew exactly what he'd say: *Possession is nine-tenths of the law*. Well, she darned well would have possessed that horse if it hadn't been for Jake Vigil's interference.

She bent down, snatched up her hat, and tried to salvage it by pushing at the inside of the crown with one fist. It was all she had left of her granddaddy, that old hat, and she felt almost as though she had desecrated something sacred by losing her temper the way she had.

"You ought to throw that thing away," Jake said in a tone of voice she'd never heard him use before. "The hat, I mean. It's not becoming—hides your hair."

His words gave Skye a sweet wrench; she prayed she wouldn't blush. He liked her hair? And what kind of silly thought was *that,* when the man was out-and-out stealing a stallion she'd had her eye on for weeks?

He ran a hand lightly down the length of the stallion's muzzle, but he was looking at Skye in an assessing way that made her deliciously uncomfortable and mad as a bee-stung grizzly with a toothache. "There is one way to settle our many differences, once and for all," he mused.

"I imagine there are several," Skye retorted. She tried to speak crisply, but her heart was skittering with anticipation and high dudgeon and profound relief that she hadn't tripped over her own tongue. Lord, but her emotions were so tangled, she didn't even hope to sort them out.

"A horse race," he said.

She stared at him. "A horse race?"

He grinned. "Yes. If you can beat me, riding this stallion," he said, indicating the bay, "he's all yours, and so is all the lumber you want for the house."

Skye could barely breathe. She hadn't lost a horse race since she was eight years old, and that time she'd been defeated by her father, one of the best riders in Virginia. "And if I lose?"

"Ah, if you lose," he said, pausing to ponder the prospect. It made him smile. *"If you lose,* Miss McQuarry, you will marry me."

Her mouth dropped open, and she closed it with an effort. Her pulse thrummed in her ears, and the whole universe contracted to a space barely large enough to contain the two of them. She even felt dizzy. The nerve of the man. The very gall. She wanted to kiss him and kick him, both at once.

For some inexplicable reason, though, she didn't do either. He'd ambushed her tongue, and it only then broke free. "You—you want to m-marry me?" she blurted, and immediately longed for death. "Why?"

He drew closer, still holding the lead line with one hand, and drew an index finger down the length of her nose. "Yes," he said. "I believe I do want to marry you, and I don't have the first idea why."

She was utterly confused. What was she doing,

standing here letting him say such forward things? Why didn't she get a gun and shoot him? Why didn't she just say, straight out, that she would have married him anyway, right or wrong, win or lose, if he just asked her?

Because she was a McQuarry, that was why. She had more than the normal allotment of pride, even when that went against her best interests, but knowing this singular truth about herself didn't help overmuch. She was paralyzed, and her tongue felt thick in her mouth.

"Suppose I told you I've been lonely for a long time?" he asked quietly. Seriously. "That I'm tired of living by myself? Suppose I said I wanted a family?"

She folded her arms and waited. It was too good to be true, all of it. There had to be something more—and there was. Her trees. *He wants my timber.* She would have laid into him, if she'd been able to speak.

"Yesterday, a little boy turned up, quite literally on my doorstep," Jake said with a sigh. "Well, at the mill, anyway. Turns out, he's mine. His name is Henry, though I think Hank suits him better."

Skye recalled the boy she'd glimpsed the day before, perched in the box of a freight wagon, and found her voice at last. She had a deep affinity for children, especially little lost boys like Henry. "It 'turns out' he's yours? Didn't you know about him?"

Jake shook his head. "I wish I had. Things might have been different, for him and for me."

"You'd have stayed with his mother?"

"I didn't leave his mother," Jake said. "She left me. After shooting me in the shoulder with my own derringer and robbing me of every dime I had. I never saw her again."

"She sent the boy to you." Skye felt her brow crumple with confusion and concern. She was still bothered about the horse and the timber, but she'd pushed those concerns to the back of her mind for the moment.

Jake nodded. "From Virginia City."

She stared at him, confounded and oddly stung. It shouldn't have troubled her to hear that there had been other women in Jake's life, before Christy—of course there had—but it did. Oh, it did. "You were in love with a woman who shot you? What's *wrong* with you?"

He laughed, though there was a somber shadow in his eyes. "*She* shot *me*. I reckon the question ought to be 'What's wrong with her?' The answer is, 'One hell of a lot.' She's crazy, for one thing, and she's a liar, for another. Of course, she's a thief, too. But she's also beautiful and clever as all get-out, and she had me buffaloed, I guess. Until it was too late, anyhow."

Skye pushed her hair back from her face with a nervous gesture of one palm. "Damnation, I don't care about her."

"Then why did you ask?"

She wanted to fly at him; the trouble was, she didn't know what she'd do when she got there—claw his eyes right out of his head, or fling her arms around his neck and hold on for dear life. In the end, she decided to stay put.

"I didn't ask about her. I asked about you." She paused, drew a deep breath, and let it out again. "You want me to marry you because your son needs a mother."

"Something like that."

"Would I have my own room?"

"No," he said without hesitation. "I told you—I want a family, and that requires a real wife. I'm not interested in playing house."

Skye turned away, hoping she'd been quick enough to hide the color burning in her cheeks. "All this happens if I lose the horse race," she said, to clarify the matter a little. She still felt dazed. Just that morning, she'd gotten out of bed without a hope in Hades of marrying Jake Vigil, and now here he was, proposing to her. She would have been overjoyed, if it weren't for one thing—the union was merely a business arrangement to him; he hadn't mentioned love. He wanted her for the plainest and most practical of reasons, and he hadn't even bothered to pretend otherwise.

"Yes," he agreed, and when she looked again, her attention drawn by the familiar creak of leather, she saw that he'd mounted his horse, keeping the bay on a long lead. It wasn't a good idea to let two stallions get into close proximity; they tended to do battle, especially when the scent of wolf still lingered.

"When?" she asked, nearly choking on the word. "Wh-when would we hold this race, I mean? And where?"

He smiled. "A week from Sunday ought to be soon enough. The road between Primrose Creek and my front gate should do as a course."

It was two miles from one point to the other, by Skye's estimation; not an unmanageable distance, certainly, for a pair of strong horses like these. But a week from Sunday! The bay wasn't even broken to ride yet, and besides, how was she going to train the animal to accept a rider if Jake insisted the stallion belonged to him? He obviously meant to take the bay back to town with him.

Jake made a gesture like tipping his hat, only he

wasn't wearing one. Skye had long since noticed that he rarely did. "Deal?" he asked.

Skye gazed up at him. The sun was at his back, like an aura, putting her in mind of pagan gods—Apollo, perhaps, riding one of his chariot horses. She couldn't make out his features. "There's a lot we haven't settled," she pointed out.

He chuckled. "Now, that's a fact," he agreed. The leather of his saddle creaked again as he bent down, extending one hand and slipping his foot out of the stirrup so she could get a purchase to mount. "Come along, Miss McQuarry. I'll see you home, so the wolves don't get you."

She hesitated, then took his hand, planted her foot in the stirrup, and allowed him to pull her up behind him. Her precarious situation forced her to put both arms around his middle to keep from falling off, and the scents of his shirt and his skin and his hair combined to tug at her from the inside. The bay stallion trotted along behind them, as docile as could be.

"You'll have to leave that stallion here," she said when they'd reached Trace and Bridget's place and she'd gotten down from his horse, "if you expect me to make a saddle horse out of him in time for the race."

Jake looked back at the captured bay, as though assessing him. Then he leaned forward, resting one forearm across the pommel of his saddle. "That's just it, Miss McQuarry. I *don't* expect you to break him. You won't make much of a wife if you get yourself stepped on, thrown, or kicked."

"I've *been* stepped on, thrown, and kicked," she snapped, annoyed at his blithe assumption that she would lose their contest. At the same time, she was confused, because she *wanted* to marry him, which meant she'd have to lose. Didn't it? "I've been around horses all my life, *Mr.* Vigil, and I can't remember a time when I didn't ride."

"Riding is one thing," he pontificated from on high, "and saddle-breaking a wild horse is another. The question is decided."

Skye wanted to throw something. "If you think you can just announce that something is decided and go right on from there, whistling a tune—"

He grinned. "Are you backing out of our deal?"

She thought of all she stood to lose if she won that race and all she stood to gain if she lost. Pride wouldn't let her sacrifice the honor of winning, and love wouldn't let her claim it. She was in a dither, though she'd have gone back and found those wolves and fed herself to them before admitting as much.

"No," she answered at some length. "Are you?"

"Not a chance," he replied. "Hank and I, we need a woman in the house." Then he turned and rode cheerfully away toward town, leading the captured bay behind him.

"What was *that* all about?" a voice inquired, from just behind her.

Skye turned to see Megan standing there, holding one of Bridget and Trace's twins. And all of a sudden, Skye began to cry, to blubber and wail like a fool.

"Whatever is the matter?" Megan demanded, her eyes narrowed.

"I've just bet my whole future on a horse race!" Skye howled.

"Well, is that all?" Megan asked, a little impatiently. "What happens if you lose?"

Skye was stupefied by her cousin's blithe attitude, but she didn't bother to say so. It wouldn't have done any good. "I'll have to marry Jake Vigil."

Megan did not look the least bit sympathetic. "I see," she said, smirking a little. "I guess you're in some trouble, then. No McQuarry *I* ever heard of ever threw a race."

Skye was glum and, at one and the same time, possessed of a strange and secret jubilance. "Not one," she whispered miserably.

Megan's expression was tentative, almost wistful. Later, Skye would think she should have guessed, right then, what her cousin was planning to do. "We'll always be friends, won't we, Skye?" she asked. "Friends as well as cousins, no matter what?"

"Of course we will," Skye said. Her uneasiness deepened measurably and would not be ignored. "Megan, what are you—?"

"Skye!" Bridget interrupted from the doorway of the house. "Megan! Come inside, won't you? I need some help with the carding and spinning."

Skye and Megan looked at each other for a long, silent moment, and it was tacitly agreed that no more was to be said, at least in Bridget's presence.

Jake smiled to himself all the way to town, where he turned the bay stallion over to one of the stable hands at the livery for safekeeping. Leaning against the corral fence, he admired the animal for a while before deciding to head home.

The moment he took a step in that direction, however, he found himself face-to-face with Zachary Shaw. Once they had been good friends, but there had been a strain between them since the marshal had married Christy McQuarry.

Zach adjusted his hat. His stance and the set of his shoulders gave clear indication that he had something to say and meant to say it, no matter how unwelcome the observation might be. "That's a fine animal," he said.

"Thanks," Jake replied without inflection. "No matter what your wife's sister might have told you, I caught that stallion myself, and I mean to put my brand on him, if matters come to that."

The marshal frowned, plainly puzzled. So, Jake thought, Skye hadn't run to her cousin's husband, the marshal, to stake a claim of her own to the bay. She went up another notch in his estimation. "What the hell are you talking about?"

Jake nearly laughed. Nearly but not quite. "Never mind that. If you have business with me, let's hear it. Otherwise, I'll be making my way back to the mill."

Shaw sighed. They were standing on Primrose Creek's only real street, two men known to have their differences. Boggle-eyed passers-by were stretching their ears in the effort to eavesdrop. "Damn it, Jake, listen to me. There are a couple of agents over at Diamond Lil's, making a lot of noise about taking over your whole operation by the end of the month. I thought you might want to know."

Jake tightened his jawline, and the joint made a faint popping sound when he released it by force of will. He glanced in the direction of the saloon, which was only one of several that had sprung up in Primrose Creek over the past few years and subsequently prospered. "Thanks," he said in a virtual growl.

"Is it true, Jake?" Zachary asked quietly. "Are you in trouble?"

There was no reason to tell his erstwhile friend about the deal he'd made with the railroad and all he stood to lose if he didn't keep up his end of the bargain. It was literally everything he could do not to storm down the street to Diamond Lil's and bang a few heads together. At last, he met the other man's gaze squarely. "No need for you to be concerned," he said coolly. "It's nothing I can't handle."

Shaw sighed. "Are you going to hold that grudge of yours until some undertaker pulls off your boots once and for all, or what?"

Jake stiffened; automatically, his right hand clenched into a fist, then relaxed again. "Malcolm tells me you're a father," he said, ignoring the question. "Congratulations." With that, he walked away, moving in the general direction of Diamond Lil's, even though it was against his better judgment.

But Shaw wasn't through with him yet. "Jake."

He stopped, refusing to turn around again, and waited.

"I didn't tell you about those railroad agents so you could head down there and tear the saloon apart. Whoever makes trouble, whether it's them or you, will end up in my jail for the night, if not longer. Clear?"

Jake didn't offer a verbal reply, but his opinion must have been obvious anyway in the sudden stiffening of his spine and the length of his strides. He reached the entrance of the saloon and was just about to push through the swinging doors and step over the threshold when Hank appeared at his side, seemingly out of nowhere.

"Pa?" he asked. The kid was still getting used to having a father—hell, Jake was just getting used to *being* one—and the word came out like a croak.

Jake closed his eyes for a moment. *Not now,* he thought. Then he looked down at his son. "Aren't you supposed to be in school?" he asked. He'd extracted a solemn promise from Hank, early that same morning, that he'd avail himself of Primrose Creek's makeshift schoolhouse.

"I ain't goin' back to that place ever," Hank announced. "There's nobody there but for a pack of runny-nosed kids and that homely teacher."

Jake, mad enough to bite through a railroad spike an instant before, now had trouble holding back a grin. At the edge of his vision, he glimpsed Zachary Shaw, pretending to look at a display of feathered hats and other female fripperies in the milliner's window. Miss Ingmire, the schoolmarm, was only seventeen herself, according to rumor, and she had trouble keeping order in class. As for the runny-nosed kids, well, Jake figured there was probably room for one more; his boy would fit right in.

He stepped aside, one hand resting on Hank's blade-thin little shoulder. "I'm afraid there are some things in this life that we don't have a choice about, and school is one of them. You'll need to read and write and cipher if you're going to run my timber company someday." Provided there still *was* a company once Hank was grown. The way things were going, they'd both end up as drifters and no-accounts.

Unless, of course, he won next Sunday's horse race—as he fully intended to do. Surely, he'd be able to persuade Skye to let him harvest the necessary timber once they were man and wife. He would run double and even triple shifts at the mill and meet the railroad's deadline. His spirits rose, and he grinned. "Suppose I told you that you were about to get yourself a mother. What do you think she'd have to say about a boy who won't go to school?"

Hank's square little chin jutted out a little, and his eyes snapped. "If she's anything like Mandy, I'll be taking to the road again, and it won't matter *what* she thinks. I ain't puttin' up with no ear-washing, neither."

Jake bit the inside of his cheek in order to maintain the sober expression he'd just managed to assume. "She's nothing like Amanda," he assured the boy. "I think you'll like her."

Hank narrowed his eyes. "She'll want me to go to school every day, though. Maybe even church on Sundays."

" 'Fraid so," Jake admitted. "Women place a lot of store by school and churchgoing. I believe the Reverend Taylor likes to cut loose with an extra sermon on Wednesday nights, too."

Hank sighed, and his shoulders slumped significantly, though Jake thought he sensed a certain excitement in the child. No doubt, he'd dreamed of being an ordinary kid many a time, with an ordinary father and mother and a set of rules to follow.

"Let's go on home," Jake said quietly. "You can make another try at school tomorrow."

Hank hesitated, then fell into step beside him.

A voice from behind stopped both of them cold. "Vigil!"

Jake turned. Two strangers stood on the wooden walkway outside Diamond Lil's, and he knew by their waistcoats and derby hats that they were railroad men. His hand came to rest lightly on top of Hank's head. "I don't conduct my business in the streets, gentlemen," he said. "You have something to say to me, you come to my office at the mill in the morning."

The taller of the two men, a thin, pockmarked fellow with overlapping front teeth, worked up a smile. "No offense meant," he said, and touched the brim of his hat in a gesture that conveyed more mockery than respect. "We'll be around to see you first thing."

"I reckon you know what it's about," put in the second agent. He was little and wiry, the kind a man had to look out for in a fight.

Jake didn't reply. He simply turned his back on the two men and started toward home again. Zachary, who evidently had stuck to Jake's heel like a chunk of horse manure, fell into step beside him. After a friendly nod of acknowledgment to the boy, he got right down to business. "It's time we put what happened behind us, Jake. Time like this, a man needs his friends."

Jake glared at him and kept walking. "I'll remember that," he said, "if I run into any."

Shaw looked downright exasperated. "Damn it," he rasped. Then, remembering Hank, he lowered his voice, as if that would keep a sharp-eared kid from hearing. *"Damn it,"* he repeated. "I'm trying to help you here!"

Jake gave a derisive chuckle. "Five minutes ago," he said, "you were threatening to throw me in jail."

"I still might," the marshal said lightly. "Even if there isn't a law against your kind of pig-headed, jack-ass approach to life, there ought to be. Now, I have another question. Two, in fact. Where did you get this kid? And did I hear him call you Pa?"

When a brisk knock sounded at his office door the next morning, an hour after he'd coerced Hank into returning to school and its many trials and crossed the street to the mill, Jake sighed with resignation. Sooner or later, he'd have to speak with the railroad people, anyway. It might as well be sooner.

"Come in," he growled.

He couldn't have been more surprised when Skye McQuarry answered his summons, clad in a yellow dress with ruffles at the cuffs and hemline. Her rich brown hair was pinned up in a loose knot at the back of her head, and her skin and eyes glowed, even as a nervous blush rose in her cheeks.

He stood so hastily that he nearly overturned his chair, and for a long moment, he just stared at her like a smitten boy, too startled to speak. She'd been pretty before, in her rough clothes and that old leather hat with the floppy brim, but she was beautiful now.

Something in his discomfiture must have given her confidence, for she straightened her shoulders and met his gaze straight on. "We need to clarify a few matters," she said. "If I lose this race—which I won't—and have to marry you, will you promise to treat me with respect? I won't put up with anything less. I expect to be a partner to you, and I will not be made to do anything I don't choose to do."

Jake Vigil found his tongue. "Yes," he said. Then he cleared his throat, still profoundly stricken by the sight and scent of her, by his sudden and fierce desire to reach out and pull her into his arms, and said it again. "Yes, Skye. I promise." He paused. "God knows, I have my faults, but I'm not the kind to take advantage of a woman." While the words he spoke were truthful, he had to admit he wasn't following her train of thought that well, stunned as he was by her unexpected appearance.

She looked as though she believed him. Could it be that she actually *wanted* this marriage? No, it couldn't be that.

"Thank you," she said, and turned to go.

"Skye?" He couldn't help himself; her name was out of his mouth like a cat slipping through an open doorway.

She faced him again and raised one eyebrow, waiting for him to speak.

"You'll want to be sure and win that race if you can," he heard himself tell her. "Just now, my prospects as a husband and provider are not exactly impressive."

She smiled again, and again he was thunderstruck. Had Christy's smile ever affected him like that? Had Amanda's? He couldn't remember feeling this way— pleasantly off-balance—in the whole of his life.

"Don't worry," she said. "Mine are excellent."

"Your—?" He was furiously embarrassed and not sure why.

"Prospects," she explained, and let herself out.

He was still standing up, still staring at the empty doorway, when the two railroad agents appeared, hats artfully in hand, manners humble.

"Sit down," he said, and tried to remember why they were there.

"About your contract with the Union Pacific," began the tall one, dragging a chair up in front of Jake's desk while his partner did the same. "There seems to be some concern among the board of directors—"

Jake sank into his own chair and shoved a hand through his hair. "Gentlemen, I gave my word that I will deliver thirty thousand railroad ties within the next few weeks, and I mean to keep it." *How?* he asked himself.

Even if Skye granted him access to her precious trees, he'd have trouble meeting the deadline, which was just a month away.

"How?" asked the second agent, crossing his legs at the knee.

"Is the order overdue?" Jake countered.

The agents reddened, and one of them curled a finger beneath his collar and tugged. "Not exactly."

That was when Jake faced the truth: the railroad was going to win either way. If they couldn't get the railroad ties, they'd have his holdings—the mountain he had fought and worked to own, the house he'd built, the equipment, and the thriving mill. Hell, maybe they'd have the whole damn town by the time they got through.

He sat back in his chair and interlaced his fingers, primarily to keep himself from springing over the desk and throttling the both of them, one gullet in each hand.

"According to our contract," said one agent, uncomfortable in the thunderous silence, "you still have thirty days. But you don't seem to be making much progress, and it would be impossible, in such a short time—"

Jake thought of Skye and of Hank. Not so long ago, he'd almost been discouraged enough to give up, count himself a fool for staking everything he had on this one deal, and move on. Now, it seemed to him, he had every reason to fight, every reason to succeed.

"You'll have your timber if I have to sell my soul to get it," he said. "Now, get out. I have work to do."

Skye went by the livery stable, after she left Jake, to look in on the bay. Sure enough, two of the hands were hard at work, trying to break him to ride, and they weren't having much luck.

She leaned against the fence, unmindful of her good dress, her dainty slippers, her carefully coiffed hair. She was so used to wearing boots, homespun skirts and blouses, and Granddaddy's hat that she forgot to fuss.

The stallion was a magnificent sight, his muscles clearly defined and powerful, his spirit so strong that Skye felt akin to him. Oh, yes, they were going to win the race on Sunday, she and the bay.

Zachary came to stand beside her at the fence, his folded arms resting on the top rail, his grin warm and full of amusement. "Well, now, who's this? Though you bear a strong resemblance to somebody I know, I don't think I recognize you."

Skye laughed. "Was that a compliment or an insult?" she asked.

"Most definitely a compliment," he replied, and his grin broadened. "Isn't this the horse you've been tracking for the last six months?"

She'd tried to keep her plans a secret, confiding only in Megan, but it was obvious that her cousin had told Christy, and Christy had told Zachary. All inclination to smile gone, she bit her lower lip before answering. "That's him," she said. "Jake Vigil got to him before I did."

"Hmmm," Zachary mused. "Almost seems like he knew you wanted that horse and got the drop on you deliberately, doesn't it? I guess he figured the bay would make a strong drawing card."

Skye felt the pit of her stomach slip. "Why should he want a drawing card?" she asked, even though she already knew. God help her, she knew.

Zachary sighed. "I guess he figures he might be able to swap you that horse for the rights to your timber," he said.

All Skye's pretty, fragile dreams collapsed in the space of a moment. She'd been deluding herself, and on purpose, too. Once she was Jake's wife, he could cut down the tallest and best trees and saw them up into railroad ties if he wanted. He'd probably lose interest in her once he'd gotten his way—he might even find an excuse to secure a divorce, though it was more likely he'd simply go right on taking his pleasure with the hurdy-gurdy women, the way other men did.

She had almost made a terrible mistake. She would not be able to endure the outrage, the humiliation of such an arrangement, not even for love.

As for Jake, well, he was *that* sure he would win the race, the arrogant scoundrel.

"Skye?" Zachary looked concerned.

"We'll just see," she sputtered, taking a handful of skirt on either side.

Zachary's worried expression changed to one of bafflement. "See what?" he asked.

But Skye was already spinning away on one heel, bent on going back to Jake Vigil's office, giving him a piece of her mind, and telling him that his devious plan had failed. The bet was off.

He didn't need to know that he had broken her heart.

Zachary reached out and caught hold of her arm, pulling her around to face him again. "Whoa," he said. He and Trace were both protective of her and Megan, as well as their wives. Much as she loved them, she often found them irritating. Did they think she was a child, helpless and without guile? "You look like you're about to shoot somebody."

Tears burned in her eyes; humiliated, she tried to blink them away.

That was enough for Zachary. He tugged her right across the street to his office. Once they were inside, he sat her down in a chair, hung his hat on a peg by the door, and poured two cups of his infamously bad coffee. He set one down in front of her on the surface of his desk and grinned. "Tell me what's the matter," he teased, "or I'll make you drink it."

Skye sniffled. "I want to report a horse theft," she said.

"What?"

"That horse was mine. I tracked it for months. I want Jake Vigil arrested for robbery."

Zachary rounded his desk and sat down heavily in his chair. "Well, now," he said reflectively, putting his feet up to rest on top of a stack of wanted posters. "This situation is getting more interesting all the time."

"You have to do something."

Zachary sighed. "Skye, I can't arrest a man without cause, and you know it. Now, I want you to calm down and promise me you won't do anything stupid."

Skye couldn't make such a promise, and it was a damn good thing she didn't. It would have been impossible to keep.

Chapter

4

The livery stable was dark, and the bay stallion wasn't in the corral.

Skye, clad for skulking in trousers, one of Trace's hats, and a dark coat, dragged a bale of hay over to a window and climbed onto it to peer inside. She had no real experience as a horse thief, since the worst thing she'd ever done was borrow her daddy's favorite gelding without asking. She'd been thrown and gotten a broken arm for her trouble, along with a blistering lecture from her furious grandfather, delivered when she'd had some time to mend and to reflect upon the error of her ways.

As her eyes adjusted to the gloom, she spotted the bay in a nearby stall. Someone had put a feedbag on him, and, in that innocent stance, he looked as if he might have spent the day pulling a buggy or trotting smartly through a big-city park with a well-dressed rider on his back.

She blew out a sigh and reminded herself that she had every right to ride the bay if she wanted; he was really hers, after all. She had been the one to track the critter, and in her heart she had laid claim to him long before Jake Vigil came along and all but grabbed him out from under her. Of course, the law—namely Zachary—definitely would not see the matter the same way.

She'd brought along her own bridle, and she tossed it through the window first, to keep herself from turning coward at the last second. Then she climbed over the sill, one leg at a time, and jumped to the straw-covered floor, hardly making a sound in the process. Although several of the horses snuffled and whinnied, she didn't hear what she had dreaded most: a human voice issuing a challenge to a trespasser. She stood very still for a few moments nonetheless, waiting for her heart to slide down out of her throat and the blood-thunder to subside from her ears. She stooped to pick up the bridle. Then, moving slowly, murmuring nonsensically in what she hoped was a reassuring tone, she approached the bay.

The animal snorted and shifted nervously between the high rails of his stall, and Skye held her breath. Orville Hayes, the old reprobate who lived in a back room and kept watch over the stock at night to earn his keep, was busy swilling spirits at the Golden Garter, as usual. Skye had paused outside the saloon on her way to the livery and dared to look over the swinging doors, just to make sure. Mr. Hayes had been at the bar, all right, bending his elbow and thereby neglecting his duties at the stable.

"Easy," she whispered to the horse. "Take it easy."

Miraculously, the stallion settled down a little.

Skye had no idea whether or not anyone had managed to ride him since his capture the morning before, but it didn't seem likely. It took days, sometimes weeks, to break a horse to the saddle, and occasionally the task proved downright impossible. If she was going to ride the stallion in Sunday's race, he had to be green-broke, at least.

"Easy," she said again. The stall gate squealed a little as she opened it. She stepped inside, one hand resting lightly on the stallion's flank in an effort to keep him from panicking, and moved alongside, trailing her fingertips over his gleaming hide until she was within his range of sight.

She patted the bay's forehead and gave him a lump of sugar from the flat of her palm, careful to keep her fingers out of the way.

When she dared, she slowly raised the far side of the earpiece into place. He sputtered a protest but didn't commence to kicking and carrying on—if he had, she'd probably have been trampled to something with the consistency of cornmeal mush—and Skye was heartened. She eased the leather strap over the other ear and balanced the bit on her open palm.

"You need a name," she said as the stallion took the questionable offering. She slid the metal bar carefully back over his tongue until it rested behind his teeth and finished buckling the bridle into place with swift motions of her hands, so long practiced as to be second nature. "How about Lancelot? Do you like that?"

The bay nickered and pranced a little, but he allowed her to guide him backward, out of the stall. It was too bad horse-thieving was a crime, Skye thought, for she certainly seemed to have the knack.

Outside, in the moonlight and the glow of saloon lamps, Skye stood, reins in hand, and spoke to the horse again in an earnest whisper. "Now, you listen here. I have to win this race on Sunday afternoon, and to do that, I need your help. I'll thank you to cooperate because, if you don't, I'm going to be a disgrace to every McQuarry who ever drew breath." She bit her lip and blinked back tears.

She could spare the timber Jake wanted, as long as it was cut responsibly, Trace and Zachary had convinced her of that, albeit with some difficulty. But now, faced with the reality, the mere thought of a lifetime passed with a husband who didn't love her was intolerable. She'd seen real love up close, between Bridget and Trace and between Christy and Zachary, the kind that flowed both ways. She wanted the same sweet secrets, the same private laughter, the same fierce passion and partnership of souls.

"All right," she said, as much to herself as to the stallion, who was still nameless since he hadn't shown any particular fondness for Lancelot. "We're in this together, you and me, and if we're going to win, we have to trust each other." With that, she closed her eyes, sent a silent but fervent prayer winging to heaven, and sprang onto the bay's back.

He stood still as death for what seemed a long while, every muscle bunched, as if about to fly apart in pieces like a clay pot left too long on the fire. Then he quivered slightly through the belly and flanks and snorted a clear warning. The next few instants would tell it all: he might buck like the devil, or he might let her ride. She knew not which, and she wasn't sure he did, either.

Her throat was dry, and her heart pounded. Gently,

she patted the animal's corded, sweating neck. "Easy," she said, and that, too, was second nature, the word her granddaddy had always used with nervous horses. "Take it real easy. I'm not going to hurt you, and I'd appreciate the same favor in return, if you can see your way clear not to throw me."

The bay was clearly the kind to deliberate, and he must have debated the question from both sides and in considerable depth, for they sat like a war monument, the two of them, for what seemed the best part of a month. While Skye waited, she tried not to imagine herself hurtling through the night air or rolling on the ground in a vain attempt to avoid four hard hooves. When he didn't rear, Skye was pleasantly surprised, and while she was congratulating herself on her way with horses, he bolted. By the time they reached the edge of town, he seemed bent on sprouting wings, like Pegasus, and taking to the air. It didn't occur to Skye to draw back on the reins and slow him down; instead, she tightened her legs around the barrel of his body and crouched low over his neck, brimming with joy.

"He's gone," Orville Hayes whined, twisting his hat in his hands as he stood blinking his rheumy eyes in the dazzling sunlight outside Jake's office. "Mr. Vigil, that fine stallion of yours is just plain *gone*. Somebody stolt him."

Jake resisted an urge to grasp the old man by the lapels and wrench him onto the balls of his feet. *"What?"* he demanded, even though he'd heard Orville's words all too clearly. "Where the devil were *you* when this happened?"

Orville swallowed visibly and crumpled the hat still

further in his nervousness. "I stepped down to the Golden Garter—just long enough to have a single drink, mind you—Lil done cut off my credit a long time ago— and when I got back—"

Jake glanced pointedly in the direction of the sun, which was well above the eastern horizon. "When you got back, you were so drunk that the stables could have burned down around your ears without your knowing," he finished, disgusted but resigned. "When, exactly, did you discover that my horse had been stolen?"

"J-just a little while ago," Orville confessed. "You ain't gonna get me into no dutch with Lil, are you, Mr. Vigil? I lose this job, I don't know what I'm gonna do—"

Jake sighed, resting his hands on his hips, and considered the situation. Orville worked for none other than the illustrious Diamond Lil; besides running a thriving saloon and brothel, the lady owned the stables and several other businesses in town, and she was hardheaded. Turning her loose on poor old Orville wouldn't get the stallion back, and besides, Jake had a pretty good idea who the culprit was, anyhow. If he found Skye McQuarry, chances were good that he'd find the bay, too.

He rubbed his chin. "I don't know," he said in a noncommittal tone of voice. "Fact is, if you worked for me, I'd show you the road."

Orville did not dare to point out that he didn't work for Jake; it would have been worse than stupid, given the circumstances. "I came and tolt you right away, didn't I?" he half whined, his countenance having slipped from fawning to outright pitiful. "I ain't even been over to tell the marshal yet."

"I'll take care of that," Jake said tightly. He didn't plan to speak to Zachary just yet himself. No, it was someone else he wanted to see. He felt a strange, elemental stir deep within him, just anticipating the coming encounter with Skye McQuarry. "You go on about your business, and I'll see to the horse thief."

"You know who done it?" Among Orville's other unredeeming qualities were a nosy nature and a tendency to gossip like an empty-headed spinster.

Jake ignored the question. "Get my horse saddled," he said, speaking of Trojan, the stallion he'd owned for the last several years. Then he turned to head for the mill, where he told his foreman he'd be gone awhile. Hank was over at the schoolhouse, and it looked as if the boy was finally going to stay put, so he could concentrate on catching up with Miss McQuarry. It shouldn't be difficult.

Ten minutes later, he was riding out of town, half amused and half furious. On the one hand, he had to admire Skye's audacity, not to mention her riding skills. On the other, he wanted to yell at her until his voice rang off the mountainsides. Damn fool woman. Didn't she know a wild horse was dangerous—especially a stallion? By now, she might well have gotten herself stomped to death or broken that stiff McQuarry neck of hers.

A rush of cold horror coursed through his system. Maybe she *had* been hurt or killed. Maybe she was already lying on the ground someplace, dead or dying. In pain.

He gave the horse his heels and reached Trace and Bridget's place in a matter of minutes. Bridget met him in the dooryard, shading her eyes from the bright sunlight with one hand. Her smile might have warmed him if he hadn't been so wrought up over Skye and the stallion.

"Jake! What brings you here? I'm afraid Trace is away from home, taking a string of saddle horses down to Fort Grant."

"I'm not looking for Trace," Jake said. He was trying to be polite, but his words came out sounding terse. "Is your sister around?"

She frowned. "I suppose Skye's around here some-where—she'd already left the house when I got up this morning. She's probably upstream panning for gold or traipsing around someplace in those woods of hers." Bridget paused, probably regretting that she'd men-tioned the timber, a known bone of contention between Jake and Skye. "Is—is something wrong?"

Jake managed to smile, though he suspected it looked as forced as it felt, just wobbling there on his face, like a bill held to a brick wall with nothing but spit. "She borrowed something of mine," he said in what he hoped was a jovial tone. "I'd like to get it back."

Bridget sighed. "Well, when you see her, you tell her to get on home, please. I need some help setting out onion starts, and it's wash day, too."

He nodded, thought briefly, and then, on a hunch, started toward the high meadow just below the timber-line, where he'd caught the bay only the morning before. Had it really been just a day since then? He felt as though he'd lived a lifetime in the interim, and he expected to battle his way through ten more before din-nertime.

She was there with the stallion, and when Jake caught sight of her, he drew up on his reins and sat back in the saddle, watching her. He was spellbound, a wan-derer come upon a graceful nymph, unable to speak or move for the awe of it. His breath caught in his throat

and lodged there like a peach pit. He felt a wild mingling of gratitude and fury, terror and pure, primitive
joy.

As he looked on, Skye rode fluidly, proudly, guiding
the stallion in a wide circle through the high, sweet
grass. She'd left the hat at home, evidently, or lost it
someplace, for her dark brown hair flowed behind her in
the breeze, as rich and wild and shining as the bay's
wind-ruffled mane.

When she caught sight of him, she did not even
break stride, though she did rein the stallion in his direction. Her smile was saucy as she faced him, easing the
splendid horse to a stop and leaning down to pat his
neck.

"I thought as much," he ground out. He was so
stricken, all of a sudden, that he couldn't manage anything more.

There was an impish light in her wide brown eyes.
She murmured something unintelligible and fond to the
stallion, and for the first time in his life, Jake Vigil
found himself envying a horse. "He needed to get used
to me," she explained, sitting easy in the saddle while
the bay danced, eager to run again, "and I needed to get
used to him. I'm sure we can win the race, he and I, now
that we're friends."

"How do you know I'm not going to have you jailed
for thieving before Sunday?" he demanded. He'd had
some trouble finding his voice, and when he did, it
came out loud as thunder.

She didn't so much as flinch at the prospect of
spending time behind bars. Of course, she wouldn't.
Zachary Shaw, the marshal, was a member of the family, and even if he *wanted* to arrest her, he'd catch hell at

home if he did. "I don't think you'd do that," she said easily.

"Just remember our terms," Jake snapped. "When I win, you'll marry me. No heel dragging, no questions asked."

Something unreadable flickered in her eyes and was gone. "I remember," she said almost sadly. Then she perked up again. "Since *I* intend to come in first, though, I'm not the least bit worried."

Jake remained firmly convinced of his own proficiency when it came to horses, but here he was, having to *coerce* a woman into becoming his bride, and that didn't set well. In fact, it was downright galling. Even facing financial ruin, he was a better catch than most of the men in town—he was strong and smart, clean and fairly presentable into the bargain, and if all his plans went to hell and he lost everything he had, he knew he could build another fortune, in another place, just by pushing up his sleeves, spitting on his hands, and getting to work. He'd be a good father to his newfound son, and to any subsequent children, and a fine mate as well . . .

Just briefly, tossing in the wake of these thoughts, he considered proposing to Skye McQuarry right then and there, just asking her to forget the race and marry him, but all of a sudden, his collar tightened like a noose, cutting off his air, and the pit of his stomach clenched painfully. Women wanted "I love you's" and promises and all sorts of pretty words, and he was no poet—he'd gone numb inside when he lost Christy. No, it had happened even before that, he realized. Something had withered within him when he saw Amanda for who she truly was, and he'd only kidded himself into believing he loved Christy.

"Mr. Vigil?" Skye prompted, brow slightly furrowed.

He realized that he'd left the conversation hanging at some length. She'd said something cocky with regard to their upcoming contest, and furthermore, she looked disappointed that he hadn't responded in kind. "I was just imagining our wedding night," he said, though he hadn't been. Until then, that is. Now his mind was full of Skye—the scent and softness of her hair, the sound of her voice, urging and then pleading and finally sighing, the limber and luminous contours of her body, bared to him in trusting abandon.

She reddened right up, and her mouth tightened for a moment, and Jake felt jubilation, in addition to the inevitable discomfort such ideas caused.

"Why wait until Sunday?" she demanded, eyes flashing. "Why don't we settle this right now? First one to town wins."

Jake considered the suggestion, and one word thrummed through his spirit, soul, and body, powerful as a tremor in the ground. *Tonight.*

"All right," he said, amazed that the sound came out whole. He fairly choked on that simple phrase, realizing, as he did, how very much hung in the balance. "Count of three?"

She aligned the stallion alongside his with such skill that for the length of a heartbeat, he actually considered that she might reach the edge of Primrose Creek proper before he did. "Count of three," she agreed.

"One," Jake said, bracing himself.

"Two," Skye continued.

"Three!" Jake yelled, and took his stallion from a standstill to a gallop in one short leap.

Skye kept up with him, leaning low over the bay's

neck, and once or twice Jake nearly unseated himself for looking at her instead of the trail ahead. God in heaven, but she was a beautiful sight, as at home on that wild horse as if she were part of him.

They rushed between copses of trees, birch and aspen but mostly pine, slapped and clawed by low-hanging branches, and came across the Qualtroughs' land, splashing through the dazzle-bright creek, neck-and-neck. Out of the corner of one eye, Jake caught a glimpse of Bridget and Megan, Christy's pretty red-headed sister, beaming and clapping their hands together. Plainly, Skye had confided in them about the wager, but there was just no telling whom they were rooting for, Jake thought distractedly. They were an odd bunch, those McQuarrys.

A two-mile stretch lay ahead, once they'd crossed the water; it was rutted and narrow in places, with steep dropoffs and sharp turns, and Jake was torn. On the one hand, he wanted to win, wanted it more than he'd ever wanted anything before, but he was aware of Skye's growing recklessness, too, and he was afraid for her. When it came to horses, the woman apparently didn't have a sensible bone in her body; she rode full-out, hell-bent-for-election, with an absence of fear that astounded him.

The town came into view, and they thundered toward it, the hooves of the two stallions pounding drumlike on the hard, dry ground. Jake waited until the last possible moment, then spurred his mount into a final burst of speed, and Skye did the same. He crossed the agreed-upon finish line a half-length ahead of her and wheeled the stallion around just in time to see the bay miss a step and send his rider soaring over his head before catching himself.

Jake watched in horror as Skye rolled end-over-end in midair, a process that seemed to take an unaccountably long time, given that no more than a few moments could have passed. Long before he'd jumped from the saddle and run toward her, she landed flat on her back, arms outspread, with a wallop that reverberated through Jake's own system.

He knelt beside her, frantic, the stallions forgotten behind him. "Skye!" he called, afraid to touch her and yet barely able to resist the urge to gather her close and hold her against his chest. It wouldn't do to move her if anything were broken, and given the spill she'd taken, that seemed pretty likely. "Are you hurt?"

She blinked up at the blue sky, as though trying to remember where she'd seen it before, and then began to breathe again, slowly and carefully. "I don't—th-think so," she said. "Just let me lie here a second—till I get my wind back." She took a few shaky breaths. "I've got to stop doing this."

He smoothed her hair away from her forehead. There were smudges of dirt on her cheeks, but somehow that only made her prettier. "I'll help you up when you're ready," he said stupidly. He had to say *something,* after all, and nothing else came to mind.

She drew in a deep breath, let it out, drew in another. Jake watched, captivated, as her shapely breasts rose and fell with the motion, then realized what a liberty he'd taken and blushed.

She sighed, though he would have sworn he saw laughter playing hide-and-seek in her eyes, and started to sit up on her own. "I guess you win," she said with a sort of breezy resignation.

Jake sat back on his heels. He'd *won.* Damn if he

hadn't forgotten all about the race for worrying about the prize. "I guess so," he said, bemused.

She was scrambling to her feet, and Jake, profoundly disconcerted, scrambled with her. He wasn't sure he'd been of any help, though, when they stood facing each other there in the dust. Her lower lip trembled, but there was a proud set to her chin.

"You don't have to do this," he heard himself say. Where the hell had *that* come from? Timber and horse be damned—if he couldn't bed this woman, and soon, he was going to calcify.

Her chin rose another notch, and her expression was solemn. She dusted off her trousers without looking away from his face. "A deal," she said, "is a deal."

Jake was at once exultant and scared out of his long-johns. "Right." He ground out the word. "A deal is a deal."

She flushed prettily, and he saw her throat move as she swallowed. "I'd—I'd like to go home first. Talk to my family—wash up a little—put on a dress—"

"I'll speak to Judge Ryan," he said. "Reverend Taylor's gone to Denver to visit his daughter."

She nodded, gathered the bay's reins into one hand, and climbed into the saddle with an ease Jake couldn't help admiring. She had courage aplenty, that was for sure, getting back on a horse right after a nasty tumble. "I imagine my sister and cousins will want to be there. Caney, too, of course."

"Two o'clock?" he said, lightheaded and a little dazed, without even a hard fall from the saddle for an excuse.

"Two o'clock," she confirmed, and he thought he saw just the faintest hint of a smile flash in her eyes before she reined the bay around and started back toward the creek.

"You lost that race on purpose!" Megan accused in a delighted whisper as she fastened the row of small buttons at the back of Skye's best dress, a pale peach organza with lace at the collar and cuffs. She'd sent away for the frock, all the way to Chicago, Illinois, with some of her first earnings from the gold-panning enterprise.

Skye assessed her image in the looking glass affixed to the wall of Bridget and Trace's bedroom, holding a fold of skirt in either hand and whirling slowly, once to one side and once to the other. She was a tomboy, had been all her life, but in that delicate dress, she thought, she looked, well, almost pretty. "You told, Megan McQuarry," she said. "I asked you to hold your tongue, and you told Christy and Bridget about the race."

Megan blushed, though not, Skye figured, from any sense of chagrin.

"Of course she did," said Christy as she and Bridget entered the room. "We're your family. We should know these things."

"Did you really lose on purpose?" Bridget asked, lowering her voice. She might have been speaking of sacrilege.

"I most certainly did not," Skye responded, perhaps a little testily. "Except for once, when Daddy outran me on a Kentucky thoroughbred, I've never been beaten in any contest involving horses."

Megan's beautiful green eyes twinkled. "Maybe Jake Vigil is worth a little sacrifice," she suggested. "He's ever so handsome, after all, and ever so rich."

Indeed, Jake was handsome, but Skye honestly didn't care whether he had two pennies to clink together in his pants pocket. Before, she'd made him into some kind of hero, straight out of an epic and impossible tale, but now she understood that he was a flesh-and-blood man, understandably wary of women, and she loved him all the more for the person he was. Deep down, she knew that he cared for her, that one day, if she bided her time, he would come to love her truly.

Besides, he'd crossed the finish line first, hadn't he?

"You really love him," Megan said, beaming. Christy and Bridget nodded, having come, no doubt, to the same conclusion.

Shyly, Skye nodded again. She felt the heat of nettled pride rise in her cheeks all the same.

"Does he love you in return?"

Skye couldn't lie, not to her family. She and Bridget and their cousins had been brought up together on Granddaddy McQuarry's farm in Virginia. Whatever their differences, they were kin. "I don't think so," she admitted.

Megan's expression changed instantly. "Then you mustn't marry him!"

"I promised," Skye replied. Her tone said she meant it, and the look on Megan's face was one of reluctant understanding.

Bridget spoke briskly, though it seemed to Skye that her blue eyes were a little bright. "Skye knows her own mind, and she always has. If she thinks she ought to marry Jake Vigil, then she's probably right."

Megan nodded. Bridget was happily married herself, as Christy was, and she probably thought Skye and

Jake's union would turn out the same way. In fact, Bridget's lack of protest gave Skye hope, for her elder sister was nobody's fool, and if she'd objected to the idea, she would have said so without hesitation and in no uncertain terms.

Megan squeezed both Skye's hands in her own. "Whatever happens," she said, "I'll be close by. You know I'd do practically anything to help you."

Skye's eyes burned with tears of affection, and she leaned forward to kiss her cousin's flawless cheek. "I know," she affirmed.

Bridget found a moment to be alone with her sister sometime later when they were about to leave for town. She held the McQuarry Bible in both hands. "I should have told you before—before your wedding day—"

Skye recalled Christy's reference to the Begats and frowned. She'd been so busy, so wrought up over the bay stallion and over Jake Vigil, that she'd forgotten. "What is it?"

"I haven't told Megan," Bridget said, by way of an answer.

Skye opened the Bible and let Bridget point out the reference she wanted her to see. Skye's face drained of color as the meaning of the inscription dawned upon her. "We're sisters?" she whispered. "But why didn't you say something?"

Bridget looked stern, then guilty, then resigned. "I guess because it's a scandal, and between our so-called fathers and mothers, this family's had enough of that."

"But why keep news like this from Megan? Christy knows, I know she does."

Bridget looked away, then looked resolutely back.

"Megan is the most impulsive, the most hot-headed of all of us. It's Christy's place to tell her, and she doesn't think Megan is ready."

Skye swallowed hard and looked at the inscription again. Then a sweet, secret peace came over her, and she smiled. "It might be a scandal, but the more I think about it, the less I mind."

Bridget smiled. "Me, too," she said. "Now, let's go and get you married off, little sister."

They took a wagon and a buggy into the town of Primrose Creek, traveling in single file like a gypsy caravan. Skye rode in the buggy with Bridget and Trace, while Caney, Megan, and Christy rattled along in the wagon, Caney at the reins, Megan and Christy in the back, juggling babies and trying to keep an adventurous six-year-old Noah from pitching over the tailgate onto the hard ground.

Judge Ryan was waiting with Jake at the marshal's office, and Zachary was there, too, an amused and mischievous grin dancing in his eyes. Jake's boy, young Hank, sat on the edge of Zachary's desk, legs swinging, expression wary. Jake looked nervous enough to come out of his skin at the first sudden move on anybody's part, and Skye's heart went out to him; she forgot her own natural trepidation, at least briefly, seeing his.

Christy kissed her husband lightly, and he took their baby son, Joseph, into his arms with the ease of a man raised in a big family. Then she walked right up to Jake, looked him straight in the eye, and said, "This is right for you, Jake. I know it is."

His jaw worked as he stared down at the woman he'd loved, no doubt recalling the day just over a year before when he'd been about to marry her and she'd left him at the altar. He didn't speak, but he gave a short, brisk nod in acknowledgment.

Christy stood on tiptoe and planted a brief kiss on his lips, in the same way as and yet quite a different way from before, when she'd kissed Zachary. "Be happy," she said.

"Let's get this shindig rolling," John Ryan, the circuit judge, said gruffly, clasping a Bible in one age-gnarled hand and beckoning both bride and groom with the other. "I've got a hanging to tend to, down in Virginia City."

Skye felt in that moment as though she were mounting the steps of the gallows herself. She considered dashing for the door, ruled the option out, and took her place in front of the judge. Jake stood uneasily beside her, while Hank gamboled over to take up a manful post at his father's right hand, visibly proud of his role in the ceremony. Megan stood up for Skye, just as they'd always planned, and when Megan married, Skye would be her matron of honor.

There, in that crowded little office, amid smiling relatives and fussy babies, with a weeping prisoner looking on from the single jail cell, Jake Vigil and Skye McQuarry were wed. The whole thing was over so fast that Skye felt sure she must have let her mind wander and missed it all. She'd heard herself say "I do," though, heard Jake do the same.

It was done, and, for Skye, there was no going back.

"You go ahead, now, Jake," Judge Ryan boomed with good-natured impatience, "and kiss that pretty bride of yours!"

Jake hesitated, then took Skye's upturned face between amazingly tender hands, lifted, and brought his mouth down upon hers. It was a brief, light kiss, and yet it set Skye's very soul atremble. She realized with a thrill of delicious terror that a number of intimate mysteries would soon be revealed to her. Jake had made it plain that if they married, she would be a real wife to him, sharing his bed as well as his life.

She was still shaken when he released her, and he smiled a sweet, private smile, with only the slightest turning-up at one corner of his mouth, and sent new joy surging through her. Yes, she thought. He would come to love her. She would see to it.

At some point, Jake had slid a ring onto Skye's finger, and for the first time, she took a moment to look at it. A band set with glittering diamonds winked up at her.

"It was my mother's," Jake said, shy again.

"It's beautiful," Skye replied softly. They might have been alone, for the others seemed far away, visible only through a dense mist.

"*You're* beautiful," he told her, and took her hand. "Shall we go home now, Mrs. Vigil, or would you rather stay here awhile with your family?"

He was family now, too, he and Hank, but she didn't trust herself not to break down and weep for foolish joy if she tried to say so aloud, so she merely nodded again.

He chuckled, and his hazel eyes were alight. "Which is it?" he prodded gently.

"Home," she managed to say. "Let's go home. But first—first, let me have a word with Hank."

Jake nodded, and Skye turned and extended a hand to her stepson. After a moment's hesitation, he accepted with his own, and she led him to one side of the room, crouching in her dress to look into his face.

"I've had some experience loving little boys," she said,

"and I think you and I will get along just fine. All I need is a chance to prove myself, Hank. Will you give me that?"

He considered the question solemnly, but she saw hope in his eyes, too, far back and frightened but there. Oh, yes, it was there, all right. "I had one ma go off and leave me. I don't reckon I need another."

"I won't leave you," Skye said, and she meant it. "Not willingly."

He narrowed his eyes. "If I got the grippe in the middle of the night and called for you, would you come?"

She blinked once or twice and swallowed. Her voice, when she spoke, was surprisingly even. "Yes," she said. "You have my word."

"Would you make me eat my vegetables all up, even if it made me sick?"

She smiled. "No," she said. "But you have to at least taste whatever I put on the table. If you don't like it, you don't have to eat it. Deal?"

Hank put out a hand again. "Deal," he said.

Five minutes later, having left the wedding in a hail of congratulations and good wishes, the bride and groom found themselves standing on the doorstep of Jake's magnificent house.

Jake scooped her up in his arms to carry her over the threshold. "The boy's spending the night with Bridget and Trace," he said. His voice, normally a baritone, seemed deeper than ever. "We'll have the place to ourselves for tonight, anyway."

Skye was looking forward to her initiation into true womanhood, for she'd long since guessed, mostly from Bridget's glowing face and tendency to sing in the mornings, and from some of her own feelings as well, that lovemaking was more than the mere duty her mother had believed it to be. Still, not knowing precisely what to expect, she was a little frightened, too.

Jake kicked the front door closed behind them. Somewhere nearby, a clock ticked in loud, measured beats, each one carrying Skye that much closer to her fate. A tangle of contradictory emotions sprang up within her. What in the name of heaven had she gotten herself into? How could she possibly bear to wait until he'd made her his own, once and for all?

He started up the grand staircase, carrying her as easily and as reverently as if she were made of the thinnest and most precious porcelain. At the top, in the hallway, he paused. A set of double doors loomed before them, slightly ajar.

"Are you scared?" He looked as though he were really concerned with her feelings, and perhaps he was. He wasn't cruel or unkind, after all. He simply didn't love her the way most new husbands loved their brides.

"A little," she confessed.

He carried her into the master bedroom, and she caught the tantalizing scents of starched linen and bay rum and of Jake himself. For the second time since they'd met, he kissed her, more deeply this time and more intensely.

The touch of his lips set her soul ablaze.

"Don't be," he said. "There are a lot of things I can't promise you, Skye. But one thing is for certain—I'll never hurt you. Not on purpose."

It was not a declaration of love, but Jake's vow brought fresh tears to Skye's eyes all the same. The contents of her own heart swelled into her throat, and only by dint of sheer desperation did she stop herself from uttering them.

Chapter

5

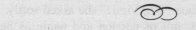

Jake undressed Skye slowly, reverently, like a man uncovering some sacred treasure, fold by fold. She was shy, like any virgin, however spirited, and kept her eyes lowered until he had taken away the last of her clothes. Then she looked up at him through those dark, dense lashes of hers, and he thought he glimpsed a spark of excitement there, even triumph. But he saw a certain sorrow, too. He turned her in a timeless pirouette, as though they were partners in some graceful minuet, and when her shapely back was to him, he saw the bruises.

He knew how she'd gotten them, of course—by sailing over the bay's head that morning, near the end of their race, and landing on the hard, stony ground made harder still by the long spell without rain.

Her right shoulder was the worst, purple and scraped, though her hip and one perfect buttock had sustained some damage, too. Jake was stricken by a sense of almost overwhelming tenderness, as though something infinitely precious had been marred, and he drew in his breath, closed his eyes tightly for a moment. Although he'd known he was attracted to Skye, even that he was fond of her, the depth of his emotions came as a vast and unsettling surprise.

Good God, did he love her? Had he really been stupid enough to fall into that trap for a third time in his life?

When he opened his eyes, she was facing him again, looking up into his face. "Mr. Vigil?" she asked softly.

He nearly smiled, full of passion and panic as he was. "Jake," he corrected. The word came out coarse as rusted iron, but quiet.

"You—you find me—unappealing?" she asked, and that look of personal misery was back in her eyes.

"No," he rasped quickly. "God, no. It's just—I should have realized—"

She frowned, still confused.

"That you were hurt. When you were thrown this morning."

Her smile was sudden and dazzling. "Oh," she said. "That. Well—er, Jake—that wasn't the first spill I've taken from a horse, and I'm pretty sure it won't be the last."

She did not seem to realize how delicate she looked to him. He felt big as a grizzly bear, awkward and inept, faced with this lovely, trusting, porcelain creature, and all the tumbles he'd taken with various local prostitutes meant nothing, in terms of experience, faced with the prospect of bedding an innocent young bride.

Cautiously, he lifted his right arm and ran the backs of his fingers down the length of her arm, shoulder to wrist, barely touching her yet eliciting a shiver. He was instantly alarmed, seized with an urge to swaddle her in quilts, like an invalid.

"Are you cold?"

She smiled a mysterious woman-smile and shook her head.

"You seem so small," he confessed.

She held his gaze intrepidly. "Well," she said, "I'm not. In fact, I'm tall for a woman. Everyone's always said so."

He thought of the bruises again. "I wouldn't want to—to hurt you."

Her eyes softened. They were like velvet as it was, those eyes, brown and rich, drawing him in, laying permanent claim to his soul. "I don't know much of anything about this," she said, and blushed a little, "except what I've seen animals do."

Maybe it was nerves that made him grin. "It's a little different with people," he said. He felt the grin fade from his face, replaced by consternation. "I reckon it might hurt, just a little, this first time."

She nodded. "Bridget told me that," she said.

"Ahh," Jake replied. Somehow, without his knowing, his hands had come to rest on the smooth, nearly imperceptible slope of her shoulders, and the pads of his thumbs made slow circles in the hollows above her collarbone. He didn't dare look at her breasts again; he was at the ragged edge of his self-control as it was, and he wasn't sure how long he could restrain himself if he were to see the nipples tighten under his gaze.

She raised her chin and carried on the conversation with the special aplomb that is woman's alone. "After that," she said, "I won't mind."

He wanted so much more for her than "not minding,"

when it came to his physical attentions, but he was dealing with a new bride, he reminded himself. Such things took time and skill, tenderness and patience. Jake had all those qualities, though he would have been the first to admit that the latter was a bit taxed at the moment. If she'd been one of the loose women over at Diamond Lil's, he'd probably be putting his shirt back on by now, but she wasn't. Dear God, she wasn't.

He swallowed hard and hoped she didn't guess that he was nervous, too. One of them, it seemed to him, ought to be in charge.

"Don't you think you should undress?" she asked logically. "After all, I'm standing here naked, and there you are, wearing everything but a hat."

He felt heat surge into his face at the idea of taking off his clothes in front of this delectable little nymph—God, he might have been an uninitiated youth instead of a man with a long and rather colorful history behind him. Reluctantly, he removed his suit coat, loosened his tie.

A groan escaped him when she pushed his hands gently aside and began to unfasten the buttons of his shirt, and the sound must have pleased her, for her dark eyes were shining as she looked up at him, her fingers busy all the while.

"I'll be a good wife to you, Jake Vigil," she said.

He kissed her then, suddenly, and with a lot of force, surprising both of them. When it was over and he'd recovered enough strength to draw his head back and look at her, he saw a bedazzled expression in her eyes. He wished he could tell her he loved her, wished it sorely, but for all his wanting, for all his passion, he knew there was a void inside him where tender sentiments should be. A place that had to be kept closed off.

"I'll protect you," he said gruffly, "and I'll always provide. No matter what."

She didn't respond but simply pushed his shirt back over his shoulders. He shed the garment, let it fall unheeded to the floor. Within a few seconds, he, too, was stripped to the skin.

He had no recollection of taking her to the bed, tossing back the covers, sprawling next to her on the smooth linen sheets. He was in a fever, a delirium, and by the time his mind cleared, even a little, they were lying on their sides, facing each other, the skin of their thighs touching. He rested a hand on the supple curve of her hip.

"Don't be afraid," she said.

Under any other circumstances, that remark would have amused him, but there, in his bed, with his brand new wife awaiting him like a feast, he was touched instead. He ran the tip of one index finger lightly from her temple to her chin, then traced the shape of her delectable mouth. The next thing he knew, he was kissing her again, and so desperate to be inside her that it took all his self-control to keep from mounting her right then.

Instead, he took his time, introducing her to every nuance of pleasure—rousing soft cries from her when he grasped her wrists together, above her head, and suckled at her breasts, sometimes leisurely, sometimes with the hunger that was already consuming him, sending the blood racing hot through his veins.

He reached her silken belly in due time and made a circle around her navel with the tip of his tongue. When he did that, she gasped and arched her back, raising herself to him like an offering. Instinct had taken over Skye's every action and movement.

Knowing that, he was lost.

He moved down, beneath the quilts and the top sheet, and slid his hands under her buttocks, lifted her to his mouth like a chalice. When she felt his tongue, quickly followed by the tugging of his lips, she sobbed his name, plunged her fingers into his hair, and begged.

He could not deny her but drew on her with more insistence, and still more, until her excitement had turned to frenzy and her buttocks were quivering in his hands. When, at long last, she stiffened against him, moist and flexing, he called upon the last dregs of personal discipline to guide her over every peak. Finally, when she sagged, sighing raggedly, to the mattress, he parted her legs gently and poised himself above her.

"Skye?" He was asking her permission, and she knew it.

She looked up at him dreamily, blinking, and a silly, beautiful smile curved her kiss-swollen mouth. "Yes," she said on a breath. "Oh, yes."

He found her entrance, slid slowly inside her. He felt the maidenhead give way, and though she flinched a little as he breached that last barrier, her breathing soon quickened, and her hips began to move in precise rhythm with his.

He was amazed.

"Oh," she whispered. "Oh, Jake—"

"Shh." He kissed her, his tongue sparring with hers.

She began to buck beneath him, fitfully at first and then with an age-old eagerness. He rode her, plunging deep, covering her face, her jaw, her neck with kisses as they rose and fell together.

And then, for Jake Vigil at least, the universe exploded, spewing stars. At the same time, Skye clung to him, her fingernails deep in the flesh of his back, and cried out in satisfaction, over and over again.

She lay still beneath him, sated, swept away, and utterly embarrassed by the echoes of her own abandon. Nothing, *nothing* Skye had ever heard, read, or imagined about the act of love had prepared her for the reality—for the fever, the need, the tender violence of it. Her throat was raw, and she was mortified, thinking she must surely have shouted right out loud in her frantic jubilance. She knew by the twisted sheets and the cool sheen of perspiration on her skin that she had been thrashing about, and she turned her face to one side.

Jake, still breathing hard, lay balanced on his thighs and forearms, careful not to crush her. "Skye," he said, and though the word was gentle, there was a command in it. "Look at me."

She looked, cheeks flaming. She'd *shouted,* she agonized silently. She'd tossed back and forth and up and down on the bed like a shameless hussy. What must he think of her?

"What," he demanded quietly, "is going on in that mind of yours?"

She lowered her lashes, and he kissed each of her eyelids, ever so softly. The warmth of his lips sent a hot thrill of fresh, unexpected fire through her, stealing her breath. She gasped and met his gaze again, her heart picking up speed like a steam engine chugging downhill. "I was just—just wondering—I mean, I've never—I'm just not sure—"

He smiled and kissed the tip of her nose. "Let's just say I'm glad you lost that horse race this morning," he said, with mischief dancing in his eyes.

Skye was glad, too, but she wasn't so far gone as to admit it. She didn't want Jake to start thinking she'd taken that spill intentionally, because she hadn't. At least, she was pretty sure she hadn't.

"I'm sorry we can't take a honeymoon trip," he said, and he looked for all the world as though he meant it. Skye was seeing a side of Jake she had never glimpsed before, as deeply as she had loved him; behind all that strength and power and obstinance lurked a passionate, skillful lover, a poet, not of pretty phrases but of caresses and kisses and whispered urgings. "Not just yet, anyhow." He rolled onto his back beside her and sighed, gazing up at the ceiling. "You might as well know, you've married a man who might just lose every cent."

She raised herself onto one elbow and peered down into his face. He was magnificent, lying there, broad at the shoulders and deep through the chest, his hair still mussed from her fingers and his aristocratic features at peace in a way she had never known them to be. It gave her a delicious sense of power to know that she'd done this for him, however unwittingly, that she'd given him the singular, womanly solace of her body.

"I don't care," she said. "If you go broke, I mean. We can live on my land."

She saw amazement in his eyes as he stared at her. "You don't care?" He sounded as though he couldn't believe what he was hearing.

"Well," she allowed, finding the strength at last to sit up, pulling the sheets modestly up over her breasts. "Of course I care. I mean, you've worked hard for all this. But it doesn't really change the important things, does it? We still have each other, and Hank. We're a family now. We have my sister and my cousins and the land at Primrose Creek."

He smiled and tugged the sheet down, smiled again when she blushed. "You, Mrs. Vigil," he said, "are a remarkable woman." He traced the circumference of a nipple with the tip of one finger, delighting in the instinctive response and the little groan Skye couldn't hold back. "Come here," he said, drawing her down into his embrace. "Let me show you just *how* remarkable."

She was lost then, utterly, completely, triumphantly lost. And, for the moment at least, she didn't give a tinker's damn about being found.

Hank stood watching Skye from the doorway of Jake's enormous kitchen one morning, some three days following the wedding, and the expression in his eyes was at once cautious and hopeful. "I didn't figure on gettin' myself another ma," he said. "Fact is, the one I had wasn't much."

Skye, who had been assessing the contents of the pantry, which were sorry indeed, wiped her hands on the apron she'd fashioned from a dishtowel and smiled down at the little boy. He'd avoided her neatly so far, except for their brief exchange after the wedding, but now he evidently felt ready to draw up some kind of unwritten treaty. He was the very image of Jake; when he grew to be a man, she expected he'd look much the way his father did now. "I see," she said carefully, keeping her distance lest she frighten the child away. He reminded her of a yearling deer, curious but watchful, too. Prepared to spring away into the underbrush at the slightest provocation. Her tone was thoughtful, almost bemused. "Well, I didn't precisely expect to get a little boy, either. At least, not right away. All the same, I'm really, truly glad I did."

"I'm *not* a little boy," Hank protested.

Skye bit back a smile. "No," she said with a ponderous shake of her head. "I don't suppose you are."

"I don't have to do what you tell me."

She dragged a chair back from the round oak table, sat down, and propped her chin in her hands. "I'm not entirely sure that's true," she said. "I do expect you to wash behind your ears and keep your teeth clean and, of course, to do your chores and schoolwork."

He made a face. "Women," he scoffed.

Skye wanted to laugh, but somehow she managed to maintain a properly serious expression. "I think we can learn to be friends if we really try."

"But you're not my ma." He plainly wanted that understood.

Jake had told Skye what little he knew about his son's past. She wondered what sort of a woman gave birth to a child, kept his existence a secret from the man who'd fathered him, and then abandoned that same child with little or no compunction. Her heart went out to Hank, though she was careful not to reveal that, either. Long experience with Noah had taught her to communicate with children as persons in their own right.

"No, I'm not your mother," she allowed. "That's true. But I would certainly be proud if you were my son."

The hazel eyes widened, narrowed again. "You're just sayin' that," he accused.

She shook her head. "Absolutely not. I never say things I don't mean. Do you?"

He studied her in silence for a long while, and she waited, content to let him speak when and if he was ready. "Sometimes," he admitted. "Sometimes I tell lies."

Skye kept her features very grave. "Oh."

"And sometimes I spit."

She nodded solemnly.

"And if I don't care for a place, then I just move on."

"Hmmm," Skye said. "Well, I hope you'll like Primrose Creek and stay right here with us. I think your father would be very disappointed if you left."

Hank's small, freckled brow furrowed briefly. "What about you? Would you be sad? If I lit out, I mean?"

"Oh, yes," she answered. "You see, we're going to have some babies around here, and they'll need an older brother to watch out for them. Oh, they'll have their cousin Noah, of course, and eventually the others will be big enough to help out, too, but that won't be the same as having a real brother, right there under the same roof and everything."

Hank looked pensive and a bit torn. Eagerness sparked in his eyes, though she knew he was doing his best to suppress the emotion. Poor, sweet thing; heaven only knew what sort of tribulations he'd gone through before coming to Primrose Creek. No wonder he was such a stalwart and serious little man.

"Did you marry my pa so's you could live in this fancy house?"

The question caught Skye off-guard and stung smartly. She hadn't married Jake for any reason other than love, though she wasn't about to explain her most intimate feelings to a seven-year-old. Jake, on the contrary, and despite his many protestations, had almost certainly married her for the timber on her land, though she didn't doubt that he regarded her highly. A man as handsome, as capable, as downright *good* as Jake Vigil could have had his pick of women.

She decided to ignore the inquiry entirely, since she'd already left it dangling so long. "There isn't much in the pantry," she said, getting back to her feet with a sigh of resolution, "but I've managed to scrape up some oatmeal and molasses. Come have your breakfast. You mustn't be late for school."

"I hate school," he said, dragging his feet as he approached the table.

Skye went to the stove, busied herself with stirring and scooping, as she'd seen Bridget do a thousand times. It was strange how such simple tasks as cooking oatmeal and looking after a child could give a person so much joy. "Well, you'll need schooling," she said, "if you hope to follow in your father's footsteps. He's a very intelligent man, you know. You've seen all his books on the shelves in the study? He must have hundreds, and it looks to me as if he's read them all—"

Hank made a great deal of noise getting into a chair and situating himself just so at the table. "Noah says you're all right," he said. "So I reckon I'll stay put awhile."

She hid a smile.

"He's about to go under, my pa," the child confided. "That's what they say at school. Then he won't want me underfoot no more. He probably won't want you, neither."

Skye was careful not to meet Hank's gaze for a few moments, for her own was glittering with a sheen of tears, quickly blinked away. "Your father will *never* give you away," she said, and it was in that moment the one thing she was truly sure of. "Never."

It was more than a rumor, though, the reference to Jake's financial situation. He'd admitted that to her himself the day they were married. She hadn't minded then, except for his sake, anyway, and she didn't now. She had land, she had timber, she had the gold that sifted down out of the mountains, settling like silt in the creek bed. She had strength and love and competence, and if she couldn't build a life from those things, she was just plain useless.

Skye set the bowl of steaming oatmeal, generously laced with molasses, before him. "Don't you go worrying, now. Your father's not beaten yet. And even if he was, why, we could start over, the three of us, just by pushing up our sleeves and getting down to work."

He looked at her for a long, poignant moment. "Their pas work for my pa, mostly. The kids at school, I mean. Everybody's real scared."

Skye dared to stroke the boy's hair, and, to her surprise, he did not pull away. For the first time, it came to her how high-handed she'd been in the beginning, flatly refusing to sell her timber to Jake or anyone else. She'd never once thought how many people would be affected by her rather blithe decision, and now she was ashamed.

Hank's words echoed in her ears all morning. *Everybody's real scared.*

Jake came home at around noon and found her in the study, with leather-bound volumes in teetering piles all around her. He looked harried and quite unsure of his welcome, but he smiled when he saw her, as though there were something amusing about a woman sorting books.

His clothes were covered with dirt, and his hair was full of sawdust, but Skye didn't care. When he pulled her close, her senses arose as one and spun their way upward in a whirlwind of sparks, like ghost leaves rising from a garden fire. He brushed a smudge from her cheek with the pad of one thumb and kissed her forehead.

"My wife," he said, as though he could not believe his good fortune.

Skye's throat closed, so great was the swell of emotion that arose within her, and some moments had passed before she managed to speak. "About the timber—" she began.

He laid an index finger to her lips. It was a gentle gesture, intended to soothe, no doubt, but it had exactly the opposite effect on Skye. She was dancing with lightning; if Jake had carried her upstairs to their bedroom, she would have gone willingly, even though it was the middle of the day.

"Never mind the timber," he said.

She blinked. "But it's yours now, at least partly—"

He interrupted with a shake of his head. "No," he said in a firm voice, and held her away from him. It was a minor distance—his hands were still cupping her elbows—but Skye felt it sorely. "The land, those trees—all of that's yours. And I know how much those trees mean to you."

Skye was speechless. Jubilance and confusion tussled within her.

"I'm the head of this household," he went on solemnly, "and I'll pay my debts and provide for my wife and child. Somehow."

"You're just being stubborn, Jake Vigil," she accused when she found the breath to speak. "You *need* that timber."

He withdrew further just then; she felt it, even though she would have sworn he hadn't actually moved. "No," he said. "What I need is to be able to look at my face in the mirror every morning when I shave without being tempted to turn away in disgust. If you want to back out—"

Skye's eyes widened, and her mouth dropped open. She had to close it again consciously. When she spoke, she was trembling with controlled fury. "Are you suggesting that I back out of this marriage? Just go home to Primrose Creek and pretend nothing's changed?"

He heaved a sigh. "Only if you want to," he said.

She stared at him. "Well," she told him, "I don't. I'm not some throwaway woman, Jake Vigil. I'm a wife, and I mean to stay that way!"

He grinned, his white teeth making a startling contrast with his dirty, rascally face. "You lost that race on purpose."

She stomped one foot. "I did not!"

He laughed. "Yes," he pressed, frankly enjoying her high dudgeon. "I think maybe you did. You *wanted* to marry me."

She *had* wanted to marry Jake, she was crazy about him, and she had been for a long time, but she would have won that race if she could have, would have left Jake Vigil and his second-rate stallion choking in the dust! With huffy little motions, she smoothed her hair, straightened her spine, dusted her hands together. "I've made cheese potatoes," she said. "For your dinner."

"Admit it," he said. "You wanted to marry me."

"All right," she said. "It's true."

He grinned and folded his arms. "Why?"

"Because I wanted lumber for a house," she lied.

He laughed. "Try again."

She flushed. "Because—I wanted—babies."

In a single motion, he swept her up into his arms.

"What about dinner?" she asked, her heart thrumming at the back of her throat.

He kissed her forehead, then bent to nip lightly at one of her breasts. "I'm not interested in dinner," he said, and started up the stairs.

The man at the Western Union office read the telegram Skye had written out and peered at her through greasy spectacles. He was a doddering old fellow, and his jaw shook with effort while he rallied his powers of speech. "This here is to the vice president of the railroad, Mrs. Vigil," he said.

She leaned forward and spoke in a cheerful whisper. "I know that," she said. "After all, I wrote it."

He was still skeptical. "You talked this over with Jake, I reckon?"

"I do not recall asking for your counsel in this matter or any other, Mr. Abbot," Skye pointed out. "That timber is mine, after all, and if I want to sell it to the railroad, I jolly well will. Furthermore, if you mention this to my husband, I will know you betrayed a confidence and report you to the Western Union people." Maybe Jake was willing to let go of everything he'd worked for by turning his back on a lot of perfectly good timber, but she wasn't about to let him. She'd sell the trees herself if he refused to do so, and the railroad would be forced to let Jake cut the ties for the tracks, since there wasn't another mill within miles, thereby fulfilling his contract.

Mr. Abbot blinked. "That beats all," he said, but he sounded subdued. Skye hadn't expected him to be the least bit daunted by her threat, since it was largely an empty one, but apparently he had taken it to heart. "Don't know what the world's coming to, when a new bride'll steal business from her own husband—"

"I'll find out," Skye warned ominously, probably overplaying her hand a little but emboldened by her success in buffaloing Mr. Abbot, "if you tell." With that, she counted out the fee for sending the wire, slapping each coin down onto the counter with a little flourish, and waited obstinately while Mr. Abbot tapped out the words that would change everything—for better or for worse.

Megan came to call first thing the next morning and took in the wonders of Jake's house with amazement. The last time Megan or any of them had been inside the mansion, Jake had been courting Christy. He'd ordered all sorts of fancy furnishings to please her back then, things it looked as though no one had touched since.

"This is even bigger than Granddaddy's place," Megan said when she and Skye were seated in the great, echoing parlor, sipping tea.

"Umm," Skye replied. The house seemed cold and imposing, and she would have preferred to live on Primrose Creek, with Jake and young Hank, of course, in the simpler place she'd planned so carefully in her mind. "That was different," she said at some length. "The farm, I mean. That house was always brimming with noise and music and—well—*life*. This place is like a museum."

Megan looked impish. "Are you complaining, Skye McQuarry Vigil? If so, I must say that you lack conviction—your eyes sparkle, and your skin glows. You look like you're going to start singing for joy at any moment." She lowered her voice and leaned forward in her velvet chair. "Is it wonderful? Being married, I mean?"

"Married?" Skye echoed, a little stupidly.

"You know," Megan persisted. *"Married."*

Color throbbed in Skye's face. "Oh," she said.

Megan would not let the subject go. "Well?"

"Yes," Skye admitted in an embarrassed rush, unable to keep herself from beaming. "And don't ask me to tell you any more, because I positively will not, Megan McQuarry."

Megan settled back, grinning. "I wouldn't dream of prying," she lied. Prying was her calling in life.

Just then, Hank burst through the front door and appeared in the parlor doorway. His eyes were enormous, and there was no color in his face at all. "There's a fire comin'!" he yelled.

For Skye, everything stopped for a moment, the world, time itself, even her heartbeat. It was the thing they had most feared, all of them, and it had come upon them. *"What?"*

"Pa sent me to tell you Mr. Hicks is comin' with a wagon. We're supposed to pack up whatever we can and head for the low country—"

Skye and Megan were both on their feet in an instant, racing toward the front door. They reached it at the same time and stared in horror at the rim of black, roiling smoke surging along the western horizon. The blaze was big, and though it was still far away, it looked as if it was headed straight for Primrose Creek.

"I'll be needed at home," Megan cried, and dashed down the walk to mount Speckles, the mare she'd left tethered to the fence. She didn't bother with decorum but planted one foot in the stirrup, swung the other leg over the saddle, and rode astride.

Skye thought anxiously of Bridget and Trace, of Noah and the twins and all the horses and cattle, but unlike Megan, she did not bolt for the homestead. She was a married woman now, responsible for a child, and if she'd gone flying off to help her sister and cousins, Bridget would have been the first to tell her to go home and look after her own.

She turned quickly and smoothed Hank's hair back from his worried face. "Where is your pa? Over at the mill?"

Hank nodded vigorously. "We'd better get movin'," he said. "Pa said he'd whup me good if I didn't mind him, 'cause there's no time to waste!"

The acrid scent of smoke reached Skye then, souring the spring breeze that had made the earlier part of the day so pleasant. Tears burned in her eyes. Perhaps it wouldn't matter now, that she'd gone behind Jake's back and offered to sell the timber on her land to the railroad. If that fire kept traveling in the same direction, there wouldn't *be* any timber.

"You go into the parlor," she said calmly, laying a hand on Hank's skinny little shoulder, "and gather as many of the books together as you can. I'll fetch blankets and food."

Hank nodded and raced toward his father's study. If he questioned the wisdom of saving books instead of other, more practical items, such as chairs and wash-tubs, pots and pans and butter churns, he didn't say so.

Mr. Hicks appeared with the wagon only minutes later, and, as the air grew thicker and sootier and more difficult to breathe, Skye wondered with real despair if all of Nevada was on fire. Still, she raced back and forth, helping to load the wagon. When it was full, she urged Hank up into the box and turned toward the mill, searching through the billowing smoke for her husband.

Jake was striding across the road, and, reaching her, he took her by the shoulders and kept on going, shuffling her along with him, until they were beside the wagon. "Head down the mountain, Skye," he rasped. "Go as far as you can tonight. I'll look for you at Fort Grant first, and if I don't find you there, I'll come to Virginia City."

Skye was horrified. It had not occurred to her that she and Hank would be leaving without Jake. It was unthinkable—they were a family, the three of them. They belonged together, no matter what.

He must have read her thoughts, for before she could speak, Jake put a finger under her chin and lifted, closing her mouth. "For once in your life," he said, "don't argue with me. This whole mountain could go up if we don't stop that fire. All the men are staying to fight it, and, frankly, we don't need anything else to worry about!"

She looked around, saw for the first time in her panic that the road was already thick with fleeing wagons and buckboards. Where, she wondered desperately, were Bridget and her children? What of Christy and the new baby, little Joseph? What would happen to the houses, the barns, the livestock?

Jake hoisted her into the wagon. "Go," he said.

She gazed down at him for a long moment, loving

him, but unable to say it, even then, for fear he would turn away. "I'll be back," she said. "Once Hank is safe at Fort Grant, I'm coming straight back."

"Don't you dare," Jake warned. His jawline looked hard, and she knew he wasn't fooling. "I mean it, Skye."

She took up the reins. "So do I," she answered, and guided the wagon around in a wide arc, joining the exodus from Primrose Creek.

Chapter
6

*A*s a McQuarry, Skye was possessed of many singular characteristics, but a propensity for blind obedience did not number among them. Her intentions were as firmly set as her jawline while she drove the team and wagon ever further, ever faster, away from nearly everyone and everything she held dear. She would go back. As soon as she could, she would return to Primrose Creek and battle the fire herself, hand-to-hand. After all, she had as much to lose as anybody else.

Smoke chased the noisy band of scrambling escapees, rolling over them like some dark, acrid tide, causing Skye's eyes to burn, as dry as if she'd opened the door of a blast furnace and peeked inside. It was hard to see the road, harder still to breathe. Deer sprang alongside the track now and then, fleeing the flames, and small animals—squirrels, raccoons, and rabbits mostly—scampered in the ruts and in the ditches, their high-pitched squeals adding to the din.

Beside her in the wagon box, Hank crouched on the floor, with Mr. Hicks's bandanna pressed to his face. His eyes were enormous with fright as he looked up at Skye, his knuckles white where he gripped the seat with one hand and the side of the box with the other.

Hurry, urged the voice of instinct, *hurry.* And Skye listened. She stood, reins in hand, feet set to hold her balance, and drove the already-lathered team harder, and then harder yet. Squinting through the smoke, when she dared to look away from the road ahead, Skye glimpsed Bridget and Christy in a shared wagon, comforting the smaller children in the back while Caney held the traces, traveling at a pace to rival Skye's own. Megan rode alongside on her spirited mare, with Noah behind her, his little arms clenched tightly around her middle.

Noah had always been Skye's special charge, and her heart went out to her nephew, finding its way through the smoke and soot and fear. He must have felt her regard, for he turned his head immediately, and their eyes connected.

She smiled at him, willing him to know that she thought he was being very, very brave.

Skye did not know how far they'd traveled, the McQuarry women and their various charges, the townswomen and theirs, when they were met by a large contingent of cavalrymen from Fort Grant. Uniforms already stained with soot, prepared for a fight that might well mean life or death to some of them, as to a great many secret and cherished dreams hiding in the hearts of all these terrified but determined women and children, Skye thought those soldiers were among the most splendid sights she'd ever seen.

They had outrun the smoke, she and the others, and while the fort was still a long way off, Skye at last could see the walls and watchtowers from her place in the wagon box. She drew back on the reins with all her might and still barely stopped the four-horse team. Caney brought the other rig to an able halt beside her.

"I'm going to unhitch one of these horses and ride back!" Skye called to her, and coughed. "Megan can turn the mare loose and drive the wagon the rest of the way—"

Caney's eyes flashed with temper and resolve. "You ain't goin' nowhere, missy, so you can just put *that* dern fool idea right out of your head! You a mama to that little boy now, and you cain't leave him!"

She risked a glance down at Hank and found him looking plaintively back up at her. Caney was right, she reflected, but ruefully. She hadn't even known he existed until just a few days before, but Hank was hers all the same, born of her heart if not of her body. She loved him with a sudden and primitive fierceness that was startling to recognize; this, she knew, was the way her granddaddy, Gideon McQuarry, had loved her and Bridget, Christy, and Megan. It was a gift, that kind of commitment to another person, for the lover as well as the beloved, and more important than anything else on earth.

She sat down in the wagon seat, holding the reins loosely in one hand, and ruffled her stepson's hair. "I'm staying," she said simply, and soon, while the cavalry hurried toward Primrose Creek, at least a hundred strong, she and Caney and the others once again set out for the fort itself.

There, they were given quarters in one of the bar-

racks, a long, spacious room cleared especially for them
and lined on either side with metal cots. A hot and
restorative—if not particularly tasty—meal was served
in the mess hall, and Bridget and Christy took informal
command of the situation, supervising the collecting
and washing of dishes, mugs, and utensils. By nightfall,
the other women of the town and its surrounding area
were settled in, hopeful if still subdued, resigned to
looking after the children and waiting for their men to
come and fetch them.

Once the meal was over, though, and the various
children of the family had been bedded down, Skye was
restless. After making sure Hank was asleep in the cot
next to the one she'd claimed for herself, she went outside under a starry spring sky.

She stood looking up for a long moment, the smell
of smoke still rife in her hair and the folds of her
clothes, even on her skin, and prayed that whatever happened to the land, the timber, and the town, the people
up there in the high country would be kept safe. Jake's
image filled her mind and brought stinging tears to her
eyes. He could so easily be killed, burned or crushed
beneath a falling tree or building, or simply overcome
by smoke. He was her husband, and though he had laid
skillful claim to her body on more than one occasion,
she had never told him that she loved him with all her
heart and soul, as well as her flesh. Her silly, stubborn
pride had gotten in the way, and now she might never
have a chance to make things right.

Despondently, she climbed a stairway to one of the
parapets, where she met and passed one of several
young soldiers making his rounds.

The place she knew as Primrose Creek, the place she

knew as home, glowed bright crimson against a background of darkness. Perhaps it was gone, all of it, even then—the home Bridget and Trace had built with love and hard work, the Indian lodge Christy and Zachary had transformed into a haven. The timber and animals on her portion of land and on Megan's. The tents and shacks and saloons, the sawmill, and Jake's grand monstrosity of a house. She closed her eyes against all those images of destruction, told herself that everything would be all right. They would survive, all of them, and rebuild as best they could. In time, the forest animals would return, and the trees would grow again.

A whisper of sound at her right side brought Skye back to the moment. She turned to see Christy standing there, a shawl pulled tightly around her slender shoulders. Although she had just given birth a few days before, and she was clearly tired, Christy's backbone was McQuarry-straight, and her chin was high as she followed Skye's gaze.

"It's the hardest thing in the world," Skye's cousin mused, "not being there with Zachary."

Skye nodded. "I can't stop thinking about Jake," she agreed.

Christy sighed. She'd wound her heavy dark hair in a bun at her nape, and it was slipping its pins, ready to tumble down her back, but she seemed heedless of everything but that distant fire and the man she loved, up there fighting the blaze with the rest of the men. "I'd give a lot to be there right now. To know Zachary and the others are all right. Bridget's frantic over Trace, too, though she doesn't think anyone can tell."

Skye smiled at the mention of her sister. Bridget was the McQuarry-est of McQuarrys. She had their granddaddy's indomitable spirit, and what she lacked in physical stature she made up in grit and intelligence. She was a wildcat at heart, Bridget was, equal to any challenge, and it was a sure bet that if she hadn't had the twins and Noah to care for, she'd have been at her husband's side at that very moment. "Don't you worry about Bridget," she said, and then touched her cousin's shoulder lightly, remembering her cousin's anxiety when the baby was about to be born and Zachary was nowhere to be found. "But what about you, Christy? Are you all right?"

Christy hesitated for only the merest fraction of a beat before nodding. "Yes," she said, her attention still fixed on the distant fire. Even from so far away, the blaze cast a moving reflection over Christy's perfect features. "A person can lose all they have, so quickly—"

There was certainly no way to refute that statement, it was patently true, but Skye slipped her arm around Christy and gave her a brief, reassuring squeeze anyway. All four of the Primrose Creek women had known tremendous loss in recent years. The farm that had nurtured them all was gone forever. Their grandmother had passed on, then their fathers and mothers, and eventually, and most grievous of all, they'd had to say good-bye to their beloved grandfather, the cornerstone of their lives. Bridget had seen a young husband march off to war, only to return in a pinewood box. Of them all, though, it often seemed to Skye that Christy always had been the most sensitive and thus the most easily wounded; she was surely thinking of Zachary again, and of what it would mean to lose him.

"We had each other, Christy. You and me and Bridget

and Megan. And Caney, too." She paused, thinking of the family Bible and the secret it contained. "Surely you'll tell Megan now? About the four of us being sisters?"

Christy shook her head, then sighed philosophically and worked up a faltering smile. That was Christy for you; she was temperamental, proud, and stubborn as a mule belly-deep in mud, but she was also one of the most courageous people Skye had ever known. None knew better than Bridget, Megan, Caney, and Skye herself how afraid Christy had been of giving her heart to Zachary, lest it be broken, but she'd gone ahead and done it anyway, and she'd been happy as a result. Through it all, she still wanted to protect her little sister.

"Everything's happened so fast," Christy said, brushing a lock of smoke-scented hair back from Skye's forehead. "I didn't get a chance."

"She deserves to know."

Christy's eyes filled with tears. "It will break her heart."

"Why?"

"She thought the sun rose and set on Granddaddy. When she finds out he lied all those years—"

"He wanted to protect all of us."

"Maybe," Christy said. "And maybe he just wanted to protect his son, the worst scoundrel of all, your— our—father." She sighed again. "I must confess, though, it's something of a relief to know Jenny wasn't Megan's and my mother. She didn't love us very much, and we always thought it was some fault in ourselves."

"Did Caney know?" Skye asked gently.

"Oh, yes," Christy replied. "Of course she did. In fact, when our dear daddy's lovely mistress came to term with each one of us, Caney was there to attend to the matter and see that no tales were spread. It was Granddaddy who gave two of us to each of his remaining sons and Granddaddy who insisted that we all grow up believing we'd been born to the parents he'd assigned us."

"I wonder what Grandmother thought."

Christy gave a chuckle that was utterly without humor. "Granddaddy loved her to distraction, but when it came to serious matters like a firstborn son so intolerable that they paid him to leave home and stay away, his word was law."

Skye nodded. "Bridget didn't tell me his name. Our father's, I mean."

"Thayer," Christy said in a faraway and very weary voice. "He was named for our great-grandfather. What a disappointment he must have been to Granddaddy and Grandmother!"

"It's odd that no one ever mentioned him, that there wasn't a portrait or a letter—"

"He was what the English call a remittance man. Granddaddy gave him his inheritance and sent him away when he was still very young."

"We had different mothers, though." Bridget had told her that much, though she hadn't been entirely forthcoming where the family scandal was concerned.

"How do you know that?"

Once again, Christy sighed. "Granddaddy left a letter. It was written on thin paper and tucked beneath the lining of the back cover on the Bible."

Skye let out her breath, feeling a little angry herself now. Bridget and Christy, being the oldest, had naturally thought they knew best, but they had been wrong to keep the secret as long as they had. Skye and Megan were not children, and they had a right to know who they were.

"I see," she said.

Christy squeezed her hand. "I'm not sure you do. There's more, Skye."

Skye braced herself, sensing that this last bit of news would be the most startling of all. "Tell me," she insisted. When she saw Bridget again, she would tell her off three ways from Sunday for hiding so much from her.

But Christy said nothing more. She merely resumed her vigil, gazing toward the fire and waiting for Zachary. Plainly, for that night at least, the subject was closed.

The heat and glare of the fire were nearly unbearable, and Jake watched with hot, itching eyes as the roof of his mansion fell in, sending a shower of sparks and flames shooting toward the smoke-shrouded sky. The mill was gone, and so was most of the rest of the town—only the marshal's office, that pitiful shack of a schoolhouse, and Diamond Lil's saloon were still standing.

Someone slapped him on the shoulder. "The worst is over," a voice said. "The fire's turning back on itself."

He recognized Trace Qualtrough, though it was God's own wonder that he could, for the man was black with soot from the top of his head to the soles of his boots. The whites of his eyes stood out, and when he smiled, Jake actually blinked at the brightness of his teeth.

"You reckon the women are all right?" he asked.

Trace nodded. "Yep."

"Your place—at Primrose Creek?"

Trace ran a forearm across his brow, and afterward he was as dirty as before. "I've been on the mountain most of the day, but Zachary rode out home as soon as we could spare him. Says everything's still standing." He had the good grace to look a little chagrined, Trace did, though Jake wasn't precisely sure how he'd been able to discern the fact, given all that soot. "You still have Skye, and the land, and her timber," Trace said, more gently. "A man's got a McQuarry woman at his side, he can do anything."

Jake thrust a hand through his hair and looked around behind him. He couldn't talk about Skye just now, couldn't even bear to think about her. It was as if he would somehow jinx her if he let her into his mind, and she and the boy would be in greater danger than they already were. "Anybody hurt?"

"Mike Finn is in a pretty bad way," Trace answered solemnly. "Reckon he breathed in too much smoke. And Malcolm's got some nasty burns on his right arm."

"They're being tended to?"

Again, Trace nodded. "Captain Tatum came up with the troops. He does the doctoring down at Fort Grant." He sighed. "There's already some talk about giving up on this town, starting over someplace else. You wouldn't be thinking along those lines, would you, Jake?"

There were folks who said Trace Qualtrough could get inside a horse's head and read its mind. Just then, Jake wondered if the man possessed the same uncanny skill where human beings were concerned. "Either way," he said, "we'll have to start over. Might as well be here as anyplace else."

Trace grinned, pleased, and slapped Jake's shoulder again. Ashes rose from the fabric of his shirt. "Might as well," he agreed.

That night, when the last blazes were out, men took turns standing watch, lest the few remaining buildings be consumed. Jake let himself be persuaded to ride out to the Qualtrough place, where he took a bath in the creek and slept in the bed that had been Skye's before they were married. The scent of her skin and hair lingered in the linens, and, comforted, he fell into an immediate, consuming sleep.

Despite the old adage that things usually look better in the morning, the plain light of day had a sobering effect on just about everybody. Most of the horses and cattle had been turned loose as the fire drew nearer, so they'd have at least a chance of escaping the heat, flames, and smoke; now, those that had survived would have to be rounded up again. Newly planted crops were either burned or blanketed in ash, and a thousand trees, most of them on Jake's own land, loomed black and brittle and spindly-limbed against the sky.

Jake had managed to keep the bay stallion tethered in the schoolyard with a few others, when the livestock was scattered to the four winds, and that morning he was glad, for, by his reckoning, the bay was all he had left—when it came to material things, anyway. Skye and Hank were safe at Fort Grant or in Virginia City, and that mattered more than anything else.

The town, when he reached it, was mostly charred rubble. He rode past the mill he'd spent five years building, past the once-grand house where he had brought his wife on their wedding night.

"Mr. Vigil?" The voice was masculine and, given that Jake knew most everybody in town, flat-out unfamiliar.

He turned in the saddle, saw a fussy-looking little man standing nearby, wearing a dusty suit and a bowler hat. "Ace Thompson," he said, extending one hand. Jake had already leaned down to accept the handshake before Thompson went on; otherwise, he probably would have kept his distance. "I'm with the railroad."

Jake swung a leg over the bay's neck and jumped down to face his visitor. Hands resting on his hips, he sighed. "Well, Mr. Thompson, it would seem that you and I are both out of luck. There's no timber and no place to mill it, anyhow. I reckon you could take my house, but that's gone, too." He folded his arms. "I'll be damned if I can come up with a solution."

Thompson looked surprised. "Well, it's true that you've suffered some serious losses here," he said. "No one is denying that. But we have the timber rights we acquired from your wife, and we'd like to lay tracks between here and Virginia City. If you'll agree to cut and plane the ties, we'll finance new equipment—"

Jake frowned. "Wait a minute," he interrupted. "Whoa. What do you mean, you have the timber rights *you acquired from my wife?*"

The other man blinked behind smudged spectacles. He wrenched them off, breathed on the lenses, and polished them vigorously with a corner of his handkerchief. "We certainly assumed you knew."

"Well," Jake growled, barely able to refrain from grabbing the little fellow by the lapels and yanking him up onto the toes of his boots, "I didn't. What the hell are you talking about?"

"Mrs. Vigil—your wife—offered to sell us whatever timber we needed."

The implications of what had actually happened struck Jake with a physical impact. How could she have done such a thing? How could she have done business with these vipers behind his back?

Thompson cleared his throat, and his glasses, Jake noticed, were still smudged. "Mrs. Vigil?" he prompted weakly.

"I know her name," Jake snapped. He was reeling inwardly. How could Skye have deceived him like this? She'd refused his offer to buy her surplus timber before they were married and then gone behind his back as soon as she had a ring on her finger and sold the logging rights out from under him. He was hot with betrayal, frantic to see his bride and demand an explanation. All the time she'd pretended to love him, she'd been planning his downfall.

"I'm sorry," said the little man. "It would seem that you were not apprised of your wife's intentions. However, I'm afraid we must insist that the deal be honored."

Jake turned away, groped for the bay, and swung up into the saddle. "Your bargain is with my wife," he said. "I won't interfere."

Thompson pushed the bowler hat to the back of his head and looked up. The sun blazed off the lenses of his spectacles, and he tugged at the hem of his suit coat with small, nervous hands. "I have more to tell you," he said.

"Sorry," Jake responded with a bitter smile. "I don't have time to listen." With that, he was gone, riding out of town.

Two hours later, he arrived at Fort Grant, and apparently the guards had seen him coming a long way off, for the towering, spiked timber gates swung open at his approach. Skye was waiting for him when he rode through, her head high, her chin out, and her eyes shining.

At the sight of him, she burst into tears. "Thank God," he heard her say, through the thrum that had filled his ears since he'd learned what she had done. "Thank God!"

He dismounted, approached her slowly. "You're all right, then, you and the boy?" he asked. A young soldier came, took the bay's reins, and led the animal away to be watered, fed, and groomed.

She nodded and dashed at her wet face with the back of one hand. She looked as though she wanted to fling herself into his arms, but she didn't. She just stood there, as if she'd been frozen, watching him. Consuming him with her eyes.

"Trace and Zachary are both fine," he said when he saw both Bridget and Christy coming toward him.

"Your mill?" Skye managed. "The house?"

"Gone," Jake said, careful to keep his distance.

Christy and Bridget reached them, and he nodded a greeting, told them their homes and husbands were safe. Relieved but obviously still very concerned about Skye, they returned to the barracks, casting anxious glances back over their shoulders as they went.

"Oh, Jake," Skye whispered. "I'm so sorry."

How he wanted to hold her, and be held by her, but he didn't dare let himself be taken in again. She was a liar, no better than Amanda; she'd sold him out for God only knew what reason, maybe spite, maybe just the sport of it. He'd thought she was so different, and he'd clearly been wrong. Well, he was a lousy judge of women, he'd proven that to his own satisfaction, and the best he could do was cut his losses and run.

"There's a Mr. Thompson in town looking for you," he said, as coolly as if he were speaking to a stranger. "He's with the railroad. Says you sold them your timber."

She swallowed, blinked once. Sniffled. She nodded again. "That's true. When you wouldn't accept it, I—"

He held up one hand. "Stop," he said. "I don't want to hear anything more."

She braced up and took a step toward him. "Well, you're going to listen to me all the same, Jake Vigil!" she exclaimed.

Jake looked nervously around, saw that life at Fort Grant was going on pretty much as usual. Soldiers were drilling, guards were patrolling the parapets, a small detachment was preparing to ride, probably headed up to Primrose Creek to relieve the troops already there. "What is there to say?" he hissed. "You tricked me, and by God, I won't take that from anybody. Especially not my own wife!"

She had her hands on her hips by then, and there was an obstinate snap in her eyes. "You're leaving something out," she retorted fiercely. "After we were married, I offered to *give* you all the timber you needed. And you turned me down! Jake, don't you see, I had to do something to keep the railroad from moving in and taking—"

He moved in until his nose was less than an inch from hers. "Enough!" he growled. "I won't hear any of your excuses!"

"You were about to lose everything you had, everything you'd worked for! The money from the sale to the railroad—"

"*Damn* the railroad *and* its money! I would have thought of something!"

Out of the corner of one eye, Jake saw a flash of pale hair and a bit of blue calico. "If you two want to have a showdown," said Bridget Qualtrough, with what amounted to towering dignity though she was a small woman, "that's certainly your business. But perhaps you wouldn't mind fighting it out in private?"

Skye reddened, and Jake felt a little ashamed himself, even though he was still convinced that he was right. He stood there, his breath coming in deep, furious gasps, and tried to calm down. That took a while, and when he thought he could trust himself not to commence bellowing again, he took his wife loosely by the elbow and, after a moment's assessment of their surroundings, hustled her toward the chapel. Bridget, having made her intercession on behalf of the McQuarry family honor, retreated, but only so far as the wooden sidewalk, where she watched them with narrowed eyes, reminding Jake of a mother hen braced to defend a wayward chick.

The small church was blessedly empty, though the door was open to a spring freeze, and Jake seated Skye on a rear pew before sitting down beside her. Maybe it was the place, maybe it was that he'd had a chance to collect the scattered fragments of his temper, but Jake felt steadier and infinitely sadder.

"I've got nothing left to offer you," he said gruffly. "No trust. No house, no business, no money."

She touched his arm, though tentatively. "We have

each other," she said. "We have Hank. And we have the land at Primrose Creek. We'll build a house and a barn and start over."

He merely shook his head.

"What about Hank?" she asked in a wretched whisper. "I promised him I'd be his mother."

"He can spend as much time with you as he wants." Jake thrust a hand through his hair and gazed at the stone floor of the little chapel, despondent.

"This is wrong," she said.

He laced his fingers together, looked briefly at the plain wooden cross affixed to the wall behind the rough-hewn pulpit. "I'm not sure how I'm going to manage it, but I will get another mill up and running, and when that happens, you and I will have a proper divorce. I'll see that you're provided for."

"I don't want your money!" she cried. She seemed to be simmering, like a pot forgotten on a hot stove, ready to rattle its lid. "Jake Vigil, you're a damn fool. I'm your wife. I'm trying to be a mother to Hank. My place is beside you, no matter what."

"You lied."

"I *didn't* lie. I simply failed to tell you—"

He held up a hand to silence her. "Please," he said. "No more."

She subsided then and sat still beside him, tears slipping down her cheeks, teeth sunk into her lower lip in what was probably an effort to regain control.

He stood. "I'd best go and speak to the boy," he said.

She didn't answer.

Before he left the chapel, he bent and kissed the top of her head in what they both knew was a gesture of farewell.

*   *   *

It was hard enough losing Jake. Losing Hank was beyond difficult. As little time as they'd managed to spend together, Skye and the boy had formed a bond, and parting was like tearing off skin.

They faced each other the next morning, woman and child, just inside the gates of Fort Grant. Jake had already loaded the wagon and climbed aboard; he was staring straight ahead, waiting for his son to join him. Together, they'd make a life that excluded Skye.

"I figure you would have made a pretty good ma," Hank said.

Skye's throat ached, and tears throbbed behind her eyes. "I'd like to go on being your friend, if that's all right with you," she managed to say. Then, with a sniffle, she rubbed her cheek with the heel of one palm.

Hank took a manful step forward and extended his little hand, as if to seal the bargain. "Friends," he said.

Skye nodded. She wanted to sweep Hank up in her arms and hold him close, if only for a moment, but she knew such a public display would embarrass him, so she didn't. "Look after your father," she said, just as he would have turned to hurry away toward the wagon.

Hank rolled his eyes in a way that might have been comical if Skye hadn't had a broken heart to deal with just then. "I don't see how I'm going to get much else done," he told her. With that, he turned and ran off to scramble up over the tailgate of Jake's wagon, nimble as a monkey.

Jake was watching Skye, and as he released the brake lever with one booted foot, he lifted a hand. Too soon, they'd be gone, out of sight.

Skye supposed she ought to wave back, but the truth

was, she didn't have the strength to do even that much. So she just stood there, dying inside, hands locked together behind her back, looking on as the only man she had ever loved, the only man she ever *would* love, drove himself and his son right out of her life.

When the gates finally closed behind that wagon, shutting Skye off from all her dreams, Bridget stepped up beside her and slipped an arm around her waist. She and Bridget had things to settle—the matter of the McQuarry secret, primarily—but just then she needed her sister. What would she have done, through all the difficulties, without Bridget?

"Come along," Bridget said gently. "I'm afraid there's something else we need to talk about."

Skye felt a swift rush of dread.

Bridget pulled her close against her side for a moment. "Megan's gone."

Skye stared. "What?"

"A freight wagon left the fort this morning for Virginia City, supposedly empty except for several canvas tarps. We think Megan was hiding under them."

"But surely she wouldn't do something like that— worry us this way—"

Bridget was steering her toward the barracks. "She left a note," she said. "Christy's in a state, and even Caney's all het up. We've got to put our heads together and work out what to do."

In the end, there was nothing they could do. Megan had left without knowing that the four of them were sisters, not cousins. According to her letter, she would be a famous stage actress before her next birthday. Skye was to keep the mare, Speckles, until she sent for it.

"Perhaps Zachary and Trace could find her," Bridget said.

Christy straightened her spine and shook her head. Her baby, Joseph, was nursing at her breast, modestly covered by a shawl borrowed from Bridget. "She's a McQuarry," she said. "We have to let her go. If we're lucky, she'll find her way back to us when she's ready."

Chapter
7

"I don't much like livin' at the saloon," Hank told Skye. "That's why I spend so much time out here." They were sitting side-by-side on a log, facing Primrose Creek, fishing for trout. It had been a month since the fire, and the small community was, if anything, more active than ever before. The railroad had brought in a crew of its own to harvest trees on Skye's land, and, according to Trace, Jake had secured a loan from somewhere and bought a new steam-powered saw, which ran at full tilt, day and night, filling the air with the screech of progress and the lingering scent of sawdust.

There had been no word from Megan.

Skye squinted against the bright sunlight winking on the moving surface of the creek and brought her mind back to the idea of Jake and Hank living above Primrose Creek's one remaining saloon. That, she decided, was just plain ironic. Neither Skye, Bridget, nor Christy had any inclination to approach the boy's mother, although Caney wasn't so reticent.

"I've got a thing or two I want to say to that woman," she'd announced after a conference on the matter.

Bridget, in the meantime, had advised Skye not to chase after Jake but to let him work things through in his own mind. She'd promised that he'd come to his senses in good time and realize that even if she had bungled things terribly, she'd only been trying to help him. So far, though, he showed no signs of doing so, and Skye hated knowing that her husband slept in that place every night. It was no comfort whatsoever that he theoretically shared quarters with his son, since Hank did indeed spend most of his time at Bridget and Trace's place, bunking in with Noah.

To complicate things further, Skye's monthly was late, and she suspected that she was carrying a child. In fact, she was certain of it. While she'd kept the news a secret from everyone so far, there would be no hiding the truth when five or six months had passed. Already, both Bridget and Caney were beginning to watch her, out of the corners of their eyes, as though they thought she would sprout something.

"I wish we could all live together, like we did before the fire," Hank said, and Skye realized how long she'd left the conversation hanging while she went woolgathering. She'd had a very difficult time concentrating on anything since her separation from Jake, though Megan's sudden flight worried her mightily. How *could* she have left without even saying good-bye?

And then there was Granddaddy's deception. It was almost more than a body could take in.

"I wish we could, too," she said sadly. Jake was an

honorable man; he would probably insist on a reconcil-
iation once he learned that he was going to be a father
again, but she didn't want him to share her life out of a
sense of obligation. And she was terribly afraid she
wouldn't have the strength to refuse him, even on those
terms, because she loved him so much. Her heart
throbbed like a bad tooth; she couldn't eat, she couldn't
sleep. All she could do was wait, it seemed. Wait and—
following Caney's brisk advice to "make herself useful"—fish for rainbow trout.

"Pa asked me about you," Hank persisted. "Just this
morning." A tug on his fishing line distracted him for a
few moments, then he went on. "He said he hasn't seen
you riding the bay stallion since you brought it back
from Fort Grant, and he wondered if you'd sold it."

Skye's disappointment was abject—how like a man
to be more concerned with a stallion than with his own
wife—but she managed to hide her reaction because she
got a fish on the line just then, a fat, gleaming trout, and
it put up a respectable tussle before allowing itself to be
caught. "You tell him I mean to breed the stallion to a
few of Trace and Bridget's mares. Once they foal, I'll
probably turn him loose. The stallion, I mean."

Hank was staring at her. "You'd do that? Let the stallion go? Let him be wild again?"

She smiled wistfully, baited her hook, and threw her
line back into the water. "Sure. He wasn't really mine. I
just borrowed him for a while." She glanced behind her
at the sprawling stands of timber, even now being
thinned by the railroad's logging crew. "Sort of the way
we borrow trees from the earth. If it's done right, the
ones remaining thrive because they're getting more sunlight and water—more elbow room, you might say."

Hank's smile was bright and sudden. "We'll see him again, though, won't we? The bay?"

"Sure," Skye answered. "Every time we look at his colts and fillies, there he'll be, big as life." And every time she looked at her baby, she thought to herself, son or daughter, there Jake would be, in the child, looking back at her. The prospect was at once a joy and a sorrow.

In the near distance, Skye heard the sound of an approaching team and wagon, and she was grateful for the distraction. She drew in her line, set her pole aside, and turned, shading her eyes from the blazing summer sun, to watch as the rig came over the knoll into the meadow where she meant to build her house.

The wagon was drawn by six mules, and though Malcolm Hicks, Caney's beau, was at the reins, Jake Vigil rode along on the seat beside him.

Skye stood her ground, folded her arms, and waited as her estranged husband jumped down from the high wagon box and came striding toward her.

He didn't speak up right away but simply looked at her, revealing absolutely nothing of his feelings—if he had any. She couldn't rightly tell whether he did or not, since he generally guarded his emotions as fiercely as a troll guarded a bridge.

"What do you want?" she was finally forced to ask. She figured they'd still have been standing there when the snows came, staring at each other, if she hadn't broken the silence.

"I've missed you," Jake confessed, but he took his time about it. He hooked his thumbs under the snaps of his suspenders.

Skye was taken aback, afraid to hope that Bridget

had been right, that the wait was over and Jake Vigil had at last realized where he belonged. With her and with Hank, right here on the banks of Primrose Creek.

She gestured weakly toward the wagon, where Mr. Hicks waited, one scarred but rapidly healing arm resting against his side. The rig was stacked high with freshly planed planks. "I didn't order any lumber."

Jake smiled. "Yes," he said, "you did. I just refused to sell it to you, remember?" He spotted his son, standing close by and listening intently. "Hullo, Hank. How about giving Malcolm a hand with the team?"

Fairly radiating curiosity, Hank obeyed. When he was out of earshot, Jake went on. "I haven't been able to think straight since we talked at Fort Grant," he began.

She put her hands on her hips. "Since *you* talked, you mean. You weren't doing much listening, as I recall."

He chuckled ruefully and shook his head. "No, I guess I wasn't. The point is, I've tried living without you, and I've been just plain miserable every moment of that time. I think about you at night, and I think about you in the morning, and all the time in between. You're the woman I want to spend my life with—I guess I knew that way back when we danced that night at the Community Hall, though I couldn't bring myself to take the chance." He stopped, drew a deep breath, and let it out slowly. "I've done a lot of thinking these past few weeks, Mrs. Vigil. I never loved Amanda, and I never loved Christy, either. Fact is, I didn't know what love was until I met you. I'm asking you to give me another chance, Skye. It's that simple."

Skye's heart had swollen to fill her throat. Words

were impossible, but tears sprang to her eyes, telling him far more than she would have chosen to reveal in an hour of talk.

Jake came near enough to take her shoulders in his big hands. "This is the first of the lumber we'll need to build our house," he said. "All you have to do is say it's all right for Hank and me to live here with you."

She swallowed painfully. "You mean—?"

He nodded. "Yes," he said. "If you'll have us."

She threw her arms around his neck, and he laughed aloud and spun her around in a dizzying circle before setting her on the ground again and kissing her soundly. When she surfaced, she heard Mr. Hicks and Hank cheering like spectators watching a sack race. She felt a little like cheering herself.

"I love you, Jake," she said, and her eyes filled again.

He brushed her mouth with his. "Thank God for that," he replied.

She took his hand, led him a little way down the creek bank, filled with sweet nervousness. "There's something I need to tell you."

He arched an eyebrow, and his expression was wary. "What?"

"You're going to be a father," she said. "Again."

"You're sure?" He nearly whispered the words.

"Pretty sure," she replied with a nod. She knew her body, knew its flows and rhythms, and there was a child growing inside her. Jake's child, and her own.

For a long moment, Jake just stood there, looking as though he'd been pole-axed. Then he let out such a shout of jubilation that Skye nearly lost her balance and fell right into the creek. He lifted her up again, this time putting one arm under her knees with the other supporting her back, and carried her up the bank and through the tall grass like a prize taken in battle.

"My wife," he told Malcolm and Hank in a voice that seemed to echo off the Sierras themselves, "is going to have a baby!"

Malcolm grinned at the announcement. Hank was beaming, and his little chest seemed to have expanded, he looked so puffed up. Skye remembered their conversation at Jake's, when she'd told him there would be babies coming and she'd need lots of help from him to look after them.

Jake kissed Skye's ear and set her gently on her feet. Then he walked over to Hank and sat on his haunches so that their eyes met, his and the boy's. "This is all right with you, isn't it?" he asked.

Hank's freckled face was shining. Since he'd come to Primrose Creek, he'd filled out considerably, and with every passing day he seemed to have more confidence in the future and in other people. No doubt, he was more certain of Jake than anybody else, which was as it should have been. "I'll teach him to spit," he said. "Unless he's a girl. Girls don't spit."

Jake chuckled and ruffled Hank's hair. "Well, most of them don't, anyway," he replied. He stood and turned to face Skye. "Now, Mrs. Vigil," he said, "perhaps you wouldn't mind telling us just where you'd like this house of ours to sit and all like that."

"I won't have a mansion," she warned. Her heart was singing, and if she hadn't been struggling so hard to hold on to her dignity, she would have danced around the meadow in great leaps of joy, with both arms outspread and her face raised to the blue, blue sky.

He laughed. "Don't worry," he said. "Right now, I couldn't afford a chicken coop, not on my own, anyhow."

"But you're willing to live here with me?" She could hardly believe her ears, even though this was just what Bridget had predicted, back at Fort Grant and several times since. And Bridget was right about most things, whether the rest of the family liked to admit it or not. "You and Hank?"

"I'm more than willing," Jake replied hoarsely, facing her again and cupping her elbows in his hands. "I love you," he repeated.

She knew her eyes were twinkling with mischief. "So you say, Mr. Vigil," she teased. "So you say. But I'm going to need proof."

He reddened delightfully, cleared his throat, and glanced back at Mr. Hicks and Hank, who were busy with the team and wagon. While Mr. Hicks began unloading lumber, whistling as he worked, Hank unhitched the horses and led them, one by one, down to the stream.

"Relax," Skye whispered, running the tip of one index finger down the front of his shirt, bumping over each button. "I can wait until tonight. But no longer than that, Mr. Vigil. Not one minute longer than that."

He laughed. "I'm persuaded, Mrs. Vigil," he replied. And then he kissed her again.

One month later
Room 11, the Comstock Hotel
Virginia City, Nevada

"You can't seriously expect to hear anything," Skye said when Jake laid his head on her bare belly. "It's far too early."

He planted a smacking kiss where his ear had been, eliciting a reluctant, croonlike groan from his bride. Although they'd been married two months by that time, they had just managed to get away for a honeymoon. They'd arrived in Virginia City that afternoon by wagon, and so far they hadn't even been outside the room to eat.

"When our baby makes a sound, I want to be there to hear it," Jake said, sitting up in the well-rumpled linens of the bed. They were just across the street from Virginia City's famous Opera House, and Jake had promised they would see at least one performance before they went home to Primrose Creek.

So far, it seemed to Skye, they'd been the ones doing all the performing, she and Jake. The strange thing was, every time they made love, it was better than the time before; it didn't seem possible, but there it was.

Skye stretched languidly and wound a finger in a lock of Jake's hair. She hoped their daughters would have his hair; her own was straight as a yardstick. "This baby will make plenty of sounds after she's born," she said. "Are you going to be there to hear that, too?"

He laughed. "Of course," he said. "When I'm not busy providing for my wife and growing family, that is." Mischievously, he began kissing her belly again.

Skye whimpered. "Jake—"

"Mmmm?"

She trembled. "I'm hungry, and you promised to take me to the Opera House."

He ran the tip of his tongue along a strategic path. "So I did. And I will. After—"

"Not after," she said, but already her breath was quickening and her hips were rising and falling in that old, all-too-familiar rhythm. "Now."

"After," he murmured.

Skye gasped. "After," she cried.

They had steaks for dinner in the hotel's fancy dining room and then crossed the busy, rutted street to the Opera House. According to the bill posted beside the ticket booth, there was an orchestra on hand to accompany a famous soprano named Nellie Baker. While Skye had never heard of the woman, she was delighted to be there nonetheless.

Inside, they found and took their seats, programs in hand. The interior of the theater was anything but rustic; the place was awash in gilt and velvet, and there were brass reflectors behind the gas footlights and paintings right on the walls themselves, just like the frescoes in Italy.

Skye was practically giddy with happiness—first the long, poignantly passionate hours alone with Jake in their room, then that delicious dinner, and now an evening of culture. At least, that was what Christy called it. Christy loved living at Primrose Creek as much as any of them, but she did tend to bemoan the lack of "genteel pursuits."

Skye was wearing a special dress, a lightweight red wool with black velvet at the collar and cuffs, made just for her and just for this occasion by Bridget and Caney. She was carrying a child, and the man she loved was beside her, loving her back. She hadn't known it was possible to have so much and wondered if it might be dangerous. Might anger the fates—

Jake must have been watching her face, for he took her chin lightly between his thumb and forefinger and scolded. "What's this? Did I see a shadow in those beautiful eyes, just for a moment there?"

She smiled, and the seats around them continued to fill with all manner of fascinating people, saddle bums and millionaires, saints and sinners, matrons and fancy women. "I was hoping we might see Megan," she admitted. "Do you think she's already moved on?"

He brushed her forehead with his lips. "Maybe."

"She doesn't know—"

He smoothed a tendril of hair against her temple. "She'll come back when she's ready, Skye," he said. "You have to believe that."

She sighed and nodded.

He touched the tip of her nose. The gesture was an intimate one—they might have been alone, for the way it affected Skye—and infinitely tender. "Things always change," he reminded her quietly. "We'll make it, though. The whole lot of us—McQuarrys and Qualtroughs, Shaws and Vigils."

The gaslights went down just then, but Skye continued to gaze at her husband, and she knew her eyes were shining. "I love you so much," she said.

"You're just saying that because you mean it," he replied.

The orchestra tuned up, and then the soprano came onstage, a tall, rotund woman, drenched in feathers and beads. She sang for an hour, and although Skye had heard better voices in the church choir, her gaze barely strayed from the woman throughout the evening. For all her bulk and for all her shortcomings as a singer, Nellie Baker conveyed high emotion in even the smallest gesture, and by the time she got to her closing number, a forlorn and sentimental song about a poor granny on the rocky shores of Ireland, vainly watching the sea for the return of her fishermen sons and grandsons, Skye was reduced to tears.

Jake handed Skye his handkerchief, and she dabbed delicately at her eyes, while the grizzled miner in the other seat blew his nose loudly into a bandanna plucked from his shirt pocket.

"That was *lovely,*" Skye sighed when the applause had ended and the lights were turned up again. "Do you think she knows Megan? The two of them being in show business and all?"

Jake grinned, raised her hand to his mouth, and kissed her knuckles. Then he laughed and pulled her to her feet. "Come on, Mrs. Vigil. We'll go backstage and ask. Then we'll take ourselves a walk in the moonlight."

No one in the cast of that evening's production knew of anyone named Megan McQuarry, and though Skye was disappointed, she wasn't surprised. For all she knew, her cousin—sister—had changed her name.

Skye and Jake made their way outside, through the crowds of vociferous theatergoers. Opinions simmered in the air and mingled with tinny piano music from the many saloons.

Skye and Jake walked away from the main street, where gambling houses and brothels, hotels, and other such places dominated, down a hill, and into a church-yard. From there, they could look out over the rough, bare grandeur of the valley. Virginia City itself had sprung up virtually overnight when the Comstock Lode was discovered; there was no timber for miles. Had it not been for the tons of high-grade silver buried quite literally beneath the streets of the town, it was doubtful that anyone would have chosen to settle there.

Skye was having a wonderful time, more than wonderful, but she would be glad to get back to Primrose Creek, back to the trees and the stream, the sizable cabin Jake had built, mostly with his own hands. Trace and Zachary had helped a great deal, of course, and so had Malcolm Hicks, but it was Jake who worked far into the night, time after time, even after a full day at the mill.

He interlocked his fingers with hers and kissed the knuckles. "I'm glad we don't live here," he said.

She laughed. "I was just thinking along those same lines."

"We can go home tomorrow, if that's what you want." He pulled her gently against him and kissed the top of her head. He smelled of good tobacco, soap, and that unique scent that was his alone.

She looked up at him. "You hated that soprano," she accused, but she was smiling.

"Not personally." He grinned. "I wasn't that crazy about her voice, it's true, but I'm willing to undergo any sort of torture if it makes you happy. Such is my love for my bride."

She rolled her eyes. "Her voice wasn't that bad. That last song was very touching."

"That last song was stupid," he said. Skye was discovering that Jake said what he thought most times, straight out. She didn't mind, though; she was used to the McQuarrys.

He smoothed a tendril of hair back from her forehead. "Did you enjoy yourself tonight?" he asked with a tenderness that made her heart soar out over the valley like a bird taking wing. "That's all that really matters."

"I enjoyed myself," she said, cocking her head to one side, and touched the cleft in his chin with a fingertip. "But I'd rather enjoy you."

He laughed aloud, and kissed her smartly. "Insatiable wench," he said.

"I've never denied it," she replied, and he laughed again.

They turned and saw the lights of Virginia City looming above them. Then, arm-in-arm, they began the climb together.

Megan

For all my loyal readers
with gratitude and love

Chapter

1

Primrose Creek, Nevada
June 1870

Dust billowed around the stagecoach as Megan McQuarry stepped down, grasping the skirts of her black-and-white striped silk dress in one hand. She'd been traveling for several endless, bone-jolting days, but she'd taken care with her appearance all along the way. She'd washed whenever the opportunity arose, which was seldom enough, and done her best to keep her auburn hair tidy and her hat firmly affixed, at just the proper angle. She was penniless, a miserable failure, with nothing but a trunk full of missed cues and frayed dreams to show for two years on her own, but she still had the formidable McQuarry pride.

She had returned to Primrose Creek in defeat, there was no denying that, but not without a certain bittersweet sense of homecoming. Coming back meant seeing her sister Christy again, after all, and her two cousins, Bridget and Skye. They'd had the good sense to stay put, Christy and the others, and now they had homes, husbands, children. Their lives were busy and full, bright with color and passion; she knew that from the letters Skye had written while she was away, always pleading with her to return to Primrose Creek.

She sighed and squared her aching shoulders, bracing herself for what lay ahead. Her kin would welcome her, she knew; they'd enfold her in laughter and love, include her in their doings, defend her fiercely against the inevitable snubs and gossip her return would arouse. But they would be angry, too, and confused, for she had left suddenly, leaving behind only a brief note of explanation.

She shaded her eyes as she looked up at the coach driver, who was unstrapping her secondhand trunk and getting ready to toss it down at her feet. She hoped he wouldn't expect any sort of recompense, because she'd used the last of her funds the day before, to purchase a bowl of stew at a way station. She hadn't eaten since.

"Be careful with that, please," she said, indicating the trunk. *It's all I have.* And it was. She'd long since sold her share of the prime timber- and grassland left to the four McQuarry women to some rancher, through a banker and a lawyer, and now she would be the poor relation, beholden for every bite of bread and bolt of calico she got until the day she went to her final rest. If only that were the worst of it, she thought.

"Yes, ma'am," the driver answered, and let the trunk fall with an unceremonious clunk onto the wooden sidewalk, raising grit from between the boards. Megan would have taken off some of the fellow's hide if she hadn't been so weary, so hungry, and so utterly disconsolate.

She was just reaching for the trunk's battered handle, meaning to drag the monstrosity across the road to her brother-in-law's office—Zachary Shaw was the town marshal—when a large leather-gloved hand eased her own aside. She looked up, expecting to see Zachary, or perhaps Trace Qualtrough, Bridget's husband, or Jake Vigil, who had married Skye around the time of Megan's flight. Instead, she found herself gazing into a stranger's face; a man with tanned skin, wheat-colored hair, and periwinkle-blue eyes grinned down at her. His teeth were sturdy and white as a new snowfall gleaming under morning sunlight.

He tugged at the brim of his weathered leather hat. "You planning to stay on here at Primrose Creek, ma'am? I do hope you aren't just passing through—that would be a sore disappointment."

Megan was used to sweet-talking men, God knew, and good-looking ones, too, but there was something about this one that caused her breath to catch as surely as if she'd just tumbled headfirst into an icc-cold mountain stream. All her senses, dulled by trouble and the long trip from San Francisco, leaped instantly to life, and she knew by looking into the man's eyes that he'd taken note of her reactions to him, and been pleased.

She was furious, with him and with herself. If there was one thing she didn't need, it was a man, however intriguing and fair to look upon that man might happen to be. "Thank you," she said stiffly, "but I'm sure my brother-in-law will collect my baggage—"

The stranger looked around pointedly. "I don't see anybody headed this way," he observed in a cheerful tone of voice. "I'm Webb Stratton, just in case you're worried that we haven't had a proper introduction."

The name slammed into Megan's middle like a barrel rolling downhill. She waited to regain her equilibrium, then put out a slightly tremulous hand. "Megan McQuarry," she said, by reflex. It was nearly too much to bear, that this man of all people should be the first person she encountered upon her homecoming. She had to admit there was a certain ironic justice in it, though.

His grin broadened in apparent recognition, and he pumped her hand, failing to notice, it would seem, that all the blood had drained from her face and she was unsteady on her feet. Mr. Stratton had bought her land, the land she should never, *ever* have sold. She cringed to think what Granddaddy would have said about such a betrayal.

"Well, now, Miss McQuarry," said Mr. Stratton, still at ease and still gripping her hand. Megan felt a grudging gratitude, for between her empty stomach and her many regrets, she wasn't entirely sure she could stand on her own. "I know your family. They're neighbors of mine."

A flush climbed Megan's cheeks. Skye, always her closest friend as well as her beloved cousin, was likely to be understanding where Megan's many mistakes were concerned, but Bridget and Christy would have an opinion or two when it came to the sale of the land. Especially when they found out how she'd been hoodwinked by a no-good man. She opened her mouth, closed it again.

"My wagon's right over there," Mr. Stratton said, nodding to indicate the end of the street. Only then did he release her hand, and she marveled that she hadn't pulled away long since. "I'd be happy to drive you and your baggage out to Primrose Creek."

She was not the sort of woman who accepted favors from men she had never met before, but Mr. Stratton wasn't exactly a stranger, and Primrose Creek certainly wasn't San Francisco. "Very well," she said. "Thank you."

She had time to consider the rashness of her decision while Mr. Stratton went to fetch the wagon. It was drawn by two well-bred paint geldings, Megan noted as she watched him approach; as did everyone else in her family, she appreciated fine horseflesh.

Stratton jumped easily to the ground, after setting the brake lever with a thrust of one leg, and Megan's attention shifted back to him, taking in his tall frame, broad shoulders, and cattleman's garb of denim trousers, chambray shirt, and buckskin vest. His hat was as worn as his boots, and, unlike most of the men Megan knew, he did not carry a gun.

Megan straightened her spine and studiously ignored the curious looks coming at her from all directions. She could almost hear the speculations—*Isn't that the McQuarry girl? The one who ran away to become an actress? She has her share of brass, doesn't she, coming back here, expecting to live among decent people, just as if nothing had happened . . .*

The sound of her trunk landing in the rear of Mr. Stratton's wagon brought her back to the present moment with a snap. He tugged his hat brim in a cordial greeting to two plump matrons passing by on the sidewalk. "Last I heard," he remarked, "it was considered impolite to stare." Caught, the women puffed their bosoms like prairie hens and trundled away. She could almost see their feathers bristling.

Megan couldn't help smiling with amusement, as tired and discouraged as she was. Webb—*Webb?*—was grinning again as he handed her up into the wagon box. He rounded the buckboard, climbed up beside her, took the reins in his hands, and released the brake lever. The rig lurched forward.

"Seems you're the topic of some serious speculation," he observed dryly as they reached the end of the street and left the busy little town behind for the timbered countryside.

Megan heaved a soft sigh. Her smile had already slipped away, and her hands were knotted in her lap, fingers tangled in the strings of her empty handbag. "Surely you've realized, Mr. Stratton—"

"Webb," he interrupted kindly.

"Webb," Megan conceded, with some impatience. She started again. "Surely you've realized that the land you bought last year was mine."

He regarded the road thoughtfully, though Megan suspected he could have made the journey over that track in a sound sleep. "Well," he allowed, after some time, "yes. I reckon I figured that out right away." He glanced at her, sidelong, and a sweet shiver went through her. "Does it matter?"

She sat up even straighter and raised her chin. "I did not like parting with my property," she said stiffly. "Circumstances demanded that I do so." That wasn't his fault, of course, but knowing it didn't change the way she felt. "Perhaps we could work out terms of some sort, and I could buy it back."

Again, he took the time to consider her words. It

annoyed her; he was well aware that she was in suspense—she could see that in his eyes—but apparently he didn't mind letting her squirm awhile. "Couldn't do that," he said finally. "I built myself a house there. A good barn and corral, too."

Megan bit her upper lip and willed the hot tears stinging behind her eyes to recede. It was going to kill her to see someone else living on her share of Granddaddy's bequest, but she had no one to thank but herself. She'd been so gullible, believing Davy Trent's pretty promises the way she had, and she was more ashamed of her brief association with that thieving polecat than anything she'd ever done. She learned some valuable lessons, but they'd come at a high price.

McQuarry that she was, the land as much a part of her as her pulse and the marrow of her bones, she had nonetheless made the sale, handed over the profits so that she and Davy could buy a small ranch near Stockton and be married. Instead, he'd swindled her, left her alone and humiliated, with barely a penny to her name.

"They expecting you? Your people, I mean?" Webb's voice was gentle and quiet, and the teasing light that had been lurking in his eyes was gone.

She swallowed hard, shook her head. "It'll be a surprise, I think," she said. "My showing up now, I mean."

He took off his hat, replaced it again. The gesture reminded Megan of her granddaddy, Gideon McQuarry. He'd had the same habit; it was a sign that he was thinking. "They'll be glad to see you, you know," Webb ventured.

Megan bit her lip for a moment, in order to recover a little. "They'll take me in," she said, very softly. It didn't seem necessary to point out that taking somebody in was a world away from welcoming them. Forgiving them.

"You were an actress," he said, with no inflection at all.

She sat up a little straighter, shot him a fiery glance. "Yes."

"What sort of roles did you play?"

She was taken aback by the question. There was no mockery in his tone or manner, and nothing to indicate that he considered her loose by virtue of her profession, as many men did. "Shakespearean, mostly," she allowed. "Ophelia. Kate in *The Taming of the Shrew.*"

He chuckled. "I don't see you as Ophelia. Just by looking at you, I'd say you weren't the type to lose your mind over a man. Any man. Now, the part of Kate, on the other hand—I can imagine that right enough."

Megan was amazed, not so much by his statements—frank to the point of being downright forward though they were—as by his knowledge of the Bard's plays. In her experience, most cowboys found them incomprehensible, if they paid any notice at all. Somewhat haltingly, she told him how she'd favored the role of Ophelia, simply because of the challenge it represented, being so at variance with her own nature. She even admitted that she would miss the stage.

Webb listened and nodded once or twice, but he offered no further comment. Shortly thereafter, the rooftop of Christy and Zachary's house came into view. Once an abandoned Indian lodge, with leaky animal hides for a roof, it had been renovated into one of the finest places around, and it was a very happy place, according to Skye's newsy letters. Joseph, Megan's nephew, was two already, and his baby sister, Margaret, was approaching her first birthday.

Megan yearned to lay eyes on those children, to feel Christy's arms around her, to be a part of the clan once again. She wished she'd never left home in the first place, of course, but hindsight was always clear as creek water. Besides, she'd learned a great deal during her brief career, learned to project confidence even when she was terrified. And God knew, she'd learned something about men—specifically Davy Trent.

Christy came out into the dooryard, hearing the noise of the wagon, shading her eyes from the late-morning sunshine. Caney—dear Caney—was soon beside her, gazing their way, but Megan could tell nothing of her mood from her countenance. Caney Blue, a black woman, had worked for Gideon and Rebecca McQuarry for many years. When the farm in Virginia's Shenandoah Valley was sold for taxes after the war, and Megan and Christy, fresh from England, had set out to claim their one-quarter shares of a twenty-five hundred-acre tract known as Primrose Creek, Caney had come along.

Christy's face kindled with joy as she recognized her sister. She clapped one hand over her mouth, caught up her skirts with the other, and ran toward the wagon, limber as a girl. "Megan!" she cried.

Megan was down from the wagon box and flinging herself into Christy's arms within the space of a heartbeat. They clung to each other, the pair of sisters, laughing and crying, while Caney stood back, smiling. Webb Stratton unloaded the trunk without a word and carried it into the house.

"Look at you!" Christy cried, beaming, as she

gripped Megan's upper arms in both hands and held her away. "You're beautiful!"

Megan didn't feel beautiful, she felt broken and soiled, used and discarded, and her throat was clogged with emotion. She couldn't speak but merely hugged Christy again, hard.

Webb came out of the house again, climbed back into his buckboard.

"Thank you," Christy told him, as warmly as if he'd gone out and searched the world for Megan and then brought her back to Primrose Creek like a prodigal daughter. "Oh, thank you."

He merely nodded, touched Megan lightly with that wildflower-blue gaze of his, and set the team in motion again, the buckboard jostling along the high grassy bank overlooking the sparkling creek.

"Where on earth have you been?" Christy demanded good-naturedly, linking her arm with Megan's and steering her toward the house. In the doorway, a little boy with bright blond hair looked on, a tiny dark-haired girl at his side.

"I'd like to know that myself," Caney put in, keeping pace. Her beautiful dark brown eyes had narrowed slightly.

So Skye had kept her promise, Megan thought, and never divulged her whereabouts. Perhaps she hadn't even told the family she was receiving an occasional letter from the McQuarry-gone-astray.

"Just about everywhere," Megan admitted, longing for sleep and tea and a nice, hot bath. Tears of happiness slipped down her cheeks as she reached the children and knelt before them, heedless of her skirts. They studied her curiously, Joseph his father in miniature,

Margaret a re-creation of Christy, with a chubby fore-finger caught in her mouth. "I'm your Aunt Megan," she said.

Joseph put out his hand in solemn greeting, small as he was, and Megan shook it. Margaret clung to her brother's shirt and edged shyly backward, out of reach.

Megan smiled and got to her feet.

Christy slipped an arm around her waist, and they entered the cool, fragrant interior of the house. It was full of light, and the floors shone with wax. Curtains danced at the open windows, and framed watercolors, probably Christy's own work, graced the walls. Hard to believe it was the same place, Megan thought, where they'd made their meals in a fire pit and slept on bales of hay shoved together for beds, those first weeks after their arrival at Primrose Creek several years before.

"I see you've met Webb Stratton," Christy said, her tone a shade less genial as she went to the wood box next to the shining cookstove and began feeding the fire to heat water for tea. Suddenly, there was a snappish tension in the air, like the metallic charge that precedes a violent storm. Perhaps Skye hadn't betrayed Megan's confidences, but the family couldn't help knowing that she'd done the unthinkable and sold a portion of the land. They would hold that against her, as they would the worry she had caused them.

"Yes," Megan replied, with a half-hearted stab at dignity. She was unpinning her hat, removing it, setting it aside atop a sturdy pinewood table. No doubt Trace had built that piece of furniture, as he had many others, in his workshop across the creek. He and Bridget had made their home in a sprawling log house, and, at last report, they'd had four children, counting Noah, Bridget's son by her first marriage.

Joseph and Margaret were hovering at a safe distance, watching Megan as though they expected her to turn a back flip or sprout wings and fly around the room. She smiled at them before taking a chair at the round oak table where the family took their meals.

"Come along with Caney, now," Caney said, gathering the children and shooing them toward one of the bedrooms. "Last time I looked, you two had left your toys scattered from here to kingdom come." No fool, Caney. She'd probably sensed the shift in the emotional weather even before Christy and Megan had.

"We were surprised," Christy said, with a false brightness that was all too familiar to Megan, busying herself at the stove, "when you sold your share of the land to a complete stranger."

Megan twisted her fingers together. "I'm sorry," she said.

"Sorry," Christy echoed. She stood in profile, high color in her cheeks, her spine straight as a store-bought hoe handle. "You're *sorry.*"

Megan sighed. She had expected just such a reception, but that didn't make the confrontation any easier. "Yes," she said wearily.

Christy slammed the tea kettle down hard on the gleaming surface of her huge iron and chrome cookstove. "You might have written."

Megan looked down at her hands, twisted together in her lap. "I did write," she said, very quietly. "To Skye. I asked her not to tell you where I was."

Christy paused, dabbed at her eyes with the hem of her blue-and-white checked apron. "Well, she certainly respected your wishes." She straightened again and drew a deep breath in a typical bid to regain control of her emotions. "That's something, I suppose." She turned, at last, and faced her sister. "Oh, Megan, how could you? How could you leave us to worry like that?"

Megan let out her breath; until then, she hadn't realized she was holding it. "I was ashamed," she said.

Christy looked stunned, as though she'd expected any answer in the world save that one. "Ashamed?" she echoed, her brow knitted prettily above her charcoal eyes. "I don't understand."

Megan forced herself to hold her sister's gaze, though she longed to look away. She could feel her face taking flame. "I was—I made a stupid mistake."

Christy crossed the room, the tea-making paraphernalia forgotten in the kitchen, and sank into a chair facing Megan. Her eyes glimmered with tears. "Oh, Megan, surely you didn't think anything you could have done—"

Megan swallowed hard. "There was a man," she said, and just uttering the words was like coughing with sharp stones caught in her throat. "I met him not—not long after I joined that first theater troupe, in Virginia City."

Christy reached across the tabletop and took one of Megan's hands in both her own. In that instant, Megan knew she could have confided in her elder sister and found understanding, but the awareness had come too late. The damage was already done. "Go on," she said, very softly.

"His name was—is—Davy Trent. He—well, I thought he was entirely another sort of man—like Zachary, or Trace, or Skye's Jake—but I was wrong."

Christy simply waited, though her grasp tightened slightly.

Megan sniffled, raised her chin. She had come this far. She would see this through. Make a fresh start, right here among these people who loved her even when she disappointed them. "I was such a fool." Megan raised her free hand to her mouth for a long moment, then forced herself to go on. Christy was silent, pale. "He—he said we were going to be married. There was a ranch for sale—we were supposed to buy it, live there—"

"But?" Christy prompted.

"He cheated me. I sold the property here at Primrose Creek, and instead of making the down payment, like we'd planned, and going through with the wedding, Davy took the proceeds and lit out." In her head, she paraphrased an old saying of her granddaddy's. *A fool and her money are soon parted.*

Christy slid forward to the edge of her chair and gathered Megan into her arms, held her. "How terrible."

"I wanted to come home then, but I was too embarrassed, and I didn't have stage fare," Megan went on when the brief embrace had ended. "I waited tables and scrubbed floors until I'd saved enough to leave."

Christy sighed. "You should have wired us that you were in trouble," she said. "Zachary and I would have come for you ourselves."

Megan shook her head. Her eyes felt hot and dry; it would have been a relief to weep, but she couldn't. "I'm here now," she said.

"And you can make a brand-new start," Christy said gently. She smoothed a stray tendril of hair back from Megan's temple. "Everything will be all right, Megan."

Megan's throat felt thick, and she dared not attempt

to say any more before she'd had time to compose herself. She simply nodded again.

Water from the tea kettle began to spill, sizzling, onto the stovetop, and both women ignored it. "Are you sure he's gone for good?" Christy pressed. "This scoundrel who fleeced you, I mean? Maybe Zachary could find him, get back your money, at least—"

Megan gave a bitter chuckle, shook her head. "He's long gone," she said.

"No doubt that's for the best," Christy said, and got up briskly to finish brewing the tea.

"Tell me about Webb Stratton," Megan heard herself say.

Christy was bustling busily about the kitchen. A pretty frown creased her forehead. "I don't know much about him," she said, with plain regret. "He's from somewhere up north, Montana, I think, though he told Zachary he'd been drifting awhile before he settled here. And Trace says he knows more about ranching than most anybody else in the high country." A sudden smile lit her face. "He's unmarried, you know. Webb, I mean. He lives in that big house all by himself."

Megan knew exactly what Christy was thinking and gave her a narrow look. "I'm not interested," she said.

Christy was undaunted. In fact, she acted as if Megan hadn't spoken at all. "I guess if we had to part with any portion of Granddaddy's land, it could have gone to somebody a lot worse than Webb Stratton."

Megan felt a slight but dizzying flip in the pit of her stomach every time she heard the man's name. She stiffened a little, in an effort to brace herself against her own susceptibilities. "I asked him to sell the tract back to me," she said. "He refused."

"I'm not surprised," Christy acknowledged. "He's got a good two-story house and a fine barn built. Fences, too, and a well. He owns another thousand acres besides. Both Trace and Zachary agree that they wouldn't sell out, either, if they were in his shoes."

"They tried to buy the place?"

"No," Christy allowed, bringing a tray to the table, "but they discussed the matter at some length, and on more than one occasion." There were cookies and dried apricots on a china plate Megan remembered from their mother's table, and the familiar flowered teapot steamed with the fragrance of orange pekoe. Megan went lightheaded for a moment, and her hand shook visibly as she reached for a piece of fruit.

Christy noticed immediately and poured tea for her sister. Then, while Megan was still grappling with the weakness her hunger had brought on, Christy returned to the pantry and fetched cheese, bread, and fresh butter. Mercifully, she left Megan to eat in peace, laying a hand lightly on her shoulder as she passed, and went to prepare a bath and a bed.

Megan ate as much as she dared and allowed herself to be led into the spare bedroom, where Caney and Christy gently divested her of her clothes and helped her into a copper tub filled with warm water. She was silent while Caney washed her hair and Christy laid out towels, scented powder, and a clean nightgown.

After the bath, Megan dried herself, used a generous amount of talcum, pulled on the gown, and crawled between blissfully clean linen sheets. For the first time in almost two years, she slept soundly, and without fear.

* * *

All the McQuarry women were beautiful, Webb reminded himself that afternoon while he worked, sweating under a shirt, buckskin breeches, and a heavy leather apron, at the forge behind his barn. To his way of thinking, it shouldn't have surprised him to find out that Megan, with her coppery hair and clover-green eyes, surpassed them all.

He threw more wood onto the fire and worked the bellows with hard pumping motions of both arms. Shoeing horses, herding and branding cattle, riding fence lines, pitching hay—all of it was hard work, and Webb reveled in it. At night, when he stretched out on that narrow bed of his and closed his eyes, he sank to a place in his mind where neither dreams nor nightmares could reach, and as soon as he woke up, the whole cycle began all over again.

He frowned as he thrust a hard metal shoe into the fire with pinchers and held it steady while it softened enough to yield to hammer blows on the anvil. Megan McQuarry had staked out a place in his thoughts and commenced to homesteading there, it seemed, for he couldn't seem to stop imagining the scent of her skin, the spirited light in her eyes, the inviting slender shape of her body. Until that morning, in town, she'd been a name on a deed to him and nothing more, but now that he'd met her, seen how proud she was, heard her talk about the plays she'd been in and the places she'd traveled, he'd gotten a real sense of her intelligence, her dignity, and the innate strength he suspected she didn't even know she had. He'd sat there beside her, on the seat of his buckboard, just listening, his thigh touching hers, and, well, something had changed.

He wrenched the shoe from the fire, laid it on the

anvil, and began to strike it hard, metal ringing against metal. On and on he worked, firing and refiring, hammering and rehammering, until the shape suited. Occasionally, he thrust the shoe into a vat of water and blinked in the hissing cloud of steam that arose around him like a veil.

He was holding the pinto mare's right rear hoof in one hand and nailing a shoe into place with the other when Trace Qualtrough rode up on his newest acquisition, a dapple-gray stallion he'd bought off a horse trader down south someplace, and swung down from the saddle.

"Stratton," he said, by way of a greeting, tugging at the brim of his beat-up leather hat. A man as prosperous as Trace could have afforded any kind of hat he happened to fancy, but he seemed partial to that one—in all the time he'd known him, Webb had never seen his neighbor wear another.

Webb nodded. "Afternoon," he said. He knew what the visit was about—he and Trace were good friends, but they were also busy men, not much given to chin-wagging sessions in the middle of the day—so there was no need to ask. Now that Megan was home from her travels, the McQuarry women and their assorted husbands would be wanting to buy back the land.

He finished driving in the last short nail, squatted to make sure the shoe wouldn't throw off the mare's balance, then straightened to his full height. He gave the pinto a swat on the flank, and she nickered and trotted off to find herself a patch of good grass.

"We'll give you a fair price," Trace said. He wasn't one to make a short story long, and that was one of the things Webb liked about him.

He shook his head. "I mean to stay right here," he said.

Trace took in the sturdy log house, the grass and timber, the cattle and horses grazing nearby. "I don't reckon I can blame you," he replied with a sigh of resignation. "Had to try, though."

Webb nodded. He knew all about trying, even when the odds were bad. Most westerners did.

"Bridget wants you to come to supper tomorrow night," Trace went on. "It's a celebration, 'cause Megan's home."

Webb knew he should refuse—common sense told him he ought to keep his distance from the redheaded Miss McQuarry, at least until he could get his impulses under control—but a neighbor's hospitality was something to be respected, and, anyway, he relished the prospect of woman-cooked food and some polite company. "I'd be pleased to pay a visit," he said.

Trace nodded. "She'll be setting the table about the time the evening chores are done, I reckon," he replied. Then he got back on his horse and, one hand raised briefly in farewell, rode away.

Webb watched him out of sight, then went down to the creek to wash. He'd get the stock fed early the next night and head into town for a real, hot-water bath upstairs at Diamond Lil's. Might even get his hair barbered and put on his Sunday suit, he reflected, and grinned to himself. The McQuarrys weren't the sort to give up easily, and if they couldn't get the land back one way, they'd try another. He wouldn't have put it past Bridget, Christy, and Skye to throw him and Megan together at every opportunity, hoping there would be a marriage.

Kneeling on the rocky bank of Primrose Creek, he splashed his face with icy water, then the back of his neck, and while the effort washed away some of the sweat and soot, it did nothing to cool the swift heat that had risen like a tide in his blood. He sure as hell wasn't going to marry into *that* outfit—he liked his women a little less opinionated—but the idea of sharing a bed with Megan McQuarry possessed him like a demon fever.

He took off his apron and shirt, drenched his chest, back, and arms with more water. Maybe he shouldn't have been so quick to accept Trace's invite to supper, he reflected, but since the deed was done, he couldn't see dwelling on regrets. He stood, snatched up his discarded clothing, and turned to head for the house.

The place was big but sparsely furnished, and entering the kitchen by way of the side door, Webb was struck yet again by the emptiness of the place. He hoped to marry one day and fill the rooms with kids, but for the moment he had to be content with his own company and that of his big yellow dog, Augustus. He still thought of his brother's wife, Eleanor, more often than he'd like, and of the children she might have given him, but she was up in Montana on the Stratton family ranch, the Southern Star, and she was likely to stay there.

He poured himself a cup of lukewarm coffee, stewing on the back of the stove since breakfast, took a sip, and winced. He wondered what kind of cook Megan McQuarry was, and then chuckled. Somehow, he couldn't picture her brewing coffee, let alone frying up a chicken or stirring a pot of oatmeal. Something had taken the starch right out of her—that was plain from her countenance and the bruised expression in her eyes—but like as not, she wouldn't stay at Primrose Creek for long, once she got her wind back. She wasn't the sort to settle down in one place; as soon as a troupe of show people passed within fifty miles, she'd take to the trail.

Webb's good spirits faded a little. He tossed the coffee into the cast-iron sink with a grimace of disgust and headed for the inside stairway.

His room, one of three sizable chambers, had a fireplace for cold nights, but the bed was nothing more than a cot, like the ones out in the bunkhouse, dragged up close to the hearth and covered with rumpled sheets and an old quilt. Just looking at it deepened his loneliness; he'd have to put in five or six more hours of work if he expected to sleep that night. There was always whiskey, of course, not to mention the friendly women who worked at Lil's, but he was in no mood for either, damn the luck.

He changed his clothes, went back out to the barn, and began the process of mucking out stalls with a pitchfork. By the time he finished, the sun had set. He entered the house again, dished up some of the beans he'd been working on for several days, and made himself eat. Then, figuring the grub had run its course, he carried the kettle outside and scraped the contents into a blue enamel dishpan with rusted edges.

Augustus meandered over to lap up his supper, and Webb smiled, patting the animal's hairy head. Bad planning on his part, he thought. The dog would have to sleep in the barn.

Chapter

2

*M*egan awoke with the first twittering of the birds and took a few moments to orient herself to her surroundings. She was home, she thought, with relief—not sharing a bed in a second-rate hotel with two other actresses or freezing on a hard bench in the back of some shoddy saloon or show house. Not carrying trays in a dining hall or scouring a filthy floor on her hands and knees. She drew a deep breath of thin, pure high-country air and let it out slowly. She was home.

She arose, washed her face at the basin on the table next to the window, then wound her already-braided hair into a coronet and donned the only really proper dress she owned, a blue-and-white flowered cotton with a modest collar trimmed in narrow eyelet. When she slipped out of her room, at the rear of the house, she found Caney already at the stove, building up the fire. Gauzy rays of pinkish sunlight seeped through the eastern windows and made glowing pools on the hardwood floors.

"I figured I'd make up some oatmeal and sausage," Caney said, and the quiet coolness of her tone injured Megan a little, for the other woman might have been speaking to an interloper instead of an old friend. "Zachary likes a good meal in the morning. Something that'll stick to his ribs."

Megan nodded, a little shyly, keeping her distance. "Is there anything I can do to help?"

Caney set a skillet on the heat with a ringing thump. "Yes'um, there is," she said with just the slightest snap. "You can sit yourself down there at that table and not get underfoot."

The words were not amicable ones, but they were familiar, and for that reason alone they reassured Megan, however slightly. She drew back a chair and sat, for no sensible person took an argument with Caney Blue lightly, not even the four McQuarry women. "I want to explain—"

Caney held up one hand. "No, miss. I won't hear no 'explanations.' All I want to know is, you gonna stay here at Primrose Creek where you belong, or go runnin' off again, leavin' us all to wonder and fret over you?"

Megan lowered her head, raised it again. "I mean to stay," she said.

Caney regarded her in silence for a seemingly endless interval, then went back to her cooking. Zachary wandered in from the master bedroom, yawning expansively, his fair hair sleep-rumpled. He was wearing trousers, a button-up undershirt, suspenders, and boots. He nodded a cordial greeting to the ladies, ambled over to the wash stand by the back door, and squinted into the little mirror affixed to the wall. With a sigh of resignation, he bent to splash his face at the basin, then whipped up a lather with his soap cup and brush, and began the morning ritual of shaving. By nightfall, Megan knew, he would have to go through the whole process again, and she found herself wondering idly whether it was the same for Webb Stratton.

Just the thought of Stratton attending to such an intimate and implicitly masculine function, ordinary as it was, made Megan feel as though a half-dozen grasshoppers were playing jump rope in the pit of her stomach. She blushed and looked down at her hands.

"Trace spoke to Webb while you were resting yesterday," Zachary said, already wielding the blade. "About selling back the land. He won't budge."

Caney offered no comment, but it was plain that she was listening. A part of the family, she was privy to pretty much everything that went on in the three households.

Megan nodded. "I know," she said.

Zachary looked back at her, over one shoulder, his face still half covered in foam, the blade in one hand. His grin was quick and boyish, and, for an instant, she envied Christy—the passionate, unconditional love he felt for her. Like Trace Qualtrough and Jake Vigil, he was devoted to his wife and family, and he didn't have any compunctions about letting the world know it.

"We've got plenty of room right here," he said. "Like as not, things will work themselves out, if you just stick around."

She blinked a little, touched by the assurance that there was still a place for her at Primrose Creek. She guessed that Zachary and Christy and all the rest of them expected her to take to her heels again at the first sign of difficulty. "I don't want to be a burden to you and Christy," she said. "I won't."

"Burden," Caney scoffed under her breath, tending to the fresh and fragrant sausage sizzling in a large black skillet.

Zachary grinned again and went back to shaving.

He had already finished eating and headed for town, wearing his badge and a well-used .45, when Christy appeared, clad in a lavender morning gown, her dark hair wound into a single thick plait, her cream-colored skin aglow with rest, good health, and some sweet, private secret. She made Megan think of an exotic night orchid, blooming in moonlight, folding back into a dignified bud by day. Joseph and little Margaret were close behind their mother, sleepy and serious in their flannel nightshirts and bare feet.

Megan's heart swelled with affection just to look at the children, her very own niece and nephew. Regret for all she'd missed seared the back of her throat, and she had to swallow hard before she could manage a hoarse good morning.

Christy paused as she passed, leaned down to kiss the top of her sister's head, and then went over to shoo Caney away from the sink, where she was washing dishes. "Go and sit down this instant," Christy told her friend.

To Megan's surprise, Caney obeyed and allowed Christy to serve her coffee and then breakfast. The children took their seats at the table, too, and tucked into bowls of hot oatmeal laced with fresh cream and molasses.

"Do you go to school?" Megan asked, gazing at

Joseph. Although he had his father's coloring, she could see Christy clearly in the set of his jaw and the level, steady look in his eyes.

"I'm too little," he said. "But I can read. I can ride, too. I've got a pony."

Megan smiled. "My goodness," she said.

"I might not ever go to school," he added after considerable rumination.

"I beg to differ," Christy stated lightly, joining the rest of them at the table and taking a delicate sip from her coffee. "You will *most certainly* go to school, Joseph Shaw."

He frowned. "I want to be Pa's deputy. I figure I won't have time for school."

Christy hid a smile, but Megan caught a glimpse of it, dancing in her gray eyes. "What use is a deputy with no education?" she asked reasonably. "Now, finish your breakfast. You have chores to do, unless I'm mistaken."

"Chickens to feed," Joseph told Megan importantly.

"And I could use a little help weeding that garden," Caney announced.

Megan made a show of pushing up her sleeves. "I might as well attend to that," she said. "Make myself useful around here."

A brief silence ensued, and Joseph was the one to break it. "There's a party tonight," he said. "Over at Aunt Bridget's place. She's going to make a cake with coconut icing."

"That was supposed to be a surprise, young man," Christy said. She was smiling, but there was something uneasy in her bearing, too. She gave Megan a nervous, sidelong glance, so quickly gone that it might have been imaginary.

Aunt Bridget? Megan thought, a beat behind. While Bridget and Christy had made their peace sometime back, they had never been particularly close, even after they buried the proverbial hatchet. They were too different from each other and, at the same time, too much alike, these two cousins.

Later, when she and her sister were working side by side in the corn patch, Megan wielding a hoe and Christy inspecting the stalks and ears for insects, dropping those she found into a can of kerosene, Christy brought up the matter of the party.

"They'll have invited Webb Stratton," she said with a sort of breezy caution. "Bridget and Trace, I mean. They make a point of being neighborly." In truth, most everyone did, for the West could be a hard and empty place, and much was made of even the simplest event.

Megan offered no comment. The summer sun felt good on her back and in her hair; even the ache in her muscles and the new calluses from the handle of the hoe were welcome.

Christy stopped, there in the corn patch, and sought out her children with her eyes. Seeing them tugging up weeds and the occasional sprout with gleeful diligence, a watchful Caney close at hand, she smiled. When she looked at Megan again, though, her gaze was somber. "There's something I need to tell you," she said.

"I suspected that," Megan heard herself say, realizing only as she spoke that she *had* sensed an undercurrent, almost from the moment of her return to her sister's home. She paused and leaned on the hoe handle, gripping it with both hands. "What is it, Christy?"

"You took off so fast, and we'd just reasoned it through—"

Megan waited, braced. Was Christy or Zachary or either of the children sick—even dying? Or was it Caney?

"Bridget and Skye thought we ought to talk about this tomorrow, just the four of us—that's why they haven't been to see you just yet—but I, well, I believe we've let it go too long as it is."

"What are you trying to say?" Megan was becoming frightened by then.

Tears welled in Christy's eyes, but, at the same time, she was smiling. It reminded Megan of spring rain showers sparkling in shafts of sunlight, Christy's smile. "Granddaddy misled us, Megan. They all did. We—you and I and Bridget and Skye—"

Megan closed her eyes, let the hoe fall, forgotten, to the ground. She felt too dizzy to retrieve it. *Don't say it,* she thought. *Don't say we're not really McQuarrys, because I couldn't bear that.*

"We're sisters. The four of us."

Megan stared at her sister, her eyes so wide they hurt. She was at once stunned and relieved. *"What?"*

"We had the same father," Christy said, her voice very quiet. "Different mothers, it would seem, but definitely the same father."

Megan couldn't grasp it. "Papa? Uncle J.R.?"

Christy shook her head. "There was another brother—Thayer. He was Granddaddy's, by a mistress."

Megan remembered her grandfather's passionate devotion to their beautiful grandmother, Rebecca. "Granddaddy had a *mistress?*"

"It was before he met Grandmother," Christy said gently. "I don't know why they never married. The point is, Thayer was a pure disgrace, and Granddaddy sent him away forever when he was twenty-two, after some dreadful occurrence involving whiskey and a duel. He said Thayer's name was never to be mentioned under his roof again, and, evidently, he meant precisely that."

Megan turned away, started down the row toward the edge of the garden, turned back. Anger was rising inside her, along with confusion and just plain fear. All these years, she'd thought she was one person, and the whole time she'd been another. She was a stranger to herself.

"Don't run away from this, Megan," Christy said, and this time she was all big sister, strong and stubborn. "Thayer McQuarry was our father, yours, mine, Bridget's, and Skye's. Granddaddy didn't want anything to do with him, but he couldn't and wouldn't turn his back on us, so he sent for us, brought us home to be raised by the sons he was willing to claim."

Megan felt sick, then jubilant, then sick again. She pressed the back of one hand to her forehead, let it fall to her side. "Dear God," she whispered.

Christy had put aside the can of kerosene; she came to Megan, sidestepping the fallen hoe, and laid a hand on her shoulder. "It isn't so terrible—is it?"

"Our mothers—?"

"I don't know anything about them," Christy admitted. "Just that they were women Thayer took up with after he left home."

"How—how did you learn—?"

Christy sighed. "When Bridget had the twins, I recorded the births in the McQuarry Bible. That was when I noticed Thayer's name and saw that all four of us were listed as his daughters, not Papa's or Uncle J.R.'s. I guess fooling us was one thing, in Granddaddy's mind, and writing a bald-faced lie in the Good Book was another."

"I was here when little Gideon and Rebecca were born," Megan recalled, and the realization stung. "You knew. You *knew,* Christy McQuarry, and *you didn't tell me!*"

Christy's gaze remained steady, though there was pain in it. Pain and honest regret. "Bridget and I talked the matter out. We decided we'd tell you and Skye when you were older. More settled. Then there was the fire, and after that, you ran away."

"You had no right to keep something like this from me!" Megan accused, stricken. She felt like the lost and wandering ghost of a person who had never truly existed in the first place. "You had no right!"

"I had no choice," Christy corrected. "You ran away!"

Megan clenched her fists at her sides. She'd never struck another human being, and she wasn't about to begin then, but that didn't mean the temptation wasn't there, for it was. God help her, *it was.* "You had plenty of time!"

"But not plenty of information. Eventually, Bridget found a letter from Granddaddy tucked into the lining of the Bible's back cover. After that, we sat Caney down and pried what we could out of her. She still hasn't told all she knows, not by any means."

Megan dashed at her cheeks with the heels of her palms. "She kept the secret? All that time?"

Christy sighed. "She believed she was doing the right thing. Our father was every kind of rascal, Megan. He eventually got himself killed, down in New Orleans. He was—he was caught with another man's wife.

Caney thought we had enough grief, the four of us, without that stirred into the pot."

Megan was silent for a long time, trying desperately to regain her equilibrium, both physically and emotionally. When she spoke again, her voice was a raw whisper. "And Skye? How long has she known?"

Christy averted her eyes, but only for a moment. "Since I had Joseph," she answered. "She and Jake were married about that time. And you took off soon after that."

Megan swallowed. She'd been so anxious to rejoin her family, but now she realized shakily, what she really needed was some time apart, a chance to work things through in her mind and heart. She stared at her sister, still astounded, trying to take it all in.

Christy spoke quickly, if calmly. "This is a shock, I know," she said. "But Bridget and Skye and I have all been much closer since we learned the truth."

"You didn't feel—angry?"

"With Granddaddy?" Christy asked, folding her arms as though she'd taken a chill. "Yes, at first. But after a while, I began to understand. He thought he was doing the right thing—the best thing. He loved us, Megan. Enough to bring us home to Virginia, to be brought up as McQuarrys. A lot of people would have turned their backs, pretended we didn't exist. That would have been a lot easier on him and just about everyone else in the family, don't you think?"

Megan's throat thickened to the point where she could barely breathe, but she nodded. She understood—she truly did—but she was a long way from assimilating what she'd learned. When she'd recovered enough to move, she turned, went back to retrieve the hoe she'd dropped, and began hacking methodically at the dirt.

Christy left her to the solace of her work.

Twilight was spilling across the hillsides in purple and blue shadows when Webb rode up to the Qualtrough house. The windows gleamed with welcoming lamplight, and, through the trees on the other side of the creek, he caught the glow of the Shaw place as well. He couldn't help thinking of the darkened, empty rooms he'd left behind half an hour before.

Trace came through the open front door, grinning in the fading daylight. "Where's that yellow dog of yours?" he asked.

"I didn't reckon Augustus was invited," Webb answered.

"Well," Trace allowed, "the least you can do is take him some leftovers."

Webb dismounted, started toward the barn, leading his horse. Trace fell in beside him.

"Mighty glad you could make it," he said.

Webb kept a straight face. "I'm not going to change my mind about selling the land," he said. "You know that, don't you?"

Trace chuckled. "Hell, yes," he said as they reached the corral gate. He worked the latch and swung it open to admit Webb and the gelding. "What I'm wondering is, do *you* know that saying no to a McQuarry woman is just the beginning of a discussion, not the end?"

Webb grinned as he led the horse through, lifted one of the stirrups, and began loosening the cinch to remove the saddle. "I reckon I had an inkling," he replied.

Trace took the saddle, hoisted it easily onto the top

rail of the fence, while Webb slid the bridle off and hung it alongside the other tack. "Megan's a fine-looking woman," he said, stepping through the gate again, fastening it when Webb was beside him.

It was all Webb could do not to roll his eyes. "Yes," he agreed, and his voice came out sounding unaccountably gruff. "She surely is."

"You must be mighty lonely, living on that big place all by yourself."

"No more than the next man," Webb answered. Which, he reasoned, was pretty damn lonely, when you thought of all the poor old cowpokes, miners, and timbermen who were living by themselves up and down the banks of Primrose Creek.

Trace thrust a hand through his hair and heaved a heavy sigh. He was a straightforward man, uncomfortable with any sort of deception, however innocent or obvious. "You could use a wife, couldn't you?" he blurted out.

Webb laughed, stopped to face his friend there in the moonlit dooryard of a happy home. "I don't know as *use* is the word I'd employ," he said. "But yes, I wouldn't mind marrying. I'm just waiting for the right woman, that's all."

"Well," Trace replied, exasperated, "maybe Megan is the right woman."

Webb considered the spellbinding red-haired creature waiting inside, with her equally lovely sister and cousins. It was no secret that Trace, Zachary, and Jake were all happy with the marriages they'd made. It was also no secret that the McQuarry females, beautiful as they were, were spirited, mule-stubborn, and overflowing with opinions that didn't necessarily match those of their mates. Such qualities were trying enough in a horse—in a woman, they could cause all manner of sorrow and travail. He had enough to do, starting a ranch, keeping it going, without that.

Didn't he?

"When did you take up matchmaking?" he asked.

He could see Trace redden up, even in the twilight. "It just makes sense, that's all. You need a wife, and Megan needs a husband."

Webb narrowed his eyes, lowered his voice. "What do you mean, 'Megan needs a husband'?"

Trace rasped out a sigh. "Not *that*," he said, and Webb knew if they hadn't been such good friends, Trace probably would have punched him one, right then and there, just for daring to *suggest* that Megan, an unmarried woman, might be in a family way. "She does have, well, a certain reputation around here."

"Ah," Webb said, and folded his arms. The sounds of laughter and clattering pots and dishes came out through the doorway, pulling at him, drawing him in. He stood his ground.

"She ran away and became an actress."

Webb almost laughed out loud. "*God*, no," he mocked. "Not that."

Trace smiled. "Well, it sure riled the ladies of Primrose Creek," he muttered, and Webb knew he wasn't referring to Bridget, Christy, and Skye. With nothing more said, the two men went into the house.

Megan seemed subdued, if not downright retiring, that evening, seated across the Qualtroughs' long trestle table from Webb; he caught her watching him twice, there in the midst of love and noise and children, and each time she flushed and looked away. Webb reminded himself that a shy McQuarry had probably never drawn breath and wondered if it wasn't embarrassment, heightening that rose-petals-and-cream coloring of hers. No doubt she knew her family had hopes of swapping her for six hundred and twenty-five acres of prime land, and, whether she was a party to the plan or not, the whole thing had to be a strain on her pride.

Thanks to his mean, sorry bastard of a father, Thomas Stratton, Sr., not to mention his elder brother, Tom Jr., Webb had long since learned not to let much of anything show in his face or bearing, and the skill stood him in good stead there among all those McQuarrys, Qualtroughs, Shaws and Vigils. Nobody needed to know that he was beginning to find the idea of marriage to Megan McQuarry intriguing, and this after all these years of thinking nobody but Eleanor could rope him in and pasture him out.

He was stirring his after-supper coffee when he felt Megan's gaze touch on him for the third time—it was like a sudden spill of sunshine, though he was sure she hadn't meant to favor him with any sort of warmth or brightness—and looked up idly to meet her eyes. She was glaring at him fit to singe his hide, and that made him grin.

She looked away quickly, and he chuckled under his breath.

"You going to be hiring for spring roundup?" The question came from the other end of the table, and a few ticks of the mantel clock sounded before Webb caught hold of the fact that it was his to answer.

He turned and saw Trace watching him, a biscuit in one hand and a butter knife in the other. "Yep," he answered, more conscious, rather than less, of Megan's presence and her regard. "I need a dozen men, at least. God knows where I'm going to find them, though."

Trace and Zachary made sympathetic noises, while Jake Vigil, the most recent addition to the family, having wed Skye McQuarry a couple of years back, looked downright grim. He ran a big timber outfit, as well as a lumber mill in town, and he and Skye had built a good-sized house on her section of land just down the creek. "Good luck," he said. "Whatever help I've been able to get, I've had to scrape up off the floors of saloons."

Skye, a brown-haired, brown-eyed beauty with a generous mouth and a quietly vibrant nature, was watching her husband with an expression of warm admiration. They had two children in their household, Webb knew: Jake's son, Hank, born of some previous alliance, and a plump baby girl of their own, blessed with her mother's good looks.

Zachary leaned forward in his chair, and, though he wasn't wearing his badge, the nickel-silver glint of it was always in his eyes. He was quick with that .45 of his, the marshal was, and even quicker with his mind. "There's been a lot of rustling and just general thieving down in the low country," he said, addressing everyone. "Bound to move up this way eventually."

Vigil uttered a sigh of resigned agreement, and Trace nodded glumly. His gaze found Webb and leveled on him. "You might want to start carrying an iron," he said. "Running that place all by yourself the way you do, you'd be easy pickin's."

Megan looked at Webb in alarm, and that cheered him. In spite of herself, she was concerned for his safety. How-do and hallelujah.

He shook his head. He hadn't carried a gun since—

well, since the day he'd learned, to his horror, that he was capable of killing a man in cold blood—and he didn't mean to start now. He had a rifle at the ranch, used for hunting and putting down the occasional sick cow or injured horse, but that was all. "No need," he said, his mind swamped, all of a sudden, with stomach-turning images of his elder brother lying broken and bleeding on the ground. Webb had thought Tom was dead, thought he'd done murder, and it still scared him to think how close he'd come to committing the ultimate sin.

"No need?" Megan echoed, speaking directly to Webb for the first time since the evening began. "There are outlaws and renegade Indians in these foothills, Mr. Stratton. There are bears and wildcats and snakes."

He took a sip of his coffee, paused to relish the taste. While his own brew might have served to strip white-wash off an old outhouse, Bridget's was delicious. "I confess to a fear of wildcats," he said mildly. "Outlaws, Indians, bears, and snakes don't scare me much, though."

Megan narrowed those changeable eyes of hers— now a tempestuous shade of sea-green—and to Webb it seemed that everyone else in that crowded, jovial room receded into two dimensions just then, no more real than figures in paintings, leaving only him and Megan fully present. "Then you're a fool," she said, and her cheeks were mottled with apricot, which meant she hadn't missed his reference to wildcats.

He smiled. "That may be so," he allowed. "Still, I'll leave the gun-toting to your brother-in-law, the marshal here, and handle things my own way."

"I'd be curious to know," she pressed, clearly irritated, perhaps thinking he was overconfident or even arrogant, "how you intend to 'handle'—say—a wildcat?"

A shrill jubilation welled up in his heart, pressed sweetly and painfully against the hollow of his throat, but he let none of what he felt show in his face. "Well, now," he said, "I guess that depends on the wildcat."

Somebody cleared their throat, and suddenly the room was full again, alive again, virtually throbbing with energy, personality, and life. Megan continued to stare at Webb for a few moments, then made a point of looking away.

Confound it, Webb thought. He didn't want to care. He couldn't *afford* to care, not about Megan McQuarry, anyhow. Much as he wanted a wife, she was an unsuitable candidate. Nonetheless, she stuck in his mind like a burr tangled in a horse's tail, and it didn't do any good at all telling himself she was an actress, an independent sort, bound to light out for parts unknown as soon as she got bored. He still couldn't run her out of his head.

Chapter

3

"**W**ell," Bridget demanded, industriously drying dishes as Megan handed them to her, one by one, "what do you think of Webb?"

Skye and Christy were nearby, Skye rocking her daughter next to the fire, Christy clearing the long table. Caney, normally a part of all their get-togethers, was in town, making supper for her beau, Mr. Hicks. The men, mercifully, had gone outside to smoke pipes and cheroots, and the other children were either asleep or chasing each other in the dooryard.

Megan took them in, one by one. Bridget, Christy, Skye. Her *sisters*. She loved them all, and desperately, but she was furious with them, too. They might as well have abandoned her in some cold and desolate place, leaving her in the dark the way they had. "What am I *supposed* to think?" she asked, as the lid began to rattle atop her temper. "That he'd make a good husband?"

They blushed, all three of them, but Megan's mind had long since moved on to another, more pressing subject. "Christy told me," she said very quietly, fixing Skye with a brief, pointed glance. "About Thayer McQuarry and his many exploits."

Bridget's smile was soft and a little rueful. "I only know of four," she commented. "Exploits, I mean. Us."

Nobody commented. At least, not on Bridget's pitiable attempt to lighten the moment.

"How could you?" Megan demanded in a sputtering whisper, and she knew that her eyes were flashing with fury and hurt. "How *could* you, any of you?"

"You didn't give us much of a chance to explain," Bridget observed, setting a clean, dry plate on the shelf next to the stove. Of the four of them, she was always the quickest to find her footing again when she missed a step, which wasn't often. "Running off the way you did, I mean."

Skye's brown eyes were round. "What does it matter now?" she wanted to know, and her tone was mildly plaintive. Family was what counted with Skye; as far as she was concerned, blood truly was thicker than water. "We're all together again. We're *sisters*. What else matters?"

"The *truth* matters," Megan said in an outraged whisper, resting her hands on her hips, the dishtowel dangling like a flag along one thigh. "*Loyalty* matters."

"You're a fine one to talk about loyalty," Bridget remarked calmly. It was hard to nettle her, but once she got her bustle in a tangle, reasonable folks took cover. "Running off like that. Leaving us all to wonder and worry."

Megan slanted a sidelong look at Skye. "Not all," she

said, and took no satisfaction in the way her cousin—
sister—squirmed.

"You made me swear not to tell anyone where you
were!" Skye blurted, and her small daughter fidgeted a
little, there in her mother's arms, then nestled close and
went to sleep. "I should never have promised—"

Bridget and Christy exchanged looks but offered no
comment.

Megan wrapped her arms tightly around herself, held
on. It was a habit she'd developed as a child, one meant
to anchor her emotions, keep her from being carried
away by their intensity. Rationally, she understood the
situation well enough, but her heart and spirit were still
assimilating the reality that she was not the person she'd
always believed herself to be. Indeed, her whole sense
of identity had been undermined. Perhaps her sisters
were content, knowing so little about their common
past, but Megan was full of questions, dizzy with them.

One by one, she considered these three beloved
strangers who were the heart and life's blood of her
family. Bridget had Trace and their flock of children;
Christy had Zachary, Joseph, and little Margaret; and
Skye had Jake, her stepson Henry, usually called Hank,
and baby Susannah. No doubt the hectic pace of their
daily lives left them little time to wonder about their dis-
inherited father, their separate mothers, and this final
loss of the parents they'd believed to be their own, faults
notwithstanding, all these years.

"The letter," Megan managed at last. "Let me see
Granddaddy's letter."

Bridget nodded, fetched the McQuarry Bible down
from its place of honor on the mantelpiece, and carried
it over to the table. Megan sat down, weak in the knees,

and stared at the giant black book as though it might contain still more shattering secrets.

It was battered and peeling, and the gold lettering impressed into the cracked leather had worn almost completely away. The corners were curled, the spine was coming loose from the binding, and the pages were translucent with age. Gently, leaning over Megan's shoulder to reach, Bridget turned the Bible facedown and raised the back cover. A vellum envelope protruded from a tear in the ancient lining.

Megan's hand trembled as she removed the missive carefully, opened it, and took out a single sheet of paper.

The handwriting, though faded, was strong, clear, and slanted just slightly to the right, and it was Gideon McQuarry's, without question. Just seeing the familiar shapes of the letters and words made her miss her grandfather with ferocious force, but she was angry, too. Oh, yes, she was angry, and her eyes were so full of tears that she couldn't see to read.

Christy took the letter, sat down beside her with a sigh. "April 17, 1862," she began in a quiet voice. "McQuarry Farm, Virginia.

"My beloved granddaughters,

"Every man must confess his sins, if he is to have any hope of heaven, and deception is certainly a grievous sin. I have deceived you, as have my sons, Eli and J.R., and their wives—they are weak people, all of them, and I dare not depend upon them to make things right when I die. For that reason, I am writing this letter, in the earnest expectation that you will find it one day and learn the truth, however belatedly. It is my prayer that you will come to forgive me in time—"

The letter went on to describe Thayer McQuarry's

birth, to an unnamed young woman of Granddaddy's acquaintance. When he married Rebecca, shortly after discovering that he was already the father of a son, Gideon had arranged to raise the boy himself. His son's mother had been relieved, and Rebecca had welcomed the child as her own.

Throughout his life, Granddaddy wrote, Thayer had been a trial, and by the time he reached manhood, he was a blight on the family honor, a blasphemer, drinking to excess, gambling and fighting with his fists, dallying with other men's wives. Granddaddy had finally paid him to leave the farm, and Virginia, forever, and, as Christy had told Megan the day before, he had forbade the remaining members of the family even to speak the man's name in his hearing. Apparently, his instructions had been well heeded, for none of the sisters had ever dreamed their grandfather had sired three sons instead of two.

Thayer had fathered four children after his banishment, and after each birth Granddaddy had sent Caney to fetch the infants home to the farm. As the wives of both his remaining sons had failed to conceive, he had given two babies to Eli and two to J.R., to raise as their own. He'd thought it might have a settling effect on his boys, giving them some real responsibility, but in the end they hadn't done much better than their elder brother would have.

Megan's throat tightened with a welter of emotions as she listened. Granddaddy might never have known their mothers' names, and if he had, he evidently hadn't recorded them, nor did he say where they had been born or, for that matter, precisely when. Even her birthday might be merely an invented date, just another lie.

She flipped to the front of the Bible, where the generations of McQuarry "begats" were recorded, and sought her own name, running a fingertip down the yellowed, brittle pages. *Megan Elizabeth McQuarry,* she read, at long last. *Born in the summer of 1850.*

She swallowed and looked up at her sisters' faces. All of them, to their credit, met her gaze steadily. "Surely *someone* can tell us—"

Christy sighed again, slipped an arm around Megan's shoulders. "I believe Caney knows," she said, "but she's already said more than she wanted to."

"I thought she'd be here tonight," Megan said, still dazed.

Bridget bit her lower lip, then nodded. "She's bound and determined to get Mr. Hicks to the altar before the first snow, and she's been spending a lot of time herding the poor man in that direction."

Megan recalled her exchange with Caney that morning in Christy's kitchen and wondered if Mr. Hicks was the real reason her friend had stayed away from the celebration supper. Caney had been furious with Megan for going off without a word of farewell, two years before, and she'd made no secret of the fact. Very likely, she had simply decided there was nothing to celebrate.

"I need to talk to her," Megan said.

"There's plenty of time for that," Skye assured her. Little Susannah, a sweet, miniature version of her mother, was sound asleep in her arms by then; she carefully rose from the rocking chair, laid the child on Bridget's horsehair settee, and covered her with a crocheted blanket. "Besides, we've all tried."

"Why wouldn't she tell us everything?" Christy ruminated, frowning. "Caney, I mean."

Bridget was at the stove, pouring hot water from a kettle into a blue china teapot. "It's possible, isn't it, that she truly doesn't know anything more?" she said.

Christy and Skye looked as skeptical as Megan felt. "She knows," they said in concert.

Bridget chuckled ruefully. "I'm sure you're right," she admitted. "I suppose there's some terrible scandal involved."

"How could it be any worse?" Megan demanded.

Bridget rolled her eyes at this, but Christy reached over, took Megan's hand, and squeezed it reassuringly.

"They could have been married to other men—our mothers, I mean," Bridget said. "Or perhaps they were women of ill repute."

Skye paled a little and glanced nervously toward her sleeping child, as though Susannah might have over-heard and been scarred by the stigma. "Bridget!" she hissed.

Bridget smiled. She enjoyed stirring embers into flame, always had. "Well, it's possible, isn't it?" she whispered. "It doesn't sound as if our dear old daddy was the sort decent women want to consort with, does it?"

"Nonsense," Christy put in crisply. Both Megan and Skye were somewhat in awe of Bridget, she being the eldest of the four and the most direct in speech and manner, but Christy suffered no such malady. "Men like Thayer McQuarry are *precisely* the sort decent women want to consort with. All we can really conclude concerning our mothers is that they probably weren't over-ly intelligent."

A silence fell while everyone absorbed the implications of this possibility, and, one by one, they dismissed it with firm shakes of the head. Stupidity was as unacceptable a quality in one's mother as a lack of moral character.

"What does any of this matter?" Skye asked. "It's all behind us. Can't we just move on from here?" Her gaze found Megan, lingered. "Maybe you're not happy to find out that Bridget and I are your sisters, not your cousins, but I think it's some of the best news I've ever heard!"

Megan's heart softened, at least toward Skye. The two of them had been close since babyhood; they'd shared cradles and prams, dolls and ponies, sorrows and secrets. She rubbed her temples with the tips of her fingers. "It's not that simple—at least, not for me."

Skye's expression was typically ingenuous. "Why ever not?" she asked.

"Why indeed?" Bridget pressed, one eyebrow raised.

Megan sat with both hands splayed atop the battered Bible, as though she might divine something more of the mystery that way. "Don't you see?" she whispered, addressing all her sisters without raising her eyes to their faces. "We know nothing at all about our mothers and *next* to nothing about our father. That means we're virtual strangers not only to each other but to ourselves."

Skye knitted her brow, and Bridget checked the pins holding her masses of blond hair in a loose bun at her nape. Christy interlocked her fingers with Megan's. "We're still the same people we've always been, Megan."

Megan nodded, but she was still troubled, still at sixes and sevens. In time, she supposed she would recover—and that was the main difference, she decided, between herself and her sisters. They had had some time to get used to an idea that was utterly new to her.

"I'm going to take some air," she said. Rising somewhat unsteadily from her seat at the table, she made for the door, and no one tried to stop her.

The breeze was cool and fresh, and it braced Megan a little, as always, cleared her head. Stars draped the sky in a silvery net, as if flung there by some celestial fisherman, and crickets took up their distinct chorus in the deep grass. The older children were throwing stones into the creek, while the men stood nearby, their voices riding deep and quiet on the clean night air.

Megan traveled in the other direction, following the moon-washed creek upstream, trying to make sense of things, sort through what she'd learned, decide where she was headed. She'd planned to stay at Primrose Creek, but now she had her doubts about the idea. It was difficult, if not impossible, for a woman to find honest work, especially in such a small community, and she wasn't at all sure she could face a lifetime under someone else's roof, even when that someone else was Christy.

She sniffled, touched the back of one hand to her cheek. The stream whispered and burbled as it danced over the colorful stones worn smooth by years, perhaps even centuries, of its passing.

"I don't reckon you can cook the way your cousin does. Can you?" The voice was Webb Stratton's; she knew that without turning around. While her first impulse was to tell him to go away, in no uncertain terms, she ignored it, because another, greater part of her was so glad of his company.

She turned, arms folded, chin high. Her face was in

shadow, and she was fairly certain he wouldn't be able to make out any trace of tears lingering on her face. *Bridget is my sister,* she wanted to say, but she didn't. The knowledge was still too fresh, too raw to share. "Yes, I can cook as well as any woman in the family. Caney taught us all—save Christy, who hasn't the proper bent for it—and she's the very best there is."

Webb stood a few feet away, easy in his skin, sure of his path through a treacherous and confusing world. Megan had once felt that way, but she'd since learned that she'd been wrong to trust her own judgment. She was as lost as any other wandering soul. "I guess I didn't figure an actress would be inclined toward domestic life," Webb ventured.

She stiffened a little, already on the defensive, even though she hadn't perceived a threat. What was it about this man that made her feel like some many-legged creature trying to dance on ice? "I'm a complex person, Mr. Stratton," she said, at some length. "Full of surprises."

"I believe you are," he agreed. "Something's been troubling you tonight. What is it?"

It was a bold question, to say nothing of a blunt one, and to her chagrin she'd answered it before she thought better of the idea. "I'm wondering if I should have come back here," she confided in low tones. "I had a place in this family once, but now I feel as though it might have closed while I was away. Maybe I don't belong here anymore."

Webb was quiet for a long time, and when he spoke, his voice was solemn. "Could be you just need a little distance."

She nodded, though her heart was already breaking

at the mere thought of leaving Primrose Creek and the people she loved.

That was when Webb took her by surprise. "I could use a woman over at my place," he said quietly.

Megan was too startled to speak. Surely he hadn't said what she thought he had—had he? What sort of person did he think she was?

He laughed, thrust a hand through his sandy hair. "I didn't mean that quite the way it rolled over my tongue," he said. "Not that you aren't real attractive that way."

Megan opened her mouth, closed it again. She wasn't sure whether she should slap Mr. Stratton across the face and walk away or stay and hear him out. Being even this close to him produced a deliciously disturbing sensation, like falling, deep in her middle, made her want to catch hold of something—or someone—with both hands. Since he was the only one there, she kept her arms locked around her middle instead.

"What I'm getting at," he went on doggedly, "is that I'd like to hire somebody. To cook and look after the house and all like that. I mean to sign on as many men as I can, like I said at supper, so there'll be a lot of plates to fill."

Megan's lips felt dry; she moistened them with the tip of her tongue. "Are you asking me to come to work as your housekeeper, Mr. Stratton?"

"Webb," he said. "And yes, that's pretty much what I had in mind."

She absorbed that for a moment. "Surely you realize that such an arrangement would arouse gossip."

"I suppose it would," he agreed evenly. "On the other hand, a job is a job. I'll pay you a good salary, and you'll have the whole downstairs to yourself." He paused. "Besides, I don't figure you for the type to turn tail and run because of a few old biddies flapping their tongues."

She'd been right, Megan thought. He was utterly sure of himself. He spoke as though she'd already agreed to go home with him, keep his house, cook his meals. What would it be like, she asked herself, sleeping under the same roof as this man, in a home built on land that had been hers? Would *still* be hers, if she hadn't been so stupid?

"How do I know you'll be a gentleman?" she inquired, mostly stalling. Webb Stratton was probably many things, but he was no fool. He had to know that if he ever forced his attentions upon her, Trace, Zachary, and Jake would hunt him down and kill him like an egg-sucking dog.

He was holding his hat, and he turned the brim slowly in both hands. His grin flashed white in the darkness. "I'm no gentleman, ma'am," he said, "but that needn't concern you. I'll confine my socializing to town."

Megan was not particularly reassured, for, in point of fact, his kindness made her feel vulnerable rather than safe. Besides, she hated the idea of his "socializing" in town.

"I will not tolerate any sort of foolishness," she warned, just in case he expected more than housekeeping.

He had been about to walk away, back toward the house, probably, to offer his thanks and say his good-byes, but he went completely still when Megan spoke. "You mean you'll take the job?" He sounded pleasantly surprised, as if he'd already resigned himself to being turned down.

"I need work," she said, "and yours is the only respectable opportunity likely to come my way."

He gave a low whistle of exclamation.

"Did you expect me to refuse your offer, Mr. Stratton?"

"Maybe," he said. "Maybe I did, deep down. Fact is, I wasn't entirely sure you wouldn't try to throw me in the creek." He glanced downstream, toward the sound of male laughter and the determined frolicking of tired children, bent on holding off sleep for as long as possible. "I promise you, Miss McQuarry—you won't be sorry you signed on with me. The work will be hard sometimes, when there are a lot of hungry cowboys looking for grub, but no harm will find you on my ranch."

She put out a hand. "Then I accept," she said.

He hesitated, took her hand in his, and shook it. A sweet jolt went through her at his touch. He was strong, his flesh callused by hard work, and yet there was a gentleness in the way his fingers closed around hers that did indeed make her feel looked after, even cherished. "I'll come for you tomorrow," he said. "You're still staying over at Zachary and Christy's place?"

She inclined her head in assent, wondering what her relations would say when she told them she was going to live with Webb Stratton as his housekeeper. No doubt they'd be pleased, not only to have her off their hands but because they'd think their plan was working, that she was going to marry the rancher and bring the lost six hundred and twenty-five acres back into the family circle once and for all.

"I'll be ready," she said, and when he left her, she sighed and tilted her head back to look up at the broad spill of sky stretching from mountain top to mountain top, speckled with stars.

She didn't rest well that night in her old bed at Christy and Zachary's house, but instead thrashed and fretted, caught in a hot tangle of dreams.

"You don't have to do this, you know," Christy said fitfully the next morning, when Megan announced that Webb would be coming by soon to fetch her. "You're perfectly welcome right here."

Megan, standing at the stove, had already made breakfast for Zachary, just to get into practice. Caney either hadn't come home the night before or was still lolling about in bed. "Christy," Megan said gently, "I might have given up my share of the land, but I've still got the pride Granddaddy left us all. I need to make my own way, and I want time to sort things through."

Christy's delicate complexion was flushed, and her gray eyes held sparks. "I declare, Megan McQuarry, your head is hard as tamarack. You belong with your family."

"I *will* be with my family. Just a few miles away, anyway." She spoke softly, for, although she was exasperated with her sister, she loved her as fiercely as ever.

Christy heaved a shuddery sigh. "There will be talk," she warned. "In town, I mean."

The rattles, creaks, and neighs of a team and wagon sounded outside, and Megan felt a wild quickening, brief but shattering, deep in her pelvis. Webb had arrived to fetch her home. *Home.* But the ranch was his place, not hers, not anymore, and she mustn't let herself forget that.

"I'm sure the gossip has already begun," she said,

recalling the two townswomen who had sniffed and pulled aside their skirts when she arrived in Primrose Creek. She heard Webb call out to the horses, heard the squeal of brakes as he set the lever. "I need to do this, Christy. I need to make my own way."

Christy started to speak again, then stopped herself and merely nodded.

Megan hurried over to Zachary's shaving mirror, peered into it, and pinched her cheeks to bring some color into her face. Too late, she realized that Christy was watching her with a curious smile.

Webb knocked politely at the door, even though it was wide open to the spring sunshine and wildflower-scented breeze, and Megan had to struggle to keep herself from hurrying across the room to greet him.

Christy did the honors. "Come in, Webb," Megan heard her sister say warmly. "I suspect Megan has already packed her things."

Megan needn't have pinched her cheeks; she could feel a high blush climbing her neck, headed for her hairline.

Webb stood just over the threshold, hat in hand, a cattleman in stance, substance, and manner. Megan wouldn't have traded his company for that of a dozen San Francisco dandies, decked out in silk shirts and polished boots—not just then, anyhow.

"Mornin'," he said, and he ducked his head a little, actually sounded and looked shy.

Megan wasn't fooled. Mr. Stratton was about as reticent as a coiled rattler, and if she didn't keep an eye on him, she was sure to be bitten. "Good morning," she said, her tone cool and more than slightly remote. "I'm ready. If you wouldn't mind fetching my trunk?"

"Point me to it," he said. Christy might not have been there at all, nor the children. It seemed to Megan that the whole world had shrunk away into a vapor, leaving only the two of them, herself and Webb Stratton, in all creation.

She indicated the doorway of her room with a hand that trembled slightly, and after glancing at Christy in an unspoken bid for permission, he proceeded to collect Megan's things from the private part of the house.

"We'll be here if you need us," Christy told her younger sister. "Zachary and the children and I. Right here."

Megan felt her throat swell with all the things she couldn't say. She nodded instead and embraced Christy, and Christy embraced her in return, holding on tightly and for a long time. The two women parted in embarrassment when they realized, simultaneously, that Webb had returned.

Megan took a last look around the house, as though she were setting out on some long journey and might never see it again, then kissed Christy on the cheek and started for the door. Webb was right behind her, easily carrying the big trunk that held all her earthly and unremarkable belongings.

He lowered the tailgate on his buckboard and placed the trunk on the wagon bed, pushing it forward toward the back of the seat. Megan stood waiting until he came to her side and helped her aboard, smooth as a gentleman escorting a lady home from a cotillion.

She gazed straight ahead as he turned the team toward his own place, afraid to look back at Christy for fear her resolve would weaken. She swallowed hard to keep from turning around in the seat to look back.

It never paid to look back. Hadn't Granddaddy said that, more times than she could count?

Webb seemed to know she didn't want to talk, and he held his peace all the way to his ranch house.

When Megan had last seen her section of the Primrose Creek tract, there had been only grass, trees, meadows, and water, with a frieze of mountains edging the blue ceiling of sky. Now the place boasted a house as fine as Bridget's or Christy's, a two-story log structure with glass windows, four chimneys, and a covered veranda out front. The barn was four times the size of the house, Megan noted, and the corral was spacious, fenced with whitewashed rails. Cattle and horses roamed the nearby pastures, grazing in the sweet grass.

She drew in her breath.

"Like it?" Webb asked. His voice was quiet, but there was a note of pride in it.

She sighed. "It's—very nice."

"You could plant a few flowers. Stitch up some curtains, maybe. If you have time, I mean."

"Yes," Megan agreed. She caught hold of her runaway emotions, gathered up her skirts, and made to climb down from the wagon. Webb caught hold of her arm and held her fast in the seat.

"Sit tight," Webb said. "I'll help you down."

She was unnerved by the idea of his hands on her waist, but she didn't have the strength to resist. "Very well," she murmured, and the next thing she knew, she was suspended between heaven and earth, Webb's strong hands clasping her sides. It seemed that she hung there, a creature of neither ground nor sky, for an eternity, looking down into Webb's eyes.

"I'll show you to your room," he said, walking away,

lowering the tailgate with a clatter, dragging the trunk across the wagon bed so he could lift it into his arms. "I reckon you'll want to spend the rest of the day getting settled."

Megan merely nodded, at a loss for words. Then she heard a dog barking exuberantly and turned to see a great yellow hound bounding toward them from the direction of the barn.

"That's just Augustus," Webb said, passing her with the trunk, headed toward the house. "He's given to a variety of enthusiasms, but he won't hurt you."

It had never entered Megan's mind that the animal would do her injury. She loved anything with four feet and fur, and Augustus most certainly fit the bill.

"Hullo," she greeted him.

He jumped up, resting his huge paws on her shoulders, and licked her face.

Megan laughed.

"Augustus," Webb growled, without even looking back. "Get down."

Augustus ignored his master and laved Megan from chin to forehead, all over again, making a jubilant whimpering sound in his throat the whole while.

Megan ruffled him behind the ears, and he dropped to all fours then, panting, to trot along at her side as she followed Webb toward the house.

The inside was cool and clean, smelling of beeswax, lamp oil, and recent wood fires. A hooked rug lay on the floor in front of the kitchen fireplace, and Augustus plopped himself down on it with a long-suffering sigh, as though exhausted.

Megan took in the fine big cookstove, the open shelves lined with canned goods, sundries, and neatly stacked blue dishes, the planed and polished floors. Although there was nothing feminine about the place, it was welcoming, in a rustic sort of way, and Megan began to think in terms of pictures on the walls, potted geraniums, and good things baking in the oven. It wasn't a long leap from there to flocks of fair-haired children, some with their father's periwinkle eyes, some with green.

"You'll be sleeping in here," Webb said, his voice echoing from a room just off the kitchen.

Megan gathered her wits and followed the sound. The room was small, but it had a high window and a little stove for cold high-country nights. The bed was narrow and looked as though it might have been hauled in from the bunkhouse, but there was a nice quilt for a coverlet, and the pillow looked soft.

Under the window was a wash stand, again very plain, topped with a basin and pitcher, white enamel, lined at the rims with red and chipped black here and there. He'd set out a towel and a bar of store-bought soap, and Megan was oddly touched by the sight. Webb had taken pains to see that she felt at home, she could tell that much.

"You can hang your clothes on these pegs," he said, quite unnecessarily, gesturing toward a row of wooden dowels nailed to a long, rough-hewn board and attached to the wall.

"Thank you," Megan said. She was wearing the only presentable dress she possessed, having refused the garments Christy had wanted to give her, unable to bear being the recipient of charity, even from her sister. What would her new employer think when he entered the kitchen one morning soon and found his housekeeper dressed in taffeta and feathers or beaded and ruffled silk? She smiled to think of it.

Webb went to the door, giving her a surprisingly wide berth as he passed, considering the fact that the room was hardly larger than a fruit crate. "If Augustus decides to come calling," he said, "just show him the way out."

Megan nodded, oddly unable to speak.

She was a wanderer, with no place of her own. So why did she feel, for the first time in her life, as though she'd finally come home?

Chapter

4

Megan's first housekeeping task was making breakfast for Webb, since he hadn't eaten, and by the time he came in from the barn, she had biscuits ready, along with thick sausage gravy. She was amused and oddly touched to see that he filled a plate for Augustus and set it on a sunny spot in the middle of the kitchen floor before starting his own meal. Megan had had toasted bread and a poached egg at Christy's, so she wasn't hungry.

She assessed the contents of the shelves while Webb and the dog ate with impressive appetite.

"This is good," Webb said between helpings. He sounded surprised. Again.

Megan allowed herself a brief smile, though she tended to concentrate purely on the business at hand, whatever it might be, and at that moment, she was making a mental grocery list. "Thank you," she said. "I can

ride, too, and herd cattle, if you have need of that."
Hadn't he and the other men bemoaned the lack of
workers in and around Primrose Creek just the night
before?

She heard him lay down his fork. "That's no work
for a woman," he said.

Megan's list blew out of her mind like feathers scattering in a brisk wind. She turned. "I beg your pardon?"
she said. Augustus whimpered once, as though sensing
the approach of something ominous.

Webb's eyes danced; plainly, her annoyance amused
him, and that realization added fuel to a kindling fire.
"What I meant was, I didn't hire you to ride herd, brand,
or check fence lines. There's plenty right here to keep
you busy."

Megan frowned. "But if you're short-handed—"

"Short-handed?" Webb echoed. "I'd have to hire three
or four men before I could call myself short-handed. I
reckon I'm going to have to ride down to Virginia City
and see if I can scare up a few cowpunchers." He paused.
"Is there any more coffee?"

She fetched the pot from the stovetop, carried it over
to the table, and refilled his cup. He and the dog had left
their plates clean, and that pleased her. Augustus probably would have eaten anything, it was true, but Webb
had enjoyed her cooking, and that gave her the first real
sense of accomplishment she'd had in a long time. Still,
she was nettled by his assumption that she couldn't
manage range work.

"Apparently, you don't understand what it means to
be a McQuarry," she said.

Webb nodded toward the chair across the table from
his. "Sit down," he told her quietly. Because the words

had the tone of an invitation rather than a command, Megan complied.

"What," he asked when she was settled, "does it mean to be a McQuarry?"

She was shaken by the tenderness of the question and by the genuine interest she saw in Webb's eyes. He wasn't just asking to be polite, he truly wanted to know. Or did he? She'd once thought the same thing about Davy, and look where *that* had gotten her. She bit her lower lip, stalling, and then sighed. "I've been able to ride since I could walk, Mr. Stratton. I can shoot, too, and I've rounded up my share of cattle, as it happens."

"Bringing the milk cows in from the pasture isn't what I had in mind," he said. "You won't be called on to do any shooting at all, and if you find yourself with time on your hands, I could use some new shirts. You sew, don't you?"

She nodded. In truth, she'd never done more with a needle and thread than put up a hem or repair a torn seam, but she could do virtually anything she set her mind to, she was certain of that.

"Good," he said. "Maybe you could drive into town later. Pick out some yard goods and the like."

She'd have to face the townspeople eventually anyway, might as well get it over with and let them all know she wouldn't be cowed by their disapproval. "All right," she agreed, and she must have sounded a little uncertain, because she saw something like sympathy in Webb's eyes.

She hated sympathy; it was close kin to pity, and Megan could not tolerate that. Years before, when she and Christy had traveled to England with the woman they'd believed to be their mother, the two of them had been promptly shipped off to St. Martha's, a venerable boarding school chosen by their English stepfather, where they had been viewed as uncouth colonials, hailing from a country where slavery was practiced. They'd been penniless into the bargain and frightfully homesick for Granddaddy and the farm, and those pupils who hadn't scorned them had felt sorry for them. Some did both.

"What's going on in that head of yours?" Webb asked forthrightly.

Once again, Megan felt compelled to raise her guard. She wasn't about to share the memories that still bewildered her at times, still ached in the corners of her spirit like new bruises. She hadn't told Skye about those hurts, or even Christy. "I was thinking that you need flour and sugar, not to mention lard," she lied. "Are there chickens?"

"Chickens?" he echoed, as though he'd never heard of the species.

"You know," she prompted cheerfully, "those creatures with beady eyes and feathers. They lay eggs and make a wonderful Sunday supper, fried and served with mashed potatoes."

Mirth lighted his eyes again. "Oh," he said. "Those. Well, no. I don't guess I've gotten around to that yet."

"We must have chickens," Megan said.

"I'll put up a coop while you're fetching what you need from town," Webb replied. "You don't mind going by yourself, do you?"

She shook her head. She'd made the trip many times, of course, and she was used to doing things on her own.

Twenty minutes later, Megan was driving toward Primrose Creek in her employer's buckboard, a list in one pocket of her dress and a fair amount of Mr. Stratton's money in the other. It occurred to her that she could just keep going, taking the funds, the team, and the wagon with her, but she never seriously considered the idea. She wasn't a thief, and she wasn't going to run away if she could help it. She'd made up her mind, during the long night just past, to set her heels, dig in, and stay put.

Some of her resolve evaporated, however, when she drew stares just by driving down the main street of town. Determined, she stopped the wagon in front of old Gus's general store and secured the team, watching out of the corner of her eye as a gaggle of women clad in calico and bombazine collected on the board sidewalk out front. She heard the whispers, and color flared in her face, but she managed a polite smile all the same. She had been an actress, after all, and a good one.

"Your eyes do not deceive you, ladies," she said, spreading her arms and executing a very grand curtsey. "Megan McQuarry has returned to Primrose Creek in all her glory."

The women muttered and looked to each other for assurance that, yes, they'd really seen this brazen creature, really heard her *dare* to speak to them in such an impudent fashion.

"Humph," said a plump, white-haired woman, barely taller than the metal jockeys that had served as hitching posts in front of the old McQuarry farmhouse. In her rustling black dress, she resembled a squat crow.

When a feminine laugh came from somewhere nearby, Megan and all the ladies turned their heads to see Diamond Lil herself looking on, from just a little way down the sidewalk. She was a splendid creature, Lil was, tall and slender, with deep black hair and amber eyes. She wore the latest San Francisco fashion in pink and gold silk, and her lacy parasol was a work of art, all on its own.

"Don't mind the welcoming committee," Lil said to Megan, as though the half-dozen townswomen were no more cognizant of her words than the street itself or the display of work boots in the window of Gus's store. "They've got nothing better to do with their time, I reckon, than to keep track of your comings and goings."

Megan stared at Lil, fascinated. She'd never seen the woman up close, though she was an institution in Primrose Creek, owning several businesses besides her infamous saloon. Then she put out a hand. "Megan McQuarry," she said.

Lil took the offered hand, shook it graciously. "Lillian Colefield," she replied. "Well, now," she said, looking Megan over. "I heard tell you were an actress."

Gasps and mutters arose from the cluster of Primrose Creek's version of high society.

Megan swept them all up in a quelling glare before meeting Lil's steady gaze again. "Yes," she said clearly.

"I've been thinking of opening a show house, next to my saloon. I might be looking to hire somebody like you."

The ladies clucked at this, like scalded hens, and Megan stifled a laugh. She'd taken a job with Webb Stratton, and she had no reason to leave, but it was nice to know she had another option. "Thank you," she said. "I'll keep that in mind."

Lil was studying the wagon and team. "That looks like Webb Stratton's rig," she said.

Megan felt the words like a punch—it was none of her business, what Webb did when he came to town, she reminded herself—but hid her reaction by broadening her smile. "I'm his housekeeper," she said in a voice meant to carry.

More murmurs among the ladies. This was turning out to be a fruitful day for them, Megan reckoned.

Lil obviously enjoyed the reactions to Megan's announcement. "Well, now," she said. "Lucky you."

Megan felt her color heighten, though she wasn't precisely sure why that should have happened. It wasn't as if there was anything going on between her and Mr. Stratton, after all. She was merely his housekeeper. "I guess I'd better get my marketing done," she said, "while I've still got work."

"You come see me if you have a mind to perform in my theater," Lil reiterated.

"I will," Megan promised. She had enjoyed acting, if not the attendant way of life, but she hoped she wouldn't end up treading the boards again, out of choice or necessity. She wanted to soak in sunshine, not the faint glow of footlights, and she was all too aware that her sisters would suffer a great deal at the hands of the ladies of Primrose Creek if she took up with the likes of Diamond Lil Colefield. "Thank you," she said once more.

Inside the store, Gus greeted her with a jovial smile. Dear Gus. He hadn't a pretentious bone in his big, bear-like body, and he'd been a good friend to the McQuarrys from the first. She well remembered the day, soon after she and her sister and Caney had arrived at Primrose Creek, that Christy had gone resolutely to town to sell their mother's brooch for desperately needed funds. Gus had given Christy fifty dollars—a fortune—for the pin and held on to it, making it clear that Christy should come back for it when she had the means. Later, when he and Christy were married, Zachary had reclaimed the piece as a gift for his bride.

"Hullo, Gus," she said warmly.

"Miss Megan," he boomed, plainly delighted. "Welcome, welcome!"

She smiled as she brought the shopping list out of her pocket. "I've come for supplies," she said. Soon, she was happily examining sturdy cotton cloth for the shirts Webb wanted, while Gus gathered the items scribbled onto a piece of brown wrapping paper and placed them carefully in wooden crates.

When she'd finished making her selections, and Gus's sister, Bertha, had cut the lengths of fabric Megan had chosen, she paid the bill in full and couldn't help noticing Gus's gratitude and Bertha's frank surprise. Times had been hard around Primrose Creek since the big forest fire two years before, when most of the town had burned, and a lot of people were probably letting their accounts go unpaid.

Gus loaded the crates into the wagon, chattering in his broken English the whole while. He had some chicks ordered from the widow Baker's farm, he said, and promised to bring out a batch as soon as they arrived. Like Lil, he had raised Megan's spirits considerably, making her feel welcome, and she was in a cheerful state of mind as she headed back toward Webb's ranch.

Webb's ranch. Best she remember that.

Reaching the far western side of Bridget and Trace's land, which bordered the acres she'd sold to Stratton, she stopped the team and wagon on a knoll and sat surveying all she had given up. A crushing wave of regret crashed over her, followed by fury, with herself and with Davy Trent. Resolutely, Megan brought down the reins smartly and got the rig moving again, jostling and jolting down the hillside toward the house Webb had built.

He'd been sawing wood in the side yard, apparently for the chicken coop, and he wasn't wearing a shirt. His suspenders dangled at his sides, and he was sweating. Megan willed herself to look away, but she found that she couldn't.

He grinned and shrugged into his shirt, leaving it to gape. His hands rested on his hips. "Looks like you laid in enough grub to last right through till next spring," he observed. He seemed pleased.

"It would be nice to have some beef and a side of pork," she said in a businesslike fashion, feeling her flesh blaze with heat as he lifted her down from the wagon. What in the name of all that was holy was wrong with her, she wondered. Perhaps she was coming down with a fever. "Do you have a springhouse?"

His hands lingered at the sides of her waist for the merest fraction of a moment, but it was long enough to send fire shooting through Megan's most private regions. "An ice house," he said. "I'll show you, after I unload these crates."

She allowed him to help, not because she was lazy or because the work was too much for her, but because she felt hot and a bit dizzy. Sunstroke, she mused. Red-haired people had to be careful about getting too much sun.

When all the crates were inside, Webb led the way to

the ice house. It was a cave, dug into the side of a knoll and lined with straw. Blocks of ice, probably hauled down out of the mountains in the height of winter, cooled the dank air. A deer carcass hung from a hook in one of the beams holding up the sod roof.

"Venison," Megan said, already planning dinner.

"Sounds good," Webb replied. He was standing in the doorway, his arms folded, watching her. Because his face was in shadow, she could not read his expression, but his voice was warm and quiet, establishing an intimacy between them that should have unsettled Megan but didn't. "How did things go in town?"

Megan couldn't resist telling him. Her smile was mischievous, though she figured he wouldn't see it in the gloom. "Diamond Lil offered me a job, acting in her new show house. I guess you'd better be nice to me—it seems I'm quite sought after."

He laughed, one shoulder braced against the heavy framework of the door. "I'll keep that in mind," he said.

Megan was conscious of the things inside the house, needing to be put in their proper places, but Webb was blocking the way out. Though there was nothing threatening in his manner—indeed, Megan felt drawn to him, not repelled—she didn't dare try to press past him.

"I—I have work to do," she said.

His grin flashed. "Me, too," he agreed. Then, to Megan's enormous relief, he turned and walked away, leaving the passage clear.

Megan dashed out as if the place had caught fire and flames were licking at her heels. Temporarily blinded by the bright sunlight, she crashed right into Webb's back and would have fallen if he hadn't turned around quickly and clasped her upper arms in both hands to steady her. She was as mortified as if she'd deliberately flung herself at him—not that she'd ever do such a thing.

He stared down at her, still holding her. Then he laughed, low in his throat, and let her go. "Watch out," he counseled. "You might just fall."

Indeed, she thought, she might fall. Maybe she already had.

Megan had been keeping house for Webb Stratton for a full three days before Skye and Caney came to pay a social call. They found her in the bunkhouse, sweeping the floor. It was a new building, never used by cowboys, although a few rats and other creatures had obviously made their nests inside. Webb had left for Virginia City that morning, hoping to hire a crew, and Megan had been working hard ever since, mostly to distract herself from the fact that she already missed him.

Not that she had any right or reason to think about the man, one way or the other. It just seemed that she couldn't help herself.

Augustus, sleeping in a pool of sunlight just inside the bunkhouse door, roused himself to greet the company with friendly, speculative *woofs* and some hand-licking. Skye laughed and ruffled his ears. Caney surveyed the newly washed window, open to the breeze, and the thin mattresses rolled up on the metal cots lining both walls.

"So you ain't forgotten how to work," the older woman observed.

Skye elbowed her. "Stop your fussing," she said, but there was long-standing affection in her tone. "You've no call to be so contrary."

Megan stood still, broom handle in hand, amazed to find herself with guests. "Come into the house," she said. "I'll brew some tea."

"I'd like to see where you sleep," Caney announced.

Megan and Skye exchanged looks, then avoided each other's eyes lest they break into giggles, the way they'd done so often when they were girls.

"I have the whole downstairs to myself," Megan said, leading the way across the yard and in through the kitchen door. Augustus trotted along at her side, his great broom of a tail swaying from side to side.

"I'll have me a look just the same," Caney said.

Megan sighed. Inside the kitchen, she paused to wash her hands and splash her face at the basin. After using the damask towel on the rod above the small table, she showed them her room, with its narrow bed, its window, its row of pegs, where her dresses hung. She had eight, none of them really suited to life on the banks of Primrose Creek, but they were her own, and she took care of them.

Caney inspected everything—the stove, the quilt, the latch on the window. There was a look of solemn concentration on her face.

"Satisfied?" Megan asked, arching an eyebrow.

Caney huffed but said nothing.

"Let's have that tea," Skye suggested, speaking brightly.

Megan smiled and nodded.

Back in the kitchen area, Skye and Caney took seats at the table, while Megan set about brewing tea.

"Where is that man, anyhow?" Caney demanded.

"I assume you mean Mr. Stratton?" Megan inquired. Caney had always been bristly, even at the best of times, and the very fact that she had come to call was reassuring. "He's gone to Virginia City to hire cowhands."

Skye looked worried. "You're staying here all by yourself?"

Megan didn't reply, since the answer was so obvious.

"I declare," marveled Caney.

"Oh, for heaven's sake," Megan snapped, reaching the end of her patience. "I'm a grown woman." Augustus came to her, toenails *click-click*ing on the wood floor, and nuzzled her right hand. "With a dog. Besides, I've been wanting time to think, remember?"

"That hound don't amount to no kind of protection," Caney protested. At least she was speaking to Megan; that was something. "You best come on back over the creek and sleep at Miss Christy's till Webb gets home."

Megan had no intention of leaving the house unattended, even for a night. She had things to do. "I'm making shirts for Mr. Stratton," she said, although she did not call Webb "Mr. Stratton" anymore or even think of him except in terms of his Christian name. "I've made patterns from newspaper and pinned them to the cloth, but I'm afraid to cut out the pieces."

Caney waved a hand. "I'll show you how to do that," she said.

It was tantamount to a hug and kiss, that statement, given the rift that had opened between Caney and the youngest of her four charges. At least, Megan *thought* she was the youngest. Now she wasn't sure of anything, where she and her sisters were concerned.

Megan set water on to heat and measured dried tea leaves into a pot. "Thank you," she said mildly, and turned her attention to Skye. "Where is little Susannah this fine day?"

Skye beamed at the mention of her daughter. "She's with Bridget."

Megan came to the table and sat down while she waited for the kettle to boil. "You're happy with Jake, aren't you?" she asked softly.

"Deliriously," Skye said, and blushed.

Megan turned her gaze to Caney. "What about you? Have you made any progress with Mr. Hicks?"

Caney's expression darkened with the approach of a storm. "Don't you mention that man's name to me. I done showed him the road."

Megan was stunned, while Skye looked distinctly uncomfortable and, at one and the same time, amused.

"What?" Megan asked, certain that she must have heard wrongly.

"I'm done waitin' for that man to marry up with me," Caney went on. Apparently, if she was going to refer to Malcolm Hicks at all, she was going to call him That Man and nothing else. "I told him, 'You go find some other woman to mend your socks and listen to your tall tales and boil up pig's feet and beans for your dinner. I'm through.' "

"But why?" Megan was truly surprised. Caney had always been so resolute, so diligent, in her pursuit of Mr. Hicks's affections. "I thought you loved him."

Caney's beautiful black eyes filled with tears. "I want to be his wife, not his woman. Unless he declares hisself and stands up with me, in front of Reverend Taylor, things ain't never goin' to change."

The kettle began to boil, and Megan got up, crossed to the stove, and, using an empty flour sack for a pot holder, removed it from the heat. When the tea was brewing, she returned to the table. "I'm sorry," she said, and she meant it. "I suppose he'll come around, though. He must miss you terribly."

"Humph," Caney said. "Where's them yard goods you were talking about?"

"I'll get them after we have tea," Megan replied gently.

"Don't want no tea," Caney replied.

Megan fetched the stack of folded fabrics from her room and set them on the kitchen table. Caney immediately spread them out to have a look, while Skye poured tea for herself and Megan. They sipped, keeping their cups at a thoughtful distance from the lengths of cloth their friend was inspecting.

"You measured that man's shoulders?" Caney asked. " 'Fore you made the pattern, I mean?"

Megan nodded. It brought on another rush of inner heat, remembering how she'd used lengths of string to chart the dimensions of Webb's upper body.

"He's a big man," Caney commented.

"Umm-hmm," Megan said, averting her own gaze only to be snagged by Skye's bright, too knowledgeable glance.

"Fine-looking, too," Skye said.

"Is that any way for a married woman to talk?" Megan challenged, but she was smiling. Webb was indeed fine-looking.

"Why do you suppose he don't have himself a wife, a man like that?" Caney speculated. She was apparently satisfied with Megan's sewing project, so far, for she'd helped herself to a pair of scissors and started cutting out a shirtsleeve.

Megan had asked herself the same question, but she'd never asked Webb, and she had no intention of doing so. It wasn't that she didn't want to know if he'd ever loved a woman—she did—but if he told her about his past, she'd have to reciprocate, and she wasn't ready to do that. Not yet.

"Maybe he was waiting to find the right woman," Skye said, her words accompanied by the *snip-snip* of the scissors and Augustus's deep, contented sigh. The dog was lying at Megan's feet, his large, soft body warm against her ankle. "Webb, I mean."

Megan blushed. "Maybe he's already got a wife someplace," she said.

"Nonsense," Skye scoffed. "She'd be here with him if he did."

Megan wasn't sure why she was arguing the point; if she were perfectly honest, she'd admit that she purely *hated* the thought of Webb being married. Which was completely unreasonable of her, of course, since Mr. Stratton's private life was no concern of hers. She was there to cook, clean, and sew, and that was all.

She sighed. "Maybe," she agreed. Whether Webb had ever taken a wife or not, there were bound to be women in his life. Hadn't he told her, straight out, that he would confine his romantic interests to the ladies who worked for Diamond Lil? It made her blood sting as though it had turned to kerosene, just thinking about what probably went on in places like that.

Caney had finished cutting out the first shirt and advanced to the second, after rearranging some of the pattern pieces to suit her. "One way you could find out, and that's to ask him," she said. "If he's got hisself a wife somewheres, I mean."

Megan was mortified. "I wouldn't!" she gasped, coloring up.

Skye smiled over the rim of her teacup. "But you do want to know—don't you?"

Megan glared at Skye. "No."

"Don't lie to me. I know you too well. You're *smitten.*"

"I am not!"

Caney made a *tsk-tsk* sound with her tongue. "You two. Carryin' on just like you did when you was babies."

Megan and Skye exchanged another glance, but this one was serious.

"How old was I when I came to Granddaddy's farm?" Megan asked quietly.

Caney paused in her snipping and looked at Megan, and her eyes were dark pools of sadness and inherited suffering. She pressed her full lips together, and for a moment, Megan thought she would refuse to answer. She had been standing to cut out the shirts, but now she sank into her chair, as though too weary to stand. "You, Miss Megan, were about two weeks old."

"Where did I come from?"

Caney was silent for a long time, but her gaze was steady. "I reckon you know you were Mr. Thayer's child, just like the others."

"That isn't what I meant," Megan said.

Caney heaved a sigh. "You were born in New Orleans. Your mama died, having the pair of you."

Both Megan and Skye went so still that they might have been statues in some Greek garden, frozen in moonlight.

"The pair of us?" Skye echoed. She'd set her teacup down, but her hands were still trembling.

Caney's eyes brimmed with fresh tears. "You're twins, the two of you. Oh, you never looked alike, that's true enough, but there's always been a special bond holdin' you together. Didn't you ever wonder about that?"

Instinctively, Skye and Megan linked hands, held on tightly, though all their attention was fixed on Caney.

"Why?" Megan breathed. "Why didn't you *say something*?"

"I promised your granddaddy I wouldn't, that's why," Caney said. "If I could go back, I wouldn't do any different. There's been enough trouble in this family."

Skye was breathing deeply and slowly, as though trying to keep her composure, and her fingers clung to Megan's. "Tell us," Megan insisted, "what you know about our mother."

"Was she—was she a lady of the—the evening?" Skye dared to ask.

Caney's face was lined with pain and reluctance and the knowledge that it was futile trying to hold the old secrets at bay. "She was an Irish serving girl," she said. Her countenance darkened again. "Sixteen years old. Prettiest thing you ever saw."

"Did our father abandon her?"

"*That* rascal," Caney said, her tone edged with an old fury. "Never you mind him. Your mama, she died the day after you were born. Wouldn't have been able to keep two little babies anyhow. She had no family, and the people she worked for had already turned her out. She'd have starved to death if Gideon McQuarry hadn't heard about her and stepped in to make sure she had a decent place to stay and food to eat."

Some of the luster had gone off that glittering summer day, for Megan at least, thinking of that poor young girl, destitute except for the kindness of a stranger, but at least she knew where she'd come from. And she was Skye's twin. The knowledge was wondrous, and, at the same time, it seemed as though she'd always known.

"What was her name?" Skye asked.

Caney sighed. "Maureen," she recalled, very softly. "I didn't know her for long. Your granddaddy sent me to look after her, down there in New Orleans. I was supposed to bring her and her baby home to Virginia, once the birth was over—nobody dreamed there was two of you—but the chile was plumb done in. Mr. Thayer, he done broke her, someplace deep inside. She hung on for a day, then she just closed her eyes and died. Saddest thing I ever did see."

Megan and Skye were both silent, envisioning the scene. Skye had borne a child, and Megan could imagine what it must be like. They understood Maureen's ordeal well enough.

"Who was born first?" Megan asked.

"Who named us?" Skye wanted to know, her words tumbling over Megan's, tangling with them.

Caney's smile was sad. "Miss Skye, you were the first one born. Five minutes later," she went on, turning to Megan, "you came along. Your mama gave you your names—she'd been saving them up, I think."

"And our father?"

"Thayer McQuarry?" Caney made another gesture with her hand, one of dismissal, angry and blunt. "That scoundrel? He'd landed himself in jail by that time."

"Jail?" Skye asked.

"He'd got himself into another duel," Caney explained. She rose back to her feet and began to cut fabric again, taking refuge in work as she had always done. "Killed a senator's son. He was hanged a month later."

Megan put a hand to her mouth.

"I wish we'd never asked," Skye murmured, her dark eyes haunted.

Caney's smile was all the more powerful for being totally unexpected. "Well, now," she said, "that's the thing with a McQuarry. They just keep on askin' until they find out the truth, even when it would be better not to know."

Neither Megan nor Skye even tried to deny that. Their granddaddy had taught them most everything they needed to know to get on in life—except when to quit.

Chapter
5

"Webb? That you?"

Webb, bellied up to the bar in Virginia City's infamous Bucket of Blood Saloon, glanced up from the glass of whiskey he had yet to touch and stared in amazement into the greasy, bottle-lined mirror. He turned and faced his younger brother, Jesse. Seven years before, when Webb had seen him last, Jesse had been just sixteen, green and gangly, but he was a man now, pure and simple. There was a stony glint in his blue eyes that troubled Webb, but the .45 riding low on the kid's hip bothered him a lot more.

"What the hell are you doing here?" he asked.

Jesse's Adam's apple bobbed at the base of his throat, went still again. He edged up to the bar and stood shoulder to shoulder with Webb, studying their reflections in the big mirror. Except for the ten years that lay between them—eventful years, into the bargain—they looked much alike. "I might ask you the same question," Jesse responded at last.

"I'm looking to hire some cowpunchers," Webb allowed. "How's Pa?" he asked when Jesse didn't speak again right away. Any mention of his family was deeply personal to Webb; he'd never discussed them with anyone at Primrose Creek, even though he considered that his home. He didn't worry about being overheard, though; the Bucket of Blood was a noisy place, even in the middle of the day, filled with tinny piano music, the click of pool balls, the arguments and celebratory whoops of its most dedicated patrons.

Jesse nodded to the bartender, and a glass was set before him. He poured a helping from Webb's bottle, raised it in a mocking toast, and drank. "Pa? Well, he's meaner than he ever was," he said.

Webb closed his eyes. *Mean* wasn't a fit word to describe the old man; he made a grizzly with a mouthful of wasps seem cordial.

"He never put a bounty on my head?" he asked after a few moments, taking a drink at last. His hand shook a little as he raised the glass, and he hoped his kid brother hadn't noticed.

"Why the devil would he do that?" Jesse asked. "He'd rather shoot you himself."

Webb sighed. "And Eleanor?" he asked very quietly. It was odd; he'd loved Eleanor Stratton, his sister-in-law, from the day she came to the Southern Star as his elder brother's bride, and once she'd turned to him for comfort and given him reason to believe she felt the same way. Now, when he tried to assemble her features in his mind, all he could see was Megan McQuarry's face.

"Same as usual," Jesse allowed. "At least, she was fine last time I was there. That was a couple of years back. I'm not much more welcome on the old place than you are, big brother."

Webb had expected Eleanor to return to her home folks back east after Tom was killed. After *he* had killed Tom, beat him to death with his bare hands. The memory brought up his gorge, and he pushed the glass away, his mind awash in blood. His brother's blood. "I'm surprised she stayed," he said at some length, and his voice sounded gruff and strange, even in his own ears. "At least I figured she'd remarry and move to town."

Jesse looked puzzled. Time had hardened him, and there was a bleak distance in his eyes that gnawed at Webb in some deep and hurtful place. He'd been all Jesse had, and he'd abandoned him. If the boy had gone wrong in the meantime, Webb would have to claim his share of the fault. "I reckon Tom would frown on that," he said.

For Webb, it seemed that all the mechanisms of heaven and earth, seen and unseen, ground to a halt in that moment. Tom was dead, Webb had knelt beside his body, in the tide of receding rage, and felt for a pulse. There hadn't been one.

Suddenly, Jesse laughed. "Good God," he rasped, refilling his glass nearly to the brim. "You thought you killed him!"

Even in the Bucket of Blood, such a remark was likely to draw attention. Webb grabbed the whiskey bottle with one hand and his younger brother's elbow with the other, then hustled him toward the swinging doors. Outside, on the sloping wooden sidewalk, Jesse still laughed. Webb dragged him into an alley, dropped the bottle to the ground, where it shattered musically, caught Jesse by the lapels of his worn shirt, and hurled him backward against a clapboard wall.

"He's alive?" he demanded. "Tom is *alive?*"

Jesse's face went cold, and he shrugged out of Webb's grip. "Yeah, no thanks to you. Took him a year to get over the thrashing you gave him."

Webb closed his eyes, but the memories pursued him all the same, glaring and fresh, acrid with the stench of blood. He'd found Ellie hiding in the corn patch that morning seven years back, her delicate arms covered with bruises, her eyes blackened. He'd raised her to her feet, led her back to the house, and attended to her wounds as gently as if she were a child. She hadn't admitted, even then, that Tom had come in drunk, sometime in the night, and taken his fists to her, but Webb had known. He hadn't been at home himself the previous evening, or he might have heard her screams. God knew he'd heard them before, and he'd intervened before, too.

"Leave him," he'd said. "I'll look after you."

She'd stared at him, dazed, and shook her head, curled in on herself like a small animal trying to shield itself from further blows. He carried her to his own bedroom, laid her down, and covered her gently. Then, coldly furious, he'd gone in search of Tom.

"They've got a boy now," Jesse said, in a more prudent tone, bringing Webb back from the ugliest regions of his mind. "Named him Tom the third."

Webb wished he hadn't dropped the whiskey, because he sure could have used a drink just then. In point of fact, he could have used a whole still. "How old?" he ground out.

"The boy?" Jesse frowned, but there was something in his eyes, a knowledge, a suspicion. A smirk displaced the frown. "I reckon he'd be about six by now. Ellie must have been carrying him when you gave Tom that licking."

Webb cursed. "Did he—does he—?"

"Does Tom still get drunk and pound on Ellie?" Jesse asked, with no discernible emotion. "No. Once she had the boy, she changed. Wouldn't take no grief from him or anybody else, including Pa. First time Tom got himself drunked up—and that was a long time coming, considering the shape you left him in—she met him at the front door with a shotgun and swore she'd kill him if he ever raised a hand to her or the kid." Jesse smiled at the memory, and there was a meanness in the expression that Webb despaired to see. "I guess he must have seen the light. There was never any trouble after that."

Webb's mind reeled; he turned away from his younger brother, turned back. "My God," he whispered, taking his hat off and then immediately putting it on again. "All this time—"

"All this time, you've been looking over your shoulder, expecting a posse?" Jesse seemed to enjoy the thought. In fact, he hooted with laughter, and Webb might have punched him in the mouth if he hadn't sworn off violence a long time before. He hadn't used his fists or carried a pistol since that day on the Southern Star, when he'd left his own flesh and blood for dead, and he still didn't trust himself.

"You think that's funny?" he asked, his voice very quiet.

It was a warning, and Jesse caught on right away, for

once. He paled and offered up a faltering, foolish smile. "Hey, Webb. It's me, Jesse. Your kid brother." He slapped Webb's shoulder. "Come on. I'll buy you a drink."

Webb had a thousand questions to ask, but he knew he would never be able to give voice to most of them. He'd confine his curiosity to Jesse himself, forget the old man and Tom had ever existed. As for the boy, Thomas Stratton III, well, he wasn't ready to think about him at all. "No," Webb said, "I'll buy *you* a steak. We have some ground to cover."

Jesse was pleased at the prospect of a free meal; he'd always been a hearty eater—the work was hard on the Southern Star and on any other ranch, hard enough to stoke any man's appetite, let alone that of a growing kid—and to Webb he looked a little down on his luck. No telling how long it had been since the boy had eaten anything but trail food, though from the look and smell of him, he hadn't been passing up the whiskey.

In the dining room of the Comstock Hotel, over slabs of beef cooked rare along with creamed corn and baked potatoes, the brothers gave abbreviated versions of their recent pasts. Jesse had left the Southern Star after a particularly nasty quarrel with the old man, and he'd been drifting ever since, stopping to punch cattle on some ranch or sign up with a trail drive whenever he ran low on money. He spoke wistfully of the home place, though, and Webb saw resentment flash in the boy's blue eyes when he said he was sure their father must have signed the land and livestock over to Tom Jr. by then.

Good riddance, thought Webb. He'd loved the land, of course he had, for he was a cattleman by blood, but he had a place of his own now, the ranch at Primrose Creek. He would build it into an enterprise to equal or even surpass the Southern Star, but that was where the similarity ended. He wanted children, sons and daughters, and if he was lucky enough to have them, he wouldn't pit them against each other the way Tom Sr. had done, that was for damn sure. Nor would he wear out three wives, planting them one by one in a desolate, windswept churchyard overlooking the muddy Missouri River, along with their many ill-fated babies, laid to rest in coffins no bigger than shoe boxes.

"Where'd you get the money to buy your own place?" Jesse wanted to know. He'd finished his steak and was starting in on a wedge of cherry pie.

Webb had saved a part of his wages ever since he'd begun drawing them when he was fourteen, and after leaving the Southern Star he'd hooked up with a couple of cattle drives out of Texas and Mexico. In time, he'd become a trail boss, and, as such, he'd gotten a percentage of the profits. He saw no need to explain all that to Jesse, who was apparently more inclined to squander whatever came his way. "I worked," he said. "I'm looking for some cowpunchers right now. You know of any?"

Jesse beamed. "Sure I do. I'll sign on. So will seven or eight of my friends, and a few strangers to boot, I reckon, if the wages are right."

"The wages are nothing fancy," Webb said, "but there's a good bunkhouse, and I've hired on a woman to cook." It seemed an understatement of phenomenal proportions, describing Megan as "a woman to cook," but hers wasn't a name he wanted to bandy about. In some indefinable way, it was nearly sacred.

"You never married?" Jesse asked, between bites of pie.

Webb shook his head. He'd loved Ellie, and they both knew it. Hell, everybody in Montana probably knew. "What about you?" he asked, though he was sure Jesse hadn't gotten beyond the stage of chasing saloon girls.

"No plans to settle down," Jesse said proudly, as though he were the first man ever to come up with the idea.

Webb smiled to himself. "I see," he said, as a serving woman came and filled his coffee cup. "Well, you round up your friends when you finish up. I'll hire on every man with warm blood in his veins and a horse to ride."

Jesse nodded. He would expect special treatment, Webb supposed, being the boss's brother. No sense in disillusioning him too soon. In point of fact, Jesse would be expected to carry his own weight, just like all the others.

He finished his pie and had a second piece, and Webb watched with amusement while that went down Jesse's gullet as fast as the first one. Then, while Webb enjoyed his coffee, Jesse got to his feet, apparently restored. "Where do we meet," he asked, "and when?"

Webb had been lucky that day, and not just because of the reunion with Jesse, the brother he'd left behind. He'd expected to have trouble hiring the men he needed, but now it seemed that fate was going to provide those, too. It made him uneasy when things just fell into place like that.

"I've got a room here," he said. "I'll talk to the men in the morning and buy breakfast for everybody who hires on. I'll get you a bed if you want one."

That smirk lifted one corner of Jesse's mouth again.

"Oh, I've got me a bed for the night," he said. "But thanks anyway. We'll see you out front."

"Dawn," Webb warned, although he was in no real position to make demands. Most of the men in Virginia City were miners, unlikely to saddle up and head out to ride herd in the high country. He'd take whatever help he could get and be glad of it.

Shortly after Jesse had nodded and taken his leave, Webb finished his coffee, settled the bill, and took himself upstairs. In his room, he lit a kerosene lamp, kicked off his boots, and stretched out on the lumpy bed to read a book he'd brought along from home. Finding himself too groggy to focus his eyes, he finally undressed, turned down the wick, and lay down to sleep.

Instead, he thought about the Jesse he remembered from seven years ago. The boy had been sensitive and skinny, with a love for books as well as horses, and he'd tried desperately to gain the old man's approval, all to no avail. There was a cruel streak in Tom Sr., and the harder Jesse strove to prove himself, the less attention he was paid.

At last, Webb dropped off to sleep, and he wouldn't have been surprised to dream about the Southern Star, about the old man, about Tom Jr., about Ellie and Jesse, even about all those lost babies. God knew he'd had a hundred nightmares about them as a boy, dreamed they were calling to him, calling and calling, thin voices piping on the harsh Montana winds.

Instead, it was Megan McQuarry who haunted his sleep. Megan, with her copper hair and impossibly green eyes, her fiery spirit and quick Irish tongue. He awakened well rested and eager to begin the long, hard ride home to Primrose Creek. Back to Megan.

He was pleasantly taken aback to find Jesse waiting for him out in front of the hotel in the predawn light, his horse saddled and ready to ride. He was sober, incredibly enough, and so were the twelve men he'd recruited to sign on with Webb's outfit. All of them had halfway decent horses and enough gear to see them through.

Webb spoke with each one, and, although he disliked a fair number of them on sight, he was running low on choices. He had cattle and horses to round up and sell to the army, and he couldn't do that on his own.

Jesse at his side, Webb turned his own mount toward the mountains and rode for home.

He was back.

Megan's throat caught with the realization, and she watched from the patch of land she'd been clearing for a kitchen garden as Webb and a dozen men rode toward the house. His face was shaded by the brim of his hat, and yet she would have sworn he was smiling.

She schooled her own expression to one of school-marmish dignity, though not before she'd forgotten herself and raised both hands to make sure her hair wasn't coming down. While the other men made for the barn, there to stable their horses before staking their claims to spots in the bunkhouse, Webb and a young fair-haired cowboy rode toward her. Augustus, barking deliriously, came bounding around the side of the house and rushed to welcome his master.

The two men stopped at the edge of the garden and swung down from their horses. Webb was indeed smiling, Megan realized, but she didn't dare presume that she was the cause of his good spirits, the way he was wrestling the dog in greeting, so she kept her own expression solemn. Inwardly, however, she was over-joyed to see Webb again; a wild surge of happiness arose and danced in her soul.

"Looks like you've been hard at work," Webb observed, indicating the garden patch with a nod of his head. He was still smiling, as though he knew her own straight face was a ruse. Maybe he'd even guessed that she'd missed him sorely.

Augustus had settled down a little, though he still whimpered in delight. Fickle dog. He'd hardly let her out of his sight from the moment Webb left the ranch, and now all his attention was reserved for someone else. Megan gathered up her skirts, suddenly conscious of the bright green silk, once trimmed with feathers at the neckline and hem. She'd torn off the fripperies and rolled up the sleeves, but the gown still looked like what it was—a fancy woman's get-up, made for a stage, a dance hall, or some such place. She saw the boy look-ing at her with frank appreciation, though she was dirty from head to foot, and blushed. "I'll get supper," she said.

Webb's gaze narrowed as he took in her dress, and she thought she saw his jawline tighten a little. He nod-ded almost curtly. "That would be fine," he grumbled.

The young man elbowed him, and he started, first in a flash of temper, then in sudden amusement.

"This is my younger brother, Jesse," Webb said. "Jesse, meet Miss McQuarry, my housekeeper."

It seemed to Megan that Webb hesitated slightly at the word *housekeeper,* as if he wanted to say she was something more, but surely she'd only imagined that. She'd been working hard since Webb had left four days before, and she'd been outside swinging a hoe and picking rocks since noon. Little wonder, then, if she was getting lightheaded and perhaps a bit whimsical. "How do you do?" she said, addressing herself to Jesse. She was still painfully conscious of the dress.

Jesse flushed. Perhaps a decade younger than Webb and not so ruggedly built, he was handsome all the same, and in time he'd be the sort of man to turn women's heads, like his elder brother. "How do?" he responded.

Webb pulled off one glove and indicated the outbuildings. "The bunkhouse is over there," he said to Jesse. "Feed and water your horse, and put away your gear. Time you're washed up, I reckon Miss McQuarry will have something on the table for supper."

Jesse looked somewhat taken aback, as though he'd expected to sleep in the house, and Megan was a little confused herself. In her family, kin was kin. They deserved—and got—the best of everything, no matter how little there might be.

"Sure," Jesse said at last, and led his horse away.

Megan ran her blistered hands down the front of her dress, painfully aware of her appearance. If only she'd known when he was going to return, she found herself thinking, she might have bathed, dressed her hair, put on something pretty. . . .

What was she thinking? She was a housekeeper, not a wife or even a sweetheart. Once again, she touched her hair. Then, embarrassed, she turned and hurried into the house, her face hot.

She went to her room, washed quickly, exchanged her dress for the one simple print gown she owned, and did what she could with her hair. Thankfully, there was fresh-baked bread, and she'd put a pot of beans and hamhocks on the back of the stove earlier in the day. There were eggs, too, from Bridget's hens, brought over the night before by Trace and Noah and stored in a basket in the ice house.

She collected those and put them on to boil, opened several large cans of fruit from the kitchen shelves, and started some biscuits. She was rushing about the kitchen when she became aware of Webb standing just inside the doorway, his hat in his hands. There was a look of curious affection in his blue eyes.

"It's a little late in the year for a vegetable garden, isn't it?" he asked.

"It's only June," she said, flustered, dashing from stove to shelf to table and back again. "There are lots of things that will grow."

He shrugged, hung his hat on a peg next to the door, and stepped inside. His clothes were filthy, and he could have used a bath and barbering, but he looked spectacular to Megan just as he was. It made her pulse race to think that he'd be sleeping under the same roof again, as of that night. She probably wouldn't get a moment's rest.

He proceeded to the wash stand, the dog prancing happily along behind him, nails clicking, tongue lolling. Webb poured water from the pitcher to the basin and began soaping and splashing his face, scrubbing his hands. Megan stood frozen, watching him, and was nearly caught gawking, turning away just in time to avoid notice.

The cowboys began to wander in soon after, led by Jesse Stratton, and they greeted Megan politely with nods and murmured "ma'am"s. They'd done their washing down at the creek, most likely, and while they were still far too dirty for decent company, they were hungry and minding their manners, for the most part, at least. She caught a few of them casting surreptitious glances her way and reckoned they'd seen her in her costume in the garden. None of them dared to make comment, of course, and they took their seats in good order, Webb at the head of the table, and tucked into the food Megan set out for them.

Watching them eat while she brewed coffee at the stove, Megan reflected that Webb had been right— cooking three meals a day for so many men was going to be more work than she'd ever undertaken before. Oddly enough, she liked the idea; like the other McQuarrys, she didn't take to idleness.

When the meal was over, she fed the few scraps to Augustus, who had waited patiently, one eye open to monitor the proceedings throughout supper, stretched out on the hooked rug in front of the kitchen fireplace. The men thanked her modestly and took their leave, including Jesse, disappearing two and three at a time into the twilight, mugs of coffee in their hands, until she was alone with Webb.

"That was a fine meal," Webb said. He lingered at the table, watching her, the light of the lanterns glowing golden in his hair.

She found herself smiling at him. "Why does it always seem to surprise you, Mr. Stratton, when I do something well?"

He had the good grace to look chagrined. He even reddened a little, along that strong jawline of his. He needed to shave, and badly, but Megan realized she wanted to touch him, just the same. She was all the more careful to keep her distance.

"I guess you look more like an actress than a house-keeper," he said.

"I didn't know you had a brother," she replied, because his remark disturbed her, and not in an entirely unpleasant way, and she needed to change the subject.

He sighed. "Ah, yes. Jesse. I ran into him in Virginia City. Turns out he left home more than two years ago."

Megan began washing dishes in a pan on the long counter under the broad eastern window, where morning light would spill in, pink and gold, when the sun rose. "Home?" she asked very quietly. "You mean the family ranch up in Montana?" If he didn't want to answer, if the question was too forward, he could pretend that he hadn't heard.

"For me," he said without hesitation, "home is right here at Primrose Creek."

She was oddly pleased by his answer, even though she grieved for this land that had once been hers. "What made you leave there?" she pressed, scrubbing away at a plate and avoiding his eyes. What caused her to be so daring? Webb Stratton's past was his own business.

He was quiet for a long while. Then, with a sigh, he spoke. "Your family is close-knit," he said. "Mine is different."

She waited.

"We never got along, Pa and me. Tom, Jr.—that's our older brother—and I could hardly stand to be in the same room together."

She felt a kinship with Webb then, for, of course, she'd known her share of familial turmoil, too. "What about your mother?" she asked gently.

"My mother," he reflected. She dared to steal a glance at him, out of the corner of one eye, her attention caught by something in his tone, and saw that he was staring off into the distance, his hands cupped around his enamel mug. He seemed to see something far beyond the sturdy, chinked log wall of the house, something that troubled him a great deal. "She died when I was five, I hardly remember her. Pa married Jesse's ma, Delia, before mine had been gone six months—in all the time I knew her, I never heard him call her by her Christian name. She was always 'woman.' "

Megan couldn't help herself. She went to stand just behind Webb's chair, laid a hand lightly on his shoulder. Took solace in the fact that he didn't pull away. "What was she like? Jesse's mother, I mean?"

He smiled, but a shadow of sadness moved in his eyes. "Delicate. Pretty. Hardly more than a girl when she first came to the ranch. She lost several babies before she managed to have Jesse, then passed on of a fever when he was just three. We didn't have a woman in the house again until Tom, Jr., went back east and married Ellie."

Ellie. Something in the way he said the name left Megan feeling stricken. She waited, not daring to speak, but he didn't say anything more about his brother's wife.

"What about you, Megan?" he asked gruffly. "Do you ever miss the homeplace, back in Virginia?"

She thought of the farm in the lush and fertile Shenandoah Valley, of her beloved granddaddy, and her heart ached for all she'd cared for, and taken so for granted, and finally lost. Once, she would have responded as Webb had and claimed Primrose Creek as the place she belonged. Now, she wasn't sure she fit in anywhere at all, and she didn't know what to say in the face of that insight.

Webb pulled her down into the chair next to his, took both her hands, and frowned when he saw the broken blisters on her palms and the insides of her fingers. His touch was comforting, and, at the same time, it sent a current of dangerous longing surging through her bloodstream.

"You've been working pretty hard," he commented gently.

She turned her head, blinking. She wasn't going to cry. She *wasn't.*

Webb got up, fetched a towel and a tin of salve, turned her hands palms upward, and proceeded to apply the medicine.

"I—I would have been all right," she said.

His eyes were as ferociously tender as a spring sky when he looked up into her face. "You don't much take to being looked after, do you?" he asked.

She drew a deep breath. "It's been my experience that it's better to take care of one's self." Davy had taught her that, single-handedly. She supposed she ought to be grateful for the lesson, but she wasn't.

His gaze searched her face, probing in a way that peeled away layers of carefully guarded defenses and at the same time infinitely gentle. "That's a hard way to live. Believe me, I know."

She drew a deep, resolute breath and got to her feet. "I'm an actress," she said. "Sometimes I can even fool myself."

He stood and examined her hands again. They were covered in salve and none too steady. "Maybe it's time you stopped doing that. Fooling yourself, I mean. You don't need to run anymore, Megan. You're home."

"Home," she echoed, as though the word were

strange to her. In many ways, she guessed, it was. It had meant so many different things during her short lifetime that she was no longer sure how to define it. "This is your ranch, Webb. *Your* home. Not mine."

He'd confided in her, and she wanted to tell him about Davy, about her rogue of a father and her poor, trusting young mother dying in a stranger's bed, but she couldn't make herself do it. She was too afraid of what she might see in his eyes if he knew the whole truth about her. Judgment would be bad enough; pity would be unbearable.

To her amazement, he lifted one hand and stroked her cheek once with the lightest pass of his knuckles. His smile was slight and sorrowful, there one instant and gone the next.

"I'm pretty tired," she blurted, for the things she felt in that moment terrified her, with him touching her that way. And caring. "I need to get some rest." And that was as much a lie as the rest of her life, she thought, because there was something about Webb Stratton that revitalized her, made her feel that she could do anything, as long as he was nearby. Why, if she'd chosen to, she could have hitched up a mule and pushed a plow all night.

"Me, too," he said. "I guess Augustus and I will turn in for the night."

She nodded, vastly relieved. "Good night, then," she said brightly, and glanced at the piles of dishes waiting on the counter.

Webb followed her gaze. "Leave those for morning," he said. Then he smiled. "That's an order."

She laughed, then saluted. "I wouldn't think of disobeying," she replied, and rose to put out the lamps before retiring.

Webb stopped her with a shake of his head. "I'll be up awhile."

She nodded, touched her hair again, and started toward her bedroom.

"Megan?"

She paused, turned to look back over one shoulder. "Yes?"

"Aren't you going to eat anything? You didn't have supper."

She'd entirely forgotten, in the hurry to prepare a suitable meal for fourteen hungry men. It amazed her, the way he noticed these small things—her missing supper, the blisters on her hands—and cared about them. During the hard years away from her family and the dark time in England before that, when she and Christy had had virtually no one except each other, she'd gotten used to keeping her chin up and toughing things out. "I'm not—not really hungry," she said, and that, at least, was true, because besides being stricken to the heart by Webb's kindness, she was also a little frightened. Depending on someone else could serve no purpose other than to weaken her, and she knew she would need all her strength to make any sort of place for herself in the world.

"Good night, then," he said.

Augustus snuffled and lay down on the hooked rug.

"Good night," Megan replied.

Inside her room, she closed her door and leaned against it, waiting for her heartbeat to slow down to a normal pace. Moonlight spilled through the window she valued so highly, silvering the floor, the narrow bed, her collection of useless theatrical dresses hanging on the wall. Through the panel behind her, she heard the stove lids rattle and knew Webb was banking the fire for the night. In a little while, he'd retire to his room upstairs, and she would creep out and finish the dishes. Then, with her work finished, she *might* be able to sleep.

She lit a lamp, exchanged her dress for a nightgown, being careful of the salve on her hands, and sat down on the edge of her bed to take down her hair and brush it. Gradually, a feeling of quiet, rather than an actual lack of sound, descended over the house, and although Megan did not hear Webb's boots on the stairs, she knew he was exhausted, and she was sure he'd gone to bed.

She slipped out of the bedroom, found that the lamps in the kitchen had been extinguished and the fire in the stove had been banked. She was midway across the room when she realized she wasn't alone—maybe it was a sound, maybe it was a feeling, but she knew.

She turned, and there, before the fireplace, where the hooked rug had been, stood a large tin bathtub, and Webb Stratton was lounging in it, one long leg stretched out over the edge. He was smoking a cheroot, and light from the hearth gilded his hair and lent a golden aura to his bare flesh.

Megan might have escaped unnoticed—he appeared to be lost in thought, gazing up at the ceiling—except that she gasped. He heard her then and turned his head. His grin shone like ivory in the night.

"Well, now, Miss McQuarry," he asked cordially, "what would you be doing out here? Not washing dishes or anything like that?"

Every nerve in her body was screaming for flight, but she couldn't move. She might have stepped into a patch of hot tar, so thoroughly was she stuck to the floor.

She saw one of his eyebrows rise.

"Miss McQuarry?" he prompted.

She managed to suck in a breath, and that steadied her a little, though her hands were knotted in front of her and her heart was trying to beat its way out of her chest. "I didn't realize you—you were here."

There was laughter in his voice, and though it was the friendly kind, Megan wasn't reassured. "I don't guess you did."

She tried to move and found that she was still frozen in place. Her knees felt dangerously weak, as though they might give out at any time, and her head was spinning. "I—well—you might have had the decency not to bathe in the kitchen!" she cried in desperation.

"It's my kitchen," he pointed out reasonably and without rancor. "Did you know the moonlight is coming in through the window over there behind you?"

She looked back and realized that her shape was almost surely visible through the fabric of her nightgown. She gasped again, clasped both hands to her mouth in mortification, and dashed for her room, slamming the door behind her.

Even then, she could hear Webb out there in the kitchen laughing. *Laughing,* the wretch. Just then, she didn't know which she wanted more—another look at Webb Stratton in the altogether or sweet, swift revenge.

Webb settled deeper into his bath, grinning long after his laughter had subsided. What a marvel Megan was, he thought. On the one hand, she seemed tough and independent, scrappy enough to take on an army of buzz saws, but there were broken places inside her, too. Private wounds that might never heal.

His grin faded. He'd been down that road with Ellie.

A reasonable man would keep his distance, find himself another woman to think about. Trouble was, when it came to Megan McQuarry, he wasn't a reasonable man.

Chapter
6

Gus set the vented wooden crate on Megan's freshly swept kitchen floor, beaming as he lifted the lid to reveal a swarming, silky, yellow mass of chirping chicks inside. She felt a deep fondness for the big man, watching as he knelt in the midst of all those tiny birds, picking them up so gently in his huge hands.

Augustus, proving himself to be of sterling character, barked once, cheerfully, came over to sniff the milling crowd, and then gave a huge huff of a sigh and went outside. No doubt rabbits would present a more interesting challenge.

Megan crouched with Gus, delighted by the baby chicks. Together, she and the storekeeper put them back into their crate by the handfuls. How, she wondered, would she ever be able to *eat* one of these dear creatures, even when they were big and ugly with their downy tufts turned to stubby feathers?

Gus seemed to read her expression with uncanny accuracy. "Is all right, miss," he said in his broad German accent. "In time, more chicks come. Always more chicks."

Megan was mildly reassured—after all, it would be a while before any of these sweet, messy little critters were real chickens.

"You give them water," Gus went on, "and the feed I brought. Keep them warm, back of the stove, until they can be outside."

Megan nodded, and Gus left the house to bring in a bag of finely ground corn meal. While he was doing that, Megan set the box of cheeping fuzz at a comfortable distance from the cookstove and put a shallow pan of water in with them. She had helped with the chickens at home in Virginia, she and Skye, and she knew they might drown in too much water or get themselves wet, fall sick, and die. Many of them would simply not survive, no matter what she did, but that was unavoidable. Chicks and puppies and colts perished with alarming frequency, as did human babies, and there was no changing the fact, no comprehending the mystery.

"You make garden," Gus observed, pleased, when Megan insisted that he sit down and have a cup of coffee before heading back to town. "You grow vegetables? Flowers, maybe?"

Megan smiled. "Just pole beans and some lettuce this year, I think. A little squash, too, and some pumpkins for pie." She sighed. "It's late for planting," she said, recalling Webb's comment the day before.

"Well, is fine-looking patch," Gus said. "Next year, you get early start. Grow everything."

Megan allowed herself the luxury of believing that she would still be at Primrose Creek come the spring, if not in this house with Webb on this land she loved so deeply, then somewhere nearby.

"Yes," she said, a bit belatedly. "Everything." Meanwhile, the chicks kept up their busy chorus. "Thank you, Gus."

His smile was the smile of a loyal friend. "You have such sorrow in your eyes, miss," he said. "You are home now. You should not be sad."

Home. The mere word filled Megan with such a sense of bleak yearning that, for the moment, she was tongue-tied.

"I just remember," Gus boomed, flushed with cheerful chagrin, patting his shirt pockets and then producing a folded slip of paper. "I bring message."

Frowning, Megan reached for the paper, unfolded it, and drew in her breath. The thin vellum stationery bore the distinctive name of Lillian Colefield—Diamond Lil.

Dear Miss McQuarry, she'd written. *I have decided to go ahead with plans to build my theater. I would like to call on you and discuss the idea, at your convenience. While I realize you may never wish to accept my offer of a leading place in the troupe, I find myself in need of advice. Please respond through Gus. Best Wishes, Lil.*

Megan was more than a little intrigued. While she had no desire to act again, and certainly no inclination to travel, she did love the theater itself. It would be nice just to *talk* about plays and sets and music with someone who shared the interest. Quickly, she found a slip of paper and a pencil and wrote her reply:

Miss Colefield,

I would be delighted with a visit. Please call any afternoon this week.

Megan McQuarry

When she'd handed the note over to Gus, he said his good-byes and left the house, stopping in the dooryard to speak to Augustus and ruffle his ears.

Once he'd gone, Megan peeled potatoes for supper, to be served with boiled venison and several tins of green beans. She was setting the table when she heard a lone rider, and, expecting Webb, she hurried to the doorway before she could stop herself.

The rider was Jesse, not Webb, and he grinned and swept off his hat when he saw Megan on the threshold, shading her eyes from the glaring rays of a sun fighting its inevitable descent toward the western horizon.

"Is everything all right?" she asked.

Jesse nodded. He was harmless, she knew, even sweet, but all the same, she didn't care for the way his gaze strayed over her body before wandering back to her face. She'd seen that look too many times, in the eyes of too many different men.

"Yes, ma'am," he said. "Webb sent me on ahead to tell you he's hired a couple more men. They'll be coming to supper."

She stepped aside to let Jesse enter the house, feeling shy. He moved past her, hat in hand, his neck glowing red.

"That dress you were wearing yesterday was really something," he blurted out, standing with his back to the fireplace. Then he went crimson to his hairline and looked so flummoxed and so very young that Megan felt sorry for him. "Fact is, I've never seen a cook like you. The ones I knew had full beards and bellies like barrels."

Megan laughed. "Thank you," she said. "I'm obliged—I think." She had guessed by then that Jesse was a little sweet on her, but she wasn't bothered by the discovery. She wasn't afraid of Jesse—she'd turned aside the wooing of bigger, stronger men, let alone boys like him, many a time—but she certainly didn't want to lead him on, either. That would be unkind. "Would you like some dried apple pie? I baked several earlier in the day."

He'd heard the chirping and was staring toward the crate of chicks, frowning. "Chickens?" he asked.

If Megan had known Jesse better, she would have pointed out the obvious nature of such a question, but she still viewed him as a relative stranger, and she needed more time to size him up. "Yes," she said. "They're too small to be outside just yet."

Jesse had been raised on a ranch, Megan knew that much about him, but he must not have been in charge of chickens. He acted as if he'd never seen one before, except breaded and fried and served up on Sunday china. Approaching the crate, he crouched to look inside. He chuckled, watching the birds scramble about.

Megan felt protective, like a mother hen. If she'd had wings and a beak, she would have clucked and flapped until Jesse Stratton had backed off a little. "They're very fragile, you know."

Jesse withdrew his hand, turned his head, and grinned at Megan, still sitting on his haunches. He did look like Webb, she found that appealing, and there was something else about him, some quality strictly his own, that inspired trust. "Sounds to me like you're already getting attached to the little beggars," he said. "I reckon you ought to get a kitten, if you want something to fuss over."

Megan felt as though she'd been accused of something, which, of course, was silly. She opened her mouth, closed it again, and watched as Jesse's grin broadened.

At the sound of approaching horses, he rose to his full height. Megan patted her hair and smoothed her skirts, without being conscious of doing so until she saw the worried look in Jesse's eyes. Caught, she blushed.

"My brother loves a woman named Ellie," he said quietly. "Think twice, Megan, before you go giving your heart away to the wrong man. You might never get it back again." With that, he went out, and Augustus scrabbled after him to greet the coming riders with a symphony of joyous barks.

She heard Webb's voice in the dooryard, caught herself smoothing her hair and skirts again. He came in just then, and the two of them stood there, squared off like a couple of gunfighters ready to draw on each other, or a pair of old friends on the verge of embracing. Megan wasn't sure which.

"Feels like a storm brewing," he said, and Megan didn't know whether he was talking about a real spate of bad weather or the crackling charge arcing back and forth between them.

Jesse came back inside then, and Megan turned her back on both of them without a word and went on with her work. She heard Webb speak to his brother in an even but firm voice.

"Go look after your horse. You left him saddled, and you know better."

She felt Jesse's reluctance to obey, rather than saw it, but he respected his elder brother and did as he was told, spurs clinking with irritation as he strode out of the house.

"Something happen that I should know about?" Webb asked when he and Megan were alone.

She didn't turn to face him but stood at the stove, trying to look busy. As it happened, the meal was ready to serve. "No," she said, and as far as she was concerned, that was the truth.

"Megan," he persisted.

She made herself meet his gaze and smile. "For some reason," she said, "Jesse's worried that you're going to break my heart."

Webb wasn't smiling. "Why would I want to do that?"

She sighed. He wasn't going to let this drop, she could see that. "He didn't say you'd *want* to, and neither did I. He did feel called upon to remind me that it's Ellie you really care about, though."

He scowled, flung his hat onto a chair. "Damn it," he muttered.

"It's all right," Megan said, though it wasn't, of course.

"It isn't all right," Webb argued. "And you know it."

"Webb—"

"I can't seem to stop thinking about you."

Megan sank into a chair. "What?"

Webb thrust a hand through his hair, then strode over to the wash stand to roll up his sleeves, douse water into the basin, and soap up his hands. He looked back at her over one shoulder, his countenance as sober as that of a hellfire preacher. "Don't pretend you don't know how I feel, Megan."

She stared at him. "How *do* you feel?" she asked. Her heart was racing so fast, she thought it might leave itself behind, and she couldn't quite catch her breath, either.

"I'm—well—" He rinsed his hands industriously, dried them on the towel above the wash stand. "*Attracted* to you."

Attracted? Did that mean he cared for her as a woman, as herself and no one else, or did it mean that he simply wanted to lie down with her? She sank her teeth into her upper lip and waited.

He faced her. "I'm not saying I love you, Megan, because I'm not sure what that means anymore. Maybe that's what I feel, and maybe it isn't, but I sure as hell feel *something,* and it's driving me out of my mind." He crossed the room, and by then he was standing so close that she could smell the piney wind in his clothes, along with trail dust and horsehide. "I've always fancied myself a pretty fair judge of character," he said, "but you've got me in a tangle. Sometimes you seem as delicate as a blade of new grass. At others, you're stronger than I ever imagined any woman could be. There's so much I don't know about you, and I figure it might take a lifetime to find it all out."

His speech had struck Megan to the heart. "I wish I knew what you mean by all this," she said, somewhat lamely.

Webb's face was still serious, though there was a mischievous light in his eyes. "I mean," he said, "that I want you to be more than my housekeeper."

There it was. Megan was dizzy with indignation and disappointment. "I may have been an actress, Mr. Stratton," she said in a furious whisper. "Some people might even say I'm a fallen woman. But I assure you, I am *not* a prostitute."

He blinked, then a crooked grin broke over his face. "I was never real good at declaring myself," he said. "I guess I thought you might be looking for a husband." He paused, cleared his throat. His eyes were twinkling. "After last night."

Megan was very conscious of the hired men shouting to each other outside, some still attending to their horses, no doubt, while others were washing at the creek. If any one of them overheard this conversation, she would perish from mortification. "That," she snapped, referring to the bathtub incident, "was an accident. I thought you were already upstairs asleep."

He chuckled, but there was something in his manner that both thrilled and alarmed Megan. Made her want to run, to him and *from* him, both at once. "It's not such a bad idea, you know," he said. "Our getting married, I mean."

Megan gaped at him. "M-married?" she echoed, utterly confounded. She felt like the last in a long chain of skaters, whipping first in this direction, then in that, never able to catch her breath or get her bearings.

He glanced toward the door. The first men were about to come in and break the curious spell that had turned Megan's reason topsy-turvy. "I guess we ought to discuss this later," he said.

Damn him, bringing up a subject like that and then just leaving her dangling. Megan could have strangled him, but she wasn't about to let him see how badly he'd rattled her. She turned away and busied herself with the task of serving supper.

Once the men were eating, she filled a plate for herself, carried it outside, and sat down on an upended crate to eat in some semblance of peace. The evening was cool, and, although the day had been a sunny one, there were clouds gathering on the eastern horizon, black and low-bellied. About to give birth to a deluge.

Presently, Webb came out with coffee and pulled up another crate. Inside, the cowboys continued to consume their suppers, talking a little, not so reticent as they'd been before. They were beginning to feel at home at Primrose Creek, she supposed, just as she was.

"Rain coming," Webb said, nodding toward the clouds. "I reckon we'll be up to our ankles in creek water come morning."

Megan's heart was skittering. He'd probably forgotten all about asking her to marry him, while she'd hardly been able to think of anything else *besides* matrimony, ever since he'd proposed the idea.

"It makes sense," he said, as though the conversation had never been interrupted. "Our tying the knot, I mean. You'd have your land back, legal as church on Sunday, as a wedding present."

Megan nearly fell off the crate she was sitting on, and she'd forgotten her supper completely. Just when she thought he couldn't surprise her, he did it again. "You'd *give* me this land, when you refused to sell it outright?" she marveled. "Why?"

"Because I want something in return," he said. He spoke quietly.

She swallowed. "What?" she dared to ask, though she was sure she knew.

Not for the first time, he surprised her. "A wife. A child. A family," he said. "That's the deal. You share my bed until you've conceived. Boy or girl, it doesn't mat-

ter. After that, you can sleep in your own room again—
if that's what you want. If we decided not to go on living together as man and wife, then I'd build another
house, up in the high meadow." He nodded in that direction, toward the land bordering the tract Megan's granddaddy had left to her.

"You cannot possibly think," she said, "that I would
let you or anyone else take my child."

"I feel pretty much the same way about the matter, as
it happens," he replied reasonably. "Guess we'd just
have to try to get along, wouldn't we? Either way, the
land would be yours, not just on paper but in reality."

"Why—why me?" Megan asked, after a long and
awkward silence.

He grinned. "Well," he said, "you're right here
handy." He glanced around, as though looking for a
bevy of women, just waiting to marry up with a high-
country rancher. "And I don't see anybody else in line
for the job."

Megan was glad she was sitting down, because if
she'd been standing up, her legs probably would have
given out. She stared at Webb. "Are you insane? Getting
married is not the same as hiring a cook or somebody to
punch cattle!" Inside the house, a sudden lull descended, alerting Megan to the very real possibility that their
conversation might be overheard, and she lowered her
voice. "You shouldn't marry anybody unless you love
them, or at least think you *could* love them, and from
what I hear, the woman you love is already married to
someone else."

The coffee mug stopped halfway to Webb's mouth,
and the grin faded away like the last light of day. He got
up, took Megan lightly but inescapably by the arm, and

double-stepped her toward the banks of the creek, where wildflowers bent their heads to sleep. The occasional rainbow flash of a trout shimmered beneath the surface of the water, and the grass, bruised by their passing, perfumed the air.

"What the devil are you talking about?" Webb demanded. He'd let go of her arm, but he might as well have been a barrier, standing in front of her the way he was, because she knew there was no way past him.

"We've already discussed this," she reminded him tersely. "Her name is Ellie, and she's married to your brother Tom."

Pain flickered in Webb's eyes, was quickly subdued. "Exactly," he said. "She's married to my brother." It was neither a denial nor a declaration, but it was enough.

Megan knew what it was to watch a dream die, and she longed to put her arms around him, though she refrained. She had pain enough of her own; if she drew Webb close, she might absorb his as well, and the burden would crush her. She wanted to ask if Ellie had loved him back, but she didn't dare.

Unexpectedly, Webb cupped his right hand under her chin, raised her face, and bent to touch his mouth to hers. At first, the kiss was not a kiss but a mere mingling of breaths. Then he kissed her without reservation, and Megan's heart leaped into the back of her throat and swelled to twice its normal size. She rose onto her toes, and her arms found their own way around his neck, and she felt something like lightning run the full length of her body and reverberate in the ground beneath her feet.

When their mouths parted, the world around her had hidden itself in a pulsing haze, and Megan had to blink several times before things came back into proper focus.

The first thing she saw was Webb's dear, earnest, handsome face.

"I've been wanting to do that for a while," he confessed, his voice gruff.

Megan felt a smile land on her lips as lightly as a butterfly. "How long?"

"Since you got off the stagecoach the other day," he said, and the grin was back.

Color climbed her neck. "There's so much you don't know about me."

He brushed a tendril of hair back from her temple with the tenderest motion of his fingers. "And there's plenty you don't know about me. With any luck, we can spend the rest of our lives getting acquainted."

She was tempted, so very tempted. She felt a powerful attraction to Webb Stratton, it was true, but what about love? She'd thought she loved Davy, and in the end, she'd come to despise him, as well as herself. That particular mistake had cost her dearly, and she couldn't afford to make another one like it. "I'm scared," she said with real despair.

He was holding her shoulders now, and behind him, the vanishing sun raised a spectacle of crimson and gold. "Don't be," he replied.

"It wouldn't be right. I'm not—there was—"

Webb's expression was so tender, so patient, that tears burned behind Megan's eyes. "There was another man?" he asked quietly.

She tried to speak, but in the end she could only nod.

He sighed, bent his head, kissed her again. "I'll make you forget him."

Megan realized she was gripping the front of his shirt in both hands, clinging to him. She forced herself to let go, because she'd made a vow long ago to stand on her own two feet, always. "That's not what worries me."

He drew her close, held her, and she felt his breath in her hair. Felt his heart beating against her cheek. "Then what does?"

She allowed herself to be held, and the sensation was like drinking cold, clear water after a long and parching thirst. Augustus had joined them at some point, and he whimpered, perhaps sensing powerful emotions, seeking reassurance. "Trusting again," she whispered. "Believing again."

He kissed her forehead. "That will come with time," he promised.

Augustus whined, still troubled.

"I'm all right, Augustus," Megan said, her voice muffled by Webb's chest.

Webb laughed and held her at a very slight distance. "If you won't say yes for my sake, say yes for my dog's," he said.

She touched his cheek. She wanted to give a husband what her sisters gave to theirs, and receive what they received in return. They loved their men passionately, all of them. Megan did not know if she loved Webb at that moment, or if she ever would, but she wanted to take the risk. She wanted a *chance* to have what Bridget, Christy, and Skye had, and here it was, but the stakes were high, and she didn't want to lose.

"What if it doesn't work?"

"It will," he said.

"But what if you're wrong?"

He sighed, but his expression was gentle. Amused.

"Then you'll have your land back, and we'll have at least one child together."

"I'll never give up my baby," she reiterated.

"Good," Webb said. "Then maybe you'll never give me up, either. Say yes, Megan."

"Yes," she whispered.

"Louder."

"Yes."

"Yes!" he yelled.

"Yes!" she shouted, and then they laughed like fools, the two of them, there beside Primrose Creek. The cowboys had gathered in the yard, and when Webb lifted Megan off her feet and spun her around in celebration of their agreement, they cheered and hooted and whooped.

Megan glanced at them, noticed that Jesse stood a little to one side, neither smiling nor clapping. A sense of foreboding shadowed her hopes briefly, like a cloud passing overhead, but she'd forgotten it a moment later. She had only to look at Webb again to lift her spirits.

He took her hand. "When?" he asked.

She wanted to go out and beat the brush for a preacher right then, but she had her family to think about. She would get married properly, wearing a decent dress, with her sisters, brothers-in-law, nieces and nephews, and Caney all in attendance. The whole town—the whole *world*—would know that she was Webb Stratton's wife. "Soon," she said. "I want to do this right, make proper arrangements."

He heaved a great and beleaguered sigh. The cowboys, except for Jesse, had lost interest in the scene and headed for the bunkhouse, where they would probably play cards, smoke tobacco, and swap tall tales.

Augustus was busy chasing an invisible rabbit through the high grass, barking as though he were truly fierce. "All right," Webb said. "I'll bunk with the boys until you and I are legally hitched."

Megan was touched by his chivalry, even though she would miss his presence in the house. She understood his reasoning, though: by tomorrow, everybody for miles around would know that they were engaged, and he didn't want people assuming they were already sharing a bed. Of course, there were bound to be those who would think precisely that, no matter what precautions they might take.

Side by side, hands loosely linked, they started back toward the house. Jesse was still there, smoking and leaning against the outside wall, braced with one foot. He smiled, but she glimpsed both anger and sorrow in his eyes.

Webb stopped to speak to his brother, and Megan went on into the house, closing the door behind her. As she was clearing the table, she heard the rasp of raised voices, although she couldn't make out any of the words.

She was washing dishes when Webb came in. He nodded to her, then went on up the stairs, presumably to gather his gear. As she was finishing up, he came down again, carrying a bedroll and some clothes. By that time, it was dark outside, and she had a lantern burning in the center of the table.

"Those chickens of yours will be moving out one day soon, I hope," he teased, watching her from over near the door.

She laughed. The noise they made was incessant, and if she didn't keep the straw bedding in the bottom of their crate changed, they'd begin to smell in short order. "About the time we get married," she promised. "Provided the chicken coop is finished by then."

Webb smiled. "I'll see to it myself," he said. He'd started the project before leaving for Virginia City to hire ranch hands, but it was only partly complete.

She simply nodded, and then he was gone. The house seemed vast without him, but she'd had a long day of hard work, and she was soon in bed and asleep, dreaming sweet, private dreams.

She awakened to chirping sounds the next morning, well before the sun had risen. Smiling, she threw back the covers and got up. After dressing, making a visit to the privy, and washing her face and hands, she made a huge breakfast of salt pork and hotcakes. Soon the long table was lined on either side with hungry men, but Megan was aware only of Webb as she worked, pouring coffee, serving second and third helpings.

When the meal was over and all the men had gone, including Webb, Megan put the dishes to soak and spent the next half an hour tending to the chickens. After that, she did some washing down at the creek, hanging sheets, shirts, trousers, and socks on various low tree limbs and bushes to dry. That done, she found a hook and line, dug up some worms, and she and Augustus went upstream to fish.

They returned with enough for the midday meal, and the crisply fried trout and thin-sliced potatoes disappeared in short order. Webb had brought several rabbit carcasses, already cleaned and skinned, and Megan had a supper stew simmering on the stove before she'd washed the last of the dinner dishes.

She'd just gone down to sit by the creek, with a book

purloined from Webb's fairly sizable collection, when a fancy surrey, drawn by two pure black horses, came over the rise on the other side, descended, and splashed across to stop perhaps twenty yards from where Megan sat.

She would have known her caller by her grand hat, parasol, and ruffled gown, even if Diamond Lil hadn't trilled a cheerful greeting.

Megan was pleased to see her, and so, evidently, was Augustus, who came back from his travels to welcome the visitor. Lil laughed, spoke affectionately to the dog, and thereby assured herself of Megan's lasting regard.

"I hope I'm not intruding," the other woman said. She was wearing cosmetics, but they were artfully applied, and the effect was attractive. Megan, who had worn paint herself on the stage, did not miss the stuff.

She linked her arm with Lil's and started toward the house. "Come along. I'll brew some tea."

Lil raised a perfect eyebrow. "Have any whiskey?" she asked. Then, at the look on Megan's face, she laughed out loud. "Just joking," she said.

They entered the house, and the chicks immediately let their presence be known. Lil walked over and peered down into the crate. "Cute little critters," she observed. " 'Course, they'll be mud-ugly in a month."

That was undeniable. Surely it was God's plan for full-grown chickens to be ugly. If they stayed cute, no one would want to serve them boiled with dumplings. "I've decided not to name them," Megan said, quite seriously.

Lil's expression was wry as she swept over to the table and gracefully installed herself in Webb's chair.

"I'd say that was a wise decision," she said. "It's pretty hard to eat anything with a name."

Megan put on the tea kettle. The rabbit stew was simmering nicely, and the aroma was pleasant. She'd make cornbread to serve with it at supper. "I'm interested to hear your plans for the playhouse," she said. "Do you really think you'll be able to make it pay? Primrose Creek is a pretty small place."

"Sit down," Lil commanded. "You make me nervous, fussing like that, and that water will boil on its own, without you hovering."

Amused, Megan sat. She liked Lil for her distinctive personality and bold—the townswomen would probably have said *brazen*—ways.

"Now," Lil went on when Megan was settled, "about the Primrose Playhouse. Everybody needs entertainment, and I think we'll get a lot of trade from the men down at Fort Grant. Too, the town's been growing ever since the fire. With more and more women coming to live here all the time, it seems to me there's call for culture."

Megan wondered about Lil's past, how such an obviously intelligent woman could have ended up running not just a saloon but a thriving brothel as well. Of course, she would never ask her, though she was dying to do just that. "Where would you get the performers? You'd want a good deal of variety, to keep people coming back."

Lil waved one elegantly gloved hand, making light of the matter even before she spoke. "Virginia City is full of singers and the like, and we can bring magicians up from San Francisco."

There it was again, the word *we*. Megan decided it

was time to speak up. "Mr. Stratton and I have decided to get married," she said.

Lil's smile was slow and thoughtful. "Well, now," she said. "Some of my girls will be sorry to hear that."

Megan willed herself not to blush, although she couldn't be sure she'd succeeded without bolting for a mirror, and she wasn't about to do that. She had no idea how to respond to Lil's statement.

Lil, unlike Megan, was not at a loss for words. She gave a sigh worthy of the stage and said, "I suppose that means you won't be interested in becoming my partner."

Megan's mouth dropped open; she promptly closed it again. "Your partner?" The kettle began to sing on the stovetop, but she paid it no mind. Listening to Diamond Lil's proposal, she forgot all about the tea she'd been planning to brew and the laundry still hanging down by the creek.

Chapter

7

*M*egan was in a distracted state of mind after Lil took her leave and so did not remember the laundry until she heard raindrops spattering on the roof and rumbling at the windows. By the time she reached the edge of the creek, the skies had opened wide, and her hair and clothes were immediately drenched as she rushed from one bush and tree to another, bunching sheets and shirts and other articles into her arms.

Augustus, eager to help, dashed around her in circles, barking in delighted panic. Unable to see past the small mountain of sodden wash clutched in her arms, she tripped over him and pitched headlong into the grass. Unsure whether this was a game or a genuine tragedy, the dog yipped and licked her face a couple of times as she sat up.

She laughed at the absurdity of the scene, and so Webb found her, sitting in the rain, surrounded by clothes and linens, her head thrown back and her dress sodden. Alone, he swung down off his horse and came toward her, frowning at first and then joining in her laughter.

He hoisted her to her feet with one hand, then helped her gather the scattered wash. By the time they reached the shelter of the house, they were as wet as if they'd both tumbled into the creek with their clothes on. They dumped the laundry onto the table and then stood there staring at each other, until Webb came to his senses and went to build a fire on the hearth. Augustus was close at hand, always ready to be helpful.

"Go and change," Webb said without looking at Megan. "You'll catch your death. Besides, the sight of you soaked to the skin is not having a wholesome effect on my character."

She hesitated, then went into her room. When she came out twenty minutes later, her hair was down, and she was wearing one of her poorly altered dresses, a pink-and-green striped silk affair entirely unsuited to Primrose Creek.

Webb, stripped to the waist, was drying himself with a towel. His expression was rueful as he took in the stage gown, and there was a glint of amusement in his eyes. "Well," he said, "that's hardly an improvement, now, is it?"

Megan's attention was riveted to the clearly defined muscles of Webb's shoulders, chest, and belly, and she raised her eyes to his face only by supreme effort. She was just about to tell him he was a fine one to talk when a modicum of reason overtook her, and she somehow managed to hold her tongue.

"Come over here and stand by the fire," he said.

"You're shivering." He was accustomed to giving orders, and Megan was *not* accustomed to taking them but this time she obeyed, drawn by the warmth of the blaze on the hearth and by Webb himself.

She went to stand next to him. "So are you," she contrived to say.

"I'll survive," he said. With that observation, he walked away from Megan and mounted the stairs, and she felt bereft, watching him go.

He returned promptly, wearing a dry shirt—not yet buttoned—and carrying a blanket. He wrapped her in the latter, pulled it snugly around her.

It was back, that rare tenderness that would be her undoing if she didn't guard against it. She tried to step away, but she couldn't, because Webb was still holding on to the blanket, and she was cosseted inside it.

"Where is everybody?" she asked, because she was adrift, and if she didn't find a way back to solid, ordinary ground very soon, she was surely lost. She was referring to Jesse and the others, though for the life of her she couldn't have clarified the fact. Her tongue felt thick, and her head was swimming.

Fortunately, Webb knew what she was talking about, and it gave her some comfort that he looked as unsettled as she felt. "I left the men with the herd," he said. "Cattle tend to get spooked in weather like this."

"Oh," she said, casting a glance toward the stove. "I've made stew for supper—"

"I'll take it out to them in the buckboard," he said.

So he was leaving, going back to the range, where he and the men had been gathering strays. His imminent departure was at once a good thing and a bad one, from Megan's viewpoint. She was a moral person, if somewhat misguided at times, and yet she did not trust herself to be alone with Webb for much longer. Getting drenched in a rainstorm had only added to his appeal, and there was a heat burning low in her middle that had nothing whatsoever to do with the fire crackling nearby.

"You're dripping," she said.

He still hadn't let go of the blanket, but he looked down. "So I am," he agreed.

Just then, Augustus gave himself a mighty shake and sprayed them both with dog-scented water. Startled, they stepped apart, and that was probably fortunate, given the way Megan's heart was thudding in her chest. She turned hurriedly, removed the blanket, and knelt to bundle Augustus into the folds.

The animal shuddered and licked her face gratefully, and she embraced him. When she looked up at Webb, she saw an expression in his eyes that made her breath lodge like a spike in the back of her throat. For what seemed like an eternity, the two of them just stared at each other, Webb standing in front of the fireplace, Megan down on one knee, both arms around the shivering dog. Finally, Webb broke the spell by thrusting himself into motion, buttoning his shirt as he went.

"I'd better get the wagon hitched and head back out to the range," he said.

Megan could only nod.

Fifteen minutes later, after she'd poured some of the rabbit stew into a smaller kettle for her supper and Augustus's, Webb returned from the barn, looking like a gunslinger in his long, dark coat, his hat dripping rainwater. He collected the large pot of stew, along with the utensils and enamel bowls Megan had gathered, and left again.

Megan felt desolate, but she had the laundry, as well as Augustus and the chicks, to occupy her mind. She got busy, draping sheets and garments over chairs, along the stair rail, from the mantels in other parts of the house. When she'd finished, she added a few sticks of wood to the fire Webb had built, fetched her sewing basket, and drew up a chair. There she sat, stitching one of Webb's new shirts together, while the rain continued to fall.

The range seemed especially barren to Webb that afternoon as he drove the buckboard back to the herd, his horse tied behind, to join the men guarding the steaming, bawling cattle. There were around a hundred head, by his count—fewer than he'd hoped for, he had to admit—and he knew the army would buy all the beef he wanted to sell, at a respectable profit. At the moment, though, he couldn't seem to take much interest in the prospect, because his mind was full of Megan McQuarry.

Megan, wet and laughing in the grass. Megan, with her red hair down around her waist and her curves showing through her dress. Megan, wrapping a dog in a blanket as tenderly as if he'd been a child. It was, he reflected, a damn good thing he had responsibilities, because, if he hadn't, he would have been back home, doing his best to seduce the woman. He had an idea she wouldn't have resisted overmuch.

The sight of Jesse riding toward him at a trot came as a merciful distraction. He had few illusions where the boy was concerned—growing up under Tom Sr.'s roof had taken its toll on all three of his sons—but Jesse was still the only kid brother Webb had, and he cared about him.

"The marshal's out here checking the brands on your cattle," Jesse said, making no effort to disguise the contempt he felt for men who wore badges. "What do you make of that?"

Webb didn't see any reason to point out that Zachary would soon be family, at least by marriage. Jesse and the others surely knew he meant to marry Megan, but he felt no real inclination to elaborate. "It's his job," Webb said. The rain was a steady drizzle now, and cold. "There's been a lot of rustling in this country lately."

Jesse looked a mite pale and a bit on the edgy side, too. "He thinks you're a thief?"

"I doubt it," Webb answered, bringing the buckboard to a stop near the lean-to that sheltered the campfire. While he was unloading the kettle of rabbit stew, Zachary rode up, mounted on a fine-looking dapple-gray stallion. Like Webb, he wore a long duster, and he was soaked all the same.

He greeted Webb with a nod, ignoring Jesse's pointed scowl.

"Afternoon, Webb," he said.

"Zachary," Webb replied. "My brother tells me you're looking at brands. Nasty day for it. Jesse, I guess you've met the marshal."

Jesse didn't speak, though he pulled his hat down low against the rain and nodded an acknowledgment.

Zachary grinned and swung down from the saddle, tugging off his leather gloves as he approached, and extended a hand to Webb. Webb responded with a firm grip.

"My wife's going to plague me three ways from Sunday if I don't come home with news of Megan," the lawman said. "How is she?"

Webb's attention was temporarily diverted to his brother, who was still sitting there with his horse reined in, gawking. The kid's ears were practically dragging on the ground. "You got something to do?" Webb inquired.

Jesse opened his mouth, thought better of whatever reply he'd been going to make, wheeled his horse around, and headed back to the herd.

Zachary took off his hat and thrust a hand through his damp hair. "Something tells me that kid hasn't got much use for me," he observed with a grin.

Webb sighed and indicated the campfire, where a pot of coffee was bubbling away. "Give him time. He's got some problems trusting folks, and not without reason."

Zachary looked after the boy, his expression serious but otherwise unreadable, but he was smiling again when he met Webb's gaze. "About Megan," he prompted.

Webb couldn't help giving a broad grin; just hearing her name made him feel as if the sun had come out, even though the rain was coming down as steadily as ever and the sky promised nothing but more of the same. "She's well." He wanted to boast that she'd accepted his marriage proposal, but the news wasn't his to break, so he would wait until Megan had spoken with her sisters. "Holding her own."

Zachary laughed. "Never met a McQuarry who couldn't do that," he said.

The conversation lagged a little, so Webb threw in "Fair cook, too," for good measure.

"Now, that"—Zachary nodded his thanks as Webb handed him a cup of hot, bitter trail coffee—"is not necessarily a family trait. If Caney ever lassos Malcolm

Hicks, I'll probably have to take up cooking myself. When it comes to getting a tasty meal on the table, my Christy's real good at other things."

Webb chuckled, sipping his own coffee and watching out of the corner of his eye while his men kept the nervous herd corralled as best they could. So far, there hadn't been any thunder to speak of, or lightning, either, but there was an ominous charge in the air, and Webb felt as edgy as his cattle. "Nonsense. The women in your family can do anything they put their minds to, and you know it."

Zachary gave a rueful, long-suffering sigh, but the happiness in his eyes was unmistakable. "I reckon that's so," he admitted.

"You having any luck tracking rustlers?" Webb asked.

Zachary heaved another sigh, and this one was somber. "Nope. Dan Fletcher lost twenty head just a week ago, though, and Pete Dennehy is out a whole string of pack mules." He shook his head. "I'll be damned if I can get a bead on this bunch."

It was discouraging, just thinking about the other ranchers' bad fortune. Twenty head of cattle were more than most folks could spare and still meet their bank notes and stay in business. Dennehy was known for the mules he raised for sale to the railroad and Western Union, and this would set him back, maybe even ruin him. Same with the others. "Sounds like you need some help," he said.

Zachary chuckled, without humor, and blew on his coffee in an attempt to cool it down a little. "Every man in this country seems to be working either in the mines or on the railroad. Not many looking to be deputized for two dollars a day."

Webb was sympathetic. It was pure luck that he'd managed to hire the men he needed to work the ranch. "I might be able to spare a few days," he said. "Maybe bring along a couple of the hands."

Zachary lowered his coffee mug and narrowed his eyes, not in suspicion but in disbelief. "You'd do that?"

"We're neighbors," Webb said. "Friends, I hope. When do you want to ride?"

Zachary studied the sky. "Doesn't look like the weather's going to clear up right away, but we'd better head out in the morning all the same. You sure you want to do this?"

"Yep," Webb replied, never one to waste words.

"Damn," Zachary marveled, grinning again.

"I guess that means you're pleased," Webb said.

"Damn!" Zachary repeated, even more cheerfully this time, and then he shook Webb's hand again with vigor. "Much obliged, Webb."

Webb nodded. His reasons for joining the posse weren't entirely altruistic, of course, and Zachary must have known that. Rustlers were a threat to all ranchers, and the smart ones would want to take hold and do something before things got worse.

The two men agreed to meet at Zachary's office in town first thing the next morning, and then Zachary tossed away the last of his coffee—with some relief, Webb thought wryly—and mounted up. He gave the brim of his hat a tug in farewell and then rode away.

Webb figured he'd stood around jawing long enough. He finished his own coffee—he wasn't real particular about the flavor, it was the jolt he liked— untied his horse from the back of the buckboard, and headed out to the herd. The sky was as heavy as before, and some of its weight had settled into the pit of his stomach.

Webb and the others had been gone two days when, in response to Megan's invitation, sent by way of Bridget's eldest child, Noah, her sisters arrived for a visit.

"You're getting married!" Christy cried when the announcement had been made, raising her hands to her cheeks, her gray eyes alight. She and Skye and Bridget had left their assorted children in Caney's care, and they were undaunted by the continuing rain.

"Yes," Megan said, as seriously, as primly, as she could.

"I'll be horn-swoggled," Bridget put in, removing her damp bonnet and shaking it by its ties before hanging it on a hat peg next to the door. "It didn't take Webb long to get the idea."

Skye beamed as she shrugged out of her cloak. Although Jake Vigil had had his financial problems in the past, especially after both his house and mill were burned in the fire that had swept through Primrose Creek two years before, he was a prosperous man, and Skye's well-made clothes reflected his success. Megan had yet to visit their house, which stood several miles downstream on the opposite side of the water; she'd had her hands full just keeping up with her work. "I'm so happy for you," Skye said, kissing Megan's cheek.

Skye, like Bridget and Christy, was gloriously happy in her marriage, and she seemed to assume that the same fate awaited Megan. Megan hoped she was right.

"Thank you," she said.

Soon, with the fire blazing, the chicks chirping, and

Augustus snoozing on the hearth, the four sisters were settled at the table, cups of tea steaming before them.

"When's the wedding?" Bridget wanted to know.

"Have you set a date?" Christy asked at the same time. She seemed a little on edge—she usually was when Zachary was away—but she glowed with well-being.

"I wanted to speak with all of you first, before we went ahead," she said, looking from one to another. "I have your blessings, don't I?"

"Of course," Bridget said.

"We hoped this would happen," Christy added.

"What will you wear?" Skye asked, her brown eyes glowing with excitement.

Before Megan could reply to any of them, Bridget spoke again. "Gus just got in a length of lovely ivory silk," she announced. "I have some lace trim in my sewing basket—"

"And I have some pearls from a gown of Mama's," Christy added eagerly, but after a beat she flushed slightly and lowered her eyes. Jenny McQuarry, the woman Christy and Megan had believed to be their mother, had never seemed to bear them any particular affection. Now, they understood her a little better.

While Megan and Skye knew at least something about their origins, knew they were the twin daughters of a servant girl, Megan doubted that Christy and Bridget had made any such discovery.

Megan reached out, squeezed Christy's hand, then looked at each of her other two sisters, lovingly, one by one. "You've all been so kind—"

"How else would we behave?" Skye replied, the McQuarry pride staining her cheeks and snapping in her eyes. "You're our sister, and we love you. This is a great occasion." She paused, drew in a breath, and rushed on. "I will buy the silk, Bridget can contribute her lace trim, and Christy her pearls. We'll all do the sewing—make a day of it. How about tomorrow, at my house?"

Megan had been wanting to visit—Jake and Skye's house had been built after she left Primrose Creek—and she was touched to the soul by her sisters' eagerness to make her wedding day memorable. "Thank you," she said with a little sniffle, quickly quelled. "Thank you—all of you."

"We're glad to have you home," Bridget said, smiling.

"I told them about our mother," Skye confessed, a bit guiltily. "How we're twins and everything."

Bridget sighed. "It's all so strange," she murmured. "I still can't believe it sometimes."

Christy nodded in agreement. "All my life, I've thought Granddaddy hung the moon, and I still believe he did what he believed was best for us. Just the same, I lie awake sometimes, racking my brain for even a scrap of gossip I might have gleaned somewhere along the way—"

"Caney knows," Bridget stated quietly, and now there was a spark of fury in her cornflower-blue eyes. "She says she doesn't, but I can tell when she's lying."

Christy nodded again. Sighed. "All we can do is make sure *our* children know *us,*" she said. "I've been keeping a journal, so that someday—"

Megan got up and poured more hot water into the plain crockery jar that served as a teapot. Webb would never have thought to purchase such a frippery when all he drank was coffee. Such was life in a bachelor's house. "I think that's a wonderful idea, keeping a diary."

"As long as you're not doing it because you don't expect to be around for a long, long time," Skye said, studying Christy narrowly.

Christy laughed. "We'll all live to be ancient," she said. "We've got Granddaddy's blood in our veins, remember?"

It was comforting to think of that. Looking around the table at each one of her three beautiful sisters, Megan could see their grandfather in all of them. "You're the reason I want to marry and have a family of my own," she said. "All of you, separately and together—I've learned what's truly important by watching you."

A silence fell, broken only by a few sniffles, quickly dispensed with.

"I still miss him so much," Skye confided, at some length, and her voice was, for that moment in time, the voice of the child she had been. "Granddaddy, I mean."

Bridget nodded. "Sometimes it seems as though he's still around somewhere, close by, looking after us. We've been through a lot, each one of us, and I'm not sure we could have survived without help."

Christy made a steeple of her fingers and frowned thoughtfully. "Granddaddy's with us, all right," she said after a brief pause, "but in here." She touched her heart. "He left us more than the land. We have his courage, and I don't care if that sounds vain." The look in her eyes dared them, or anyone, to challenge her, and they all smiled, because it only proved she was right.

After that, they discussed Megan and Webb's wedding, agreeing that it ought to be held right there, in the house the newlyweds would share. They made plans to begin work on the dress the next afternoon at Skye's and decided that Bridget should bake several of her coconut cakes to serve after the ceremony.

Twilight was coming on, and the rain had decreased into a soggy mist by the time they all got into Skye's surrey and took their leave.

Megan stood in the dooryard, the loyal Augustus panting at her side, until they were clear out of sight.

Then, feeling a little lonely with her sisters gone and Webb out riding with Zachary, she went back inside, lit more lamps, and put some leftover soup on to heat. She and Augustus would have their supper, and then she'd gather the damp laundry hanging all over the house, to be pressed in the morning. After that, since she had the house to herself, she would take a lovely bath in steaming hot water.

The plan went off without a hitch, but barely. She had just gotten out of the bath, dried herself, and put on a flannel wrapper, donated by Christy, when the door opened and Webb stepped into the kitchen, looking wet and exhausted. He glanced at the tub, still full on the hearth, and grinned in a way that tugged at her heart and made her want to fuss over him. "What are you doing here?" she asked. "I thought you were out with the posse."

"No luck," he said. "We'll be heading out again in the morning." He let his gaze drift over her. "I just wish I'd gotten back a few minutes sooner."

She rather liked his teasing, though she was enough of a lady not to admit as much, at least while she was standing there in a wrapper and nothing else, with her feet bare and her hair trailing, still damp, in spiral curls around her waist. She raised her chin and tried not to smile. "Have you eaten?" It was hard to be businesslike in such a state of dishabille.

"Had some jerky out of my saddle bags," he said. He took his sweet time, hanging up his hat, pulling off his leather gloves, shedding his coat. "It was no feast, but I'm full."

"Coffee, then?" she pressed, but cautiously.

He sighed. "That sounds fine," he said, and crossed to the hearth.

While she was brewing fresh coffee, he dragged the bathtub to the side door and emptied it into the mud, then hung it in its place again.

"Are the men coming in later?" she asked, getting a mug down from the shelf, fetching the sugar she knew he liked to add.

Webb was in front of the fireplace again, crouching there, scratching Augustus behind the ears and murmuring to him. Augustus sneezed heartily, as if to let it be known that he, too, had endured a cold, wet, and difficult day.

"They'll be spending the night in camp," Webb answered. "I'll go and join them. I just stopped by to look in on you and say that I'm going back out with Zachary tomorrow. We might be gone several days this time."

Megan set the cup and the sugar bowl down on the table. She'd forgotten, by then, that she was not properly dressed, and later she would wonder about that. For the moment, she was busy worrying. "You're going to be a deputy?"

"Just until this business is settled," he reiterated quietly. "There's been a lot of thievery around here lately. Zachary needs help."

She could hardly beg him not to offer much-needed assistance to her sister's husband, but she wanted to. Her mind was spinning with images of Webb being shot or injured, or simply catching his death in the damp weather. "I see," she said, and bit her lower lip.

He smiled. "I'm glad you're here, Megan," he said gruffly. "I'd forgotten what it was like to have a woman around."

Megan blushed, though she knew his comment was not meant to be a disrespectful one. "There's—there's something I need to know," she said, taking herself by surprise. "Did she love you? Ellie, I mean."

He gazed at her steadily for what seemed a long time. Then he answered. "I thought so once," he said, and she believed him. "It was all wrong, though—I see that now, though I was too young and hotheaded back then to get my mind around the idea. A thing that's wrong at the start can't be expected to turn out right in the end, can it?"

She shook her head. "No," she agreed. "This is all so confusing—feeling these things—finding out that Bridget and Skye are my sisters—"

He arched an eyebrow, and she realized she hadn't told him about Granddaddy's elaborate scheme to keep his family together, and no one else had, either. While he sat at the table, sipping hot, fresh coffee, she explained it all, or what she knew of it, anyway.

At the end of the story, he gave a low whistle of exclamation. "A man's got to admire that kind of gumption," he said. "Seems like it skipped a generation, though—passed from your grandfather to you and your sisters."

"I always wonder about that. How such fine people

as Gideon and Rebecca McQuarry could produce the sons they did."

He leaned over, kissed her lightly, innocently on the forehead. Harmless as it was, that kiss took fire and blazed through her blood. "And I'll always wonder," he replied, "how a son-of-a-bitch like my old man could have had a fine son like me."

They both laughed.

"Maybe we can make sense of things, if we work together," Webb said, more seriously. "What do you say, McQuarry?"

She almost said it then, almost admitted that she was beginning to love him, against all will and reason. The words welled up from within her, as if springing from the root of her soul, but she held them back. What did *she* know about love? She'd already proven herself to be anything but an expert on the subject, believing Davy's lies the way she had. "I say we ought to try," she answered very softly, and she knew her eyes were shining, that she hadn't entirely hidden what lay in her heart.

"I'd better go," he said, nearly sighing the words. "Do you know what a temptation you are, in that night-gown, with your hair down?" He let a strand slide between his fingers. "Soft."

Megan closed her eyes, swayed slightly. What was it about this man that made all the strength in her body seep down into her feet and then soak into the floor? No one, certainly not Davy, had ever affected her in such a way.

He kissed the top of her head. "Good night," he said, and stepped back.

"Good night," she managed. She didn't want him to

go, not because she was frightened of being alone, not because she would be diminished without him, but because she was so much more vividly alive when he was nearby. He brought a shape and a substance to her life that simply were not there without him.

He cupped her cheeks in his hands. "I could stay."

She called upon all her McQuarry determination. She wanted their marriage to be right, from the first. "Better if you go," she said.

His blue eyes were remarkably tender as he looked down at her, and at the same time they blazed with a heat that rivaled the flames on the hearth. "You're right," he said with a sigh. "I hate to admit it, but you're right."

Having said that, he bent his head and kissed her with a sort of reverent hunger. Once again, the floor undulated beneath Megan; once again, she held on to the reins of her emotions, but they were slipping. Fast.

"Go," she gasped when she drew back.

He nodded, went back to the door, and took his hat and coat down from the pegs on the wall.

Megan's head cleared, and she remembered that he was rejoining the posse in the morning. "You'll be carrying a gun, won't you?"

"I can borrow a rifle from Zachary if I need one," he said.

She nodded. "Be safe," she said.

He didn't answer, didn't promise he wouldn't be hurt, and that troubled Megan, irrational as it was. Of course, he couldn't make a vow like that—no one could—but she still wanted to hear it. She wanted to storm the gates of heaven itself, pounding with her fists, demanding to know that no bullet would find Webb Stratton while he searched for rustlers or at any other time.

When he'd gone, she latched the door, put out all but one lamp, and retreated to her room, with its narrow, lonely bed. Augustus padded after her and curled up on the floor at her side with a long and philosophical sigh. She was deeply moved, sure he sensed her loneliness and wanted to lend what comfort he could.

"He'll be all right," she told the dog, rolling onto her side and bending down to stroke his silken coat.

Augustus whimpered, as though he had his doubts, but his presence was comforting to Megan, and she soon drifted off to sleep.

She awakened to a low growl and sat up, blinking. She'd secured the main door, but there was someone in the house, all the same. Webb? No—Augustus would have gone to greet him; instead, he lay on his belly, forelegs in front of him, making that grumbling sound.

Before she could arise, she saw a man's form take shape in the shadows of her doorway—she'd left it open in case Augustus wanted to leave again during the night—and although a scream rose in her throat, she strangled on it. She was literally too frightened to cry out, or even to move.

Augustus's growl turned to a snarl. He raised himself onto his haunches, and even in that thick darkness, Megan could see that his hackles were up. His teeth gleamed, more ominous than the fangs of a snake.

The shadow man stiffened. "Settle down, boy," Jesse said. A gun whispered against leather as he drew.

"*Jesse?*"

Augustus slumped to the floor, but Megan was still annoyed, and frightened, too.

"*No,*" she said, urgently and with force. "If you kill

this dog, Jesse Stratton, you'd better be ready to kill me, too."

She heard the pistol slip back into its holster. Augustus didn't move, but Megan knew he was poised to spring. Knew he would have gotten himself shot in the attempt to protect her, the dear, foolish thing.

She sat up, pulled on her wrapper, struck a match, and lit the lantern on the little table next to her bed.

Sure enough, Jesse was standing in the doorway. "I didn't mean to scare you," he said, and, remarkable as it was, Megan believed him. He looked pale and sick, and that aspect of his appearance alarmed her more than any threat to her own safety could have done.

"What is it?" she demanded, bolting to her feet. "Has something happened to Webb?"

Jesse thrust a hand through his hair, in a gesture very reminiscent of his older brother. "No," he said. "Not yet."

"What do you mean, not yet?" Megan reached down to stroke Augustus's head, hoping to calm the animal, but she was far from calm herself, and the dog must have sensed that. Like a child, he took his cues from what she did, not what she said.

"It's all a trick," Jesse said miserably. "All of it."

Megan's stomach dropped, bounced into the back of her throat. "*What* is a trick, Jesse? Damn it, *tell me.*"

"Those men Webb hired. My friends. It's them Webb and the marshal have been looking for. They're here to steal the herd."

Chapter

8

Megan's heart lay heavy and cold, half frozen with fear. For a long moment, she was so furious, so stricken, that she couldn't say a word to Jesse, but, being a true McQuarry, she soon found her tongue. She thrust both palms hard into his chest, not giving a damn that he was half again as big as she was.

"You betrayed your own brother?" she demanded. "How could you do a thing like that? Webb trusted you, welcomed you. He gave you a job!"

Jesse looked downright gray, and even younger than he was. His eyes seemed huge, and his Adam's apple bobbed as he swallowed. He was obviously ashamed, and remorseful, too, but as far as Megan was concerned, the damage was done. "I'm sorry. I didn't think—"

"You didn't think," Megan mocked, shoving him backward into the kitchen, toward the main door. "Damn you, Jesse, if I had the time, I swear I'd take a

587

buggy whip to you. You go out to the barn and saddle a horse for me—this instant—and don't give me any backtalk!"

Jesse backed, blinking, over the threshold, into the damp, windy night. "A horse? You can't—"

She pushed him through the opening and slammed the door in his face. "Saddle that horse! Now!" she yelled through the heavy panel, then hurried back to her room and began pulling on the first clothing that came to hand, a black velvet evening gown, trimmed in pink sateen, that she'd worn on the stage. It was highly impractical for the task at hand, and heavy, too, but it would provide warmth and a degree of shelter from the weather. As she dressed, she regretted being so prideful as to refuse her sisters' repeated offers to lend her clothing.

When she and Augustus reached the barn, perhaps ten minutes later, Jesse was leading out a little bay mare, chosen from the string of horses Webb kept to train and sell. Even in the relative darkness, she saw the startled expression on Jesse's face when she mounted, nimble as a monkey, Webb's rifle in one hand, and nudged the mare into motion with her knees.

"Where the hell do you think you're going?" Jesse shouted through the rising wind. The rain had stopped for a little while, but Megan knew the worst of the storm was yet to come.

"Never you mind where I'm going," Megan yelled back. "You go and fetch Jake Vigil," she said, pointing to the rise on the other side of the creek. "Then Trace Qualtrough. Tell them what you told me."

Jesse was trying to mount up, too, but the process was a protracted one, since his slat-ribbed sorrel gelding had turned fitful and taken to dancing a fancy sidestep that had Jesse hopping along with one foot in the stirrup and one still on the ground. "You're heading out to the herd!" he accused, as fresh, ice-cold rain began to slice down upon them. "You let me do that. *You* go fetch those fellers, whoever they are!"

"Do as I tell you," Megan called over one shoulder, reining her horse westward, toward the place where Webb had told her the herd was gathered, "and maybe I'll try to talk the judge out of hanging you for thieving!"

She thought Jesse might pursue her, and maybe he considered it, but when she reached the edge of the woods and looked back, she saw him and his horse splashing across the creek. She prayed he would obey orders—having no real reason to believe he would—because she was going to need Jake and Trace's help to stop those rustlers from driving off the herd. She wished she had her own mare, Speckles, but she, like the land, had been sold long ago. As she rode, she silently cursed the day she'd laid eyes on Davy Trent.

Because the sky was overcast, Megan could barely see, but she followed Augustus, who made an intermittent yellow flash as he ran through the trees. She was slapped and battered by low-hanging branches as she raced on, moving as fast as she dared, and once, when the mare stumbled in a ditch, she nearly dropped the rifle. Her teeth were chattering, mainly with cold, though she might have admitted to a measure of fear, depending upon who was asking.

Thunder began to rumble as she rode higher and higher toward the top of the ridge. Sure enough, the herd was there, sheltered in the small canyon below, and when she gained the vantage point, lightning spiked across the sky and danced on the ground, illuminating the milling cattle and the rustlers in a series of brilliant, blue-gold flashes. Augustus hunkered down on the wet ground, growling.

"Quiet," Megan commanded, though there was no likelihood that he'd been heard.

The terrified cattle were bawling fit to raise the dearly departed, churning round and round like whirlpools in a flooded river, and the men riding herd shouted to each other in hoarse, worried voices. With every strike of lightning, every boom of thunder, the creatures, two-legged and four-legged alike, became more agitated.

Megan thought of the discussion she'd had with her sisters that afternoon and hoped they'd been right, figuring that Gideon McQuarry was still looking after them all, from wherever he was. "Granddaddy," she murmured, "if you're listening, if you're looking on, I need your help, and I need it pretty quick."

There was no blinding insight, but it did come to her that Granddaddy had always believed in action. *Do something,* he'd often said, only half in jest, *even if it's wrong.*

Her arm was aching from the weight of the rifle—there was no scabbard on her saddle—so she rested the weapon across the pommel, in order to balance it while she descended the hill. Augustus, perhaps heeding her instructions to keep his own counsel after all, perhaps merely as frightened as she was, trotted alongside, nose skimming the ground every now and then.

It hadn't occurred to Megan that if the lightning had revealed the herd and the rustlers to her, the reverse might be true as well. When the whole hillside lit up and the herd began to scramble through the opening of the canyon, the cattle trampling and goring each other in the process, she saw two men riding up the trail toward her. At the rate they were traveling, there was no question that they'd seen her and that their intentions were bad.

Well, Granddaddy, she thought, with resignation, *I did something, like you said, and it was wrong.* Then she raised the rifle, cocked it, and sighted in. She didn't like the idea of gunning anybody down, for any reason, but she'd do it if she had to, to stay alive.

The cattle began to run, bellowing now like souls being driven into the flames of hell, and Augustus shot forward like an Indian's arrow, racing toward the approaching riders, barking.

The dog was sure to be killed, and Megan knew that even if she was lucky enough to live through this night, she'd never forgive herself. She'd had few enough friends in her lifetime, and Augustus had been one of the best.

Her finger was on the trigger, ready to fire, when another bolt of lightning revealed that one of the riders was Webb, and the other was Zachary. She was so relieved, and so utterly horrified by what she had nearly done, that she didn't release her grip fast enough when she lowered the rifle, and a shot pinged into the ground.

The mare, already scared halfway out of its hide, reared straight up, pawing at thin air as though to claw a hole in it, and sent Megan slipping backward to topple over its rump and land with stunning force on what should have been soft ground, even mud, given the recent rain. Conscious of the danger of being kicked or dashed to shreds under those panic-driven hooves, she hurled herself to one side, bruising herself even more as she rolled over the fallen rifle.

Before she could get her breath, Webb was kneeling on the ground beside her, pressing her down by the shoulders when she tried instinctively to rise. "Are you hurt?" he roared. She wasn't, but it might not be prudent to say so.

Megan hesitated as long as she could, but her mental inventory had already indicated that she was just fine. "No," she said. "No, I don't think so."

Webb got up then and, taking one of her hands, wrenched her unceremoniously to her feet. "Then go home! It might have escaped your notice, but we're just a little busy here!"

Megan seethed. Remarkable, she thought. Here she'd risked life and limb, trying to save *his* blasted cattle, and how did he repay her? By jerking her up off the ground and shouting at her. "I'm not going anywhere!" she yelled back, just on general principle. Heading for home was the reasonable thing to do, she supposed, but she felt anything but reasonable just then. She was mad enough to spit. "Jesse just told me that the men you hired are rustlers!"

Webb bent down so that his nose was almost touching hers. "I already know that," he growled. "Now get your bustle back on that horse and *go home,* or I swear I'll take you across my knee right here!"

Zachary had caught and settled the anxious mare, and he led it over to her. "We've got our hands full here, Megan," he said, "and the best thing you can do to help is stay out of the way, so we don't have to worry about you."

The rain started again just then, with fresh force, and Megan felt as though someone had upended a bucket of cold water over her head. She ached in every joint and muscle, and she was mortified into the bargain. She wasn't a man, that was true, but she could ride and shoot as well as most of them, and Webb needed her help—he was just too hardheaded to admit it. On top of that, he wasn't even grateful that she'd tried to save his mangy cattle from a pack of rustlers.

By that time, the herd was in full stampede. In that rugged country, they could easily kill or injure themselves; probably a number of them already had.

Megan looked from Zachary's face to Webb's, which was hidden by the night and the brim of his hat, then turned in defeat, gripped the saddle horn, and mounted the mare. Zachary handed up the rifle.

"How did you know?" she asked. "About the rustlers, I mean?"

"Figured it out the other day, when I was checking brands," Zachary answered. "Listen, Megan, maybe you ought to pass the night with Christy. Tell her we'll be all right."

Tell her we'll be all right. The words echoed in Megan's mind as she watched the two men get back on their horses and head straight for the heart of chaos. *Tell her we'll be all right.*

"They'll be *all right,*" Caney said half an hour later when Megan was seated before the kitchen stove in Christy's kitchen, wearing one of her sister's nightgowns, wrapped in a heavy blanket, and still shivering so hard that her teeth chattered. Instead of following his master, Augustus had accompanied her on the ride through the trees and over the creek, evidently following some canine code of honor, and Christy was drying his coat with one of her good towels.

She looked pale—naturally, she was worried about Zachary—but her gray eyes were fierce with anger. "What were you thinking of, Megan McQuarry, chasing off after a pack of outlaws all by yourself like that?"

Caney handed Megan a cup of tea, laced with honey and a dollop of whiskey, and tried to hide a smile. "I reckon she thought she was going to help some way," she said, in her smoky voice. "Didn't you, girl? I declare, you'd have been better off, the four of you, with a little less of your granddaddy's cuss-headedness."

"I couldn't just sit there at home and do nothing, knowing Webb was about to lose everything," she said, well aware that it was a lame excuse. Nonetheless, it was all she had. She looked at Caney, then Christy. "Could I?"

"*You* wouldn't have, if you'd known," Caney told Christy.

Christy's eyes glittered with tears. "It's bad enough that I have to worry about Zachary all the time. I don't need to be fretting over my sister, too!"

Caney's smile broadened, but there was something broken in it, something fragile. "Seems to me you ought to have some of this doctored-up tea, too," she told Christy. "Come on and sit by the fire, and give that poor dog some peace. You keep rubbin' him like that, you're going to wear the skin right off him."

Christy's hair was trailing down her back. She was clad in a heavy nightgown, a flannel wrapper, and a pair of Zachary's woolen socks, and still she was beautiful enough to attend the ball at some castle and distract the

Prince from Cinderella for good. She got to her feet and did as she was told, and Caney handed her some tea of her own. "I don't know why I had to fall in love with a lawman," she fussed. "Why not a farmer, or a banker, or a storekeeper?"

Caney laughed, but, even in her present state of mind, Megan saw the sorrow in her friend's eyes. "We don't choose love," she said. "Love chooses us. And it don't much matter what our druthers might have been."

Megan took a steadying sip of the stout, blood-warming brew, and though it seemed that her spirit had stayed behind on that hillside with Webb, her heart went out to Caney. "I guess things aren't going too well with Mr. Hicks," she said softly.

Caney sighed and joined Christy and Megan at the table. "He's a stubborn man, my Malcolm." Megan saw tears in Caney's eyes, and that was a rare occurrence, despite what they'd all been through over the past decade or so, what with the war, and Granddaddy dying, and the farm being lost to Yankees. "I'm at my wit's end, where he's concerned. I tried cookin' for him. I tried fussin' over him. I tried ignorin' him. And nothin's changed, nothin' at all."

Both Christy and Megan were still, sensing that something was coming, something about to break over them with as much force as the storm tearing the night sky asunder. Neither of them wanted to hear, but they could no more prevent it than they could change the weather.

Caney blinked and dashed at her eyes with the sleeve of her woolly robe. Her gleaming, abundant hair was subdued into a crinkly braid, thick as rope, and for what might have been the first time in her life, Megan saw her clearly. Because Caney had cared for her and for her sisters, because she'd been at the farm as far back as any of them could remember, they'd thought of her as old. Now, Megan realized that Caney probably wasn't even forty, and that she was beautiful.

"Any sensible man would be proud to have you for a wife," Megan said, in a hopeless effort to forestall the inevitable.

"About time I moved on," Caney said. "Three of you are married, and you're spoken for, Miss Megan. Webb's a good man, and he'll make a fine husband." She smiled a misty smile. "I wouldn't make a habit of crossin' him, though, if I was you." A throaty chuckle. "But then again, if I *was* you, I probably would."

Both Megan and Christy had stiffened in their chairs, and they were both weeping silently and without shame.

"None of that," Caney scolded. "I done spent my life lookin' after you four. It's my turn to kick up my heels."

"Why can't you stay at Primrose Creek?" Christy asked, making no attempt to dry the tears on her cheeks. "You can kick up your heels all you want, right here."

But Caney shook her head. "I love Malcolm Hicks. Love him with my whole heart. I can't stay because I can't bear seein' him all the time and knowin' he don't think enough of me to make me his wife."

Megan and Christy looked at each other in despair, but neither of them had any idea how to respond. No matter what joy the four McQuarry women might find with husbands and children and each other, Caney's going would leave an empty spot in each of their hearts.

Megan reached out to take one of Caney's hands, and Christy took the other. And they just sat there, the three of them, holding on and, at the same time, trying to let go.

*   *   *

Megan awakened in a twist of sheets, soaked in perspiration and gasping from some dreadful dream, still crouching like a monster just beyond the reach of her memory. It was a moment before she realized that she was back in her room at Christy and Zachary's place, a moment more before she heard deep and even breathing.

Still, she thought it was only Augustus, but in the glow of lantern light coming in through her door, open just a crack, she saw a man's form sprawled in the room's one chair. She didn't need to see clearly to know it was Webb—her heart told her.

He was safe. Thank God, he was safe.

"Go back to sleep," he grumbled.

Megan pretended to be indignant, though she wasn't sure how well she succeeded, because the truth was, she was glad he was there. Gladder than she'd ever been about anything. "I don't have to take orders from you," she pointed out.

He laughed, then yawned expansively. Megan wished they were already married, so that he could lie beside her on the bed, maybe hold her in his arms. "We'll discuss that later," he said. "Right now, I haven't got the gumption it would take to settle the matter."

"There are other beds in this house," she whispered, because she didn't have the strength for a debate, either. Not at the moment, at any rate. "Why are you sleeping in a chair?"

"I'm not sleeping," he pointed out with some regret. "And I wanted to be close to you. Make sure you didn't go sneaking off to confront the whole Sioux nation or try to haul in a few outlaws for the reward."

She smiled in the darkness. He wanted to be close to her.

He yawned again. "Megan?"

"What?"

"Don't ever scare me like that again. I damn near had a heart attack when I saw you out there, in the middle of a storm, with the whole countryside crawling with outlaws."

She was silent. After all, she couldn't make a promise she wasn't sure she could keep.

"Megan." He was quietly insistent.

"I'll try," she said, with little or no hope of success.

He chuckled again. "I guess that'll have to be good enough, for now anyway."

She swallowed hard, dropped her voice to a whisper. "What about Jesse? Have you seen him?"

"He must have taken to the hills."

"He tried to do the right thing, Webb."

"He was a little late."

"He's your brother."

"Go back to sleep."

She persisted. "Come and lie here with me. You'll never get any rest in that chair."

"I'd never get any rest lying next to you on a bed, either," he replied dryly. "Except maybe the permanent kind, if Zachary, your sister, or Caney came in here and shot me for a rascal."

She closed her eyes, trying to think of something to say, and the next thing she knew, there was light at the window, and the smells of freshly brewed coffee and frying bacon filled the air. The chair beside the bedroom door was empty, and Megan wondered if she'd only dreamed that Webb had returned, had sat there keeping watch over her well into the night. Suppose he hadn't come back at all but instead lay trampled or shot, somewhere in the canyon?

She hastened out of bed and into a practical brown cotton dress either Caney or Christy must have laid out for her to wear. She swallowed her pride and put it on; the garment fit loosely across her breasts, since Christy had a more womanly figure, but just then fashion was about the last thing on Megan's mind.

She wrenched on her stockings and shoes, did what she could with her hair—which wasn't a great deal, given that it was still damp from her flight through the rain the night before—and dashed out into the kitchen.

Christy was there, along with Joseph and little Margaret, who were tucking into their breakfasts with uncommon relish. No doubt they were eager to go outside into the sunshine after being confined to the house for several days by the dismal weather.

Megan opened her mouth to ask about Webb, but Christy answered before she could get the words out.

"He's fine," she said. "So is Zachary. Right now, they're trying to round up what's left of the herd."

"What about the rustlers?" Megan asked. She thought of Jesse again and wondered what would happen to him.

"They got most of them last night. Six of them are in jail."

"Zachary and Webb arrested *six men* by themselves?"

Christy poured coffee and set it down on the table, indicating that Megan ought to take a seat. "Jake and Trace were there, too, along with Mr. Hicks and Gus and several other men from town."

Even after the scene with Webb the night before, there on the hillside, Megan found herself wanting to ride out and find him, make sure he was unhurt. It made no sense, thinking that she could protect him, but there it was. The drive to be near him was deeper than anything she'd ever felt before.

"What are we going to do?" she asked in a small voice.

Christy smiled gently. "Do? Why, we're going to head over to Skye's place, just like we planned, and start stitching up your wedding dress. We all went to town for the silk right after we left you yesterday."

"It's dangerous, caring for a man—"

Christy came to stand beside Megan's chair and laid a hand on her shoulder. "Take my advice," she said. "Think about the wedding. It's a lot better than fretting."

Megan nodded, but only after she'd weighed her sister's counsel.

"Where's Caney?" Joseph wanted to know. "She don't burn the bacon."

"Doesn't," Christy corrected. Megan noticed her sister didn't defend her own cooking skills. "And Caney's busy. She's going on a trip."

Joseph narrowed his eyes. "Where?"

"Young man," Christy sighed, "there are times when I wish you weren't quite so precocious. Finish your breakfast." She rounded the table, ruffled his hair. "We're going to Aunt Skye's house, and we mustn't be late, because there is a great deal to be done."

Joseph's eyes widened. "Will Hank be there?"

"I would imagine he'll be at school," Christy said. Her expression was tender, though her voice was firm. She knew Joseph would be mightily disappointed if he didn't get to see his cousins before the day was out.

"I want to go to school," he said.

"I thought you wanted to be a deputy instead," Christy replied. Margaret was waving her spoon back and forth over her head, and Christy reached out and gently stayed the small, plump hand. It touched Megan deeply, watching her sister with her children; Christy was a good mother, as Megan had always known she would be.

"Changed my mind," Joseph said seriously. "Deputies have to work outside all night, in the rain. Pa told me so this morning." He might have been a miniature man, the way he spoke, instead of a child not yet three years old. If he was that smart at his tender age, Megan reflected, Christy and Zachary would have their hands full bringing him up.

Christy patiently wiped Margaret's hand clean with a checkered table napkin, then gave her back the spoon. Over the heads of her children, Christy met Megan's gaze and smiled. Plainly, for all the uncertainties in her life, she was completely happy. Furthermore, she seemed to have every confidence that Megan would be, too.

The house Skye and Jake shared with their young family was much smaller than the mansion Jake had owned in town before the fire swept through and burned the place to the ground, but it was still impressive. The walls were white clapboard, and there were green shutters at the windows. Crimson roses grew on either side of the flagstone steps leading up onto the spacious veranda, and there were two gables on the second floor.

The place's resemblance to Granddaddy McQuarry's Virginia farmhouse filled Megan with a bittersweet sense of nostalgia.

She and Christy had walked the short distance from Christy's, Megan carrying Margaret while Joseph and Augustus tagged along behind.

Skye came out onto the porch, her brown hair swept up into a loose chignon, her smile bright with pleasure at the prospect of company. She was holding little Susannah in her arms. "Where's Bridget?" she asked.

"She'll be along," Christy said.

"And Caney? Is she coming, too?"

Christy and Megan exchanged a look. This was no time or place to tell their sister the bad news, they tacitly agreed. It was a special day, and there was no reason to spoil it.

"She's busy," Joseph said. Fortunately, he didn't add that Caney was going on a trip. Hank had come through the open doorway, behind Skye, grinning in welcome.

"No school today?" Christy asked, raising an eyebrow.

Skye smiled, somewhat mysteriously. "The latest schoolteacher ran off last week. Married a peddler." Schoolmarms came and went like good weather in Primrose Creek. As soon as they got there, some man was sure to start courting them, there being a shortage of marriageable ladies, and it didn't matter a whit whether they were pretty or homely as a bald chicken.

"What are you going to do?" Christy asked, concerned.

"Go fishing," Hank replied happily, before Skye could answer, and all of them laughed.

The inside of Skye's house proved to be as appealing

as the outside, its shiny wooden floors scattered with bright braided rugs, its furniture store-bought. The curtains were of pristine white lace, and a large, splendid oil portrait of Skye hung over the parlor fireplace. She looked like a member of high society, depicted in ropes of pearls and a gauzy rose-colored dress with lots of ruffles and lace.

Following Megan's gaze, Skye blushed prettily. "Jake commissioned that," she said. "I told him it was a foolish extravagance, but he insisted. The last thing I have time to be doing is sitting around all gussied up while somebody paints my picture, but he brought a man all the way from San Francisco to do just that."

"Yes," Christy said, taking off Margaret's cloak and bonnet before attending to her own. "And that fellow stole our *last* schoolteacher."

"Maybe you ought to hire a man," Megan suggested. Skye and Christy both laughed, though she'd been serious.

Within the hour, Bridget arrived with her tribe of children, and soon the older cousins were chasing around outside in the high, fragrant grass, while the little ones played quietly on the floor near Skye's grand dining room table. Megan was measured, fitted, and measured again, but over the course of the morning, the wedding dress began to come together, and, by midafternoon, it was finished except for the lace trim and the pearls. Bridget would add the former, taking the gown home with her that evening, and Christy the latter, after collecting it from Bridget in the morning.

Megan and Christy walked back, Megan once again carrying Margaret, while Joseph pretended to be leading them all safely through the wilderness. When they arrived, the lanterns were lit, and Zachary was there. Plainly exhausted but freshly bathed and shaved, he was at the cookstove, stirring a huge skillet full of hash.

"Supper's about ready," he said with one of his patented grins. "How's the wedding dress coming along?"

Megan glanced around, looking for Caney, knowing already that she wouldn't find her. Christy had made the same deduction, judging by the look in her eyes, but, surely for the children's sake, she made no mention of this noticeable absence.

"Nicely," Christy said, barely missing a beat. "Megan's going to be the prettiest bride this side of Paris."

He'd set the table. He was an unusual man, Zachary was, but then, so were Trace and Jake. Although he nodded, the glow in his eyes was strictly for Christy, and a glance at her flushed sister convinced Megan that the message was getting through, whatever it was. She wondered if she and Webb would ever have a relationship half as deep and gratifying as the one these two shared.

Megan wasn't going to ask about Caney, at least not in front of her niece and nephew, but she had no such compunction where Webb was concerned. She opened her mouth to speak, and before she got the question out, he strolled in from a back room, where he'd evidently washed, shaved, and changed clothes. Although he looked weary, and even a bit gaunt, he had clearly come through the ordeal unscathed, at least physically.

"Zachary invited me to stay for supper," he said.

Once again, Megan felt that humbling urge to run into his arms. It was getting familiar, that feeling, and so were some others that were much more difficult to define. "The cattle?"

He sighed. "We lost twenty head," he said.

She remembered Jesse and felt guilty for not thinking of him first.

Webb didn't wait for her to ask; he'd seen her next question in her eyes. "Jesse's running scared right now," he said, "but I reckon he'll be back one of these days. He's not a bad kid."

Megan might not have understood Webb's loyalty to his brother if she hadn't had three sisters she would have loved no matter what. "You're not going looking for him?"

"No time," Webb said with obvious regret. "I've got my hands full with only three ranch hands to ride herd."

"Not all the men were in league with the thieves, then," Megan remarked.

"No," Webb agreed. "Not all."

They ate companionably, a family gathered for an ordinary meal, and afterward, when Webb rode home, Megan went with him, sharing his horse, sheltered in the curve of his strong arms, while Augustus ambled along beside them.

Webb didn't speak to her all during the ride home, but Megan wasn't troubled by that, because she knew he was thinking about Jesse. When they arrived at the ranch, he sent her into the house while he went to the barn to groom the horse he'd been riding and saddle a fresh one. Without saying good-bye, he left again, headed for the canyon and what remained of his herd, and Megan watched from the doorway until he was out of sight.

Chapter

9

*W*ebb was chilled, bone-weary, and about halfway discouraged as he rode through the evening wind, headed for the piece of range land where what remained of his herd was grazing. The sky was starless, a great, dark void, but there was a crescent moon and the rain had moved on. God knew they needed all the moisture they could get, but he was glad for the respite all the same.

His mind, meanwhile, kept straying back to the ranch house, back to Megan. He envisioned her moving from room to room, perhaps making tea at the stove, or searching the shelves for a book in the parlor, or maybe getting ready for bed. He found himself lingering on the last possibility; he couldn't help remembering the night before, when she'd so innocently asked him to lie down beside her.

He'd have given just about anything if he could have squared that with himself and accepted the invitation, but his sense of honor had gotten in the way. He'd developed a lot of self-control over the years, but not enough to stretch out on a mattress beside Megan McQuarry without touching her.

He adjusted his hat and sighed. In a few days, they'd be married, he and Megan. He could wait that long. Couldn't he? He was still debating that with himself when he broke through to a small clearing and a rider came out of the trees on the other side. Startled out of some very private thoughts, he automatically reached for the pistol he hadn't carried in better than seven years.

"Webb!" Jesse reined in that broken-down cow pony of his in a thin wash of moonlight, standing in his stirrups.

Webb was at once overjoyed to see the kid and hot to wring his neck. Which only went to show that he hadn't really changed, even though he'd long since hung up his gun. He rode to the middle of the clearing and waited without a word. Jesse had come looking for him, and it was Jesse's place to speak first.

The kid flashed a nervous smile, but he didn't come any closer. Webb estimated the distance between them at fifty yards or so. "I guess you heard I was the one who told Megan them men was planning to steal your cattle," he said. His voice had a shaky quality, though he was trying to sound as though he thought he deserved some credit.

"I don't suppose it occurred to you to tell *me*," Webb observed.

Jesse's horse was fitful, but he kept the reins short. He didn't retreat, but he didn't come any closer, either. "I'm heading back up to Montana," he said. His tone still had a bluff quality. "I stay around here, I'll either be hanged or shot."

Webb understood his worries. Zachary hadn't said what twists and turns the law might take in a case like this one, and even though six of the rustlers Webb had hired on his brother's recommendation were in jail awaiting a military escort to Fort Grant, there were still three of them on the loose. One or all of them might come gunning for Jesse, just on general principle. "I reckon you should have thought of that before."

"Ain't you going to ask why I did it?"

Webb would have smiled under other circumstances. "No," he answered, "I figure I already know. Things were hard for you after I left the Southern Star, weren't they, Jesse? Without me there to take your part, Pa and Tom Jr. must have given you a pretty hard time."

Even at that distance, Webb saw Jesse's face contort with emotion. The boy said nothing, but as Webb rode closer, he noticed that Jesse's breathing was quick and shallow, and his eyes were overly bright.

Soon, they were facing each other like jousting knights on the field of battle, their horses side by side. Webb reached out with his left arm and took the back of Jesse's neck in an affectionate hold. "I shouldn't have left you behind," he said. "I'm sorry."

"You thought you'd killed Tom Jr.," Jesse said, and when Webb let go of him, he looked the other way for a few moments and sniffled.

"Yeah," Webb said. "I surely did. You want to know the worst thing of all? That's exactly what I meant to do. When I went at him that day, I *wanted* to kill him."

"You aren't the only one who ever felt that way," Jesse allowed.

"You sure you want to go back to him and Pa, after being out on your own?"

Jesse thrust out a hard breath, sniffled again, and ran his shirtsleeve across his face. It softened Webb, that gesture; he'd seen his kid brother do that often, when he was a little fella, trying not to cry. "I got to go back," he said with considerable resolution. "At least long enough to prove them wrong about me. I've got some things to prove to myself, too."

If he'd had the time and the leisure, Webb might have done the same thing. "Watch your back," he said. "And send me a telegram when you get as far as Butte."

"You ain't vexed with me?"

Webb nearly smiled. "I didn't say that," he replied. "Given what I did to Tom Jr., I guess it makes sense that you'd want to step lightly around me. I've changed a little since those days, though, Jesse. I've had enough years to wonder what kind of man has that kind of violence in him."

Jesse put out his hand. "Anything you want me to tell Pa?"

The brothers clasped hands for a moment. "Yeah," Webb said. "You can tell the old coot that if I never see him again, it'll be a week too soon. Same goes for Tom Jr."

"What about Ellie?"

Webb grinned. "You tell her I'm happy," he said, "and I wish her the same."

At long last, some light came into Jesse's face. "That Megan, she's going to make you a fine wife."

Webb nodded. "Good-bye, Jesse," he said. "If you want to head back this way, when things have had time to cool down a little, there's a place in the bunkhouse for you."

"Thanks," Jesse said. Then he reined his horse around and rode off, disappearing into the trees on the opposite side of the clearing.

Webb's mind was on the long ago and far away as he rode on toward the herd, but only briefly. The past had no more meaning for him; he'd broken free of it a long while ago, without consciously realizing that, and now that Megan McQuarry was a part of his life, he was only interested in the present and the future.

Megan was wide awake before dawn and determined not to pass another night with chickens in her kitchen. After feeding herself, Augustus, and the chicks—all but three of which had survived—she carried the crate out into the barn and set it on a bale of hay while she fed the horses, taking time to visit a bit with each one of them, the way she would have done with a neighbor.

When the sun was up, she inspected the chicken coop from the inside. The walls were up, and there was even a latch on the door, but only about a third of the roof boards had been nailed into place. Another spate of rainy weather like they'd just had, and the whole project would be ruined.

Shaking her head, Megan found a ladder, a hammer, and some nails in the barn, beside the salvaged lumber Webb had set aside for the purpose. Far from new, the wood was silver-gray with wear from years of sun and wind, rain and snow. The lengths were uneven, too, but for the time being, Megan was only concerned with providing proper shelter for the chicks. If the coop looked too strange when she was finished, she would simply climb up again and saw off the ends.

It was hot work, roofing a chicken coop, and far more difficult in skirts than it would have been in trousers. Nonetheless, Megan spent the morning clambering up and down the ladder, nailing boards in place, getting slivers in her knees. She was finished and sitting on the ridge of the roof, lamenting the gaps where the warped planks didn't fit together, when she got to daydreaming about Webb Stratton and what it would be like to give herself to him, come their wedding night.

As if she'd conjured him, Webb appeared, riding along the creek's edge.

Startled, as chagrined as if he could see into her mind and read her thoughts, she lost her balance and slid straight down one side of the roof on her backside. Unable to catch herself, she scooted right off into midair and fell to the ground with a plunk.

Fortunately, she had not broken her tail bone. *Unfortunately,* her buttocks and the backs of her thighs were prickly with splinters.

Webb reached the yard and, having seen the spectacle, dismounted and sprinted toward her. "Are you hurt?" he demanded. "Good God, you could have broken your neck——"

Megan's eyes filled with tears of humiliation and pain. "I'm hurt," she said.

Instantly, he crouched beside her. "Where? How?"

She scraped her upper lip with her teeth. She didn't want to tell him, but she had to, because this was one problem she couldn't solve by herself. "My—the place where I sit—slivers—"

Although a smile lurked in his eyes, he kept a suitably serious expression. "Now, that," he said, "is a shame." Gently, he helped her to her feet. "Come on. I'd better start pulling."

Megan balked, even though she felt as though she'd sat herself down in an ants' nest. "You could go for Skye, or Christy, or Bridget—"

"And leave you with pieces of wood festering in your hide? Not likely."

Megan simply didn't have the strength to protest further; the only thing greater than her embarrassment was the stinging in her flesh. Augustus accompanied them into the house, whining in sympathy all the while. Megan felt a little like whining herself, but she managed to refrain.

"Let me have a look," Webb said, closing the door.

Megan's face flamed. Try though she might, she could not think of a way out of this dilemma. "This is dreadful," she said, sounding a little like Augustus.

Webb, on the other hand, was all business. "Lift up your skirts," he said.

Utterly abashed, Megan did as she was told. Webb crouched behind her and very carefully lowered her drawers. His only comment on the state of her posterior was a low whistle.

"Is it bad?" Megan dared to inquire. Surely this situation could not get worse.

She was wrong, as it turned out. "Depends on your perspective," he said. "Bend over the table, so I can see."

"I most certainly will not!"

"Megan, you've got more splinters in your backside than I've got cattle. Some of them are in delicate places. Now, do as I tell you, and let's get this over with."

Blushing quite literally from head to foot, Megan leaned over the table, her eyes squeezed tightly shut. In addition to the slivers, and a not inconsiderable breeze, she felt Webb's gently probing fingers, and the sensations *that* produced would probably cause her to find religion.

"You wouldn't—you wouldn't tell anyone about this, would you?" Megan asked, flinching as Webb extracted a particularly stubborn bit of wood.

He chuckled. "Now, who would I tell? I gotta say, though, after this, we might as well already be married."

Megan's face couldn't have been hotter if she'd dipped it in kerosene and lit it with a match. "Perhaps you think this is funny, Mr. Stratton, but I don't!"

Again, that low, brief laugh. "I don't imagine you do," he said. "And, now that you mention it, I *do* think it's funny."

"That is reprehensible!"

"Nonetheless—"

"Are you trying to make this worse?"

"Nope," he said reasonably. "I just figure one of us ought to enjoy it."

Megan considered kicking him, the way a horse might do, and decided against the idea. After all, who knew how many slivers were still protruding from her backside like quills from a porcupine, and she didn't relish the idea of trooping miles along the creek bank, knocking on Skye's door, and starting the whole process over again. "None of this would have happened," she said, "if you'd finished putting the roof on the chicken coop."

"I reckon that's true," he said, with no discernible guilt.

Augustus raised his paws onto the table's edge across from Megan and made a low and mournful sound in his throat. "Your master has no sense of delicacy," she said.

"At least," Webb observed, from behind and below, "his master has the wits not to slide down the roof of a chicken coop on his hind end."

Megan reconsidered kicking him and decided against it again, fearing that he might retaliate in some way. "Can't you hurry?"

"Yes," he answered, "I guess I could. But I might miss a few of these little devils if I did."

In time—roughly the life span of a biblical patriarch, by Megan's calculations—Webb announced that he'd gotten the last of the splinters, and she was ready to rejoice, not to mention right her clothes, when he stopped her. "Not so fast, darlin'," he said. "I still have to paint you with iodine. Otherwise, you might get an infection."

"*Iodine!*" The word shot out of Megan's mouth like a bullet. "That burns!"

"Yep," Webb agreed. "It'll dye your backside orange, too."

"Oh, thank you."

He had the gall to pat her right on her bare bottom. While she was still fuming, he rose and went to a shelf near the stove for a small medical aid kit containing bandages and the like. When Megan pressed her palms to the tabletop to hoist herself upright, he shook his head. "Don't," he warned. "If you pull up your drawers, I'll just have to pull them down again."

Megan was certainly no prude—she'd spent much of her life on a farm, after all—but that statement disconcerted her so much that she thought she'd choke on her tongue. Webb merely went back to his previous enterprise, this time dabbing on iodine. Every touch of the stuff stung like fire, and there must have been a hundred places where the skin was broken. Finally, finally, it was over.

Webb eased her drawers up over her knees and hips, then lowered her skirts. "You'll want to be careful about sitting down for a while," he said.

Megan would not, *could not,* look at him. Instead, she headed for the stove and started the process of brewing tea.

"If I were in your position," Webb said from near the fireplace, "I'd want whiskey."

"Well," Megan replied sharply, still refusing to meet his gaze, "you're not, more's the pity."

"You know, I must have missed it when you thanked me."

Megan's backbone stiffened like a ramrod. "*Thank you,*" she said acidly. She supposed she should be grateful for what he'd done, but she had yet to achieve that noble state of mind.

Suddenly, he was behind her again, but this time was very different. He stood close and slipped his arms loosely around her waist. "I'm sorry," he said quietly, and with a touch of amusement lingering in his tone. "I shouldn't have teased you. You were real brave."

The way he was holding her was somehow far more intimate than the sliver pulling had been, and instead of resisting, she longed to lean back against him, and that

made her furious with herself. She tried to answer—
even then, she wasn't sure what she would say—but it
was as though her tongue had swollen to fill her mouth.
It simply refused to work.

He turned her gently around, raised her chin to look
into her face. His smile was tender, his eyes alight with
a weary joy. He kissed her forehead, and it seemed to
Megan that all of time and creation came to a halt, that
she and Webb were somehow outside both, in a realm all
their own.

Webb was the first to speak. "I've got to get back to
the herd," he said presently, with great reluctance.

Megan nodded. He wasn't even gone yet, and
already she missed him. Which seemed incredible,
given that only minutes before, she'd considered planting one heel in the middle of his face.

He started to move away, then stayed. "Megan—"
He paused, started again. "About the wedding—how
long do we have to wait?"

Megan could only gape at him for a long moment.
Then, careful not to trip over her tongue, she asked,
"Wait?"

He smiled, traced the length of her nose with the tip
of one index finger. "Yes," he said. "I figure this
Saturday would be good. Agreed?"

Saturday. She was going to be Webb Stratton's wife
in just a few days. It seemed too good to be true.
"Saturday," she agreed with a shy nod.

He leaned down and kissed her mouth in a leisurely way that left her trembling inside. Then, eyes smiling
again, he said, "Stay off the roof of the chicken coop."

She laughed and whacked his chest with the heels of
both palms.

A few minutes later, he'd ridden away, and she and Augustus went outside to reclaim the crate of chicks from the barn and settle them inside the new coop. After spreading straw on the dirt floor of the little hut and setting out feed and water, she set the birds free in their new home. Augustus was waiting on the other side of the chicken house door when she came out, and he greeted her as eagerly as if she'd been away for days.

As she walked back toward the empty house, however, loneliness filled her in much the same way twilight was filling the high valley. She missed Webb, of course, but the loss of Caney was just coming home to her, and she ached with the knowledge that she might never see her good friend again. When she was married on Saturday, Caney would not be there with the rest of the family, and that was hard to imagine, though she understood how hard such an occasion might be for the other woman.

If only Mr. Hicks would come to his senses, go after Caney, and bring her home.

"Miss Caney Blue!"

Caney, riding through the woods on a mule borrowed from Trace Qualtrough, recognized the voice, and she tried to pick up the pace.

"Woman," Malcolm Hicks said, drawing alongside her on one of Jake Vigil's fancy horses, "I am talkin' to you."

"You ain't got nothin' to say that I want to hear," Caney answered. That wasn't true, of course, but she was through hoping for things that weren't going to happen. For the past several years, she'd cooked and sewed for Mr. Hicks. She'd walked with him and let him hold her hand, and when he was down sick after the big fire, from breathing smoke, she'd looked after him for a solid week, with the whole town gossiping. And in all that time, whenever she brought up the possibility of holy matrimony, he'd found some way to distract her.

He reached down and grabbed hold of the mule's bridle. He was a handsome man, with sleek bright skin, dark as a night sky, and the kindest pair of eyes Caney had ever looked into. He was broad in the shoulders and strong as the horse he rode, and just looking at him made Caney feel weak all through, even now, when she'd made up her mind not to have a thing to do with the no'count rascal ever again.

"You can't go leavin'," he said.

"You just hide and watch," Caney spat back. If she didn't act tough, she was going to break down and cry like a baby. The only thing she'd ever really wanted in all her life, besides a red petticoat with black satin bows stitched to the ruffles, was this one cussed man, and he didn't want to be married.

"I love you," he told her earnestly, and by the way his brow was furrowed, she thought he might mean it.

She was so stunned, she couldn't find a thing to say.

"I said I love you," he repeated in a louder voice, apparently under the impression that she hadn't heard him the first time.

"Talkin' is easy," she managed. "It's *doin'* that signifies."

He thrust out an enormous sigh. "If you don't want to stay and marry me, I can't force you to do it. I'm a poor man, Caney Blue. I can't give you much besides a little company house over by the lumber yard and my name. A woman like you deserves a whole lot more."

"Maybe I do," Caney said softly, her eyes prickling with tears, "but all I want, Malcolm Hicks, is to be your missus, right and proper."

"Then come back with me. Reverend Taylor will marry us up tonight."

Caney's heart soared. She would have Mr. Hicks for her own after all, and maybe some babies, too. "What took you so long, Malcolm?" she asked, right there in the middle of noplace, sitting astride a mule.

He averted his gaze, looked back. "I had a wife once. I told you that." His eyes were wet, but he didn't seem shamed by it. He didn't even try to wipe his face. "Becky and me, we was slaves on the same place. She was carryin' when the *master* decided she was distractin' me from my work and ought to be sold. Sold." He stopped, and a great shudder went through him. "He sent her away, and I never did find her again, though I tried. The good Lord knows I tried." He fell silent again, and memories contorted his fine, proud face. "Then, just before I came here to work for Jake Vigil, I met up with a feller I knew back in Georgia. We worked in the fields together. And he told me my Becky had died in that new place, having our child."

Caney was too stricken to weep. She managed to put out a tentative hand, touch Malcolm's arm. "I'm so sorry," she said.

Malcolm shook his head, caught up in memories. "I swore I'd never let myself care for any woman again the way I cared for Becky. It just hurt too much."

"What happened to the child?" Caney asked. She knew it was a painful question, and none of her affair into the bargain, but she had to know.

"That's the worst part," Malcolm said. "I never did hear. That baby would be ten years old now if it lived. I got to spend the rest of my life wonderin'—wonderin' if I got a son or a daughter. Wonderin' if my child's got food in his belly, a place to lay his head. And I ain't never gonna know for sure."

Caney reached up, touched his cheek tenderly. Now her face was as wet as his. "You just listen here to me, Malcolm Hicks. You *is* going to be wonderin', but I'll be right there wonderin' with you, if that counts for anything."

He leaned down until his forehead touched against hers. "Don't you leave me, Caney. Don't you *ever* leave me."

Caney vowed that she wouldn't, and two hours later, when she and Malcolm stood in front of Reverend Taylor exchanging their vows, she made the same promises all over again, in different words, though it wouldn't have been necessary. Once Caney Blue gave her word, it was solid as a mountain and didn't need giving a second time.

She'd never been happier in her life, not even with Titus, the husband she'd liked and respected but never quite loved. All the same, it stuck in her mind, her conversation with Malcolm. It was a fearful trial to be left wondering about lost kin—Malcolm had suffered for a long time. And so, because of her, had Bridget and Christy, Skye and Megan, her girls. She'd finally broken down and told Skye and Megan about their poor mama, but Bridget and Christy didn't know where they came from, except that they'd both had Thayer McQuarry for a papa. She wondered if they were strong enough to hear the truth.

* * *

Gus arrived in the morning, quite unexpectedly, with a loaded wagon and a broad grin. Megan went out to greet him, waiting while he drove the rig across a shallow place in the creek. Augustus ran up and down the bank, barking with elation, and it seemed to Megan that she was perfectly happy in that moment beside the sun-dazzled stream. She was going to marry Webb. She had a family and friends, with and without fur, and she would live out the rest of her life on the land her grand-daddy had left to her. A person couldn't ask for more without being downright greedy.

"What have you brought?" she demanded good-naturedly, smiling and shading her eyes with one hand.

"I bring wedding present," Gus called down, his round face filled with delight. He loved being the bear-er of glad tidings.

The wagon bed was covered with a canvas tarp, and Megan was more than curious. Whatever Gus had brought, it was big, and it was bulky.

"Is gift from Diamond Lil," he added when Megan didn't ask.

The reminder of Lil Colefield and the agreement they'd made took some of the starch out of Megan; with all that had happened, she'd forgotten her promise to help get the show house started. She had given her word lightly, and now she would have to keep it. No longer smiling, Megan lifted a corner of the tarp and peeped underneath, but all she could see was a finely carved section of wood.

"Is bed," Gus said. "I bring mattress in afternoon."

Megan's face warmed a little, but after bending over a table for half an hour while Webb pried out slivers, it took more to embarrass her. "Diamond Lil sent us a *bed?*"

Gus didn't reply directly, probably because the answer was lying right there in the back of his wagon for all the world to see. He tossed back the tarp to reveal a beautiful bed frame of carved mahogany, with four pineapple posts. It would have to be assembled, but Gus had brought his tool box along, no doubt for that very purpose.

"You show me where to put," he said.

Megan had been in Webb's room upstairs, though only to make the bed and sweep, of course, and she'd seen the cot he slept on. Obviously, that would not do for a married couple. She turned to lead the way and to hide the added heat that had climbed her neck to glow in her cheeks. She wondered what Webb would have to say about such a gift and how he'd react when she told him about her unofficial partnership with Lil.

Gus was bull-strong, and after he'd surveyed the master bedroom and they had decided that the frame ought to go between the two big windows opposite the fireplace, he carried in the gigantic piece of furniture, piece by piece, and assembled it. Watching from the doorway, Megan couldn't help anticipating her first night in this room, as Webb's wife, and all those that would follow. Whatever problems they might face, and surely they would have their share, here was their sanctuary, the heart of the house, where they would talk, sharing their hopes, dreams, and fears, or *not* talk, on those inevitable nights when they were fractious with each other or simply too tired to string words together into sensible sentences.

"It's beautiful," she said when Gus had finished. She

would ride to town, as soon as she could, and thank Diamond Lil for the gift in person. She probably should not have accepted something so expensive and so personal in the first place, but she didn't have the heart to disappoint Gus that way, let alone Lil Colefield. "Thank you, Gus."

She offered him coffee after that, but he refused politely, saying he had to get back to the store. He would bring the mattress, he reiterated, sometime in the afternoon.

He was as good as his word, arriving several hours later with the promised item, and he was still seated at the table, enjoying coffee and plum cake, when Webb showed up, dirty from the trail but otherwise in good spirits. The closer Saturday came, Megan had noticed with some satisfaction, the more cheerful he became.

"Hullo, Gus," he said, pleased, offering his hand after hanging up his hat. "What brings you out here?"

Before Gus could answer, Megan did. "Gus brought us a bedstead. It was a gift from Diamond Lil." She couldn't wait to ask her future husband how the saloon owner and madam of a notorious brothel had known he didn't own a proper bed, and she saw by the faint flush in Webb's tanned face that he was dreading the question.

His discomfort amused her a little, partly because of the sliver episode and partly because, when she finally told him about her promise to Lil, she wouldn't be the only one with some explaining to do. "Well, now," he said, and rubbed the back of his neck. That was all, just "Well, now."

In good time, after inspecting the chickens, who were sprouting real feathers and growing at an astounding rate, and talking horses with Webb for a while out in the barn, Gus finally climbed back into his wagon and headed home.

Webb came into the house, carried a basin of water out onto the kitchen step, took off his shirt, and began to wash himself industriously. The splashes beaded in his hair and on his skin, glittering with fragments of refracted sunlight.

"What prompted Diamond Lil to give us a bed?" he asked, drying himself with the towel Megan provided.

"I was going to ask you that very thing, Mr. Stratton," she replied.

"I might have said something," he admitted.

"To Lil?" Megan inquired lightly.

He shook his head, thrust a hand through his damp hair. "One of the girls. They gossip just like all females." He paused, sighed, rested his hands on his hips. The gesture, usually an indication of stubbornness, seemed almost defensive. "Megan, I won't deny that I've spent time upstairs at Lil's. A man gets real lonely out here without a wife. But I won't be going back there, ever—I give you my word on that."

She hid a smile. "Not even to the saloon?"

He grinned. "I didn't say that," he pointed out.

Her turn. She drew in a deep breath, let it out slowly. "Lil is building a show house," she blurted out, just to get it over with. "She asked me to be a silent partner and help her get started, and I said I would."

Webb's face was unreadable, but he wasn't smiling, and that wasn't a good sign. "You're going to be an actress again?" he asked. He'd brought one foot to rest on the top step, and now he leaned, both arms folded, against his raised knee. "Seems to me that won't leave you much time to be a wife and mother."

Dread rose within Megan, but she did a good job of hiding it. Or, at least, she thought she did. "There might come a time when I'm called upon to play a part or two," she admitted, "but mostly I'll just be helping to arrange the entertainments."

"I see," Webb answered, and everything about him indicated just the opposite to be true.

"Webb, I promised," Megan said.

He looked her up and down. "We've made a few promises to each other, you and I," he said, "even if they were unspoken."

"And I'll keep them."

He was quiet for a long time, tilting his head back, looking up at the blue summer sky. When he met Megan's gaze again, he said the one thing that made it impossible for them to agree. "I guess you'll have to make a choice or two before Saturday, won't you?"

Chapter

10

"**D**on't be bull-headed," Christy said the following afternoon, when she and Bridget came by to give the wedding dress a final fitting. Megan was standing on a chair in the center of the kitchen, while Bridget knelt, pinning the hem into place, and Christy adjusted the seams. She had just explained her quandary concerning Lil and the new show house, describing her promise and Webb's ultimatum.

Bridget looked up. "Just tell Miss Colefield you made a mistake."

Megan's conscience was giving her as much trouble as the slivers in her backside had done, maybe more, and she expected she'd be a lot longer in the healing if she made the wrong choice. She heaved a frustrated sigh.

"Hold still," Christy scolded, giving her a pinch on one side of her waist to make the point. Her gray eyes were direct and perhaps a little fierce. "What do you really *want* to do, Megan?"

Megan bit her lower lip and willed the tears burning behind her eyes into full retreat. "I want to marry Webb," she said. "I want to live in this house with him until I'm an old, old lady. I want a flock of babies. But a part of me wants what Lil's offering, too."

Bridget tugged hard at the elegant, rustling skirts of the magnificent dress. Between her touches of lace and the dozens of tiny pearls Christy had stitched to the bodice and the cuffs of the full, billowing sleeves, that gown was as fine as any she could have bought in Richmond before the Great Strife. "All of us have to make choices sometimes," she said. "Nobody can do everything."

"Do you have any idea how busy you'll be, once you have children?" Christy argued. "Good heavens, Megan, you're already responsible for cooking meals and cleaning the place, not to mention everything *else* that goes with being a wife. You purely won't have the *time* to do a proper job in either place. And if I know you, you'd wear yourself to a nub trying, all the same."

"He's never said he loved me," Megan confided in a small voice.

Bridget and Christy looked at each other before focusing their gazes on Megan's face. "Have you ever told Webb you love *him?*" Christy asked.

Megan swallowed. "No," she said.

"Why not?" Bridget wanted to know.

Megan sniffled and barely caught herself from touching the back of one hand to her nose. "I'm not sure it would be honest."

They both stopped working. Bridget got to her feet,

and Christy stepped back, frowning. "What?" Christy demanded.

"What I mean is," Megan began, wincing once and wringing her hands, "I feel all sorts of things for Webb Stratton, but I don't know if it's love. It's not like anything I've ever felt before."

Again, a cryptic glance passed between the two elder sisters. "What, exactly, *is* it like?" Bridget asked.

Megan felt much the way she had when she'd been bent over the kitchen table with her bare bottom in the air, but she needed Bridget and Christy's help, so she bore it with as much grace as possible. Nonetheless, her face was hot, and there were grasshoppers springing about in her stomach. "Sometimes it's like nothing and nobody else exists, except for Webb and me," she said in a whisper, though the three of them were quite alone, except for Augustus, who was snoozing on the hearth. "I know I can live without him, but I also know it would be a darker, thinner, more hollow life. And when he kisses me—"

Both Bridget and Christy leaned forward, the better to listen.

"When he kisses me," Megan went on, "I always feel as if I'm going to faint. My insides catch fire just like dry timber, and I ache to beat all."

A smile crept across Christy's mouth. "You love him," she said with quiet confidence.

Bridget's cornflower-blue eyes sparkled. "Oh, yes," she agreed. "You most definitely do."

"What do I know?" Megan wailed. "I thought I loved Davy Trent!"

Bridget raised one eyebrow and folded her arms. Obviously, she had no idea who Davy was and what had happened between him and Megan. Just as obviously, she had her suspicions. She didn't ask, though. She just stood there with her usual authority, waiting to be enlightened.

"Did he make you feel the same things Webb does?" Christy asked carefully. "This Davy person, I mean?"

Megan felt as though Christy had just flung a bucket full of dirty mop water all over her, unprovoked. "Of *course* he didn't!" she hissed.

"There you have it," Bridget said solemnly, addressing Christy rather than Megan. The pair had been embattled for much of their lives, and yet they shared an alliance that set them apart from the rest of the family in a subtle and unique way. "Webb is the one for her."

"Yes," Christy agreed. "I think you're right."

"Does it matter at all here what *I* think?" Megan cried softly, and Augustus whimpered and got to his feet, as though he thought she might need rescuing.

"What *do* you think?" Christy reiterated.

Megan burst into tears. "I won't be able to bear it," she sobbed, "if he calls off the wedding. It's bad enough that Caney won't be there!"

"The dilemma seems simple enough to me," Bridget said. Sometimes it made a body want to stick pins in her, the way she was always so damnably certain of everything. "Marry him, Megan. What does the Good Book say? 'It's better to marry than to burn'?" She paused for effect, and Megan remembered that she wasn't the only one in the family with a sense of drama. "If you ask me, you're about to go up in flames right now. As for Caney, she'll come back when she's ready. Just you wait and see."

"You really think so?" Skye asked softly.

Bridget nodded. "We're her family," she said.

Despite Bridget's claim that the matter of Webb's decree was settled, Megan felt like a hound who's just chased a rabbit round and round the same bush for half an hour without catching it. She was as confused as ever; they hadn't settled anything. Still, she was comforted by the prospect of Caney's eventual return.

Christy handed her a dish towel, that being the first thing that came to hand for the purpose. "Here. Dry your face and blow your nose before you ruin that dress," she ordered.

Megan wiped her eyes, but that was as far as she was willing to go. After all, she had to *use* that dish towel. "You two were absolutely no help at all," she accused.

Bridget smiled. "You don't need our help anyhow," she said. "You already know what you have to do."

Megan realized that indeed she *did* know. She was going to have to choose between love and honor, in this case, and she would follow her heart and choose love. She would tell Webb what she'd decided, as humbling as that would be, then go to town and make her apologies to Diamond Lil. No doubt the saloon mistress would want her four-poster pineapple bedstead back.

She nodded. "You're right," she said. "Both of you. Jupiter and Zeus, I hate that."

Christy and Bridget laughed out loud, their voices as beautiful as distant bells on a Sunday morning, and returned to the task at hand.

He'd been unreasonable, Webb thought, saddle-sore and sick to death of looking at cows and cowboys. Sure, it was unusual for a married woman to be in business, but Megan was no ordinary female. That was one of the many reasons he loved her.

He sighed. Yep, he loved her. What he'd felt for Ellie had been mere infatuation; he'd known that for a long time. It was Megan he wanted to share his life with, Megan he wanted to bear his children, Megan he wanted to lie down beside, every night until he died. Still, he was a proud man, and it would be a bitter pill, having his wife go into business with the town madam. Sweet heaven, he'd be joshed damn near to death over that, and he might even have to take up fighting again.

"Rider!" the lookout—one of Jake Vigil's lumberjacks, borrowed until more men could be hired—shouted to Webb, pointing up the ravine.

Webb lifted his gaze and knew immediately that the visitor was Megan. He spurred the gelding into a trot and headed straight uphill.

He and Megan met midway.

"Webb—" she began.

"Megan—" he started.

They laughed. "You go first," Webb said. It was good just to look at her, just to hear her voice. A homecoming of sorts.

"No," she said. "You."

He sighed, the reins lying easy in his gloved hands, which rested on the pommel of his saddle. "I still hate the idea of your working in town," he said. "It's going to look like I can't provide for my own wife, and God knows what the gossips will say. All the same, I had no right forcing you to choose." He paused, searched the horizon for inspiration, and looked back at her. "What it comes down to is, I'll take you any way I can get you."

She blushed prettily, and joy shone in her eyes.

"Webb," she said, in a tone so tender that it had the effect of a caress. Then she shook her head. "I won't be working with Lil, not unless she runs into a real emergency," she said. "Part of this ranch will be mine, and that will be more than enough to keep me busy, when you figure in a husband and babies."

Something leaped inside him. He almost said it then, almost said right out that he loved her. It didn't seem like the proper place to make such a declaration, though, there in the middle of noplace, with cows and a few saddle bums for witnesses. His voice came out hoarse. "I'm for starting that first baby as soon as possible," he said.

She went even pinker, but the tears were gone, and her eyes were still shining. "That's something we can agree on. Will you be home for supper tonight?"

Webb knew he shouldn't leave the herd. He was short-handed as it was, and the weather was still uncertain. If he lost any more cattle, he'd have a problem, and not a slight one. "I'll be there," he heard himself say.

His reward was a smile, that sweet, sassy Megan McQuarry smile that always made his gizzard shimmy up into his windpipe. "I'll be waiting," she said.

Lordy, he thought, and sat there in the saddle like a lump on a log, watching her ride away.

When, resigned, he reined his horse around to go back to work, he saw Trace and Zachary coming toward him on horseback, with Jake Vigil and Malcolm Hicks close behind.

When they got within shouting distance, he saw that Trace and Zachary were grinning from ear to ear. Damn pleased with themselves.

"Figured you could use some more help with these

dogies," Zachary said, indicating the cattle with a toss of his head.

Webb was at a loss for words. He'd been on his own a long time, even before he'd left the Southern Star, in many ways, and now he was going to have brothers, the kind a man could count on in good times and bad.

"You do want some help, don't you?" Trace inquired, still smiling.

"God, yes," Webb said at last.

Jake rode forward, put out a hand. "I hope you appreciate this," he said, his eyes bright with amusement. "Malcolm here got up out of his marriage bed to lend a hand."

Webb had never seen a black man blush, but he reckoned that was what Malcolm did just then. He sure did curse.

"He and Caney got themselves hitched in secret," Zachary said, standing in the stirrups to stretch his legs. "I'll allow that I envy him her cooking."

Malcolm smiled at that. He did look happy, Webb thought. "My missus can spare me for a little while," Hicks said, "But it don't work the other way."

"What we need to do," Webb said, his voice a little unsteady, "is drive these cattle closer to the house. Now that twenty or so of them are gone for good, the high meadow will serve as grazing land, at least for a few weeks."

"Makes sense," Zachary agreed.

Within half an hour, with four extra hands to help, Webb's herd was on its way up out of the ravine, toward higher ground, and Webb himself was on his way home.

To say walking straight into Diamond Lil's infamous saloon in broad daylight drew stares and whispers would be an understatement, but Megan did so with her shoulders squared and her head held high. She had something to say to the woman, and it had to be said face-to-face.

Just past the swinging doors, Megan paused and waited, blinking, for her eyes to adjust to the dimmer light. She saw a long, narrow room with sawdust-covered floors and high, murky windows. The bar seemed as long as the railroad tracks between New York and Philadelphia, laid out straight as the crow flies, and the mirror behind it must have cost as much as the rest of the building. There were tables with green felt tops, and a few early customers were hunkered over glasses of whiskey, like freezing men trying to absorb the heat of a faltering bonfire. The infamous "girls" who worked upstairs were nowhere to be seen, somewhat to Megan's disappointment.

The bartender stopped wiping the glass in his hands, and his mouth dropped open. "I'll be jiggered," he said.

"I'm looking for Lillian Colefield," Megan said clearly, though her voice was shaking. The McQuarry women had a reputation for boldness, but this was new ground, even for them.

"Well, here I am," Lil said, appearing in a doorway at the back of the room. It looked like three miles, the distance between where Megan stood and that door. "Come on back to my office, and we'll jaw awhile." She took in the staring patrons of the bar. "You fellas just shove your eyeballs back in your heads and go on about your business. Haven't you ever seen a decent woman before?"

Megan might have been walking in knee-deep mud as she made her way through that saloon. If word ever got back to Caney, wherever she was, she'd get a lecture that would blister both her ears. On the other hand, what else could she have done? Stood in the street and yelled for Lil to come out?

Lil's office surprised Megan; she'd expected silk and satin, sumptuous cushions and fainting couches, perhaps, and velvet draperies with tassels. Instead, the place was utterly plain, with just a desk, a couple of chairs, and shelves full of books and ledgers. A little stove stood in the corner.

"Sit down," Lil said, taking her own seat behind the desk and folding her hands loosely. She wasn't dressed like a madam, either, Megan noted. Her dress was brown bombazine, unadorned, and without cosmetics, her face reflected the hard life she'd led. A smile tipped up the corner of her mouth. "What brings you here, Miss McQuarry?"

Not for the first time in her life, Megan wished she could be two women, one of them Webb's wife and the mother of his children, the other helping to build the Primrose Creek Playhouse into something the community would be proud to claim. She sat up very straight and took the plunge. "I'm afraid I cannot be your partner after all. I'm sorry."

Lil arched one eyebrow. "Webb put his foot down, did he?"

Megan's face flared, and her backbone lengthened another notch, as if she'd grown an extra vertebra. "I made the decision myself," she said firmly. It wasn't entirely true, of course, but that was beside the point. "Thank you for the beautiful bed. I suppose you'll be wanting it back now."

Lil laughed. "You keep the bed," she said. "It's my gift to the both of you."

Megan didn't know what to say, now that she'd stated her intentions regarding the partnership. She hadn't had much experience conversing with brothel owners, her scandalous career as an actress notwithstanding. "Th-thank you," she faltered, and then realized that she'd repeated herself.

Lil took a cheroot out of a box on her desk and, before lighting up, offered one to Megan, who refused with a shake of her head. The older woman sat back in her chair and regarded her visitor through a haze of blue-gray smoke. "You've got a good mind and a lot of gumption. Not many women would walk right into Diamond Lil's saloon in the middle of the afternoon."

Megan's smile was rueful. "I was an actress. I'm accustomed to being talked about."

"Are you?" Lil countered quietly. "I never did get used to it, myself."

Megan wanted to ask Lillian Colefield how she'd become Diamond Lil, but it would have been prying, and, like the other McQuarrys, she did her best to confine snooping to members of her own family. She sighed. "It's hard. I'd like to be like them—the 'good women' of Primrose Creek—but I can't seem to get the knack of it."

Lil smiled. "Oh, they'll come around in time, once you're safely settled down. You won't be such a threat to them then."

Megan frowned. "A threat?"

"Yes," Lil drawled, drawing on her cheroot with frank enjoyment and exhaling the smoke in a way that seemed almost elegant. "They look at you, pretty as a flower garden after a long winter, and smart to boot, and they see all the things they'll never have or be. Once you're married, they'll be able to convince themselves that you'll end up just like them, sooner or later. I don't think that will happen, though."

Megan's eyes were wide. "You don't?" she asked in a hopeful voice.

Lil smiled. "You're different. Like the other women in your family. Challenges only make you stronger. Somebody breaks your heart, you'll learn to love more, and better. Your grandfather would have been proud of you."

Megan's breath caught in her throat, fairly choking her. Everything in this woman's tone and bearing implied that she'd known Granddaddy, but that was impossible, wasn't it?

"I was born and raised in Richmond," Lil went on. "I met your grandfather only twice, and not under pleasant circumstances either time, but I could tell he was worth ten of that son of his, charming as my Thayer was. I adored him, even though he did me wrong more than once."

Megan could barely speak. The coattails of an idea flickered at the edge of her thoughts, but she couldn't quite grasp them. "You knew—?"

"Your granddaddy paid me to leave the state of Virginia forever after Christy was born, and I did. He'd come to claim Bridget when she was a week old, and I let her go, too. Thayer was long gone by the time Christy came along—I heard he'd gone to New Orleans, one jump ahead of somebody's husband." Lil paused, and her eyes were fixed on something in the invisible distance. "I knew I couldn't give my babies the kind of life I wanted them to have, not the way I lived, but it was hard to let them go all the same."

Megan closed her eyes. "Why are you telling me this?"

"I've kept my secret for twenty-odd years. I reckon I'm just tired of carrying the load."

"Why did you come here—to Primrose Creek?"

"I knew your granddaddy had a tract of land out here. He'd taken it as security for a debt, I believe. I worked my way west and decided to take a look at the place before heading on to San Francisco. I liked it here, saw the potential, and stayed instead."

"Bridget and Christy are—are you daughters." Megan was still trying to absorb the fact.

"Yes," Lil said. She looked so weary, so beaten down, in that moment that Megan felt sorry for her. "Imagine my delight when the four of you showed up here."

"Didn't you ever want to tell them? To see them?"

"I do see them, all the time. Primrose Creek is a small town. As for telling them about myself, well, I couldn't quite bring myself to look them in the face and say their mama was a saloon keeper and, once, a whore. Besides, that was what your granddaddy paid me for— to stay out of their lives. In spite of what most folks think of me, I'm not without honor."

Megan felt dizzy. "You're the secret Caney's been keeping all this time," she said.

Lil nodded. "She wasn't pleased when she realized who I was, but she and I weren't entirely in disagreement. She thought, as I did, that my daughters ought to be left to believe what they'd been told all their lives."

Megan rose shakily to her feet. "And now?"

Lil spread her elegant, long-fingered hands. Close up, Megan could see things in her countenance and her appearance that reminded her of both Christy and Bridget—grace, for example, and courage and intelligence as well. "I guess that's up to you," she said.

All too aware of the burden that had been laid on her shoulders, Megan rose shakily to her feet. "You've put me in a fine position," she said. "Do you expect me to explain everything to Christy and Bridget, so you don't have to do it?"

Lil looked sad. "Think what you like," she said.

Megan had no answer for that, no answer for anything. She simply nodded in farewell, turned around, and walked out of the office and straight through the saloon without looking to either side.

She'd been home less than half an hour, still moving in a daze, when Caney showed up, driving one of Jake Vigil's rigs. If she hadn't already been in a state of shock, seeing her dear friend would have done the job.

"You came back!" she cried in relief and delight, standing in the doorway and gripping the framework with one hand. Caney would attend her wedding after all. Maybe she'd even changed her mind about leaving Primrose Creek to start over someplace else.

Caney smiled as she set the wagon brake and climbed down. "Mr. Malcolm Hicks came to his senses, right enough," she said, holding out her left hand to show a narrow gold band. "We got ourselves married. Been honeymoonin' ever since."

Megan shouted for joy, and the two women embraced, but when they went inside, Caney's aspect changed.

"What was you doin' in Diamond Lil's this afternoon?" she demanded, taking Megan by the upper arms.

"You know about that?" Megan asked, and gulped. "A-already?"

"The whole town knows!" Caney snapped. Despite her flaring nostrils and narrowed eyes, Megan realized, Caney wasn't so much angry as frightened. "Place is buzzin' like a hive full of scalded bees. What in the world was you thinkin' of?"

Megan wouldn't have explained herself to anyone else on earth, not even Webb. "I was going to be Lil's partner." At the look on Caney's face, she hurried on. "She's building a show house. Anyhow, I had to tell her I'd changed my mind."

"That's all?" Caney asked. "That's all that happened?"

Megan couldn't lie, especially not to this woman who had been a second mother to her. "No," she said. "She told me about—about Bridget and Christy."

"Lord have mercy!" Caney gasped, and spread one hand over her heart in such a way that Megan was momentarily terrified for her. "I got to sit myself right down!"

Megan took Caney's arm and ushered her to a chair at the table. Then she brought her a cup of cold water and watched protectively while she sipped. When Caney looked up, her eyes were dark with pain.

"I suppose you plan to tell them."

"I think they ought to know," Megan said quietly. "But I'm not sure it's my place to tell them, or yours, either."

"How you gonna keep a secret like this?" Caney asked anxiously. "It'll chew you up inside."

Megan sat down in the chair next to Caney's and took the other woman's strong hands into her own.

"What about you? This must have been a terrible burden for you to carry all these years."

"It wasn't so hard at first. I believed it was best. But now you're grown women, the four of you." She let out a long, shaky sigh. "It's my place to tell them the truth," she said after a brief silence, during which a myriad of emotions crossed her face. "Christy and Bridget deserve to know. It's goin' to throw them some, though."

Megan nodded. "Yes," she said. "But the truth is always better than a lie, isn't it? And they have Trace and Zachary to lean on. Frankly, I think they'll be glad to finally know, once they get over the initial shock."

Caney pulled free and covered her mouth with one hand, clearly fighting back sobs, maybe even hysteria. Her eyes were huge and round, and she looked ashen. *"Glad?"* she mocked, but not unkindly, when she'd gained some control. "To find out they have a whore for a mama?"

Megan stiffened. "Lillian is a lot more than a—a woman of the evening, Caney. She's strong, and she's smart, too. Just look at all she's accomplished." She stopped, remembering the interview in Diamond Lil's plain office, revelation by revelation. "She gave Christy and Bridget to Granddaddy because she wanted them to have a real family and a home."

Caney lowered her eyes, raised them again. They were filled with fire. "We've all had hard times," she said. "And we didn't take to whorin' to put food on the table!"

Megan stroked Caney's cheek, so glad to have her back that she couldn't begin to express what she felt. "Who knows what made her what she is? Maybe she thought Thayer was going to marry her, in the beginning. Maybe she loved him."

Caney laughed and sniffled at the same time. "You suppose they'll forgive me, my Christy and Bridget?"

"I don't think there's anything to forgive," Megan said softly. "We all know you were merely trying to protect us."

Caney rallied significantly after that. "What kind of manners you got, girl? You ain't even offered me a cup of tea, and here I am, back to stay."

Megan kissed her friend's forehead. "Thank heaven," she said. "I don't know what any of us would do without you."

"Stop your carryin' on," Caney commanded, bluffing, "and make that tea."

Megan lay in her narrow bed in the small spare room downstairs, off the kitchen, staring at the ceiling and thinking of her wedding day. Her splendid dress, carefully pressed and hung on the wall, seemed to glow in the moonlight, like the garb of an angel.

"I found him, Granddaddy," she whispered. "I found the man I know you always wanted for me, and we're going to make a family, right here at Primrose Creek."

There was no reply, of course, but Megan still felt a sense of Gideon McQuarry's presence. He'd be there, the next afternoon, when she and Webb were married, she was sure of that.

Smiling, she closed her eyes and drifted off to sleep.

The new bed felt as if it was an acre across, Webb reflected, as he lay with his hands behind his head, smiling into the darkness. Come tomorrow night, Megan would be there with him, and that would make all the difference.

He wanted her, there was no question of that, and he wanted her soon. But he knew she was going to bring a lot more to his life than pleasure; she already had. She'd brought laughter and hope and feelings Webb had never experienced. Before she came, his life had stretched before him, vast and empty. Now, it looked like the land of milk and honey.

Saturday morning arrived, right on schedule.

At long, long last, Megan's wedding day had come, and she had the dress and the bridegroom to prove it.

Christy and Bridget and Skye fussed over her happily, upstairs in the room she would share with Webb after that night. Clearly, Caney had not yet told the two elder sisters about their mother; Megan would have been able to see signs of it if she had, and there would not have been this sense of merry chaos.

"You are beautiful," Christy said, and smiled. Her eyes glittered with joy and pride. "It just doesn't seem possible—our little Megan, a bride."

Bridget assessed Megan proudly. She'd arranged her hair, weaving in baby's breath and buttercups, and Skye's contribution was the bouquet of daisies, bluebells, and wild tiger lilies she carried, gathered from the meadow above the stream bank only minutes before. "Lovely," she agreed.

A knock sounded at the bedroom door, and Skye hurried over to open it just a crack, peering out into the hallway. "Webb Stratton, you know perfectly well you aren't allowed to see the bride!" she scolded, but there was a smile in her voice.

"I just wanted to make sure she hadn't climbed out the window and headed for the hills," he replied. "Reverend Taylor's here, by the way, and he keeps pulling out his pocket watch and saying he's got a salvation sermon to give this afternoon."

Skye looked back at Megan, who nodded.

"We'll be right down," she said.

"Bring Megan," Webb replied, and then Megan heard his boot heels on the wooden stairs just down the hall.

"Are you ready?" Christy asked.

Megan nodded. Each of her sisters embraced her, Christy first, then Bridget, then Skye, who threw in a kiss on the cheek for good measure.

"Let's go," Megan said after drawing one more deep breath.

Skye descended the stairs first, then Bridget, then Christy, who was to stand up for Megan as a witness. Megan followed slowly, relishing the moment, wanting this day to last forever. The house gleamed, and the people she loved best in the world were gathered in the parlor, including Caney. Her new husband, Malcolm, stood proudly at her side.

Megan's gaze ricocheted to Webb's face. Standing with Zachary at his right side, he watched her with frank admiration and a sort of wonder that caused her heart to overflow. She loved him. She *loved* him! First chance she got, she'd say so, right out, too. Something that personal had to be said in private, that was all.

Reverend Taylor cleared his throat, and Megan took her place shoulder-to-shoulder with Webb, there in front of the fireplace. The preacher began to read, and Megan answered when she was called upon, her voice whisper-soft. So did Webb, though he sounded gruff instead. He was, Megan suspected, as nervous as she was, and somehow that was comforting.

Finally, the reverend pronounced them man and wife, and Megan was overwhelmed by the enormity of it all. It was a good thing Webb turned and took her into his arms then to kiss her, because she figured she would have swooned dead away if he hadn't been holding on to her.

The touch of his mouth on hers was as gentle as the brush of a feather and, at the same time, as hot as fire. When the kiss ended, she looked up at him, blinking and a little stunned, and everyone else in the wedding party laughed and applauded.

Congratulations rained down on the bride and groom, and there were more hugs, more kisses, more tears and laughter. Megan set her wilting bouquet aside on a table, and Augustus, always one to observe any occasion to excess, snatched it and ran furiously around and around the parlor. Then he dropped the flowers in a colorful tumble at Megan's feet and looked up at her with so much unreserved adoration that she couldn't resist bending down to kiss the top of his furry head and ruffle his silly ears.

When the cake—Bridget's famous recipe with coconut frosting—was served, Megan made sure Augustus got a good-sized piece, like every other guest at the wedding.

It was nearly sunset when the well-wishers left, tearing themselves away, family by family, until Webb and Megan were completely alone.

Webb cupped her chin in one hand. "If it isn't Mrs. Webb Stratton," he said, and grinned. Then he took out his pocket watch, flipped open the case, and considered the time.

"What are you doing?"

"Calculating when our first child will be born. I put it at nine months and two hours."

Megan blushed. "That soon?"

He lifted her up into his arms. "That soon," he confirmed, and headed toward the stairs. Augustus padded after them and whimpered once, disconsolately, when the door of the master bedroom closed in his face.

"*T*here's something I—I need to tell you," Megan murmured, gazing up into her husband's face as he gently removed the pins from her hair, one by one, and set them atop the bureau. "Before—"

He let her hair fall around his fingers, his hands gently cupping her skull on either side, his callused thumbs tracing the prominent ridges of her cheekbones. There was a quiet, knowing expression in his eyes. "I'm listening," he said, his voice gruff.

She drew a deep breath, let it out slowly. "I love you."

He was silent for a few moments, apparently absorbing those words, weighing them in his heart and mind. "Now, that's interesting," he said. "I was about to say the same thing to you."

She felt her eyes go wide. He was standing so close that she could feel the heat from his body, sense the strength in his arms and legs and chest. Unlike many men, he never wore oil or pomade in his hair, and he smelled deliciously of pipe smoke, summer winds, and a subtle, teasing scent that might have been store-bought soap or cologne or something entirely his own. "When did you know?" she asked when she could get her tongue to cooperate with the effort.

"Oh, I reckon I've been in love with you right along. I only admitted as much to myself a few days ago, though."

She nodded, shaken and certain that if he weren't resting his hands on her shoulders, she would surely have risen right off the floor, like a stage sprite harnessed to an invisible wire. "I don't exactly know how to do this," she confided, whispering, as though they were in the midst of a crowd instead of their own bedroom, on a ranch several miles from town.

He arched an eyebrow and grinned slightly, gave her shoulders the lightest possible squeeze. "This?" he teased, pretending not to know what she meant.

She swallowed. "Lovemaking," she replied, even more quietly than before.

His brow crumpled, but there was still a blue light dancing in his eyes. "Oh," he said. "I understood you to say you were a woman of experience."

He would find her wanting, she was sure he would, as soon as he discovered how little she knew about the act of love. She was utterly mortified and quite unable to speak.

"Ah," Webb said, as though enlightened by her silence.

She felt her face ignite with embarrassment. "It—it only happened once, and I—well—it was terrible—"

He was combing her hair with his fingers now, and

she felt his breath on her forehead. "Did you feel the way you feel right now?"

She paused, considered the question, and then shook her head. She couldn't have spoken, though; her throat had drawn shut again, like a tobacco pouch with the strings pulled tight.

He smiled, tilted her chin, and looked straight into her eyes. "Let me show you," he said, "how a woman *should* be loved."

A sweet, hard shiver went through her, partly disquiet but mostly anticipation. She nodded, still stricken to silence, to let him know she wasn't scared. She closed her eyes when she felt his hands slide down from her shoulders along her arms to her hands. He raised one to his mouth and brushed the knuckles with his lips, then did the same with the other, taking his time. The very slowness of the gestures stirred exquisite sensations in the most sensitive parts of her body.

After a few delicious moments, he turned her around, so that her back was to him, and began unfastening the cloth buttons that held her wedding gown closed. When the dress was open to the waist, Webb slipped his hands inside, boldly caressing her breasts.

Megan groaned and let her head fall back against Webb's shoulder.

He chuckled, as though amused by her response. It was a heavenly misery, and, to compound matters, he slipped his thumbs inside her camisole, brushing her nipples until they hardened like creek stones. She gasped, and he continued his teasing, bending to kiss her temple and then nibble at her earlobe. By the time he got to her neck, she was dizzy with wanting, but this, she soon discovered, was only the beginning.

While he continued to tease her nipples with one hand, Webb slid the other down over her bare belly, leaving the nerve endings jumping under her skin as he went. He made a circle around her navel, with just the tip of his finger, and continued to nibble and nip at her earlobe. Involuntarily, Megan thrust her hips forward, and that was when he reached beneath the waistline of her petticoat and bloomers and found the warm, moist delta where her thighs met.

She stiffened, her back curved.

"Shhh," he murmured against her ear, and she sagged against him, gave herself up to the fierce pleasure of his touch. Surely, she thought, half-blind with need, it must be a sin to feel like this, to want something—some*one*—so badly.

He eased the dress down over her shoulders and let it fall to the floor in a rustling circle, soft as flower petals. Then, because her knees were threatening to fail her, he curved one arm around her middle and held her against him. Now, in addition to the fury he was stirring with his fingers, she felt the length and heat of him pressing into her lower back. She began to thrust her hips into his hand, seeking something she couldn't have explained.

He kissed her bare shoulders, one and then the other. "Not so fast," he said in a rasp. He turned her to face him once more and began removing his own clothes, his eyes linked with hers the whole time. She ached to have him touch her again but was too proud to say so. Instead, she raised trembling hands to take off her few remaining garments.

She had no memory of lying down on the bed, no idea whether she went under her own power or Webb carried her. She was aware only of her own responses, and of Webb, and of the pinkish-gold light of a fading sun pooling around them.

Webb was naked, and he was glorious. She wanted to touch him everywhere, not only to give him pleasure, though she certainly wanted that, but because he fascinated her. In the combined glow of sunset and her love, he looked like some gilded creature, more of heaven than earth. He was strong, and yet he handled her with infinite tenderness, even reverence.

He kissed her, again and again, and she kissed back. Webb's lovemaking was not something to be endured but something to be reveled in, surrendered to, celebrated. When he cupped one of her breasts in his hand and tasted the nipple, already taut from stroking, Megan arched her back and gave a long, shuddering sigh. Groping, she plunged her fingers into his hair, then let them wander up and down his back in a frantic search.

He moved to her other breast and enjoyed it thoroughly before finding his way to her belly, where he dipped the tip of his tongue into her navel as though he'd found honey there. She shivered again, moaned in her throat.

She thought it was over then, that he would take her, because he moved her knees apart and centered himself between them. She closed her eyes and braced herself for pain, and instead encountered an ecstasy so forbidden that she had never even imagined it before, let alone experienced it. He found her most delicate and private place and took suckle there, on the nubbin of flesh that throbbed against his tongue in frantic welcome.

She cried out, a great, triumphant, groaning shout, and wove her fingers into his hair again, holding him close and closer, even as she tossed her head back and forth on the pillow like a woman in a fever. If he didn't stop, she would die, and if he *did*, she would die. She'd raised herself onto the soles of her feet, seeking him, and he braced his hands under her buttocks and held her high to his mouth. He was insatiable, relentless, and utterly wonderful.

Fierce satisfaction swelled and billowed, swelled and billowed within her, like the sails of a ship catching the wind. On and on it went, while Megan flung back her head and tried to stay with her bucking body. Webb slipped her legs over his shoulders and took her to what was surely the end of the journey. Sobbing, her body still flexing long after all her strength was spent, Megan held nothing back.

It was not the end, she was startled to discover when Webb finally lowered her gently to the bed, but merely the beginning. He lay as close as a second skin, his arms around her, and soothed her while she regained her senses. Then he gently spread her legs again and mounted her, and she was amazed to feel herself catch fire again the instant he entered her. As his thrusts grew more urgent, more powerful, she moved with him, stroking his back, holding his face, drawing him down, again and again, for her kiss.

When release came, it swept them both up into a golden fury, and, for a time, their bodies belonged neither to them as individuals nor to each other but to the same forces that spawned stars and fires, mountains and floods. Megan was flung so far heavenward, so fiercely, that she never expected to return from the skies and be herself again.

After several such encounters, sleep finally claimed

the lovers, and when Megan awakened in the morning, she was alone in their marriage bed. She sat upright, unaccountably frightened that Webb had abandoned her, but he was standing at one of the windows, hands braced against the sill, gazing out. He wore trousers and boots, but his chest was bare, and his suspenders dangled below his hips. Megan thought he looked delicious.

"Good morning, Mr. Stratton," she said, stretching.

He turned his head, grinned at her. "Don't tempt me," he warned. "I might just come back to bed and have my way with you."

Megan did not lower her arms. Although she was covered by the top sheet, she was naked underneath, and, of course, Webb knew that. "Do you suppose we've started that baby?" she asked, batting her lashes once or twice. She knew they were thick, and one of her best features.

He crossed to her, leaned down, and placed a noisy kiss on her mouth. "Stop it," he growled. "I've got a ranch to run. I can't be lolling around in bed with my wife all day."

She slipped her arms around his neck. "Can't you just—loll—for a little while?"

He laughed. "No," he answered firmly. He touched the tip of her nose with an index finger. "Tonight, however, is another matter." With that, he tugged down the sheet, took a leisurely sip at each of her breasts, and then left her to contemplate her situation.

She got up, muttering, and hastily washed and dressed. Webb had already started breakfast when she got downstairs, and Augustus, waiting for his share of the sausage and the eggs from Bridget's chickens, spared her only a single glance, the ingrate. Apparently, he'd already forgotten the piece of wedding cake she'd given him.

"Shall I bring dinner up to the meadow?" she asked Webb. Although the sun was up, it was still very early, and there was a kerosene lantern burning in the middle of the table. It gave the room a cozy glow, as did the small fire Webb had built on the hearth, and Megan felt sinfully contented.

Webb gave her a sidelong glance, skillfully turning sizzling sausage patties in the big iron pan. "The men have probably got a rabbit stew or a pot of beans on the fire," he said. "Why don't you just spend today resting up for tonight?"

Megan moved behind her husband, slipped her arms around his waist, let her cheek rest in the space between his shoulder blades. He'd put on one of the shirts she'd sewed for him, and she could smell his singular scent through the cloth. "You *are* confident," she said, and laughed softly.

He turned, drew her close, kissed her. "Last night, you seemed to think that confidence was justified," he drawled. "If I remember correctly, you were tearing my hair and sobbing and pleading for more."

It was all true, of course, but it was insufferable of him to remind her in the broad light of day. "Webb Stratton!" she gasped, mortified and flattered and excited, all of a piece.

"Just wait until tonight," he said, and when, laughing, she flailed at him with both fists, he grasped her wrists and subdued her with a kiss that left her sagging against him. Then he swatted her bottom, seated her at the table, and served her breakfast.

*   *   *

Christy and Bridget sat in Bridget's parlor, their eyes swollen, hankies clutched in their hands. "They've been this way for days," Skye confided in a theatrical whisper. Megan had been married a full month, and well occupied most of that time. Now, seeing the state her sisters were in, she felt guilty for being so happy.

"Caney told them," Megan guessed.

Skye's brown eyes widened. "You *knew?* About Diamond Lil and—and our papa?"

Megan nodded, then sighed. "Lillian told me the day I went to see her about our partnership."

"And you didn't say anything?" Skye hissed.

Both Christy and Bridget were glaring at her accusingly, and Megan realized that they had overheard. She straightened her spine, squared her shoulders, and marched across the room to stand between their two chairs. She rested her hands on her hips, feeling very matronly now that she was an old married woman of thirty days. "Stop feeling sorry for yourselves," she said crisply. "You're a disgrace, the pair of you!"

For once in their lives, her elder sisters were speechless.

"Your mother is alive." She gestured wildly with one hand in the general direction of town. "She's barely two miles from here. Don't you have questions you want to ask her? Don't you have things you want to say?"

Bridget's jawline tightened. "You bet your bustle I do," she said, rising out of her chair, then sitting down again.

"Well?" Skye prompted, spreading her hands.

Bridget's lower lip wobbled, but only slightly. Her posture was as proud as ever. "I'm not sure where to start."

"Start?" Christy whispered miserably, and dabbed at her eyes again with a wadded handkerchief. "Our mother is a *prostitute*. That's not a beginning, it's an end!"

"Oh, for heaven's sake," Megan said. "There are worse things, you know."

"What?" Christy sniffled, plainly mystified.

"What if she'd kept you? Raised you in a series of saloons and brothels? She cared enough to give you both up, to give you a family and a good home," Megan said, losing patience. Always the youngest, the pet of the family, she wasn't used to taking charge in moments of crisis. She rather liked it. "Do stop behaving like a pair of babies!"

"I'm going to town to speak to my mother," Bridget said decisively, rising again, looking down at a profoundly stunned Christy, who was still in her chair. "Are you coming or not?"

Never one to be bested, even at something she didn't want to do in the first place, Christy bolted to her feet. "Of course I am," she replied. Then Bridget turned to Megan and Skye.

"Will you please look after the children?" she asked.

Megan nodded. Since Christy had brought little Joseph and Margaret along to this crying fest, all the kids were close at hand.

The two daughters of Lillian Colefield did not trouble themselves with a change of clothes, nor did they splash their faces with cold water or attend to their hair. No, they crossed the bridge over the creek in single file, then set out for town, arm in arm, like a two-woman army marching on an unsuspecting city.

"You suppose they'll be all right?" Skye asked, peering after their sisters as they ascended the steep bank on the other side of Primrose Creek.

"I'm more worried about anybody who might get in their way," Megan replied, and laughed. The morning was a happy one, spent playing games in the yard with the nieces and nephews, and when Bridget and Christy returned, after two hours, they were dry-eyed and introspective. Neither of them wanted to give an account of their interview with Diamond Lil, and Megan and Skye weren't foolish enough to ask. In fact, they wisely took their leave, Skye with her two children, Megan with Augustus, who had come to escort his mistress back along the creek path. She was pleased by his attentions, as always, and stopped several times to throw a stick and then praise him outlandishly for fetching.

She was smiling when she rounded the last bend and saw the familiar horse standing in the dooryard, reins dangling. Webb was home.

Augustus ran to his master, barking with glee, and Webb laughed as he bent down to ruffle the animal's loose, gleaming hide.

"You're back early," Megan commented, quite unnecessarily. She was Webb's bride, and she shared his bed, and still her heart leaped every time she laid eyes on him, whether close up or from a distance.

He straightened, grinning. "I got to hankering for my wife," he said.

Megan bit her lower lip and waited.

He extended a hand, and she crossed the distance between them without further hesitation. He kissed the backs of her knuckles, one by one, sending hot shivers throughout her body. Then he whisked her up into his arms and carried her not toward the house, as she had expected, but in the direction of the barn.

"What—?" she managed.

He gave her a long, deep kiss, without slackening his pace. "There are a thousand places I mean to have you," he said when at last he raised his mouth from hers, "and the hayloft is one of them."

The inside of the barn was cool and shadowy, rife with the scents of animals and hay and saddle leather. Augustus, by that time, had lost interest in the activities of his master and mistress and trotted off on some errand of his own.

Webb set Megan on her feet in front of the ladder leading up into the loft. She met his eyes, briefly, and then began to climb.

*M*egan stood in the dooryard, watching as the woman drove the livery rig, a dusty buggy, deftly across the shallow creek. There was a young, fair-haired boy on the seat beside her, about the same age as Bridget's Noah and Skye's Hank. Even from that distance, Megan somehow knew that the child's eyes would be periwinkle-blue.

As the wayfarers drew nearer, Megan could see that the woman was like a cameo come to life. Her skin was a flawless shade of ivory, her eyes some dark shade of purple or brown. *Ellie,* Megan thought, full of amazement and despair.

In her spotless traveling suit, made of lightweight, cream-colored linen, Ellie Stratton made Megan feel as though she'd stitched all her own garments together from potato sacks. She'd been meaning to sew some new dresses, but, what with one thing and another, she just hadn't had time.

The other Mrs. Stratton drew back on the reins and smiled, though there was a certain caution lurking in her eyes, as though she might be unsure of her welcome. "I guess you must be Megan," she said.

Megan barely returned the smile, and she could only speculate about what was visible in her own eyes. She felt such a tangle of things, she couldn't begin to sort them out. Unfortunately, Christian charity wasn't among them. Whatever Ellie Stratton wanted, she'd been Webb's first love, and Megan dreaded seeing them together. "Hullo, Mrs. Stratton," she replied.

Ellie winced slightly. Augustus had ambled over to investigate, and the boy was looking at him with interest. Interest and those blue-purple eyes Megan had been so certain he would have. "Just call me Ellie," she said. "If you wouldn't mind."

Megan nodded and then smiled at the boy, who was still watching Augustus with fascination. "He's friendly," she said. "You can pet him if it's all right with your mother."

"Go ahead, Tommy," Ellie told the boy.

Tommy climbed nimbly down and put out a tentative hand to Augustus. The dog responded with a long slurp of his tongue, and a delighted laugh bubbled from the little boy. Ellie alighted, much more gracefully than her son had done, and stood facing Megan.

"You're just as pretty as Jesse said you were," Ellie said. "Is—is Webb at home, by any chance?"

Megan was about to say that he wasn't, when they all turned at the sound of a rider coming across the creek. It was Webb.

Megan's knees nearly buckled with relief at the mere sight of him, but, at the same time, she feared the moment when he recognized Ellie, the woman he'd once wanted for his wife, and the boy.

Ellie was on her way to him even before he'd reached the yard. When he swung down from the saddle and embraced her, she put her arms around his neck.

Megan stood rigid, watching. Waiting. She was only vaguely aware of the boy and dog, now running round and round in a huge circle, both of them barking.

Ellie and Webb parted, but she was beaming up into his face. Her joy in seeing him would have been obvious to anyone, although Webb's state of mind was not so easy to read. He took her elbow in one hand and started toward Megan, leading the horse along behind.

Megan called upon all her theatrical ability just to smile.

"I guess you've met my brother's wife," Webb said. Was she mistaken, or had he put a slight emphasis on the last three words?

"And I've met Megan," Ellie said, as though it were the most natural thing in the world for a first love to come calling at the hot tail end of a July afternoon. She gestured for the boy to come to her side, and he obeyed, albeit with reluctance. Seeing him with Webb took Megan's breath away, so great was the resemblance. "Tommy, this is your Uncle Webb."

Webb crouched, facing the child. "Hullo, Tommy," he said.

"Hullo," Tommy replied uncertainly. He might have moved a fraction of an inch closer to his mother, though there was no telling for sure.

Webb stood up, and his gaze caught Megan's and held on. No smile. "Let's all go inside," he said.

Megan knew her fears were irrational, for the most

part, but that didn't stop the inward shiver that coursed
through her just then. Was Webb going to tell her that
this was his boy, his and Ellie's? The resemblance was
amazing, but then, Jesse looked very much like Webb.
Perhaps Tom Jr. did, too.

They entered through the main door, and Megan
immediately made for the kitchen. She put on a pot of
coffee and cut slices from a pan of yellow cake she'd
baked earlier to serve at supper. She set a plate on the
floor for an appreciative Augustus and put three others
on an old cupboard door that she liked to use as a tray.

Webb was seated in his chair near the fire, the very
place where he'd often said, jokingly, that he meant to
pass his old age. Ellie and Tommy sat side by side on
the settee, and Ellie's feelings for Webb were evident in
her eyes in a way they had not been before. Try though
she might, Megan still couldn't make sense of Webb's
expression; it was closed, unreadable.

"Never mind the coffee," he said when Megan had
set down the tray and started back toward the kitchen.
"Sit down and catch your breath."

Catch your breath. Megan wasn't so sure she was
ever going to breathe easily again—not, at least, while
Ellie Stratton was there in her parlor, making cow eyes
at *her* husband. Megan sat and took some pleasure in
the fact that her chair was the mate to Webb's, and close
enough that she could have reached out a hand to touch
his arm or his knee.

All the same, her heart was pounding.

Ellie fiddled with the drawstring bag in her lap
and brought out a sheaf of papers. She leaned over to
hand them to Webb, and, although the move could
not have been described as coquettish, it nonetheless

made Megan want to pull out the other woman's hair.

Silently, she instructed herself not to be such a ninny, but it didn't do much good where her feelings were concerned.

Webb took the papers, unfolded them, scanned the words therein. Megan saw his jawline tighten.

"I'm sorry to tell you this way," Ellie said gently. "Your pa died six months ago. Tom Jr. took over the Southern Star, but one third of it is yours, and one third is Jesse's. We didn't know where you were till Jesse came home."

Webb handed back the papers. "They can split the difference," he said. "Tom Jr. and Jesse. I've got a ranch of my own, right here."

Megan wondered if the dizzying range of emotions she was feeling showed in her face or countenance, but since no one but Augustus was looking at her anyway, she guessed it didn't matter.

"I'm afraid it isn't that easy," Ellie replied. "The will is written in such a way that if one son refuses his share, the other two lose theirs as well. And on top of that, you have to live there, all three of you, and work the place the way your father did."

Webb got up and turned his back to stand at the front window, looking out at the land he loved as much as Megan did. He'd poured a lot of himself into making that ranch what it was. "They can fight that in court, break the will. Tom Jr. and Jesse, I mean. It's unreasonable to insist that we all live there."

Ellie's face was filled with pain and memories of pain. "Yes, it's unreasonable. That was your father, in a word." She paused, murmured to the boy that he ought to go and eat his cake on the stoop, which he gratefully did, and then went on with a sort of despairing tenacity. "Tom Jr. won't last the year, Webb. The doctor says his liver has been eating itself away for a decade. Jesse can't handle that place on his own; he's too young. So even if they convinced a judge—"

Megan watched, her heart pounding so loud she was sure it must be audible, as Webb turned from the window. With both his elder brother and his father gone, Webb might well want to return to the Southern Star. After all, he'd been born on that ranch, and his mother was buried there. Perhaps that was home to him, not Primrose Creek.

"What about you and the boy, Ellie?" Webb asked. "What's your place in all this?"

What, indeed? Megan wondered, and hoped nobody had noticed that she was sitting on the edge of her chair.

Ellie lowered her head for a moment, and when she looked up, her eyes were shimmering with tears. Crying always made Megan look puffy and mottled, with her delicate redhead's coloring, but this woman managed to weep gracefully. She might have been a fallen goddess, wrongfully toppled from her pedestal in some pagan temple. "I told Tom Jr. that Tommy and I wouldn't stay around and watch him drink himself to death, and I meant it."

Megan closed her eyes tightly, braced herself. Ellie had come searching for the brother she truly loved, and the boy would probably provide any further inducement that might be necessary.

"What do you mean to do, then?" Webb wanted to know. Megan could not tell anything at all from his tone, but when she realized he was standing behind her chair, when she felt his hand come to rest lightly on her shoulder, a jolt went through her.

Ellie's gaze was steady. Level. "We'll get to that later," she said, showing the tensile strength underlaying her nature. "Right now, I'm trying to protect my son's future. Tom Sr.'s will is specific. If Tom Jr. dies, the ranch becomes yours and Jesse's, in equal shares. You'll still have to live on the land, both of you. If one of you chooses not to accept the terms, then, like I said, the property will be forfeited. If that happens, of course, then Tommy will have nothing when he comes of age."

Megan felt chilled through and through, and her stomach was jumpy. She was glad she hadn't tried to eat any cake, because she might have disgraced herself by clapping one hand over her mouth and running out of the room.

"That mean old son-of-a-bitch," Webb murmured. "God in heaven. The man's dead and buried, and he's still trying to run all our lives."

"My family isn't wealthy, Webb," Ellic said. "A share of that ranch is all Tommy will ever have."

Webb sighed. "He looks like a sturdy little fella. I imagine you're underestimating him, Ellie." He squeezed Megan's shoulder once more, reassuring her only slightly, then turned and walked back to his desk. She heard him pull back the chair and sit down, knew he was reading his father's will in depth this time, word by word.

"I'll get that coffee," Megan said, and bolted, because she couldn't stand the tension anymore, couldn't bear just sitting there, with everything she cared about hanging in the balance.

"I don't want any, thank you!" Ellie called after her,

and Megan already knew that Webb would refuse a cup, but she went about the task anyway because it gave her something to do with her hands, and she sorely needed that.

Minutes later, standing in the kitchen doorway watching Tommy and Augustus bounding tirelessly about the yard, Megan heard Webb and Ellie talking, their voices rapid and earnest. She couldn't make out the words, but the tones said a lot, Ellie's high and timorous, Webb's low and hoarse. Despair filled Megan, as though she were flooded to the neck with brackish water.

Presently, Ellie appeared, her eyes showing evidence of more exquisitely lovely tears, her chin high. She nodded to Megan, as cordially as she could, and stepped past her into the yard. "Come along, Tommy," she called. "We'll miss the stagecoach to Virginia City."

Tommy waved to Megan and to Webb, who was standing silently behind her, but his most sincere farewell went to Augustus. Ellie climbed gracefully into the buggy and took up the reins without looking in their direction at all, waited for her son, and drove away.

"You're going," Megan said, without turning around to face her husband.

"I have to," he replied, and walked away.

Megan stood on the threshold for a long time, hugging herself, struggling not to cry. Damn Webb Stratton, anyway, if that was all their marriage meant to him. She'd get along just fine without him.

When she went upstairs, not bothering with supper, Webb was at his desk in the parlor, wearing his reading spectacles and going over a stack of ledgers and loose papers. He looked up when she paused on the first landing, and their gazes locked, but neither of them spoke.

It was late when he came to bed, but Megan had not slept. She wasn't sure she would ever sleep again.

"Why?" she asked. Despite the spareness of the question, he knew full well what she meant.

He sighed. "Because of the boy."

Her heart turned brittle and trembled, on the verge of shattering. "Yes," she said. "Because of the boy."

Webb spoke gently, in a hoarse voice. "He's my nephew, Megan," he said. "Not my son. But whatever my differences with the kid's father, I can't just turn my back and let him lose everything. I feel some responsibility toward Jesse, too."

Did he expect her to be reasonable? She couldn't, not where their parting was concerned. She said nothing.

Webb knew she was crying, of course, since the bed was shaking. He turned her into his arms, pulled her against his chest. "I'll sell off the herd," he said, "and you can stay in town or with one of your sisters. There's enough money to see you through—"

She pushed away from him. "No, Webb," she replied tartly. "If I can't go with you, and I suspect I won't be invited, then I'm not leaving this ranch. You promised to sign the place over to me if anything happened to—to us, remember?"

His sigh was gusty, a raw sound, fraught with pain. "It's a long, dangerous trip from here to Montana, Megan."

She turned her back again, and this time, he didn't touch her. "Not too long and dangerous for Ellie, I see," she said, and hated herself for jealousy so evident in her voice. "Well, I'll have you know, Webb Stratton, that I traveled to and from England on a small ship without any trouble at all." *Other than a week of seasickness each way,* chided a voice in her mind. "Furthermore, I came west with Caney and Christy in a wagon, and we ran into just about every hardship a body can come up against."

"Ellie made the trip for her son."

"She made the trip for you," Megan insisted, and Webb did not deny that. In fact, he was typically straightforward.

"She hoped Jesse had been mistaken about my marrying you, that there might be a chance for her and me once Tom Jr. passes. I told her different."

"But you're leaving with her."

"No, Megan. She and the boy are going back east to live with her folks. I'm headed up to Montana to work this whole thing through with my brothers. I'll be back in a few months, I promise."

Megan felt both relief and doubt. Relief because she knew Webb didn't make promises lightly, and doubt because nobody was more aware than she was of the bonds between family members. "I don't believe you."

He chuckled, but there was no humor in the sound. "That's apparent," he said. Then he stroked the length of her side with his left hand, and, in complete contrast to her emotions, a rush of need went through her, powerful as a flash flood spilling into a dry creekbed.

Against her will, against her better judgment, she turned to him, this man who was leaving her. This man who might never be back, no matter what he said to the contrary.

Their lovemaking was fierce that night, a thing of sorrow as much as passion, a holding on and a letting go. Even as her body spasmed with almost unbearable pleasure, Megan sobbed.

The next day, Webb went to town and came back with a paper transferring ownership of the ranch at Primrose Creek into Megan's name, along with an envelope full of money drawn on his account at the bank. They didn't speak all day, except in broken sentences, and poor Augustus, sensing that something fundamental had shifted, was beside himself. That night in bed, however, Webb and Megan made love as wildly, as desperately, as they had the night before. It was almost a form of combat rather than communion, but it was no less satisfying for that. Megan knew Webb was as deeply affected as she was, but none of that made any difference. Webb was leaving, and soon, and Megan grew more convinced with every passing moment that he wouldn't return. She'd already suffered too much loss to believe in happy endings where things like that were concerned.

On the third day after Megan's world cracked down the middle and began to come apart, Webb arranged by wire to sell the cattle to the army at far less than the going price, and he managed to hire enough men to help drive the beasts as far as Fort Grant. He would ride on from there alone.

It would have changed everything if he'd taken her with him, but he wasn't going to do that, and she wasn't being given a say in the matter. She might have followed Webb, forced him either to take her along or waste time doubling back to bring her home again, but she had a very personal and private reason for not doing that.

So she tried to resign herself to losing the only man she would ever love.

On the morning Webb left, with all his cattle and a

half-dozen cowhands, Megan stood at the edge of the high meadow, watching. Augustus, confused, ran frantically back and forth between Webb's horse and Megan, yipping sorrowfully.

"Go on home, boy," Webb said to him. "Go home with Megan."

Megan was blind with tears when the dog trotted back to her, glancing over his shoulder, once or twice, lest Webb summon him, as he came. She couldn't wave; she couldn't even find the strength to say good-bye. So she just stood there, like a tree stump, and watched as Webb rode away.

Soon, there was nothing left to see but a roiling cloud of dust in the distance, nothing left to hear but the incessant bawling of all those cattle. Megan turned, a whimpering Augustus at her side, and made her way back down the hill and along an old trail toward the house.

She stood in the dooryard for a while, looking around her at the land her Granddaddy had left her. She'd gotten what she wanted—it was hers again, and hers alone, and she would never let it go.

Drying her eyes on the hem of her apron, she went inside to put on a pot of tea.

Fat flakes of snow drifted past the window over the kitchen work table, and Caney, spreading slices of dried apple in a pie shell, turned with a beaming smile to Megan. "The young'uns will love this," she said. "They always like a good snow."

Megan, kneading bread at the table near the fire, smiled. "Trace made them all sleds," she said, referring to the many cousins living up and down Primrose Creek. "They'll be looking for a slippery hill."

Caney's expression turned somber. She was well along with her and Malcolm's first child, and pregnancy had rendered her more exotically beautiful than ever before. "You hear anything from Webb?" she asked in a small voice.

Megan figured her sisters had probably put Caney up to asking the question, since she'd made it clear she didn't want to discuss the matter with them. She'd had two letters from him in the months he'd been gone, one saying that Tom Jr. had died and he and Jesse were trying to sort things through with a pack of lawyers, the other containing a bank draft and a promise, neither of which carried much weight with Megan by that time. She hadn't written him back, because she couldn't do that without telling him about the baby, and she wasn't about to beg or use weakness to get what she wanted.

Caney abandoned her pie-making and crossed the room to take Megan into her arms. Their protruding stomachs bounced against each other, and both women laughed, though Megan had already given way to tears. Kindness always did that to her, always broke down her defenses.

"If I didn't have this here baby in me," Caney said, rocking Megan back and forth the way she'd done for years and years, "I declare I'd go find that man and take a horsewhip to him."

Megan sniffled, straightened her spine, and dashed at her cheek with the back of one hand. "If he doesn't want me and our baby, then we don't want him, either. I'll hire somebody to run this ranch and go to work for Lil in her new show house."

Caney put a finger under Megan's chin and lifted.

"Does Webb even know about this chile, girl? Or were you too proud to tell him?"

Megan used her apron to mop her face, which was as wet as if she'd stuck her whole head into a pail of water. She had suspected her condition before Webb left for Montana, but she hadn't said a word. "I couldn't," she said. "And it isn't a matter of pride, Caney. He would have stayed—yes, I'm sure he would have stayed—but against his will and for all the wrong reasons."

"He got a right to know, Megan," Caney insisted. "Might be growin' inside you, but that babe belongs to him, too."

"I'll tell him—sometime," she said.

Caney made a clucking sound with her tongue and shook her head. "I think you ought to write him. I'll leave the letter off for mailin' when I get back to town."

Megan shook her head. Then she turned her back, went to the basin, and thoroughly washed not only her hands but her tear-stained face, too. That done, she went back to the table, put the dough into buttered pans, and set it to rise on a table near the hearth.

Caney was still working on her pies—they were having a family dinner that night, at Bridget's to celebrate Noah's birthday—when all of a sudden she let out a long, low whistle and crowed right out loud. Augustus got up from his rug in front of the fire and gave a lazy *woof, woof.*

Caney turned, gesturing wildly, her face wreathed in a glorious smile. "Git over here, girl, and look out this winder!" she cried.

Frowning, her heart picking up speed, Megan obeyed, wiping her hands on a dish towel as she went. When she reached the window, looked out, and saw a man on horseback crossing the creek, she drew in her breath. Although the horse, a strawberry roan, was unfamiliar, and the rider wore a long coat and a hat with a wide brim pulled down low against the freezing wind, Megan knew him instantly, and her heart rushed out to meet him.

"Webb," she whispered.

"Speak of the devil," Caney cried joyously, raising both hands into the air and shaking them in a sort of unspoken hallelujah. Immediately, she bustled over, took her cloak down from one of the row of pegs next to the door, and put it on. "I got me news to pass!"

Megan didn't even think about a coat. She just opened the door and stepped out into the snowy chill, barely noticing when Caney tried to pull her back. Augustus dashed by, a golden streak shooting across the snow, barking so hard he was bound to be hoarse come morning.

Webb rode to the middle of the yard and climbed down. The dog jumped up, his forefeet resting on his master's chest. Webb laughed and ruffled the animal's sides with gloved hands, but his eyes rose to rest on Megan.

"Lord o'mercy," Caney clucked, tucking a cloak around Megan, "you'll catch your death. Then what good will it be, your man comin' home at long last?" She glared at Webb. " 'Bout time," she snapped. Then stomped off through the rising snow in an energetic huff. Just like that, she collected her mule and rode off.

Webb didn't speak, and neither did Megan. She just stood there, afraid to believe he was really back, not an apparition or a figure in a dream. How many nights had she tossed in her lonely bed in the spare room, unable to sleep in the one they had shared, dreaming just this dream? How many times had she awakened, already weeping because she knew it wasn't real?

He faced her, laid his hands on either side of her huge belly. "When?"

"February," she managed to say.

A grin broke across his wind-chapped face. He needed a bath and a shave and a thorough barbering, and he was the most beautiful sight Megan had ever seen. "Guess I got here just in time," he said.

"You're back to stay?" She hardly dared put the question, the answer was so important.

He nodded. "If you'll have me. I settled my business up in Montana, just like I said I would, and now I'm home for good." He propelled her toward the house. "Go on inside before you take a chill. Caney'll have my hide if you do."

She hesitated, then nodded and obeyed, but she stood at a side window, still wearing her cloak, and watched as he led his horse into the barn, watched till he came out again and started toward the house. Only then was she truly convinced that she wasn't imagining everything.

He saw her, grinned.

Her heart tumbled end over end, like a circus acrobat doing somersaults.

He came in, pulled off his gloves, removed his coat and hat, and hung them up like he always had, then moved toward her. "If I can't hold you in my arms, Megan, and lay you down in our bed, I don't know that I'll live much longer. I've missed you so much."

"Whose fault is that?" she demanded, but she was weakening, and he knew it.

"Mine," he said. Then he held out one hand to her. She took it.

He led her inside, lifted her off her feet, and carried her up the stairs, along the hallway, and into their bedroom. The room was cold, going unused the way it had, and once they had divested each other of their clothes, they scrambled under the covers.

Webb slipped beneath the blankets to caress Megan's stomach, to kiss and nibble at her flesh. Then he was between her legs, parting her, slipping his hands under her bottom. When he tasted her, she cried out. When he indulged, she all but lost her mind. At last, she reached a crescendo that flung her mind in one direction and her spirit in another, and she sank, whimpering, to the mattress.

He murmured to her, kissed her all over. By the time he reached her mouth, she was desperate again. The instant he slid inside her, with touching care, she exploded in satisfaction, but his appeasement took a while. When it overtook him, he stiffened upon her, shuddered violently, and groaned her name like a dying man crying out to heaven.

He fell beside her, and they lay in exhausted silence for a long time, arms and legs entwined, while shadows crept across the room.

"You won't be going back to Montana?" Megan ventured presently. She had to know.

"Maybe for a visit sometime," Webb answered. "Jesse's got a good foreman, though. He'll make a go of the place."

"So the two of you managed to have your father's will overturned?"

Webb sighed. "Yeah," he said. "But the old man

didn't make it easy. That's why I was gone so long—there was a lot of wrangling to be done."

Megan snuggled closer still and traced a finger tip down the middle of Webb's bare chest. "If you were a gentleman," she said, "you'd get up and build a fire."

He moved under the blankets again, began kissing her belly. "Who said I was a gentleman?" he countered, his voice muffled. He found her breasts, nibbled at one peak as though it were some delectable delicacy. "Besides, I think things are getting pretty hot right here in this bed. We've got a fire going already, Mrs. Stratton."

She couldn't disagree.

Soon, in fact, she couldn't speak at all.

Epilogue

There they are, my beautiful granddaughters—fiery Bridget, face glowing in the firelight, plainly adoring her husband and that pack of rascally children she and Trace have produced. I well recall the day Trace Qualtrough came to Primrose Creek, on foot and carrying a worn-out saddle over one shoulder, meaning to look after his best friend's widow. They've made them a place to be proud of, since then.

Then there's Christy. She presented the greatest challenge to my matchmaking skills, setting her cap for Jake Vigil the way she did, when it was really young Zachary Shaw, the marshal, she was meant to marry. Things have certainly come right in the end, though not without considerable doing on my part. There are two perfect children in that family, with another on the way, though Christy and Zachary don't suspect it yet.

And Skye. My brave, lovely Skye. She's met her

match in Jake Vigil, and between the two of them, they'll build an empire. No, sir, I've got no worries where they're concerned. Their love is as sturdy as the trees bristling on these hills.

Finally, little Megan. Of course, she's not so little anymore—a grown woman, in point of fact—and a beauty into the bargain, with that glorious red hair of hers. She and Webb, they're as well suited as me and my Rebecca were, and that's saying something. Megan's baby will be a girl, as beautiful as her mama, and just as smart and spirited, too. Fact is, they'll have them a flock of girls, the Strattons will, with a couple of boys coming along later, to bring up the rear.

There's snow falling outside, coming down soft and pretty from a heavy sky. Noah, Bridget's boy, he's just about ready to come unstrung, he's so excited about his birthday. He'll grow into a fine man, though not without giving his folks a gray hair or two in the process. Makes me smile to think about it.

Here are Caney Blue and her fine bridegroom, arriving late for the festivities. Happiness has been a long time coming to Caney, and to her husband, too, but they've finally reached a place of peace and plenty, these two good people. Caney's baby girl will grow up right here, with the rest of them.

Darned if Lillian Colefield herself didn't just follow Caney and Malcolm into the house. She's worn pretty well over the years, given all she's gone through. I never expected to see her again, but things do have a way of coming full circle, especially in matters of the heart. I'm glad they've all found each other. Glad I can go now, and meet up with my Rebecca.

She's been waiting a long time.

POCKET BOOKS HARDCOVER
PROUDLY PRESENTS

Last Chance Café

LINDA LAEL MILLER

Available April 2002

Turn the page for a preview of
Last Chance Café. . . .

Last Chance Café

*T*he tiny brass bell above the door tinkled in the same annoyingly cheerful way it always did, that night when the whole slow and sleepy course of his life did a sudden 360. Chance Qualtrough probably wouldn't even have bothered to give his stool at the counter a quarter turn and take a look if it hadn't been for the odd sliver of heat that caught somewhere in the innermost regions of his heart and took a tight stitch there.

He glanced over his shoulder, and there she was, coated in snow, skinny and scared, with a little kid clasping either hand. He squinted, taking in the rug-rats—girls, judging by their small pink jackets, fuzzy mittens and the pom-poms on their knitted hats, and probably not old enough for school. Despite an instinctive reluctance, Chance raised his gaze to the woman's face.

Her eyes were brown, and there were strands of blond hair—that dishwater shade that's invariably natural—peeking out from under her snow-crusted baseball cap. She was a stranger to Primrose Creek, Chance was sure of that, and yet, as he looked at her, he had the damnedest feeling that they were old friends.

He was still chewing on that insight when Madge Beardsley, who owned the Last Chance Café in partnership with her brother, an ex–rodeo clown named Claude, rushed over to greet the new crew of refugees. "Why, look at you," Madge fussed, fluttery as an old hen. "Half frozen to death!" She peered past them, through the glass door, apparently looking for a vehicle. "You get stuck somewhere?"

The woman shivered visibly and then, finally, released her hold on the little girls' hands. "My—my truck broke down, out on the highway—"

"Good heavens," Madge exclaimed, herding her charges toward the one empty booth remaining. There were a lot of folks stranded at the Last Chance that night, most of them locals, though a few were just passing through, and the place was pretty lively. "You don't mean to tell me you were all alone out there, in this weather—"

The blonde smiled and nodded, and Chance was chagrined to realize that he was still watching her. She must have sensed that, for she glanced briefly in his direction, and the smile faded. Fumbling a little, she concentrated on unbundling the kids, then herself. Madge draped their coats and hats over the old-fashioned soda cooler, since the pegs on the wall were already bulging, and poured three big mugs of hot cocoa, with extra whipped cream on top, without even being asked.

"What's your name, honey?" Madge demanded of the wayfaring stranger, setting out the mugs. Both kids stared at the mounds of sweet froth on top, their eyes wide and brown, like their mother's, and one of them hooked a finger in the stuff and slipped it in her mouth.

"Hallie," the woman answered, a little hesitantly. "Hallie O'Rourke. These are my daughters, Kiley and Kiera."

Madge beamed at the kids. "Twins," she remarked, delighted. "How old are you?"

"Five," said the one who'd swiped a taste of whipped

cream. "I'm Kiley, and that's Kiera. I was born first, so that means I'm bigger, even if it doesn't show."

Kiera tossed her sister a resentful look, but offered no comment.

Still embroiled in a drama that was, any way you looked at it, none of his damn business, Chance wondered where *Mister* O'Rourke was, and what the hell had possessed the man to let his family run all over the countryside in weather like this. He turned back to his coffee and pie, trying in vain to set Hallie O'Rourke aside in his thoughts, like a newspaper article he'd already read. He was aware of her in every cell of his body, and all the spaces in between, with a vengeance. It was spooky.

He tried not to listen in—God knew, there was plenty of noise in the café to distract him, what with the jukebox cranked up and the Ladies Aid Society over there in the far corner, playing cutthroat canasta—but he might as well have been sitting at Hallie's table.

One of the kids spoke up. "Hallie? Can I have a cheeseburger?"

Chance shook his head and took another sip of his coffee. What was this world coming to? he wondered. Families out joy-riding in the middle of a blinding snowstorm. Little kids calling their mothers by their first name, as if she were a playmate and not a parent. Madge gave Hallie a vinyl-covered menu, then trotted off to refill cups along the length of the counter and cut slices of banana cream pie for a flock of truckers over by the pinball machines.

"You can split one with Kiera," Hallie replied, in the meantime.

"I want my *own* cheeseburger. All to myself."

"We have to be careful with our money, sweetheart. You know that."

"I think we should go home. We'd have lots of money if we just went home."

Hallie couldn't have been more than thirty, but the way she sighed, she might've lived a century since breakfast. "We can't do that," she said patiently, and she sounded like she was about to break down and cry. "We'll find a place to live. A wonderful place, I promise."

"I need to piddle," the other child interjected. Chance sensed that, small as she was, Kiera was used to heading up domestic peace-keeping missions. Poor kid.

"Let's go, then," Hallie said, and they all trooped down the hall to the rest rooms.

When they returned, Madge was just setting three plates on their table. Cheeseburgers and french fries, all around. Chance watched Hallie's reflection in the age-streaked mirror behind the cash register.

"I didn't order all this," she said, sounding a little desperate.

Madge glanced in Chance's direction, probably blowing his cover. He'd offered to pay for the food, though he didn't want anybody else to know it. "Don't worry about it, honey," Madge told the young mother. "It's covered."

The kids were already tying into the food in a way that made Chance wonder how long it had been since they'd had a decent meal, but Hallie stood stiffly beside the booth, her chin high. She spoke in an agitated whisper. "I wasn't looking for charity!"

Madge recovered her aplomb, gestured to take in the crowd of customers filling the café to the baseboards, then smiled at Hallie again. "You ever wait tables, kiddo? I could use some help. I've about run my feet off, the last six hours, and that snow doesn't show any signs of letting up." As if to lend veracity to her story, a sudden wind shook the front door and made the fan rattle in the ventilator behind the big cookstove in back. The storm had begun in the early afternoon as a mere skiff, not an unusual phenomenon in the high country in mid-October, and worked itself into a hissy-fit of apocalyptic proportions. "You'd be doing me a favor," Madge finished.

Silently, Chance blessed Madge and her kindly heart, and took another sip of his coffee. She might have told Hallie that he'd staked her and the kids to the cheeseburgers and let it go at that, but she'd chosen instead to honor the other woman's pride. When Hallie didn't say anything, Madge leaped back into the breach.

"You just have yourself some supper and quit your worrying. You can work off the bill by pouring coffee and helping me clean up later."

Hallie sighed again, gave a brisk little nod of agreement, then sank gratefully into the booth and started to eat. Madge rounded the counter, picked up the coffee pot, and gave Chance a long wink as she topped off his cup. He glared at her for almost giving him away, though he knew there was a smile lurking in his eyes, and she chuckled and shook her head. She was caught in a time warp, Madge was, circa 1955. She wore her drug-store red hair high and hard, and her lipstick was crimson. Her pink dress was right out of an *I Love Lucy* episode, as were the oversized pearl baubles clipped to her earlobes, and the sensible shoes on her feet.

The weather got worse over the next hour, but the crowd began to dwindle all the same. Chance's cousin Jase Stratton, the sheriff, showed up with his four-wheel-drive and, without so much as a howdy-do for Chance, began squiring the members of the Ladies' Aid Society to their various homes, four at a time. The truckers went on down the road, their rigs equipped for hell and high water, and young Ben Pratt, a budding entrepreneur, started a little taxi service with his snowmobile.

Chance, who drove a good-sized truck himself, remained where he was, on his usual stool at the Last Chance Café, nursing his eighteenth cup of coffee and watching surreptitiously as Hallie O'Rourke showed herself to be a diligent worker. The kids, full of cheeseburgers and fries, were asleep on the vinyl seats in their booth, Madge having covered them with crocheted afghans she kept in the rear storeroom.

When Hallie came to a stop across the counter from Chance, coffee carafe in hand, he started a little, caught off guard, and she favored him with a wary smile. "Too much of this stuff is toxic, you know," she said.

He gave his cup a little push in her direction, to indicate that he wanted more poison. He'd head for home soon, try to get a few hours of sleep. No need to hurry, though, since there was nobody there waiting except the dogs and the horses, and they had each other for company. "Thanks," he said, when she broke down and poured the java. It was bottom-of-the-pot stuff, potent enough to fuel a tractor.

She put the pot back on its burner and started wiping down the counter with a cloth. Chance didn't flatter himself that she was lingering on his account. The café was warm and bright with light, and her kids were asleep. She had no place else to go, except back out into the storm.

He thought about his aunt Jessie's log house, standing empty across the creek from his own place, and inspiration struck. It seemed sudden, but he reckoned the idea had been sneaking up on him right along. "You need somewhere to stay?" he asked.

She froze right where she stood, Hallie did, and her eyes narrowed. He was glad she'd set the pot down, because she looked like she wanted to douse him with something, and scalding-hot coffee would not have been his first choice.

Chance laughed, held up a hand. "Hold it, ma'am," he said. "You just jumped to a wrong conclusion. My aunt's away in Kansas City, looking after an ailing friend, and I've been keeping up the chores over at her place. You know, making sure the pipes don't freeze, and feeding her livestock. Fact is, I've got enough to do on my own spread, without spending half the day on the other side of the creek." He watched as Hallie's brown eyes widened out again, this time with cautious interest. "You know anything about horses?" he asked, pressing his advantage, slight as it was. "Aunt Jessie's got three of them, and they need to be tended twice a day."

She hesitated, and he knew somehow that she wanted to lie, to say she knew all there was to know about equine management, but couldn't bring herself to do it. "No," she admitted, with a little sigh.

"Well, it's not too hard to learn," he allowed. Was he crazy? Whoever she was, Hallie O'Rourke was on the run, and maybe in big trouble. And here he was offering to let her stay in his aunt's house, unsupervised. Hell, she could strip the place bare, burn the furniture for firewood. "I could show you the basics."

Hallie bit her lower lip, and eagerness flared in her face, like a flash of muted light. She glanced at her sleeping kids. "No strings?" she ventured.

Chance met her gaze squarely. "No strings," he promised.

She hesitated again, then nodded. "Okay, then," she said, and went back to her counter-wiping.

Madge, a guardian angel clad in pink nylon, stood with her hands resting on her ample hips, smiling at Hallie. "Chance Qualtrough?" she said. "He's all right. His people have been out there on Primrose Creek since pioneer days. They done all right for themselves, all of them."

Hallie ran her hands down the thighs of her worn jeans and glanced over her shoulder at the cowboy still parked on the same stool at the counter. He was good-looking, with his dark blond hair and blue eyes, and he didn't seem dangerous, but Hallie had learned to be careful. Learned it the hard way. She tried to ignore the little twinge of envy she felt, hearing that his roots ran deep into the Nevada soil. "Does he hang around here a lot?"

Madge chuckled, a fond, raspy sound. "No more than any of the other regulars," she said. "He likes to take his breakfast here, and I've never seen a body that could hold more coffee. He's got himself a nice little ranch and a few cattle. Trains horses for a living. Takes on the hard cases."

Hallie barely knew one end of a horse from the other, and to her, the concept of training an animal extended to sit, stay, and fetch, and no further. She looked at Chance for a fraction of a second too long, and he caught her at it, and winked. She turned her head quickly, but she suspected he'd seen the color rise in her face. His lazy grin lingered in her mind like an echo.

Madge laughed again. For all her lack of sophistication, she didn't seem to miss much. She took one of Hallie's hands and gave it a motherly pat. "You look after Jessie's place; that'll give you somewhere to light for a while. Get your bearings and the like. I could use you here at the café, that's for sure. It's just minimum wage, but the tips are decent."

Hallie couldn't speak for a few moments. Just a couple of hours ago, she'd been stranded on a snowy highway, essentially homeless, with two children, one ratty suitcase, and one hundred and twenty-eight dollars to her name. When the truck gave out, she'd laid her forehead on the steering wheel and breathed deeply until she was sure she wouldn't cry, and offered a desperate, silent prayer for help. Now, after a two-mile walk in the cold, carrying one or both of the twins the whole way, she'd stumbled into this place, met these people. Kiley and Kiera had eaten their fill, and they were warm now, and safe. Dreaming little-girl dreams as they slept. She had a job, and a place to stay. Maybe God hadn't misplaced His hearing aid after all.

"Well?" Madge prompted. "Have I got me a waitress, or not?"

Hallie smiled and put out a hand to seal the bargain. "You've got a waitress," she said. "Thanks, Madge."

Madge was all business. "I'll look for you around eleven-thirty tomorrow morning, weather permitting. You can work lunch and supper." She paused, briefly worried. "I don't mind tellin' you, it makes for a long day. We don't get out of here till midnight sometimes, me and Claude, but you can knock off around eight o'clock. Meals are included, of course, and you can bring the kids with you as long as need be. They seem well behaved."

Hallie felt a little rush of pride, hearing her daughters praised. She's done *something* right. And she'd found a job and a place to live. Okay, maybe she wasn't exactly rising out of the ashes of her life, phoenix-like, but she could see a glimmer of light, faint as a distant star, through the wreckage. There was reason to hope. "They're the best," she said.

Madge smiled wearily. "Let me just fix you up a little care package to take out to Jessie's place. Lord, she'll be pleased to know the house isn't standing empty." The older woman peered through the kitchen doorway, hands braced on the framework. "You better fire up that truck of yours, Chance," she said. "Get the heater going. Don't want Hallie or those little girls coming down with pneumonia before they even get to Jessie's."

He nodded, pulled on his battered hat, and tugged at the brim, a real gent. Hallie felt a stir, part anticipation, part fear, as she digested the fact that she and her children were about to ride God knew how far, to God knew what kind of place, with a virtual stranger. Under normal circumstances, she wouldn't even have considered taking a risk like that, but now, on that snowy October night, there in the high country of northern Nevada, she was fresh out of choices.

Madge put together a box of provisions—bread, milk,

cheese, a small can of coffee, eggs, a package of breakfast sausage and half a pecan pie—while Hallie woke the twins and shuffled them back into their coats.

"Where are we going?" Kiley wanted to know.

"Is there a bed?" Kiera added.

Before Hallie could come up with an answer to either question, Madge was right in there, pinch hitting. "You're going to a real nice place," she told the kids. "There's a hill for sledding, and a barn, too. In the summer, you can swim and fish for trout in the creek."

Hallie bit back a protest. By summer, they'd be long gone, she and the twins, miles from Primrose Creek, Nevada, with new identities and new lives, but she couldn't afford to discuss that with anybody, no matter how kind they seemed. "There's a horse there," she said, a little tightly. "We're going to take care of it."

The look in Kiera's eyes made her wish she hadn't mentioned the horse. *"Really?"* the child whispered, in sleepy awe.

"Wow," Kiley said, pushing Hallie's hands aside to zip up her own jacket. "Do we know how to take care of horses?"

"We're going to learn," Hallie answered, and then Mr. Qualtrough was back from the parking lot, snow-dappled and bringing a chill wind along with him.

He led the way out, carrying Kiley in one arm and the groceries in the other, while Hallie, having donned her own coat, followed with Kiera. His truck was parked a few yards from the door, humming with power, spewing white vapor from the tailpipe. The headlights turned the steadily falling snow into a shower of golden coins.

With a sort of rangy grace, the cowboy put down the box, opened the passenger door, set Kiley inside, then helped Kiera and Hallie in after her. When Hallie had buckled the appropriate seat belts, he set the provisions on her lap, shut the door again, and went around to the driver's side. A few seconds later, they were pulling out onto the still-unplowed highway, headed away from town.

Hallie held Kiera on her lap and slipped an arm around Kiley, who was huddled beside her. "You're sure your aunt won't mind?" she asked, mostly to make conversation. She was a person who appreciated solitude, but right now she couldn't deal with silence.

He fiddled with the radio, found a country oldies station, and settled back to concentrate on his driving while the voice of Johnny Cash joined them in the warm darkness, a familiar, rumbling base.

"Mind?" he answered, at his leisure. "She'll be doing back flips for joy. Aunt Jessie believes no house is complete without a woman in it."

"You said she was in Kansas City?"

Chance nodded, squinting as he navigated the nearly invisible road. "Her college roommate lost her husband about six months ago, then found out she was dying of cancer herself. Jessie went back to help out."

"I see," Hallie said. She wondered what it would be like to have a friend who would do something like that, just turn her own life upside down to be there when you needed her. "I guess she's not married herself, then. Jessie, I mean."

Chance shook his head. "She's the independent type," he said, with neither admiration nor scorn. They crept over a wooden bridge, the same one Hallie and the kids had crossed on foot on their way into town earlier. "What about you, Hallie? Are you married?"

"Independent type," she answered, and smiled a little.

He chuckled. "Me, too," he said. They traveled on in silence for several minutes. Johnny Cash finished walking the line, and Marty Robbins came on, crooning "El Paso." A shape loomed, snow-mounded, at the side of the road. "That your truck?" Chance asked.

Hallie nodded. She'd left her suitcase behind, having her hands full with the children.

Chance pulled in behind the battered pickup. "I suppose you have some stuff in there?"

"A suitcase," she said.

"That's all?"

Kiley spoke up. "Elmo's there, too," she said. "I bet he's cold."

Chance grinned, got out of the truck, slogged through the blizzard to the other rig, and pulled open the door. He was back within a few moments, bringing Elmo, a stuffed toy, and the suitcase containing the few things Hallie had taken time to pack before making her escape.

"I'll come back and have a look at the engine in the morning," he said, after handing Elmo to Kiley and stowing the suitcase in the space behind the seat. "Maybe I can get it running again."

Hallie figured the truck was a hopeless case, but she was too tired to say so, and she didn't want to worry the twins. "Okay," she said. Then, hastily, she added, "I don't have money for parts, though. Or labor, either."

He simply shook his head, shifted his own truck back into gear, and rolled out onto the highway.

"How can you see?" Hallie asked. The windshield looked almost opaque to her, and the snow was coming down even harder than before.

"I could drive this road in a coma," he said. "Lived here all my life."

A row of mailboxes appeared in the white gloom, and they turned onto a bumpy road. Hallie sensed, rather than heard, the sluggish burble of the creek flowing alongside. At last, they stopped in front of what looked like a two-story log house.

"Wait here," Chance said. "I'll switch on some lights and turn the furnace up a notch or two."

Hallie waited, holding tightly to her daughters, relishing the delicious heat flowing from under the dashboard. A light winked on, then another, and something awakened in Hallie's heart, bittersweet and hopeful. Unconsciously, she laid a hand to her chest, as if to keep the feeling from escaping.

"Where's the horse?" Kiley asked, all business.

Hallie chuckled. "In the barn, probably," she said.

"Can I ride him?" Kiera put in.

"No promises," Hallie answered.

Kiley sighed with temporary resignation, settled against Hallie's side, and nestled there. Hallie relished having her close, having both her children safe within the circle of her arms. She'd learned, in recent months, to appreciate the simple blessings.

In due time, after the radio had pumped out two more of Johnny Cash's ballads and a Patsy Cline medley, Chance returned from the house and opened the door on Hallie's side.

"It's still pretty cold in there," he said, "but the furnace has kicked in, so the place will warm up pretty quickly, I think. I laid a fire for morning."

Hallie's throat tightened a little, with gratitude and relief. "Thanks," she managed.

He reached in, taking Kiley in one arm and Kiera in the other, and favored Hallie with a brief grin. "We'll see if you're still singing the same tune after you've met Trojan," he said.

"Trojan?" Hallie queried, literally following in Chance's footsteps as they trudged toward the house.

"He's a miniature horse. Known in some quarters as Jessie's Folly," he said, pausing on the rough-hewn porch. "She's got a couple of full-sized ones, too. A mare named Dolly and an old gelding she calls Sweet Pea. Wonder the poor fella doesn't die of embarrassment, hung with a moniker like that."

Hallie tried to imagine herself feeding these animals, cleaning up after them, grooming them. The prospect was overwhelming. She'd never even looked after a goldfish.

Then they were inside the house, with its two-story rock fireplace, its hooked rugs and rustic furniture. Colorful weavings graced several of the otherwise plain log walls. There was a desk across from the fireplace, with a plastic-covered computer on its surface.

The floor was fashioned of gleaming planks, mellowed with age, and a gigantic loom, surely antique, stood in one corner, framed on all sides by windows. A set of stairs led to a mezzanine of sorts, lined with a total of six doors.

"The kitchen's that way," Chance said, pointing to an archway to their right, "and that's the downstairs bathroom there, at the base of the steps. The bedrooms are all on the second floor, and there's another bath up there. You'll find sheets and towels and all that in the linen cupboard, and you should have hot water by morning."

Hallie turned in a slow circle, there in the middle of that plank floor, trying to take it all in.

Kiera headed for the bay windows overlooking the front yard. "This," she said, with authority, spreading her tiny arms wide and twirling with sudden exuberance, "is where the Christmas tree goes."

Hallie's heart ached. "This isn't our house, honey," she reminded the child. "We're just visiting."

Out of the corner of her eye, she caught a glimpse of Chance. He was turning his hat in his hands, and looking somber, but if he wanted to say something, he held it back.

"No," Kiera insisted. "We belong *here*."

Hallie was too tired to argue the point. She turned to Chance. "You'll show me what needs to be done?" she asked. "For the animals, I mean?"

"First thing in the morning," he agreed, a little gruffly. "I'll be over as soon as I finish my chores."

"Good," she said, walking with him to the door. "And thanks." She nearly choked on the word; she hadn't had much cause to use it in a while, and she'd gotten rusty. "Thanks for everything."

He smiled. "Lock the door behind me," he said, and she nodded, and he was gone.

She fastened the latch, went to the nearest window, and watched as Chance became a shadow, and finally disappeared, leaving no trace except for the faint gleam of taillights and the whir of his truck's engine. Then she turned to face her children, summoning up another smile.

"Well," she said, "what do you say we make up a bed and get some sleep?"

The girls, wide awake again, would probably have preferred to stay up all night exploring, but by the time Hallie had chosen a bedroom for the three of them to share, made up the large four-poster bed, seen to the brushing of teeth, the washing of faces, the putting on of pajamas, and the saying of prayers, they were both exhausted again.

They crawled between the cool, crispy sheets, quilts mounded on top of them, Hallie lying in the middle, with a child cuddled against each side. Soon, both Kiera and Kiley were sound asleep, but Hallie, weary though she was, stared up at the rafters and wondered. Had her luck turned at long last, or was this run of good fortune just a cruel prelude to yet another disappointment, another battle, another headlong rush for safety?